The Witchwood Crown

Book One of The Last King of Osten Ard

TAD WILLIAMS

HODDER &
STOUGHTON

First published in Great Britain in 2017 by Hodder & Stoughton
An Hachette UK company

This paperback edition published in 2018

1

A CIP catalogue record for this title is available from the British Library

Paperback ISBN 978 1 473 60324 0

Printed and bound by Clays Ltd, St Ives plc

Hodder & Stoughton policy is to use papers that are natural, renewable
and recyclable products and made from wood grown in sustainable
forests. The logging and manufacturing processes are expected to
conform to the environmental regulations of the country of origin.

Hodder & Stoughton Ltd
Carmelite House
50 Victoria EmbankmentL
ondon EC4Y 0DZ

www.hodder.co.uk

Dedication

After much consideration I've decided that this book really must be dedicated to the three people who have done the most over the years to lead me back to Osten Ard.

My publishers Betsy Wollheim and Sheila Gilbert have politely nudged me for ages, reminding me approximately every seventeen minutes that everyone else but me was certain that the prophecy at the birth of Josua's and Vorzheva's twins was meant to set up a sequel, and that they'd really love to see me write it. (Actually they were quite patient. But they did remind me from time to time. Occasionally they threatened me with sticks.) And their nudging came not just from business reasons, but also because they thought I could do something wonderful with it.

My wife and partner Deborah Beale also kept after me over the years with equal sweetness and patience, being sensitive to my process (which for peak efficiency requires months at a time spent almost entirely napping) while asking me at courteous intervals why *exactly* I couldn't ever write a sequel to *Memory, Sorrow, and Thorn.*

Prompted by one such conversation, I finally sat down to think carefully about why I couldn't do it. The reason had always been that I needed to have a story first, otherwise it would feel as uninspired to me as opening a franchise operation. Every book starts as a story for me—but I didn't have another Osten Ard story inside me. So in my mind I shot down possibility after possibility— lame, derivative, self-parodying—because I wanted to show Deb (and by extension, everybody who'd ever asked me about a sequel) why a sequel just wasn't going to happen. But by the time a long day or so of thinking had passed, I realized I *did* have a story to tell, and by the time I described it to Deb I was getting pretty excited about it. Not too many weeks later, I was actually writing it.

There are also about nine hundred other ways Deb has supported this book, from reading and analyzing the manuscript in draft (with her usual acumen) to generating publicity from our dining table like P. T. Barnum in a bathrobe. Figuratively speaking, her fingerprints are all over the book.

Sheila and Betsy also contributed in many, many ways from the publishing end, including their usual loving attention to editing the manuscript in process and to creating the look of the thing.

So I dedicate this book to all three of them—Sheila and Betsy and Deborah.

Betsy and Sheila, thanks for everything, your friendship by no means the least. I'm really happy (and, I'll admit it, a bit damp-eyed and sentimental) to be sharing this particular publication with you—finally.

Deborah, you are the one. For these and so very many other things, thank you.

Acknowledgments

It's always extremely hard to properly acknowledge all the people who contributed to a book, but with this one it's even harder, because so very many people kindly contributed their time and effort to make it possible.

Here are as many of them as I can be certain about, since the process started more than two years ago. If you're one of the deserving and I failed to mention you here, definitely consider yourself thanked, but please write to me so I can make sure to get a proper acknowledgment into the next book.

First off, my sincere gratitude to all who took the time to read a very long, very early manuscript and give me their impressions and suggestions, or who worked to make sure the index was comprehensive, accurate, and also jibed with the previous books. Each name represents hours of work that I didn't have to do!

Charlotte Cogle; Ron Hyde; Ylva von Löhneysen; Eva Maderbacher; Devi Pillai; Cindy Squires; Linda Van Der Pal; Angela Welchel; and Cindy Yan.

You guys are my heroes. Thanks and thanks and thanks.

As always, I need to mention those who have done the most for me for the longest. The crucial help that my wife Deborah Beale and my publishers Sheila Gilbert and Betsy Wollheim provided for this book is discussed in the dedication, but I wanted to say again how much they rock my world.

My agent Matt Bialer has been his usual smart, helpful, and amusing self throughout this process. You're in a rut, Matt.

Lisa Tveit has managed no matter what befell to keep my website (and other online aspects of my career) wonderful and working—as always, thank you so much, Lisa.

MaryLou Capes-Platt, who is copyediting the new Osten Ard books, is both a stern taskmistress and a charming muse, commenting in the margins of the proofs, giving me happy little reactions when I do well or gently pointing out when my writing is sloppy, confusing, or otherwise not up to par. Her sharp eye and wit, and her kind heart have strongly influenced the final version of the story.

Isaac Stewart has not only contributed brilliant new maps, but spent long, difficult hours trying to get all the details exactly right so that they match the geography from the earlier books as well. (He had help with this, but I'll get to that in a moment.) The results are obvious—and gorgeous.

Michael Whelan's doing the paintings for these books—'nuff said, really—and as always, he worked really, really hard to take what's in the story and expand it with his great talent into more than I could ever have imagined.

Joshua Starr has labored long and hard to keep me on schedule and (more or less) out of trouble—as have many other people at DAW Books and Penguin Random House. Josh makes coping with the eye-crossing minutiae of publication a pleasure. Many thanks, Josh!

And my British and German publishers, Oliver Johnson at Hodder & Stoughton and Stephan Askani at Klett-Cotta, read and supported this newest Hideously Long Tad Book with their usual kindness and savvy. I am very fortunate in my publishers worldwide.

And of course I must mention those most loyal and kind friends a writer could have, the gang on the *tadwilliams.com* message board, many of whom are already listed here by name—but by no means all. Let's party in the Mint, dudes. I'm buying.

Last, but decidedly not least, I have to thank two people who have put in so much work on this return to Osten Ard that I hardly know where to begin to praise them.

Ron Hyde has basically become the official Osten Ard Archivist, not just reading and consulting on the manuscript, but putting in many hours with Isaac Stewart and the maps too, as well as answering questions from me at all times of the day or night, because I wrote the original books thirty years ago, and Ron knows the details of the land and its history better than I do. Trying to keep all the details consistent in a million words written that long ago (and a background even larger, also constructed back then) with what will probably be another million words when I finish the new ones, is a Herculean task. Without help like his, I'd be writing this acknowledgment about two years from now.

Ylva von Löhneysen has also gone above the call of duty and probably even sanity to help this book come into existence, doing many of the same things as Ron and making other contributions of her own, reading all the drafts, commenting extensively, and her own vast knowledge of Osten Ard to help keep me on the right track. (Yes, Ylva also knows more about my creation than I do.) She sent me notes constantly during the rewrite process with reactions to this or that scene she had just read, helping me keep my courage (and page production) up, not to mention aiding with ideas and suggestions that, like Ron's and the others mentioned above, in many cases directly influenced the version of The Witchwood Crown you hold in your hands.

I salute you all. I could not have done it without you. May blessings shower upon you.

Author's Note

Many of you reading this are already aware that this book is part of a return to Osten Ard, a world I created in an earlier set of books. If you weren't aware, don't panic, but read the following:

You do *not* need to have read the earlier works to enjoy the new series—it takes place some three decades later, and I have done my best to explain crucial pieces of information within the current story—but of course you may want to go back and read them anyway. (I did. I had to, to write the new ones.) You can find a synopsis of the previous series, *Memory, Sorrow, and Thorn* in several places, including the DAW Books website, *dawbooks.com*, or on my own website, *tadwilliams.com*.

There will NOT be a test.

The first series, *Memory, Sorrow, and Thorn*, consists of these books:
The Dragonbone Chair
Stone of Farewell
To Green Angel Tower (divided into Part One and Part Two in the mass market editions)

The new books, titled as a whole *The Last King of Osten Ard*, will be the following:
The Witchwood Crown
Empire of Grass
The Navigator's Children

as well as two short novels not directly part of the new story, but with many of the same characters and historical events from the other books. The first of these, *The Heart of What Was Lost*, is already published. The second, tentatively called *The Shadow of Things to Come*, is not yet written, but will probably be published sometime before *The Navigator's Children*.

Foreword

Rider and mount glided down the slope through stands of
Kynswood trees, larches, shiny-leaved beeches, and oaks festooned with dangling catkins. Silent and surprising, the pair appeared first in one beam of bright
sunlight then another at a speed that would have startled any merely mortal eye.
The rider's pale cloak seemed to catch and reflect the colors all around, so that
an idle or distracted glance would have seen only a hint of movement, imagined
only wind.

The warmth of the day pleased Tanahaya. The music of forest insects pleased
her too, the whirring of grasshoppers and the hum of busy honeymakers. Even
though the smell of the mortal habitation was strong and this patch of forest
only a momentary refuge, she spoke silent words of gratitude for an interlude
of happiness.

*Praises, Mother Sun. Praises for the growing-scents. Praise for the bees and their
goldendance.*

She was young by the standards of her people, with only a few centuries
upon the broad earth. Tanahaya of Shisae'ron had spent many of those years in
the saddle, first as messenger for her clan's leader, Himano of the Flowering
Hills, then later, after she had made her worth known to the House of Year-
Dancing, performing tasks for her friends in that clan. But this errand to the
mortals' capital seemed as if it might be the most perilous of all her journeys,
and was certainly the strangest. She hoped she was strong and clever enough to
fulfill the trust of those who had sent her.

Tanahaya had been described as wise beyond her years, but she still could
not understand the importance her friends placed on the affairs of mortals—
especially the short-lived creatures who inhabited this particular part of the
world. That was even more inexplicable now, when it seemed clear to her that
the Zida'ya could no longer trust any mortals at all.

Still, there was the castle she had been seeking, its highest roofs just visible
through the trees. Looking at its squat towers and heavy stone walls, it was hard
for Tanahaya to believe that Asu'a, the greatest and most beautiful city of her
people, had once stood here. Could anything of their old home be left in this
pile of clumsy stone that men called the Hayholt?

I must not think of what might be true, of what I fear or what I hope. Horse and rider moved down the slope. *I must see only what is. Otherwise I fail my oath and I fail my friends.*

She stopped at the edge of the trees. "*Tsa*, Spidersilk," she whispered, and the horse stood in silence as Tanahaya listened. New noises wafted up the slope to her, as well as a new and not entirely welcome scent, the animal tang of unwashed mortals. Tanahaya clicked her tongue and Spidersilk stepped aside into shadow.

She had a hand on the hilt of her sword when a golden-haired girl dashed into the sunlight, a basket of winter flowers swinging in one hand, daffodils and snowdrops and royal purple crocuses. Tanahaya's senses told her the child was not alone, so she stayed hidden in the shadows between trees as a half-dozen armed soldiers followed the child in gasping, clanking pursuit. After a moment, Tanahaya relaxed: it was clear the mortals did not mean to harm the little one. Still, she was surprised that mortal soldiers were so heedless of danger: she could have put arrows in most of them before they even realized they were not alone in the Kynswood.

A mortal woman in a hat with a brim as wide as a wagon's wheel followed the armored men into the clearing. "Lillia!" the woman cried, then stopped and bent to catch her breath. "Do not run, child! Oh, you are wicked! Wicked to make us chase you!"

The child stopped, eyes wide. "But Auntie Rhoner, look! Berries!"

"Berries! In Marris-month? You little mad thing." The woman, still trying to catch her breath, was handsome by mortal standards, or so Tanahaya guessed—tall, with fine, strong bones in her face. By the name the child had given her, Tanahaya guessed this must be Countess Rhona of Nad Glehs, one of the mortal queen's closest friends. Tanahaya did not find it strange that a noble of high standing should be minding a child, though others might have. "No, you come back with me, honey-lamb," the countess said. "Those are owlberries and they'll make you sick."

"No they won't," the child declared. "Because they're forest berries. And forest berries have lots of magic. *Fairy* magic."

"Magic." The woman in the hat sounded disgusted, but even from such a distance Tanahaya's sharp eyes could see the smile that played across her face. "I'll give you fairy magic, *mu' harcha*! You wanted to search for early flowers, and I brought you. We have been out for hours—and by Deanagha's spotless skirts, look at me. I am filthy and bepricked with nettles!"

"They're not nettles, they're berry bushes," said the golden-haired girl. "That's why they have thorns. So nobody will eat the berries."

"Nobody wants to eat those berries but birds. Not even the deer will go near them!"

The heavily armored soldiers, still struggling for breath in their heavy mail, faces gleaming with sweat, began to straighten up. The girl had clearly led them a long, wearying chase over the hillside. "Should we grab her, your ladyship?" asked one.

The countess frowned. "Lillia, it is time to go back. I want my midday meal."

"I don't have to do anything unless you call me 'Princess' or 'Your Highness'."

"What silliness! Your grandparents are away and I am your keeper, little lion cub. Come now. Don't make me cross."

"I wish Uncle Timo was here. He lets me do things."

"Uncle Timo is your sworn bondsman. No, he is your helpless slave and lets you get away with everything. I am made of harder stuff. Come along."

The girl called Lillia looked from the countess to all the dark bushes full of pale, blue-white fruit, then sighed and slowly walked back down the slope. If its handle had been any longer, her basket would have dragged in the loamy soil. "When Queen Grandmother and King Grandfather come back, I'm going to tell on you," she warned.

"Tell what?" The countess frowned. "That I wouldn't let you run away by yourself in the forest to be eaten by wolves and bears?"

"I could give them berries. Then they wouldn't eat me."

The woman took her hand. "Even hungry bears won't eat owlberries. And the wolves would rather eat *you*."

As the small party vanished back down the deer trail into a thick copse of oak and ash trees farther down the slope, Tanahaya watched with a kind of wonder. To think that little creature named Lillia would reach womanhood, perhaps marry and become a mother and grandmother, grow old and even die—all in not much more than one of her people's Great Years! It seemed to Tanahaya that being mortal must be like trying to live a full life in the space between falling from a high place and hitting the ground, a rush through wind and confusion to death. How did the poor creatures manage?

For the first time it occurred to Tanahaya of Shisae'ron that perhaps she might learn something from this task. It was an unexpected thought.

So this young creature was Lillia, she told herself, the granddaughter of Queen Miriamele and King Seoman—the objects of Tanahaya's embassy. She would be seeing that proud little bumblebee of a girl again.

Bumblebee? No, butterfly, she thought with a sudden pang. *A flash of color and glory beneath the sky, and then, like all mortals, too soon she will become dust.*

But if the fears of Tanahaya's friends proved accurate, she knew, then the end for that butterfly child and all the rest of the Hayholt's mortals might come even sooner than any of them could guess.

As she reined up again to examine the castle, she could still hear the faint rattle of the retreating soldiers and the golden girl's voice, no words now but just a musical burble rising from the forest below. The wind changed, and the stink of mortals, of unwashed bodies and unchanged garments abruptly deepened; it was all she could do not to turn around and retreat. She would have to accustom herself, she knew.

Tanahaya had never liked the squat, cheerless look of men's buildings any more than she cared for men's odor, and the Hayholt, this great castle of theirs, was no different. Despite its size, it seemed nothing more than a collection of carelessly built dwellings hiding behind brutish stone walls, one wall set inside another like a succession of mushroom rings. The entire awkward structure perched on a high headland above the wide bay known as Kynslagh, as though it were the nest of some slovenly seabird. Even the red tiles that roofed many of the buildings seemed dull to her as dried blood, and Tanahaya thought the famous castle looked more like a place to be imprisoned than anything else. It was astounding to realize that a few mortal decades earlier—an eyeblink of time to her people—the Storm King's attack on the living had ended just here, only moments from success. She thought she could still hear the great crying-out of that day and feel the countless shadows that would not disperse, the torment and terror of so many. Even Time itself had almost been overthrown here. How could the mortals continue to live in such a place? Could they not feel the uneasy dead all around them?

Watching the girl had brought her a moment of good cheer, but now it blew away like dust on a hot, dry wind. For a moment Tanahaya's hand strayed to the Witness in her belt-pouch, the sacred, timeworn mirror that would allow her to speak across great earthly distances to those who had sent her. She didn't belong here—it was hard to believe that any of her race could in these fallen times. It was not too late, after all: she could beg her loved ones in Jao é-Tinukai'i to find someone else for this task.

Tanahaya's impulse did not last. It was not her place to judge these short-lived creatures, but to do what she had been bid for the good of her own people.

After all, she reminded herself, *a year does not dance itself into being. Everything is sacrifice.*

She lifted her hand from the hidden mirror and caught up the reins once more. Even from this distance, the stench of mortals seemed unbearably strong, so fierce she could barely stand it. How much worse would it be when she was out of the heights and riding through their cramped streets?

Something struck her hard in the back. Tanahaya gasped, but could not get' her breath. She tried to turn to see what had hit her, simultaneously reaching to draw her sword, but before it cleared the scabbard another arrow struck her, this time in the chest.

The Sitha tried to crouch low in the saddle but that only pressed the second arrow more agonizingly into her body. She could feel something like a cool breath on her back and knew it must be blood soaking her jerkin. She reached down and broke the second shaft off close to her ribs. Free of that obstruction but still pulsing blood around the broken shaft, she threw herself against Spidersilk's neck and clung tightly, aiming now only for escape. But even as she clapped her heels against the horse's side a new arrow hissed into the animal's neck just a handspan from Tanahaya's fingers. The horse reared, shrilling in pain and terror. As Tanahaya struggled to hang on, a fourth arrow took her high in her back and spun her out of the saddle. She fell into air, and for a mad moment it seemed almost like flight. Then something struck her all over and at once, a great, flat blow, and a soundless darkness rushed over her like a river.

PART ONE

Widows

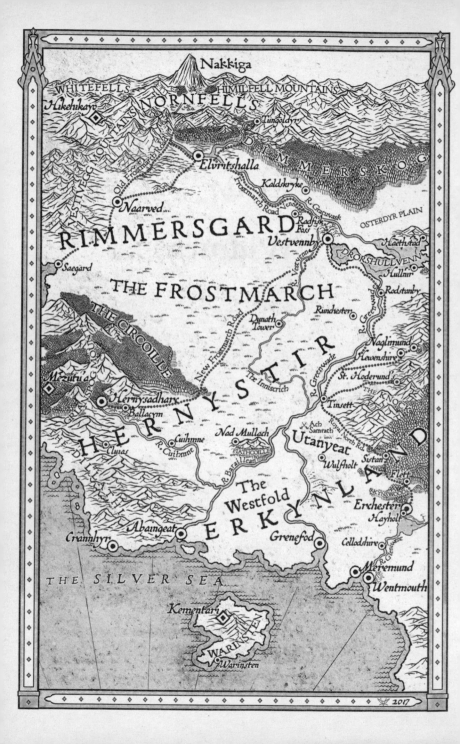

Locusts laid their eggs in the corpse
Of a soldier. When the worms were
Mature, they took wing. Their drone
Was ominous, their shells hard.
Anyone could tell they had hatched
From an unsatisfied anger.
They flew swiftly toward the North.
They hid the sky like a curtain.
When the wife of the soldier
Saw them, she turned pale, her breath
Failed her. She knew he was dead
In battle, his corpse lost in the desert.
That night she dreamed
She rode a white horse, so swift
It left no footprints, and came
To where he lay in the sand.
She looked at his face, eaten
By the locusts, and tears of
Blood filled her eyes. Ever after
She would not let her children
Injure any insect that
Might have fed on the dead. She
Would lift her face to the sky
And say, "O locusts, if you
Are seeking a place to winter,
You can find shelter in my heart."

—HSU CHAO
  "The Locust Swarm"

1

The Glorious

The pavilion walls billowed and snapped as the winds rose. Tiamak thought it was like being inside a large drum. Many people in the tent were trying to be heard, but the clear voice of a young minstrel floated above it all, singing a song of heroism:

> *"Sing ye loud his royal name*
> *Seoman the Glorious!*
> *Spread it far, his royal fame*
> *Seoman the Glorious!"*

The king did not look glorious. He looked tired. Tiamak could see it in the lines of Simon's face, the way his shoulders hunched as if he awaited a blow. But that blow had already fallen. Today was only the grim anniversary.

Limping more than usual because of the cold day, little Tiamak made his way among all the larger men. These courtiers and important officials were gathered around the king, who sat on one of two high-backed wooden chairs at the center of the tent, both draped in the royal colors. A banner with the twin drakes, the red and the white, hung above them. The other chair was empty.

As a makeshift throne room in the middle of a Hernystir field, Tiamak thought, it was more than adequate, but it was also clearly the one place King Seoman did not want to be. Not today.

> *"With hero's sword in his right hand*
> *And nought but courage in his heart*
> *Did Seoman make his gallant stand*
> *Though cowards fled apart*
>
> *"When the hellspawned Norns did bring*
> *Foul war upon the innocent*
> *And giants beat upon the gates*
> *And Norn sails filled the Gleniwent . . ."*

"I don't understand," said the king loudly to one of the courtiers. "In truth, my good man, I haven't understood a thing you've said, what with all this shouting and caterwauling. Why should they have to lime the bridges? Do they think we are birds that need catching?"

"*Line* the bridges, sire."

The king scowled. "I know, Sir Murtach. It was meant as a jest. But it still doesn't make any sense."

The courtier's determined smile faltered. "It is the tradition for the people to line up along the bridges as well as the roads, but King Hugh is concerned that the bridges might not stand under the weight of so many."

"And so *we* must give up our wagons and come on foot? All of us?"

Sir Murtach flinched. "It is what King Hugh requests, Your Majesty."

> *"When armies of the Stormlord came*
> *Unto the very Swertclif plain*
> *Who stood on Hayholt's battlements*
> *And bade them all turn back again?*
>
> *"Sing ye loud his royal name*
> *Seoman the Glorious!*
> *Spread it far, his royal fame*
> *Seoman the Glorious!"*

King Simon's head had tipped to one side. It was *not* the side from which he was being urgently addressed by another messenger, who had finally worked his way to a place beside the makeshift throne. Something had distracted Simon. Tiamak thought that seeing the king's temper fray was like watching a swamp flatboat beginning to draw water. It was plain that if someone didn't do something soon, the whole craft would sink.

> *"He slew the dragon fierce and cold*
> *And banished winter by his hand*
> *He tamed the Sithi proud and old*
> *And saved the blighted, threatened land . . ."*

Murtach was still talking in one royal ear, and the other messenger had started his speech for the third time when Simon suddenly stood. The courtiers fell back swiftly, like hunting hounds when the bear turns at bay. The king's beard was still partly red, but he had enough gray in it now, as well as the broad white stripe where he had once been splashed by dragon's blood, that when his anger was up he looked a bit like an Aedonite prophet from the old days.

"That! That!" Simon shouted. "It's bad enough that I cannot hear myself think, that every man in camp wants me to do something or . . . or not do something . . . but must I listen to such terrible lies and exaggerations as well?" He turned and pointed his finger at the miscreant. "Well? Must I?"

At the far end of the king's finger, the young minstrel stared back with the round eyes of a quiet, nighttime grazer caught in the sudden glare of a torch. He swallowed. It seemed to take a long time. "Beg pardon, Majesty?" he squeaked.

"That song! That preposterous song! 'He slew the dragon fierce and cold'—a palpable lie!" The king strode forward until he towered over the thin, dark-haired singer, who seemed to be melting and shrinking like a snowflake caught in a warm hand. "By the Bloody Tree, I never killed that dragon, I just wounded it a bit. I was terrified. And I didn't tame the Sithi either, for the love of our lord Usires!"

The minstrel looked at up at him, mouth working but without sound.

"And the rest of the song is even more mad. Banished the winter? You might as well say I make the sun rise every day!"

"B-But . . . but it is only a song, Majesty," the minstrel finally said. "It is a well-known and well-loved one—all the people sing it . . ."

"Pfah." But Simon was no longer shouting. His anger was like a swift storm—the thunder had boomed, now all that was left was cold rain. "Then go sing it to all the people. Or better yet, when we return to the Hayholt, ask old Sangfugol what really happened. Ask him what it was truly like when the Storm King's darkness came down on us and we all pissed ourselves in fear."

A moment of confused bravery showed itself on the young man's face. "But it was Sangfugol who *made* that song, Your Majesty. And he was the one who taught it to me."

Simon growled. "So, then all bards are liars. Go on, boy. Get away from me."

The minstrel looked quite forlorn as he pushed his way toward the door of the pavilion. Tiamak caught at his sleeve as he went by. "Wait outside," he told the singer. "Wait for me."

The young man was so full of anguish he had not truly heard. "I beg pardon?"

"Just wait outside for a few moments. I will come for you."

The youth looked at the little Wrannaman oddly, but everyone in the court knew Tiamak and how close he was to the king and queen. The harper blinked his eyes, doing his best to compose himself. "If you say so, my lord."

Simon was already driving the rest of the courtiers from the pavilion. "Enough! Leave me be now, all of you. I cannot do everything, and certainly not in one day! Give me peace!"

Tiamak waited until the wave of humanity had swept past him and out of the tent, then he waited a bit longer until the king finished pacing and dropped back onto his chair. Simon looked up at his councilor and his face sagged with unhappiness and useless anger. "Don't look at me that way, Tiamak."

The king seldom lost his temper with those who served him, and was much loved for it. Back home in Erkynland many called him "the Commoner King" or even "the Scullion King" because of his youthful days as a Hayholt dogs-body. Generally Simon remembered very well indeed what it felt like to be ignored or blamed by those with power. But sometimes, especially when he was in the grip of such heartache as he was today, he fell into foul moods.

Tiamak, of course, knew that the moods seldom lasted long and were fol- lowed quickly by regret. "I am not looking at you in any particular way, Maj- esty."

"Don't mock me. You are. It's that sad, wise expression you put on when you're thinking about what a dunderhead one of your monarchs is. And that monarch is nearly always me."

"You need rest, Majesty." It was a privilege to speak as old friends, one that Tiamak would never have presumed on with others in the room. "You are weary and your temper is short."

The king opened his mouth, then shook his head. "This is a bad day," he said at last. "A very bad day. Where is Miriamele?"

"The queen declined any audiences today. She is out walking."

"I am glad for her. I hope she is being left alone."

"As much as she wishes to be. Her ladies are with her. She likes company more than you do on days like this."

"Days like this, I would like to be on the top of a mountain in the Trollfells with Binabik and his folk, with nothing but snow to look at and nothing but wind to hear."

"We have plenty of wind for you here in this meadow," Tiamak said. "But not too much snow, considering that there is still almost a fortnight of winter left."

"Oh, I know what day it is, what month," Simon said. "I need no remind- ing."

Tiamak cleared his throat. "Of course not. But will you take my advice? Rest yourself for a while. Let your unhappiness cool."

"It was just . . . hearing that nonsense, over and over . . . Simon the hero, all of that. I did not seem such a hero when my son . . ."

"Please, Majesty."

"But I should not have taken it out on the harper." Again, the storm had blown over quickly, and now Simon was shaking his head. "He has given me many a sweet hour of song before. It is not his fault that lies become history so quickly. Perhaps I should tell him that I was unfair, and I am sorry."

Tiamak hid his smile. A king who apologized! No wonder he was tied to his two monarchs with bonds stronger than iron. "I will confess, it was not like you, Majesty."

"Well, find him for me, would you?"

"In truth, I think he is just outside the tent, Majesty."

"Oh, for the love of St. Tunath and St. Rhiap, Tiamak, would you please stop calling me 'Majesty' when we're alone? You said he was nearby?"

"I'll go see, Simon."

The minstrel was indeed near, cowering from the brisk Marris winds in a fold of tent wall beside the doorway. He followed Tiamak back into the pavilion like a man expecting a death sentence.

"There you are," the king said. "Come. Your name is Rinan, yes?"

The eyes, already wide, grew wider still. "Yes, Majesty."

"I was harsh to you, Rinan. Today . . . I am not a happy man today."

Tiamak thought that the harper, like everyone else in the royal court, knew only too well what day it was, but was wise enough to stay quiet while the king struggled to find words.

"In any case, I am sorry for it," the king said. "Come back to me tomorrow, and I will be in a better humor for songs. But have that old scoundrel Sangfugol teach you a few lays that at least approach the truth, if not actually wrestle with it."

"Yes, sire."

"Go on then. You have a fine voice. Remember that music is a noble charge, even a dangerous charge, because it can pierce a man's heart when a spear or arrow cannot."

As the young man hurried out of the pavilion, Simon looked up at his old friend. "I suppose now I must bring back all the others and make amends to them as well?"

"I see no reason why you should," Tiamak told him. "You have already given them all the hours since you broke your fast. I think it might be good for you to eat and rest."

"But I have to reply to King Hugh and his damned 'suggestions,' as he calls them." Simon tugged at his beard. "What is he about, Tiamak? You would think with all these nonsensical conditions, he would rather not have us come to Hernysadharc at all. Does he resent having to feed and house even this fairly small royal progress?"

"Oh, I'm sure that's not so. The Hernystiri are always finicky with their rituals." But secretly Tiamak did not like it either. It was one thing to insist on proper arrangements, another thing to keep the High King and High Queen waiting in a field for two days over issues of ceremony that should have been settled weeks ago. After all, the king of Hernystir would not have a throne at all were it not for the High Ward that Simon and Miriamele represented. Hernystir only had a king because Miri's grandfather, King John, had permitted it under his own overarching rule. Still, Tiamak thought, Hugh was a comparatively young king: perhaps this rudeness was nothing more than a new monarch's inexperience. "I am certain Sir Murtach, Count Eolair, and I will have everything set to rights soon," he said aloud.

"Well, I hope you're right, Tiamak. Tell them we agree to everything and to send us the be-damned invitation tomorrow morning. It's a sad errand that brings us this way in the first place, and today is a sad anniversary. It seems pointless to dicker about such things—how many banners, how high the thrones, the procession route . . ." He wagged his hand in disgust. "If Hugh wishes to make himself look important, let him. He can act like a child if he wants, but Miri and I don't need to."

"You may be doing the king of Hernystir a disservice," said Tiamak mildly, but in his heart of hearts he didn't think so. He truly didn't think so.

"Can we swim in it, Papa?"

The black river was fast and silent. "I don't think so, son."

"And what's on the other side?" the child asked.

"Nobody knows."

It was a mixture of Simon's dreams and memories, made partly from the time he had taken young John Josua down to Grenburn Town near the river to see the flooding. In the wake of the Storm King's defeat the winters had grown warmer, and in the years after the fall of the tower, spring thaws had swollen the rivers of Erkynland until they overflowed their banks, turning fields on both sides of the Gleniwent into a great plain of water, with islands of floating debris that had once been houses and barns. John Josua had been nearly five years of age when Simon took him to Grenburn, and full of questions. Not that he had ever stopped being full of questions.

"Don't cross the river, Papa," his dream-son told him.

"I won't." Simon didn't laugh, but in life he had, amused by the boy's solemn warning. "It's too wide, John Josua. I'm a grown man but I don't think I could swim so far." He pointed to the far side, a place where the fields were higher. It was farther than Simon could have shot an arrow.

"If I went across, would you come after me?" the child asked. "Or if I fell in?"

"Of course." He remembered saying it with such certainty. "I would jump in and pull you out. Of course I would!"

But something was distracting him, some dream noise that he knew he should ignore, but it was hard not to notice the hard-edged baying of hounds. All his life since the weird white Stormspike pack had chased him, Simon had found that the noise of howling dogs chilled his blood.

"Papa?" The boy sounded farther away than he had a moment before, but Simon had turned his back on the river to look out across fields that were darkening as the sun disappeared behind the clouds. Somewhere in the distance a shape moved across the ground, but it moved like a single thing—no hunting pack, but a single hunting *thing* . . .

"Papa?"

So faint! And the little prince was no longer holding his hand—how had that happened? Even though it was only a dream, though Simon half-knew he was in bed and sleeping, he felt a dreadful cold terror rush through him, as if the very blood was freezing in his brains. His son was no longer beside him.

He looked around wildly but at first saw nothing. In the distance the mournful, scraping noise of the hounds grew louder. Then he saw the little head bobbing on the dark river, the small hands lifted as if to greet some friend—a false friend, a lying friend—and his heart shuddered as though it would stop. He ran, he was running, he had been running forever but still he came no closer. The clouds thickened overhead and the sunlight all but vanished. He thought he could hear a terrible, thin cry and the sound of splashing, but although he threw himself toward the place he had last seen the child, he could get no closer.

He screamed, then, and leaped, as if he could cross all that uncrossable difference by the sheer strength of his need . . . of his regret.

"Simon!"

A cool hand was on his forehead, not so much soothing him as holding him back, prisoning him. For a moment he was so maddened with terror that he reached up to strike the obstacle out of his way, then he heard her gasp, surprised by his sudden movement, and he remembered where he was.

"M-Miri?"

"A bad dream, Simon. You're having a bad dream." When she felt his muscles unknot, she took her hand from his head. She also had an arm around his chest, which she loosed before letting herself back down beside him in the disordered bed. "Shall I call for someone to bring you something?"

He shook his head, but of course she couldn't see him. "No. I'll . . ."

"Was it the same dream as last time? The dragon?"

"No. It was about John Josua when he was little. Of course—I haven't been able to think of anything else for days."

Simon lay staring up into the darkness for a long time. He could tell by her breathing she had not gone back to sleep either. "I dreamed of him," he said at last. "He got away from me. I chased him but I couldn't reach him."

She still didn't speak, but she put a hand against his cheek and left it there.

"Seven years gone, Miri, seven years since that cursed fever took him, and still I can't stop."

She stirred. "Do you think it is any different for me? I miss him every moment!"

He could tell by her voice that she was angry, although he did not know exactly why. How could the priests say that death came as the great friend when instead it came like an army, taking what it wished and destroying peace even years after it had withdrawn? "I know, dear one. I know."

After a while, she said, "And think—we have the ninth of Marris every year from now until the end of time. It was such a happy day once. When he was born."

"It still should be, my dear wife. God takes everyone back, but our son gave us an heir before we lost him. He gave us a great deal."

"An heir." The edge in her voice was brittle. "All I want is *him*. All I want is John Josua. Instead we are lumbered with *her* for the rest of our lives."

"You said yourself that the Widow is a small price to pay for our granddaughter, not to mention our grandson and heir."

"I said that before Morgan became a young man."

"Hah!" Simon wasn't actually amused, but it was better than cursing. "Scarcely a man yet."

Miriamele took a careful breath before speaking. "Our grandson is seventeen years old. Much the same age that you were when we were first wed. Man enough to be taking his fill of the ladies. Man enough to spend his days drinking and dicing and doing whatever takes his fancy. You did not do the same at that age!"

"I was washing dishes, and peeling potatoes and onions, and sweeping the castle, my dear—but not by choice. And then I fought for Josua—but that was not really by choice, either."

"Still. With ne'er-do-well companions like the ones he has, how will Morgan grow? He will bend to their shape."

"He will grow out of this foolishness, Miri. He must." But Simon didn't entirely believe it. Their living grandson sometimes seemed as lost to him as the son who had been swept away into the black river of death.

After another silent time in the dark, she said, "And I miss our little one, too. I mean our granddaughter." Miriamele put her arm across her husband's belly, moving closer. He could feel the tightness in her muscles. "I wish we hadn't left her home. Do you think she's being good for Rhona?"

"Never." He actually laughed a little. "You worry too much, my love. You know we could not bring Lillia. It's still winter in Rimmersgard and the air will be full of ice and fever. We brought the grandchild who would benefit from being with us."

"Benefit. How could anyone who has already lost a parent benefit from watching a good old man die?"

"Prince Morgan needs to learn that he is not just himself. He is the hope of many people." Simon felt sleep pulling at him again, finally. "As are you and I, my wife." He meant it kindly, but he felt her stiffen again. "I must sleep. You, too. Don't lie there and fret, Miri. Come closer—put your head on my chest. There." Sometimes, especially when she was unhappy, he missed her badly, even though she was only a short distance away.

Just as she began to settle her head on his chest, she stiffened. "His grave!" she whispered. "We didn't . . ."

Simon stroked her hair. "We did. Or at least Pasevalles promised in his last letter that he would take flowers, and also that he would make certain Archbishop Gervis performs John Josua's *mansa*."

"Ah." He felt her stiff muscles loosen. "Pasevalles is a good man. We're lucky to have him."

"We are indeed. Now we should both sleep, Miri. It will be a busy day tomorrow."

"Why? Is Hugh finally going to let us in?"

"He'd better. I'm losing my patience."

"I never liked him. Not from the first."

"Yes, but you don't like many people at the first, dear one." He let his head roll sideways until it touched hers.

"That's not true. I used to." She pushed a little closer. The wind was rising again, making the tent ropes hum outside. "I had more love in me, I think. Sometimes now I fear I have used it all."

"Except for me and your grandchildren, yes?"

She waited an instant too long for Simon's liking. "Of course," she said. "Of course." But this anniversary had always been blighted since their son had died. Small wonder that she was bitter.

Somewhere during the wind's song, Simon fell asleep again.

2

The Finest Tent
on the Frostmarch

He had been following his father for a long time, it seemed, although he did not remember when or where they had begun. The sky had grown dark and the familiar tall shape was only a shadow in front of him now, sometimes barely visible as the path twisted through the deepening twilight. He wished he wasn't too old to hold his father's hand. Or was he?

He did not know how old he was.

"Papa, wait!" he cried.

His father said something, but Morgan couldn't understand him. Something seemed to be muffling his father's voice, doors or distance or simply distraction. He hurried after, out of breath, short legs aching, trying not to notice the sounds in the trees that seemed to follow him, the strange voices hooting as softly as the ghosts of doves. Where was this place? How had they come here? So many trees! Were they in the forest of Grandfather's stories, that dark, unknowable place full of odd sounds and watching eyes?

"Papa?" He raised his voice almost to a scream. "Where are you? Wait for me!"

The trees were everywhere and the moonlight was so faint that he could hardly see the path. As he hurried around each bend in pursuit of his father's ever-dwindling figure the roots seemed to writhe in the mud beneath his feet like moon-silvery snakes, grabbing at him and tripping him. Several times he stumbled and nearly fell, but forced himself on. The entire forest seemed to be twisting around him now, the trees spinning and drooping like exhausted dancers. He stopped to listen, but heard only the ghastly, breathless hoots from above.

"Papa! Where did you go? Come back!"

He thought he heard his father's measured voice float back to him from somewhere far ahead, but he could not tell if he was saying "I'm here!" or "I fear . . . !"

But fathers were never afraid. They stayed with you. They protected you. They weren't afraid themselves.

"Papa?"

The path was gone. He could feel the roots moving beneath his feet as the branches reached down to enfold him and smother the light.

"Papa? Don't leave me!"
He was alone—abandoned and crying. He was just another orphan, a stray.
"Papa!"
No answer. Never an answer. He fought to get free, but the trees still clung.
It was the same every time . . .

Morgan, Prince of Erkynland and heir to the High Throne of Prester John's empire, tumbled off his cot and onto the ground, fighting with the cloak that tangled him. Half lost in the dream-forest, he lay for long moments on the damp rugs, his heart thundering in his chest. At last he sat up, trying to make sense of where he was and what had happened. He was cold even with the blanket still clinging to his neck like a spurned lover, and something nearby was making a nasty, rasping noise. Morgan peered worriedly into the darkness, but after a moment realized the sound was only the snoring of his squire, Melkin.

Well, praise be to God that somebody can sleep.

Memory came slouching back. He was on the royal progress with his grandfather and grandmother. He and Melkin were in his tent in the middle of some field outside Hernysadharc, the capital, and it was cold because spring was still a fortnight away. Tonight there had been a meal and too much talk. Also too much wine, although now he was wishing he had drunk more of it—a great deal more, to chase the chill from his bones, the deep, feverish body-cold of another foul dream.

His eyes were wet, he realized, his cheeks damp. He'd been crying in his sleep.

Papa. I couldn't catch up to him . . . There seemed to be a hole where his heart should be, as though the wind were blowing right through him. Angry, he wiped his face with his sleeve.

Weeping like a child. Idiot! Coward! What if someone saw me?

Wine was what he needed. Morgan knew from experience that a large cup of sour, reliable red would warm the cold hole in his vitals and push the dream out of his thoughts. But he had no wine. He had drunk all that had been offered while he dined with the king and queen, but it hadn't been enough to give him a dreamless night.

For a moment he considered simply trying to go back to sleep. The wind was blowing chill outside, and the camp was full of people who would gladly scurry to his grandparents with the tale if they saw him out staggering around at this hour of the night. But the memory of that endless forest track, of the horror of never being able to catch up to his father, was too much.

Wine. Yes, it would be good to hear the foolish arguments of his friends, an ordinary, reassuring thing. And it would be even better to be drunk again, drunk enough this time that he would not hear the voices in the forest, would not feel the chill of being left behind, perhaps would not even dream.

Morgan dragged himself to his feet and pushed his way out of the tent in search of accommodating oblivion. He had a good idea of where to look.

No royal proclamation or official announcement of any kind designated the tent shared by the Nabbanai knights Sir Astrian and Sir Olveris as the home of the makeshift tavern. The presence of seasoned drinker Sir Porto and a reasonably constant supply of wine was enough.

The sprawling royal camp was dark, but a pair of lanterns made the tent seem nearly festive. Old Sir Porto stared down into his cup and nodded. "Bless us when we are weak, O Lord," he said in his most doleful tones. "And save some blessings, if You please, because soon we will be weak again." He took a long swallow, then wiped his damp mouth and scruffy white beard with the back of his hand. "That is the last," he said. "God be kind, what I wouldn't give for a little of that red stuff from Onestris they keep back at the *Maid*. A man's vintage, that is. This . . . this grape water is scarcely old enough to know of the existence of sin."

"One does not need to know about sin to enjoy it," said Sir Astrian.

"Please, my lord," said the young woman on Astrian's lap. She was struggling hard to stand, but having no success. "I will be punished if I don't get back to my work! Let me go."

Astrian did not loosen his grip, and kept her on his knee with small adjustments of balance. "What?" he demanded. "Would you return to the shocking boredom of the ostler's wagons?" He reached up and pulled at the girl's bodice until her bosom threatened to overspill.

"My lord!" She snatched to hold up the fabric, and his hands, unchecked, strayed elsewhere.

The tent flap jiggled but did not open. Something good-sized was caught in it, and the poles of the tent swayed as though in a gale.

"The heir to all the lands of Osten Ard appears to be tangled," said Sir Astrian. "Somebody set him free and be rewarded with a sizeable estate."

"I will give you a sizeable boot in your arse," said the voice whose owner was writhing in the flap like a butterfly trying to escape its cocoon. "As soon as I find you."

"Someone go to our noble prince's aid—make haste!" cried Astrian. "I would myself, but at the moment I am engaged in fierce battle." He finally managed to pull down hard enough to overcome the young woman's resistance and her bare breasts sprang into view. Instead of surrendering and trying to cover herself, though, the girl redoubled her efforts to escape, cursing and flailing.

"*The bubs, the bubs!*" sang Sir Astrian. "*The bubs, the bubs, in all Nabban did ring! On the day they hanged our Redeemer, though no hands did pull the cord, The bubs in every tower tolled, to prove Aedon our lord!*"

With help from dour, black-haired Sir Olveris, Prince Morgan finally emerged from the tent flap. Morgan's hair, a shade too brown for golden, clung in strands across his face, damp with melting snowflakes. His brows, a shade darker and thicker than his hair, rose in slow, slightly distracted dismay as he saw the serving girl fighting to free herself. "God's Eyes, Astrian, what are you doing? Let the poor girl go. And someone pour me a cup of something strong." He looked around. "What? No succor for your lord? I call you traitors."

"We have finished the last, Highness," said Porto, guiltily wiping his upper lip. "The place is as dry as the dunes of Nascadu."

"God curse it!" Morgan seemed genuinely upset. "Nothing to drown a night of foul dreams? Ah, well—distract me, then, Astrian. You owe me another game and I am ready to take my money back. And this time we are not using your dice, you cunning near-dwarf."

"Cruel words," said Astrian, grinning. The ostler's maid was still trying to get off his lap and looked ready to weep. "I am not the tallest man in this kingdom, true, but I am not so low as you make me. My head reaches Olveris's neck, and since there is nothing of much use above that point, he and I are as good as even."

"Sweet Aedon!" Morgan lowered himself carefully onto a wooden stool, scowling ferociously. "Are you still mauling her? I said let the girl go, Astrian! If she doesn't want to be here, let her be on her way." He kicked at Astrian's leg, then folded away his frown to show the young woman a smile made slightly less courtly by the extreme redness of his face. "He begs your pardon, lass."

"Of course I do, my prince." Astrian released his prey just as she was straining away from him, so that she would have fallen to the ground if Olveris had not caught her and held her up until she gained her balance. The tall knight said nothing, as was his wont, but rolled his eyes at Astrian as he returned to his own seat atop a wooden chest.

"My apologies for Sir Astrian," Morgan said to the girl. "He is a rude fellow. And what is your name, my dear?"

She was as red-faced with exertion as the prince was with drink and her eyes were wide as a frightened horse's, but when she had pushed herself back into her bodice she did her best to curtsey to Morgan. "Thank you, your Highness. I am Goda, and I only came here to tell these . . . men that Lord Jeremias said they were to have no more wine. As it is, he said, they have already drunk much of what was meant for the return journey." Despite the angry force of her words she was near tears.

"It is a good thing that there will be mead in Hernysadharc, then." Morgan waved permission for her to go. She lifted her skirts and almost ran from the tent.

"If they ever let us into the city." Porto's voice was doleful as a funeral bell. "Soon, we will die of thirst here in this field."

"I must say, Highness," Astrian said, "*you* look as though you've already found a bit of something to ease this sad journey. Did you bring it back to share with your brothers of the road?"

"Share?" Morgan shook his head. "I had to spend the longest evening of my life at the royal table with my grandmother and grandfather, having my sins . . .

my sins and yours, that is . . . listed for me in exis . . . excu . . . exquisite detail. Then I tried to sleep, and . . ." He scowled and waved the idea away with his hand. "It matters not. I deserved every drop I could guzzle, and it was still nowhere near enough." He sighed. "Still, if there's nothing left to drink, we might as well gamble." With the young woman now long gone, Morgan let himself slump, revealing what he truly was—a very young man who had drunk too much.

"So you bring us nothing, Highness?" asked Porto.

"I swallowed everything I could reach at my grandparents' table. But it wasn't enough. No, they all just kept *talking*. And it was about nothing—the bloody Hernystiri king, and the royal blacksmith's need for scrap to turn into horse nails, and the complaints of the local Hernystiri farmers that their lands are being pillaged by the royal progress. And after putting up with that all evening, I am beginning to be sober again. I do not favor sobriety." He looked to Astrian. "By the way, speaking of pillagers, I cannot help noticing a haunch of something on the spit over your fire. It looks rather like the remains of a fat farm pig."

"No, no, a free wild boar of the hills, Highness," Astrian said. "Isn't that right, Porto? He led us a fierce chase."

Porto looked more than a bit shamefaced. "Oh, aye, he did."

"All over his pen, I have no doubt." Morgan frowned. "God save us, the boredom!" But the prince looked more haunted than bored. "Oh, and there was a messenger arrived from Elvritshalla right in the middle of it all. The Rimmersmen beg us to make good speed after we leave Hernystir. It seems the duke is not dead yet."

"But those are excellent tidings!" said Porto, sitting a little straighter. "Old Isgrimnur still lives? Excellent news."

"Yes. Huzzah, I suppose." Morgan gave Astrian a hard look. "Why are we not dicing, fellow? Why is my money still in your pocket?"

"My lord," said Porto, "I do not mean to scold, but Duke Isgrimnur has been one of your grandparents' greatest allies. I fought with him for the Hayholt more than thirty years ago, and again at the cursed Nakkiga Gate."

"You still call it 'fighting'?" Astrian smirked. "I believe the name for what you did was 'hiding'."

Porto scowled. "My dignity does not allow me to respond to such wretched untruths. Were you there, sir? No. You were a mere imp of a child then, vexing your nursemaid, while I was risking my life against the Norns."

Astrian's loud laugh was his only reply.

Porto struggled to his feet, scraping his head against the top of the tent. It was said that of all the knights who had ever fought to uphold the High Ward, only the great Camaris had been taller than Porto. However, that was where the comparison ceased. "What is this, then—laughter?" the old soldier demanded. "Shall I call you Sir Mockery? What is this?" He pulled a pendant out of his collar, a smooth female shape carved in rounded blue crystal. "Did I not take this from one of the fairies after I slew him? This is Norn stuff, the true article. Go ahead, mock—you have no such prize."

Sir Olveris said, "I doubt not that you took it from one who was face-down and dying, old man. And then finished him off with your sword in his back."

Prince Morgan jumped in surprise. "By the bloody Tree, Olveris, you are silent so long, then you speak from the shadows without warning. I thought for a moment we were haunted!"

The black-haired man did not reply. He had exhausted himself with such a long speech.

"Enough with tormenting Porto," the prince said. "Come now, Astrian, is it to be Caster's Call or Hyrka? I will not let this day end without some good result, and beggaring you would make me very happy. I have not had a good day with the bones since we crossed the border into Hernystir."

"There are no borders out here," said Astrian as he gave the prince's dice a good, long look, weighing them on his palm and then letting his fingers probe the pips for boar's bristles or painted lead. "These will do," he said, handing them back.

"What do you mean by that nonsense?" the prince asked. "No borders?" He rolled his first number. "A ten, sir—two hands. You may bid as you explain your remark."

"It is only this, Highness," said Astrian. "We crossed into Hernystir days ago. Rimmersgard is still twenty leagues away. Who do you suppose lives in Ballydun, the walled city just to the east?"

Morgan shrugged, watching Astrian make his point with a six and a four. Everything the knight did had a compact grace to it, most definitely including his use of a sword, where his speed and nimbleness more than made up for his small stature. He was frequently named—and not least by himself—one of the best swordsmen in any land. "Hernystirmen, I suppose," Morgan said. "Knights, nobles, peasants, all the regular sorts of people."

"Rimmersmen, your Highness. They settled there after some war hundreds of years ago and never moved again. Most of the folk there are of northern blood." Now it was Astrian's turn, and he immediately rolled stones— "ballocks" as soldiers termed it, a pair of ones. He swept the small pot from the chest serving as a table. "I *do* like your dice, my prince. Now, did you notice that village we passed this morning? Not that you looked as if you were seeing much."

"My head was pounding and ringing like your damn Nabbanai bells. Yes, I suppose I saw it. Some children and others came out to wave at us, yes?"

"Exactly. And do you know what language they speak there?"

"No, by the eternal Aedon, how would I know that?"

"They speak Hernystiri, of course—we are in Hernystir, after all." Astrian grinned. "But *their* blood is that of Erkynland, just like yours, and there are many Erkynlandish words in their speech. Do you see?"

"Do I see what?" Morgan had lost the second throw as well, and his improved mood was beginning to fail again. "That nobody here seems to know what language they should speak? 'S'bloody Tree, man, how is that my concern?"

"Because it shows that borders are nonsense, at least most of the time. There are a few—such as the boundaries between Northern Rimmersgard and the Nornfells—that mean something real, because they are fiercely defended on both sides. But here on the Frostmarch all are mixed up together—Hernystiri, Rimmersmen, Erkynlanders. The people here speak a jumble of different tongues. They remember feuds that go back hundreds of years, but they speak in a way that would make their ancestors see blood before their eyes."

"Do not jest about the Nornfells," said Sir Porto. "You were not there at Nakkiga. You did not see those . . . things, or hear them singing with voices like sweet children, even as they killed and died."

"I do not jest at all," said Astrian. "God grant the White Foxes stay in the north where they belong. But the rest of the peoples of Osten Ard are mixing like the wax of different colored candles, melted and swirled together. Soon there will be no difference between a Rimmersman and a Hernystirman, or between a Nabbanai lord and a Thrithings barbarian. That is the curse of peace."

"Peace is no curse," said old Porto.

"I would love to do some deeds worthy of a prince," said Morgan sadly as he watched another pile of coins disappear into Astrian's purse. "Not a large war, perhaps but it has been more than a score of years since we fought the Thrithings-men and I see no threat to hope for. It is a bad time to be young."

"Porto would say it is never a bad time to be young," said Olveris from the back of the tent. "He would also say it is never a good time to be old."

"I can speak for myself, sir," said the tall knight. "I am not so ancient, nor so drunk, that I must be interpreted like a Naraxi island-man." His face drooped a little. "Nevertheless, Olveris is not wrong."

"Will there ever be another war?" Morgan asked.

"Oh, I rather think so," said Astrian. "Men do not manage well with too much peace. Someone will find a quarrel."

"I can only pray that you're right," said Morgan. "Hah! Look at those beauties—a pair of ale wagons! *This* pot is mine." He swept the coins toward him, but one slid off the chest and onto the dark ground. He got down on his knees to search for it.

"To be honest, Highness, I grow a little bored with dicing," said Astrian.

"Of course you do, now that I am beginning to win my money back!" Morgan straightened up in triumph, the wayward coin in his fist. "What else have we to do, in any case? It must be rising midnight, and you told me the wine is all gone."

"Perhaps," said Astrian.

"Perhaps?" Morgan grimaced. "Anything but 'yes' has an ugly sound, for I could happily drink more."

Sir Porto stirred. "I marvel at your stomach, young master. It must be from your mother's side. Your late father, I recall, never drank anything stronger than the weakest, most watered wine . . ." His eyes widened in distress. "Oh, Highness, forgive me. I forgot what day it is."

"Fool," said Olveris.

Morgan shook his head as though in anger, but said, "Don't chide old Porto. What should I care? The dead are dead—it does no good to think on them too much."

Porto still looked shaken, but now a little surprised as well. "Ah, but I am sure he watches you from Heaven, Prince Morgan. If it were me . . ." He fell silent, caught up by a sudden thought of his own.

"Only you could so deftly crush a conversation, ancient fool," Astrian told him. "We speak of wine, then you chime in with death *and* Heaven, the two chief foes of a man's drinking pleasure."

Morgan shook his head again. "I said leave him be, both of you. If my father is watching over me, it would be the first time. No, truly—I will tell you a story. Once when I was but young, I went to his chambers to tell him I had saddled and rode my horse all by myself. When he came to the door, he said I must tell my master he was not to be disturbed."

"I do not understand," said Porto, frowning.

"He thought I was some page boy sent by Count Eolair." Morgan smiled at the joke but did not seem to find it truly funny.

"Perhaps he had the sun in his eyes," Porto said. "I am all but blind when the sun shines in my face . . ."

"It wasn't the first time he did not know his own son, nor the last." Morgan looked down for a moment, then turned to Astrian. "We were talking about wine. Why? Do we have some left after all?"

Sir Astrian smiled. "As it happens, a few local girls we met promised they would meet us tonight in the birch grove at the edge of the field. I told them if they brought wine they might even meet the true prince of all Osten Ard."

For a moment Morgan brightened, but then an unhappy shadow passed over his face. "I can't do it, Astrian. My grandparents want to be ready to ride into Hernysadharc tomorrow morning as soon as the invitation is received. They told me to be in my tent by the end of the second watch."

"They want you rested, am I not right? So you may present yourself to the Hernystiri as befits a prince?"

"I suppose."

"Then what do you think would be better, to go sourly and soberly to bed after I have finished taking more money from you, or to have an enjoyable time with some local wenches and to wet your dry throat enough to allow you a happy, peaceful sleep?"

Morgan laughed despite himself. "By God, you could argue the Ransomer down off the Holy Tree, Astrian. Well, perhaps I will go along for a little while, then. But you must promise to help me get back to the royal tents. My grandfather is already furious with me." He made a face. "*He* had adventures. *He* slew dragons. But what does he expect of me? Endless, horrid ceremonies. Sitting still all day while fools drone on about justice and taxes and hides of land, like the buzzing of bees on a hot day. It is enough to send anyone to sleep, whether they have drunk any wine or not." He stood, brushing the worst of the dry grass and dirt from his clothes, although it was hard to tell by lamplight whether he had improved his appearance much. The sleeve of his jerkin had a woeful tatter, and the knees of his hose were both now damp and darkened with mud. "Olveris, Porto, are you coming?"

Olveris appeared suddenly from the shadows like something lifted from a box. Porto only shook his head. "I am too old for this foolishness, night after night," he said. "I will remain here and think about my soul."

"That is the part of you least worth exercising, old man." Astrian rose and stretched. "And now, Highness, if you'll follow me, I believe some ladies await us."

"It amazes me how such a short fellow cuts such a figure with the women," the prince said, looking on his friend with more than a little pride.

"Huh," said Olveris, looking down at the prince, who was in truth less than a handspan taller than Sir Astrian. "I see *two* short fellows."

"Silence, beanpole," said Morgan.

"There is no need for amazement, Highness." Astrian was grinning. "As with swordplay, the weapon must only be well-employed and long enough to reach its target." He made a mocking bow and swaggered out, pointedly leaving Prince Morgan and Sir Olveris to follow him.

After they had gone, Porto rose with a series of pained grunts and began to look around in case someone had left something to drink. After long moments of fruitless search, he sighed, then followed his comrades out between the tents and toward the distant birch grove.

The prince knew he had waved to the guards standing watch. That much was certain. Everything had been fine up until then. But now he seemed caught like a fish in a net, and it had happened quite by surprise.

He was having a particularly difficult time with tent flaps today—that much, at least, was beyond argument.

Morgan pawed at the heavy cloth, turning, trying to find the edge. No luck. He took another step forward, but now there seemed to be fabric on both sides of him. What madman would make a tent with two flaps? And when had they substituted it for the perfectly good tent he'd already had? The prince cursed and pawed again, then picked up as much of the flap as he could reach and lifted it, staggering forward with the weight of the heavy fabric on his head and shoulders. The stars appeared above him.

For just a brief moment he wondered why there were stars inside his tent, but then realized that he had somehow worked his way back outside. He had an overwhelming need to piss, so he undid his breeks and sent forth a mighty stream. He watched it feather in the stiff breeze until it dwindled and died. He decided he should try the flap again.

Ah, yes. I have been drinking. It explained a great deal.

This time he solved the puzzle after only a short interval of grunting and fumbling, and made it two steps into the tent before he smashed his shin against some obstacle. The pain was so fierce that he was still hopping on one foot swearing like a Meremund riverman when somebody flipped open a hooded lantern, bathing the interior of the tent in light.

"Where have you been?" demanded his grandmother, the queen. Morgan almost fell down before remembering two feet on the ground made for better balance. The shock of the sudden light and Queen Miriamele's voice had not yet passed when she added, "And what are you thinking, child? Fasten your clothes, please."

He scrabbled to pull his breeks closed. Drink had made his fingers as clumsy as raw sausages. "I . . . Majesty, I . . ."

"Oh, for the love of all that is good, sit down before you trip on something else and kill yourself."

He sank onto the chest that had so recently and cruelly attacked him. His shin still throbbed. "Am I . . . is this . . . I thought . . ."

"Yes, you young fool, this is your tent. I was waiting for you. God, you are stinking drunk. And stinking is the word."

He tried to smile, but it didn't feel like he was getting it right. "Not my fault. Astr'n. Astr'n challenged Baron Colfer's men to contest." For a long time Morgan had thought that the man he was matching cup for cup was Baron Colfer himself. He had been surprised that the baron was so young and so muscular, and that he had the Holy Tree tattooed on his forehead. It hadn't been until Morgan had fallen to his knees vomiting and the baron's men had been cheering loudly for someone called "Ox" that he had realized the baron himself was not present.

He wouldn't have felt so bad at this moment if he had managed to win. That would have made the scolding worthwhile.

"You have no idea how lucky you are that it was me waiting for you, not your grandfather. He already thinks you are becoming an embarrassment."

" 'M not an em . . . embearsamint. 'M a prince."

His grandmother rolled her eyes to the heavens. "Oh, spare me. Is this what a prince does to honor the day of his father's birth? Drinks until the morning hours? Stumbles back in, half-dressed, smelling of vomit and cheap sachet? Could you not at least spend your time with women who can afford a decent pomander? You stink like the end of Market Day."

Yes, there had been a few girls. He remembered that now. He and Astrian had been walking them back to their village, for their protection—Olveris was off protecting an older woman he'd met—but then things had become a bit confusing, as the walk turned into a game of hide and seek. Then there had been wet grass. Somebody had been named "Sofra," he thought—a very friendly someone. After that he had been back in camp, trying to get past the demon tent-flap. Waiting for his lazy squire to wake up and help him . . . which reminded him. "Where's Melkin?"

"If you mean your squire, I sent him out a short while ago to get me a blanket—a clean blanket. I didn't expect to be waiting so long, and I was getting cold."

She sounded very, very unhappy. "Please, Majesty. Gra'mother. I know you're angry, but . . . but I can explain."

Queen Miriamele rose. "There is nothing to explain, Morgan. There is nothing interesting or unusual about anything you have been doing, except for the fact that you are heir to the High Throne." She moved to the tent flap. "We will only be a day or two in Hernysadharc—where the people are already whispering about you and your friends, I am told—then we must travel to Elvritshalla in Rimmersgard to say farewell to one of the finest men your grandfather and I have ever known. You will not simply be a visitor there, you will be all they will see and remember for years of the man who will one day lead them—the man to whom even the king of Hernystir and the duke of Rimmersgard must kneel. Will you make yourself an ugly joke as you have done in Erchester and all during this journey? Will you earn the people's loyalty or their scorn?" She flipped shut the hood on the lantern, leaving only her voice to share the darkened tent with him. "We leave early tomorrow. Isgrimnur still lives, but for how long no one knows. You will be on your horse at first light. If you are timely and presentable, I will not tell your grandfather about this. Remember, first light."

Morgan groaned despite himself. "Too early! Why so early?" He tried to remember what Astrian had said, because it had made sense at the time. "I only drank wine so I could sleep better and not . . . I mean, so I could be a good prince. A better prince."

There was a long silence. The queen's voice was cold as a blade. "Your grandfather and I are tired of this foolishness, Morgan. Very, very tired."

The queen seemed to have no trouble with the flap, passing through and out into the night without a sound. Morgan sat on the chest in darkness and wondered why things were always so much easier for everyone else.

3

Conversation with
a Corpse-Giant

The waxing moon was nearly full, but curtained by thick clouds, as were the stars. It was not hard for Jarnulf to imagine that he was floating in the high darkness where only God lived, like a confessor-priest in his blind box listening all day long to the sins of mankind.

But God, he thought, did not have that corpse-smell in His nostrils every moment. Or did He? *For if my Lord doesn't like the scent of death,* Jarnulf wondered, *why does He make so many dead men?*

Jarnulf looked to the corpse stretched at the side of the tree-burial platform nearest the trunk. It was an old woman, or had been, her hands gnarled like tree roots by years of hard work, her body covered only by a thin blanket, as though for a summer night's sleep instead of eternity. Her jaw was bound shut, and snow had pooled in the sockets of her eyes, giving her a look of infinite, blind blankness. Here in the far north of Rimmersgard they might worship at the altar of the new God and His son, Usires Aedon, but they honored the old gods and old ways as well: the corpse wore thick birch bark shoes, which showed she had been dressed not for a triumphal appearance in Usires the Ransomer's heavenly court, but for the long walk through the cold, silent Land of the Dead.

It seemed barbaric to leave a body to scavengers and the elements, but the Rimmersfolk who lived beside this ancient forest considered it as natural as the southerners setting their dead in little houses of stone or burying them in holes. But it was not the local customs that interested Jarnulf, or even what waited for the dead woman's soul in the afterlife, but the scavengers who would come to the corpse—one sort in particular.

The wind strengthened and set clouds flowing through the black sky, the treetop swaying. The platform on which Jarnulf sat, thirty cubits above the icy ground, rocked like a small boat on rough seas. He pulled his cloak tighter and waited.

*   *   *

He heard it before he could see anything, a swish of branches out of time with the rise and fall of the wind's noises. The scent came to him a few moments later, and although the corpse lying at the far end of the platform had an odor of its own, it seemed almost healthy to Jarnulf, matched against this new stink. He was almost grateful when the wind changed direction, although for a moment it left him with no way of judging the approach of the thing he had been waiting for since the dark northern afternoon had ended.

Now he saw it, or at least part of it—a gleam of long, pale limbs in the nearby treetops. As he had hoped, it was a corpse-giant, a Hunë too small or too old to hunt successfully and thus reduced to preying on carcasses, both animal and human. The sinking moon still spread enough light to show the creature's long legs flexing and extending as it clambered toward him through the treetops like a huge, white spider. Jarnulf took a slow, deep breath and wondered again whether he would regret leaving his bow and quiver down below, but carrying them would have made the climb more difficult, and even several arrows would not kill a giant quickly enough to be much use on such a dangerously constrained battlefield—especially when his task was not to kill the creature, but to get answers from it.

He was frightened, of course—anyone who was not a madman would be—so he said the Monk's Night Prayer, which had been one of Father's favorites.

> *Aedon to my right hand, Aedon to my left*
> *Aedon before me, Aedon behind me*
> *Aedon in the wind and rain that fall upon me*
> *Aedon in the sun and moon that light my way*
> *Aedon in every eye that beholds me and every ear that hears me*
> *Aedon in every mouth that speaks of me, in every heart that loves me*
> *Ransomer, go with me where I travel*
> *Ransomer, lead me where I should go*
> *Ransomer, give me the blessing of Your presence*
> *As I give my life to You.*

As Jarnulf finished his silent recitation, the pale monstrosity vanished from the nearest tree beneath the edge of the platform; a moment later he felt the entire wooden floor dip beneath him as the creature pulled itself up from below. First its hands appeared, knob-knuckled and black-clawed, each big as a serving platter, then the head, a white lump that rose until light glinted from the twin moons of its eyes. For all its fearsomeness, Jarnulf thought the monster looked like something put together hurriedly, its elbows and knees and hairy limbs sticking out at strange angles. It moved cautiously as it pulled itself up onto the platform, the timbers barely creaking beneath its great weight. Its foxfire eyes never left the dead woman at the far end of the wooden stand.

Jarnulf had seen many giants, had even fought a few and survived, but the superstitious horror never entirely went away. The beast's shaggy, powerful limbs were far longer than his own, but it was old and smaller than most of its kind. In fact, only the giant's legs and arms were full-sized: its shrunken body and head seemed to dangle between them, like those of some hairy crab or long-legged insect. The *Njar-Hunë*'s fur was patchy, too: even by moonlight Jarnulf could see that its once snowy pelt was mottled with age.

But though the beast might be old, he reminded himself, it was still easily capable of killing even a strong man. If those grotesque, clawed hands got a grip on him they would tear him apart in an instant.

The giant was making its way across the platform toward the corpse when Jarnulf spoke, suddenly and loudly: *"What do you think you are doing, night-walker? By what right do you disturb the dead?"*

The monster flinched in alarm and Jarnulf saw its leg muscles bunch in preparation for sudden movement, either battle or escape. "Do not move, corpse-eater," he warned in the Hikeda'ya tongue, wondering if it could understand him, let alone reply. "I am behind you. Move too quickly for my liking and you will have my spear through your heart. But know this: if I wanted you dead, Godless creature, you would be dead already. All I want is talk."

"You . . . want . . . talk?" The giant's voice was nothing manlike, more like the rasping of a popinjay from the southern islands, but so deep that Jarnulf could feel it in his ribs and belly. Clearly, though, the stories had been true: some of the older Hunën could indeed use and understand words, which meant that the terrible risk he was taking had not been completely in vain.

"Yes. Turn around, monster. Face me." Jarnulf couched the butt of his spear between two of the bound logs that formed the platform, then balanced it so the leaf-shaped spearhead pointed toward the giant's heart like a lodestone. "I know you are thinking you might swing down and escape before I can hurt you badly. But if you do, you will never hear my bargain, and you will also likely not eat tonight. Are you by any chance hungry?"

The thing crouched in a jutting tangle of its own arms and legs like some horribly malformed beggar and stared at Jarnulf with eyes bright and baleful. The giant's face was cracked and seamed like old leather, its skin much darker than its fur. The monster was indeed old—that was obvious in its every stiff movement, and in the pendulous swing of its belly—but the narrowed eyes and mostly unbroken fangs warned that it was still dangerous. "Hungry . . . ?" it growled.

Jarnulf gestured at the corpse. "Answer my questions, then you can have your meal."

The thing looked at him with squinting mistrust. "Not . . . your . . . ?"

"This? No, this old woman is not my grandmother or my great-grandmother. I do not even know her name, but I saw her people carry her up here, and I heard them talking. I know that you and your kind have been raiding tree burials all over this part of Rimmersgard, although your own lands are leagues away in the north. The question is . . . why?"

The giant stared fixedly at the spear point where it stood a few yards from its hairy chest. "I tell what you want, then you kill. Not talk that way. No spear."

Jarnulf slowly lowered the spear to the platform, setting it down well out of even the giant's long reach, but kept his hand close to it. "There. Speak, devil-spawn. I'm waiting for you to tell me *why*."

"Why *what*, man?" it growled.

"Why your kind are suddenly roaming in Rimmersgard again, and so far south—lands you were scourged from generations ago? What calamity has driven your evil breed down out of the Nornfells?"

The corpse-giant watched Jarnulf as carefully as it had watched the spear-point, its breath rasping in and out. "What . . . is . . . 'calamity'?" the giant asked at last.

"Bad times. Tell me, why are you here? Why have your kind begun to hunt again in the lands of men? And why are the oldest and sickliest Hunën—like *you*—stealing the mortal dead for your meals? I want to know the answer. Do you understand me?"

"Understand, yes." The thing nodded, a grotesquely alien gesture from such a beast, and screwed up its face into a puzzle of lines. "Speak your words, me—yes." But the creature was hard to understand, its speech made beastlike by those crooked teeth, that inhuman mouth. "Why here? *Hungry.*" The giant let its gray tongue out and dragged it along the cracked lips, reminding Jarnulf that it would just as happily eat him as the nameless old woman whose open-air tomb this was. Even if it answered his questions, could he really allow this in-human creature to defile an Aedonite woman's body afterwards? Would that not be a crime against Heaven almost as grave as the giant's?

My Lord God, he prayed, *grant me wisdom when the time comes.* " 'Hungry' is not answer enough, giant. Why are your kind coming all the way to Rimmers-gard to feed? What is happening back in the north?"

At last, as if it had come to a decision, the beast's mouth stretched in what almost seemed a smile, a baring of teeth that looked more warning than wel-come. "Yes, we talk. *I* talk. But first say names. Me—" it thumped its chest with a massive hand—"Bur Yok Kar. Now you. Say."

"I do not need to tell you my name, creature. If you wish to take my bar-gain, then give me what I ask. If not, well, our trading will end a different way." He let his hand fall to the shaft of the spear where it lay beside him. The giant's gleaming eyes flicked to the weapon, then back to his face again.

"You ask why *Hojun*—why giants—come here," the creature said. "For food. Many mouths hungry now in north, in mountains. Too many mouths."

"What do you mean, too many mouths?"

"*Higdaja*—you call Norns. Too many. North is awake. Hunters are . . . everywhere."

"The *Norns* are hunting your kind? Why?"

"For fight."

Jarnulf sat back on his heels, trying to understand. "That makes little sense. Why would the Hikeda'ya want to fight with your kind? You giants have always done their bidding."

The thing swung its head from side to side. The face was inhuman but something burned in the eyes, a greater intelligence than he had first guessed. It reminded Jarnulf of an ape he had once seen, the prize of a Naarved merchant who kept it in a cage in the cold courtyard of his house. The beast's eyes had been as human as any man's, and to see it slumped in the corner of its too-small prison had been to feel a kind of despair. *Not everything that thinks is a man*, Jarnulf had realized then, and he thought it again now.

"Not fight with," the giant rasped. "They want us fight *for*. Again."

It took a moment to find the creature's meaning. "Fight for the Norns? Fight against who?"

"Men. We will fight men." It showed its teeth. "*Your* kind."

It was not possible. It could not be true. "What are you talking about? The Hikeda'ya do not have the strength to fight mortals again. They lost almost everything in the Storm King's War, and there are scarcely any of them left. All that is over."

"Nothing over. Never over." The giant wasn't looking at him, though, but was staring raptly at the body of the old woman. Thinking again about supper.

"I don't believe you," said Jarnulf.

Bur Yok Kar turned toward him, and he thought he could see something almost like amusement in the ugly, leathery face. The idea of where he was, what he was doing, and how mad it was, suddenly struck Jarnulf and set his heart racing. "Believe, not believe, not matter," the corpse-giant told him. "All of north world wakes up. They are everywhere, the *Higdaja*, the white ones. They are all awake again, and hungry for war. Because *she* is awake."

"She?"

"Queen with the silver face. Awake again."

"No. The queen of the Norns? No, that cannot be." For a moment Jarnulf felt as though God Himself had leaned down from the heavens and slapped him. In an instant, everything that Father had taught him—all his long-held certainties—were flung into confusion. "You are lying to me, animal." He was desperate to believe it was so. "Everyone knows the queen of the Norns has been in a deathly sleep since the Storm King fell. Thirty years and more! She will never awaken again."

The giant slowly rose from its crouch, a new light in its eyes. "Bur Yok Kar not lie." The beast had recognized Jarnulf's momentary loss of attention, and even as he realized it himself, the giant took a step toward him. Although half the length of the treetop platform still separated them, the creature set one of its huge, knobbed feet on the head of his spear, pinning it flat against the tethered logs. "Ask again. What name *you*, little man?"

Angry and more than a little alarmed at his own miscalculation, Jarnulf rose and took a slow step backward, closer to the edge of the platform. He shifted his balance to his back foot. "Name? I have many. Some call me the White Hand."

"White Hand?" The giant took another shuffling step toward him, still keeping the spear pinned. "No! In North we hear of White Hand. Big warrior, great killer—not skinny like you." The creature made a huffing noise, a kind of grunt; Jarnulf thought it might be a laugh. "See! You put spear down. Hunter, warrior, never put spear down." The giant was near enough now that he could smell the stench of the rotting human flesh in its nails and teeth, as well as the odor of the beast itself, a sour tang so fierce it cut through even the stiff, cold wind. "Ate young ones like you before." The corpse-giant was grinning now, its eyes mere slits as it contemplated the pleasure of a live meal. "Soft. Meat come off bones easy."

"I am finished with you, Godless one. I have learned what I needed to know." But in truth Jarnulf now wanted only to escape, to go somewhere and try to make sense of what the creature had told him. The Norn Queen awake? The Norns preparing for war? Such things simply could not be.

"*You* finish? With *me*?" The huff of amusement again, followed by the carrion stench. Even as the giant leaned toward him its head still loomed high above Jarnulf's, and he was now within reach of those long, long arms as well. This monster might be old, might have to scavenge its meals from burial platforms, but it still weighed perhaps three times what he did and had him trapped in a high, small place. Jarnulf took one last step back, feeling with his heel for the edge of the platform. Beyond that was only a long drop through sharp branches to the stony ground.

Not even enough snow to break my fall, he thought. *Lord, O Lord, make my arm strong and my heart steadfast in Your name and the name of Your son, Usires the Aedon.* As if reminded of the cold, he adjusted his heavy cloak. The giant paid no attention to this small, insignificant movement; instead, the great, leering head bent even closer until it was level with his own. Jarnulf had nowhere to retreat and the corpse-giant knew it. It reached out a massive hand and laid it against the side of Jarnulf's face in a grotesque parody of tenderness. The fingers curled, each as wide as the shaft of the spear that was now so far out of his reach, but Jarnulf ducked beneath its grasp before it caught at his hair and twisted his head off. Again they stood face to face, man and giant.

"White Hand, you say." With Jarnulf's spear pinned to the platform beneath its foot, the beast was in no hurry. "Why they call you that, little Rimmersman?"

"You will not understand—not for a little while, yet. And I was not born in Rimmersgard at all, but in Nakkiga itself."

The cracked lips curled. "You not Higdaja, you just man. You think Bur Yok Kar stupid?"

"Your problem is not that you are stupid," Jarnulf said. "Your problem is that you are already dead." Jarnulf looked down. A moment later the giant looked down too.

Beyond the hilt in Jarnulf's hand a few inches of silvery blade caught the starlight. The rest of it was already lodged deep in the monster's stomach. "It is very long, this knife," Jarnulf explained as the giant's jaw sagged open. "Long enough that the blood does not stain me, which is why I carry the name White Hand. But my knife is also silent, and sharp as the wind—oh, and cold. Do you feel the cold yet?" With a movement so swift the giant had no time to do more than blink, Jarnulf grabbed the hilt with both hands and yanked upward, dragging the blade from the creature's waist to the bottom of its ribcage, twisting it as he cut. The great beast let out a howl of astonishment and pain and clapped its huge hands over the wound even as Jarnulf threw himself past it, still holding fast to the hilt of his long knife. As he tumbled into the center of the platform the blade slid back out of the beast's hairy stomach, freeing a slide of guts and blood. The monster howled once more, then lifted dripping hands to the distant stars as if to fault them for letting such a thing happen. By the time it came staggering toward him, innards dangling, Jarnulf had regained his spear.

He had no time to turn the long shaft around, so he grabbed it and charged. He rammed the rounded butt-end of the shaft into the bloody hole in the giant's midsection, freeing a bellow of agony from the creature that nearly deafened him. The logs beneath them bounced and swayed, and snow pattered down from the laden branches above as the giant thrashed and howled and plucked at the spear-shaft, but Jarnulf crouched low and braced himself, then began to push forward, hunched over the spear as its butt-end dug deep into the monster's vitals.

The corpse-giant staggered backward, arms swinging like windmill vanes, mouth a hole that seemed too big for its head, then it suddenly vanished over the side of the tree-burial platform. Jarnulf heard it crashing through the branches as it fell, then a heavy thump as it hit the ground, followed by silence.

Jarnulf leaned out, keeping a strong grasp on the edge of the platform. His head felt light and his muscles were all quivering. The giant lay sprawled at the bottom of the tree in a tangle of overlong limbs. Jarnulf could not make out all of it through the intervening branches, but saw a pool of blackness beneath it spreading into the mounded snow.

Careless, he berated himself. *And it almost cost me my life. God cannot be proud of me for that.* But what the thing said had startled him badly.

Might the giant have lied? But why? The monster would have no reason to do so. The Silver Queen was awake, it had said, and so the North was coming awake as well. That certainly explained the giants now pushing down into Rimmersgard, as well as rumors Jarnulf had heard of Hikeda'ya warriors being spotted in places where they had not been seen for years. Certainly the border was as active as he had ever known it, with Nakkiga troops and their scouts everywhere. But if the giant had actually spoken the truth, it meant that Jarnulf had been wrong about many important things. He had stepped onto a bridge he thought safe only to find it cracking beneath him when it was far too late to turn back.

So Father's murderer is not gone—not lost in the dream lands and as good as dead, but alive and planning for war again. That means everything I have done, the lives I have taken, the terror I have tried to spread among the Hikeda'ya . . . has all been pointless. The monster is awake.

Until this moment Jarnulf had believed he was God's avenger—not just God's, but Father's as well. Now he had been proved a fool.

He watched from the platform until he was quite sure the giant was dead and his own limbs had stopped trembling, then he tossed his spear over the side and began to climb down. The wind was strengthening, bringing snow out of the north; by the time he reached the ground Jarnulf was dusted in white. He cleaned the blood and offal from his spear, then used his long, achingly sharp knife to cut off the giant's head. He set the monster's head in the crotch of a wide branch near the base of the burial tree, the eyes lifelessly black and stretched wide in their last surprise, the fanged mouth gaping foolishly. He hoped it would serve as a warning to others of its kind to stay away from human settlements, to find some easier forage than the corpses of Rimmersfolk, but just now defending the bodies of dead men and women was not what dominated his thoughts.

"We men beat back the witch-queen and defeated her." He spoke only to himself, and so quietly that no other creature heard him, not a bird, not a squirrel. "If she has truly returned, this time men like me will destroy her." But Jarnulf had made promises to himself and God before, and those pledges had now been proved nothing but air.

No, save your words for fitter things, he told himself. *Like prayer.*

Jarnulf the White Hand tipped the long spear across his shoulder and began walking back to the part of the snowy woods where he had left his horse.

4

Brother Monarchs

As if to crown the entrance of the High King and High Queen, the sun had emerged from behind the morning clouds and was spreading its light generously across the hills of Hernysadharc. Even the disc of gold atop the Taig's distant roof glittered like a coin spun into the air, as though the great hall celebrated their arrival as well.

Simon was fidgeting with a golden coin of his own—a medallion of unusually large size and uncomfortable edges that held his cloak and was currently rubbing against his neck. His friend the Lord Chamberlain had insisted that he wear it.

"Remember, you *are* the High King and High Queen," said Jeremias, pushing the pin through the heavy cloak with enough force to make the high king wince. "I didn't come all this way to see you two looking like beggars."

"Then you should have stayed at home," Simon growled. Waiting had put him out of temper. The hurt on Jeremias' round face was so profound that Simon almost apologized, but the edge of the medallion was still digging painfully into his jowls and he resisted the impulse.

"I am the Royal Chamberlain, in charge of the king's and queen's household," Jeremias said stiffly.

"That household is in Erkynland," Simon pointed out. "We are in Hernystir."

"The household is wherever you and the queen are . . . Majesties." Jeremias put a little twist on the last word to make Simon feel it. The king knew it was difficult sometimes for his childhood friend to live happily with the distance that now yawned between them, even when Jeremias was close enough to breathe on his cheek, as he was doing now. "In the old days, they say old King John would travel from castle to castle for a year before coming back to the Hayholt, so you have little to complain about. There. Now please don't fiddle with it. It looks splendid."

Simon stared into the hand mirror one of Jeremias' servitors held before him. "It looks like I am ready to be buried. The Heavens know I couldn't do much else wrapped up like this."

"Some might think that was not a very nice joke," his wife told him, frowning. "In fact, some might think the king is taking his own bad temper out on everyone except the one who caused it."

Now it was Simon's turn to send a warning look. Neither of them were happy with Hernystir's King Hugh at this moment, but such things were not to be shared in front of any but the most important advisers. "Enough, Lord Chamberlain," Simon said, gently lifting away Jeremias' hand as he tried to give the medallion one last burnishing with a kerchief. "You are right and I apologize, I suppose. It looks splendid."

"I should hope so," said Jeremias, his face red from effort.

The royal procession slowly climbed the main road through the city of Hernysadharc, past waving and cheering Hernystiri lined up on both sides, many crowded on overhanging balconies, or even perched precariously on sloping roofs. The houses and shops had been done up in festive style, bright banners and fresh paint so that sunlight seemed to jump back into the air as soon as it landed, full of new life. Simon and Miriamele rode side by side as they always did—monarchs together, not monarch and royal spouse. In the early days Simon had been the stickler for that distinction, but as the years had rolled past Miriamele had become increasingly determined to remind people that she herself was the daughter of a king, however blackened his name might now be, and also the grandchild of Prester John, founder of the High King's Ward that gave them dominion over much of Osten Ard.

"Hugh should have come to meet us at the gate," the queen said, in words so quiet only Simon could hear them. "I will tell him so myself."

"Give him a chance, my dear." Simon waved his hand at the crowd. "You see he has brought the people out for us."

"He could not have kept them inside," she said. "And why shouldn't he bring them out? We are High King and High Queen. He is only a king himself because his great-grandfather did my grandfather a favor, so Hernystir kept its crown."

"Still, he is a king for all that, and kings have their pride. As do queens."

"Do not make it *my* complaint, Simon." Her voice was firm but her look contained love and a little amusement as well as irritation. "You are too kind and you hate a fight, but there are people—and I suspect Hugh is one of them—who take that for weakness."

"Yes, I do hate a fight. Let's not have one now." He waved to the cheering Hernystir-folk again. Near the road, a group of small girls were leaping up and down, waving colored ribbons that curled and snapped like a frayed rainbow. "Look at them. It makes me miss Lillia."

"Our granddaughter would be out in the road, trying to lead the procession." Simon smiled. "Yes, she would."

Miriamele sighed. "Sweet God give me strength." She squinted up the road, lined as far as they could see with well-wishers. "We will not reach the Taig until nightfall at this rate."

"Patience, my dear. Patience."

"No more for me, thank you."

Count Eolair covered his goblet with his hand and kept it there until the servant had gone away. He would have enjoyed a little more wine, and after a long day in bright sun after a fortnight of clouds and dark days he certainly deserved another cup or few, but Eolair's sense for conflict, as trained as the nose of a hunting hound, suggested restraint. Queen Miriamele's and King Simon's Lord Steward, more commonly known as the Hand of the High Throne, did not want a haze of wine slowing his thoughts tonight.

The scene itself could scarcely have been more familiar to him, of course. The wooden palace called the Taig had been Eolair's second home for much of the early part of his life, when he had become first a messenger to kings and eventually an esteemed advisor. The atmosphere in the Great Hall, where ancient wooden carvings of animals and other totems hung from the rafters, was unquestionably festive, the bright colors of the Hernystiri gentry in their best clothes mingling with the sounds of tipsy laughter and the succulent smell of roast pork. But something was off-kilter here. Queen Miriamele and King Simon were out of sorts with the delays and confusions King Hugh had put them through, of course, but Eolair could not help feeling that something deeper and more troubling was going on.

A few seats away, Queen Miriamele was being entertained—"distracted" she would doubtless have termed it—by Lady Tylleth, an attractive widow who was almost certain to become King Hugh's wife. Many at the Hernystiri court thought her too old, nearly thirty years, though her children by her husband, the late Earl of Glen Orrga, showed that at least she was fertile. In fact, with her handsome, womanly figure, glossy chestnut hair, and high color, Lady Tylleth looked a bit like Eolair's idea of the Hernystiri goddess Deanagha, or even great Mircha herself, the mistress of the rains.

The high queen made a stark contrast to dark Tylleth. Miriamele's golden hair was largely silver now, worn in simple plaits under a modest circlet. Her cheeks were pale, her green eyes shadowed, and Eolair was worried for her. This was the first time the king and queen had faced the anniversary of Prince John Josua's birth while away from home. Eolair did not blame Queen Miriamele in the least for her irritation at being marooned in conversation with King Hugh's mistress.

In fact, as Eolair watched, the queen seemed to have lost patience entirely with Tylleth's chatter and was trying desperately to draw King Simon's eye. Her husband saw, but Hugh was leaning close to him, talking with quiet animation, and Simon could only shrug to show his helplessness.

Eolair shifted on his seat and felt his joints complain at him for sitting too long on a hard bench. He was beginning to wish he had accepted that offer of more wine, if only to ease his old bones. The day seldom passed now that

Eolair—once among Hernystir's best riders and swordsmen—did not marvel at what age had done to him.

I have become Time's poppet, he thought sadly. *She plays with me as a child with a doll, pulling off a piece here, another there, dragging me through the mud, then carrying me back to sit at some mock-banquet.*

But this gathering was no child's performance of grown-up ways. It was deadly serious business, the monarch of Hernystir welcoming his liege-lords, the king and queen of Erkynland. Simon and Miriamele ruled over Hugh's Hernystir and most of the rest of Osten Ard by the authority of the High King's Ward, the empire that Miriamele's grandfather John of Warinsten had created with his strength and his sword. But even at the best of times, some of the lords of the High Ward's component nations had chafed under John's rule.

Eolair could not help wondering whether Hugh was becoming such a man. Or did something else explain his odd behavior in keeping Simon and Miriamele waiting so long outside the city? And even after they rode in, Hugh had waited to meet them until they had reached the Taig itself, which suggested less than perfect subservience on his part. But Hugh had been changeable and headstrong all his life, something Eolair knew better than most.

Hugh's father Prince Gwythinn had been one of the first to die in the great war that had made Simon and Miriamele monarchs. Gwythinn had been killed and mutilated by renegade Rimmersmen serving Miriamele's father, King Elias of Erkynland, who had been corrupted by the lying promises of Ineluki the Storm King. Gwythinn's body had been left for his kinsmen to find. When his father King Lluth had died in battle against the Rimmersmen not long after, only Lluth's daughter Maegwin and the king's young wife Inahwen had remained to lead their shattered people. Then madness had taken Maegwin, and with her, nearly all that remained of Eolair's hope for his native land.

The Storm King's attack on the countries of men had failed at last, but in the chaos that followed, the ruined, headless nation of Hernystir struggled to hold itself together. Over the first few months a surprising number of nobles asserted slender if not completely spurious claims to the throne, and it seemed only civil war would settle their rivalries. Then a sort of miracle occurred. Everyone had been certain that the line of royal blood had ended with Maegwin until a young woman of the court was pushed forward by her mother and father to tell her tale and show the infant she had been sent off to bear in secret—Prince Gwythinn's bastard.

Gwythinn had not married the young woman before his death, but he had made certain promises to care for her, and her family had his ring and letters to prove it. The court was anxious to have a royal family again, so the child's claim was backed by the wiser nobles—not least of whom was Eolair himself—who did not want their suffering nation to tumble into war again so soon. So, in the end all fell into place for the infant Hugh ubh-Gwythinn. When his mother died from a fever a few years later, young Hugh was given to the king's widow, Inahwen, who did her best both to raise him for kingship and to rule as his regent, with help from Count Eolair whenever he could pull himself away from Simon and Miriamele and the court of the High Ward in Erkynland.

And here sat Hugh tonight, Eolair thought, a man now more than thirty years of age but still with much the look of the changeable, energetic child who had gusted through the Taig like a spring gale flinging open the shutters. Still the same large, round eyes that could look so innocent, so surprised by any accusation. Still the same curling dark hair that would never lie flat, but bounced with every shake of his head, every loud laugh. The round cheeks of his childhood were gone, his handsome face grown thin, but it was still easy for Eolair to remember the monarch's charming youth.

So why did this older Hugh make him so uncomfortable?

King Hugh caught him staring. "Eolair! My noble Eolair *Tarna*, better-than-uncle! Why do you look so downcast? Must I beat the potboy for sloth? Boy! Bring the master of Nad Mullach more wine!"

Eolair smiled. "No, Majesty. I have been amply and regularly served and your table is splendid. I am only thinking."

"Bah. Thinking. You will sadden us all." Hugh held high his cup, waiting until the roar of drunken conversation diminished in the high wooden hall. "Instead, we should all rejoice! This is a rare feast indeed, when we are joined by our brother and sister monarchs!"

Eolair saw Miriamele's head lift at the same moment as Simon looked down at the table. Neither of them had failed to notice Hugh's choice of words.

As the cheers fell away and people began to wave for their cups to be refilled, the dowager queen Inahwen rose quietly from her seat. Hugh noticed. "Dear lady, why do you leave us?"

"I beg forgiveness, Your Majesty, but I feel a bit weak and the wine is too much for my head. I mean the High King and High Queen no disrespect, of course. I am suddenly unwell." Inahwen didn't look Hugh directly in the eyes, but her shoulders were squared as though she expected some kind of violent response, which seemed odd to Eolair: if she was not the king's true parent, Inahwen was the closest thing that Hugh had.

"Ah, then I beg forgiveness myself for putting you through a tiresome evening, dear stepmother." Hugh smiled. His expression seemed quite ordinary, but Inahwen turned her head as though it hurt her to see it.

"Not tiresome at all, Majesty," she said. "How could it be, in this best and highest of company?" She smiled and inclined her head in a bow toward Simon and Miriamele, but it appeared to Eolair that the dowager queen was having difficulty keeping her lip from trembling.

"Please don't stay on our behalf, Queen Inahwen," Simon told her. "But we will have a chance to see you before we leave, I hope?"

Inahwen assured them of it, and made her way down the length of the table. King Hugh now clasped Simon's shoulder, pulling the High King back into conversation. Eolair took the opportunity to rise and follow Inahwen out of the great hall.

"Poor, poor queen," said Lady Tylleth.

Miriamele was not sure she'd heard correctly. "I beg pardon?"

"The poor dowager queen. She does not like these gatherings." The dark-haired woman laughed. "I do not blame her. They can be tedious. The king loves his company, but some of the older folk at court weary of long evenings."

Miriamele was not so much younger than Inahwen that she enjoyed hearing this woman speak of "the older folk." "Your queen did much to save this king-dom during the Storm King's War and after it."

"Of course, of course!" Tylleth laughed again, as if it was a little strange anyone should take offense. "All the more reason she should rest now, with Hugh on the throne." Lady Tylleth gave every appearance of being as attractive and stupid as a peacock, but Miriamele could not shake the certainty that some-thing deeper and perhaps darker was going on beneath the surface.

Do not let your petty jealousies get in your way, she chided herself. *Think of the wise words of holy St. Yistrin—"God gives us all youth, and then takes it away again." What have you gained to offset that loss? Patience? Perhaps a little wisdom? Then be patient, and perhaps you'll also be wise.* This banquet was work to be got through, just as much as reviewing the verdicts of the assizes or examining the exchequer with Pasevalles. She did her best to smile and said, "Pardon me for being clumsy, Lady Tylleth, but is there not concern still here in Hernystir about the succession?"

Tylleth waved her hand at this tiny matter. "Oh, believe me, Hugh has bas-tards enough if the need of an heir arises before he and I have made one."

Miriamele found this young woman more than a little disconcerting. "You seem unworried."

"We will conceive. The gods have promised me." Her eyes, darkly lined in a style Miriamele thought of as almost exclusively southern, showed not a trace of doubt. "I hope I do not insult you by speaking of my belief in the gods of my own people—your Aedonite piety is well-known even here in Hernystir."

Miriamele could only shake her head, although she could not help feeling that something less than complimentary had been delivered. "Of course not. The king and I have never tried to force our own faith on others." She did her best to smile. "And of course we pray that Heaven will bless you both with a healthy child." Miri could not help wondering whether the woman was a little mad. Was she really certain that making an heir would be so easy, even with divine help? Miriamele and Simon had only managed one child in all their years together, and that child was dead. Had John Josua not married while still young there would be no male heir. The High Ward itself would be in danger, all its nations ready to plunge back into chaos when she and Simon died, as they someday must.

God grant I go first, she thought suddenly. *I will not have the grace to put up with them all if Simon is gone. He was always the patient one.* Miriamele turned to look for her husband. *Sometimes too patient.* At the moment, Simon was looking more than a bit like one of the weary old ones himself, smiling stiffly as King Hugh poked and prodded him, the younger monarch prattling on and on about hunting or something else that her husband could not care less about. Put to work in the Hayholt's steamy kitchens from a young age, Simon had not enjoyed the sporting education most kings received. Nor did he much like the noise of belling hounds—and neither did Miri.

"Majesty?" Tylleth asked. "Have I said something that upset you?" But the hint of a smile seemed to lurk at the corners of the woman's mouth. Something about this wife-to-be put Miriamele on edge, there was no escaping it. She was suddenly filled with a powerful desire to be anywhere else. "No. Of course not, Lady Tylleth. It has been a long day, that's all."

King Hugh's heavy chair scraped on the floor—stone flags now, not the strewn rushes of the old days. Despite the ancient carvings still hanging in pride of place from the rafters, even the honest old wooden Taig was beginning to resemble something different—perhaps one of the palaces of Nabban. "A toast!" Hugh cried. "Let us raise our cups once more before the evening slips away! To our beloved fellow monarchs, who grace us with their company, King Simon and Queen Miriamele."

"*King Simon and Queen Miriamele!*" shouted those still sober enough to get names and titles in the right order. The uproar was followed by an expectant silence. Simon looked to his wife, who nodded. He put a hand on the table and hoisted himself to his feet.

"To King Hugh and the throne of Hernystir," Simon said, raising his own cup. "Long may the Stag of Hern's house graze in these beautiful meadows. And I hear that the king is soon to be married as well." He nodded toward Lady Tylleth, who straightened in her seat. "May the union be ever blessed." The packed hall echoed to more toasts, more cheers.

Something else was needed, but Miriamele tried not to make it too obvious. Accustomed by years of practice, Simon caught her expression and, to her grim satisfaction, understood it.

"*And,*" he said, silencing the murmur and the returning hum of talk, "I would also like to make one more toast. This is a night of joyful reunion between old allies, and meetings with new friends, but as you know, it is not such joyful business alone that brings us here. The queen and myself are bound for Elvritshalla with the sad task of saying goodbye to a dear friend and a faithful ally, Duke Isgrimnur. Raise your cups in his honor, please."

"Duke Isgrimnur!" many cried, but the response was more muted than to the previous toasts, and Miriamele distinctly heard someone down the table say, "One less frostbeard!" Before she could demand to know who had uttered such a vile remark, Simon caught her eye and shook his head. For a moment she felt almost as much anger toward him as toward the fool who had insulted the dear old duke, but Simon had earned her trust many times over. *Patience*, she told herself. *He's right. Not here, not this evening.* She took a breath and did her best to let her fury seep away, just as wine spilled during the toasting was now soaking into the linen tablecloth. She could not help wondering whether the red stains could ever be completely washed out.

He caught up to her in the lower ward outside the great hall.

"Queen Inahwen! Highness!"

Inahwen's maid continued a few discreet steps ahead as her mistress turned. For a moment Eolair saw not the mature, almost elderly woman who had left the hall, but Inahwen as he had once known her, golden-haired and fair of skin, threatened by shadows all around.

"*You honor me, Count Eolair,*" she said in Hernystiri.

The soft burr of his mother tongue reminded him of several things, not least the ticklishly warm feeling of Inahwen whispering it into his ear, so long ago that it seemed like another life. "*Please, lady, in your mouth a title seems something shameful, at least for me. It has been too long, Inahwen. You look well.*"

Her smile did not have much conviction. "*I look like what I am—an old woman, old and in the way.*"

"*Never.*" But her words struck him. "*In the way of what? Do you object to the king's upcoming marriage?*"

She glanced at her maid, who was pretending to look up at the stars a short distance away, and at the two guards who had accompanied them from the great hall. "*Oh, no. Who could object to the king's happiness? But come to the Queen's Little House and talk with me a while. I have no wine worth serving you, but there might be a little mead left from the midwinter festivities.*"

"*I have not had proper mead in months—no, two years, my good lady, since I was last in Hernysadharc. I would be honored.*"

The Queen's Little House was in truth not so little, a square, three-story structure in the modern style near the outer wall of the Taig. Eolair sat in a deep chair in the parlor as the maid was dispatched to the kitchen in search of mead.

"I have a bottle here we can start with," said Inahwen, producing a ceramic jug from a sideboard and pouring it into two small glasses of fine workmanship. "It's made from Circoille clover honey."

Eolair took his glass and sniffed it as they settled into chairs by the fireplace. "Lovely. Then what use have we for the other?"

"The use of giving my maid something to do for a few minutes. You asked me a question. I gave you an answer. Did you believe it?"

He was almost amused to see this version of Inahwen. "You have become a plotter, then, my dear? What happened to the shy, truthful young woman I once knew?"

She gave him a sad look. "You mock me, sir."

"No. Not at all. Talk to me, then. Do you dislike the idea of the king's marriage?" He thought it would not be surprising if Inahwen felt protective toward
Hugh, and Tylleth was certainly no subservient virgin bride.

"Marriage is a necessity. Do you know how many children he has fathered
without benefit of one? Seven. Seven that are known. Can you imagine the
furor if he died without a chosen heir?"

The mere idea of a half-dozen claimants to the Hernystiri throne was
enough to make Eolair suppress a shudder. "Yes, I think I can. So the marriage
will be a good thing, then?"

"If he wed someone else, it would be." And although they were alone in the
spacious room, she lowered her voice. "But not to that little witch."

Eolair could not help being startled by the harshness of her words. "She is so
bad, then? Or is it her father whose ambitions reach too high? He was a loyal
bondsman to King Lluth, as I remember."

"No, her father is trustworthy enough—a fat old gentleman farmer now that
his fighting days are past, fond of meat and drink and bragging about his cattle.
He gained much land when he married Tylleth to the Earl of Glen Orrga. It is
the daughter herself, Tylleth, that I fear." The dowager queen pursed her lips.
"She is a witch."

"You've used that word twice. Does it mean more than your dislike?"

Inahwen looked down at her glass for a moment. The firelight filled the
room with long, dark shapes that moved as though in anticipation of something. "I do not know, Eolair, but I have heard many rumors and some of them
are frightening to me."

"What do those rumors say?"

"If I tell you, you will be certain my wits are gone." She shook her head.
"Some say Tylleth has brought back a very old, very evil worship."

"Worship?" He was puzzled. "I am not sure I understand, my lady, nor
would I believe it anyway. You of all people should know that king's favorites
often attract ugly tales."

Inahwen grimaced. "Yes, some cruel things were said of me also. But nobody ever accused me of reviving the rituals of the Crow Mother."

"The—" Eolair could scarcely believe he had heard it. "The Maker of
Orphans—the Morriga?" Even indoors beside a fire, a shiver traveled up his
backbone. "Nobody would be so mad. It took Hernystir hundreds of years to
destroy that horrid cult."

"Still, that is what I am told, and by those who have no reason to lie to me.
They say she has become fascinated with the Dark Mother, and she and some
followers try to summon her."

"Why?" Eolair had not thought of Morriga the Crow Mother in years. No
Hernystirman had openly sacrificed to her since before King Tethtain's day,
three centuries gone. The last of her worshippers, a filthy, inbred remnant in
the northern deeps of the Circoille forest, had been destroyed by Lluth's father
King Llythin long before Eolair's own parents were born. *Surely not even a*

self-absorbed creature like Lady Tylleth could hope to revive such a fearsome practice, he thought. "Why would she do such a mad thing?"

"How should I know? They say she claims the Morriga came to her in dreams." Now that they were sitting by the bright light of the fire, he thought Inahwen looked pale and exhausted. "I hope it is only some passing fashion, Eolair—the pastime of bored courtiers. But I remember my grandmother's tales of the Morriga's followers from when she was a girl, how frightened people in her village were, how they would walk a long way to avoid the gaze of one of the Crow Mother's worshippers."

Eolair felt a pang of uneasiness, but would not show it. "Surely, even if there is any truth to this rumor, Lady Tylleth thinks of it only as an amusement— something to shock the Taig's elders." He essayed a smile. "Elders like you and me."

"Perhaps," said Inahwen, but with no answering cheer. "But this I can swear to you, dear Count—Hugh has not been the same since he took up with her. He was always flighty, always changeable. You remember that, surely?"

"I do indeed. There were many times in his boyhood I wished I could take him across my knee."

"I wish you had. I wish someone had. But now . . . I don't know, Eolair. He has changed, and it frightens me. The way he looks now, always as though he has some delicious secret! It is as though she has convinced him of something, something that makes him think he is beyond danger. Surely you can see that! Everything he did today, everything he arranged, was meant to snub the High Throne in some way or other. That was not the Hugh I watched grow. That child might have been spoiled, perhaps, headstrong . . ." She frowned and fell silent. A moment later the maid came in, unsteadily bearing a large jug.

"Found it, Mistress," she said.

"Do you hear that?" Inahwen tried to smile. "Mistress. Not even 'Highness' any more."

The maid looked stricken. "My apologies, Highness, I . . ."

"Put it down, child." Inahwen waved her to set the jug on the low table. "Now take yourself to bed. The count and I have almost finished our talk. He can let himself out."

The maid nodded and set down her burden before scurrying toward the stairs.

Eolair waited until the door closed on the landing. "Is there anything else I should know? Or can do?" He reached out and touched the back of Inahwen's hand. "I would see you happier."

"Speak to the gods, then. Only their plans matter, not ours."

He looked at her fondly, at the lines on her once-smooth face that told the story of the miseries and the passing moments of happiness. Not enough moments of happiness.

Not enough for either of us, he thought. *And certainly not enough that the two of us shared.* During the great war against the Storm King, both of them had lost someone who could never be replaced, Inahwen her royal husband and Eolair King Lluth's daughter Maegwin. Eolair had not realized how much he cared for brave, bedeviled Maegwin until she was gone. Was he making the same error now with Inahwen?

There is so little comfort in this world, he thought. *Have I been foolish to let duty guide me always?*

"Lady . . ." he began, but she was already shaking her head.

"I can guess a little of what you're thinking, my brave Count. There is no use in it. We are what we are, and our roads ran side by side for only a short while. But you will always be dear to me, Eolair."

"And you to me, Highness." He finished his second cup of mead, and felt it in his legs as he stood to return to the great hall. "I will think carefully about the things you've said, and I will do some asking of my own. And rest assured, Queen Miriamele and King Seoman will know your fears." He bent and kissed her hand with careful attention. "May the gods take good care of you."

"Of all of us, dear Eolair." She finally smiled, but it was a half-hearted thing. "It is so strange to see you with your hair all gray! I cannot even think how I must look to you. Yes, may the gods watch over us closely, because we are all in need of the gods' good care."

5

Awake

She blinked. Tzoja always blinked when she stepped out of the great Nakkiga Gates, and her eyes always watered. Freezing winter had imprisoned her under the mountain for months: even the cloud-smothered white ember that was the northern sun dazzled her to blindness.

She signaled to her escort to wait until she could see properly. The household guards halted at a carefully calculated distance, demonstrating both her high status as a magister's property and their own mute indignation at having to protect a mortal, any mortal, even their lord's most valued concubine.

When her full sight returned, Tzoja led the four silent Hikeda'ya guards down the cracked, discolored stairs onto the Field of Banners, anciently a place of triumphant celebration, currently the home of the so-called Animal Market. The air outside the mountain was painfully fresh and cold, but rich with smells from the nearby Sacred Grove, pine and lemony birch and honey-sweet daphne. Even the reek of the fermented fish, sold from jugs all over the market, was almost welcome, because it reminded her of her old, simple life in Rimmersgard before the Norns took her. And as always, simply being out in the light and air, even surrounded on all sides by her fellow slaves and their corpse-pale overseers, Tzoja was thinking about freedom. Even though she had conceded long ago that it would never happen, she still dreamed about escape.

As she made her way down the untidy rows of mortal vendors and mortal buyers, she stopped to look at some gloves offered for barter on a crumbled stone table while the woman who had made them squatted beside it to stay out of the wind. In the early years of her captivity, one of Tzoja's fancies had been to keep hidden a set of cold-weather clothes in case the chance for escape ever actually came. A warm, sturdy pair of fur-lined gloves like this would be much better than the ones she had hidden away, along with the gold coins and clothes and other useful things. But Tzoja could no longer convince herself that she would leave the mountain even if she were given the chance; Nezeru's birth had changed all that.

She set the gloves back on the stone. The Clan Enduya household guards fell in around her once more. The crouching woman did not even look up.

The Animal Market had gained its name because nearly all the buyers and sellers were mortals, and that was how the Hikeda'ya thought of Tzoja's kind. The market sprang to life each year during the Wind-Child's Moon and came back once each moon during the warm season. Mortal serfs and slaves from the outermost Hikeda'ya lands came to trade goods with their own kind, both those who lived in the mountain itself and those who sheltered in the new settlements outside it, a tumbledown collection of shelters tossed up in recent years on the bones of Nakkiga-That-Was, the long-deserted Hikeda'ya ruins outside the mountain's gates.

Most of those who came to the market were overseers buying cheap blankets, clothes, and food for both mortal and changeling workers. A few of the more fortunate mortals like Tzoja herself, mostly body slaves and other pets of the Hikeda'ya nobility, came looking for luxuries—scents, drinks, and foodstuffs more suited to their human tastes than what was given to them by their masters. But although most of the goods were meant only for mortal slaves and the poorest Hikeda'ya—no Norn of any standing would be seen mingling with the human herd—Tzoja was still constantly reminded that she now lived among the fairies.

Mingling with the hundreds and hundreds of mortals (and the smaller contingent of armed Norn guards keeping watch over the market) were a large number of the only slaves the Norns considered lower than mortal men and women—the changeling Tinukeda'ya in all their weird variety. There were carry-men, of course, manlike beasts of burden almost as tall as wild giants, with immense, muscular shoulders and tiny, empty-faced heads that showed no alteration of expression even when they stumbled under their monstrous loads. But Tinukeda'ya came in many other shapes as well, from the small, scuttling hairy things that worked on the highest mountainside farms in other parts of the Nornfells to the slender, mournful-faced delvers, who, despite their spindly appearance, could not just dig faster than either humans or Norns but also shape stone with the delicate ease of a man carving soft wood. Tzoja watched a pair of these delvers with bleak amusement as they bargained almost silently with a gem-seller: the owl-eyed creatures' flinching hurry to be out of the sun and back into soothing darkness was the exact opposite of her own desires. But body shape alone meant nothing, not here: her Norn captors themselves, although more manlike than any of the changelings, were as different from Tzoja as a wildcat from a rabbit.

She should have been used to it by now. *How long can you live in such a place and still feel that you are caught in a terrible dream?* But it was an empty question, because she knew the answer was *forever.* Or at least until she died.

Tzoja did her best to banish such dire thoughts so she could enjoy her scant time in the sun, but it was not easy. Pointless as it was, she knew that the dream of escape would never completely leave her—she had spent too many years under the open skies ever to be able to surrender. Still, all she had to do was look around to be reminded of how hopeless such thoughts were. The slave folk never looked up at the Norn guards, and barely raised their voices above a whisper even when they were bargaining with other mortals. Back in Rimmersgard, where she had lived so many years in such ignorant happiness with Valada Roskva, the Rimmersgard matriarch and healer who had given her a home, the noise of the entire market would have been suitably respectable from a crowd gathered for a funeral. Even so, inside the mountain that was now and forever her home, so many mortal voices at once would be considered an unbearable, traitorous clamor, and would be quelled by swift violence. So the slaves barely whispered even out here, beneath open skies.

What good is freedom that cannot be used? she wondered. *Is the poor gift of life worth so much?*

But of course it was not her own life that held her in thrall. And because she had given birth to that beloved life, Tzoja knew she was doomed to live and die among a people stranger to her than the beasts of the field, and would never know real peace.

Even Tzoja's Hikeda'ya lord and lover Viyeki, who was unlike his kindred in so many other ways, and who had been more considerate of her than any other of his kind would ever have been, did not understand Tzoja's restlessness. The magister seemed to consider it an endearing but inexplicable mortal oddity, as a child might laugh at a dog chasing its tail, seeing only the low comedy and not the horrible futility. And Viyeki was by far the best of them.

It took a long time to walk up and down the crooked rows, and snow was beginning to flurry before she had finished, but Tzoja was determined to stay in the light as long as possible. The market was large—the site had once been the Norns' Field of Banners, a broad ceremonial ground in front of the mountain gates, last used for its intended purpose centuries past, when most of the north had been ruled by the Hikeda'ya. The Rimmersmen who had come to Osten Ard out of the lost west had changed that beyond all recognition, long ages before Tzoja had been born. The thick-bearded warriors had conquered all the way down through Erkynland, killing Norns and their Sithi kin in great numbers, and killing countless mortals as well. After the Northmen came, her mistress Roskva had taught her, the Sithi had deserted their old cities and fled to the forests, while the Norns had withdrawn here, to their mountain capital and last stronghold, swearing never to give it up, to fight until the last Hikeda'ya was dead. After living two decades amidst these fierce immortals, she did not doubt they would do just that.

And what if war does come again? she could not help wondering. *Whose side will I be on? My own people's? Or my daughter's?*

The guards were giving her hard looks now. It was clear they thought it time to go back to the mountain, but Tzoja knew the weather might turn again and the deep snows return, which would mean no more outdoor markets for several moons. She ignored their looks and continued to walk up and down the rows all the way to the market's outermost reaches, bartering Builders' Order scrip for hazelnuts and cloudberries, dried turnips, parsnips, and wild celery, even a selection of dried river fish, mostly perch and pike, all of them things that reminded her of her days in Roskva's order, of her happy time as a free woman, now so long ago. At last, as the sun dropped toward the western peaks and the Dragon Guard began to close the market, she reluctantly signaled to her escorts that she was ready to return.

If I had a basket big enough, I would take back a piece of the sun. Then I think I could put up with anything.

She wouldn't even need much of it to take with her, she told herself: her life in the mountain would last barely a fraction of her master's, though he was her elder by centuries. She often wondered if any of the immortals would remember her after she was gone, any more than they might recall a single fallen leaf.

But what of Nezeru? Will my daughter, who may live almost as long as her father, still remember me when hundreds of years have passed? And what of Viyeki? Will a great lord like him recall that he once loved a mortal? Why stumble on when the end will be the same—darkness and silence?

The sun had dipped. The outer city and marketplace were growing so cold that her own vaporous breath obscured her sight. She shivered. It was past time to return, and she dared not make Viyeki unhappy with her. Not even her death was hers to choose, because she had given a hostage to Fate—her only child.

Back inside, then, to the quiet, endless halls of stone. Back to the incomprehensible rituals, the masked faces, and the constant knowledge that even after giving birth to a praised young warrior, Tzoja herself was still considered scarcely more than a beast.

Ah, beautiful, brave Nezeru, my child, she thought. *Though you cannot understand me, and though you despise my mortal weaknesses, I love you still. For you I will go on living in the dark.*

Did she love Viyeki, her daughter's father, too? Was there something more in her feelings for her many-centuried master—her *owner*—than mere gratitude to someone who had allowed her freedoms that few of her fellow slaves enjoyed? Who had shown her real kindness, and even what seemed like tenderness, as unusual as that was among the Hikeda'ya?

Tzoja had no answer for that. She bade a grudging farewell to the sun, then turned back toward the tall, forbidding mountain gates, but in a small act of rebellion she made her Hikeda'ya guards carry the things she had chosen for herself.

Deep inside the mountain, Viyeki sey-Enduya, Queen's High Magister of the Order of Builders, was reading in his garden, lingering over a poem by Shun'y'asu:

As the silence of birds just before dawn,
So the silence of the living heart
Just before death.
Then comes the light.

Silence, yes, Viyeki thought. *Before death, it is indeed a rich gift. Afterward, though, it will be freely available even to the poorest of us.*

Shun'y'asu's poetry had been important to Viyeki's master Yaarike, the former high magister of the Order of Builders. This volume had been the old noble's favorite book—a gift to Viyeki from his own hand—and reading the words almost brought Yaarike sey-Kijana back to stand over him once more, austere but with moments of sudden humor, yet always full of secrets.

Viyeki, like most of his people, valued silence, but it was not what he loved best about his garden. The district of noble compounds on Nakkiga's second tier was already quiet but for the occasional shuffle of servants' feet or the muted clatter of a troop of armored guards on patrol: his house was already a refuge from noisy surroundings. It was not silence but solitude that Viyeki coveted.

By the standards of the city inside the mountain, the high magister's garden was both luxurious and vast, as befitted the leader of one of the most important orders. A shaft led straight up from the chamber's rocky roof, all the way through the mountain's stony hide and out to the sky by way of an angled entrance in Nakkiga's icy flanks that allowed sunlight to bounce down its polished sides and create a single bright column at the center of the garden chamber. At this season, melt water splashed continuously from a crevice in the garden wall into the rectangular pond, luring birds in from the outside sky. On a good day like today, as many as a half dozen mountain sparrows and a few black and white choughs might be splashing in the shallows, shaking out their feathers and calling back and forth in creaky voices barely louder than a whisper. Even the birds of Nakkiga seemed in perpetual mourning.

He heard another sound now, softer even than the birds' gentle calls—an intake of breath. Viyeki, recognizing his secretary Yemon by that sound alone, carefully slipped the book of poetry he had been reading under his other book, the traditional magister's copy of *The Five Fingers of the Queen's Hand*. Yemon seemed loyal to Viyeki, but he would have been a fool to seem anything else, and Shun'y'asu's poems had long been forbidden by the palace. Although Viyeki's copy of *The Color of Water* had been given to him by his master Yaarike, who was considered a great hero, it was still unwise for anyone to see Viyeki reading it, or any other book that the queen's Hamakha Clan considered suspect.

Especially now. Especially today.

"I interrupt you, Master." Yemon did not sound particularly apologetic, more as though he secretly hoped it were true.

Viyeki looked up, mirroring Yemon's rigorously empty expression with his own. "Not at all. Tell me your errand."

Small, stolid Yemon was an excellent secretary, clever and observant and without any close family of his own to distract him from duty. He was also ambitious, and almost certainly planned on replacing his master Viyeki someday (as was true of any but the dullest underlings in every royal order in Nakkiga). It would have been foolish for his master to expect anything else, but there was no need for Viyeki to hasten Yemon's advancement by being caught with a copy of Shun'y'asu. He risked a brief downward glance to make sure the forbidden book was not visible.

"Your appointed time at the palace is at evening bell, Master," Yemon reminded him, although they both knew Viyeki would sooner forget his own name than a summons from the Mother of the People. "Shall I have the litter ready in the hour before, or do you wish to leave the house sooner than that?"

"I will not need the litter. I will walk."

He did not have to see him to know that Yemon had infinitesimally raised an eyebrow, as he always did when his master did something he thought oddly sentimental or foolish, a hair's-breadth movement as telling as a hiss of contempt. "Indeed, High Magister. I will have the guards ready an hour before the bell."

"Thank you, Yemon. You may go."

Queen Utuk'ku's summons, of course, was the reason Viyeki had gone searching for solitude, and why he had been tempted into taking out the forbidden book. Although the poet was long, long dead, Shun'y'asu of Blue Spirit Peak had written in sorrowful yet dancing words of just such moments as this, of trying to choose between perfect duty and the importunities of conscience. Viyeki had stood atop such high and frightening places before, but he had never learned to like them.

This time his dilemma was a simple one, at least in its root: Viyeki had been summoned to the highest honor any Hikeda'ya could have, a meeting with Queen Utuk'ku, the immortal ruler of his people and mother of the race. But he did not want to go. In fact, the high magister had to admit to himself, he was afraid.

The messenger had arrived at the door only an hour before with the summons to the royal palace. It would be his first time waiting on the queen since she had awakened from the deep, decades-long sleep called *keta yi'indra*, and also his first time meeting her since he had been elevated to high magister of the Builders. The thought of the coming audience filled him with dread, in part because his loyalty to his old master Yaarike meant that Viyeki had kept secrets even from the palace itself. Viyeki had made difficult decisions during the years of the queen's sleep, always trying to do what was best for his monarch and his people, but he knew as well as anyone that good faith and good intentions were no defense against the queen's unhappiness. The pits in the Field of the Nameless were full of the scorched bones of those who had meant well but failed to please her.

He sighed and called out for a servant. Moments later a bent, older Hikeda'ya whose name Viyeki always had difficulty remembering crept in on silent, bare feet.

"Please remind Lady Khimabu that I am called to attend the queen herself at the evening bell, may she reign over us always," Viyeki told him. "I do not know when I will return, because I will be at the disposal of the Mother of All, so please give my wife my most sincere regrets and bid her dine without me."

The servant bowed and withdrew. The interruptions had long ago sent the birds swooping back up the shaft, so the pond was again still. For a moment Viyeki hoped he might calm his thoughts once more and try to find a measure of peace, but the garden now seemed corrupted, the shaft of falling light too harshly bright, the pond too shallow, as though the darkness that had been lurking in his heart since the summons now touched his eyes and ears as well.

Why do I fear the one who has given us so much? What is wrong with me that I cannot unreservedly love and trust our queen, who protects us against a world that hates us?

Viyeki could find no answer to that. He stood, straightened his clothing, and went in search of his mortal concubine, hoping that she had returned by now from the market outside the gates.

As they lay naked in her narrow bed, the great stone bell in the distant Temple of Martyrs tolled once for the mid-hour.

"I must rise again," said Viyeki.

"I look forward to that."

"Don't be wicked, Tzoja. I am called to the queen." But he did not wish to leave her embrace. Her warm skin against his seemed a sort of magic that defeated worry. How strange, he thought, that this mortal slave, this savage, short-lived creature from despised Rimmersgard, should be able to bring him peace when nothing and no one else could.

"Then you must go, of course," she said. "Surely you won't refuse?"

"Refuse?" Viyeki almost laughed, but the surprise of it was like a stumble while walking on a thin bridge above an abyss—even to be amused was to be reminded of the depths that yawned beneath him. "I know you are ignorant of many things, little mortal, but any other of my people would strike you for that. Refuse the queen? I might as well tear my heart out of my breast and step on it."

"But surely you have nothing to fear from her, my great lord. While she slept, you have done everything she would wish and done it well." Tzoja sat up a little, resting on one elbow, and her breasts settled against his arm. Viyeki reached out and let his finger trail across them. How innocent she was! And how little she knew of the thorny tangle that was life in the queen's service. "Even I have done my part," she said brightly. "Did I not provide her with a warrior for our great Order of Sacrifice?"

"Do not jest!"

Tzoja frowned. Her dark hair was disarranged and damp with sweat. She shook the strands out of her face. "I didn't intend to, my lord. Together we made a daughter so clever and capable that she was chosen to be a Queen's Talon at a younger age than any other. Your true wife cannot make such a claim—although she treats me as if *she* birthed Nezeru and I only order supper for you."

"Enough," said Viyeki. Why did everyone seek to trouble him today? "We will speak of this no longer. Our laws come from the Garden itself and are not to be disputed. If anyone hears you speak this way you will die in pain and there will be nothing I can do to save you."

Tzoja fell silent. Viyeki nodded his approval. Mortals, even the cleverest ones, were like the birds of the meadows, chattering and piping at all hours. But this one still charmed him, he had to admit, even as the first signs of her mortality began to show on her face and body. Even in the brief bloom of her youth she had never possessed anything like the icy beauty of his wife Khimabu, but something in her had drawn him from the first. Tzoja's youth was fading now, in the same way the end of summer taught the edges of the leaves to curl, but the thing that had drawn Viyeki—the thing that even now he could not name—still burned in her every glance, every movement.

Is it that mystery itself that fascinates me? he wondered. *Or the terrifying pleasure of something stolen, something forbidden?* After all, if any of his underlings saw him this way, talking freely with a mortal animal as if she were the equal of a Hikeda'ya, they would denounce him immediately.

Thus the problem with climbing to a great height, he thought, weary already, and with the true ordeal still ahead. *All the more can look at you with envy, and the height of the waiting fall grows with each upward step.*

He rose from her bed and began to dress.

"I will miss you, my lord," she said. "My days are lonely."

He ignored her. She always said such things after they coupled. He did not know how to respond, any more than he would if his warhorse or hunting owl should speak to him the same way.

When he had pulled his robe tight and belted it, Viyeki patted himself to make sure he carried no weapon or other implement forbidden to the queen's visitors. He wholeheartedly approved this ban, but it also seemed a bit foolish: after all, who would be so mad as to dare attack Utuk'ku the Ever-Living? And not only because of the constant presence of her personal guards, the Queen's Teeth, the finest warriors in Nakkiga. No, the most daunting of all Utuk'ku's defenses was the queen herself. Nobody living could even guess at the limits of her power. The Hikeda'ya's immortal monarch inspired the reverence of all her people, but she inspired fear as well and in even the most potent of her underlings.

Viyeki was still annoyed with Tzoja for her irresponsible questions; he left her rooms without the usual sentimental exchange she so valued.

The royal summoner's torch bobbed before him, serving more as a ritual banner than a source of light. Trailed by his secretary Yemon and a small contingent of his household guards, Viyeki followed the messenger up the great open stairway toward the third tier and the palace, past the dimly glowing expanse of the

White Gardens, which stood on a high stone island midway between the tiers. Viyeki had always found the fungus gardens soothing. Once he had even brought Tzoja to see them, but instead of understanding, his mortal concubine had been disturbed by the forest of snaking, dead-white stems, the delicately spreading fans and huge parasol caps that nodded in even the smallest shift of air. She had told Viyeki they made her think of writhing worms in a shovel full of dark, moist earth, and had pressed him to take her out again after only a short time. He had been disappointed, almost irritated, at her inability to recognize the sublime beauty of the place, but Tzoja was only a mortal, after all. Small wonder she saw death and decay in everything.

Still, Viyeki would have given much to be walking in those gardens now, even with an unappreciative companion.

As the royal messenger led them upward, an almost imperceptible breeze lifted a cloud of spores that drifted to the summons party and swirled with every step they took. He found himself recalling what the poet Lu'uya had written about this very spot:

"When earthstar and snowtongue send up their seed, I walk the naked night, constellations dancing around my feet."

More than a dozen Great Years had passed since Lu'uya's death—almost eight mortal centuries—but what she had written of the White Garden was still true. The unchanging nature of Nakkiga was its greatest beauty.

As they drew closer and closer to the palace, uneasy thoughts followed Viyeki's every step like Sun'y'asu's beggars. He wanted to believe this summons was only part of ordinary protocol, the awakened queen summoning her highest ministers to an audience, but Viyeki knew that he had greater crimes on his conscience than simply reading forbidden verses.

He had colluded with his master Yaarike and others to hide the things they had done while Utuk'ku slept. What did it matter that they had acted for what they believed was the good of the Hikeda'ya people? The queen was not merely power, she was justice itself, the spirit and conscience of the race. How could he stand before her and not confess everything he had done or had even thought of doing? And if he did, how could his punishment be anything less than the end of honor and the utter destruction of himself and his family?

Breathe and grow calm, Viyeki sey-Enduya, he urged himself. *You are a noble of the Hikeda'ya and a child of the sacred Garden. Even if death itself awaits you, do you wish to meet it like a cowering child?*

High Celebrant Zuniyabe stepped up to meet him as Viyeki entered the palace's front gate. At first it seemed an honor that ancient Zuniyabe had come himself instead of sending an underling, but today the masked high celebrant did not speak a word to Viyeki, only made a ritual gesture of respect before signing for him to follow. Viyeki showed no reaction to this ominous silence, of course, but only made a sign of assent and let the masked Zuniyabe lead him.

A guide through the royal palace was always necessary for visitors, although that guide was seldom anyone so elevated: the *Omeiyo Hamakh* was a maze in truth as well as in name, an unfathomably complicated puzzle of carved chambers and corridors, of slender bridges and apparently pointless staircases that led nowhere, a vast mystery that could never be untangled by chance alone. Only the highest Celebrants knew their way to the heart of the labyrinth where the queen waited.

As venerable Zuniyabe led him deeper and deeper into the maze, Viyeki could only think of who had summoned him, of who sat waiting at the heart of this web of stone. *Utuk'ku the eldest, the Mother of All, the heart of our race.* The honorifics he had learned in childhood presented themselves to his fretful mind, one after another. *Wise beyond wisdom. Strong beyond strength. Immortal. All-Seeing.*

At last they reached a corridor full of doors, each as plain and unprepossessing as the rest. Zuniyabe paused and laid his gloved hand on Viyeki's sleeve. "Now I leave you," said the High Celebrant, any expression hidden behind his ivory mask. He pointed to one of the doors. "She waits." Zuniyabe made a courteous but abbreviated bow, then turned away.

For perhaps the half-dozenth time since leaving his house, Viyeki commended his soul to the Garden. *Begone, beggars,* he commanded the useless, plaguing thoughts as he opened the door and stepped through into shadows. *Didn't the old heroes say that one is only truly alive when death is close?*

The darkness behind the door was not as complete as he had first thought. A single torch burned at the far end of a corridor of featureless stone, above a door as simple as the one he had just entered. For a moment he mistook the row of unmoving figures on either side of the hallway for statues, but then he saw they wore the unadorned, face-hiding helmets and snowy white armor of Utuk'ku's personal guard, the Queen's Teeth. These were no stone carvings; unmoving silence was their ordinary state.

Viyeki's father Urayeki was a court artist, always sober and correct with his noble subjects but more high-spirited at home with his family, and on occasion almost fanciful. When Viyeki was a child his father told him that the Queen's Teeth were actually the spirits of warriors who had fallen in the queen's defense, their bravery earning them the privilege of guarding her for all eternity. Viyeki had eventually learned the truth, but the memory remained. And though they might not be spirits, none except for those in the highest precincts of the Maze and the Order of Sacrifice knew much about the Teeth, how they were chosen and trained, where in the great palace they were housed, or even any of their names. A drunken commander of Sacrifices had once told Viyeki that the queen's elite guards surrendered their tongues to the knife during the ceremony when they donned their sacred helms of white witchwood.

What a world it must have been when witchwood was so plentiful, Viyeki thought as he passed between the rows of silent, helmeted sentries. Little of it still grew, and the sacred groves were now all but empty. *Only the queen herself remains undying and unchanged. Everything else that belongs to the People falls away, grows slack, crumbles to dust . . .*

As he reached the end of the corridor the door there opened, though none of the guards had moved and no one stood behind. Viyeki stepped across the threshold, back into space and light.

Faces. They were the first thing he saw, spread across every wall of the vast chamber and stretched across its ceiling as well—huge faces, some staring nobly, some grimacing in agony; and every face belonged to the same person. Viyeki had seen those features a thousand times on monuments and murals. He knew them as well as those of his own family. It was Drukhi the White Prince, the queen's martyred son, who stared at him from all directions, most of the portraits rendered in *srinyedu*, a sacred weaving art that the Hikeda'ya had brought with them from the Garden, though even the tile floor displayed different moments of Drukhi's foreshortened life. In the middle of the chamber, under the eyes of all those weeping, suffering Drukhis, a spherical, filigree frame surrounded a massive bed, both supported by a single plinth of black stone. And at the center of the bed, like an egg waiting on a nest, sat the silver-masked form of Utuk'ku herself.

Viyeki was in the queen's own state bedchamber.

Shocked nearly witless by this realization, he dropped to his knees so quickly that he hurt himself against the hard floor, then pressed his head down on his hands in a pose of utter subjugation. He waited, eyes closed, but when someone finally spoke, the voice was not the queen's.

"Greetings, High Magister Viyeki. You are welcomed into the presence of the Mother of the People."

Still face down, Viyeki clenched his teeth. He knew those harsh tones all too well, and he did not like hearing them now. What was Akhenabi doing here, alone of all the queen's ministers?

"Her majesty speaks, and we all obey," Viyeki replied carefully. "Her majesty spoke and I obeyed."

"Rise, Magister," said the Lord of Song. "No need for excessive ceremony. The queen does not wish it."

"All thanks to the Mother of the People," he said, "and thanks to you for your welcome as well, Lord Akhenabi." Viyeki climbed to his feet but still avoided looking too directly at the slender, shrouded white figure on the great bed. The high magister of all Singers made an easier, if more unpleasant, object for his attention.

"You may address the queen," Akhenabi instructed him, as though Viyeki were some new-minted acolyte. "You are permitted."

It was all Viyeki could do to turn toward his ruler, though he still could not gaze at her directly. His heart was racing like a stone bounding downhill. He had been elevated to high magister during her long sleep, and had never met her face to face. He had not thought he would be so overwhelmed by the queen's presence, but every childhood story, every bit of his people's long history under her rule, had suddenly risen inside him like a flood and swept away his other thoughts. What did it matter what he believed or intended? Viyeki's entire existence belonged to the mind behind that shining, imperturbable silver mask; his life was utterly hers. How could it ever be otherwise?

Still, he could not help noticing that the Mother of All seemed a surprisingly small figure in the great bed with its spherical canopy of filigreed witchwood. Despite its great size, the canopy was as delicate as fine jewelry, as boldly beautiful as a ring of ice around the moon. Viyeki realized after a little discreet study that it was meant to resemble the porous casing around a witchwood kernel. And by that shape, he then realized, the canopy announced that the queen herself was the *kei-in*, the holy witchwood seed from which everything else sprang—the beginning of the Hikeda'ya people, as well as the source of all their race's gifts. Small wonder this was where she held audiences with her servitors.

That seed of all growth, the ageless queen, reclined on cushions in the center of the bed, her lower half covered by blankets. As always, Utuk'ku wore mourning colors—gown and gloves and hooded cloak of icy white—but the eyes that stared at him from the holes in her shining mask were as dark as the emptiness between stars.

She was staring at *him*, Viyeki abruptly realized—and *he* was staring back at the Mother of the People. Horrified by this accidental effrontery, he pressed his forehead against the tiles once more. "I offer the Garden a thousand thanks every day that you have returned to us, Majesty."

An ivory mantis in a cage on the queen's nightstand turned its head at Viyeki's sudden movement, then resumed cleaning itself. The silence stretched. At last he looked up, stilling the urge to blurt out more praise and more thanks, because that would suggest weakness or guilt, both bad things to show before the queen. At last Utuk'ku nodded, a tiny dip of the head that was the first movement he had seen from her. Her words, when they came, were not spoken from her mouth, but leaped directly into his thoughts like molten metal poured into his ears, abrupt, shocking, and painful.

"When you walk long enough in the wastelands of sleep," the queen said, *"you discover that the stars are eyes."*

Viyeki had no idea what her words meant. "Yes, O Mother of All."

"The queen is still not entirely well after her long sleep, Magister Viyeki." Akhenabi's harsh voice sounded more amused than anything else, but as always with Eldest, whether the queen, the Lord of Song, or one of their shrinking number of peers from the earliest years after arriving here from the Garden, it was impossible to guess what was hidden by the masks they all wore. Where the queen's features were forever hidden behind smooth silver, Akhenabi concealed his face behind a wrinkled, nearly translucent tissue of pale leather covered all over with tiny, silvery runes, the whole stitched directly to the Lord of Song's own skin at the sides, mouth, and the holes for the eyes. Whispered rumors said his mask had been the living face of one of Akhenabi's rivals. "With the help of my Singers, the Mother of the People is recovering swiftly from her great exertions in the War of Return, may she live forever in glory," Akhenabi continued. "But the welfare of our race cannot wait for the queen's full health, so neither will she. She wishes me to speak to you about the projects your Builders have begun in the lower levels."

"I am honored to make my report to our beloved monarch," Viyeki said with a small revival of confidence: if the queen wanted to know about his work, perhaps this was not his day to be punished after all. "As High Magister Akhenabi can confirm, Great Queen, we are expanding the city on Nakkiga's lower levels to make room for all the new slaves and halfblood workers." He spoke with a certain satisfaction: he and his order had worked hard for their queen and their people during her long sleep. "Two hundred of my Builders lead the effort, commanding a thousand mortals and almost half that number of Tinukeda'ya—carry-men, delvers, and others. We will finish in time for Drukhi's Day."

"Enough," said Akhenabi abruptly. "All this detail is meaningless, because the queen commands the work to stop now."

For a moment, Viyeki could draw no breath. "But . . . but we—!" he began.

"Do you dispute with the queen, Magister?"

"I . . . no, never! I would not dream of it," he said, struggling to find words. "But so much work has already been done!"

"That is unimportant, Magister Viyeki," declared the Lord of Song. "The Mother of All has different employment in mind for you and your Order."

Viyeki watched his most important undertaking as High Magister, the greatest source of his pride, crumble away in a moment, as though some foolish apprentice had struck at the wrong flaw in a stone facing. "Of course," he said after a pause to collect his startled thoughts. "Our lives are hers, always."

"Queen Utuk'ku is pleased to hear that," said Akhenabi. "Because while our monarch was deep in the *keta-yi'indra*, some of her nobles made decisions that are rightly reserved to the Mother of All alone. Rebuilding the old city outside the mountain gates, for instance. Or taking mortals as concubines simply to create more children—more *halfblood* children!"

Viyeki felt an icy fist close on his heart.

"In fact, Her Majesty was astonished to discover all that had changed during her *yi'indra*," Akhenabi went on, his voice carefully pitched to show his contempt for any who would try to alter the queen's will. "Things never done since the Eight Ships landed had been ordered in *her* name while she slept! Yes, Magister, our queen is unhappy—*very* unhappy—especially with any nobles who made these decisions while claiming the good of all as their reason, but in fact to benefit their own bodily lust and greed."

Of course the Lord of Song himself had been involved in every decision he now recited; but Akhenabi had not lived to be the queen's oldest and most powerful courtier by taking the blame for mistakes.

Viyeki was beginning to believe his execution might be the purpose of the audience after all. *So does Akhenabi intend to sacrifice me to preserve his own life, with Tzoja his unwitting excuse? But if I am given to the Hamakha torturers, I know things about the Lord of Song himself that Akhenabi might not wish the queen to hear. Could he only be warning me, then? Might he even be reminding me*—the thought was bizarre but compelling—*that we have common cause, a need to protect each other's secrets now the queen is awake?* In the midst of so much strangeness, this seemed perhaps the oddest idea of all, that Viyeki might be forced into permanent alliance with the Lord of Song. His old master Yaarike had been right—there was no stranger mistress than power.

"Thus, Magister," said Akhenabi sharply, "you can see why with so many other unwanted changes revealed to our beloved mistress upon her awakening, the queen does not wish to see her Order of Builders laboring for the greater comfort of slaves. Our race will not dwindle without them or the halfbreeds that treacherous nobles have forced upon us. The only thing our beloved queen has not decided is whether some of these mistakes were honest ones or whether they were all attacks on her sovereignty. Do you grasp this, High Magister?"

"Of course," Viyeki said. "I am grateful that she has shared her thoughts with an object as humble as myself."

"Good. And the queen wishes you to summon back those Builders who are working to shore up the old walls as well. All your order will be given new labors."

This was even more surprising than ending the expansion of the slave quarters. The old walls and their guard towers were some of Nakkiga's best defenses against the mortals, and all of them were badly in need of repair.

"I am not certain I understand," he said carefully. "Do we speak of the walls around Greater Nakkiga, the walls that surround our old city and territory outside the mountain? Because while the queen slept, the murdering Northmen won their way to our very doorstep precisely because those walls were in disrepair, but now we have almost made them safe again."

"You waste time just as your workers waste efforts on those useless walls, *Builder*." Akhenabi pronounced the order's name with scorn. "The queen says we no longer need to protect ourselves from the mortals."

Viyeki was astonished. "We . . . we do not?"

"No." The Singer's voice grew harsher. "Soon the mortals will need to protect themselves from us instead. The most recent War of Return is not over. But this audience nearly is." Akhenabi spread his gloved hands in a signal that demanded attention, but Viyeki was so stunned by his words that he could not have spoken if he wished. "The queen commands that all building in the lower levels and at the outer walls of Nakkiga must stop. You will see to that personally, Magister Viyeki. Later you will receive word of what new works your order will undertake. Is that understood?"

It did not appear he was going to die, or at least not at this moment, but beyond that Viyeki could scarcely grasp what he had just been told. Was this a plot of Akhenabi's to snatch even more power? Did the magician only pass along the queen's wishes—did Utuk'ku truly mean to go to war with the mortals again?—or did he somehow press his own ideas in her name? Akhenabi was subtle beyond Viyeki's understanding, but surely the Lord of Song knew how

hopeless such a war would be. Even with the new generation of halfbreed warriors, the Hikeda'ya were still vastly outnumbered by the Northmen on their
borders, let alone the rest of the mortals in all their ugly, wasp's-nest cities
scattered across the known world.

"I understand," was all he said out loud. "I will do whatever my queen
wishes, as always, and I thank her and the sacred Garden for her confidence in
me."

"One last thing that our beloved Mother of All wishes to make clear," declared the master of the Singers. "From now on the queen commands that all
mortal breeding-women will be kept in the lower level pens with the rest of
the slaves unless needed, and then returned there afterward. Do you hear this,
High Magister?"

Viyeki could only nod.

"Good. The queen's confidence in her noble ministers, like her love for her
people," said Akhenabi, "is wonderfully deep. But not endless."

A door opened in the wall. Akhenabi glanced at it, then back to Viyeki; the
meaning was clear.

Viyeki bowed and said, "We all sleep until the Queen wakes us," then performed his rituals of leavetaking before backing out of the vast white bedchamber.

Outside, his thoughts as disordered as if he had taken a bad fall, it was all he
could do not to stumble down the palace stairs and corridors like a drunkard.
He could make no sense out of what had just occurred. Did the queen truly
know what was happening, or did she still wander in dream while only seeming to have wakened? Was Akhenabi an enemy or an unlikely ally, and was
Viyeki really meant to send his favorite, Tzoja, out of his household entirely?
Most disturbing of all, what on earth could the Lord of Song have meant by
saying, "The War of Return is not over"? Were those merely words meant to
inspire? Then why abandon the work on the outermost walls? Viyeki had feared
many things from this audience, but had not imagined confusion as its main
product.

His household guards and his secretary were waiting for him outside the
palace gatehouse. Yemon could have no idea what had happened during his
audience, but recognized that his master's thoughts should not be interrupted,
so he accompanied Viyeki all the way back to the residence in silence. Neither
did he ask any questions when they were finally through the doors of the house
itself, because Viyeki left them all suddenly and without further orders, shut
himself in his study and latched the door behind him.

His wife Khimabu could not rouse him when she was preparing to go to
bed—Viyeki told her loudly and angrily to go away. And much later, when
Tzoja knocked softly at the study door and called to him, the mother of his
child received no answer at all.

6

An Aversion to Widows

Even several days after they had departed Hernysadharc, the queen was still angry.

Spring was coming on quickly even as they traveled farther north, the snow reduced to patches upon the open meadows, in treetops, and on the upper slopes of the hills; the breeze carried warm hints of grass and flowering things. It all should have made for a pleasant ride, but Miriamele could not shift the mood that had seized her.

"Your Majesty looks a bit fierce," her husband said. "Frightening, a lesser man might even call it."

Simon was only trying to amuse her, she knew, but she was not in the mood. "If you must be told, I am still furious with that preening, giggling bitch, Tylleth."

"Then you think she is a real danger?" Simon's look said he truly wanted to know. Miri felt a sudden wash of gratitude that she had found such a man, one who cared what she thought because he trusted her and loved her, not because of the crown on her head.

Could I rule with any other? I cannot imagine such a world.

"If she were merely some chattering magpie of a courtier Hugh was bedding, no, I would not," she told him. "But she has him wrapped around her finger. And you heard what Eolair said. Witchcraft!"

Simon frowned. The two of them were riding a short distance behind the vanguard; for once they had the chance to speak privately. "Perhaps. But even so, don't be so quick to put all the blame on her," he said. "Hugh has changed since I first knew him, and not for the better."

"Doubtless. But you didn't speak with her as much as I did. Although not for lack of the woman trying to get you to notice her."

Simon frowned. "Do you think so?"

"Think so? Blessed Elysia, she was all but rubbing her bosom against your arm when they showed us around, sliding against you like a cat in heat."

"I did not notice."

"You don't convince me—how could any man fail to notice that woman's breasts? She was all but carrying them around on a cushion and calling them the crown jewels."

Simon grinned and for a moment was a boy again. "Well, then, you're right, my dearest—I did notice. It embarrassed me, because I knew you were looking. I promise you, I care nothing—"

"That is not the point. Don't be thick."

"Ah, wife. You still retain your power to charm me."

"Stop. I won't be put off by your good mood. That woman frightens me. Even Inahwen—gentle Queen Inahwen!—calls her a danger. She is trying to raise demons! As Pryrates did!" Both of them had almost met death at the red priest's hands; she knew Simon would not pass over it lightly.

"Yes, yes, I heard everything Eolair had to say." Simon shook his head. "But we already have plenty of other problems, my dear. And Hernystir may be under the High Ward, but they are also a kingdom in their own right. What should we do? Seize the king's mistress and put her on trial for trying to raise demons? Aedonite rulers passing judgement on pagan nobility for witchcraft? Many of the Hernystiri are already chafing at being ruled by foreign Aedonites. We might as well send in the questioners of the Sacred College."

"Don't blind yourself, Simon," she said, more harshly than she intended. "Not everyone means well, as you do. You are too naïve sometimes."

"Please don't treat me like a child, Miri." For the first time, her husband's equable mood soured. "Don't instruct me as if I was still a scullion. Not after all these years."

After that, they rode for a while in silence. She was sorry to have scolded him, but not enough to apologize. Her husband's inclination to trust was part of the reason she still loved him so powerfully, but that didn't mean she was wrong.

Miriamele had already conceived a deep dislike of Hugh's intended before Eolair had told them of his conversation with Queen Inahwen. Certainly Lady Tylleth's easy familiarity—as if Miriamele, a queen herself and the daughter and granddaughter of kings, were nothing more elevated than an elder sister—had set her teeth on edge. But the woman also seemed amused by everything going on around her, not like Miriamele's dear friend Rhona, who genuinely could not help finding things funny, but in the superior way of someone who treasured a secret that everyone else would be shocked to know. Hearing about Inahwen's fears had only solidified Miriamele's own concerns. Still, Simon was right about one thing—the High Throne had many other problems more tangible and more pressing. The horrible mess of the Northern Shipping Alliance's near-war with the old meddler Count Streawé's daughter, the Countess of Perdruin, had the potential to throw trade into chaos up and down Osten Ard, to name only one.

But as she thought of such things, Miri found a core of sadness inside herself that had little to do with the affairs of state.

"It was hard, being away from home on his birthday," she said, the first words either she or Simon had spoken in some time. "I did not expect it to be so hard after all this time. But it was."

Her husband accepted the offered peace. "For me, too, my dear. I sometimes feel like a cat." He saw her look and smiled sadly. "I mean, Old Shem the groom used to say that he had to watch the stable cats carefully, because if they had a small spite, a rat bite or wound from another cat's claws, all would seem well and healed on the outside, but the wound would still be festering under the skin. Sometimes it would kill them weeks later, when they seemed to have been long past it."

"Now that's a lovely, reassuring thought."

He flushed. "I meant only that grief . . . that sometimes we have not healed as well as we thought, my love."

She saw that she was doing it again, biting at him when she most needed their old companionship, the thing that bound them together from the very beginning as surely as the love they later came to feel. The subject of John Josua especially brought it out in her, as though her husband somehow bore the blame for that agonizing loss instead of being another victim. "I'm sorry. You're right. It is hard sometimes. I thought it would be easier as the years went on. I suppose most of the time it is. But when it isn't . . ."

"I try to remember all the good that came from his life, cut short though it was. I remind myself of the good things we still have . . . Morgan, and Lillia."

"Do you count the Widow too?"

He smiled, but there was a pained twist to it. "Idela is the mother of our grandchildren. And I don't think she is as dreadful as you sometimes paint her."

"John Josua should not have married so young. And he should not have married *her*."

"He loved her. No one could talk him out of it, Miri. You know that."

"But we were his mother and father! We should have—!" This time she swallowed the words before they could come out, then violently expelled her breath. "All the saints, give me strength! I cannot bear to hear myself." She bent forward in the saddle and ran her fingers through her horse's mane, trying to distract herself. She saw Eolair riding a short distance away, close to them now but not too close. "Everything seems sad or frightening to me today," she told her husband. "Isgrimnur, John Josua's birthday, and that mad, rude performance in Hernystir. Hugh treated us like unimportant old relatives. And spending three days with that witch he's going to marry only made it worse. Demons or no demons, that Tylleth probably killed her husband, you know. People certainly think so."

"People think many things. Often they are wrong." This time, Simon's smile looked a bit foxy. "Perhaps you simply have an aversion to widows."

She glared, but she knew it was only a jest. "There is Eolair. Ask *him* to tell you again what he thinks of her. And what Queen Inahwen thinks."

She said it loudly enough that the Hand of the High Throne looked over to them, his expression carefully empty. "Did you call me, Majesty?"

"You have been riding beside us for a while, good Count," she said. "I can see you are waiting for us to stop talking."

"I do not want to trouble Your Majesties or interrupt your conversation."

"Call it saving us from ourselves, then," said the king. "Miri and I are both out of sorts. Come, ride here beside us and tell us what's on your mind."

Eolair looked at Miri, who nodded. "Very well, then," he said. "I have had a messenger from Hernysadharc just now. Pasevalles' dispatch came after we had left, so Hugh sent it on by fast rider."

"Very kind of him," said Simon flatly.

Eolair was the last man in Osten Ard to miss something simply because it was unspoken. "Majesties, I still do not know what King Hugh was thinking to keep you waiting at the gate," he said. "I apologize again on behalf of all my countrymen for such strange, discourteous behavior. Queen Inahwen was surprised and shamed that the king kept you waiting so long outside the walls. She told me so."

Simon waved his hand. "Inahwen is kind—she always was. I am not too troubled. Men are men, whether king or kitchen worker, as I should know better than anyone. Hugh may be a bit overexcited by his own grandeur, as well as by the prospect of marriage. As for Lady Tylleth . . ." Simon had just noticed the halves of the broken seal that bound the folded papers in Eolair's hand. "Well, enough of her for now. What does Lord Chancellor Pasevalles have to say?"

"Do you not want to read it yourself, Majesty?"

"I know you too well to think you would have broken that seal if the letter was not addressed to you, good Eolair, and I also know you will have read it carefully and probably more than once, because you are someone who 'never has time for clean hands,' as my old taskmistress Rachel the Dragon used to say. So please, tell us what is on Pasevalles' mind, or at least the things we need to know."

Miriamele nodded. When they were young, and the fact of their sudden power was like a waking dream, Simon had tried to be all things to all people, unable to refuse a favor or to turn his back on a cry of need. Miriamele, raised in her father's courts in Meremund and then the Hayholt, had already known that a monarch who could not stand aloof sometimes was a miserable monarch indeed. It had taken years, and the elevation of several old, trusted friends to the most important positions in court, but her too-kind husband had finally learned he could not be all things to all people.

Eolair undid the flattened roll and, as Miriamele had expected, immediately found the first thing he wished to discuss, several pages in: He prepared for any and all of his duties, no matter how small, with the anguished care of a general outnumbered and at bay.

"After much talk about the dedication of the new chapter house and the work on the library—as well as a few other matters I will save for later, like the League's complaint about Yissola's latest *outrages*, as they deem them—the Lord Chancellor gets to the business at hand." Eolair's rueful smile pulled his strong, weathered features into a droll face, and Miriamele remembered when she had thought him perhaps the most handsome man in all of Osten Ard. "I do wish our friend Pasevalles could be persuaded to put the most important business at the beginning of the letter, but he still writes like a child of a provincial court, full of flowery greetings and formal phrases even in a dispatch." Eolair's eyes widened a little. "Forgive me, Majesties. I did not mean to sound as if I was criticizing the Lord Chancellor. He is an able man and a fine administrator . . ."

Simon laughed. "You need not worry—we know you admire him."

"Indeed. Your Majesties are lucky to have him, and he will take good care of the Hayholt and Erkynland in your absence."

"But you were not so certain of that when we made the decision to travel to Rimmersgard, were you?" Simon said. "Come, I am teasing you, old friend. I know you were only doing your duty. It is a difficult thing to take away the king and queen from their court for so long. But we should get back to the business of Pasevalles's letter."

"Let me just read this to you," said Eolair, moving the heavy parchment until he found an appropriate distance from his eyes. *"But, my gracious lords and lady, I fear the news from your great southern duchy of Nabban is not so good . . ."* he began.

"He can be a bit wordy, our Pasevalles, can't he?" Simon remarked when Eolair had finished.

"But the essence is clear enough," said Miriamele. "Duke Saluceris is struggling more than ever with his brother, and Drusis as always is champing at the bit to push the boundaries of Nabban farther out into the Thrithings. And the rest of Nabban, also as usual, is waiting to see which of them wins the contest, as though it were no greater matter than a horse race."

"Drusis claims that he wants only to protect Nabbanai settlers from raids by the Thrithings-men," said Eolair. "But that is the substance of the discord, yes, Your Majesty. I will summarize the rest of Pasevalles' points. He believes the desire to push out into the grasslands is too strong among the houses of Nabban's Dominiate, and in the country as a whole, for Duke Saluceris to openly forbid his brother these aggressive actions, and he is also not certain that the duke could survive an open struggle with Drusis in any case."

"Does he truly mean 'survive'?" asked Miriamele, alarmed for the first time. "Surely these are mere disagreements. The Benidrivine House is the house of Camaris the Hero himself, and Saluceris is the lawful duke of Nabban, not just by their own laws, but under our Ward. By the love of the saints, Simon and I crowned Saluceris ourselves in the Sancellan Aedonitis, in front of God and all Nabban!"

"All true," said Eolair. "And I do not imagine Drusis would move directly against his brother and flout so much law and custom. But assassination, if it could not be directly laid at Drusis's door, would still make him the next duke, since Saluceris' son is still a child. I hate to say so, but as Your Majesties know, murder has long been a favored method of gaining power in the south."

Simon made a frustrated noise. "Well, this is a puzzle and no mistake. But what can Miri and I do? It would be heavy-handed to send troops to Saluceris when he has not asked for such a thing." He looked around at the column of armored men marching behind them and the vanguard of mounted knights. "Not that we have any troops to spare just now, with the planting season hard upon us. Maybe Duke Osric is right when he says we need a larger standing force . . ."

After the king had paused long enough that it was clear he had finished his thought, Count Eolair gracefully took charge of the conversation once more. "Let me be clear, Majesties. Lord Pasevalles does not ask you for a solution at this moment, but merely wishes you to know what the news from Nabban tells him, so that any change will not come as a complete surprise."

"In other words," said Miriamele, "he wishes us to share his worry and his helplessness."

Eolair frowned just the smallest bit. "I'm afraid that is often a loyal subject's duty in such cases, my queen."

Miri knew she was being unduly cross, but the sun and the spring scents she had hoped to enjoy were fading beneath all these fretful shadows of statecraft.

"You look as though you are thinking hard, my clever wife," said Simon. "You have been in Nabban far more than I have and your family is still powerful there. What should we do?"

Miriamele shook her head. "Clearly my Nabbanai kin are busy adding fuel to the fire, almost certainly for their own purposes, and I would not trust my cousin Dallo Ingadaris even to hold my reins for fear he would steal my horse. But there are still many other Ingadarines I trust. I'll write to them and see how things appear from where they sit, and whether the fight between brothers is as dangerous as Pasevalles suspects."

"We've already heard enough of this Drusis to think ill of him," Simon said. "He's an arrogant, troublesome fellow, no doubt. But surely one man cannot provoke an entire nation into war by himself."

"It seems unlikely," said Eolair. "But stranger things have happened. In any case, as Your Majesties pointed out, we cannot send troops when they have not been requested—the Nabbanai would rightly resent it. And this is only one letter. Pasevalles is from Nabban himself, so perhaps he feels its storms more strongly than the rest of us would. But when we return—well, perhaps greater attention to Nabban would not go amiss. They are a numerous and often quarrelsome people. I beg the queen's pardon if I offend."

After a moment's silence, Miriamele said, "Offend? No, Eolair, I say it often enough myself. But we've barely begun this journey and already I see troubles growing everywhere." The sun, though its beams still sparkled on patches of snow and the sky was empty of clouds, seemed to have grown dimmer. "I wish we were home."

"We all feel that way, my love," Simon told her. "At least, at times like this."

He Who Always Steps On Sand, why did you lead your child to such a strange place?

The gods of Tiamak's childhood in the Wran were nowhere near as powerful and ever-present as the deity his employers worshipped, but there were times he couldn't help thinking that a little closer oversight from them might still be in order, especially on this royal progress into cold northern lands.

He pulled his cloak tighter. He would never become used to drylander clothes, but he was inexpressibly glad to have the right sort of garments for these chilly northern lands instead of what he had worn in the first part of his life, seldom more than a breechclout and occasionally a pair of sandals. Even thinking about what it would be like to cross into frigid Rimmersgard in such near-nakedness made him shiver, although several of the riders nearest him had taken off their helmets to enjoy the early spring sunshine.

Sunshine, he thought. *Back in our swamp, no one would have called such thin gruel "sunshine." It is not hot enough here to lure even a cold turtle out onto a rock.*

It was not that Tiamak missed his marshy home, exactly; even in Village Grove he had been an outsider, a strange young man who had learned to read and write and had gone to Ansis Pellipé in Perdruin to study—an actual city! But he missed the security he had felt as a child in the swamp, beneath the spreading branches and heavy leaves, when everything had been known and familiar. Now it seemed that the more years passed, the more strange the world became.

Not too many years from now I will truly be old, he thought. *Will the world be completely strange to me then?*

Tiamak had never been this far north before, that was part of it. Not only the cold air, but the very size of the sky seemed foreign, the broad expanse of blue so wide that he almost felt as though he stood atop some terrible high plateau instead of on a broad plain of streams and snow-dotted meadows. But the snow was finally vanishing with the warming days, Tiamak reminded himself; he should remember to say a prayer of thanks. At the same time last year, as his comrades never wearied of telling him, this part of Osten Ard had been hip deep in swirling, mounding snow, the skies gray as lead.

So that is a good place to start with my gratitude, he told himself. *Thank you, He Who Bends the Trees. Thank you for any sun at all and not too much snow!*

He might have felt differently, he suspected, had they not been called north by such a sad circumstance, the imminent death of Duke Isgrimnur of Elvritshalla. Had it been anything less, though, he would probably not have accompanied the king and queen. But Isgrimnur had been Tiamak's friend as well. Along with Miriamele, who was then only a young girl, they had faced impossible, almost unbelievable odds together and survived. That alone would have obligated Tiamak to travel to this unsettling part of the world, but over the years his friendship with Isgrimnur had become something more, something completely unexpected. The sulfurous duke, big as a house, as he had first seemed to Tiamak, had proved to be as wise as he was loud and as subtle as he was brave. They had stayed in touch by letter, only a few per year stowed in the diplomatic posts that passed between Elvritshalla and the Hayholt, but enough to keep the friendship very much alive.

And in fact, for most of that time it had been a three-part friendship, because Isgrimnur's wife Gutrun had always carefully gone through her husband's letters, adding in the words the duke had forgotten in haste, correcting the occasional woeful mistake of grammar (Isgrimnur was equally bad in his native Rimmerspakk, she had often told Tiamak) and adding her own comments full of useful news and funny stories about her husband. The news of Gutrun's death several years ago had been one of the saddest days of Tiamak's life. He had spent very little time in her actual company, but in her husband's letters, peeping out from between his scrawled lines, she had made a home for herself in Tiamak's heart.

It was so hard to lose her, he thought. *And now the duke. Why does She Who Waits To Take All Back wait so long? Why must the reaping wait until we have grown so used to the world, when the pain will be sharpest for both the dead and their survivors?*

Tiamak adjusted himself on the hard carriage seat. He had not become so much of a northerner now that he liked to ride a horse, nor was he large enough to comfortably ride one for long even if he wished. He had a donkey they kept for him in the stables back home, an unpleasant but reasonably steady creature named Scand, but there was no question of Tiamak riding the beast on this trip, where it would struggle every moment to keep up with the horses. Instead, the little man sat beside the driver atop the carriage meant for the king and queen— not that they had used it yet as anything more than a moving cabinet for their clothing and other belongings. Back at the Hayholt, Tiamak only rode Scand when he wished to be outside, and almost always in the company of young Princess Lillia and her pony. The royal granddaughter was nearly as pig-headed as the donkey, but Tiamak loved her in a way he would never have imagined possible, more even than he had loved his sisters' children, as much as if she had been of his very own flesh.

It was not solely his loyalty to Simon and Miriamele that made it so: Tiamak liked the heir Prince Morgan well enough, but there was something about the little girl that pulled and tugged at his heart, and when she called him "Uncle Timo" he was quite helpless. Even if there had been anything left for him back in the Wran, even if the elders there had begged him to come back and be their chief, Tiamak knew he might not have been able to leave the little girl behind. He wanted to watch Lillia grow, see that clever mind fill with more and more understanding, watch her learn to put that powerful ambition to some higher task than simply forcing her slave-uncle Tiamak to build complex waterwheels for her in the mud of Kynswood streams.

But losing Isgrimnur or missing little Lillia were not the only sources of

Tiamak's discomfort. When the news came to the Hayholt about the duke, Tiamak had just begun his great work. Planning it had been the work of years, but instead of seeing it finally come to fruition he was here, a hundred leagues away from the castle and weeks from returning, knowing his work had all but stopped in his absence.

And I am no longer young, he thought sadly. *Who knows how much time I have to complete this sacred task?*

It was only a library, most people would say, a collection of books and scrolls, the kind of thing Isgrimnur himself might well have thought a strange waste of space and time, but it was to be the first true open library ever built in the northern lands, and to Tiamak, who as a child had wondered if he might ever own a real book, it meant the world. Conceived to honor Miriamele and Simon's late son, Prince John Josua, the unfinished library was already precious to Tiamak, who had cared for that young man very much. John Josua had loved books and learning as much as the Wrannaman did, and he had ambitions to make it a great center of scholarship in the young prince's name.

But until we return from Rimmersgard, I can do nothing to aid the work except send the occasional letter to the master mason and pray for patience—

A sudden gust from the faded blue mountains to the north pimpled Tiamak's exposed skin, and although the wind had been blowing all day, the strength of this chill surprised him, pushing deep into his very substance, bones and innards. Without even thinking, he made circles of his forefingers and thumbs to repel bad luck, as he had done when he was a child.

If I were back in Village Grove, he thought, *I would be certain that She Who Waits To Take All Back had just breathed on my neck, reminding me that she has plans none of us know about.*

Which was true, of course, as it always was. He was letting sadness over Isgrimnur make him fretful, jumping at shadows, cringing from sharp breezes.

While Tiamak was trying to gather back together his hopeful thoughts about the library, he heard someone come riding swiftly up behind him. He looked down from his high seat to see one of Eolair's servants pacing the carriage on a tall, dark horse.

"Your pardon, Lord Tiamak," the rider said. "The Lord Steward bids me give you this. It came with the dispatches from Erkynland."

Tiamak looked it over as Eolair's servant rode away, and his heart lightened a bit. He knew who it was from instantly because of the odd seal pressed into the red wax: instead of a heavy metal stamp or a signet ring, his wife Thelía always pressed a small dried flower into the melted wax. Because she had sent the letter several months back, in Feyever, she had chosen one of the first wildflowers that bloomed in Erkynland every year, a bright yellow bloom called sunlion or sometimes coltsfoot. He knew she would have picked it herself as she gathered herbs and simples in the castle gardens, and it should have warmed him just to see its sunbeam petals, still bright despite its long travels, but he was still feeling the effects of the chill that had surprised him a few moments earlier.

He unfolded the letter and began reading, hoping for good news, or at least an absence of anything worrisome. Her opening words were in her usual, conversational tone—Thelía seemed interested only in sharing various workaday matters, a few decisions on the library materials she hoped he would be able to write back about, and a question about wild marjoram and what he knew of its use in his boyhood home in the Wran. But then he reached the final paragraph.

One last thing, my patient husband, a small but odd and interesting tale.

I was called in your absence to practice physick on one of the kitchen workers, an old fellow of Hernystiri blood who had fallen into a fit on the floor of the buttery. I do not know if you know him. His name is Riggan, and he is a thin, gnomish fellow, three score years old or even more, with large, bleary eyes and rough skin. He was not badly hurt, but his command of the Westerling tongue is poor, so I asked Countess Rhona to help me. She asked him in his own speech what had happened, and he said, "I hear the Morriga talking to herself. Every night and I cannot sleep."

Countess Rhona looked a bit startled, I thought, and told me the Morriga was an ancient Hernystiri goddess of death and battle, no longer worshipped among her people but still feared, still blamed for nightmares and other foul things. Then, before I could ask another question, this Riggan said something else in that tongue, and this is what I thought would interest you. His words were, "She summons us back. She summons us all back. She is the silver-masked Mistress of Tears." Now I ask you, husband, does that not sound as though the Norns' Queen Utuk'ku, once a real, living menace to all mankind, has somehow become a demon-fable for kitchen workers? The Sithi friends of the king and queen thought her power was utterly destroyed when the Storm King was defeated, and I pray that is true. If she is now nothing but a legend, a fading nightmare, then I thank our merciful God for preserving us all from her evil.

I did not want to spend long with the man Riggan once he seemed recovered, because he disturbed me more than a little, with his strange face and goggling, fishlike eyes, and it was also disquieting to see calm, wise Countess Rhona look so pale at hearing the name of the Morriga—the 'mother of all demons' as Rhona named her. My Aedonite sisters would call this man's malady the work of the Devil, but my learning has been so shaped by yours, dear Tiamak, that I suppose it instead only the confusion of an illness of his mind with tales he might have heard in childhood. In fact, I deem it proof of what you always say, my wise husband, "Truth and falsehood walk a long way together before they go their separate ways . . ."

Had he received her message just a few days earlier her tale of the kitchen worker's fit would have been a mere curiosity to turn over in his spare moments; but instead this story of a madman who dreamed of the Norn Queen made Tiamak feel like a traveler abroad at night who hears something following him through the trees. On the night the royal party had left Hernystir, Count

Eolair had told Tiamak and the king and queen of Queen Inahwen's worries about Lady Tylleth—that she and some the courtiers were worshipping the terrible ancient goddess, the Morriga, and now here was that name again.

It has to be chance, Tiamak told himself—Eolair himself had said that stories of the goddess were as old as Hernystir itself. But even as he soothed himself, his earlier chill returned, and this time without any cold wind to blame.

The silver-masked Mistress of Tears . . . A deep dread clutched at his heart. *Something is coming that will threaten all,* he thought helplessly—*my library, the royal children, the throne. I can feel it.* He took in a long, shaky breath, his heart fluttering behind his ribs like a trapped bird.

The driver flicked his whip to keep the horses together, oblivious to anything but the jingle of harness and the thump of hooves. The sky was still blue overhead, the sun still shone, but Tiamak felt as though he had stepped on what should have been solid ground and found nothing beneath him but yawning emptiness.

7

Island of Bones

The other four members of the Queen's Hand sat silently on the beach below, waiting for the ship to come. They had already waited on the graveled strand for hours, still as statues while the wind strengthened and the afternoon died with the sun, and would likely sit that way without moving for many hours more, but Nezeru had never before seen the ocean. She had been so taken by its immensity, its vitality, its ever-changing surface and colors that she had climbed the cliffs above the isolated beach to get a better view.

It was not only the size of the ocean that fascinated her, astounding as it was: the snowfields north of the great mountain back home seemed equally boundless. It wasn't the colors, either, as magnificent and unexpected as they were, the startling jade translucence of the waves, the grays and blues and blacks and ragged whitecaps, because to Hikeda'ya eyes the great icefields of the Nornfells were full of color, too. No, it was the *alive*-ness of the sea that stunned Nezeru, the constant motion in different directions, the intersection of wave against wave that could turn water into weightless froth and throw it high into the sky. And it was not just the water itself that was alive: seabirds rose and sank on every swell, or drifted above the waves in rotating clouds, their squawking cries filling her ears, filling the sky. Most of them were hunting the silvery fish that sparkled in almost every wave. Life was everywhere. Nezeru knew that if she gathered a sack of Nakkiga barley the size of a house and dumped it onto the snowy ground outside her mountain home, not a thousandth of this array of living things would come to it. There would be crows, a few waxwings, and with nightfall the rats and mice, but the land around Nakkiga could boast nothing like this chaos of noise and movement.

She crouched on the hilltop and watched the sun dive down toward the sea, where it tipped the waves with copper. As the last sliver of the daystar dropped behind the horizon it flashed green, and as that moment came and passed Nezeru happened to look down at the cliff face beneath her feet. Something pale sat only a few arms' lengths below her, shining in the day's last light.

Nezeru did not hesitate, but swung herself over the edge and then let herself down the steep rock face, testing each hold before giving it her weight because the sandstone cliff was old and crumbling. In moments, she was dangling by one arm and balancing on the ball of one foot beside a bird's nest and its lonely occupant, a single pale, brown-spotted egg.

A seagull's nest, she decided as she examined the frowsy accumulation of sticks and feathers and mud. Few gulls made it all the way inland to Lake Rumiya beside the great mountain, but those who did were of keen interest to the Hikeda'ya and their servants, whose diets were always limited by the bitter cold and frosty ground of their native land. Nezeru knew very well both the look of a seagull's nest and the taste of the birds and their eggs.

She carefully lifted the speckled thing, testing its weight. It seemed early in the year for egg-laying, but there was no question that something warm and alive slept inside. For a moment she considered taking it—Hand Chieftain Makho was very sparing with food—but after hours standing atop the cliff, Nezeru felt almost like a guest in this place. Also, the nest held only one egg, which made it seem something to be admired rather than used. It was an odd feeling—one that most of her training refuted—but Nezeru gently set the egg back down in the nest.

The light was waning as she climbed back up the cliff, the sky above her bleeding its violet into growing black. She paused to look out to the west where the sun had sunk and the last light of day was fighting and failing. Far out on the horizon, so distant it would have been invisible to less keen eyes than those of the Hikeda'ya, she saw the pale geometry of sails. She glanced down to the beach, but felt certain that the approaching ship must still be hidden from Makho and the rest. As she scrambled to the top of the bluff, pleased to be the one bringing news, a swirl of air brought the sharp and sudden smell of danger.

Nezeru peered above the edge; a boar had appeared, out for its evening forage. It was unaware of her, at least for the moment, but she knew that ignorance would not last long. At first she thought it must be a large male, since it looked to be at least three times her own weight, with viciously sharp tusks as long as her fingers, but the scent and the time of year suggested it was an older sow, in which case it was probably protecting piglets and would be especially aggressive. Worse, to make climbing easier, Nezeru had left her sword and bow with her pack down on the beach.

As she pulled herself onto more or less level ground she slipped her knife from its sheath, although it didn't give her much confidence. A dying boar pierced by a heavy spear could still drive itself on sturdy, strong legs up the shaft toward its attacker and rip out a hunter's guts before collapsing.

Nezeru had killed before, and not just animals, but wanted no part of this if she could avoid it. This creature had not sought her out. It might have young to protect. Still, the stink of the sow was powerful, even against the prevailing ocean breeze and its blend of complicated smells. If the creature had recently farrowed, it might not accept anything less than a fight to the death or Nezeru's running for her life, and a Sacrifice did not run—especially not one of the Queen's Talons.

It saw her. *It will swing its head side to side to strike with those tusks*, she thought. *My knife is not long enough to reach its heart, but a well-aimed thrust might take it in the eye—*

Before she had time to finish the thought, the boar scrambled toward her, back legs shoving hard against the loose, cold dirt, grunting and squealing as Nezeru dodged its first lunge. It turned on her again with such surprising quickness that she had time only to leap up and put her hands on its shoulders, hard bristles digging into her skin as she vaulted into the air. The boar threw up its snout to catch her as she went over, swinging its great head; the muddy tusks missed Nezeru's belly by less than a hand's breadth.

She landed and spun, knife out. The boar moved sideways, doing its best to keep Nezeru trapped against the edge of the precipice. Vegetation was so sparse here that she knew if she was forced over the edge she would find nothing to grab, nothing to arrest her fall all the way down to the stony beach. Still, leaping over the huge beast had barely worked the first time; if she tried it again, her belly or her leg might well be torn open by one of those deadly ivory scythes.

She quickly checked the distance to the cliff's edge behind her, then crouched, knife extended now, tracking the boar's head from side to side. Nezeru decided she would go for the animal's eye, or perhaps if she was lucky and avoided the first slash of the tusks, make a quick attempt to rip open the belly or the throat. "Are you sure you want this, Little Mother?" she asked. "I would not take your life except in defense of my own."

The angry red eyes gave no hint of similar sentiments. The wild sow shook her head and let out another grating bellow. An instant later the huge pig was thrown sideways to the ground as if struck by lightning. It let out a shrieking squeal that sounded like the terror-cry of a thinking being, then began to crawl unsteadily away toward the undergrowth, dragging a long spear shaft through the bloody dirt.

Kemme, one of Nezeru's fellow Sacrifice warriors, strode forward and set his booted foot on the sow's ribs to yank his spear free. The boar screamed again and its legs kicked, but he seemed to have torn a hole in its guts and the animal's last struggles ended quickly.. He wiped the head of his spear on the bristling hide, then looked up at Nezeru with poorly hidden distaste. "The ship is here," he said. "Chieftain Makho orders you down to the beach." He set his spear on his shoulder, turned, and walked away without a second glance at the twitching animal.

"But what about the boar?" said Nezeru after a moment, when her surprised, swirling thoughts had turned back into words.

"We have enough to eat." Kemme was clearly displeased to have to explain himself to a younger Sacrifice. "A war-hand, especially one made up of the Queen's Talons, does not drag food around with them as helpless mortals do."

"But there will be mortals manning the ship," she said. "Surely they can find some use for the meat." She did not know if she could carry the dead beast down the hill by herself, but she was willing to try. It was better than wasting it.

Kemme did not even bother to look back at her. "Leave it," he said.

The ship was anchored far out in the bay. As Nezeru reached the bottom of the cliff a few paces behind Kemme, a longboat rowed by a half-dozen bearded men was already nearing the beach. She had no real fear of mortals, but simply seeing so many of them together lifted her hackles. Their hand chieftain Makho was speaking with Ibi-Khai of the Order of Echoes, but Nezeru kept her distance, in no hurry to be reprimanded for dallying on the hilltop. She was wondering where the fifth member of their hand had gone when she felt a presence behind her, as though someone or something was about to touch her. She whirled, drawing her knife again. The blade stopped an inch short of the halfblood Saomeji's throat.

The magician did not blink or lift a hand to defend himself, but his pale lips curled in an expression that might have been amusement. "We could not find you," was all he said. Unlike the rest of the Talons, the Singer did not wear his cloak with the black side out, now that they had left the snows, but continued to wear the white as proudly as if he were in the Singers' Order-house back in Nakkiga. For someone who was as much of an outsider as Nezeru was, Saomeji never seemed to fear setting himself apart from the rest of the company.

"Thank you, hand-brother," she said, making her words as neutral as possible. She was determined not to give him undue respect, although she feared him as she feared all his order. No, it was *because* she feared him that she would give him nothing. "I was only atop the cliff, watching for the ship."

Saomeji held her gaze. He had strange, golden eyes, though his skin was as white as that of any pureblood. "Traitor's eyes" they were called back in Nakkiga, because the eyes of the Sithi, the Norns' kinfolk, were that same color, though the two tribes had been gone their separate ways for a very long time. Such ancient features were scorned among the Hikeda'ya, even though they predominantly occurred in the oldest clans. As another halfblood, Nezeru wondered how much Saomeji had suffered for having a mortal parent. Even to ask him, though, would be to create a kind of intimacy in which she had no interest.

As she and Saomeji joined the others, Makho stared at her so hard it made her uneasy, his eyes as unfeeling as a hunting eagle's. Nezeru had admired him since she had first joined the Order, and had always done her best to emulate his pure-mindedness and his mask of stony indifference, but she feared that no matter how hard she tried, the human side of her heritage would keep her from being accepted by him or the others as true Hikeda'ya. Halfbloods were plentiful now in Nakkiga, and they always matured far more swiftly than their pureblood counterparts, though they seemed to live nearly as long. Nezeru had become a death-sung Sacrifice at an age when her untainted peers were scarcely ready to join an Order, let alone be granted its highest honors, but the confidence of the insider could never be hers. She was half-mortal, and her father, though important, was not even of the Order of Sacrifice; only deeds could overcome such a heritage and lift her out of the crime of her diluted blood.

The rowers pulled their longboat up onto the strand. Like most mortals who lived near the ocean here in the north, they looked to be of Rimmersgard blood, but unlike their kinfolk farther south who had long ago given up the seafaring life, these so-called Black Rimmersmen still made their living upon the water, trading along the coast and even harrying and robbing any ships of other nations that strayed too far out of safe southern waters. But that was not the only reason these people were scorned by their Rimmersgard kinsmen. The Black Rimmersmen had been bound up with the Hikeda'ya for centuries, many of them captured and kept like animals, forced to labor for their Hikeda'ya masters. Slave or free, though, they were usually hated as turncoats by their own mortal kind.

At a sign from Makho, the Queen's Talons climbed silently into the boat and the staring, clearly frightened mortals rowed them out to the waiting ship.

The captain of the *Hringleit,* a gray-bearded mortal with a face browned and cracked by the elements, tried his best to act as though these passengers were nothing unusual. But Nezeru knew that there had been little direct contact between the coastal lands and Nakkiga since the end of the Storm King's War decades ago. These mortals might even have convinced themselves they were no longer the queen's slaves—until Makho and the rest of the Talons appeared in the coastal village and demanded passage to the outer northern islands. The thought filled Nezeru with sour amusement.

The captain certainly seemed to know these waters well, because they sailed through the night. As the dark hours passed and Nezeru watched, the stars wheeled across the sky overhead in their familiar constellations, the Gate, the Serpent, the Lantern and the Owl, as if they had come to remind her that no matter where she voyaged, she was still beneath the protection of the Garden.

When morning came, the land had utterly disappeared and everything beneath the gray sky was water. Nezeru slept for a while without closing her eyes, letting her thoughts drift.

She rose back to awareness to find the sun higher in the sky but still far from its noon prominence. A short distance away her chieftain Makho was sharpening his witchwood sword Cold Root against a polishing stone. She had watched him do it a hundred times since they had left Nakkiga in the previous moon, and still it fascinated her, the rigor of his attention, the unshakable sameness of his actions. The sword was well worth the care, of course, a blade of impeccable lineage: fellow Sacrifice Kemme had once told her, in tones of veneration, that it had belonged to a brother of Ekimeniso himself, the queen's revered but long-dead husband. More recently it had been wielded by one of Makho's nearer kin, General Suno'ku, the beloved hero who had died in the Nakkiga Siege.

Nezeru did her best to watch without too much obvious staring—it was a very bad time to break their leader's attention; Makho had slapped Ibi-Khai's face once for coughing when Cold Root was unsheathed. As she watched the chieftain's long, pale fingers moving across the blade, she found herself almost falling into the pattern of the witchwood, its gray lines like whorls on a fingertip, so delicate as to be almost invisible. Each witchwood sword was as individual as its wielder: the pattern of the grain differed with each tree. Even discounting ornament, no witchwood sword would ever be the same as another.

They were rarer than ever now, since witchwood itself was ever more scarce. Nezeru had heard whispers that the groves were lifeless places now, that only a few of the trees still grew, and that these had been moved for safety's sake to a garden inside the royal palace. Some of the whispers even said that these last trees were dying, too. Nezeru thought that such a loss would be almost a greater tragedy than the ancient dispossession of her race from the Garden or the evils that mortals had done to them in these new lands. The People still survived, and if they were strong, the Hikeda'ya might last until the world itself was unmade, but with the witchwood gone there would never be another sacred blade smithied; the great, damaged gates of Nakkiga would never be properly rebuilt. Old witchwood could not be forged anew. When it was broken the spells were unbound and it became no different than any other object of the weary, mortal earth.

By the second day on the mortals' ship, Nezeru began to see islands, some little more than clumps of rock that barely pierced the sea swells, others large enough to have vegetation of their own. One cold, windswept atoll was even decorated with wooded hills and a settlement of thatched houses near the shore.

"What people live here, in such a place?" she asked Makho as they passed it, but the chieftain ignored her.

"*Qosei*, we call them." The Singer Saomeji was very close to her, almost beside her ear, and this time she had not heard him approach. "They are much like the trolls in the eastern mountains or the mortals of the south, the swamp dwellers."

She wondered why the Singer seemed so eager to speak to her. Did he have some interest in her beyond their comradeship—beyond the Queen's sacred mission? She was grateful that he was another halfblood and thus had no right to force her to couple with him as Makho and the others did.

"Yes, they are like the trolls and the savages of the Wran," said Kemme, a scarred, hard-eyed veteran of the battles for Asu'a and the Nakkiga Gate. "They bleed, they die. And someday they and all the rest of the mortals will be scraped from the Queen's lands." He turned and strode away up the deck. The mortal crew hurried to get out of his way. Nezeru made to follow him, but Saomeji moved with graceful precision to block her path. "We have some time still before we reach the Island of the Bones."

"The sooner we can perform our task for the Mother of All, the happier I will be," she said, but for once she was interested in what he said. This was the first time she had heard anything of the nature of their mission, and the name of the island was unfamiliar to her.

Saomeji still had not moved. "If you would learn more of the Qosei or anything else of this place in the world, I would be pleased to share my knowledge with you."

"You are kind," she replied, "but I am sure such learning would be beyond me." Her father had always told her that the followers of Akhenabi, Lord of Song, were as deadly and secret as adders, subtle beyond the understanding of the other orders. Everyone in Nakkiga knew that the Order of Song was the Queen's favorite, its spellwielders and loremasters more valued even than the ancient Order of Celebrants or Nezeru's own huge and powerful Order of Sacrifice, but Nezeru could not imagine exchanging the warrior's way just for power. She had fought too hard in the first place to become, not just a Sacrifice but also the first of her kind to be named a Queen's Talon. Who would exchange such honor for a life of shadows, and ugly secrets? "I am trained only for a single task," she told him, making her voice firm, "—to kill the queen's enemies."

Saomeji may have guessed at her thoughts. "Do not scorn my knowledge, Sacrifice. A sword is no use without a hand to hold it, and a hand no use without the thoughts that guide it. My blood is no more pure than yours, and yet I have risen high already."

"My presence here shows that I am not scorned by my own order, either. Still, I thank you, Singer, for enlightening me about the natives." She inclined her head in the smallest acceptable acknowledgment, then slipped past him.

On the fourth day under sail, far out in the stone-gray sea, they reached the largest island they had yet seen. It was topped by a great mountain, the peak a broken cone dusted with snow. A half-dozen or so smaller hills clung to its sides like weary children, all of them blanketed at their bases in mist. Nezeru saw few tall trees, but everywhere that the land had not been cleared it was covered with green grass and thick undergrowth. A sizable settlement stood on the nearest plateau, several dozen sod-roofed houses surrounded by tiny earth-bound clouds that became sheep as Nezeru's ship drew closer, with herds of deer roaming farther up the slopes.

Dozens of small, brown-skinned people came down to the water's edge to watch as their ship anchored in the bay, and although the faces were more reserved than joyful, the men, women, and children watched the Hikeda'ya come ashore without fear. The islanders were small, though not as small as the mortals of the Trollfells, but as if to make up for the sameness of the landscape they were nearly all dressed in colorful clothing of woven wool and hide.

As Makho and the ship's captain walked into the village the crowd followed them into the center of the cluster of sod houses. When they stopped, an old man in a suit of bead-decorated hides walked slowly out of the largest hut. In one hand he held a scepter made from an antler, in the other a curved bone knife, its surface acrawl with carvings. As he approached, the old man waved these implements in the air and began to speak in a guttural tongue that was like nothing Nezeru had heard.

The ship's captain translated for them. "The elder welcomes you. He says it is an honor to meet the Knowing One's people. They have prepared a feast in your honor. Tonight you will stay in his lodge and then climb Goaddi tomorrow."

Makho was expressionless. "No. Tell him we wish to see the bones now."

A little taken aback, the captain translated this to the elder and the other villagers. The old man waved his staff again, this time using it to point toward the towering peak above them.

"He says the shrine is high on Goaddi and it is almost evening. The paths are too dangerous in darkness. Also, you may frighten the guardians of the shrine by arriving unexpectedly."

"It does not matter," said Makho. "This is what our queen has ordered. Her words are our law. If we cannot reach this place tonight, we will spend the night on the mountain and continue in the morning."

Nezeru did not know whose bones Makho spoke of, or what value there was in seeing them, but as she examined the strange, small folk surrounding them and the exultant, endlessly varied greens of the island's vegetation, she felt an unexpected pride. Who would have dreamed that a mere halfblood child could travel so far from Nakkiga and see such things? If she had not followed her heart into the Order of Sacrifice she would now be piling stone on dull stone as part of her father's Order of Builders, or perhaps have become a second wife for one his underlings. What would High Magister Viyeki think now, after trying so hard to keep her from submitting to the Order of Sacrifice, if he could see his daughter serving the Mother of the People here at the farthest edge of the world? Surely he would be ashamed at his own timidity. Surely he would have to admit that his daughter had chosen well.

Led by islander guides, they climbed most of the way to the top of the mountain before darkness fell. The villagers who led them were surprised to see the strangers making such fast time, but of course they knew nothing of the training all Queen's Talons received; the nights and days of endless hardship that built upon their natural hardiness and made each of them, even the Whisperer and the Singer, fit and fierce as beasts. When it was too dark to continue, or at least too dark for the mortal guides, Makho commanded them to make camp for the night.

As she made a comfortable place for herself against a hummock of grassy ground in a spot shielded from the worst of the wind, Makho appeared. "I have been looking for you." But he barely looked at her. "I will couple with you tonight. Await me."

He did as he had promised, coming to her when the moon was high. Nezeru did not feel flattered but neither could she complain: one of the burdens of her mixed blood was that she was available to pureblood men, because it was the duty of all Hikeda'ya to help the race grow so that they would become numerous enough to destroy the queen's enemies and bring harmony to a world badly in need of it. It was even more necessary because pure-blooded women had not made many children with halfblood males—although not, some of the noblemen complained, for lack of trying.

Makho made her take off all her clothing before he mounted her. Nezeru did not feel cold, and she certainly was not encumbered by modesty, but she wished he had not ordered it so. A part of her feared being watched by one of the others, especially Saomeji, although she could not say precisely why. If there had been any enjoyment for her in the act it would have been soured by that discomfort, but in any case, enjoyment was never in view.

Her mother Tzoja had once called this intimate connection of two people "lovemaking," which Nezeru thought as soft and silly a mortal idea as she had ever heard—as soft and silly as her mother herself could be. Tzoja had also tried to comfort Nezeru after she had been disciplined by her father, even when Nezeru herself tried to shrug off the embraces and the pointless apologies. There was nothing of love in what she did with Makho, Nezeru knew, only duty, but that was more than enough. The Hikeda'ya were few now. Their mortal enemies were many and bred like pink frogs, spawning in their thousands every year: soon the world would be full of them and the People and even the Garden itself would be forgotten as if neither had ever existed.

Certainly there was nothing unduly affectionate in Makho's treatment of her. His coupling, like his body, was as hard and smooth as witchwood. When he finished it was in utter silence, and when he rolled off her, it was as though Nezeru herself had suddenly disappeared, even as she lay in the moon's blue-white light with his fluids and her own sweat drying on her skin. But she felt she had the right to ask him at least one question.

"What bones?"

He looked at her. His voice told her he had all but forgotten her presence already. "Bones?"

"You told the mortals we came to see the bones."

Makho turned away from her. "The queen sent us to find the bones of Hakatri."

For a moment she could not say why the name sounded so familiar. Then, suddenly and shockingly, it came to her. "Hakatri? Do you truly mean the brother of *Ineluki the Storm King?*"

"Is there another?" This time Makho's scorn was unhidden, and he would answer no more questions.

8

A Meeting on Lantern Bridge

The last days of Marris-month blew by on cold Frostmarch winds as the royal progress made its way north across the plains of Rimmersgard toward Elvritshalla. The journey seemed inchingly slow to Morgan, since the great procession stopped at the landholdings of some of the most powerful nobles and also in some of the larger cities, like high, windy Naarved. Each time they did, his grandparents explained the reasons for the visit, anxious for Morgan to learn their statecraft; but each stop seemed so much like all the rest, full of speeches and dull ceremonies, that he lost track. The broad, unfamiliar landscapes and wide sky that had first engrossed him became ordinary and dull as the journey dragged on and on. Even the fair faces of young Rimmersgard women began to lose interest for him. As Marris passed and Avrel blew in, Morgan spent more and more time lost in his own brooding thoughts.

Often, lulled into near-sleep by the monotony of the spare northern landscapes, he found himself thinking of his dead father, something he had done his best to avoid during the journey, though not all the memories were unhappy ones. A solitary evergreen in an empty waste, bent and shaped by the wind, reminded him of the carefully crafted shapes in the Hedge Garden back home, and that brought back to him the day when his father had lifted a much smaller Morgan up onto his shoulders so he could see those hedge animals more closely. From his new vantage they had all seemed more plant than beast, the eyes and mouths so carefully shaped from boxwood branches dissolving into mere whorls of green, but instead of disappointment, child-Morgan had felt exalted. The view from atop his father's shoulders made him feel as though he had suddenly become a man, a tall man. Seeing not just the tops of the hedge animals, but over the garden wall into other parts of the Inner Bailey, had given him an exciting sensation of power and possibility.

Someday I will be this big, he had thought. *Someday I will be able to go anywhere.*

"Take me outside, Papa!" he had demanded. "Take me out. I want to see if I'm as tall as the castle walls!"

His father had laughed, enjoying his excitement, and then carried him to the massive old Festival Oak at the garden's far end to let him feel its centuried bark, so covered with cracks and bumps that the young Morgan could imagine it was a dragon's armored skin.

But that had been before Prince John Josua had lost interest in his wife and young son, before he had become so immersed in his old books and his writing that he scarcely joined Morgan and his mother even for meals. Even when he was with them in those later days, he had seemed always to be thinking about something or somewhere quite different.

It was hard to mourn the way his grandparents did, with careful conversations and quiet ceremonies. Morgan felt his father had left him years before he died.

Now that they had reached the hilltop, Simon and the rest of the mounted company could look down the river's course and see almost the whole of the Drorshull Valley. Even several days into Avrel, snow was still piled so thickly that in many places everything but village and farmstead roofs were buried; even the church spires that marked out each settlement seemed to be standing on tiptoe.

"Look," said Morgan, pointing. "Is that it?"

The royal progress had been following the course of the river for several chilly days, through cold rains and painful flights of gravelly sleet, but it seemed they had finally reached their destination—a huge, walled city at the far end of the valley, where the Gratuvask split into two channels. Set on the peak at its center was a keep surrounded by four stocky towers, each crowned with a steep, conical roof.

"Elvritshalla," Simon said. "Praise God, we've finally arrived. I haven't seen the place for so long!"

Even so early in the gray afternoon, the city smoldered with lights like a field of live coals. "What are those other lights, Grandfather?" Morgan asked. "The ones stretching over the river?"

"That is the Lyktenspan—'Lantern Bridge' in Westerling," the king explained. "The lanterns are hung along its whole length. Most of the time they are lit at sunset each evening and extinguished when the sun rises, but it looks like they've lit them early today—perhaps because of us!"

"I would not be surprised," Miriamele said. "We are the High Throne, after all. It is not as though we visit every sennight."

"It's a very nice bridge," Morgan said dutifully, but Simon thought it a poor compliment. He had loved the Lyktenspan since the first time he had seen it: the distant rows of lights always seemed to float above the river like something magical.

"Did you know," he told his grandson, "that there are times in winter when the lanterns burn for days straight, because the sun never rises?" He frowned at Morgan's dubious look. "Don't scoff, lad, it's the truth. In summer it is the opposite—the sun stays in the sky for days."

Morgan was obviously doing his best to stay on his elders' good sides, but his youthful pride, just as obviously, made him fear being the butt of some hoary old joke. "Is that really true, Grandmother?" he called to the queen.

"Unlike some of the things your grandfather says, yes, it actually is. Duchess Gutrun used to speak of how the winter made her fret because it felt as though the sun had actually gone away for good. But do not ask me why such a thing should be."

"It is because the vault of the sky is curved, I think," Simon said. "Something of that sort. Morgenes once explained it to me."

"Ask Lord Tiamak," the queen suggested. "He doubtless has learned something from his many books that can explain it, Morgan."

"I will, Grandmother." But the prince could not hide his lack of enthusiasm at the prospect of being lectured on the workings of the firmament, and Simon felt a prickle of irritation. What did it take to engage the lad? Morgan would inherit the rule of this land and most of the known world, yet he acted as though it were all some unwanted chore. It was hard for Simon not to blame Miri. She was always worrying about their grandson, trying to protect him from his own mistakes. He certainly understood why—how could he not, after the terrible loss she had suffered, they *all* had suffered?—but protecting the boy from the consequences of his mistakes seemed like the wrong idea.

Yes, he lost his father. But I lost both my mother and father before I was born, and I had no loving grandparents, no younger sister, none of the things that Morgan has. I had blistered hands from hard work in the kitchen, and I had Rachel the Dragon pinching my ears. Would the boy trade his condition for mine?

Simon took a breath. "It would not harm you to learn a bit more about the history of the nations under our High Throne . . ." he began, but Morgan saw his direction and changed the subject.

"Why is the bridge so high over the river? I've never seen a bridge so tall."

Simon had to admit it was a sensible question, and his annoyance faded. His grandson was no fool, at least. The Lyktenspan was set on a row of tall stone arches so that it stood far above even the leaping froth thrown up by the turbulent river.

"That's because when the spring thaws come, the Gratuvask climbs over its banks and rises a man's height or more, and stays there for weeks," Simon explained. "The water rushes down from the mountains so fast that it's full of white foam. And cold! I remember Isgrimnur talking about it. *'It isn't water, it's melted ice,'* he used to say. *'And it hasn't melted much.'"* He laughed.

Morgan had an unusual expression on his face, as though he was doing his best to understand a new idea. "You and Grandmother talk about the duke very often, Grandfather. You must have loved him. I'm sorry I never knew him."

Simon was a bit surprised by Morgan's words, worried that they were meant only as distraction, but after a moment he nodded and smiled. "Duke Isgrimnur was a great man," he said, then corrected himself. "He *is* a great man, and we may yet greet him before this day is over. Isgrimnur is the best friend Erkynland and the High Ward ever had, a man who saved my life and your grandmother's life many times over. I have prayed God would let him see you once more, now that you are grown, and not just because you will inherit the High Ward from us one day and rule over his people. It would mean much to the queen and to me if that good old fellow could give you his blessing."

The perpetual rush and roar of the river filled their ears as they followed its course along the floor of the valley, past tidy farms and prosperous villages all but hidden under snow. In places the drifts were still piled so high that the houses were marked only by the smoke wafting from their chimneys. Morgan seemed to be enjoying the sights, but Miriamele just wanted the ride to end, in part to escape the cold, but in the largest part because she desperately wanted to see beloved Isgrimnur still alive.

The prince seemed most impressed by the house-sized chunks of ice floating past them down the churning, fast-moving Gratuvask. Miri could not help smiling at the look of wonder on Morgan's face, and remembered her husband at a similar age, a kitchen boy seeing things that even the hardiest travelers had never experienced—the Sithi's beautiful, ruined city of Da'ai Chikiza, the great stone pillar of Sesuad'ra . . . he had even fought a dragon, like someone in an old story! He might not want to speak of it now, might feel some strange modesty, but that did not change the fact that the king was no ordinary man.

Even in his middle age, Simon still stood almost two hands taller than Morgan, but Miri thought they were more alike than not. Stubbornness? Morgan had inherited a full measure of it from Simon, but as her husband liked to point out, Miriamele was no sapling bending to the wind herself. And of course trying to get Morgan's father John Josua to do anything he hadn't wanted to do had been like trying to pull a badger out of its den. And Morgan's mother Idela was not much more tractable, although she pretended to be. No, if she was going to be fair, the queen had to admit that Morgan's stubbornness was a family affair, generations in the making.

For a moment, as she watched them silhouetted against the lights of the bridge, Miri could picture her husband and grandson as the wings of a triptych, like the life of Usires that stood behind the altar in the royal chapel at home. There on one side was Simon the patriarch, tall, with gray in his red beard; on the other stood Morgan his descendant, still callow enough to think drinking and womanizing was proof of something other than drinking and womanizing. But the center panel was missing, that which should have been her son, John Josua, and which should have united the two on either side. Her child, her beautiful child, who had grown to be such a tall, clever young man, was now only a shadow even to his own children. His death had left a hole in their lives that could never be filled, no matter how she and the rest of the family pretended.

Her heart aching again, she tried to pray, but her own measure of the family obstinacy rose up and thwarted her. No matter what the priests claimed, how could such a loss be God's will? Why had the Creator, whom Miriamele had always tried to serve, stolen her only child?

The royal progress had dispatched riders to alert the city to their approach. They had disappeared across the bridge and into the shadow of the gates more than an hour before, but still had not come back; Miriamele was beginning to wonder if something had gone wrong. She couldn't imagine what the problem might be—thanks to the old duke, Rimmersgard was the High Ward's most faithful ally: it seemed unlikely they would suffer the same kind of problems that had plagued the Hernystir visit.

"Ah! Look there!" Morgan announced. "Someone is riding toward us. See, he has just mounted the bridge from the far side."

Simon squinted. "Oh, to have young eyes again! Is it one of our messengers?"

Morgan shook his head. "Too far away to tell, but I don't think so. Something odd about the rider. Still, there is only one."

"Odd?"

"I can't say more yet, Grandfather. May I ride forward to get a better look?"

"No," said Miriamele firmly. "No, Morgan, you may not."

Simon gave her a look full of unspoken meaning—he thought she was being too cautious, she could tell. "I think he might—with the queen's permission, of course. But only if he takes a troop of the Erkynguard with him. Remember, Morgan, these are some of our oldest allies and we have no reason to doubt their good will."

"What if something happens to him?" Miriamele demanded. "He is our heir!"

"What if we all die in our beds from the Red Ruin? What if we are struck by lightning?" The king realized he had become loud and lowered his voice. "Be fair, Miri. When people told you to hold back, to do nothing dangerous, what did *you* do, my love? Rode off into the night on your own, with nobody but a thieving monk for a companion."

She did her best to push down unqueenly anger. "Are we not allowed to learn anything from our own mistakes then? Should we let our children and grandchildren make the same errors without saying a word?"

"Making those errors may be the only way they will learn the lessons we did, my dear one," Simon said. "Certainly for all Morgenes or Rachel tried to teach me, it never quite made sense until I had ignored their good advice and done something impressively stupid instead." He put on his most innocently harmless face. "Come now, wife. Let Prince Morgan ride out with the Erkynguard to find out who is coming to meet us."

As was often the case, Miri found herself caught between wanting to kiss her husband and briskly rattle his pate. Instead, she shot him a look that made it clear the larger discussion had not ended, but at last gave her reluctant consent.

While Morgan was gathering an escort of Erkynguards, Simon called for Rinan, the minstrel. Ever since he had scolded the young harper some days earlier, her husband had gone out of his way to be kind to him.

When at last the musician was located, he looked anxious as a cat in a room full of drunken dancers. "Majesty?"

"I want you to ride with me, harper," the king told him. "Somebody find this lad a horse!"

"Of course, M-Majesty. I would be honored."

"You are not still frightened of me from the other day, are you?" Simon shook his head. "Don't be. I need your help."

"Majesty?"

"You really need to think of something new to say, son. And you can leave that stringed thing hanging on your back. I don't want your music—I want your eyes." He saw the startled look. "Good God, I'm not going to *take* them from you! I want you to see what I can't from this distance, with evening coming down."

"Yes, Majesty."

Morgan and his Erkynguard escort rode out, and soon reached the beginning of the Lyktenspan while the queen and king watched. At the center of the bridge a dark shape was moving toward them, though at such a distance Miri could make out little more than a blot of moving shadow.

"What do you see, harper?" the king demanded. "By the Tree, lad, talk to me!"

For a moment the young minstrel only narrowed his eyes and leaned forward. "The rider from Elvritshalla," he said at last, "is . . . is . . . well, there is something strange about him, Majesty."

"People keep saying that! What in the name of blessed Saint Sutrin does that mean? Strange *how*?"

Miri was amused despite herself. "You really must calm yourself, husband. Let the poor man answer you."

Simon scowled. "Go on, then. What do you see?"

The harper was still squinting. "He is quite small, I think. Now that our soldiers and the prince are getting closer. Yes, he is small. And . . ." Rinan licked his lips. "Majesty, I swear to you, that is no horse he is riding. It looks— it is hard to make out, but I would swear—" He turned to the king and queen with a look of shame and guilt. "Majesties, please do not punish me, but I think that the one coming from Elvritshalla is riding . . . some kind of *dog*."

The king was not a violent man, although over the years he had broken a few things in his angriest moments, as the servants in the Hayholt could attest, but Miri knew he had never struck and never would strike one of his subjects. Still, when King Simon swore in loud astonishment, she saw young Rinan brace himself for the blow he must have felt sure was following such a ridiculous pronouncement. But the harper looked even more surprised when his liege lord suddenly spurred his horse toward the bridge as though leading a battle charge, leaving the queen and the harper to watch him go. Several of the Erkynguard even cried out in surprise, but when they would have pursued Simon, Miri lifted her hand to hold them back.

As the echo of hoofbeats faded, Rinan turned to the queen. "Majesty?" he managed at last. "Did I do wrong? Majesty?"

"I beg your pardon?"

"Forgive me, my queen—but what just happened? Is the king angry?"

She smiled. "Oh, do not fear, young man. All of that was nothing to do with you. He is hurrying to meet an old friend."

Morgan and his guardsmen had just reined up their mounts, filled with surprise and not a little superstitious dismay at the apparition before them, when they heard the clatter of hooves coming up the stone bridge behind them. Already unnerved by the odd little man riding toward them on a huge, white wolf, the sound of swift pursuit startled Morgan's horse so badly that he had to fight to stay in the saddle. His balance finally regained, he yanked his sword out of its scabbard, wondering if he would now have to fight to the death like some ancient hero. Caught up in the moment, several of the Erkynguard drew their blades as well.

"Put up!" someone shouted. "Put up your blades! It is the king coming!" The wedge of men on the bridge milled in confusion as they struggled to make a way between them for their fast-moving monarch. Morgan could only watch as King Simon, standing in his stirrups, gray-shot red hair flying, sped through their midst. He scarcely glanced at Morgan as he careened past.

"Grandfather . . . ?" Morgan called. "Majesty?"

But both the king and the wolf-riding apparition had stopped in the middle of the bridge and were climbing down from their mounts, paying attention to nobody but each other.

"Binabik!" his grandfather shouted, then pulled the small figure into his arms like a father whose child has been returned to him after a long, frightening absence.

"Friend Simon!" cried the little man, who was scarcely higher than the king's waist, and then laughed as the king whirled him around so violently that Morgan was frightened they both might tumble off the bridge into the freezing Gratuvask. The prince spurred his horse forward, partly to be sure they stayed on the bridge, partly to better make sense of what was happening. Clearly this must be his grandfather's troll friend, a nearly legendary character.

"My people are saying that to meet an old friend is like the finding of a welcoming campfire in the dark," the little man said, slightly breathless from the king's powerful embrace. "Just the sight of your face warms me, Simon."

"It is wonderful to see you, Binabik," Simon said happily, finally setting him down. "But why have only you come out to greet us?"

"In Elvritshalla, the spools and cranks of the Frostmarch Gate somehow are not working to open it. A great many horses and riders are there waiting to honor you, but they are being caught on the far side. Only noble Vaqana and I were small enough for squeezing through." He patted the monstrously large wolf, a creature of shaggy, spotless white who seemed utterly at ease with the humans that surrounded her, although the same could not be said for most of those humans. "But have no fearfulness, old friend," Binabik said. "I think they will be repairing it by the time your people are reaching there. Where is Miriamele, your beloved? She is well, I am hoping?"

"She's back there on the bridge, clucking her tongue at me for riding off like a madman," said the king, smiling so broadly that Morgan thought he looked demented. "Ah, but it is good to see you." Simon looked at the wolf, now seated and calmly grooming. "And you said this was . . . ?"

"Vaqana, ever loyal," said the troll. "Yes, one of noble Qantaqa's descendants, she is being. And it is so very good to be seeing you, too, friend Simon, after too many years!" Binabik grabbed a thick tuft of snowy fur and climbed onto the wolf's broad back, which bore it with the patience of long experience. At last the small man noticed Morgan. "Ha! I think I am seeing a face that is now much changed from my first seeing of it. Is this truly being your grandchild?"

King Simon smiled and nodded; for a moment, Morgan could almost convince himself his grandfather looked proud. "Yes, indeed! I'm sure he does look a bit different. This is Prince Morgan, our grandson and heir."

"Look at him, a grown man!" crowed the troll. "As we also say on Mintahoq, *hanno aia mo siqsiq, chahu naha!*—as easily be trying to catch an avalanche in a thimble as to make the seasons stand still."

The king turned to his grandson. "Morgan, this is Binabik of Yiqanuc, my dearest friend. You have not seen him since you were a child, more than ten years ago. Do you remember?"

Morgan was about to say no, but then a scrap of memory fluttered up—a group of small men and women, and Morgan himself brought to meet them. He had seen dwarves at the court many times, but these had been something different, with dark, serious faces and strange clothes, and they had frightened him. "A little, I think."

"Well, you will meet no better man in all Osten Ard, of any height." The king seemed happier than Morgan had seen him in a long while. "And your good lady wife, Binabik? She is well? And your child?"

"Both are being well, and both are also being with me, but the girl has been growing from child to woman. And she has brought her *nukapik*—her marrying friend. We all were riding here together, the others on their rams, myself on bold Vaqana." As he scratched behind the wolf's ears, Binabik's brown face creased into a broad smile surrounded by wrinkles that showed it was a frequent expression for him. "You will see them all tonight, I am thinking. Well, perhaps not the rams, who will be resting and eating."

"And how is Isgrimnur?"

"The duke still is alive, praise to Sedda our Dark Mother, but he is very old and his weakness is growing. Still, he will be pleased to see you, friend Simon, so very pleased."

At that moment, Morgan was startled again by a screech from somewhere at the other end of Lantern Bridge, near the walls of Elvritshalla; his horse was startled too and had to be calmed.

"And that, if I am making a good guess," said Binabik, "is the sound of the city's Frostmarch Gate being at last opened. Come, Simon-king and almost grown Morgan-prince! Isgrimnur's son Grimbrand and the duke's subjects have all come out for welcoming you—it was only that I was slipping out first and spoiling their plan. Come!"

Morgan was quite happy to be out of the cold Frostmarch winds at last and inside the city walls. All of Elvritshalla seemed to have lined the streets to see the royal party enter, or at least lined the main road between the gates and the duke's palace atop the stony hill at the center of the city. People shouted and waved torches and lanterns, others hung from upper floor windows, and despite the late hour, all cheered loudly as King Simon and Queen Miriamele rode by, as if the High Monarchs had come to make their dying duke well again.

No one seemed to recognize Morgan himself, but the prince was not too unhappy about that. He had worked hard to please his grandparents of late, but the last thing he wanted was to be dragged into more of the endless rituals and court functions that would fill the next few days. He wanted instead to find Astrian and the rest as soon as possible, then find a place to drink, some warm, dark refuge hidden away from the numbing boredom of official life. As he observed the mostly fair-skinned citizens of Elvritshalla he noted more than a few young women as tall and comely as anything that even Erchester, capital city of the High Ward, had to offer, many of them with hair as golden as a shiny, unspent coin. He had believed he was weary of northern girls, but suddenly he felt less certain. In fact, Morgan was beginning to look forward to conversing with some of the duke's young female subjects.

My subjects too, some day, he thought suddenly. *When I am king.* It was a strange but interesting thing to consider.

"There you are, my prince!" Sir Porto rode up beside him. The old knight had a scarf wrapped around his throat and lower face, as if he had ridden through a howling blizzard. "It is good to be here, yes? I have not seen the place for many years—not since the days after the siege, when we came this way with Duke Isgrimnur."

"And I have heard that story so many times I could tell it myself and be no less truthful than you," said Morgan. "More so, probably, since according to Astrian half your tale is invented and the rest is exaggeration."

Porto gave him a hurt look. "The Nabban-man knows nothing about it and only seeks to tease me. He was a suckling babe in his mother's arms when I fought the Norns."

Morgan grinned. "To be quite honest with you, it is not fighting Norns I want to know about just now, you old villain. Where does one go to find a decent spot for drinking and singing and not having to put up with all the nonsense that my grandparents came for?"

Astrian rode up, looking as well turned out as if he had just set forth instead of having suffered the same long ride as the rest of the company. "My prince! I was afraid you had already gone with your family to the castle."

"I'm trying to get Porto to tell me where the good spots in this city are, since he claims to have been here before."

"Claims?" Porto lifted himself to his full height in the saddle, which made him look like a stork trying to take off from a chimney-nest. "I promise you that even after so many years they will not have forgot Porto of Ansis Pellipé in the better taverns of the Kopstade!"

"Now we are getting somewhere," said Morgan. "What is this Kopstade?"

"The market and its surroundings," the old knight said. "We have passed it already, Highness. It was near the gates."

"Then let's turn back."

"My prince, I think not." Unusually, it was Astrian preaching moderation. "Not tonight, at least. You will be expected to partake in at least a few . . . formalities with your grandparents. The old duke, all of that . . ." He waved his hand in a vague way.

"No!" Morgan realized he had almost shouted it. He could feel himself reddening. "No, I don't need to watch some old man die. It's none of my business—he's my grandparents' friend."

Astrian shrugged. "As you wish. But at the very least, Highness, you must find out where you are to be housed before you spend an evening out. Elvritshalla Castle is not a small place. You'll need to know how to find your way to wherever you will be sleeping."

"Sleeping? Who wants to sleep?" Morgan gave him a bitter look. "It is cruel to break my heart this way, Astrian, and I certainly didn't expect it of you. All I want is a tankard of beer and a bit of a laugh."

"Still, Highness, it was you who warned us your grandparents were angry with you." Astrian looked up as Olveris approached, guiding his war horse through the procession that crowded the wide road. "Come help me, my friend," Astrian called to him. "I am trying to convince our good prince that this first night, at least, he must appear to honor the king's and queen's wishes."

Olveris made a face. "Astrian calls for good behavior? We clearly have taken a wrong road and wound up in the land of Faerie."

"Do not make such a jest!" said Porto, alarmed. "Not here in the north. Because the fairies are closer and fiercer than you think. In the morning, you will be able to see Stormspike Mountain in the distance."

"As long as it stays distant," said Morgan.

It was coincidence, of course, but just as the prince finished speaking a cold wind blew down the street, whipping the banners on the houses, making Morgan shiver even through his armor and surcoat.

"It is a pleasure to see you again, Sisqinanamook," Miriamele said as they stood together around the fireplace in a low-ceilinged but sumptuous antechamber in the ducal residence. Simon knew that after weeks of repeating these words across the length and breadth of Hernystir and Rimmersgard, this time she truly meant them: Miri had always been fond of Binabik's wife, since the days they had all fought together.

Sisqi bowed her head, clearly pleased to hear Miriamele use her full name. "As it is for seeing you, great queen."

Miri waved the title away. "You came all the way from your mountains to see Isgrimnur! Bless you!"

"We could not be doing other," Binabik said. "The best Rimmersman we ever had the luck of knowing."

Miri smiled at that. "And Simon says your daughter is here in Elvritshalla too. I so look forward to seeing her. She must be a grown woman now!"

Sisqi smiled. "Grown is Qina, yes. And here with her man, too."

"Is she married?" Simon asked.

"Soon," said Binabik. "When again they reach Mintahoq, Qina and Snenneq will go together to Chidsik Ub Lingit—do you remember that place, friend Simon, where you once were pleading to Sisqi's parents for sparing my life?—and then they will bind together their hands before the ancestors and our people."

The door to the duke's chamber swung open and Grimbrand came out to greet them. With his dark hair and his broad face and figure, Simon thought he looked more like his father than his older brother Isorn ever had. Still, it was strange to see how much gray and white now flecked Grimbrand's beard.

By the Ransomer's Tree, when did we all grow so old?

Grimbrand had been too young to fight in the Storm King's War, and had spent the time of his family's exile with relatives. He had grown into a just and thoughtful man who possessed many of his father's best traits. It was good to know that at least one of the lands of the High Ward would be in good hands. "He has just woken up, Majesties." Grimbrand's smile was weary. "I think if you all go in at once it might be too much. May I take the High King and High Queen first?"

Simon turned to Binabik. "With certainness," said the small man, smiling. "Go in."

"Tiamak should be here, too," said Miriamele. "He and the duke love each other well. But he is still searching for our grandson, Prince Morgan."

"Come then," said Grimbrand. "The others can join you shortly, and if your grandson's absence is anything serious, I will send men to look."

"Oh, please don't," said Miriamele hurriedly. "I'm certain we will find him quickly enough."

"As you wish, Majesty." Grimbrand beckoned them toward the door.

The duke's chamber was much as Simon remembered from his last visit ten years ago or more, still kept as a sort of shrine to Isgrimnur's beloved wife Gutrun, Grimbrand's mother. Candles burned everywhere, but especially on a low table in front of a painted portrait of her. Her chair and her sewing chest still sat beside the room's largest window, which to Simon's surprise stood open. The Rimmersfolk did not seem to mind an airiness that would have terrified Erkynlanders. At the center of the room, the canopy of the huge bed fluttered in the night air. Simon could not help thinking of a ship drifting out to sea, its sails filling with wind.

But the Rimmersmen no longer take to the waves, Simon remembered.

Two priests who had been praying at the foot of the bed rose and left the room. For a moment, as he and Miriamele approached the bedside, Simon was confused. Surely this sleeping stranger could not be Isgrimnur! It wasn't possible that this old man propped on the pillows, unable to hold his head up, was their friend the duke, one of the largest and strongest men Simon had ever known. This almost-stranger's cheeks were sunken, his hair and beard snow-white and sparse, and his neck seemed far too frail to have ever lifted a head as noble as Isgrimnur's.

The old man's eyes fluttered open. For a moment they could not seem to fix on anything, and roved from the ceiling to the walls. Grimbrand stepped forward and kneeled beside him.

"Is . . . is that you, Isorn?" The voice was a ragged ghost of the duke's booming tones.

Simon guessed that Grimbrand had been called by his dead brother's name many times in the last months, because he did not bother to correct his father. "Sire, some friends of yours are here to see you. Queen Miriamele and King Simon have come all the way from Erkynland."

And now the rolling eyes touched Simon's, and the man inside the worn, spent body seemed finally to take control. Isgrimnur frowned, squinted, and then his eyes opened wide. "By the good God, it *is* you." His gaze slid to Miriamele, and he smiled. "You have both come, God bless you and keep you. Come, give me your hands. We'll not meet again on this earth, I fear, so give me your hands."

Simon and Miriamele each moved to one side of the bed, and each took one of the duke's hands. Simon, whose eyes were already filling and threatening to overspill, thought the old man's bones felt fragile, like eggshells. "Of course we've come," he said, struggling against his suddenly treacherous voice. "Of course."

"God bless *you*, Uncle." Miriamele had always called him that, although there was no blood relation. "Bless you for waiting for us." She fell silent, tears running down her cheeks.

"How goes the High Ward?" Isgrimnur asked. "Is all . . . well?"

"All well, Uncle," Miriamele said.

"Good. Good." So many words seemed to tire him out. The duke closed his eyes and for a moment only breathed, his chest rising and falling. "And Josua? Prince Josua? Is there any word?"

Simon swallowed. The subject of Miri's uncle, their son John Josua's namesake, was a painful one. "I'm afraid not. We have long searched for him, his wife Vorzheva, and their children, but we can find no trace of them."

Isgrimnur shook his head. "Ten years—no, twenty! Twenty years. I fear he must be dead after such a long time."

Simon squeezed the duke's hand, but gently, very gently. "We will never stop searching."

"I will not be here to see him found." Isgrimnur opened his eyes again. "Simon, is that you? Tell me that is truly you. I have so many dreams lately, I scarcely know whether I am awake or not."

"Yes, it's me, Isgrimnur. The same scruffy boy you found on the Frostmarch near St. Hoderund's, long, long ago."

Isgrimnur smiled a little. "Scruffy! You rate yourself too high. I remember you as skinny and frightened as a wet cat!" His laugh became a cough, but he waved his hand to reassure them. "No, I am all right. The cough is nothing. It is the weight on my chest that is getting more difficult to bear." He let his head sag back into the pillows. "Simon. Good boy. No, I forget myself. You are king! High King!"

"Do you forget his wife?" asked Miriamele, but in a tone of gentle mockery.

"Never, my queen." Isgrimnur's hand tightened on Simon's. "I ask you a favor. I ask you both. You must promise me."

Simon did not have to look at his wife to know what to answer. He used his free arm to wipe the tears from his cheeks. "Anything, Duke Isgrimnur. We owe you more than we could ever repay. As do all the kingdoms of men."

"Gutrun and I were godparents to Prince Josua's children. With Josua and Vorzheva both gone, I fear for those children . . ."

"They would no longer be children," Simon said gently. "They were born the year the Storm King was defeated."

"Even so." Isgrimnur's reedy voice took on something of its infamous growl. "Is it your habit to travel so far just to interrupt a dying man?"

It was hard not to smile. "Sorry, my lord Duke. What would you have us do?"

"Find them. If you cannot find their parents, find the children. Do for them what Gutrun and I were promised to do, but failed—find them and keep them safe. See that they have what they need for a happy life."

"We have looked for them and we will keep looking, old friend. One day we will find them."

Isgrimnur stared at him as though he did not know whether to believe him or not. "Do you promise it to me?"

"Of course," Simon told him, stung and sad. The king looked to Miriamele. "We promise you on the honor of our house and yours."

"Gutrun would have sent me after them long ago, but her illness . . ." The duke shook his head. "I will see her soon, thank God and all the blessed saints. I will see her soon!"

"You will, Uncle," said Miriamele. "She is waiting for you."

"And Isorn, too." Isgrimnur's lip trembled. "So long since I have seen their beloved faces . . . !" The old man's eyes were red. "So long . . ."

"You are tired, Father," said Grimbrand from the foot of the bed. "There are others waiting to see you, but perhaps they should come back after you've rested."

"Others?" Isgrimnur seemed to find a reserve of strength. With a last squeeze he let go of Simon's hand, then Miriamele's. "What do you mean?"

"Other friends are waiting for you outside," Miriamele said. "Count Eolair, and Binabik and his wife . . ."

"Binabik? The troll is here? Send him in! Send them all in!" The duke even managed to work himself up a little higher on his pillows. For the first time, Simon could truly see their old friend in the feeble, sharp-boned scarecrow stretched on the bed. "Aedon and his angels can wait for me. They will have me for a long time."

Binabik and Sisqi entered first, small as children. Behind them came somber Eolair, accompanied by Tiamak, whose limp always slowed him. The Wrannaman stepped aside to whisper to Simon, "I cannot find Morgan, Majesty. Binabik's daughter and her friend are looking, too."

Simon had to take a deep breath to contain his temper. "Did you check the alehalls?"

"There are dozens just along the main road," Tiamak whispered. Simon looked to his wife and shook his head. Her mouth set in a thin line.

"Go and see Isgrimnur," Simon said quietly. He patted his old friend on the shoulder, although inside the king was boiling like a pot forgotten on the fire. It was not Tiamak's fault that their grandson was a scapegrace.

"And wait, who is that?" Isgrimnur's voice was again growing thin, his breath short, but he lifted his head high off the pillow. "Is that Tiamak? Is that my Wrannaman?"

"It is indeed, Duke Isgrimnur." Tiamak hobbled to the old man's side.

"Miriamele, come back." Isgrimnur lifted his hand to her. "Come back. Look, Grimbrand, do you see the three of us?" He nodded toward Tiamak and the queen. "Do you see us?"

"Of course, Father."

"Looking at a feeble ruin like me, you would not know it, but we three crossed half the known world. From Kwanitupul across the Wran, then across all the Thrithings to the Farewell Stone, on foot. We even went down into the foul ghants' nest together and we came out again! There's a story, eh? That's the equal of any tale you'll ever hear, I'll wager. And Sir Camaris, the greatest warrior of any age, was with us!"

"And Cadrach, too," said Miriamele. "Poor, sad, mad Cadrach."

"You were as brave as a she-wolf," Isgrimnur told her. "You were . . ." He had to stop to catch his breath. He coughed for a while before he could speak again, and had to do it with his son begging him to save his breath. "A noble tale," he said, wheezing. "Someone should make a song of it."

"Someone has," said Simon, laughing. "Several. Dozens! Good lord, have you avoided the songs up here? I would have moved our court to Rimmersgard long ago had I known!"

"The song . . . the song . . ." Isgrimnur had seemed keen to say something, but trailed off. "What were we saying?"

"That we are together again," said Miriamele, and bent to kiss him on his hollow cheek. "And nobody can take those times from us."

"Bless you," said Tiamak quietly. He was weeping unashamedly, holding Isgrimnur's hand against his face. The old man hardly seemed to notice.

"I think . . . I think I must sleep . . . for a little . . ."

"Of course," said Miriamele, straightening up. "We will come to see you later, Uncle, when you are rested."

"We will be here for days," Simon said. "Never fear—there will be plenty of time for news and old tales, both."

Binabik stroked the old man's hand, then placed his own fist against his chest, a troll gesture that Simon knew signified all that was in the troll's heart. Sisqi bowed her head, then the two of them turned and walked out of the room.

Eolair was next. He kneeled beside the bed and kissed the duke's hand. "It is good to see you, my lord," was all he said before he too rose and went out. Simon was about to bid the old man goodnight when he saw a familiar face in the antechamber beyond. "Morgan!" he said in a loud whisper. "Come here!"

"Our grandson is here?" asked Miriamele. "Thank God."

The prince's eyes had the look of something hunted as he entered the bed-chamber. "I have been trying to find you," he said quietly, looking at anything and everything but the old man on the bed. "This place is a maze!"

"This place, or the Kopstade?" Simon fought down his unhappiness. "Just come here."

Isgrimnur's eyelids had been sagging, but as Simon bent and kissed him on the cheek, he opened them again. "Simon, lad? Is that you? Are you truly a king, or did I dream all that?" He seemed to fight a little for breath. "I have so many dreams . . . and it all mixes together . . ."

"You did not dream it, Duke Isgrimnur. And Miriamele and I rule in large part because of you, your son Isorn, and a few other noble souls. And now I want you to meet the heir to the High Throne, Prince Morgan. I hope you will give him your blessing."

"Prince Morgan?" Isgrimnur looked surprised. "You brought an infant all this way?"

"No, look, Uncle," said Miriamele. "He is grown now."

"Kneel down, boy," Simon whispered to the prince. "Take his hand."

Morgan looked as though he would rather be almost anywhere else in the world than this draughty bedchamber, but he reached out and enfolded the duke's crabbed, bony hand. For a moment Isgrimnur only stared at the ceiling, but then he seemed to come back to himself and looked searchingly at the heir where he knelt beside the bed. "Bless you, young man," the duke said. "Do as God would have you do, and you cannot help but succeed. Listen carefully to your mother and father."

Morgan looked to his grandfather in confusion, but Simon shook his head to silence him. "Thank you, Isgrimnur," the king said. "We've done our best to make him ready."

"I'm sure you've done very well," said Isgrimnur. "He's a fine young man." But the old duke's eyes had fallen closed again. "Bless you, son," he said, his voice faint and weary. His fingers released the prince's hand. "May Usires and . . . and the saints watch over you and . . . keep you safe."

"You are tired, Isgrimnur." Simon nodded to Morgan, who sprang up as though released from a trap. "We will go now and let you rest. We have only just arrived—there will be time to talk again later."

Isgrimnur's eyes half opened, looked first on Simon, then Miriamele. "Don't forget what you told me," he said with surprising intensity. "Don't forget our godchildren, Deornoth and Derra. It was my last promise to Gutrun, and I could not look her in the eye when we meet again unless I know you will work to repair my failure."

"We won't forget, Uncle," said Miriamele. "We will never forget."

"Good." He closed his eyes again. "Good. All is good . . ."

When they could see he was sleeping they left him, with Grimbrand still sitting at his father's bedside. The two priests had reappeared as if by magic, and were again kneeling at the foot of the bed, murmuring the words of the *Exsequis*.

Simon did not know what time it was, only that the midnight bells had rung long ago, drawing him up from sleep for a moment. He thought he had been having the dream of burning that had troubled him so many nights in the last months, but all he could remember for certain was a face made of smoke, a face that alternately wept and laughed and spoke to him in a tongue he had never heard.

"Who's there?" He sat up, feeling for the dagger he kept at his bedside, but then remembered he was not in his own bed, not even in his own country. "Who is it?"

"Only me, Majesty. Tiamak." The little man came farther into the room. "You heard me speaking to the guards. Is the queen asleep?"

Simon looked at Miriamele, who lay sprawled in the covers like an exhausted swimmer. "She is. Should I wake her?"

"I leave it to you, Majesty. Simon. But I have news."

For the first time, Simon realized there was something strange about Tiamak's voice. "What news?" But Tiamak had been crying again, and Simon thought he knew.

"Duke Isgrimnur. That good old man . . . he died an hour ago. His son has just told me. Forgive me for disturbing you, but I thought you would want to know. I thank She Who Waits to Take All Back that we were in time to see him once more."

Tiamak went out. Simon looked at his sleeping wife. Suddenly the weight of the great old castle around him, of Rimmersgard itself, foreign and yet a part of him, as well as the expectations and fears of all their subjects in all the lands, seemed like a weight too heavy to bear. Even with Miriamele only inches away, Simon felt more lonely than he had felt in many years.

He wondered if he would ever sleep well again this side of the grave. Perhaps those who had gone on, like Isgrimnur, were to be envied after all.

9

Heart of the Kynswood

Lord Chancellor Pasevalles had spent most of his morning listening to a group of fat, wealthy merchants complaining about Countess Yissola of Perdruin and her attempts to wrest control of shipping in Erkynlandish waters back from the Northern Alliance. To hear the merchants speak, the lady was part demon, part pirate, and the worst parts of both. He had done everything he could to mollify these men, but what they really seemed to want was to complain, as they had been doing for a long time, and clearly intended to continue doing. Pasevalles was trying to look interested, whatever mayhem he might have been privately contemplating, when the messenger from the Nearulagh Gate guardhouse found him. The merchants didn't stop talking even when Pasevalles leaned aside to listen to the guardsman, and might not have noticed his divided attention if he had not loudly interrupted them.

"I'm sorry, my lords, but something very important has come up. I must leave you, but I promise that your concerns will all be relayed to the king and queen."

"We do not merely want our concerns *relayed*, Lord Chancellor," said the fattest merchant of all, Baron Tostig, who had bought his title from a distressed landowner with the profits of a lucrative trade in wool and hides. "We want the High Throne to do something!"

"And so the High Throne shall, I'm sure—but *not* before the king and queen return to Erkynland." It was hard to keep patience with men like these, creatures intent only on their own ledger books and never on any larger issues. But Pasevalles had been well schooled in patience long before he had agreed to act as Hand of the Throne while Count Eolair traveled with the king and queen. "But I told you the truth, my lords—I am needed. Father Wibert, will you show the gentlemen out?"

As his secretary rounded up the herd of merchants—most of them still bitterly advertising their grievances—Pasevalles hurried to find his cloak. He made his way across the Inner Keep to the stables and borrowed one of the post-horses, fresh and already saddled. Only moments later he was riding out through the Nearulagh Gate, where the Erkynguard all gave him vigorous salutes. The chancellor was well-liked by the guardsmen, who knew he had taken their side when Duke Osric, the Lord Constable, would have reduced their numbers.

He cantered down Main Row, through the city, and out into the warren of streets that had sprung up there with the growth of Erchester. He could not help being impressed by the way the place had changed just during his time at the Hayholt. Twenty years earlier, Erchester had ended at the city walls, but today it sprawled far beyond them, with buildings both ramshackle and surprisingly well-made standing shoulder to shoulder all across Swertclif, although most of the roads were little more than well-worn tracks still muddy from the winter rains. When Pasevalles had arrived, some years after the Storm King's War, no more than ten thousand people had lived in the castle and town, despite it being the capital of all Osten Ard. He felt sure that today there must be at least five times that many. Someday in the not too distant future the new residents outside the city proper would demand the protection of their own wall.

The only place in the outer city where houses were not squeezed higgledy-piggledy along the walls like mushrooms was on the western side, where the royal forest called the Kynswood lay stretched like a sleeping beast. It was becoming harder every year to keep the forest safe from Erchester's growing population, not just to keep a few deer for the king's and queen's table, but to prevent the wholesale cutting of trees for timber, since the Kynswood was a great deal closer than the mighty Aldheorte. Only the previous Autumn the king and queen had been compelled to double the number of royal foresters, and even so King Simon hadn't liked it much: *"But what if a man is starving?"* he had asked. *"Should he be hung for trapping a hare?"*

"If starving men know they can find a meal in the royal forest," the queen had told him, *"then there will soon be no hare in the forest, or deer, or boar, or anything."*

The king and queen made an interesting pair, Pasevalles thought, seemingly as different as husband and wife could be. Simon was proud of his lowly birth and upbringing, and if given his way would have spent most of his time in the stables or the kitchens, gossiping with the servants. But the queen had been born to the old royal house, and was comfortable with most of the privileges of wealth and noble blood. She was also very fierce about protecting what she felt was right: When she sat in judgment she was fair-minded, but in no way the soft touch for a sad story that her husband was.

Once he was beyond the outermost neighborhoods of Erchester, Pasevalles guided his mount off the Kynswood Road and down into the trees. He knew his secretary Wibert would be furious when he learned that the Lord Chancellor had gone outside the city without guards, but there were times when Pasevalles did not want to wait and this was one of them.

It was not easy to find the spot, but at last he saw a flash of red and white through the trees below him—the two rampant dragons, emblem of the royal house. He tied his horse to a branch and made his way down the slope. A pair of Erkynguards and a royal forester with a feather in his cap were waiting with a fourth man, a thin fellow in a ragged jerkin who looked as though he had been sleeping rough for some time.

"Don't hang me, my lord!" the thin man squealed as Pasevalles finally reached them. "I only found it—I never did nothing!"

Pasevalles could see the unmistakable shape of a human body half-buried in the leaves at their feet. He turned to the man with the feather. "Your name, Forester? Then tell me what has happened here."

The forester had the lean, weathered look of one who, had he not been given this post, might have been poaching with the man begging for his life. "Natan am I, Lord Chancellor. My lad and I were on our rounds when this fellow ran out, screaming like the White Foxes had come back. Said there was a dead 'un in the woods. A woman."

"Was he carrying anything? Any game?"

"I weren't!" cried the ragged man, bursting into tears. "I were only lost!"

Pasevalles knew better, but he waited for the forester's reply.

"No, lord. His hands were empty. His bag, too."

The steward turned to the weeping man. "And what is your name? Be truthful or I will know it, and things will go hard for you."

"Dregan, lord, but I done nothing wrong! I swear on St. Sutrin's holy name!"

Pasevalles shook his head. "You may go. But I hope I never hear your name again, Dregan. And if you are caught in the royal forest again—well, you may wish we *had* hanged you."

The ragged man got to his feet with many cries of gratitude, then ran back up the hill toward Erchester. The Erkynguards watched him go with the sulky expressions of dogs denied a chase.

"Begging your pardon, lord, but you know he was in these woods for only one thing," said the forester Natan.

"Of course, but if we'd beaten him, he'd be back in a few nights. As it is, he has told me his name. That will give him pause a bit longer." Pasevalles stepped closer to the body, then sank to his knees beside it. "So he brought you to see this. Then what happened?"

"I sent my boy to fetch the guards."

"And we sent a messenger to you, Lord Chancellor," said one of the Erkynguardsmen, almost proudly.

"Fine. You all did as you should." He leaned closer, brushing away the damp leaves that clung to the body. He could see a little less than half of the face, but that was strange enough, thin and high-boned and less pale than he would have imagined. What was stranger was that he could see no other sign of decay despite the body likely having been in place for days, at least by the amount of forest debris that covered it. The corpse looked to be a woman's. "I don't see any sign of what . . ." he began, then the royal forester jumped and swore behind him.

"That eye!" he said. "It twitched! I saw it!" He took a few stumbling steps back.

"Don't be foolish," Pasevalles began, then he saw it too, the faintest tremor in the exposed eyelid. His heart jumped a little in his chest. "Merciful Aedon, I apologize. You are right."

There was only one thing to do. Pasevalles began to dig away the mulch that covered her. After a moment, the Erkynguards got down beside him to help, although the forester stayed a careful distance away.

When they had uncovered her completely, one of the guardsmen made the sign of the Tree on his breast. The other stared for a moment, then did the same.

"Is it . . . is it a fairy, my lord?" the second guard asked.

"A Sitha, you mean? Or a Norn?" Pasevalles sighed. He had half-anticipated something like this ever since the king and queen had set out for Rimmersgard, some major crisis that would push aside the things he had planned to do during their absence. "I guess that she is Sithi, although I have never met one myself." He took the soiled cloth of her sleeve in his fingers and felt its smooth weave, slippery as southern island silk. Now that she was uncovered, he could see a shallow movement of her chest. "God save us, she still breathes. Help me." He rolled her onto her side and sucked in his breath at the sight of three broken arrows that had pierced her, as well as all the dried blood they had let out of her slender body. "Quick," he told the forester. "Run to the city and find someone with sailcloth or a heavy blanket—something we can use to carry her. And have a cart ready when we get her up to the top."

"Carry her where, my lord?" asked one of the guards as the forester scrambled away up the slope.

"Back to the Hayholt. It's our misfortune that Master Tiamak is with the king and queen, but I will find someone to take care of her. Did she say anything, make any sound that you heard?"

"No! We thought she was dead, my lord."

"And so she should be. Any mortal would have died from those wounds long ago."

Princess Lillia was waiting for him in the outer throne hall when he pushed through the doors from the Garden Court.

"I heard the noon bell a very long time ago," the girl said. "You didn't tell the truth. You said you would tell me a story when noon came, and I've been waiting and waiting—"

"I am so very sorry, Highness." Pasevalles held the door for the guards and their burden. "But we found this woman sick in the forest, and I must help her. Do you know where Lady Thelía might be?"

"She went to the market today," said Lillia. "I wanted to go but Auntie Rhoner said I couldn't."

"Ah. Well, I have a bit of a problem and need some help, Highness. Would you please go and ask Countess Rhona to come to me?"

"I don't have to do that! I'm a princess!"

Pasevalles took a long breath. "No, you don't, you're right," he said. "My apologies, Princess." He turned to the guards as they staggered up carrying the blanket with the wounded Sitha. "Put her down there, men," he told them. "We'll be taking her somewhere else when we find a clean room."

"Who's that?" asked Lillia, eyes wide. "Is she dead?"

"No, but she's badly hurt." He turned back to the men. "One of you go find the Mistress of Chambermaids, and the other go fetch Brother Etan, the apothecary. Look for him in the herb garden behind the mews." He turned back to the princess. "And I promise I'll tell you that story soon. But you want me to help this poor lady, don't you?"

Lillia frowned, but kept staring at the indistinct figure in the blanket-sling. "Suppose. Maybe I *could* go tell Auntie Rhoner for you." The princess was clearly of two minds, but at last she tucked her hands behind her back and skipped slowly off to find her more-or-less nursemaid, the countess.

"Here you are! What are you doing hiding in one of the guest chambers? I have been searching and searching!" said Rhona. "You are a popular man today, Lord Chancellor—both princesses, mother and daughter, desire your company." She took a step into the room and stopped, eyes wide, when she saw the figure stretched on the bed. "By the Black Hare, what is this?"

"A Sitha-woman, found nearly dead in the Kynswood," said Pasevalles. He needed a moment before what she said sank in. "*Both* princesses? I know Lillia wants a story, but what does her mother want?"

"What Princess Idela wants is a mystery to me, as always." Countess Rhona was the one who began the joking custom of calling Idela "the Widow," because she still wore black so many years after Prince John Josua's death, despite few other signs of actually being in mourning. "But what of this poor woman here?"

"She has arrow wounds—several—and she lay among the trees for days, but still lives. Now you know as much as I do."

"She still lives?" The countess bent over the motionless body, seeming caught between fascination and pity. "And you are certain she is a Sitha?"

"Look at her. What else could she be?"

"One of the White Foxes, just as easily. By the good gods, are you sure it is wise to bring her into the Hayholt?"

"There is nowhere else we could keep her alive—and safe, too, if she lives. Someone tried to kill her, Countess! And no, she is not one of the White Foxes—no Norn has golden skin like that. She is only paler than usual."

The countess had a faraway look in her eyes. "I was a young girl when the Sithi came to Hernystir. Their tents filled the fields as far as the eye could see, and the cloth was every color on the gods' Earth. My mother said it was like the olden days come back."

"Did your mother also tell you how to keep one of them alive?" Pasevalles immediately regretted his surly tone: Rhona was a valuable ally, the queen's best friend and a member of the Inner Council. "I'm sorry, Countess. I beg your pardon. I seem to have left my manners out in the Kynswood."

She smiled. "No need to apologize, Lord Chancellor. I can imagine this day has tested you, and it is scarcely past noon. But what did you want with me? I am not much use as a healer or bedside nurse. Did you send for Lady Thelía?"

"I am here, my lord, I am here!" Brother Etan, his youthful face red and shiny with sweat, staggered through the doorway. "I am sorry it took me so long—I had to run back to my room for my things." He quickly examined the woman on the bed. "Goodness! The guard was right! A Sitha!"

"She has three bad wounds. The arrowheads are still in them," Pasevalles said. "And she has been exposed in the forest for several days. Oh, and Lady Thelía is gone to the market. Can you do anything for this poor creature, Brother?"

The monk mopped his face with the sleeve of his robe. "I cannot answer until I see what I can see."

Pasevalles pointed to the two chambermaids who had been waiting discreetly in the corner of the room since they had finished preparing the sickbed. "For now, these good women will help you to nurse her, Brother. If she wakes or tries to talk, please send one of them for me immediately, no matter the time of day or night. The victim herself may be the only one who can help us unpick this crime. Because make no mistake, this was no accident. Whoever shot her intended murder."

"But why?" asked the countess. "And why is she here? We have not seen the Sithi inside our walls for years."

"And we would not have this time, had a poacher not stumbled onto her where she lay, half covered by forest leaves," said Pasevalles. "Brother Etan, I leave you to your work. Remember, if she wakes or speaks, send for me with all haste."

"Of course, Lord Chancellor."

Countess Rhona walked with him down the long hall of the Royal Gallery. "She was dressed for riding," the countess said at last.

"Yes, she was. I half-suspect she is a messenger from one of the king's and queen's friends among the Fair Folk. That is one of the reasons I am so desperate to be there if she speaks. It has been so long and the Sithi have been so silent. King Simon and Queen Miriamele would never forgive me if I let this messenger die."

The countess took his arm. She was the wife of Count Nial of Nad Glehs, an important noble; she had a fine wit and a keen observer's eye, and she and Pasevalles agreed on court matters far more often than they did not. "You take too much upon yourself, my lord," she told him. "You have done all you can."

"But that is the problem with royalty," he replied, "although I hasten to say that our monarchs are different than most. But still, they do not easily relinquish responsibility. Once disappointed, they will seldom bestow it again in the same place."

Countess Rhona laughed. "As I said, you take too much upon yourself. But I still do not know why you asked me to come to you. Clearly it was not because of my skills as a healer."

"Ah, of course, I'd nearly forgotten. This morning you said you were going to send a message to your husband with the post rider. Is your noble lord, the count, still at Hernysadharc?"

"He will not leave before Elysiamansa is celebrated here." She smiled sadly. "I miss him."

"Of course. I wonder if your messenger would also carry another message— one that your husband might discreetly deliver for me . . . ?"

"There you are, Lord Pasevalles!"

He turned to see Princess Idela and two of her ladies moving toward them along the gallery, having likely just come from the chapel. Pasevalles felt a stab of irritation. Prince John Josua's widow was a comely young woman who had made plain her desire for his attention, although he suspected that was mostly a matter of court politics. It flattered his vanity, but it definitely made his life more difficult.

"Your Highness, Ladies," he said, bowing. "You honor me."

"Oh, good day, Countess," said Idela with a smile for Rhona. "I trust Lillia hasn't given you too much trouble today. Where is she?"

Only Pasevalles noticed the small hitch before the countess answered. "She is lying down, Princess. She tired herself out this morning trying to convince her pony to wear a hat."

"Oh, the little dear." The princess who would never be queen turned back to Pasevalles. "I have something most important to discuss with you, Lord Steward—and yet it seems you are avoiding me. Am I so frightful, that you flee me like an ogre out of a nursery tale?"

Rhona took that as a hint that she should find other things to do. She gave Pasevalles a look of commiseration as she took her leave.

He hid his annoyance beyond a smile. This day of all days! "Never, Princess. But less pleasant duties have been playing the tune all day, and I have been forced to dance to their measure."

"And what could be of such importance, Lord Chancellor?" There was no question where little Lillia had learned to pout when denied anything, but Pasevalles did not want to explain about the Sitha woman. Idela would insist on being involved, and Pasevalles wanted to keep control of the situation. He would tell her later.

"Nothing of great weight, Highness." He took a breath, doing his best to push his worries from his mind. He had set everything in place, and for the moment could do nothing more. Now it was up to the Sitha to live or die. "How can I help you?"

"It is this library of Master Tiamak's. Well, it is the king's and queen's library, I suppose, but you know what I mean. The little fellow seems to do nothing else these days."

"Not at the moment, as you know, since he is with them on the journey to Elvritshalla."

"Yes, but that is why I want to speak to you. Lord Tiamak seems most adamant that all the old books in the Hayholt must be found and written down and put in his library." She shook her head. "All of them!"

"I am sure that he does not mean to take your own books, my lady." Idela was known to spend much of her time reading the Book of the Aedon, or at least memorizing appropriate phrases that she could use to point up the failings of others. "It is the rare books, Princess, the old ones, that Tiamak is so anxious to protect." The longer the conversation lasted, the more he was feeling the tug of other duties. Idela, who was used to being waited on and cosseted, was clearly puzzled by his distraction.

"Yes, and that's just it," she said. "My John Josua had many books, as you know. So many books! Sometimes I despaired of his attention. Even when Morgan came, the midwife could scarcely get him to lift his nose from one of them long enough to leave the room."

"Your husband would have been a great scholar, Highness—*was* a great scholar even in his short time. He had a rare gift." Which was true, but he doubted Idela's ambitions for John Josua had tended in that direction.

"There is a collection of books that Tiamak has not seen. I would not even open them myself—only the good Lord knows what horrors are in them, what ancient blasphemies—but they look very old to me. Some are only rolls of parchment tied with string. I wish you would come by and look at them. If they belong in this library he and the king and queen are building, the Wrannaman is welcome to them."

"I beg your pardon, lady, but why me? Surely Master Tiamak should be the judge of what belongs in the library."

"Oh, but that little man is so greedy! I do not trust him to take only those that are truly old and valuable. And I do not want to lose my husband's possessions. They are all I have left."

Pasevalles knew that what she really wanted was to have him to herself for a while out of the public eye, and to draw him deeper into her circle. Idela was not entirely satisfied being only the mother of the heir, and was an active participant in the Hayholt's incessant contests of power and influence. But was that all? She had certainly pursued him for much of the last year, seeking him out, asking his opinion. Pasevalles was beginning to wonder whether she had some deeper interest in him. She was not an astonishing beauty, but she was certainly comely, with large eyes and a fine, straight nose much like her father Osric's. A man seeking to improve his position could do worse than a dalliance with the prince's widow.

As long as that man could keep her sweet, he reminded himself. That was a less certain proposition. Her power depended on something that could not be undone, so she was immune to most forms of persuasion.

In any case, it was a knotty problem, and not one Pasevalles wished to spend time on now.

He took the princess's hand and kissed it. "You do me too much credit, Highness. I am ignorant of most such matters of scholarship—my schooling was more the rough and tumble sort one gets in a backwater court like Metessa. But I will put my mind to your problem and come to you with a solution very soon. Will you give me your leave to resume my less interesting duties?" And he smiled, hoping it would serve as a reassurance no matter what she truly planned.

"Of course, good Pasevalles. You are the best of men. Go and do what you must do. I know that the king and queen must have left you a dreadful burden to carry in Eolair's absence."

And you are a significant part of that burden, lady—or might become that if I do not deal with you carefully. "You are too kind, Princess." He made a bow, then left her. Behind him he heard Idela and her ladies giggling softly among themselves, like fairy music on the wind.

10

Hymns of the Lightless

Nobody who lived in Nakkiga could be completely surprised to find soldiers at their door, but Viyeki had not expected a troop of the feared Hamakha Wormslayer Guards to arrive at his house in the middle hours of the night to demand that he accompany them. Faceless in their helmets, stern and utterly formal in their speech, the soldiers made no threats but it was clear that he had no choice except to go with them.

Viyeki knew all too well that such invitations were generally the formal precursor to an execution. Despite his overwhelming shock, he still could not help wondering why, if he had fallen from her grace so completely, the Mother of All had given him an audience and new orders just a few days earlier. Could this arrest be some private scheme of Akhenabi's instead, using the queen's authority to remove him? If so, it seemed to be a new tactic: ordinarily, the Lord of Song's enemies simply disappeared, or succumbed to sudden and mysterious ailments.

Still, the guard chieftain had a summons that bore the queen's seal, which meant Viyeki could only go with them and try to prepare himself for whatever might follow.

Viyeki's secretary Yemon was suspiciously absent from the household, so he directed his second cleric to ask the Hamakha guards to wait a short time for the dignity of his office. He bade his servants dress him in his magisterial robes, his great outer tunic, his sashes and belts, and did his best to stand unmoving as they did so, keeping limbs, face, and breathing respectably calm.

"Where am I being taken?" Viyeki asked as his ornamented collar was tied in place.

"That is not for me to say," the Wormslayer chieftain replied. "Only that you are to make haste to come with us, High Magister."

At that moment his wife burst into the room, startling one of Viyeki's servants into dropping the magister's ceremonial mattock. As the tool clattered on the stones, the Wormslayers calmly leveled their spears at her. "What happens here?" she demanded. Despite the dishevelment of her nightwear, Khimabu eyed the Hamakha guards with contempt. Viyeki noticed that she also darted a glance at his bed, no doubt to see if Tzoja had been with him. "Why do these people trouble us, husband?"

"I truly do not know, my lady wife, but it is a lawful summons in the queen's name. We will trust to the wisdom of Our Mother that all will be resolved as it should be. I have done nothing wrong." He looked at the empty features of the chieftain. "Is that not correct?"

The leader stared forward, unblinking. "It is not for me to say, High Magister."

"Ah, yes. So you mentioned." Viyeki snapped his fingers, and his servants stepped forward to help him with the last of his clothing, the heavy over-mantle. "How should I call you, officer? Do you have a name?"

"I am a chieftain of the Silent Court of the Hamakha Clan," the officer said. "That is all you need to know."

Such stiffness—such rote prosecution of duty! thought Viyeki. He wondered if the chieftain might be a halfblood like his daughter Nezeru; they were common these days, especially in the ranks of the Sacrifices and clan guards. How many of the Wormslayers here on his doorstep were the fruits of such couplings? They seemed to make up most of the soldiery these days—but were they, as his master Yaarike had once hoped, truly Hikeda'ya, through and through? Or were they merely crude imitations, attack dogs dressed up in the finery of the Garden?

What does it matter, he asked himself with a touch of dark amusement, *if they are only here to lead me to execution? Even a trained hound could do that.* "Very well . . . Chieftain," he said. "I am ready to accompany you."

As he stepped out the front door, past his household guards and into the wide, silent street, his wife followed them to the doorway. "Husband!" she called. "Do not disgrace our family."

"How could I, kind Lady Khimabu," he replied, "with your faithful support to hearten me?"

The last he saw of her—the last he might ever see of her, he could not help thinking—was her long pale shape in the doorway, ordering the servants back inside before the other denizens of the Noble Tier saw the family's shame.

Whatever hopes Viyeki might have entertained that this was merely another summons to the palace vanished quickly. Instead of climbing the great staircase to the sacred Third Tier and the *Omeiyo Hamakh*, his guards led him downward instead into the labyrinth of the city. They passed across the deserted New Moon Market and along the edge of the ghostly, web-festooned Spider Groves as they made their way outward toward the edge of Nakkiga, through the mist clouds thrown up by the thundering Tearfall, then past the massive vertical column of Tzaaita's Stone. At last they reached the Heartwall Stair and followed it down to the levels stacked below the city. Viyeki had given up trying to guess where he was being taken, because each new destination he could think of seemed grimmer than the last.

The first level was filled with the community temples and mass burial grounds of the lower castes, the *sojeno nigago-zhe* or "little gardens of memory." Hikeda'ya who were too poor or too humble to have family tombs, but too proud to see their dead thrown into fiery crevices or left on burning ash heaps in the Field of the Nameless, had built the shared memorial parks, each full of symbols of the Lost Garden, each with its single, silver-faced Guardian, a simple upright stone figure presiding over those places of rest as the Queen herself ruled the waking world. As they passed, Viyeki could not help envying the sleepers in these humble shared graves: he feared he was fated for an even less exalted resting place.

But it quickly became clear to him that even the throat-burning sparks and the smoky gray winds of the Field of the Nameless would not be lowly enough for him: His guards passed the Fields and continued to descend, escorting him down, level by level, into the most profound depths. He thought he had been prepared for shame and execution, but it seemed the soldiers were leading him, not to the simple, swift ignominy of a disgraced noble's death, but toward something altogether more disturbing.

Is it to be the Chamber of the Well, then? Viyeki felt his knees go weak at the thought of that ominous place, a vast natural vault of naked stone hidden deep in the heart of the mountain. The infamous chamber contained both the Well and the Breathing Harp, objects of terrible, legendary power. It was all he could do to stay upright.

Trust the Queen, he told himself with more than a touch of desperation. *Remember the Garden. Trust the Way.* But the old, reassuring refrain now felt as hollow as the ageless and unknowable mountain deeps that were slowly enfolding him.

Lower and lower they guided him, by stairs so infrequently used that they were completely dark and the soldiers had to hold his arms as they all inched down the steps together. Viyeki felt as though he climbed down the throat of some vast, impossible beast, and it was more than just frightful imagining: with each step the air was growing steadily warmer and thicker, and the very stones around him seemed half alive.

Once, as a young acolyte, Viyeki had been lowered by harness into one of Nakkiga's deepest interior chasms. That throat-clutching, disorienting darkness had felt a little like this, but the smothering air here seemed to quiver to some slow, heavy pulse, a vibration he had never felt before, like the beat of a giant heart.

Remember the Garden. It was all he could do, all he could afford to think. *Trust the Way.*

The fear Viyeki had been trying to suppress since the dragon-helmeted soldiers first appeared at his door eased fractionally when they reached the convergence of stairways known as the Hawk's Path. Several sets of stairs entered the wide, helical stairwell from different levels, and for the first time he could see that he was not the only well-dressed figure being escorted down the spiraling steps to the Chamber of the Well. Viyeki could not yet recognize any of his fellow nobles because of a curious thickness to the air here, as though they all swam through brackish water, but he counted at least a dozen different escorts winding their way downward. Was it possible that so many important Hike-da'ya would be brought together all at once for obliteration? That seemed too reckless for a planner as careful as Akhenabi.

At the base of the Hawk's Path the different groups crowded together, wait-ing to enter a single narrow doorway, from which light of several unusual colors played across their faces—sickly yellow, deep crimson, and cadaverous gray-blue. Viyeki's guards urged him forward, and for the first time he could see that his fellow guests (or prisoners) were not only magisters like himself but also lesser officials, dozens of clan leaders, influential clerics, and other import-ant members of the ruling caste, both male and female. If Akhenabi intended to imprison or execute them all, Viyeki thought wonderingly, it would mean the destruction of nearly the entirety of Nakkiga's ruling elite.

Then Viyeki saw that one of the others being led toward the arch by a troop of Hamakha guards was High Marshal Muyare sey-Iyora himself. Muyare was one of the most respected nobles, leader of all the queen's armies, and though he was certainly one of Akhenabi's chief rivals, he was also far too powerful to be led meekly through Nakkiga as a prisoner: Viyeki felt certain the marshal's sol-diers would never have let him be taken against his will from the order-house of Sacrifice. But even though the marshal must have come willingly, there was a deep bleakness to the commander's expression that left Viyeki uneasy.

The crowd surged forward. As Viyeki and the other high officials and sol-diers crowded through the archway and onto a single wide staircase leading down into the Chamber of the Well, the heat and the sense of smothering seemed to close in on him. When he put his foot on the first step, it felt as though he stepped not simply into another chamber in great Nakkiga but out into pure space, some absolute emptiness that could not be understood. For a moment Viyeki could not tell down from up, and he wavered in something close to blind terror until he felt someone take his arm and heard a quiet voice.

"Are you well, Magister?" It was Luk'kaya, leader of the Harvesters and one of Viyeki's few allies among the ordinal elite.

"I thank you, High Gatherer, but it is nothing," he said, although secretly he was grateful for her presence. "A misstep, that is all."

Despite the many nobles and guards descending together, the narrow stair-well was nearly silent but for the feather-soft rustle of their footfalls. The smothering air seemed to grow even thicker and closer, but Viyeki found as he descended that with self-control he could breathe normally, if more shallowly than usual.

Viyeki had never entered the sacred Chamber of the Well in all his long life, and as he emerged from the last stairwell into the cavern he could not help staring around in fearful fascination. Arched galleries ringed the chamber both at the bottom and higher up, but what drew his eye was the hole in the center of the cavern floor, a ragged gouge surrounded by a circular lip of carved, inlaid stones—the mouth of the Well. The radiance that oozed from it seemed like something heavier than mere light, lying close along the stony floor while leaving the reaches above the upper galleries lost in shadow. By its dull ocher gleam, Viyeki thought he could see faces gazing down from the dark openings in the walls above him—or at least things that looked like faces.

The Well itself blazed like the maw of one of the mountain's flaming crevices, but its thick light seemed to come from a source even older than the mountain's internal fires—a bleak, yellowish glow that might have lit the world before even the stars first began to burn, and which made everything in the great chamber seem to lean and loom. A shape hung in the column of wavering light above it, something real as blown glass yet insubstantial as smoke, an object Viyeki could not entirely understand or even completely see. This was the Breathing Harp, a sacred object brought to Nakkiga from lost Kementari when the immortals had fled the sudden ruination of that great city. From some angles the harp seemed near enough for Viyeki to touch, but even a slight tilt of his head reduced it to vanishingly faint scratches on the air, lines that were barely there at all, but with spaces between them that seemed to open onto limitless vistas and made his eyes ache. When Viyeki finally pulled his gaze away, the Harp seemed to linger before him like a shadow wherever he turned.

But even the Well and the Harp could not hold his attention for long, because like any of his people, when Viyeki saw the slender, silver-masked figure sitting still and pale as a statue on her great chair of black stone, he found it nearly impossible to look at anything else.

Mother of All, give strength to your servant. The sight of the queen brought old words of worship to his mind. *My life is yours. My body is yours. My spirit is yours.*

If this is *an execution,* Viyeki thought then, *even a wholesale destruction of the noble caste, then at least my death will be at her command.* It was a strangely reassuring idea. Dying, he would at least know that order prevailed—that the Mother of the People, not Akhenabi, still ruled in Nakkiga.

The Lord of Song was present, of course, standing to one side of the queen's throne, facing the Well. Its weird pulsing light, which painted Utuk'ku's white mourning garb with earthy yellows and strange blues, fell onto the darkness of Akhenabi's hooded robes and vanished, so that the powerful Singer seemed to stand in his own shadow, only his mask of dried flesh and painted runes clearly visible.

More surprising to Viyeki, though, was the figure on the other side of the throne—Jijibo the Dreamer, a descendant of the queen so rarely seen outside of the palace as to be almost a legend in the rest of Nakkiga. Utuk'ku and Akhenabi were motionless as they watched the crowd assembling, but scrawny Jijibo was in perpetual, twitching motion, his fingers convulsively flexing and his wide mouth working as he muttered unendingly to himself.

Viyeki knew from experience that the Dreamer's words seemed to leap from his thoughts to his tongue without even the faintest consideration for propriety or courtesy or even ordinary sense. Most of Nakkiga's nobles considered Jijibo helplessly mad—a rare but not unknown affliction among the People—because he wore mismatched garments and talked to himself aloud, though often incomprehensibly. But the Dreamer had a talent for devices and plans that pleased his ancestor the queen, so he was suffered to go where he wished and to do largely as he pleased. Viyeki's Order of Builders, in particular, often had to deal with his sudden demands for this or that space or materials they had planned to use themselves, but as a relative and favorite of the Mother of All, Jijibo was outshone perhaps only by mighty Lord Akhenabi himself, so Viyeki's order seldom had any recourse but to let the Dreamer have his way.

Because his vision had been blocked by so many others, it was not until Viyeki reached a position in the crowd directly facing the queen's throne that he saw a group of figures already kneeling at the queen's feet as though to receive honors from their monarch—but their slumped postures and bound wrists told Viyeki more than he wanted to know about the nature of the reward they expected.

As the last of the Nakkiga nobles crowded into place behind Viyeki, the Lightless Ones began to sing in the unknown deeps below the Chamber of the Well, soft, strange cries as alien as bitterns booming in a marsh but also as complex as speech. Some said the Lightless Ones had lived in the depths even before the Hikeda'ya came to the mountain, some that their ancestors had traveled from the distant Garden on the Eight Ships with Queen Utuk'ku and the Keida'ya, but in truth nobody could say for certain whether they were many creatures or one thing with many voices. If the queen knew the Lightless' full tale, she never spoke of it.

As they all waited in near-silence, Viyeki could feel fear and tension growing in his fellow nobles, as though they were a single flock of birds that might suddenly startle and take wing. Clearly most of them were as confused as he was, frightened by the unexpected summons, by the Hamakha guards who had led them here and the squadron's worth of battle-armored Queen's Teeth guards who stood behind Utuk'ku's throne.

If we are not all to be executed, Viyeki thought, *then there must be grave news indeed if the queen brings us all to the Well to hear it. Are we under attack? Have the mortals come again to besiege us?*

Akhenabi spread his arms, his long sleeves hanging like the wings of a bat. "Silence for the Queen," he said. "Hear the Mother of All."

No one had been speaking above a whisper, but at the Lord of Song's words the room grew silent in an instant. Utuk'ku leaned forward, her eyes glittering in the slots of her mask.

I need you, my children.

Her words were not spoken aloud, but flew straight into the minds of all those present like a sudden thunderclap, a crash of overwhelming fury that for a long moment turned Viyeki's own thoughts into shards, splinters, powder.

I am weak, the queen told them, although the force of her thoughts brought tears of pain to Viyeki's eyes. *My strength has been spent in the defense of our race. The sacred sleep from which I just awakened will be my last—there is no further help for me there.*

Many of the nobles around Viyeki began to moan, whether in pain like his at the force of the queen's words, or in fear at what they signified, but Utuk'ku did not pause. *Only with the aid of all your hearts and hands can I survive the present danger,* she told them—*can we all survive.*

Several of the gathered nobles, overwhelmed by the force and terror of this message, now dropped to all fours and pressed their faces against the cavern floor like sacrificial beasts awaiting slaughter. Jijibo the Dreamer laughed and did a gleeful little loose-jointed dance beside the queen's black stone chair, as though he had never seen finer entertainment.

Akhenabi raised his arms and spread his gloved hands and the observers quieted. "Our beloved queen has fought so long and hard for us," the Lord of Song declared, "both here and in the lands beyond life, that she is weary— terribly weary. So she asks me to speak for her." He raised one arm higher and curled his fingers into a fist. "Heed your queen! We are in peril! But before we can protect ourselves from the new dangers that threaten, we must put our house in order. There are those among us who took advantage of the queen's *keta-yi'indra*—traitors who tried to use her long sleep for their own advantage." He paused, and his masked face looked out blankly over the crowd of nobles and soldiers. "Libertines. Thieves. *Traitors.* And now they will face justice."

A pair of tall Queen's Teeth stepped forward and grabbed the first kneeling figure, dragged him to his feet, and then turned him around to face the crowd of nobles. His features, though battered and bruised, were all too familiar. It was Yemon, Viyeki's secretary.

The magister's terror returned like a blast of icy wind. Every sense, every nerve, urged him to flee, but his limbs would not respond; he could only stand and wait and watch. *So it is to be death for me after all,* he thought. *Akhenabi has found someone to inform against me. Farewell, my family. I hope the disgrace is not too great to be endured. Farewell, Nezeru, my daughter and heir.* But in that moment, instead of his lawful wife, it was the face of his mortal lover Tzoja that came to him. He hoped she and their daughter would not be punished for his mistakes.

One by one the other prisoners kneeling before the queen were dragged to their feet, named, and then forced around to face the watching crowd. To Viyeki's increasing confusion, almost none of them held any higher rank than Yemon—a few clerics, another magister's secretary, a Sacrifice commander who had only recently been named a general. The most important of them was Nijika, a Host Singer Viyeki remembered from the days of the Northmen's siege of the mountain. Like Yemon, she had new wounds on her face and head, and had obviously suffered since being seized, but she stood expressionlessly in the grip of the Queen's Teeth while the watchers murmured and stared and the Lightless Ones throbbed in the deep. After she had been named and displayed to the watching crowd, Nijika and all the other prisoners were forced back onto their knees again at the foot of the queen's great stone chair.

"In these terrible times, we face dangers both from within and without," Akhenabi warned. "While the People's beloved Mother slept, these wretched creatures you see before you conspired to flout her will. They instigated laws and directives that went against our oldest traditions, weakening their own people and making a mockery of the very memory of our Garden."

Viyeki was stunned by the Lord of Song's words. Surely no one gathered here could believe that this small coterie of minor officials had instigated the idea of giving half-mortal bastards the right to join important Hikeda'ya orders like Sacrifice and Song. It had taken the combined power of Marshal Muyare and Viyeki's master Yaarike, as well as Akhenabi himself and several more of the most powerful nobles, to create such sweeping changes. Had the great Singer somehow managed to convince the queen of such an obvious untruth? Or was something else going on?

The first prisoner, Yemon, was now dragged on his knees right to the queen's feet. He whimpered, but when he would have turned away in shame and terror from the queen's shiny, masked face, strong hands grabbed his head and held it so he could not move. Viyeki expected Akhenabi to read a list of charges against the prisoner, but instead the Mother of the People reached down and touched Yemon's forehead with her white-gloved hand. The hapless secretary began to quiver harder and harder, until it seemed some huge, invisible predator shook him in his jaws. The guards abruptly let go, as though they had found themselves holding something hot. Yemon began screeching, broken, wordless cries, even as the chant of the Lightless grew louder and the air in the cavern grew warmer and thicker.

Now a strange shadow slipped across the prisoner from the place where Utuk'ku's hand touched him, rippling slowly outward, spreading down his head and over his body like ink spilled on a blotter. Yemon's shrieks subsided into little more than whistles of escaping air, then he abruptly dissolved into a cascade of ash or black dust; Viyeki barely restrained a cry of disgust and horror.

While the crowd watched in rapt, uneasy silence, the next bound figure was dragged forward to the queen and the scene was acted out once more, and then again with each of the accused traitors. By the time the last prisoner, Host Singer Nijika, was dragged to Utuk'ku's throne, she had to kneel in the drifting remains of her predecessors.

Nijika did not wait for death in silence, or whimper as Yemon had done. Instead, she proclaimed in a loud, clear voice that all the gathered nobles could hear, "*Hikada'yei!* I do not know precisely what I have done, but if my queen and my master say I am guilty, then I am guilty beyond question. Know only this, as my last and truthful words. I love my queen more than my own life, more than the honor of my family, clan, or order. I swore when I became one of her Singers that I would gladly surrender my life for her, and the manner of that surrender is of no import now. I die without regret, because it is my Mother's wish."

Light from the Well played across Utuk'ku's silver mask as the queen paused, and for a moment Viyeki thought she had been touched by the Singer's words and might pardon her. Then the queen reached forward, but instead of touching Nijika's face, she placed her fingers on the Host Singer's breast, as if in blessing, and the Singer threw her head back in some unknowable pain or ecstasy. The queen leaned farther forward. Her hand seemed to pass into Nijika's body. The prisoner cried out, a moan of uttermost extremity like nothing Viyeki had ever heard, then the blackness swept over Nijika like wildfire and she crumbled into a mound of dark motes indistinguishable from those who had died before her. But as this ashy powder settled to the cavern floor and the wisps of smoke dissipated, Viyeki saw that the queen held something in her hand. It was Nijika's heart, still wet, but blackened in places as though it had been pulled from a fire.

Here, Song-Lord. Utuk'ku's thoughts, though directed at Lord Akhenabi, pierced Viyeki like darts of ice. *Keep this with honor in your order-house. Her circumstances may have made her traitor, but the host singer's heart remained true.*

The Lord of Song accepted the burned thing from the queen, nodded in apparent gratitude, and then stepped back. "So ends the conspiracy," he announced. "So must it always come to those who betray our queen and people."

Many of the audience in the Chamber of the Well now cheered and called out their thanks, praising the queen and Akhenabi for preserving them from the traitors, but Viyeki could not help noticing that Muyare, marshal of all Sacrifices, leader of the queen's armies, was not one of those caught up in the moment. The great warrior stood with eyes downcast, his arms at his side, and Viyeki realized that whatever was happening here, it was not yet over.

"Hear me now, as I speak for the queen!" intoned Akhenabi. "Hear now why you are all needed, why your strength and loyalty are our only defenses against destruction!" He raised his arms again, waiting for the shocked murmurs of the onlookers to fade to stillness. "Yes, destruction! You all know of Ineluki Storm King, who fought the mortals until they destroyed him, then returned from death to fight them once more, before being destroyed forever in the War of Return—the same war that forced our queen into the healing sleep from which she has only now awakened."

As Akhenabi spoke the queen looked upward, past the Well and the Breathing Harp, her masked face staring into the farthest heights of the chamber, where cold from above met the damp warmth from the mountain's depths and flakes of snow had begun to swirl.

"When Ineluki of the Zida'ya was still a living king," Akhenabi continued, "defending the great fortress of Asu'a from the ravaging Northmen, he turned to our queen for help in his struggle against the mortals. She sent him the finest hearts of the Order of Song, five of our eldest, wisest, most skilled Singers. These five lords of Song—Karkkaraji, Sutekhi, Ommu, Enah-gé, and Uloruzu, may they all be remembered as long as the Garden itself!—were afterward called the Red Hand. Adding their strength and knowledge to Ineluki's, they bent the walls of time and space and sung up ancient powers and dreadful spirits, but not even the Red Hand were powerful enough to defeat the swarming Northmen and their iron weapons. In desperation, Ineluki sought for a weapon so devastating that it would scour the plague of mortals from the face of our land forever . . . but his summoning failed and he was destroyed. The five Red Hand perished and died beside Ineluki. Asu'a fell to the mortal invaders."

A cry of grief and loss went up from the crowd, as if the old and familiar story were being told for the first time. Even the Lightless Ones seemed to hear it with dismay, and their alien voices thrummed in counterpoint from the depths.

"Thus passed the last kingdom of our kind from these lands," said Akhenabi, "—the last, that is, but for our home, this mountain of Nakkiga. Ineluki's Zida'ya kinsmen scattered to the woods and other hiding-holes. We Hikeda'ya sealed ourselves behind our great gates as the tide of mortal men swept across all we had known and loved. But Ineluki, though his earthly shell had died, was not truly gone. His anger was so strong that he lingered in the Places Between as a spirit of helpless rage—until our queen found him again." He bowed and made an elaborate gesture of gratitude toward silent Utuk'ku. Most in the crowd imitated him. "Yes," he went on, louder now, "our queen risked her own precious life to search for him in those dark regions where life itself is the enemy. And when she found what remained of him—a small, deathless flame of rage—she brought him to sanctuary in the endless corridors of the Breathing Harp. Together, our queen and Ineluki Storm King summoned back the spirits of the Red Hand as well."

We thwarted the true death for you! The queen's thoughts were ragged, but so powerful that many of those listening cried out to hear them. *All for you! And now that death stalks me in turn!* Some of the Hikeda'ya were slack-mouthed and moaning.

"And so we prepared to strike at the mortals once more, and the War of Return continued," said Akhenabi. "But again treachery overcame us! This time those of our own race—Ineluki's own cowardly kinsmen—sided with the mortals. The turncoat House of Year-Dancing led the remaining Zida'ya against us, and less than half a Great Year ago we were defeated at the very gates of Asu'a. Ineluki Storm King, that great heart, that sacrifice for his people, was delivered to Unbeing and is forever lost to us—one of the bravest of all our kind, unmade. And when Ineluki and the Red Hand failed this time, our beloved queen was also nearly destroyed."

Some of the gathered Hikeda'ya cried out in fury and shook their fists in the air, as if the treacherous Zida'ya were here with them in the depths of Nakkiga and could be punished.

"Futility!" cried Akhenabi. "Ah, such a bitter taste! There is no poison to match it. But do not underestimate our queen, who loves and protects us always. Because in the grim aftermath of that failure, as she wandered lost in the *keta-yi'indra,* great Utuk'ku was still searching for a way to destroy our treacherous enemies. *And she found one.*"

The cries of anger ceased. The great chamber fell silent. Even the Lightless seemed to pause and listen.

"Ineluki was gone, and most of his Red Hand, too," the Lord of Song continued, "but one who had sacrificed all for us and for the queen still lived! And Utuk'ku, the Mother of All, found that fearless spirit in the lands where sleep and death meet."

Although it was Akhenabi who spoke, all eyes were now on the motionless queen.

"Yes, for despite all the mortals could do," Akhenabi declared, "Ommu the Voiceless, one of the greatest of all our kind, had not entirely perished in the Storm King's destruction. Try to imagine such devotion, Hikeda'ya," Akhenabi cried. "Already murdered once by mortals, returned from death to fight again for our kind, and then murdered once more by those same cruel mortal hands—and yet still Ommu of the Red Hand would not die!" Murmurs of horrified wonder rose from the crowd. "Full of secrets from the Places Between, still burning for the vengeance that has been denied us, Ommu the Whisperer did not surrender. And even as I speak, she still clings to existence in the dreadful lands beyond life! And in this very hour—but only with your help—the queen will bring Ommu back to us."

Although he was as stunned by this as the rest, Viyeki was also full of doubt. Even if the bizarre tale of Ommu's survival was true, what could death have taught the undead Singer that it had not already shown her the first time she died? How would bringing back one of the Red Hand change the Hikeda'ya's fortunes when the queen and Ineluki themselves had not managed it? And why had Viyeki and the rest of Nakkiga's elite been brought here to the Chamber of the Well?

"We will prepare for her return," Akhenabi announced.

As he spoke, a squadron of Queen's Teeth appeared from one of the chamber's outer archways. Four of them carried an open ceremonial litter with a young woman of the Hikeda'ya swaying inside it. She was dressed in a robe as rich as one of Utuk'ku's own, an ornate masterpiece of patterned spinsilk, and her jet hair was elaborately curled and pinned as if for a wedding, but despite her rich clothes and considerable beauty, Viyeki did not recognize her. As the guards set the litter down by the edge of the Well, her head wobbled. She did not seem to see anything around her—not the assembled nobles, not the Breathing Harp, not even the queen herself.

She has been given kei-vishaa, Viyeki realized. *She walks in dream. But why? Who is she and what is happening here?*

"Bow your heads, Hikada'yei!" commanded Akhenabi. "Lend your queen the strength of your hearts, and today the Mother of the People will bring back one whom the mortals could not unmake, for all their trying." His voice grew softer; Viyeki thought the Lord of Song mimicked regret. "But that return is not without cost, and Ommu's passage will not come without pain to us all. Praise loudly loyal Marshal Muyare, High Magister of the Order of Sacrifice, who at our queen's request gives Ya-Jalamu, his own granddaughter, to be the Opener of the Way."

"Praise Muyare!" someone shouted. "May the Garden remember and bless him always!"

"Praise the queen!" cried someone else. "Praise the mother of us all!"

Viyeki could feel everything the others felt, the fear and exhilaration of the queen's struggle on their behalf, but some of his doubts remained. The girl might only be one of Muyare's several granddaughters, and part mortal at that—Viyeki had heard her mother was a human slave, like his own Tzoja—but it seemed hard to believe that the marshal had surrendered her willingly to such a terrible fate, no matter how exalted the purpose. Muyare was a powerful man, with all the armed might of the Order of Sacrifice at his command: only an order from the queen herself could have made him do it.

"Respect this noble gift of the high magister!" Akhenabi proclaimed. "Revere Muyare's loyalty and his granddaughter's honorable sacrifice, which will open the door for Ommu's return to us. The queen declares that in Ya-Jalamu's name, an entire new league of the Order of Sacrifice will be created—the League Seyt-Jalamu!"

A shout of approval and gratitude went up from the assembled nobles, but Muyare still gazed steadily at the ground before him, as if the sacrifice Akhenabi was praising brought him only pain. He clearly could not bear to look at his granddaughter's face, though she would not have known him in her *kei-vishaa* dream.

"Now our queen needs your silence!" Akhenabi announced, and the chamber grew quiet. Even the throbbing of the air seemed to diminish. Only the Lightless Ones continued as they had been, their distant song droning and echoing beneath the great chamber. "She also needs your hearts and your thoughts," said the Lord of Song. "Only with the return of great Ommu can our queen resist those who would attack and destroy us. If our people are to survive, we must bring the Whisperer back from death to help our beloved queen fight for our survival.

"It is time for the Opening of the Way."

Now Viyeki heard another note join the music of the Lightless, soft at first, but rising in pitch and volume until it wound through their croaking hymn like a single bright thread in a dark-hued tapestry: it was one of Akhenabi's Order of Singers, kneeling beside Ya-Jalamu's litter. More Singers joined, and it sounded as if the icy mountain winds had all been given tongue, each syllable so sharp and cold that they seemed to pierce the bodies of all those listening and turn their inner organs to frost.

Why perform such a ritual in front of us all? Viyeki wondered. *The Order of Song never display their powers this way. Why now?*

The answer came when he felt something touching his thoughts, a probing pressure that soon became an altogether more commanding intrusion. It was the queen, he realized, taking control of his mind and the minds of his fellow nobles, weaving them into one thing, using their strength and her own together to pierce the veils that bounded life. The magister resisted from pure reflex, but only for a moment—his strength was nothing against the queen's. Within moments he and the others were no longer individual Hikeda'ya, but were being shaped into a single tool in Utuk'ku's matchless grip. He could feel something of the queen's emotions, her fixed determination and even her chilly satisfaction as she caught them all up and wove them together.

"Do not resist the Mother of All!" Akhenabi declared as if he had sensed Viyeki's unwillingness. "Now, silence. Silence for the Word of Opening."

The song abruptly grew louder, more painful to the ear, the words harsh as hammerblows. Then, as if someone had thrown open a door to fierce winter, darkness swept over the chamber and the cavern suddenly seemed to plunge into a terrible cold. But what Viyeki could feel through Utuk'ku's thoughts was a thousand times worse. Beyond the cavern in which they stood, beyond their sacred mountain, beyond life itself, he could sense a lurking chill so deep and so cold that nothing alive could approach it. Only Queen Utuk'ku, armored in the song of Akhenabi's minions and wielding the thoughts of her subjects like a weapon, dared to match herself against that ultimate, life-swallowing darkness. Viyeki could feel his own heart beating so fast he thought it must burst from the terror of that ultimate shadow, but at the same instant it seemed to be happening impossibly far away. He felt like a single bubble among thousands in one of Nakkiga's frothing hot lakes.

Now Muyare's granddaughter began to writhe against her bonds, head back and mouth agape as though she were drowning. It was hard for Viyeki to see through the deepening gloom—even the ocher light of the well seemed to be shrinking, dying—but as the song gained strength the young woman's movements atop the litter became more rapid and erratic, until her head was whipping violently from side to side. Marshal Muyare let out a loud groan, and even seemed as if he might go to her, but one of his Sacrifice generals put a hand on his shoulder. The marshal grew still again, face stolid, but Viyeki could tell that beneath the stony pretense Muyare was as desperate as a trapped animal.

The light of the Well had faded until it seemed as dim as the glow of a distant, dying star. Ya-Jalamu's blind eyes turned helplessly toward the watchers and her mouth opened in a shriek of pain that never broke free. Caught up in the song and helpless, Viyeki thought he saw his own daughter Nezeru there, calling to him for help that he could not give.

That is the other purpose of this, he realized in despair. *Not just to bring back Ommu, but so Akhenabi can show us that only he has the queen's favor, that he alone now decides who lives and dies. Muyare's granddaughter, my child—no matter how powerful the noble or the clan, the Lord of Song wants it known that he can reach out to take whoever he chooses and the queen will support him.* Viyeki looked to Utuk'ku, who watched the girl's suffering without any sign of pity, and he felt something break inside him, something that had been there all his life—a belief, a trust.

That could be my own daughter, was all he could think, over and over. *It could be Nezeru.*

Ya-Jalamu was thrashing harder now atop the litter; for a moment it seemed the force of her agonized struggle might break the heavy bonds that held her. Then her bones began to glow. First the skull bloomed behind the girl's face, a hot light that made her pale skin glow like the oiled parchment of a lantern. Next her grasping hands became things of fierce radiance, and smoke began to rise from garments torn and disarranged by her struggles. Within moments her clothing curled and darkened, becoming smoke and ash even as it lay against her ivory skin, until the marshal's granddaughter was all but naked, legs and arms wreathed in flame, all her secrets exposed to the staring multitude.

Then Ya-Jalamu's flesh itself caught fire—it licked upward even from her mouth and nostrils and the corner of her eyes—then, in an instant, all her skin blazed into light. She threw her head back and steam gushed from her sagging mouth. Shivers of burning red climbed out of her throat to splash flame in all directions over the litter, but the conveyance was made of ancient, cured witch-wood, and mere fire would not harm it. Only the girl burned.

It was all Viyeki could do to keep his knees locked, to remain upright. He felt as though he were ablaze too, but instead of his flesh it was his thoughts, his certainties, that were burning away into ash.

Very soon there was nothing to be seen of Ya-Jalamu but a faint movement in the depths of the fire, a flutter of ash, a pair of black sticks waving. The heat was so intense that the air shimmered and grew untrustworthy, but Viyeki still had not felt it, and the Singers crouched around the litter seemed not to feel it either. A few paces from the heart of the blaze, Queen Utuk'ku stared down on the spectacle from behind her featureless mask; Viyeki could no more guess at her thought than he could have supposed the desires of a distant star. But a part of his own thoughts still resonated with the queen's, and as he stared at her he felt something *come through* from the dark reaches beyond the world he knew. Something from that lifeless place was forcing its way out of the cold and blackness, into the world of the living.

As the flames began to die down the center of the blaze was visible once more, but instead of the blackened wreckage Viyeki expected to see there, a scatter of cindered bones, something else sat in the queen's litter, something whole and strange—a figure of shifting red light, wreathed in smoke.

"*Ommu k'rei!*" cried Akhenabi. "Ommu the Whisperer, you have again returned to us from death! May your wisdom and strength help preserve your people—the people you twice gave your life to protect!"

As the queen's grip on his thoughts loosened, Viyeki slowly collapsed to his knees in exhausted terror, as many others around him had already done. He could not look at the shape in the litter directly: it was too strange, too angular, and seemed both far away and terrifyingly close at the same time, as though it had not entirely emerged into his own world of length and distance.

Only when Akhenabi and his Singers rose and surrounded the shape did Viyeki realize that he had been holding his breath for so long he was nearly faint. He let it out with a ragged sigh. Some of his fellow nobles had fallen insensible to the cavern floor. Others had prostrated themselves, amazed and full of veneration to see their queen cheat Death itself, and exhilarated by the small part they had played in it.

Then, just when even the Lightless Ones had fallen silent, and it seemed that the ritual had ended, the shape in the litter suddenly began to thrash in a wild but silent spasm of movement and red light. Viyeki could feel it, though, a quivering touch on the membrane that separated the Chamber of the Harp from the regions beyond life, a violence against its tension, as though a doomed fly struggled against a web, and Viyeki himself was one strand of that web. Mist swirled, obscuring the litter and its occupant. He was surprised—could it be that Ya-Jalamu somehow still fought for the body Akhenabi stole from her? Brave heart, brave woman! A few heartbeats later, though, he thought he could feel something much different, something powerful that was trying to follow Ommu out into the living world—an old and angry thing, full of hate. His heart sped ever faster, until he feared it might burst.

The light of the Well flared for a moment, bright as an earthbound sun, then dimmed as a great, soundless cry of anguish made the assembled nobles grab at their heads in pain and horror. At the same moment a palpable sense of something *ending* swept through the chamber, as though all the strands of the web of thought that connected them had snapped at once: it was clear that the Way that they had opened into outer darkness had just closed again.

Ommu! Ommu she'she mue'ka! The queen had not spoken for some time, and these sudden words boomed in Viyeki's head like a blacksmith pounding at an anvil, their gloating strength bringing tears to his eyes again. *She has come back! The Whisperer! Praise her!*

"Yes, praise her!" cried Akhenabi. "With Ommu's help our great queen will be able to avenge all that has been done to us. We will burn the mortals from the face of the land! We will claim the Witchwood Crown!"

The glow of the Well abruptly faded to its ordinary brightness. Akhenabi's minions wrapped the glowing thing in lengths of white cloth, wrapping it round and round as though it were just another a corpse being prepared to wait for the Garden's return. But this thing *lived*, though its movements seemed those of an infant, the twitching of something that had not yet mastered its own limbs. The flames were gone but the shape itself still glowed, so that the Singers of Akhenabi's order seemed to be swaddling a molten stone.

After a time they finished their work and stepped back from the litter. Though the figure that swayed there was wrapped head to foot in bandages, ruby light leaked between the wrappings each time it moved. Akhenabi stepped up and draped a ceremonial Singer's robe across the figure's shoulders, then tugged the hood forward to hide the faceless head, so that nearly all the glow was hidden. Those nobles who had not lost their wits and fallen senseless to the ground watched, listless and stupefied, but their expressions seemed almost ashamed.

The queen's guards now lifted the litter and carried it and its shrouded passenger toward the arched doorway. The rest of the white-helmeted Teeth stepped forward from behind the throne and began to drive the confused and largely unspeaking elite of Nakkiga back across the cavern toward the stairs. It was not entirely clear what had transpired here in the Chamber of the Well, but Viyeki sensed that all of them had been made part of some grave bargain whose end remained unknown.

What truly happened? he wondered. *Do we face such a terrible threat that a horror such as this, the murder of an innocent, was our only choice? Then why have we not begun to prepare against another siege?*

Full of such dubious, almost certainly treasonous thoughts, he did not notice Jijibo the Dreamer approaching until the queen's odd descendant reached out and took his arm. Exhausted and anxious, Viyeki recoiled.

"Congratulations!" said Jijibo, grinning. "*Hea-hai*, but just look at him! He's been thinking too much and now it's made him ill!"

It took the bewildered Viyeki a moment to realize Jijibo was talking in his bizarre way about Viyeki himself. "What do you mean, congratulations?" he asked.

"He really doesn't know," said Jijibo, wriggling with pleasure. "Your family has been noticed, Magister Viyeki! Yes, your family has been noticed in some very high places!"

Viyeki had no idea what the queen's strange relative meant, but the words still chilled him. "I'm afraid I don't understand."

"No, you don't, do you? Not yet. But then again, it is not always good to be noticed, is it? After all, look at *that* one!" Jijibo pointed to something behind Viyeki, then turned and trotted away up the stairs, laughing and talking to himself.

Confused, Viyeki looked back and saw Marshal Muyare being led out of the Chamber of the Well by his officers, some consoling him over his loss, others congratulating him on the singular honor he had been given. The high marshal did not look at any of them, but stared ahead helplessly, as lost and baffled as if he had been struck by lightning.

11

The Third Duke

People had dressed warmly, and the great chapel of St. Helvard's Cathedral smelled of furs and grease and torch-smoke. Miriamele had thought she was impervious to the reek of many people pressed together, but she was feeling dizzy.

Frode, the Escritor of Elvritshalla, was ancient and not particularly swift of foot. As he ascended to the pulpit the queen found herself wanting to help push him up the stairs, but reminded herself that patience with others, especially the old and infirm, was one of the virtues the Aedon had most emphatically preached.

When he reached his spot, the escritor took a pair of lenses in a frame from his gold vestments and perched them on the bridge of his long, thin nose.

"Morgenes used to have something just like that," Simon whispered to her. "It's called a 'spectacle'."

Frode looked out over the gathering, which, in addition to the visitors from the south, comprised several hundred of Rimmersgard's most important people, and cleared his throat. To Miriamele, it felt like the trumpet of an invading army. She had never liked funerals, and she liked them even less at her age, when they were no longer rare occurrences.

"Long ago," the escritor began, his voice reedy but surprisingly strong, "these lands were a wilderness, a place where darkness of all kinds ruled. Before we came to Rimmersgard, our people lived across the ocean in Ijsgard, a green land in the west, and although they prospered there, they did not thank God for their fortune but worshipped instead the pagan demons of their fathers. Because of their heedlessness, the Lord sent a great catastrophe. The greatest mountain of that land burst into flames and fell down upon their chiefest cities, and all the skies went dark. Then Elvrit Far-Seeing led his people in their many ships through that darkness and across the ocean to this land, and thus were his people saved. And he built in these lands a great kingdom for himself, and his children ruled after him. The mightiest of those was Fingil, and during his life he ruled from the Himilfells south to the Gleniwent, and was called 'Fingil the Great'."

Fingil the Great, Miriamele thought. *Or as the people called him who had lived here before the Northmen came, Fingil the Bloody-Handed. What does any of this nonsense have to do with dear Isgrimnur?* She looked sadly at their old friend's coffin, draped in the banners of his house and of Elvritshalla, with the ducal crown perched atop them all.

"But Elvrit's people brought their old gods into this new land," the escritor went on, "and still did not heed the words of our Lord, the true God. So the Lord sent unto them a punishment, the great dragon who came into the Hayholt and destroyed King Ikferdig, Fingil's successor, driving our people back into the northernmost lands, home of Norns and giants and other grim enemies.

"And although Aedonite priests like our St. Helvard tried to save our people from the Lord's wrath by leading them to the true faith, it was King John of Erkynland, the mighty Prester John, who slew the great dragon and finally brought the Lord God to his proper seat in Rimmersgard.

"Later John fought the last king of Rimmersgard, Jormgrun Redhand, who carried the relics and token of the old gods into battle, and at Naarved Prester John defeated him.

"And then John in his wisdom chose that good man Isbeorn from all the other nobles to rule the people of this new-conquered land—but only if Isbeorn would cast away his false gods and accept the true God, who sent his son Usires to die that Man might live forever.

"Duke Isbeorn *did* embrace the true God—praise the Highest—and afterward ruled long and well. His son Isgrimnur ruled even longer than his father had, granted a long life by the God he served so faithfully, and today it is that life we celebrate.

"Our beloved Duke Isgrimnur fought the Lord's battles up and down the length of Osten Ard. He battled the barbarians of the Thrithings and the terrible Storm King at the very gates of the Hayholt, John's capital, helping to save it and the Aedonite people—perhaps *all* people—from destruction. And then Isgrimnur pursued the Norns all the way to their foul seat in the Nornfells, driving them into hiding with so much loss that they have not troubled mankind again.

"Now our beloved duke is with the Lord once more. Now he sits at the right hand of a master even greater than King John Presbyter. But he has not left us unguarded. His son Grimbrand will take up the Sea Rover's Crown and rule over all the lands of Rimmersgard under John's High Ward in the name of John's heirs, King Seoman and Queen Miriamele. Two dukes Rimmersgard has been given under God's leadership, and now a third to come, another godly man, and peace has prevailed."

Here the escritor paused to remove his lenses and polish them on his stole. Miriamele felt a tickle of hope that the long afternoon might be coming to an end, at least the part that took place in the smoky, drafty cathedral. As far as she was concerned, it could not end too soon: the days since the duke's passing had been filled with every kind of obligation. She had met so many northern nobles she could no longer remember what Grimbrand had told her about a single one of them.

"But let us remember that God's favor is only granted to the righteous," Escritor Frode resumed in a ringing voice. "As Grimbrand follows his father and grandfather as the third Duke of Elvritshalla, let us remember that we must all follow him in the ways of the Lord. For only by God's hand can our people survive and prosper."

To the queen's relief, he then led the congregation in the final prayers of the *Mansa sea Cuelossan*. She reached out for Simon, wanting to feel her husband's warm, real presence. He jumped a little, perhaps startled to be reminded of what was going on around him, but after a moment folded his large hand around hers.

"It's bloody strange, if you ask me," Simon said as they followed the duke's effigy out to the dock.

"In the old days the Rimmersmen used to burn all their dead," she explained.

"Yes, and in the old days the Rimmersmen used to kill Erkynlanders as well. Not to mention Sithi and everyone else."

"Ssshhh! Do you want Grimbrand to hear you?" The duke's heir walked only a few yards behind them with his wife and children. Behind them came Isgrimnur's daughters, Signi and Ismay, and their husbands, Valfrid and Tonngerd of Skoggey. Signi was a grandmother herself now, Miri realized. She was overwhelmed once more by the realization of how the years had spun on so swiftly since they had last visited, since Signi had been a pink-cheeked bride and Grimbrand a youth with his first beard. But it had been a long time since anyone had thought him a youth; he had waited long, patient years to take his father's place. Grimbrand was a good man, and she felt sure Rimmersgard was in trustworthy hands, but it still felt strange beyond understanding to be following the great straw funeral effigy of Elvrit's ship *Sotfengsel*, and to know that their friend Isgrimnur was truly gone.

"How did it come to be that we are the old ones now, Simon?"

"Same way it always does." The sun was coming out now after a gray morning full of snow flurries—snow that had now all turned to puddles of water. Her husband squinted. "People tell you what to do. You do your best, but you don't always succeed. Then one day, you realize that you're the one doing the telling."

"Yes, but nobody is listening. Look at Grimbrand's son, Isvarr. See how respectful he is? But where is *our* grandson? I have not seen him since the cathedral, slouching in the back. Morgan should be with us. At the very least, his disappearance is an insult to Isgrimnur's memory."

Simon set his teeth. "I don't want to talk about Morgan. If he's crept off somewhere with his so-called friends again, I'll deal with him later. As it is, I'm so angry I'm half-tempted to leave him out on the Frostmarch to find his own way home."

Miriamele was frustrated with her grandson too, but it was slowly turning to a kind of desperation. No matter what they said or did, the boy seemed to go out of his way to disappoint them. "This is what I meant, husband. How did we become the old people, always furious with the young? It was not like we were so well-behaved when we were of such an age. You were beaten more often than a lazy plowhorse for not doing what you were told."

Simon made a face. "Shem would never have done to a plowhorse what Rachel used to do to me. With a broomstick! On the backs of my legs!"

"Ssshhhh!" said Miriamele, surprised into laughter despite the solemn occasion. "Not so loud. I daresay you had it coming."

"Says the girl who ran away from the Hayholt against her father's wishes, then from Naglimund against her uncle's, and then from our camp against *everybody's* wishes—even mine."

"You didn't try to stop me, you liar. You invited yourself along."

"I wanted to protect you. Even then . . ." His face suddenly changed, the lines of his brow deepening. "Even then I loved you more than anything, Miri."

She was touched but also saddened. "I know. And we have made a good life, haven't we? When it is our turn to be trundled off to Swertclif, we won't have any regrets, will we?"

He frowned. "How could we not have regrets? Is there nothing left you want to do?"

"I don't know, my love. Sometimes I wonder whether the ideas I had when I was young weren't just foolishness. The things that seemed so clear then . . . well, they aren't nearly so clear now."

Simon looked up to see the effigy ship being lowered to the water. "We're here. I still think it's damnably strange to make a puppet out of straw and burn it."

"Don't curse. Everybody has their customs."

"But the Rimmersfolk hate the sea."

"Because it has swallowed their home," she said. "And no matter what it has done, you can't defeat an ocean." They stopped and waited for the rest of the procession to come to a halt.

When the boat was floating at the edge of the wide Gratuvask and the straw figure that represented Isgrimnur's body had been laden with funeral gifts, a black-robed priest walked up the bank to offer the torch to Simon and Miriamele. As agreed, they declined, directing him to pass it to Grimbrand instead. The duke's son, his wide frame and greyshot black beard making him look eerily like the man they were all mourning, walked carefully down the muddy bank to the edge of the water, and with a prayer no one else could hear, tossed the torch into the boat. The priests then pushed the flimsy craft out into the water.

"*His ship, to the sea!*" cried Escritor Frode. "*His soul, to the sky!*"

The straw boat caught quickly, and the effigy of the duke soon vanished in flames. As the burning boat drifted out into the current, for a moment it seemed that a piece of the setting sun had fallen into the great river.

My father, my uncle Josua, Camaris, Isgrimnur—nearly all our elders are gone, Miriamele thought. *They have left us a world, but have they left us enough wisdom to protect it?*

A wind swept down from the mountains and sent a scatter of sparks from the burning straw glittering across the river's back, to fall at last hissing into the water.

"Ah, ah, you forgot to toast St. Gutfrida." Sir Astrian was laughing so hard he could hardly speak. "Fill another one for the prince!" A few of the Northmen in the alehouse were laughing and catcalling too, but others looked a little less than pleased to have the day of the duke's funeral turned into a drinking and toasting contest. Morgan was annoyed in turn by their disapproval. Hadn't they already toasted the late duke with great thoroughness? Weren't the Rimmersmen supposed to be such great folk for drink? How could anyone have a funeral and not bend an elbow?

Astrian took a new ale bowl and scooped up a healthy helping, sloshing some on the table as he did so. Olveris looked at the puddle, his long face sad. "You are wasting perfectly good drink."

"No, I am sharing it with the gods of the north." Astrian folded Morgan's hands around the wooden bowl. "Do it properly this time, Highness."

"But they are Aedonites here," said Morgan, staring at the liquid sloshing back and forth in his unsteady hands. "Aren't they? Yes, they are. The old gods are . . . old."

"Not as old as Porto!" crowed Astrian.

At the sound of his name, the ancient soldier groaned and lifted his head from the pillow of his arm. He peered, slit-eyed, at the prince. "Highness, what are you doing here? We thought you were with your family."

"Oh, be quiet, Porto, you old broomstick," said Astrian. "He's been here for an hour."

"A man can only be sad so long," Morgan declared. In truth, it had been that bore of an Elvritshalla courtier who had driven him away from the funeral feast, Thane Somebody-Or-Other. The old fool had visited the Hayholt once years ago, and, braced with this experience, had spent far too long forcing his patchy memories of Prince John Josua on John Josua's son. In an attempt to silence him, Morgan had even said, "I scarcely remember my father,"—a terrible lie, but it had only sent the courtier into further windy wheezing about the wisdom and nobility of the late and lamented John Josua, and the tragedy of his early death, to the point where Morgan had felt his only choice was either to knock the man's head off or escape to a suitably quiet place and try to forget the yammering fool completely.

"Come now, my prince," Astrian urged. "Leave the old beanpole Porto to his rest and his dreams of faded glory. Drink up!"

"Right, then." Morgan lifted the bowl high. "A toast to St. Gutfrida, may she watch over all tradesmen."

"*Travelers,* not tradesmen," Olveris said. "You will have to drink another if you're not careful."

"There are surely worse fates," said Astrian.

"So. A toast to St. Gutfrida, may she watch over all travelers." Morgan brought the bowl to his lips and downed the whole thing, although there was a bit of choking and spluttering at the end that Astrian tried to convince him would necessitate yet another bowl. "No, by God," the prince said. "Now it's your turn. I am going to piss."

"Not here," said Sir Porto. "Begging your pardon, Highness, but not here, if you please."

"What, do you imagine I am some Thrithings barbarian?" Morgan rose, not without a bit of work, and staggered toward the door of the ale hall. It was strange how quiet this and the other taverns were today, the drinkers silent and almost sullen. It was not as if the duke's death had been a surprise, not at Is-grimnur's advanced age.

As he passed the innkeeper's daughter, a buxom young woman who looked as if she knew a few interesting things, Morgan spun to watch her walk. This maneuver did not turn out well, and he had to grab at a table for support, vexing a group of men sitting there. "My very deepest apologies," Morgan told them, and bowed, which did not turn out much better than the spin. By the time he had reached the door he had caromed off more tables, as though someone was using a prince to play ninepins.

Damned Frostmarch baron, he thought, more than a bit dizzy now. *Tell me about my own father, why don't you? Oh yes, can't shut him up. But was he there? Did he hear my father moaning and weeping in his last fever? See the look of fear on his face . . . ?* Morgan shook his head, trying to rid himself of the evil memories that had settled on him like snow sifting down from the gray sky, but memories did not melt as swiftly as snowflakes.

It was a great relief to empty his bladder against the outside wall of the alehouse, but Morgan could not escape the feeling he was being watched. He turned and found a hairy white monster staring up at him, fangs gleaming, red tongue lolling.

He did not even realize that his knees had buckled and that he was now sitting on the slushy ground until the little man standing beside the wolf extended a hand to him. "Vaqana is not a danger," he said. "She did not mean to be frightening."

Which was easy enough to say, but a little harder to believe, at least for Morgan as he stared at the wolf's powerful, grinning jaws just inches from his face. "You're that troll," he said at last. "Grandfather's friend."

The little man nodded and smiled. "Binabik, I am being called—yes, a troll. And your grandfather's friend, yes, and forever. And you are being Prince Morgan."

"Believe so. Are you sure he won't bite?"

"He?" The troll looked around. "Ah, it is Vaqana you are meaning. She. No, she will not bite." He looked up. Several locals were watching their conversation, and not all of them looked particularly friendly. "She will not bite unless I am telling her, Bite," the troll corrected himself.

Morgan ignored the offered hand and climbed slowly to his feet, just in case the wolf was not as committed to pacifism as her master. He noticed that he had not done up his clothing quite as well as he'd thought, and paused to remedy the situation, grateful he had not pissed himself completely at the unexpected sight of the white wolf. He felt quite sober now. Terror might have been the cause, but he told himself it was the cold wind. Living in such a chilly, gray place, it was a miracle these Rimmersgard folk ever chose to be sober.

Finished with the laces on his breeks, he regarded the troll and the grinning wolf. "Umm," he managed at last. "Ah. I have to go back to my friends now." He knew he should say something else, because his grandparents were bound to hear of the meeting, so he added "I give you good day," with all the drunken articulation he could muster. But the little man would not stop staring at him. The troll's eyes were brown and quite disturbingly intent.

"I was seeing you in the church earlier, when they spoke for Duke Isgrimnur," Binabik said. "You had a look of sadness, was my thought. Were you knowing that good old man well?"

Oh, God save me, Morgan thought. *He knows I'm drunk, and he's forcing me to talk to him on purpose.* "I never met the duke before the day he died," he said. "No, once, I think, when I was a boy. He was big, and he had a loud voice." Unlike the lie he had told about his father, this was true: Morgan had not accompanied his grandfather on his last trip north, and almost all his knowledge about the Duke of Elvritshalla came from his grandfather's long and doubtless exaggerated stories.

Binabik's smile was wider this time. "Loud voice, with certainty! Like a great ram bellowing at his rivals. But there was being more to Isgrimnur. Much more."

"I don't doubt it." Morgan wanted only to escape back into the lamplit dark and the company of ordinary people—and ale. Why did everyone insist on talking to him about dead people today? "Still, I should find . . ."

"My family and I have been walking about the city in this evening, once the duke's funeral was ended," said Binabik. "Your grandmother the queen had worry that we would be abused by the people here, because for long years these folk and mine were being each other's enemies, and still there are many *Croohok*—Rimmersmen—who are not liking to see trolls. But I like learning always, and seeing and doing is being the best way for that learning. Are you not thinking the same?"

"Huh? I suppose. Yes." Morgan was a hair's breadth from turning his back and going inside. "Yes, learning . . . is certainly good."

"I am glad we have agreeing," Binabik said, nodding and smiling. "Because here is coming my daughter Qina and Little Snenneq, her *nukapik*—her 'be-trothed,' you would be saying. Qina has a weariness of the city now and would return to the place where we sleep, but Snenneq still has a desire to learn more of Rimmersgard ways. It would be a kindness for you to show him something of this place."

"Show him . . . ?"

"Yes, Prince Morgan, this place where you and your friends are resting and eating would be something he would like, I think. Little Snenneq is loving to join in such pastimes, and is considered very skillful at singing, games, and contests." Binabik must have seen the expression of horror on Morgan's face, because he quickly added, "You are not to be fearing. Snenneq has coins of his own."

"But . . ."

"Ah, and here they are coming to us now." Binabik turned and waved to a pair of figures approaching through the narrow, night-dark street. Both were dressed in thick hide jackets and both seemed small to Morgan, although one was much smaller than the other—the troll's daughter, he guessed: he could tell by the curve of her hips and an indefinable something in her round face that the smaller one was female.

Morgan had seen dwarfs in Erchester and occasionally the Hayholt, mostly with troops of traveling players, but trolls seemed to be different. They were stocky and short-legged, but otherwise their proportions were more like that of other folk. The troll's daughter had a pretty face with almond eyes and smooth tan skin, and she was even shapely, as far as could be told under such heavy garments, but she stood no higher than Morgan's own little sister Lillia. By contrast, the top of the young male troll's thatch of black hair reached almost to Morgan's breastbone.

"Ah, Qina my daughter, you are here!" said Binabik. "Come and greet Prince Morgan. And this fellow is being her friend Little Snenneq."

"It does pleasure to meet you, Highness Morgan." Qina crossed her arms before her chest in a gesture Morgan didn't understand. Was she bowing, or did it mean something else? He was still dizzily full of juniper-scented ale and seemed to have missed his chance to flee, so he gave her a sickly smile and nodded and mumbled the sort of thing he did when he was talking to people he didn't know but his grandparents were watching.

Little Snenneq did not look particularly awed to be meeting a prince of the High Royal Household, but crossed his arms the same way Qina had, bobbed his head like a quail, and announced, "Ah, of course. This is a momentous meeting."

Morgan had no idea what that meant either. As Binabik spoke rapidly in the troll tongue to the new arrivals, the prince cast his eyes desperately toward the alehouse door, hoping one of his friends might come out to look for him. He felt a small, cool pressure on his hand and looked down to see that Qina had removed her glove and was squeezing the tips of his fingers. "Hmmmmm . . . ?" he said, rather helplessly.

"I taught to her the handclasp of friendship that you *utku*— 'lowlanders' as we say in Yiqanuc—are using," Binabik explained.

"Friendship and thank you," she said, still holding the end of his hand in her small, solid grip. "For showing to Little Snenneq more of this place. Because of my wearying now, it is kindness and you are showing to be a true primp."

"Prince," said Binabik gently.

"*Prince*," said Qina, blushing a little and finally letting go of his hand. "You are a true prince."

Escape impossible and all other resistance now thoroughly dismantled, Morgan could only wait as the young troll woman rubbed cheeks with her betrothed, then followed her father back down the long street in the direction of Elvritshalla Castle, the massive white wolf pacing beside them. Loiterers who might otherwise have been calling abuse at the trolls took one look at Vaqana and slipped away.

Morgan was not entirely certain what had just happened, but he was already wishing it hadn't.

"And so we will entertain ourselves like true Rimmersgarders now, eh?" announced his new companion, his grin so wide it seemed to squeeze his eyes shut. "The prince and Little Snenneq! Bring out ale and stinking fish!" Then, as they made their way back inside, the troll suddenly said, "My someday father-in-law is a very good man."

The prince did not reply. Most of the alehouse denizens had looked up when they pushed open the squeaking door, and many of them looked displeased by his new companion.

"Because I told him it was needed for you and I to meet," the troll went on. "I am going to help you, you see."

"Help me?" By the love of all the saints, Morgan wondered, how far back into this poxy place were his friends sitting? Surely he hadn't traveled such a distance on the way out. "How are you going to help me?"

"As I told my father-in-law to-be, the Singing Man Binabik, I will help you to find your destiny, just as he was doing for your illustrious grandsire, the king Seoman."

The prince made a firm decision to ignore everything this little moon-mad creature said from that point onward. Also, his grandfather's tiny friend Binnywick had deliberately picked Morgan out for this suffering, and he would neither forget nor forgive.

Olveris was right—little people can't be trusted.

"And who is your new companion?" asked Porto when Morgan finally discovered the table in the opposite dark corner from the one in which he'd been searching. The old knight squinted. "He has not the look of the Rimmersgarders I've seen. One of their country cousins from up north?"

"This is . . ." Morgan couldn't precisely remember. "Snow-Neck. Or is it No-Neck . . .?"

"Snenneq," the troll said. "Little Snenneq, they are calling me, because it was also the name of my father and grandfather."

Astrian was plainly delighted to meet someone shorter than he was. "No-Neck it is! And what will you have to drink, Sir No-Neck? Some milk, perhaps? With a bit of bread dipped in it to suck upon?"

Snenneq smiled a polite, yellow-toothed smile. "Not a child. I am Qanuc."

"No-Neck the Ka-Neck!" Astrian crowed. "You must join our merry band!"

Even Olveris grinned at that. But not everyone in the dim alehouse was as happy. Morgan could hear more than a few angry words from the surrounding tables about the troll's presence.

"They think they can go anywhere," someone complained.

Why am I lumbered with this little goblin? Morgan wondered. *Probably get me beaten half to death by these bearded ice-bears.* He couldn't completely remember what other wrongs had been done to him today, but he felt certain that this was only the most recent of many. "Give him something to drink, Porto, and for God's sake be quick."

The old knight poured a bowl for the new arrival, but stared at Little Snenneq so intently that he spilled more than he poured. Sir Olveris watched mournfully as it puddled on the splintered table. "I've seen your kind," Porto said at last as he pushed the ale toward Snenneq. "Trolls. Your folk met us on the road back from Nakkiga."

It was obvious many people in the ale-house were listening, because a fresh round of whispers began at this word, although not so obviously hostile this time.

Snenneq nodded. "True. Our Herder and Huntress had sent them to help the fighting against the Hikeda'ya, but they came after the siege was ending."

"Hikadikadik. Says No-Neck from Ee-Ka-Neck," said Astrian, a bit too loudly. He was unusually drunk. "And why would they send such as you to fight the Norns?"

Little Snenneq looked at him and smiled again, although it vanished more quickly this time.

"Never doubt them," said Porto, the fumes of reminiscence beginning to rise from him. "The little troll-men fought fiercely in Erkynland. I saw them there, in battle."

Olveris rolled his eyes, but Astrian sat forward. "Truly?" he asked. "Did they run among the White Foxes, kicking their shins? Or perhaps hid in the Norns' saddlebags and then sprang out to attack?"

"I made that joke about *you*, Astrian," Morgan complained. "About kicking the shins of your enemies. That's mine."

"Ah, but about me it is merely comic exaggeration," the knight said. "My question to this fellow is an honest one."

"There were times that the winds blew so hard and the snows fell so thickly on the Hayholt from the Storm King's magic that we could see nothing," Porto said, ignoring Astrian and warming to his tale. "But those little fellows—well, they could find their way through anything . . ."

"Then why can't they find their way back to the place they came from?" brayed a very large, bearded Rimmersman at a nearby table. His friends laughed loudly, toasting him with their slopping bowls. "We have no need of them here."

Little Snenneq smiled again, but there was something quite different in it this time, a certain hardness to his eyes that Morgan recognized. Astrian got that look sometimes when he was in his cups and angry. Morgan's grandfather Simon wore it sometimes as well, usually when someone spoke about the strong taking cruel advantage of the weak.

Morgan was suddenly wondering whether it might be time for their little party to move on.

The big, bearded man was sitting down. Little Snenneq waited patiently at the man's elbow until he was noticed.

"What do you want?" the red-faced man demanded. He put down his bowl, his fingers already curling into fists.

"I am hoping that you now will play a game," said Snenneq mildly. "With me."

The man goggled at this small, black-haired interloper. "Game? What does that mean?"

"Are you wrestling with just arms and hands here?" asked the troll. "So I think."

Morgan did not remember everything his grandfather had told him about the troll-folk, but he thought he would remember if they had been gifted with superhuman strength, or if they could grow back an arm once it was ripped off, as a lizard could grew a new tail. "Sno . . . I mean, Snenneq," he called. "Why don't you come back to the table—?"

"Arm wrestling?" The big Rimmersman laughed loudly and mimed with his bent arm. "Like this? There's not a man here who could best me, including any of that puny lot of yours." His gaze slid from Astrian to Porto and lingered on Sir Olveris, who was not quite as tall as old Sir Porto but far more well-muscled, then he spat on the straw covering the floor. "I am Lomskur the Smith. I broke a bullock's neck with my hands when I was but a boy. I won't waste my time on any of your friends." He scowled at Morgan, who edged back a bit farther on the bench. "I don't want the duke's men to put me in chains for troubling that cream-faced boy. So go back to your foul mountain, ice-goblin, before I throw you there."

Several of the others laughed and cheered, but one warned, " 'Ware, Lomskur! That's the High King's heir."

The big man snorted. "I'm not troubling His Very Highness, am I? It's his lapdog that's troubling me."

"Qanuc are not dogs for anyone." Little Snenneq wasn't smiling any more. "Is this meaning that Lomskur is feared to hand-wrestle with me?"

"You?" The bearded man was genuinely astonished, but it seemed to make him even angrier. "Look at you! I could use you to pick my teeth."

"No. Just hand-wrestle." The troll vaulted onto the bench beside Lomskur with surprising nimbleness and extended his arm. "Here. Now."

Lomskur's friends and acquaintances in the alehouse were all shouting, most in favor of crushing the troll on the spot, but the bearded man stared at Little Snenneq's outstretched hand. "For true?" He frowned. "No tricks? I don't want to get a troll knife in my gorge when I only came in here to pass the time."

"No tricks. On the honor of the prince." Snenneq kept his arm out.

Morgan started to rise but Astrian reached out and grabbed his tunic, holding him back. "Let it be, Highness," he said softly. "Do not spoil the joke—whatever it may turn out to be."

Lomskur turned and straddled the bench to face the troll. It took a while—each one of the bearded man's legs looked as wide as a normal man's waist. Finished positioning himself, he thumped his elbow down on the table, making the crockery jump. The troll did not sit down, but knelt on the bench opposite Lomskur so that he could rest his elbow and still reach the other's hand. The difference in their sizes was so great that the Rimmersman had to grasp the small man's hand at an angle, with his arm low to the table; the troll's hand almost disappeared inside the Rimmersman's grasp.

The bearded man suddenly began laughing. "You are no coward, I see. If you live, little snow-beetle, I will buy you a pitcher all for yourself, to wash away the pain."

Snenneq nodded, still not smiling. "And the same I will be doing for you. If you live."

Everybody in the place seemed to be watching now. Even the ostler had come out from the back room, and stood, worriedly wiping his hands over and over on a dirty cloth.

"Start!" yelled one of Lomskur's cronies.

It should have been over in an instant, and nearly was. With a scowl on his red face, Lomskur bent Little Snenneq's arm until the back of the troll's hand quivered just a finger's breadth above the table. Most of the Rimmersmen in the alehouse were so certain of the outcome that they dared not turn away to take a drink, certain they would miss the ending, and instead fumbled blindly for their bowls. But Snenneq did not collapse. He made what looked to Morgan like a few small adjustments of his knees and back and shoulders, and although Lomskur leaned far to his left to keep the pressure on, somehow the very small man withstood it. Snenneq shifted again and pushed his elbow closer to Lomskur's, and for some reason the tiny change of angle brought an expression of discomfort and surprise to the big man's face.

Moments became longer moments. The faces of Lomskur and Little Snenneq settled into fixed masks of effort. Every time it seemed the much bigger man must finally overcome the resistance of the smaller, the troll moved again—never more than a little, but always enough to keep the giant on the other side from being able to force his hand down against the table.

The spectators were beginning to worry now, not so much at the incredible spectacle of a troll holding off a man almost three times his size, but over the notion that a trick must be involved. Some shouted to look under the table, that the little man was bracing himself in some way, or being otherwise helped to cheat, but of course Morgan and the rest hadn't moved from their own table, and Snenneq's legs were still curved beneath him on the bench. The whole thing seemed a sort of magic, and more than a few of the drinkers looked around with superstitious alarm, as though the sequel might be a Norn raiding party or a dragon or some other legendary menace crashing through the door.

At last, and to the complete astonishment of everyone, Morgan and his friends most definitely included, Lomskur began to tire. Sweat coursed down his face and dripped from his beard, and his face turned the color of a baked Aedonmansa ham. Little Snenneq began to lean back, slowly pulling Lomskur's hand toward him, increasing the angle of their mutual grasp until the big man's entire arm was stretched only inches above the tabletop.

Then, with almost no warning, the troll twisted his wrist sharply to one side and Lomskur let out a bellow of pain; a split-instant later the back of the Rimmersman's hand was pressed against the tabletop.

For a moment the room went silent. Lomskur was clutching his wrist, in too much pain to say anything; Morgan and his fellows were too startled even to cheer.

"By all that's holy," said Astrian wonderingly, "why did I neglect to wager on this?" As Lomskur squeezed and chafed his aching wrist, Little Snenneq dropped down from the bench and walked to an ale cask that stood beside the ostler. A couple of large stone tankards had just been filled for someone else and then left on the cask until their foamy exuberance subsided. The troll pulled a coin out of his hide jacket and dropped it on the barrel top, then took a tankard in each hand and walked back to Lomskur's table. He held one out to the big man, who looked up at him with reddened eyes and an expression of utter bewilderment.

"I was promising to buy for you an ale," said Little Snenneq.

Lomskur goggled at him for a moment, then his already red face became even more enflamed, as if he were a baby about to howl, and he lashed out, knocking both the ale tankards out of Snenneq's hands. "Cheat!" he roared. "Little devil! I don't know what trick you played, but . . ."

Without finishing his sentence, he swung a huge fist at Snenneq's face. The troll dropped beneath the blow so neatly that for a moment Morgan thought the little man's head had been knocked cleanly from his shoulders. Lomskur swore loudly and tried to drop on him. Morgan had no doubt that if he did, no trick in the world would save the troll from being crushed to death, but Snenneq had somehow already rolled out of the way, grabbing the handles of the two overturned tankards as he went. Lomskur, on his knees, seemed to have lost the use of words completely. He snarled and swung, but Snenneq kept dodging. Lomskur grabbed a heavy bowl from a table and flung it at him, but the troll simply ducked. Now the Rimmersman clambered to his feet once more, roaring like a wounded bear, but something glinted in his hand.

" 'Ware!" Morgan shouted. "He has a knife!"

Many of the customers nearest the door decided this would be a good time to leave, but the rest of the crowd seemed unable to move or look away as the huge man swiped at the troll with a long, crude-looking blade. None of Lomskur's friends or fellow Rimmersmen made any move to stop him, although they could hardly be blamed.

At first Little Snenneq simply backed away, but he was beginning to run out of room. Lomskur, despite his lumbering, clumsy steps, was steadily backing the troll into one corner of the room. Even using the two heavy mugs as shields would not protect Snenneq when that happened, the prince knew, and for the first time he realized what kind of utter disgrace he would be in if something happened to one of his grandfather's troll friends.

The bearded man's blade lashed out and cut through the troll's jacket. Morgan thought he saw blood. "Enough!" he shouted. "Put up, man! The heir of the High Throne commands you to lay down your weapon!"

But Lomskur, if he even heard, was too far gone in rage now to care about princes. Someone ran outside and began calling for the city guard, but Morgan felt certain no soldiers would arrive to end this before someone was hurt or killed. "Astrian! Olveris!" he shouted. "Help the little fellow!"

"It is his fight," Astrian said. "He challenged the man."

"But the man has a knife!"

"Even so." Astrian had not even taken his eyes off the fight. "It is *you* we are meant to protect, my prince, not any troll who wanders down out of the mountains."

Frustrated and frightened, Morgan was about to draw his own blade and try to even the odds, but he never had the chance. The next time the big man jabbed the knife at him, Little Snenneq did not duck or dodge again, but instead brought the two mugs together and hammered Lomskur's hand from either side. The big man dropped the blade, cursing loudly, blood suddenly welling from his knuckles. A moment later the troll flung himself down at Lomskur's feet and crashed one of the heavy stone mugs against the Rimmersman's kneecap. With a howl of agony, Lomskur collapsed. He did not try to rise again, but rolled back and forth, screeching and holding his leg.

"I was only at buying him an ale because I made a promise," said Little Snenneq with a distinct tone of irritation, then brought the other tankard around in a wide arc and slammed it against Lomskur's temple. The big man dropped on the floor like a sack of grain and lay silent.

Suddenly Rimmersmen were rising all over the room, but Morgan didn't think they looked as if they were coming to congratulate the victor. Snenneq calmly backed toward Morgan's table, a move that the prince did not approve of much, because the angry crowd was following him. Morgan wondered whether these unhappy people remembered that he, Morgan of Erkynland, was the heir to the High Throne. He hoped so.

"Enough! Stand back!" Astrian sprang up, and his sword rang as it slid from his scabbard. "Back, you northern scum. I will gut the first one of you who takes another step toward the prince." However drunk he had been earlier, the knight gripped his sword as steadily as a jeweler would hold his chisel over a large, uncut gem. The people in the alehouse stopped short and watched him, silent and sullen. Astrian nodded at them, like a teacher pleased with his clever students. "Highness," he said in a pointed tone, "I suggest we take our leave of this establishment."

"I agree with your suggestion." But as Morgan backed toward the door he noticed that Little Snenneq still stood between their table and the disgruntled patrons. "You! Troll! You'd better come with us."

"I am being owed my copper back for those two ales," the little man said, frowning at the empty tankards he still held. "And I was not even given the courtesy of drinking mine."

"Let it go." Morgan beckoned. "We're leaving. You should leave with us."

Little Snenneq shook his head in frustration, but set the tankards on the table and joined the prince and his friends. Porto and Olveris had their blades out now too. Nobody opposed them as they backed out into the narrow street and slammed the door behind them.

"Goodness," said Sir Porto. "They have not changed much since I was a young man, these Rimmersgarders."

"When you were a young man," said Astrian, sheathing his blade, "the Rimmersmen were still in the lost West."

"But how did you do that?" Morgan asked the troll. "How did you beat that big lout?"

The little man shrugged. "No tricks. It is like stick-fighting—balance, that is the story to tell. And another word that I am not knowing, but it means changing the strength of the pulling, and the direction. Feeling what the other man is doing. No tricks, no secret. With only a small effort, I can be teaching it to you. I have much to teach you, Prince Morgan. We will be famous friends."

Morgan stared at him. "You keep saying things like that. What on the wide, green earth are you talking about? We have only just met."

"I am fated to be your companion, Morgan Prince." The troll nodded vigorously. "This I feel certain to be true, and I have the blood of a Singing Man in me. That is what I will be one day, and because of it, I have knowing of things." He bobbed his head again, as if this stream of nonsense proved something.

"Dear God, no," said Astrian, amused. "If you're his companion, the prince wouldn't need *us* any more. What would Olveris and I do for entertainment? But we *will* allow you a temporary apprenticeship in our noble guild, Sir

Ogresbane, as long as you have enough of those coppers to keep us in drink. Do you approve, Olveris? Porto?"

"What?" said Sir Porto. "I beg pardon, Your Highness, but there are some men coming out of the tavern behind you. Several of them. And is that the city guard they are waving to . . . ?"

"Sadly, there are urgent matters that require our attention elsewhere," Astrian declared, and led them off into the dark streets.

They had a long walk back to Elvritshalla Castle. As he grew more sober, Morgan began to feel sickly certain his grandparents would hear about this latest fuss. Of course, by the time they did, he had no doubt it would all have somehow become his fault. *But what did I do wrong? Nothing. I tried to help Grandfather's friend, the famous troll Binny-whatsit. Is it my fault he saddled me with a tiny madman?*

The unexpected sight of the tiny madman lifting a skin bag and squirting himself a mouthful of some liquid chased Morgan's gloomy thoughts away. "What is that you're drinking?"

Little Snenneq held out the bag. "Try if you wish, Morgan Prince. I am of course preferring this to the weak ale the *croohok* drink," the troll said. "Little more than weasel-piss, that is being."

Morgan lifted the bag and squeezed a long draught into his mouth.

A short time later Olveris and Porto helped him back onto his feet, to the hooting sound of Astrian's laughter. Morgan could not speak for a while because he was still wheezing and coughing, but when he finally could, he asked—still with a certain breathlessness—"What *is* that?"

"*Kangkang*," said Little Snenneq. "It has real goodness, eh? And when the *burruk* is coming, the . . . bilch? Belch?" He laughed. "Oh! but it is burning like fire, like the breath of a dragon. A fine drink for a man's life, it is." The troll reached up and patted Morgan on the elbow. "Did you know that my grandfather was fighting beside yours at Sesuad'ra, as Sithi call it—the famous Battle of the Frozen Lake? My grandfather was killed there. But I am not blaming you for that, Morgan Prince." The troll patted him again, reassuring him. "Despite that sadness, we can be to each other friends. And now you are to be spending more time with me, you will be learning oh so many useful things."

"Just remember always to bring your purse," said Sir Astrian, reaching out to try some *kangkang* for himself. "Thirst is an expensive mistress."

12

The Bloody Sand

The morning sky seemed so bright between the branches, and the world so full of new sights and smells and sounds, that Nezeru found it hard to keep her attention on what was before her. The mountainside forest was shrill with birdsong. The colors, more shades of green than she had imagined existed in the world, seemed to crash against her eyes like the sea flinging itself onto the rocks of the shore.

She had seen so much in such a short time since leaving Nakkiga, first the plains and headlands that had seemed to throb with life, then the ship and the impossibly wide ocean, and now on this island mountainside the mad cacophony of colors, a thousand different trees and vines crawling over each other to stretch toward the sun. It was almost hard for her to believe that it was all happening to her, a halfbreed, perhaps the youngest Talon ever gifted with the Queen's trust.

Yes, see me now, Father! she exulted. *At the order of the queen herself, we seek the bones of Hakatri, brother of the Storm King!* It was like a story—a new one, a tale whose ending she had not heard time and again.

"You make too much noise," Makho the chieftain growled. "I hear your every footfall."

The Queen's Talons, their guides from the village, and their translator, the ship's captain, had begun climbing again by dawn's first light, when the mortals could see. Makho was clearly disgusted at being delayed by mortal frailties, but the islanders had warned that the shrine, as the ship's captain called it, was guarded against strangers and there was no way to tell them of the Hikeda'ya's arrival beforehand.

As the sun rose higher and Nezeru grew more used to the rioting greenery, the slopes on either side of the mountain trail continued to produce more astonishing colors; crimson, cup-shaped flowers like falling blood drops, great swaying banks of yellow mountain olive, and lavender-blooming heathers that clung to the slopes like a fur mantle, delighting Nezeru's eye. The Singer Saomeji insisted on naming them all, breaking in on her pleasure to identify marsh marigold in wet ditches, moss campion and saxifrage, as if naming something added to its pleasure, or knowing was somehow better than simply *seeing*.

The sun was still well short of noon when they reached the summit and what the mortal captain called "the place of the bones," a large, low, circular stone house with a sod roof. Many more of the small, brown people came out of the building to greet them, all of them males with shaved heads and wearing similar clothing, yellow and blue robes belted at the waist by colorful scarves. To Nezeru, some seemed no more than children, and it was these who watched the approach of the Hikeda'ya and their escort with the greatest curiosity. Then, as Makho and the rest approached the low front door of the building, a final small group came out, two shaven-headed men helping a third who was the strangest, oldest mortal she had ever seen, his skin so full of wrinkles he might have been made of jerked meat.

The Rimmersman captain stepped forward and made a long speech in the villagers' tongue that had the old man nodding and smiling. When the captain finished, the wrinkled old man replied at some length.

"The head priest welcomes you," the captain explained. "He says he is very pleased that the People of the Bones have come to this place to pay their respects, and he wishes to let you know that he and his priestly ancestors have honored and cared for them for more years than the meadow has grass blades, and will do so until the sun falls from the sky."

Nezeru understood now that this place was some kind of religious shrine, and that all these men and boys were either priests or in training to become priests, like order acolytes back home. But how had mere mortals become the stewards of Hakatri's remains?

Makho was not one for decorated speech. "Tell him we will see the bones now."

His abruptness caused more than a little consternation among the priests, but at last they led their Hikeda'ya visitors inside the building. A few hides covered with swirls of paint hung on the walls, but otherwise the large main room with pounded dirt floors was dark but for the firepit in the center and the smokehole in the roof. The place smelled of many things, mortal human bodies not least, but Nezeru could also detect sweet oils and the charred dust of flowers and plants, small offerings, burned over many years, whose cloying scents had infused everything.

The old chief priest said something, gesturing with his hand.

"The fire always burns," the captain translated. "That way the sacred bones are always in the light."

The collection of brown bones was piled in a shallow pit just beyond the fire—a skeleton, neatly stacked, with the skull placed on top. The bones were oddly pitted, filled with holes as though someone had attempted to make them into musical instruments, then put them aside again, unfinished.

The old priest spoke. "He says, '*Behold,*'" the captain translated. "'*These are the bones of the Burning Man.*'" His fellow priests made a kind of moaning sound, but precise and measured, as though part of a long-practiced ritual.

"See the scars made by the dragon's blood," said Saomeji. He spoke quietly, but there was exultation in his voice. Nezeru, too, was awed to see the actual remains of Hakatri, the Storm King's brother—Hakatri the Dragon-Burned, revered by both Sithi and Norns. Together Hakatri and his younger brother, who would one day be known the world over as Ineluki the Storm King, had slain the black worm Hidohebhi, but the curse of Hakatri's unhealing wounds had driven him out of the lands of his people and neither Zida'ya nor Hikeda'ya had ever seen him alive again. Could these bones truly be his? Nezeru looked to Makho, but saw no doubts in the chieftain's expression.

"These are what we came for," was all he said. "Mortal, tell the priest that our great queen needs them, so we will take them now."

The captain stared at him, his bearded face so pale he almost looked like one of Nezeru's band. "But I c-cannot say that," he stammered. "They will kill us!"

Makho looked at him with contempt. "It is possible they will try. No matter. Tell them."

"Please do not make me say these words, immortal ones," the captain begged.

"Tell them!"

The priests had been watching in apprehension, understanding something was wrong, but when the captain translated Makho's words they cried out in agony. The old priest pulled free from his two helpers and limped forward until he stood between Makho and the bones. He raised trembling arms. His high-pitched voice was full of agitation and anger. But when the captain started to translate, Makho waved his hand for silence.

"I do not need to know his objections. They are unimportant. The Queen of All has sent us for the bones of her kinsman. Tell the old man that his people have cared for them well and they have the queen's gratitude. That should be enough for them."

But the captain had barely begun speaking when the old priest let out a cry of anguish, then turned and threw himself across the bones where they lay on their bed of sand, shielding them with his scrawny body. Makho stared at him, then looked at the other priests and acolytes now shoving in through the door, their faces dark with anger.

Makho had his sword in his hand so quickly that Nezeru did not see him draw it; a moment later it swept out and the ancient priest's head rolled to one side. Before the severed neck had pumped twice, Makho used his foot to shove the body away from the bones so that the blood only seeped onto the stones and into the crevices between them. The old priest's comrades cried out in horror.

"Singer, gather noble Hakatri's remains," Makho ordered. "We return to the ship."

Even as Saomeji hurried to comply, the nearest of the dead priest's helpers leaped at Makho with a shout of fury, only to be sliced through to the backbone by an offhand flick of Cold Root, the chieftain's witchwood blade. More priests began streaming into the temple-house, screaming as if they had lost their minds, grabbing at the Norns with the clear purpose of tearing them to pieces. Kemme immediately killed two with one thrust of his spear, spitting them like meat on a skewer.

"Some of those outside are running for help," Ibi-Khai called from the doorway.

Nezeru felt something tighten around her neck and yank her backward. One of the shaven-headed priests, small but wiry and strong, had pulled Nezeru's own bow across her shoulder and over her head and was now trying to strangle her with the string. She got one hand between the bowstring and her neck at the last moment, but the mortal had his knee in her back and was pulling as hard as he could. She was separated from the rest of her comrades by the swirl of attackers, and could not get leverage on the string to loosen it, so she groped for her knife with her free hand and cut the string. As the bow fell uselessly to the floor, Nezeru spun and slashed through the priets's sacklike garment, opening his belly. He sagged, a look of surprise and disappointment in his suddenly mild eyes.

Three more dead priests now lay at Makho's feet, but he seemed almost oblivious to the grief-maddened mob. "Nezeru, Kemme, go after those who fled," he directed them. "Do not let them reach the village or they will raise the alarm and the rest will swarm us like ants. Saomeji, you must keep the bones safe as we go. We may have to fight our way down to the water."

"*Rayu ata na'ara,*" Nezeru replied, the ancient phrase that signified "I hear the Queen in your voice." She had to leap over one of Kemme's fallen victims, who writhed in the doorway, trying to lift himself up with both of his arms gone and the severed ends gushing blood like a mountain cataract.

Outside, Kemme had drawn his bow; as Nezeru emerged from the building she saw him let the first arrow fly. One of the fleeing mortal priests stumbled, fell, and did not get up. A scant moment later Kemme loosed a second shaft and another escaping priest stumbled, then dropped.

Only a few of the fleeing priests were still visible on the side of the hilltop Kemme had already chosen as his field of fire, so she left them to him and headed after the others. She no longer had a bow of her own, just her sword and knife, but that only meant she would have to outrun them, something that should not be difficult for one of the queen's death-sung Sacrifices. Following them would be even easier: The scent of the escaping mortals hung in the air, animal clouds of terror and exertion.

She sprinted swiftly down the slope, her feet barely touching earth, and ran down the first fleeing priest within a hundred paces. He was mature and larger than Nezeru, but nowhere near as fit as a Queen's Talon. When he stopped to gasp for breath he saw her coming, grimaced in resignation, and snatched up a large deadfall branch. From the way he held it he was no stranger to a fight, and the last thing Nezeru wanted was to waste time trading blows with him, because she could smell another mortal farther down the hill. A long struggle with this one might allow time for the other to get to the village and tell his people what had happened.

"Blood of the Garden, guide my arm," she prayed quietly, balancing her dagger. Then, before she was close enough for the big priest to swing his make-shift club, she let it fly. The priest dropped the branch and sank to his knees, clawing at the knife that now stood in his throat; by the time she had taken three more steps he was on his face, barely squirming, his blood matting the grassy earth. Nezeru put her foot on his head and shoved it to one side, freeing a last, rattling gasp from his torn throat. Then she retrieved her knife and hurried down the mountainside after her other quarry.

The scent of the next mortal's terror was strong, but his sweat smelled curiously sweet. It also took a longer time than she had expected before she could finally hear him crashing through the undergrowth a few dozen yards below her. The fugitive was moving with surprising speed, which gave her a moment of worry. No mortal priest could have been trained and strengthened in all the ways Nezeru had been during her years in the Order of Sacrifice, so how could this one pass through the tangled brush and close-standing trees so easily?

Then, as she emerged into the open and could look out over the expanse of mountainside below her, she finally saw her quarry's shaved head glinting in the sunshine like a raindrop on a leaf. It was a child—one of the young acolytes. Nezeru knew little of mortals, but thought this one could not have been much past the age when boys first left their mothers to follow their fathers into the field or forest.

A moment later the boy vanished behind trees once more, bounding down the sloping hillside. Nezeru sped her pace, but could see that he was far enough ahead that if she did not reach a clear spot quickly where she could take him down, he would be in shouting distance of the village before she could stop him.

She hurried toward the next open view, risking several falls that would have ended the pursuit entirely, but at last reached a place that overlooked a large part of the slope beneath her. She held a knife behind her ear waiting for the boy to appear, watching a gap as wide as a door frame between two trees. Nezeru had been one of the best in her entire rank with a throwing knife, and these blades had been a gift from her father—a beautifully balanced pair of antique daggers forged by Tinukeda'ya craftsmen. Now all she had to do was wait.

It did not take long. The child made enough noise as he hurried downward that she could almost have hit him with her eyes closed. When he appeared in the opening between the two trees Nezeru let out a loud cry of triumph, cal-culated to freeze him for a sufficient instant.

It did: at her shout the boy stumbled and almost fell, turning a look of blind terror toward the hillside above him as he fought to regain his balance. He was indeed small, his legs still too short for adulthood, his shaved head too large. In the fractional instant he swayed there between the framing trunks she could even see the curve of his childish belly and his eyes full of tears. Perfect. All she had to do was let her blade fly.

But she did not throw it.

A moment later the little acolyte regained his footing and was gone again, racing down the path. She heard his footsteps grow fainter even as his scent began to fade on the breeze.

Nezeru was astonished at herself. She had failed—she had not even tried! Why had she let down her comrades and betrayed her queen? She didn't know, but something about the child—his small size, his . . . *realness*—had shocked her in a way she had not foreseen.

I've betrayed my people. That was all she could think. She could have killed the boy easily, ended the threat of his escape, but she had not done it. It was as though her own body had turned traitor without explanation.

Nezeru could not understand what had happened. All she could do was climb back up the hill to join Makho and the others. She was a traitor, and deserved death, that was the simple truth.

But Nezeru did not want to die.

"But if you saw his eyes, how could you fail your shot?" Makho was furious, as well he should have been. The five Talons were hurrying down the mountainside now, the mortal captain following them as best he could, although the sound of his cursing was already nearly too weak to hear.

"I told you, my knife struck a vine and went astray." Nezeru had never lied to her fellow Sacrifices before. It was a bizarre sensation, like discovering that despite what everyone said, she could actually walk upon thin air. But as with walking on air, she could not believe it would last, and the knowledge of what would happen when the truth of things reasserted itself terrified her. *It is bad enough that I failed—but to evade punishment like a coward by lying to my hand chieftain . . . ?* She felt as though she, not the wrinkled mortal priest, had been the one whose head had been cut off. Everything she had thought, everything she had believed, had been dashed to pieces in an instant.

"Let us not waste time talking!" pleaded Saomeji. He was carrying the bundle that contained the bones as he ran, cradling them as a mother would cradle an infant.

"The Singer is right," said Makho. "We will speak of your failure later, Talon Nezeru. Now we must be silent. The mortals may not wait until we reach the village to attack us."

He was right: the mortals did not wait. Before the afternoon sun had fallen all the way behind the mountain the Talons were attacked by a group of men from the village. Unlike the priests, these had armed themselves with bows and arrows, with knives of bone and stone clubs. Sadly for them, they were not fighting other mortals but the trained soldiers of the Queen of the North; Ibi-Khai took an arrow wound in his arm and Nezeru herself only avoided having her skull smashed by throwing herself between an attacker's legs and hamstringing him from behind, but in the end the armed islanders fared no better against the Queen's Talons than had the unarmed priests; nearly two dozen bodies lay on the ground when the village men finally retreated, and none of the corpses belonged to the Hikeda'ya.

The day was all but over by the time they reached the base of the mountain, the sky purple as a bruise, but the village was bright with fires as Nezeru and the rest of the Hikeda'ya came down out of the heights. A mass of villagers waited on the beach of the bay where the Black Rimmersmen's ship *Hringleit* lay at anchor. The sailors had seen what was happening and had rowed their shore boat beyond the range of the villagers' arrows and stones to wait. Nezeru wondered how long it would take to swim out that far.

Then she had no time to think of anything, because the villagers fell upon them in a great crowd, most of them screaming with rage. It was nothing like the armed attack on the mountainside: there were women and even children among these desperate attackers, some barehanded, but others swinging heavy stones or digging tools. In the dim light Nezeru even saw some of the women stabbing at her companions with bone sewing needles, the only weapons they had been able to find.

In the chaos of fighting her way down to the beach Nezeru had to take what came, but she did her best not to kill children or women unnecessarily; instead she pushed them away or knocked them witless with the pommels of her sword and dagger. Saomeji beside her, clutching the sacred bones against his chest, seemed to have no such compunctions. Each time an islander approached him, his bare hand darted out like a striking snake; everywhere it touched there was a flash and a thump of air, then the smell of burning flesh as another assailant collapsed to the ground. And veteran Sacrifices Makho and Kemme were like deadly whirlwinds, destroying everything that drew near them, turning living flesh into lifeless lumps so swiftly Nezeru could not always make out what they had done. At last Makho fought his way down to the edge of the beach, his face covered with bloody scratches, his long white hair pulled free of its elaborate coiffure and whipping in the breeze like a ragged banner.

The longboat began to row toward them. Makho turned and grabbed Saomeji, then shoved him out into deeper water. The Singer lifted the bones high above his head as he waded out, paying little attention to the villagers' crude arrows splashing around him. Makho followed, backing into the bay until the waters reached his waist, protecting Saomeji's escape.

Nezeru had fallen behind the others, and now had to fight her way clear of a group of older men and women to get down to the strand. She batted their withered arms aside as if they were tree branches swiping at her face. Kemme was in the shallows ahead of her, still dropping bodies in a wide semicircle described by the length of his blade. The beach was strewn with corpses, many with black arrows jutting from throat or belly or back. The Whisperer Ibi-Khai stumbled along just behind Kemme, holding his wounded arm close to his side, head down to make a smaller target as he splashed toward the shore boat. For a moment Nezeru thought they had escaped, but then she saw the ship's mortal captain stumble out of the forest and collapse, clearly all but exhausted. The villagers saw him and several of them moved to surround him.

Can the ship sail without its captain? Nezeru wondered. She hastened back through the shallows and leaped into the midst of the villagers, her sword slashing and biting. As the islanders fell away from their victim in surprise, several holding bloody wounds, Nezeru dragged the captain back onto his feet and pushed him ahead of her into the surf. She waited until he was up and moving again before following him. The rest of the queen's hand had almost reached the longboat, with Saomeji and his precious burden in the lead.

My fellow Talons will leave me here, she suddenly realized. *As they should. The queen would want it so. If I cannot get to the boat, they will leave me here.* She knew what being captured by the furious villagers would mean. However these people might have come to have Hakatri's relics, it was clear that they worshipped them.

We have stolen their god . . .

Something struck her full in the back, an impact so sudden that for a moment she thought she had been arrow-shot. Then she felt hands pulling at her hair, nails scraping her face, and heard the wordless howls. Her sword had tumbled to the sand just beyond her reach, but she managed to curl her fingers around one of her throwing knives and pull it from her harness. She stabbed backward, catching something with meat on it. Somebody screeched just behind her ear and the grappling arms loosened for a moment. Nezeru smashed backward again, this time with the pommel of the knife, guessing where her enemy's head must be, and felt the satisfaction of impact. The burden fell away from her. Nezeru crawled forward until she could reach her sword, but even as her fingers closed on the hilt she was attacked again, and had to turn and try to push her assailant away. The figure was small but fat around the middle, something she had only an instant to note before she managed to roll out from under the grasping, mad thing. She could hear Makho out across the water, calling to the sailors to hurry, but she could hear other, angrier cries from much nearer and knew that whoever had attacked her would soon have help.

Finally free, she staggered upright and saw that her attacker was a young woman with dark hair in a wild tangle and eyes red with tears. The woman's hands curved into claws as she caught up to Nezeru again, trying to swipe at her face. Nezeru thrust with her blade through her attacker's robe and into the rounded body, then pushed the blade deeper. The woman's eyes bulged and she opened her mouth as if to speak; blood was on her tongue and her teeth. Then she fell heavily onto the red sand and a blood-spotted bundle rolled out of her robe. A baby had been strapped to her chest. Nezeru's sword had pierced them both.

My father, Lord Viyeki, I am sorry, was her first thought. *How shamed you will be to have such a daughter.*

A bone-tipped arrow snapped into the sand near her foot, scarcely a hand's breadth from the dead woman's slack face. Nezeru turned and ran into the water.

13

Lady Alva's Tale

"**Enough of weeping**, friends," Simon declared loudly. "Since the good old duke died, it seems like that's all we've done for days. To-night will be different—by royal command, we will drink and laugh!"

"We hardly need a royal command for that, husband," Miriamele pointed out. "And in any case, it's not truly a royal command unless I add my voice."

"Well?" He took a long drink from the cup that had already been twice refilled by helpful servitors. "Do you?"

"Do you need to ask?" she said. "With all our friends here? Yes, husband, I agree that we have wept more than enough. Let us put away our grief for one night and celebrate Isgrimnur's life."

"And our own lives, too," said Eolair, smiling. "For we have all endured much to be here today."

"And some would even say the world is a better place for it," said Tiamak, wiping beer froth from his mouth. "Isgrimnur contributed much to that."

Simon was amused—he could almost believe that the usually abstemious Wrannaman was getting a bit tiddly. "You speak truth, Brother Tiamak—and I salute what Eolair said as well. We are all friends here, but we are friends with a history few can match." He looked around the hall where the duke's great-grandchildren frisked on the rug-draped floors and a large, comforting fire burned in the hearth. "Friends . . . and the family of friends, who are as good as family—or do I mean as good as friends? Never mind." He raised his cup. "Let us drink also to the new duke, Grimbrand, the new duchess, Sorde, and all Isgrimnur's fine family!"

The others echoed him. Isgrimnur's daughter Signi and her husband had brought a large array of children and grandchildren to the gathering, and Duke Grimbrand's son Isvarr and his fair-haired wife had contributed four towheaded boy-beasts who seemed to do little except shout, run, and wrestle. Two of Isvarr's sisters and their husbands also had broods of their own. It was hard to tell exactly how many children were present, but it was not a small number.

Look at all Isgrimnur's grandchildren and great-grandchildren, thought Simon with a momentary pang. *What a fine, big family he and Gutrun made.* He looked to Miriamele to see if she shared his mood, as she so often did, but his wife was on a bench by one of the fireplaces talking to Sisqi and Duchess Sorde and she looked happy enough.

Just me, he thought as he drained his cup. *Just me being a mooncalf.* "God bless old Isgrimnur!" he shouted, then waved for one of the servants to come fill his cup again.

"And with that," said Grimbrand, rising, "I think it is time for my clan to head back to our chambers and leave our distinguished guests to their own conversations. You have much to discuss, I think, and even more to remember." He bowed to Miriamele, then beckoned to his wife.

As the new duke and duchess and their large party of children and servants went out they paused to greet an older couple in the doorway.

"Sludig!" Simon stood up so quickly he nearly knocked the pitcher from the serving-boy's hand. "God bless you and keep you, you old badger, I have been looking for you since the funeral!"

The Rimmersman, who had broadened considerably since the days they had marched across the north together, spread his arms. "Am I allowed to embrace the king and queen?"

"The king would be angry if you didn't." Simon let himself be enfolded in the northerner's bearlike grasp. "Miri! Come see who's here! It is Sludig the Dour, masking as the Earl of Engby."

"*Jarl* of Engby," Sludig told him, smiling deep in his beard as he returned the embrace. His whiskers were still mostly yellow, despite all his years, but he truly had grown a bit wider than when the king had seen him last. "We also say 'thane' here instead of 'baron'. We have not been entirely enslaved by Your Majesties' overcivilized southern ways."

"Ha!" said Sludig's wife. "My husband has largely given up beer for Perdruinese wine brought north to us at great expense, so do not pay too much heed to his bragging about northern pride."

"Thank you for telling me," Simon said. "And welcome, Lady Engby." Simon had met Sludig's wife for only a few moments at Isgrimnur's funeral, but had liked her instantly. She was younger than her husband, a tall, broad-shouldered woman with an open, friendly face and a swift wit.

"'Alva', please, Your Majesty, or 'Lady Alva' if you must. My old man is right about one thing—we're not so civilized up here as some others."

"Lady Alva, it is so good to see you again," said Miri from her bench beside the fire. "Come and have a proper talk with me while the men bellow drunken lies at each other."

"Are all those stories of the old days truly made up?" Alva asked with false innocence. "I suspected as much, you know. Dragons and fairies and deeds of heroism that only they witnessed—what nonsense these men like to talk!" But her words were belied by a sudden seriousness that crossed her face like a shadow, and Simon did not miss the quick glance that traveled between husband and wife.

If there was something bothering them, Sludig was not going to be the one to broach it. "Can you credit that?" he said, gratefully accepting a large flagon of beer from a servant. "Treacherous woman. *She* is the one for dragons and fairies, far more than me—she's practically a witch! Alva grew up in the superstitious north and has not an ounce of Aedonite piety, for all the time she spends in church."

"Oh, good," said Miriamele. "Someone worth talking to, then. Come and join us, Lady Alva, and hurry!"

Simon steered Sludig toward the men, who were occupying their own set of benches on the other side of the massive hearth. Now that the children and many of the servants had left with the duke's family, the great hall had grown quieter and seemed larger, at least to Simon. *But the north always makes me feel that way,* he thought. *Dark so early, and so long—and the cold! And knowing that there are things out there in that darkness who do not love us, of course.*

Binabik leaped up with a glad cry and hurried toward Sludig to embrace him, something that could have been comical because of their different sizes had it not tugged so strongly at Simon's heart. "If we had managed nothing else," he said to the others as they watched this reunion, "we would still be remembered for allowing a Rimmersman and a troll to find a love to make the poets sing." He was rather pleased with this, and repeated it loudly.

Sludig gave him a sour look. "Your Majesty still likes to make jokes. I will not apologize for what I feel for this little man."

Binabik grinned. "Or I for what I feel for this large one." He called to his wife. "Sisqi! Sludig is here!"

"She knows, I think," Eolair said. "She is talking to Sludig's lady even now."

"Look at us all," said Sludig, spreading himself gratefully on a bench beside Binabik.

"A little fatter, some of us," Simon pointed out.

"Some of us, Majesty, are not all legs and nose, like a stork," growled Sludig. "It is only right for a man to become more substantial with age. But a great scarecrow like you, king or no, is something that only frightens the children."

"Hah! You are still too sober to make sense. Drink up!" Simon found himself a spot on another bench where he could watch the others talk from a little distance. With Sludig's arrival, he felt as though a circle had closed and something was completed. The old friends, who had known each other since the days of the Storm King's War, were quickly lost in reminiscence, talking of old terrors and of equally distant moments of joy and wonder. The beloved voices washed over him.

Someone sat down beside him. "Are you being well, friend Simon?"

"I am well indeed, Binabik, and so much better for seeing you and hearing your voice. Where are your daughter and her man tonight?"

"You may believe or not believe, old friend, but they are with your Prince Morgan. Little Snenneq has taken a liking to the prince, and they are spending much time together."

Simon did not want to think too much about his errant grandson. "Are you happy with him as a match for your daughter? Snenneq, I mean."

Binabik laughed. The familiar sound warmed Simon, made it seem for a moment as if time really could be cheated. "It would be making no difference at all if I did, I am thinking. Qanuc women are making their own minds up about the partners they are wanting, as Sisqi did when she was choosing me over her parents' wishes." The expression the little man wore as he looked to his wife made Simon's chest ache a little. Did he and Miriamele still gaze at each other that way? He hoped so. "But, as it happens," Binabik continued, "I am also liking Snenneq. True it is that he is having too much pride, as the talented young often are having—'a man who only wants to step on unbroken snow,' as we say on Mintahoq. Yes, sometimes Young Snenneq is being a bit of a braided ram."

In the moment of silence, Tiamak's voice rose above the others. "No, no, Eolair speaks the truth. I am a married man now."

"By our good lord, I wish you well of it!" said Sludig. "What is the woman's name, so I may pray for her poor soul?"

For a moment Tiamak seemed to bridle, then he heard the laughter of the others and realized Sludig was jesting. It was hard to tell with the Rimmersman sometimes. In his younger years Sludig Two-Axes had been a serious, often sour-faced man, but age—or perhaps Lady Alva—seemed to have mellowed him. "You are a wicked man, Jarl Mischief," Tiamak said, wagging his finger, "but I will tell you anyway. Her name is Thelía."

"Is she Nabbanai?"

"That is where she was born, yes. I met her in Kwanitupul. She had been a nun."·

"A nun?" Sludig looked around in mock astonishment. "So this little fellow stole one of the Aedon's brides right out of a nunnery? No wonder Isgrimnur thought him a fit partner for clambering through ghant-nests!"

"You mock too much," Count Eolair said gently. "Lady Thelía was no longer under the convent roof when Tiamak met her. She was serving as a healer in the poorest parts of Kwanitupul, working with the Astaline Sisters. A very noble woman."

"And all the nobler for marrying Tiamak, no doubt," Sludig said. "At least she seems to have taught him to wear shoes! But the count is right—I make too many jests. Tiamak, I am truly happy for you. A good marriage can redeem even the wickedest fellow, and you were already one of the best of men."

Tiamak smiled. "I could not agree to *that*, my good jarl, but I can agree that both you and I have been lucky in our mates."

"Hear, hear!" said Simon, lifting his cup. "A toast to all married men! And a cheer for the best of women, their wives!"

"Methinks the king has had too much to drink," the queen said; and yet, she was glowing.

Elvritshalla Castle had fallen out of sight, blocked by the imposing, nearer shape of the cathedral, as the prince and the two trolls made their way by diffident moonlight down to the lake that lay at the heart of the city. The snow had stopped falling but the north wind still cut like a knife. "I think it's time for a little more of that *kangkang*," said Morgan. "One swallow is not enough to ward off this chill."

"No, with sorrow, Morgan Prince," said Little Snenneq. "Afterward, I was saying, and afterward it must be. Not only is there some risk, but you also will need a clear head to appreciate the cleverness of my device."

A day spent with the trolls in the castle was one thing—Morgan had quite enjoyed drinking fiery *kangkang* and trying to puzzle out Snenneq's and Qina's strangely amusing speech. Wanting more, he had even declined the chance to accompany Astrian and the rest down to the Kopstade tonight. But following Little Snenneq through bitter cold wind to the arse-end of Elvritshalla was another matter, and Morgan was already regretting his choice.

This end of the city was mostly dark, with only an occasional lantern to paint the angles of the streets and buildings, and a few fires burning in the small, high-roofed houses. Morgan, who had spent most of his time in Elvritshalla evading the guards his grandparents arranged for him, suddenly began to wonder what might happen if he and the trolls were set upon by robbers in this dismal section of the city. Was that why Little Snenneq wouldn't give him any more of the reviving liquor? Because the troll expected a knife fight with angry Rimmersmen? The Northmen certainly didn't like Little Snenneq or his kind very much.

Morgan didn't have the chance to ask, because Snenneq put out his arm and waved the prince to stop. "No farther. Not yet. Soon there is an icy downslipping. I have been here already, because I am a great one for learning and preparing. Is that not so, Qina?"

His betrothed, who had been following them as quietly as a shadow, nodded her head vigorously. "Preparings, yes," she said. "And there are learns, too. Many of them my *nukapik* is having. Oh and most yes." Morgan thought he could see her smile.

"Because that is how it must be. I will be Singing Man of all Mintahoq one day. Learning is my duty. Wisdom is my destiny!" He turned to Morgan. "You see, not only princes are having these destinies."

Morgan could only shake his head in confusion. "Why did we stop? Is it time to go back?"

"Ah. Not for going back, but so I can be showing you my cleverness." Little Snenneq shrugged off his pack and rummaged in it, then began to pull things out that made jingling noises as he piled them on a stone. "Put these on," he said, and tossed a clinking something onto the snowy ground beside the prince.

"What are they?" Morgan lifted one and it poked painfully into his finger. The object looked like nothing so much as an iron horseshoe, but longer, and the bottom and sides were covered with sharp spikes almost the size of house nails, each as long as the first joint of his finger. Long rawhide straps dangled from the spiked irons like some foppish decoration.

"Climbing spikes they are, of course." Snenneq was strapping on a pair of his own, deftly weaving the straps up from his feet, through various tie-rings, then to his ankles like the ribbons twined around a Maia-tree. "We use them most time only for traveling in the highest of mountains, but it is icy where we go next. Also, they will be part of my surprise."

Morgan stared helplessly. He could not for the life of him make sense of how the things were supposed to be used and he wasn't certain he wanted to use them anyway. Qina saw his dismay and came to help, showing him how the flat parts pushed against the soles of his boots, and how the straps should be wound around his feet and ankles, then tied above his calves. It took several tries before Morgan could figure out how to climb to his feet while wearing the odd things without tripping or gouging himself, since spikes protruded not just from the bottom but the sides as well.

"Ha!" said Snenneq. "You are looking like a tall troll for certain, Morgan Prince. Are you now ready?"

"Ready for what?"

"Good. Follow, then, and I will show you." And just like that, Little Snenneq slid between two piles of rubbish that had once been dwellings, but had long since tumbled down and been cannibalized for their useful bits by the locals.

"It is not a fall to death," said Qina reassuringly. "You go, Prince friend. Lowlander can climb down here without frightened."

As she promised, what lay beyond the edge of the city here was not a steep cliff, but rather a descending slope of mostly flat stone, cracked and heaved up in places. Beyond it lay a great misty openness whose details Morgan could not quite make out, flat and white as a fallow field covered with snow.

"What . . . ?" he asked, then felt his foot begin to go out from under him. The sheets of rock on which he stood were covered in ice. He did not fall completely over, but saved himself only at the expense of a crack to his knee and scraped palms.

"Do not talk with Qina!" called Snenneq over his shoulder from farther down the slope. The husky young troll was scrambling with surprising ease across the icy surfaces, headed toward the misty white flatness below, and his words were faint in the wind. "Her words, however full of sense, will bring you distraction and tumbling. You must instead be watching your feet!"

Limping and grumpy, Morgan made his way as carefully as he could down the glassy, treacherous stones. Little Snenneq was definitely right about one thing: using the climbing irons demanded keen attention on such a surface, because the spikes on the bottom of them were small. In most situations, he discovered, it was better to use the longer side spikes to wedge his foot into spaces between stones, so he could move slowly and balance himself. Still, even managing after a while to stay consistently upright did not make the journey enjoyable. The worst part was watching little Qina, who stayed behind him all the way—clearly by choice—looking sympathetically at him from the depths of her furry hood each time he fell. She herself had not even donned the iron spikes, but made her way over the icy stones in just her soft boots, like a particularly graceful bear cub.

As he neared the bottom of the slope, the silhouettes of the wall towers and the castle rising high against the waning moon, Morgan could finally see that what he had first taken for a vast, snowy field was in truth a lake covered in ice, right in the center of the city. He had heard someone mention it, but that was not the same as coming upon such a wide and silent place in the middle of a dark night, accompanied only by trolls.

Little Snenneq had reached the bottom of the hill long before, and sat waiting for them, beaming in pleasure as though he had created the lake himself. "Bridvattin, this water is called. Here the Little Gratuvask river bends upon itself, and so was forming this lake. At the center is an ancestor house."

"A what?" Morgan peered out toward a small island in the middle of the lake, where a low tower and several other roofs could just be seen through the fog. A few small lights burned in the windows, but otherwise it was only an angular collection of shadows. "Ancestor house?"

"Yes, with certainty. A place where your people come together to pray to the ancestors."

"A church, you mean," Morgan said. "Actually, I think it's a monastery."

"Monastery." Little Snenneq sounded it out, repeated it. "A good word. In any case, it is here I will show you the main part of my cleverness. Look!" He lifted up his foot. Morgan could see nothing of interest. "For sliding on ice," the troll said, waggling his leg.

The crescent moon gave just enough light for Morgan to see that something like a knife's blade had replaced the climbing spikes on the bottom of the troll's sheepskin boot. "Ice skates?" asked the prince, mildly nettled. "That's nothing new. People here skate on ice all the time. We even do it down in Erkynland."

Snenneq shook his head. "You are not seeing the beauty of what I have crafted. Here, sit down. Give me your foot."

Morgan grunted in a put-upon way, but sat on a slippery stone and raised his leg. Little Snenneq scrambled over and began pulling on Morgan's side-spikes. After a moment, and a clicking and clunking that tickled the bottom of Morgan's foot even through his boot, the troll lifted his hands. "Do you see? With my idea, the climbing irons can be taken away and turned around—as so—and when they are again rightly affixed—they are blades for ice sliding!"

"Ice *skating*." But Morgan could not help being impressed. In a matter of moments the troll had changed the shoe spikes into the blade of a skate. As he watched Snenneq do the same with his other foot, he suddenly realized what this meant.

"Do you mean we are going to skate here? On this lake?"

Snenneq almost chortled. "Do not worry! I am sure the church men in that ancestor-house will not mind."

Morgan had a feeling that the troll didn't know many Aedonite priests. "But . . . but I've never skated."

Qina finally appeared. For some reason the female troll had stopped and retreated back up the slope, and now she was dragging a heavy branch much longer than she was.

"Not to fear, Morgan Prince," said Snenneq. "I will teach you. I am a rare teacher. I have taught Qina many things!"

"Many, yes," she said, settling herself and her long branch on a stone near the edge of the lake. "So I do not slide on ice tonight. I sit here. If you fall into cold wet, Prince Highness—" she patted the heavy branch—"this for you to pull out."

If Qina herself did not want to get on the ice, Morgan wanted to even less. His grandfather and grandmother had told him many frightsome stories of how treacherous ice and snow could be in the far north. But Snenneq was already hurrying him out onto the glassy surface of the lake. "Now do as I am doing. Your knees must be bending!"

Morgan did his best, but each time his feet went out from under him and he fell, he could swear he heard the ice fracturing beneath him. It was hard fully to appreciate the wonder of skating on an ice-mantled moonlit lake when all he could think about was the freezing black water that lurked beneath the ice.

"Oh, poor luck!" Snenneq said for perhaps the fourth or fifth time, so cheerful that Morgan wanted to kick him, but he had to concentrate instead on getting back up without falling over again. "Do not fear to fall, Morgan Prince! That way true learning is found! And that is why our creators gave to us hindquarters of flesh and protecting fat! Do wolves have such fundaments? Do sheep? No, only people, who learn by each tumble."

Morgan wished he had gone to the Kopstade with the others, even if their evening had ended in a brawl. By now, he could have been comfortably drunk, and even being pummeled by angry Rimmersmen would surely be less painful than Snenneq's ice sliding.

"By the Good God, I think I've broken my knee *and* my arse at the same time! How is that even possible?"

"Do not fear, Morgan Prince. You are doing well for a first try!" At least the troll was enjoying himself. "Yes, wave your arms, so, around and around, to keep from falling! Try to slide here to me, farther out. Of course I am knowing your knee pains you, but do you see? Such a good teacher I am that you are already learning! Soon you will be ice sliding like the most nimble Qanuc!"

"But I keep the long stick here," Qina assured Morgan in a voice too low for Snenneq to hear. "Just for careful."

The conversation had ranged widely over both past and present, from dragon fighting to cow breeding. As part of the estate at Engby, Isgrimnur had given Sludig and his wife several hundred head of long-bodied, short-legged northern cattle, and the creatures had become Sludig's obsession.

"You would never credit it," he kept saying, "but in their way, they are as interesting as people!"

"I suspect that may have more to do with the people you meet than the cows you raise, Baron," Tiamak said, which made everyone laugh. But Sludig did not reply for some moments.

"To speak honestly, it is not the *people* in Engby who worry us," he said at last.

"Remember, husband, this is a happy gathering," said Alva.

For Simon, the pleasant haze of beer and company dispersed a bit. Based on the looks Sludig and his wife shared now, he had not been mistaken: something deeper and darker was disturbing them. "What do you mean?" asked Simon. "Not people?"

Sludig shook his head. "Truly, let us talk of something else, Majesty. Let us talk of your grandchildren. I hear Morgan is man-sized now. I would like to see him!"

"I would like to see him too." Simon frowned. "At least now and then." He knew he was being led away from something, and he didn't like it. "Tell me what it is that worries you, Sludig."

"Nothing for Your Majesties to fret yourself with. The north is always strange. Perhaps a bit stranger this winter, that's all."

"Is it about the White Foxes?"

"Husband," said Miriamele in a tone Simon knew all too well. "Sludig does not want to speak about it now."

"Begging your pardon, but the queen is right," Sludig said. "Not when all are drinking good wine and ale and sharing tales of old times. But while you are still here in the northlands we should speak of these other things . . . and we will."

They returned to other stories, other subjects, but the mood had changed, and Simon for one could not summon back his earlier carelessness. "This is the cruel trick of being a king," he said at last to Binabik. "You can have anything you want, but you spend all your time worrying."

"That, I am fearing, is not just true for monarchs, but for most who live long enough to become grown men and women." He smiled. "What is your worrying now, friend Simon? Is it what Sludig was saying, or is it still the silence from the Sithi that troubles you, as you were telling to me before?"

Miri had come to stand behind him for a moment; Simon could feel her cool hand on the back of his neck. "The silence from the Sithi is something that worries us both," she said, "but it troubles Simon the most."

"It should trouble everybody." Simon thought he sounded loud, so he tried again in a softer voice. "We haven't heard a word from them in several years."

"How strange that is being!" Binabik shook his head. "Not even words from Jiriki or Aditu? They have sent no messengers?"

Simon shrugged. "Nothing. And we have sent them many messages, or at least tried. Perhaps it's their mother Likimeya who wants it this way. She was never very happy with us—was she, Eolair?"

The count, who had fallen out of the other conversation, started. "Certainly Likimeya was not friendly to us in the way Jiriki and his sister were," he said at last. "But after meeting her, I would not say she hated mortals, either. *Cautious* is the way I would put it. And after what her people have gone through at mortal hands, who could say she is wrong?"

Simon made a sour face. "Spoken like the diplomat you are, carefully generous to all sides. But what do you truly think?"

Eolair shrugged. He looked uncomfortable. "It is not entirely fair to ask me to shed the habits of a lifetime in a matter of moments, Majesty. But I suspect there may be something at work we do not know, some argument among the Sithi themselves. I cannot see any reason for such a silence otherwise."

Miriamele nodded. "I think you may be right, Eolair. And from what Simon has said about his months with them, they also seem to keep time differently than we do."

"Still, it is strange, this so-long silence," Binabik said, but then noticed his daughter Qina, who had appeared as if from nowhere and stood silently in the chamber doorway. He beckoned her to him and they had a murmured conversation, then she nodded shyly to the others and went out again, quick and quiet as a mouse.

"The young ones are back from their adventuring," Binabik said. "Morgan the prince is tired and sore, Qina says, so he is going early to bed."

Miriamele looked worried. "Is he unwell?"

Binabik smiled. "A mere tumble of small nature, Qina says. Bumped and bruised a little, and shamed because of it, but otherwise without harm. He is in good hands with my daughter and her *nukapik*, who studies the healing arts. I do believe they are all becoming friends."

The queen looked uncertain, but Simon sidled over to her. "The boy's fine. They went out for a walk, he had a little fall. Probably had too much to drink. Don't embarrass him by rushing off to look in on him. The trolls will take good care of him."

She did not seem entirely convinced, but she sighed and let herself be guided back to a chair by Sisqi. Soon the conversation turned back to the Sithi.

"We Qanuc have not been much meeting with the Zida'ya—the Sithi-folk, as you are calling them—in recent years," said Binabik, "but we have also been seeing no great change in their dealings with us. Do you agree, Sisqi my wife?"

She nodded emphatically. The other conversations had now ended, and all by the fire were turned toward each other. "Many Sithi coming to Blue Mud Lake only three summers gone," she said. "They giving us news of many things, and sharing meals with us then. They sang." Simon could hear the change in her voice as she remembered. "At night, beneath all stars. It had so much beauty!"

"But nothing was being said by them of silence between the Zida'ya and their friends in the Hayholt," Binabik added, a frown creasing his brow. "Still, these were being ordinary Sithi—I mean not of the family of Year-Dancing that we are knowing best, Aditu and Jiriki and their kin."

"All we can do is be patient, I suppose," Simon said. "We have sent them many messages. One day, perhaps they will answer." But he could not keep the deep sadness out of his voice. Once, he had held out great hope that the Sithi and mortal men could be reconciled, but it had been many years since a better friendship between their peoples had seemed anything but a foolish, idle dream. He stared at the fire, watching the flames and thinking of his last, terrible night in Jao é-Tinukai'i with Jiriki and the rest, the night the Norns had attacked their Sithi kin, the night Amerasu Ship-Born had died.

The others were thinking their own thoughts; for long moments the room was silent but for the crackling of the fire. At last the king turned to Sludig. "I'm sorry I've made a muddle of the festive mood, old friend, but now you might as well tell me what you've heard of the Norns. Is it just rumor or something more? The north is always full of tales that the White Foxes are coming again, that I know. That hasn't changed since the days of the Storm King's War. Grimbrand said there were many stories this winter, but he did not think it was so much different from other years."

"Simon, don't," said Miriamele. "You agreed."

Sludig shook his head. "Perhaps your husband is right, Majesty. And perhaps things are different here in Elvritshalla—it is a large, well-guarded city. Engby, where we live, is farther north—closer to the Nornfells. But I should let my wife tell the story, since it is hers."

They turned to Alva. "What story?" the queen asked.

Alva looked a little surprised. "I had not expected to . . . it will seem foolish, or at least parts of it will . . ." Several of the others urged her to speak. "Very well," she said finally. "But it seems a poor way to end an evening of good fellowship." She turned to Sludig. "Send the squire back to our chambers for it, will you, my husband?"

Sludig called for a young man who had been waiting outside in the hall's antechamber. The young man bowed as he was given his quiet orders, but he was struggling to keep something else from his face—distaste or even fear, Simon thought.

"What is this mystery?" he asked.

"I beg your Majesties' patience," Lady Alva said. "All will be revealed soon enough. But here is what I must tell you first.

"Elvritshalla, Kaldskryke, Saegard, all these places are much like Erchester, cities with towns and villages all around. If you stand upon almost any road nearby, within an hour you will hear a farmer's cart or the sound of hooves as a royal messenger rides past, or glimpse hunters or charcoal burners making their way through nearby woods. But in Engby where I grew up, and where Sludig and I now live, if you walk away from the houses you can continue on for days without seeing another living human soul. Some of the older roads will not see a traveler for a year or more. But that does not mean that you will be alone.

"In the north, we have always known that the land of the White Foxes—the Norns—is close to our borders. There is a valley just beyond ours to the northeast that has been called the *Refarslod*—the Fox's Road—as long as anyone can remember, going back to my great-grandmother's day, because the Norns have always used it."

"Hold a moment, please, Countess," Tiamak said, his usual shyness pushed aside by his curiosity. "Engby, your home, is far east of where we sit here in Elvritshalla—east even of Kaldskryke, is it not? Why would Norns travel so far that direction? Nothing lies to the east of the Dimmerskog forest except snow and emptiness."

"I am not meaning to take offense where I am suspecting none was meant," said Binabik a bit sternly, "but by 'nothing' I hope you are not speaking of Yiqanuc, land of our people?"

Tiamak was dismayed. "Forgive me, no! Of course not, Binabik. But the mountains of Yiqanuc are far away, many, many leagues, and I had not heard of the Norns being seen in the Trollfells."

"They are not," Binabik admitted. "Not since the most ancient of days, before great Tumet'ai vanished in the ice."

"That truly is puzzling," said Eolair. "The two ways the Norns have always traveled to the south, at least when mustered for war, are down the old Northern Road in the shadow of the western mountains or down the wide Frostmarch Road, that leads past this city and through the eastern heart of Rimmersgard on the way south."

Simon was a bit dazzled. "All this map-reading and such. I don't understand. Miriamele, does this make any sense to you?"

"A little, I think," she said, "but I am still waiting to hear Alva's story."

"And me," said Simon. "It's only that I've had too much drink for patience. Go ahead, Lady Alva, please."

"I hope you will be patient enough for this," she told them. "Because I must tell you of a dream I had when I was a girl."

"Tell, then," Simon said. "I have had many dreams myself that turned out to be true."

"Then we have that in common," Alva said. "I have always had dreams of things that later come to pass. Small matters, mostly—things that are lost, visitors unlooked-for, messages from those who have passed on that make sense only to those who knew them."

"It is true," said Sludig. "All in Engby know of Lady Alva's dreams."

"Once when I was but a girl," she went on, "I dreamed that St. Helvard himself came to me, dressed in robes of white, as I had seen him portrayed on the walls of our church. He led me out of my parents' house and through the snows. In the dream there was a great storm, but I could hear other voices in the wind, singing and laughing. They were beautiful, but also frightening, and somehow I knew I was hearing the White Foxes, the ice demons I had been taught to fear since I was old enough to understand.

"In the dream, Helvard led me up a hill and across its crest to the far side, so that I could look down and see the Refarslod laid out below me. A ghostly army walked it, barely visible through the hard-blown snow, but what I could make out was spiky with spears and banners. In truth, all I could see clearly were their eyes glowing like the eyes of beasts, and they were beyond counting.

" *'They march to a city that never was,'* the saint told me. *'They seek to win the everything that is nothing.'* And then I woke up, shivering in my bed."

Simon was shaking his head. "I don't understand," he said at last. "You say this dream came to you when you were a girl?"

"I used to have many strange dreams," Alva said. "But no other like that one."

"Why do you look so puzzled, husband?" Miriamele asked.

"The wise woman Geloë used to say I was closer to the Road of Dreams than many people, Miri, but I don't . . . of late I haven't . . ." Simon paused. "I've just realized something. I've stopped dreaming."

"What?" The queen was not the only one who stared at him as though he had begun babbling nonsense.

"It's true! I only realized it now. I can't remember the last time I dreamed. It's been days—no, weeks!" Simon turned back to the baroness. "Lady Alva, I apologize for being distracted. I will try to make sense of it later. But I still do not understand—you said this dream came to you when you were a child. Why do you tell us now?" He looked from her to Sludig. "Am I misunderstanding?"

"No, Majesty," said Alva. "Because I have not finished. We were going to wait and tell you this later, but it seems the moment is now." She gave a little shrug. "Here is the rest. I have remembered that dream of St. Helvard all my life, with no sign of it ever coming true. In truth, the Norns seemed to have entirely stopped using the Refarslod they had traveled for generations. But just in the last few years such stories have begun to be told again. People are once again seeing strange things around and on the ancient fairy road. Then, scarcely a month before Sludig and I came to Elvritshalla, one snowy night several dozen cattle escaped from one of our barns. My good husband took several men and went in search of them. Nearly half of the cows were found wandering, but the others had simply vanished."

"I started back with some of the men," Sludig said, "leading back such cattle as we had found. My foreman, my wife, and several of our men stayed behind, searching for stragglers." He nodded to his wife. "Now you speak, Alva."

Sludig's squire re-entered the chamber, but stood patiently waiting while his master and mistress continued their story. Simon could see the young man was carrying a bundle of cloth, handling it with the exaggerated diffidence of someone tasked to bear something foul-smelling or foul-feeling.

"It does not matter who tells the tale—the end is the same," said Lady Alva. "We could ill afford to lose so many cattle, so we searched long after we should have gone back. As twilight fell, we came upon a group of strangers at the far eastern edge of our lands. It was snowing and hard to see well, but at first it seemed as though they were all sleeping—an odd thing to be doing in a snowstorm, you will agree. But when we got closer we saw that they were all dead, several of them besmeared in blood. More surprisingly, though, they were not men."

"Norns?" asked Simon. "Were they White Foxes?"

"Yes, but not all of them. Some of the dead were equally strange in face and form, but golden-skinned."

"Golden?" Simon looked at Miri, then at Binabik. "You mean they were Sithi?"

"Perhaps, but I cannot say it certainly, since I had never seen any of the Fair Ones before," Lady Alva told him.

"But your husband has—he most definitely has!" said Simon. "What were they, Sludig?"

"I never saw the bodies, Majesty. My wife and the men hurried back to fetch me, but when we went back to where they had found the dead, they were all gone."

"Gone?"

"Someone had come while we went to fetch the rest of the men," explained Lady Alva. "They had carried away all the bodies and brushed away most of the tracks. But they had not had time to remove all traces—blood could still be seen in the snow. And something else as well, half covered in the drifts." She turned to Sludig. "You show them, husband," Alva said. "I cannot bear to hold it, myself."

Sludig took the bundle from his squire and unfolded the thick cloth. "This is what we found." What he held out was a dagger of strange design, with a faint coppery sheen, its hilt made from a single piece of polished stone. At the top, just below the pommel, was a thin ring of what Simon at first thought was another kind of stone, shiny and gray. Then he saw that the gray stone had a grain. "God's Bloody Tree," he swore, pointing at the gray stuff with a trembling finger. "Is that . . . *witchwood*?"

"A bronze Nakkiga dagger, that is being," said Binabik, peering at it. "And, yes, the decoration is witchwood."

The Aedonites all made the sign of the Tree. Sisqi touched her hand to her heart, as did her husband.

"I know what that marking on the witchwood signifies," said Tiamak. "Do you see it carved there?" He was obviously reluctant to touch the dagger, and only pointed at the ring of gray stone below the pommel and the tiny spiral rune carved there. "I have seen it in old books. It identifies the Order of Song— the Norn Queen's chief sorcerers."

Simon stared at the knife. It was such a small, simple thing, but he felt cold and heavy in his chest, as if a stone hung there instead of a warm, beating heart. He had not felt an apprehension like this since John Josua's death. He turned to

Miriamele, but his wife had gone very pale. "So not just Norn warriors, but Norn wizards, too?" Simon said. "And fighting against the Sithi? Are the White Foxes going to war with their kin again? If so, all the immortals seem to be keeping it secret from us. But fear not, friends—if our enemies are up to something again, we will remind them of what happened last time."

He spoke with a certainty that he was nowhere close to feeling. He had hoped that a few of his companions might chime in with similar boasts, or at least a few brave, reassuring words, but the room had gone silent but for the crackling of the fire.

14

Ghosts of the Garden

"Nezeru, come and kneel before me."

It was the first time Makho had spoken to her since the *Hringleit*'s captain had returned them to the mainland shore, then hurriedly cast off again, clearly happy to have survived with ship and crew intact.

She walked across the rough camp the Queen's Talons had made on the bluff above the ocean. For once, Saomeji did not even look up to see her pass, too fascinated by the sacred bones in his care, which he had been examining for hours like a jeweler who had found a cache of gems from the Lost Garden.

Nezeru stopped and stood before Makho but did not meet his eye.

"I said *kneel*." The hand chieftain reached out and shoved her down. She hung her head and waited for what would come next, trying not to imagine. *Useless speculation gives power to fear,* her father had always said, and although Viyeki might not know much about her life as a Sacrifice, the magister understood the need to confront power with a clear head. But although Nezeru knew her father's advice was good, she could not stop her heart from speeding or her skin from prickling. The Order of Sacrifice was no stranger to battlefield executions and her crime had been one of the most terrible.

"Sacrifice Nezeru Seyt-Enduya, after being given a clear order, you failed the Mother of All," said Makho. "Because of that, the members of this hand were forced to fight for their lives. Our mission for the queen might have been compromised or even defeated. Useful Hikeda'ya warriors might have been killed through your fault. Do you deny it?"

How could she? "No, Hand Chieftain. My crime is great."

"Do you have any explanation?"

That she had decided at the last moment she could not kill a defenseless mortal child? How could that be an explanation? She might as well say she had simply gone mad. "No, Master."

"The sacred ghosts of the Garden hear you. It is they who judge you, not me. Now look up." Makho waited until she lifted her eyes. "Do you know what I am holding?"

All other activity in the camp, even Saomeji's study of the sacred bones, had stopped. Nezeru felt a chill all over her body. "That is your sword Cold Root."

So it was to be death. She would do her best to take it bravely, as befitted one of the Queen's Sacrifices, but she grieved at what it would do to her father's pride and position, let alone to her mother Tzoja, who would be devastated. Nezeru did not weep, though: Sacrifices did not shed tears from pain or fear. No matter her crimes, she would go to her end still loyal in *that* way, at least.

Makho turned the heavy sword over. A bone grip protruded from the leather on the back of the scabbard, just beneath the hilt. He pulled on it and a long, thin branch of witchwood slid free of its own small sheath. Makho held it close to her face. "And do you know what this is?"

Nezeru shuddered. She had been ready for death, or at least as ready as she could be, consoling herself with the idea that it would at least be swift. "That is the *hebi-kei*, Hand Chieftain Makho. The serpent."

Makho waved the long, flexible branch in the air, watched it dance against a gray sky of almost the same color. "Yes, the serpent. And for your crime, you are sentenced to feel its bite. Kemme! Come here and strip this Sacrifice."

Kemme was beside her in an instant. He yanked at her jerkin, barely bothering to undo the straps; within a few moments Nezeru was naked to the waist. At Makho's nod, Kemme grabbed her arms and dragged her swiftly to a pine tree at the edge of the campsite clearing. He set her face against it, then grabbed her arms and held them from the other side so that she could not move. The rough bark scraped her breasts and cheek. She could not see Makho, but she could hear him walking back and forth behind her. Kemme was carefully keeping his face empty of any expression, but she could tell by how tightly he held her wrists that some part of him relished this duty.

"I could take your life," Makho said. "But apparently your gifts are unusual, and both the queen and the High Magister of Sacrifice gave permission for you to join our hand, so I will spare you for the judgment of my superiors. But you have endangered our most sacred mission and that cannot go unpunished. The snake shall strike twenty times."

Twenty times! Nezeru's legs became shamefully weak and her knees suddenly could not hold her. Had it not been for Kemme's powerful grip she would have slumped to the ground. Even a dozen strokes of the *hebi-kei* could kill.

"If you are truly of the blood that makes a Queen's Sacrifice, you will walk beside us tomorrow morning when we ride out for Nakkiga," Makho said. "If not, we will leave you to die. The bones of great Hakatri are far more important than any one of us. Is she held tightly, Kemme?"

"Aye."

"Then let the serpent bite." Nezeru heard his footsteps getting closer. Suddenly overcome with an animal terror she had never felt before, she struggled, but Kemme was too strong. The tree trunk must be scratching her nipples until they bled, she knew, but in her fear she hardly felt it. "Hold steady, Sacrifice," Makho hissed. "Show courage."

She gained a little control of herself and managed to stop squirming.

"You owe the queen your body," Makho intoned, and then the first blow of the *hebi-kei* fell.

She only dimly heard the loud crack it made, because a bolt of fiery pain leaped through her entire back. Nezeru writhed in agony and almost cried out, but she was afraid to open her mouth, afraid she would vomit with her face pressed against the tree. The pain, which had seemed at first so fierce it would stop her heart, only grew worse as the moments passed.

"You owe the queen your heart," said Makho, and struck again.

Stars seemed to burst and die inside her head, and her bones felt as if they would snap, so hard did she try to push forward, away from the lash, but Makho only waited a few moments, then calmly continued.

"You owe the queen your spirit."

The serpent bit her again, another poison wound, deep and foul. She had never felt pain like this, not even in the worst days of her training, the Fire Ordeal or the Ice Ordeal or the Hall of Spears. She tried to suck air into her body but it would not come. She could not see. Everything was red mist.

"You owe the queen your life."

Again and again Makho struck, and each time Nezeru thought she could take no more, that the next blow would separate her shrieking spirit from her agonized flesh forever. Somewhere near the end a great darkness bloomed in her head like one of the holy black flowers of Nakkiga's high meadows, filling everything, bringing silence, bringing blackness.

In dreams her mother Tzoja followed her through a lonely forest of dead trees and damp, dark earth, calling for her, but Nezeru did not want to be found.

Leave me alone! she wanted to shout. *You've cursed me with your mortal ways! With your weakness!*—but her mouth was full, and her limbs would not obey her. Earth. Her mouth was filled with earth. She was buried in the dirt and only the mortal woman who had brought her into the world still searched for her. But the weight of the heavy soil was too much, and even though Nezeru had changed her mind, even though she wanted now to be found, she could not move, could not speak, and her mother's voice grew ever more faint . . .

She woke in horrible, blazing pain to discover a weight on top of her. She tried to cry out, but a hand was over her mouth. A moment later, a stinging slap rocked back her head.

"Be quiet, halfblood! Would you disturb everyone's rest? We set out in the morning!"

It was Makho. For a moment, confused and in terrible pain, Nezeru continued to struggle. The chieftain dropped his hand from her mouth to her neck and squeezed until she stopped fighting, but kept his weight on top of her. She felt him untying the laces on her trews.

"Wh-what are you doing?"

"Having you." He yanked her clothing roughly down around her knees. "Do you think punishment means you escape your duty to your people?"

The pain was everywhere, each muscle and sinew shrieking as if they had been burned black. She could barely think, but she felt that if he took her now, it would kill her heart stone dead in her breast.

"No!" she gasped out. "You can't!"

"You tell me no?"

He slapped her again, but it was so much less than the pain of her wounds that she barely noticed.

"I could kill you for that—"

"No, Makho, it is . . . I am . . ." She could think of no other excuse, no other way to stop him. "I am with child. We dare not chance harming it."

His hand had been raised a third time, but now it halted in mid-air. His face was still contorted in a snarl. "With child? Do you tell the truth?"

It was too late to take back the lie now. "Yes."

"Why did you not say anything before?"

"I only knew it with certainty yesterday on the ship. I began to suspect when we were on the Island of Bones."

"You took twenty strokes of the serpent without telling me this? You risked the life of a new subject for the Mother of All?" He seemed to want to beat her again. "Selfish she-crow!"

"I did not think—it all happened so quickly . . ."

He grabbed her arms and yanked her up into a sitting position. He was not particularly rough, but sudden movement still brought agony from her wounds. "Is the child mine?"

Panic rolled over her like an avalanche. The deception had popped out of her mouth as quickly as the decision not to kill the fleeing boy on the mountainside, but the results would be just as long-lasting. *O Mother of the People, what am I becoming?* Still, she had no time to consider consequences: if she took too long answering, Makho would begin to doubt her story. "I . . . I think it must be, Hand Chieftain. I have coupled with no one else since we left Nakkiga during the last moon." Nor with anyone else for some time before that, she knew, but there was no reason to complicate things with too many details. *Even when you are forced to tell a lie,* her father had once said in a moment of unusual candor, *tell one that contains as much simple truth as possible, so you will have fewer invented details to recall later on.*

Nezeru realized that, almost by chance, she had chosen the one falsehood that could genuinely change her situation. Nakkiga's ancient laws had changed after the terrible losses they had suffered during the failed War of Return, and the Hikeda'ya now encouraged nobles to couple with mortals or halfbloods. The blood of mortals was more fertile than that of the immortals, somehow, and their offspring, even with a pureblood Hikeda'ya parent, reached maturity at a startlingly early age. Nezeru herself had solved Yedade's Box and begun her path through the Order of Sacrifice at an age when many true Hikeda'ya children were still infants, and she had reached a high level of achievement in her order when pureblood Norn children born the same year remained babes in arms. The one thing that all Hikeda'ya knew was that new births were a sacred necessity. Makho's ability to use her or even punish her had now been sharply curtailed, all to protect the children the Hikeda'ya so badly needed.

But there was no child.

"Dress yourself, Sacrifice," Makho told her. "Despite your punishment you may ride, not walk, but you still will do everything else your position demands and that I order."

"Of course, Hand Chieftain Makho."

He was clearly disappointed, but Nezeru didn't think it was only because he could not couple with her. "We set out when dawn touches the treetops, Sacrifice. Be ready—you will receive no special favors. The Hikeda'ya do not pamper those who breed our new Sacrifices, lest we create a generation of the weak." Then he walked back across the campsite, leaving her alone. She pulled her trews back up, then wrapped herself in her cloak and turned her back on the places where the others lay.

Now I am twice a liar, she thought, floundering in the enormity of her crimes. *If the truth of either of them is discovered, it will seal my execution.*

Despite having avoided the humiliation and agony of being taken against her will, Nezeru felt as though she had lost something unspeakably important. Tears filled her eyes for the first time since the habit had been driven from her in early childhood. She felt like a husk, like something left behind. She lay wretched and unsleeping for a long time afterward, unable to understand how her life had gone so badly astray.

Later, Nezeru could scarcely remember the first two days of riding after her session with the *hebi-kei.* The hours blurred into one long fever dream—in fact as well as in feeling, because a malady had gripped her in the night and would not let go. The trees swayed before her as if in a high wind, although she could scarcely feel a breeze. Her skin, especially on her back, felt as though red-hot ants swarmed across her. None of the others would speak to her, and though Makho might avoid harming her outright, he lived up to his promise of doing her no favors. Among the Hikeda'ya, pain and even death were small sacrifices compared to the greatest sacrifices of all, the queen's decision to leave first her home in the Garden, and then later to separate from the rest of her family, all for the good of her people. All Hikeda'ya knew that, for more than a hundred Great Years—many thousands of seasons as the fleeting mortals counted them—Queen Utuk'ku had survived the loss of both her husband and son, living on without them all these long years because the People needed their monarch, and that was the only measure by which suffering could be considered.

"Everything we have, we have because of our queen," her father had always told her. *"Just look at all the gifts she has given to me, and through me, to you. We owe her*

more than our lives. We owe her our very thoughts. Never doubt, she knows when you are not grateful and it disappoints her."

Nezeru had never actually seen Utuk'ku, who had been slumbering all her short life and had only recently awakened, but she had seen the queen in dreams and imagination a thousand times. In those dreams the queen's expressionless silver mask somehow seemed to convey her monarch's sadness better than a living face ever could—sadness at Nezeru's unfitness, her diluted heritage, her failures to hide her feelings properly and curb her temper. How much greater would Utuk'ku's sorrow be now, to see how the halfblood had failed her?

She left the Garden for us, her father often said. *The holy Garden. How can we give back to her anything less than all we have to give?*

"Makho says that I may clean your wounds," said Saomeji on the third night, when the Talons had finished their meager meal. "Will you let me see them?"

Nezeru was strangely reticent about showing herself to the Singer, not least because she could not guess whether he had some way to discover the lie she had told about carrying a child, although that was not the only thing about Saomeji that disturbed her. Perhaps her discomfort with him was because he was a halfblood like herself, but had *not* failed the Mother of All—a halfblood who had not lied to his chieftain, and who did not face shameful death several times over if the truth about him was discovered.

Reluctantly, she undid her jerkin. Though she removed it with great care, still it tugged at the healing skin of her back, each tug a knife stab. She threw the jerkin aside, but lifted her cloak to cover her breasts. Had she not felt so sick and so pained, Nezeru would have been sourly amused at her own modesty, something more befitting a lady of the Nakkiga court, some pampered noble, not a halfblood and certainly not a Sacrifice. The men and women of the Order of Sacrifice bathed together, ran naked in the snow together. Her body was only a weapon in the queen's service. How could she be modest about something that was not her own?

But somehow the nakedness that had felt wholesome in the order-house of Sacrifice felt different in front of this Singer. She could feel Saomeji's breath as he leaned close to examine her wounds. "Deep but healing," he said. "The bite of *hebi-kei* is cruel but clean." He sounded so matter-of-fact she could almost forget it was her own ruined flesh he spoke of until he dabbed at one of the weals with a dampened cloth and a bolt of hot misery crackled through her. She gasped and nearly dropped her cloak. "Ah," he said. "Still tender. But this must be done, Sacrifice Nezeru. My mentor taught me that a deep wound untended is a death unlooked-for. And it would be a shame for you to have come so far only to fall before we see the gates of home again."

After he had finished cleaning her wounds the halfblood Singer took something from inside his voluminous robe and removed the lid. "Ice moly," he said of the pale substance in the small bone pot. "Precious. It is my own."

"Why should you waste something precious on one such as me?" Saomeji had said nothing about the supposed child as he worked, so she guessed that Makho had not told him. It was doubtless safest just to assume so and remain silent, but she had asked the question without thinking.

"Why waste it on you?" said Saomeji. "Because I see something in you that intrigues me, Sacrifice Nezeru."

She did not want to share anything with him, not even conversation, and for the moment it was easy to avoid talking: as he rubbed the paste into the longest, deepest cut, Nezeru had to bite her lip to keep from crying out. If she thought cleaning the wounds had been painful, she had been a fool. The ice moly felt like a handful of gravel being rubbed into the fissures in her raw, oozing flesh. But after a few moments she felt a coolness there, where before she had felt only hot agony; it did not make the pain go away but pushed it to a slightly greater distance so that she could regard it with a more philosophical mind.

Saomeji was talking again. "I do not know many others who share my . . . encumbrance. Unlike Makho and these other purebloods, I spent my earliest childhood alone, without even the company of my fellow halfbloods. I suspect you did too. Perhaps we have things to share . . . even to teach each other."

Nezeru was having trouble concentrating on what he was saying. The soothing coolness in her back was making her realize how many hours, how many days that she had been forcing herself to take each step, to survive through the anguish of each moment. For the first time since the whipping she just wanted to let go and sleep. But what was he prattling on about? Was he offering some kind of friendship? What could it mean if he did?

"There, hand-sister—that should help." He tucked the little pot back into a hidden pouch in his white robe. "I will tell Makho that your wounds are healing. And perhaps you will think over what I said."

It was all too much, and suddenly the world and the night were pressing down on her like a great weight. Nezeru did not even pull her jerkin back on, but simply tugged her cloak around her and lay down on the cold, stony ground to sleep.

As they continued eastward along the base of the mountains the cold winds returned, scattering snow, and although the chill striking down from high peaks did nothing to relieve the ache of her wounds, Nezeru found that it helped in other ways. The swirling white felt like a curtain she could draw around herself, something to keep her thoughts private. She was glad, because those thoughts had grown strange.

She knew why she had lied about being with child—the idea of Makho forcing himself upon her when she was nearly dead from the whipping had been too much to bear. But she still could not say, even to herself, why she had hesitated to kill the young mortal on the island of bones. She had understood the danger as well as Makho himself, had known how much more difficult it would be to escape the island if the villagers were warned. And the child himself had almost certainly died anyway, along with most of the rest of his people, so her hesitation had accomplished nothing. And the most maddening part was that she had seen in that instant of hesitation all the likely consequences, seen them as clearly as if they had already come to pass. Yet she had not buried her knife in the fleeing boy's back.

Destroying those who would destroy you is your solemn duty as a Sacrifice. If laying down your life for our queen is a joy, how much better to take the lives of the queen's enemies? Nezeru had learned these lessons with her runes and numbers in her very first year at the order-house. She knew them as she knew her own name. But the first time the chance had come, she had bridled and failed. Why?

It is my blood. It must be. Somehow the mortal half, the part of me that is weakness and confusion, thwarted the better part.

It was not the anger of Makho and the others that filled her with shame, she saw now; it was the knowledge of her own impurity. It was the mortal in her, her mother's *shu'do-tkzayha* blood, the blood of thralls and slaves. Look at how that Black Rimmersman captain and his men had stood by while women and children of their own mortal race fell beneath the blades of the Hikeda'ya! Only a weakness in the blood could explain such cravenness, such cowardice. If her own family were attacked, Nezeru knew that she would fight until she was killed and die with her teeth in an enemy's throat. But how, then, had she failed to stop a single child to protect her people?

And now she had lied to her superior—a terrible, impious lie—simply to save herself discomfort. She had falsely promised to produce a child, a new subject for the queen, the thing the Hikeda'ya valued most. What madness had overtaken her?

I am at war with myself, she realized. *If I am to be the queen's woman, if I am to bring honor to the Order of Sacrifice, I must kill that weakness in my blood, that mortal weakness. It is the only way.*

It was a long trek back to Nakkiga through the hilly lands along the base of the mountains the Hikeda'ya called Shimmerspine and the mortals called the Whitefells. The Talons sheltered for one night in a sentry outpost of the Order of Sacrifice, a cavern hollowed deep into the stony hillside and almost impossible to see from the valley below. The warriors stationed there were on long detail, and thus strange to Nezeru—their service had begun long before she had received her sacred calling—but Makho and Kemme knew many of them, and spent the evening drinking the quicksilver liquor called *analita,* and Ibi-Khai was closeted with the fort's chief of Echoes for hours. Even Saomeji spent a brief time with his order counterparts, although as with most of their kind, Singers were solitary by nature, so the conversation did not last long. Only Nezeru found herself completely alone, but after what had happened on the island she felt no desire for fellowship and telling tales. She was also certain many of the tales would be about her, so she found herself a spot far from the sounds of conversation and did her best to rest.

In the morning, Nezeru thought that their Sacrifice hosts were looking at her differently: every Hikeda'ya soldier of the outpost, whose path crossed hers, seemed to examine her with interest, although with some it seemed more like contempt. She was shamed anew: she had little doubt that Makho and Kemme had told them of her failure and her punishment, and although her wounds were finally healed enough for her to move with some of her old grace, it felt as though everyone could see them through her garb. She could not help wondering if Makho had told them about the child she claimed to carry as well. Her belly would never grow, but her lies felt larger with each passing day, her crimes harder to hide.

"We have new orders," Ibi-Khai informed them when Makho had gathered the Talons in preparation for leaving. "They were passed to the Chief Echo here in the sentry post, with my Magister's binding truth-word to prove them. We are not to go back to Nakkiga, but instead we are ordered to take Hakatri's bones to Bitter Moon Castle."

All the Talons were surprised by this change in plans, and none were happy, especially not Makho, who Nezeru felt sure had been looking forward to a triumphant return to Nakkiga, not a trip to an isolated border fortress. Still, any message authenticated by the High Magister of the Order of Echoes came with the implied authority of Queen Utuk'ku herself, so all the Talons' faces were cloaked in respect. Only Saomeji dared to show anything else, and his look was close to triumphant. As they made their way out of the fortified cavern, past the files of armored and helmeted Hikeda'ya soldiers, he leaned close to Nezeru, his golden eyes bright, and said, "It seems my masters have snatched this triumph from the lords of your order."

She did not know what he meant, but she wanted no more to do with him than was strictly necessary, so she did not ask.

After leaving the outpost, Makho's hand rode on fresh horses for several days through the mounting snows, following a more southerly route than they would have, until at last, on a morning when the sky was clear, they saw Bitter Moon Castle on the horizon. The fortress was a squat mass of granite at the top of Dragon's Throat Pass, built in the days of Hikeda'ya power to watch over one of the most important routes in and out of Nakkiga. The Talons had a hard climb up narrow, winding paths to get there, and Nezeru was not the only one whose body ached by the time they reached the top of the pass and the great cleared area in front of the castle walls.

To her astonishment, as they approached the forbidding structure, its gates swung open and a great procession moved out onto the plain toward them, a hundred Sacrifices or more, a few riding but most marching to the rhythm of muffled drumbeats. The troop was led by something Nezeru could not quite make sense of, a massive sledge pulled across the snow by a team of panting wolves. A huge, cloth-covered bundle the size of a small cottage was lashed to the sledge.

Makho signaled the rest of the Talons to stop and wait. This was clearly no ordinary greeting party. Nezeru wondered what might be on the sledge. Was it meant for them?

The odd procession came to a halt before them, but a single white-robed rider continued forward on a tall, ice-white horse. As this figure neared, a sensation of helplessness swept over Nezeru, a terror stranger and more subtle than anything she had ever felt—like Saomeji's ice moly, but chilling thoughts instead of wounds. She sank to her knees in the snow, waiting for the tall shape to dispose of her in whatever way it chose; within moments, the other members of the hand, even Makho the chieftain, had done the same.

"Where is the Singer of this hand of Talons?" asked the hooded rider in a voice like the scraping of ice on stone. Given time, Nezeru felt sure such a voice could reduce a mountain to rubble.

"Here! I am your humble minion, great Lord of Song." Saomeji hurried forward to abase himself before the rider. "It is my joy to live and die for you and our queen, Master."

"Pretty words," said the rider. "Perhaps you shall have the opportunity to do both, and sooner than you think. Do you have the bones, little Singer? Hakatri's precious bones?"

"I have carried them all this way."

Makho stood up, although Nezeru thought he might have stumbled a little in his haste, which was astonishing in itself. "Here! By what right do you seize the queen's prize?"

At his movement several Hikeda'ya soldiers from the front of the procession stepped toward the Talons, pikes lowered, but the smallest movement of the white rider's hand stopped them. "By what right?" the tall figure said. "Child of our long exile, I *am* that right." He reached up a white-gloved hand and pushed back his hood. Nezeru's heart skipped and barely righted itself.

"Lord Akhenabi!" Makho's voice was squeezed and faint. He fell back onto his knees and pushed his face against the snow. "Magister, I did not know it was you! I beg your forgiveness. I did not know . . .!"

Nezeru could only stare as her heart fluttered and bumped in her chest like a trapped thing. Akhenabi! She felt her skin tighten, her hackles rise. The High Magister of the House of Song was a figure of terrifying legend among the Hikeda'ya, the queen's closest confidant and counselor. One of the first born in this land after the Eight Ships had arrived from the lost Garden, the great magician had been a power in Nakkiga since longer than any but Utuk'ku and a few other ancients could remember.

And like the queen, the Lord of Song went always masked. All the Hikeda'ya's first generations wore masks by tradition, but Akhenabi's was the strangest Nezeru had ever seen, made of a thin, pale material that clung to his face and neck so closely that it mimicked the movements beneath. Only his eyes, the holes of his nostrils, and his mouth showed through, but the mask clung so closely to those that it might have been a second skin.

Akhenabi turned back to kneeling Saomeji. "You. Bring the bones to me."

The Singer carried the bundle forward with careful, reverent steps, then kneeled beside Akhenabi's stirrup and lifted it high in the air. Akhenabi reached down his long arm for it, then unwrapped the cloth in which the bones were shrouded. His masked face did not change or show any emotion, but Nezeru thought she could feel the satisfaction beating out from him like the heat of a fire.

"So. You have done well." The Lord of Song turned his masked face to Makho and the rest of the Queen's Talons. "So well that the Mother of All has gifted you with a new quest—a second vital task. You should be very proud."

Makho took a moment to speak. "Of course we are proud, great one. Serving the queen is everything to us. But may we know what this task is?"

"Your own Echo has been told what is needed," rasped the Lord of Song. "The knowledge has already been placed in his head, and he will lead you where you must go, Hand Chieftain. To your eternal honor, you are given this service by the Queen herself." He paused and nodded, as if savoring something. "You and your hand are to find a living dragon and bring it back. Our queen has a use for its blood, but the beast must be alive when we take that blood."

"A *living* dragon?" Makho was clearly astonished, but with a visible effort of will, he mastered himself. "Are we not to return to Nakkiga first, Magister?"

"Did I not say this is the queen's wish? Do you question me?" The angry scrape of Akhenabi's voice made Nezeru tremble though she was not its target.

"No, great one!" Makho bowed his head, but the chieftain had never lacked for courage, and there was still a sign of stubborn resistance in the straightness of his back. "It is just that I had planned on our return, so I could deliver one of my Talons for discipline. She nearly compromised our retrieval of the bones. How can I trust her with this new task?"

Akhenabi's masked face turned to the rest of the hand where they kneeled behind Makho, and lit on Nezeru with a chilly finality she could feel in her innards. "You," he said. "Come to me."

Her heart seemed to be racing downhill now. It was nearly impossible to make her legs work, worse even than the first day after her whipping. When she managed to get her feet beneath her at last, she staggered forward and then sank to her knees once more, staring at the horse's slate-colored hooves instead of at the Lord of Song.

"Look up, Sacrifice. Look at me."

She did, and had to restrain a sound of startled horror. Akhenabi's mask was not simply draped over his face, she now saw, but had been stitched at the eyes and mouth and nostrils with tiny knots—stitched, she felt sure, to his very skin. The pearly, translucent mask itself was painted with runes almost as small as the knots, faint silvery letters she could not read, symbols that only showed when the starlight fell on them at an angle, so that as the Lord of Song examined her, they appeared and disappeared across his cheeks and forehead.

"No, my eyes," he demanded. "Look into my eyes."

She did not want to—by her oath and her death-song, she did not want to!—but she could not resist that harsh, powerful voice. Her gaze met his. For a moment the dark wells of the magician's eyes seemed to grow smaller, until they were no larger than the puncture a bone needle would make, but at the same time Nezeru felt herself falling forward into them as though they were gaping holes in a dangerous, icy pond.

For an instant she tumbled helplessly into that darkness, then the magician's empty black eyes were somehow *inside her* instead, digging carelessly through her thoughts. Everywhere they roamed she lay naked and unprotected, as if some great pair of hands held her and touched her in any way their owner wished. Her lies, her treacherous, cowardly thoughts, even the corrupt flow of her mortal blood—Nezeru was certain that the Lord of Song could see them all. She could hide nothing.

At last, Akhenabi turned from her, and she toppled forward into the snow, limp and barely sensible, resigned to death.

"There is no need to return her to Nakkiga," the Lord of Song declared. "She will suffice for what comes next."

Nezeru was astounded. How could the great Akhenabi not have seen her deepest secrets? But he *had* seen them, she was certain—she had felt the subtle, inhuman touch of his curiosity push in wherever it wished. So why was she not being punished?

"But, great lord," protested Makho, "—a living dragon? How will a single hand, even of Queen's Talons, manage to capture and bring back such a creature? Hakatri, whose bones we have brought to you, was one of the greatest of the Zida'ya, but the worm Hidohebhi burned him unto death."

"So you would say five of our kind cannot equal the deeds of one of the Zida'ya?" Akhenabi hissed, and his voice was like the crack of the *hebi-kei*. Makho tried to meet his eye but could only hold that dark gaze for a split-instant. "You let fear of failure make you a coward, Hand Chieftain. But the queen herself demands your success, and Utuk'ku is always generous. She has sent you a gift to help you complete your task." Akhenabi raised his hand again and the wolf-team drivers whipped their animals up onto their feet and drove them forward. The great sledge creaked and groaned for a moment, frozen in place, then the ice cracked and the huge runners slid across the ground until it reached Akhenabi and his white horse.

"Give Chieftain Makho the goad," Akhenabi ordered. One of the sledge's drivers came forward and handed Makho a rod of bright vermillion crystal. "Now take up the goad, Hand Chieftain." The Lord of Song spoke as though enacting some ritual only he knew. "Wait until you feel it warm in your hand, then say the word 'Awaken'."

Makho stared at him for a moment, then at the sledge and the covered mound tied at the center of it. He lifted the crystal rod. *"Awaken."*

For a moment, nothing happened. Then the ropes on the sledge began to rustle and creak as they were pulled tighter. One of them snapped with a report that made even Makho start. Then a second broke, then a third, and the covered mass began to quiver. Now the great wolves harnessed to the sledge all began to moan, loud, whining noises of unease. An instant later the heavy tent-cloth ripped like parchment and fell away as the thing on the sledge rose, trailing broken ropes that seemed no larger than spiderwebs.

Even Saomeji was surprised—Nezeru heard him murmuring beneath his breath. It sounded like prayers.

The giant crouched, blinking. It was by far the biggest of its kind that Nezeru had ever seen, nearly twice the height of mortals or Hikeda'ya, covered in grayish-white fur except for its jut-browed face, which was hairless and covered in leathery, dark gray skin. A wide gray ring of witchwood encircled the beast's neck.

"Look! Do you see the yoke he wears?" asked Akhenabi. "The queen herself put it on him. It binds him to the service of the one who holds the goad. But use it sparingly or he will become inured to the pain and difficult to master."

The giant looked blearily from side to side. It hunched its shoulders and growled so loudly and deeply that the watching Hikeda'ya twisted in discomfort at the sheer power of it. The beast then leaped down from the sled, landing so hard Nezeru felt the ground shudder. The wolves began to howl with redoubled excitement and terror.

"Bind him to your will!" Akhenabi almost sounded amused. "Bind him quickly, Hand Chieftain, or he will tear you apart!"

"How?" shouted Makho.

"Hold the goad firmly! Think of your hands closing on his neck. Think of choking him as you tell him what you want." Now Akhenabi actually laughed, a terrible, scraping sound. "Or be sure the monster will kill you all!"

"Stop, giant!" shouted Makho. He thrust the rod toward the creature. "Down on your knees."

The giant growled, the sound so low that it made Nezeru's heart bounce behind her ribs, but it did not otherwise move.

"Down!" cried Makho.

The creature groaned and clawed at its neck, but after a moment sank slowly to its knees, massive, black-nailed hands flexing in frustration.

"He is Goh Gam Gar, oldest of his kind," said Akhenabi. "He is your new companion—although I doubt he will be your friend. Now go, and bring back the blood of a dragon. The Queen of the World awaits your success."

15

Atop the Holy Tree

It was a warm day out and a hard climb up hundreds
of narrow steps, but Lord Chancellor Pasevalles considered it well worth the
trouble.

I am like a cat, he thought with quiet amusement. *Always happiest when I can
perch in some high place and look down on everything else.*

He stepped out onto the top of the Tower of the Holy Tree, and his troubled
mind was immediately soothed by the cool air swirling in from the Kynslagh.
He put his back to the morning sun and peered down from the western side of
the tower, but other than an assortment of castle livestock grazing on the green
and castle-folk going about their assorted employments there was little to see.
He wondered what those curiously foreshortened men and women would think
if they knew they were being watched from on high. Then another thought
came to him: *Is this what God sees from his high heaven? No wonder He cares so little
for us. We are scuttling things.*

After a while the sun slipped behind some clouds. Shrouded from the glare,
his sweat from the climb now dried, Pasevalles began to walk the rectangular
tower-top, something he did whenever he could find the chance, in search of
that catlike feeling of peace. Holy Tree Tower had been built in the years after
the Storm King's War, when the Hayholt's two tallest structures had both become useless. Hjeldin's Tower—the squat, brooding cylinder of stone he looked
down on now—had been sealed up at the order of the king and queen, and
Green Angel Tower, which had soared far above everything else, had collapsed
in the final hours of the struggle. A castle without a tower was like a rich man
without eyes, a target for thieves and bandits, and so a new tower had been
constructed against the wall of the Inner Keep, a high place where sentries
could stand and look over the innermost lands of the king's and queen's protection—the heart of the High Ward.

Pasevalles gazed at the secretive mass of Hjeldin's Tower, its premises forbidden to all for many years. Then he continued along the tower battlements until
he could look down on the spot where mighty Green Angel Tower had once
stretched to the sky. *What a thing it must have been,* he thought, *to have stood atop*

it—twice this height or more!—and looked out across the world. No cat, no matter how ambitious, could be displeased with such a perch!

Even the rubble of Green Angel Tower was long gone, hauled off to rebuild the ruined parts of the castle after the last, dreadful battle; all that had remained for many years were the faint marks of its foundations. Now even those were gone, the ground filled and leveled, and foundations laid for a new hall that would become the royal library. Lord Tiamak thought a monument to learning would be a fitting use for the place where the Storm King had almost managed to tear open the world and turn it inside out, but Pasevalles was not so sure.

Learning itself cannot stop destruction or repair its ravages, he thought, suddenly caught up in old sorrows. *It can only make certain that you understand how much you have truly lost.*

He straightened, stretched. Those were not the kind of thoughts he wished to have now. He had carefully, deliberately put those bad days in the past and turned his back on them. He had work to do now—a kingdom to care for.

He heard footsteps and voices. The sentries, whom he had sent off to find themselves a drink and a late morning meal, were climbing the stairs back to their posts. Pasevalles took a long breath and tasted rain coming. The king and queen would be back in a few weeks and there was much to do.

Still, he regretted having to descend the stairs, not because of the wearying journey, but because he hated leaving the quiet and isolation of the heights. He had not realized before how lonely it was to rule a kingdom, as he had been doing in the royal couple's absence. And it was lonelier still when you were surrounded by the voices and faces of all the people that wanted something from you.

"God give you good day, Lord Chancellor!" said the first sentry onto the tower top. His beard was shiny with butter, and crumbs were caught in the sleeves of his hauberk. "Did you have yourself a breath of fresh air?" The second one climbed up behind the first, then they both turned toward him and clutched their pikes in formal salute.

"I did," Pasevalles said, smiling. "Enjoy the view, men. You do not know it, but you have a better job than mine."

As he stepped into the stairwell, he saw the two sentries exchange puzzled looks.

Pasevalles had climbed many more steps by the time he reached the residence hall of the Inner Bailey and the bedchamber where he had installed the wounded Sitha. He was given no time to rest, though: instead of the sentry who should have been standing guard at the door, two frightened chambermaids huddled there, faces pale as cooked fish, and he could hear men shouting beyond the door. He drew his knife and hurried forward.

"What has happened?" he demanded.

One of the maids said, "Oh, my lord, she is awake—and angry!"

He sprang past her and threw open the door to discover the even more surprising spectacle of Brother Etan and an armored Erkynguard wrestling with a naked woman. "What is the meaning of this?" Pasevalles shouted.

Brother Etan had several long scratches on his face, and blood dripped from his chin. "She woke and attacked me!" He struggled to keep the Sitha's long nails from scoring him again. "Help us, your Lordship! By my vow, she is ungodly strong!"

The guardsman had his arms around the woman's slender waist and was doing his best to hold her down on the bed while she slapped at his helmeted head. Etan had managed to catch one of her arms, so Pasevalles threw himself forward and caught the other. The monk was right—the woman, who had seemed nearly dead only a couple of days earlier, was astonishingly strong, and the sweat that coated her limbs made it difficult to find and hold a grip. At last Pasevalles pushed her arm down onto the mattress and lay atop it, but he could still feel her pulling and twisting beneath him like some powerful serpent of the far southern swamps.

"Lady!" he cried. "Lady! You are among friends! Stop fighting us! We will not hurt you!"

He turned his head sideways to see her better, and was nearly rewarded with the loss of his nose as she bit at him savagely, her teeth snapping shut only a thumb's width from his face. "Redeemer save us, is she mad?" he shouted.

"Does it matter?" croaked Etan. The collar of his robe had been pushed halfway over his face so that he seemed to have shrunk to the size of a child. "Mad, sane, either way she is fierce. Call more guards!"

But the Sitha, as though Pasevalles' words had traveled to her slowly, over a long distance, at last began to calm. He risked another look and saw her head sag back and her astounding golden eyes roll up beneath the lids. She went limp then, and for a moment all four of them, three good sized men and one slender woman, lay on the bed, struggling for air together.

Pasevalles felt something wet, and rolled a little to the side to see what it was. "By the Aedon, this is blood! Everywhere! Etan, is this all yours?"

The monk groaned. "It feels like it, Lord Steward, but I fear it's hers. She has reopened the wounds I stitched closed. May God help us, we must close them or she will bleed to death."

Pasevalles loosened his grip on her arm to see whether she would resume her struggle, but her pale golden face and limbs had gone slack. He sat up. "Get something to tie her down," he told the guard. "Not rope, something softer. The ties from those curtains." He watched the guardsman hesitate in front of the window, taking off his helmet to peer at the window fittings like a cow ordered to jump a tall fence. "God curse it, man, don't stare!" Pasevalles cried. "Rip them down!"

The soldier returned with an expression of deep unease on his perspiring face and a curtain tie in each hand. Pasevalles snatched them from him and, although she was no longer resisting, tied the Sitha's ankles to the footboard of the bed, pulling the makeshift ropes tight before knotting them. Brother Etan tilted the upper half of her body onto its side so he could examine her bleeding wounds. She seemed quite insensible now, but Pasevalles was not going to rely on this strange creature, who only looked like a mortal woman, to remain passive for very long, so he sent the bemused guard for ties from the chamber's other set of curtains, then used one to bind her wrists together before dismissing the guard back to his post. The large man all but ran from the room, giving one last wide-eyed look before closing the door.

Pasevalles would have preferred to tie both the Sitha's arms separately, as he had done with her legs, but he did not want to interfere with Brother Etan, who was stanching the blood still seeping from her wounds. He sat on the floor and held her bound wrists instead. "What do you think?"

"Think? I think I know nothing about the Fair Folk, Lord Steward. She has lost much blood." The monk shook his head. "As have I! But she had lost far more before she came here, and she survived that."

Her nakedness was disconcerting—in repose she looked much like an ordinary, slender young woman. Pasevalles was about to reach down and pull the coverlet up over her lower body when the Sitha-woman's eyes fluttered open again. For a moment, they seemed to rove unfixed, then they narrowed. She tried to fling herself off the bed again, but was hindered by her bound ankles and only succeeded in bucking off Etan, who tumbled onto the floor on the far side of the bed and cracked his head against the stone flags so loudly that Pasevalles could hear it. Meanwhile, it was all Pasevalles could do to hold onto the curtain tie knotted around her wrists. She cried out in what he guessed was her Sithi tongue, but the stream of rapid, fluid sound meant nothing to him.

"Lady!" he cried again, as Etan slowly crawled back onto the bed, a red lump already showing itself above his eye, "Lady, stop! We will not hurt you! You have been wounded, and you must not fight us!"

It took a moment, but he saw something like understanding pass over her, and her features softened, but she still fought against the restraints.

"Where . . . where are they?" she said in perfectly understandable Westerling. "Where are my things?"

"Things? Lady, stop fighting, we mean you nothing ill. Do you mean your saddle bags? We brought them with you. Here! Brother Etan, they are in the corner. Bring them to her!"

The monk half ran, half stumbled to the corner, holding his head as though it might come off if he let go. He found the white leather bags and carried them to her. She snatched them away and began to paw through them despite her wrists being tied together. Pasevalles had gone through the bags himself when she had first been brought here, and knew that other than a few small tools, a roll of very strong twine wound from fine hairs, and a carved wooden bowl, they did not contain much. He also could not avoid the sight of her nakedness without looking away altogether, and although Brother Etan had done just that, Pasevalles felt a kind of fascination.

The Sitha was slender, long-backed and narrow-hipped, but firm muscles moved beneath her smooth, evenly golden skin, and Pasevalles knew as well as anyone could what strength was in them. Her tangled hair was silvery, wet with perspiration and blood. Her face, subtly different from a mortal's, tilted oddly at cheek, forehead, and chin so that it seemed almost feline. She might have been some heathen goddess of the hunt, running unclothed beneath the moon at the front of a savage pack. Had she been a mortal woman, he would have guessed her to be less than two dozen summers old.

He was staring at her small breasts, Pasevalles realized. He felt a sudden clutch of confusion and looked away.

"It is not here!" the Sitha suddenly wailed. "Is this all you found? Where is Spidersilk? Have you seen him?" Some blood was dribbling anew from the wound in her chest, and Etan was trying to stanch it with a cloth.

"Spidersilk? Who is that? You were alone when we found you. We thought you dead," said Pasevalles.

"My horse! Where is he?"

"We found no horse. The bags were hung willy-nilly, half-hidden in a bush. Doubtless the horse ran and they caught there."

She swayed, then dropped the bags as suddenly as if they had caught fire. She looked at Pasevalles and her eyes again were unfixed and confused. He could see that she was now struggling to remain upright. "Was there . . . did . . . was there aught else?"

"No, my lady. But we will search again, if you tell me only what you have lost."

She sank back onto the bed and drew one forearm over her eyes, as if she no longer wished to see what surrounded her. "No . . . I must go there . . ."

"You are in no fit shape for that." Pasevalles waved to Etan to resume binding her wounds. He reached out himself and pulled the coverlet up from the floor and draped it across her lower limbs, then pulled it up to her collarbone, and felt a kind of relief when he had done so. Her damp skin seemed to glow like honey in the bright noon light that blazed through the uncurtained windows.

She said something in her own tongue that he could not understand; her voice had become heavy and slow as syrup. She opened her mouth to speak again, but instead her head rolled to one side and her eyes closed.

Pasevalles stared. "Is she . . .?"

"She still lives, God be praised," said Etan. "But she has cruelly tired herself—and me, too, I must say, not to mention nearly breaking my skull. I will bind the wounds again."

"When you've finished, I will watch her for a while in case she wakes," Pasevalles says. "You must rest. But first, I will beg a favor of you. It is something I was to do myself, but I have not the heart."

Brother Etan looked as though he would have preferred to be released without more duties, but he only nodded and, from somewhere in his deep weariness, pulled up a smile. "Of course, Lord Steward."

The monk was a patient old soul in a young body. Pasevalles decided he would remember that. "You have my gratitude, Brother. You must go and wash yourself first, though—tend your wounds and put on something less blood-spattered, too. The lady to whom I am sending you, you will not have to fight with." He laughed, despite his own great weariness. "Or at least, not the kind of fight we have just had. But she may be less than sweet when she finds I have sent you in my place."

"As long as she keeps her nails to herself," said Etan, "I will thank God and be content." He began wearily gathering up his medicaments, which had been scattered widely about the chamber, but stopped to ask, "What of the Sitha lady's possessions, from her saddle bag?"

"I will gather up those," Pasevalles said. "You have done enough here, Brother."

His knock echoed for a while. Brother Etan waited, then knocked again. At last, a pretty young woman opened the door.

"Her Highness is expecting you," she said, but she looked as if he was anything but what had actually been expected.

Etan followed her in. The retiring room was handsomely appointed, draped from high ceilings to floor in tapestries depicting the famous tale of Sir Tallistro of Perdruin; it was many times the size of Etan's own cell in the monk's dormitory at St. Sutrin's. Princess Idela sat in a tall chair beneath one of the windows with her sewing on her lap. The sun touched her red hair and made it seem almost a fiery halo.

"Your Highness," Etan said, getting down on his knees and touching his shaved head nearly to the floor. "Your pardon, but Lord Pasevalles said that you sought advice on some books belonging to the late prince, your husband. I am Brother Etan."

"Very kind of you, Brother. I know you—I have seen you about the palace." But she did not look entirely pleased by the chance to meet him. "And how is our lord chancellor? Not ill, I trust?"

"No, Princess. Only weary from a long day's labors and with still more duties before him. But he was anxious to send help to you as soon as possible, even if he could not come himself."

"Lord Pasevalles is too kind." Her tone suggested otherwise. "Will you have some wine, Brother?"

Etan hesitated. "Ordinarily I would thank you but decline, my lady. Today, I think, I will take up your kindly offer. The Lord will forgive me, I hope."

She signaled to one of her ladies. "Then be seated, please." As Etan turned to look for a suitable chair, the princess saw the raw, red marks on his cheek for the first time. "Merciful Elysia! Surely those are fresh wounds on your face! Are you badly hurt, Brother? What happened?"

He reached his hand up to his scratches. In the strangeness of being sent to the mother of the heir, he had forgotten them. "Oh! Nothing of import, Your Highness. An ill woman I was treating became confused and violent."

She gave him a shrewd look, perhaps guessing that Pasevalles' absence might have something to do with the patient in question. "I'll have one of my ladies tend those, by your leave."

"Oh, they are truly nothing to worry about."

"Still." She signaled to a dark-haired woman, who put down her sewing and left the room. "Begga is skilled in healing—she trained with a northern *valada*-woman. Ah, here is the wine."

As the young woman brought in the tray, cups, and ewer, then filled them, Etan watched the princess. Poised and upright in her dark green gown, Idela had beautifully smooth, pale skin, and delicate hands and wrists to go with her slender, pretty face. A sprinkling of freckles on her nose and bosom had been obscured by powder, but the heat of the day rendered the disguise less effective.

Etan realized he was staring at the creamy expanse of flesh above her bodice and felt himself flush. Idela gave no sign she had noticed, except what might have been the wisp of a smile at the corner of her mouth.

"Let us drink the health of the king and queen," she said.

"And their safe return." Etan took what he hoped was a dignified sip, and was astonished at how many flavors he could taste. This was certainly not the sour stuff he and his brothers drank at the refectory table on feast nights, nor the over-sweetened Nabbanai sack he had occasionally shared at the archbishop's table. He took another, longer swallow.

"Ah, here is Begga," the princess said. "Loosen your cowl, Brother. It is a privilege to give aid to a man of God."

Already the young Rimmerswoman was running her cool fingers on his cheek, gently touching the long scratches. To cover a new rush of heat to his face, Etan took another drink. "My lady is too kind."

"Nonsense. I wish we could help Lord Pasevalles as well. You said he has had a wearying day."

"I think every day for him is wearying, Highness. His responsibilities are great, especially in the absence of the king and queen."

"Ah, yes. I miss them both so." She sipped from her own cup, and her tongue came out for a moment to take a drop left on her lower lip. When she noticed him looking, she smiled shyly. The young Rimmerswoman was rubbing something onto Etan's cheek, and the sting was strangely mixed with a growing chill where the skin had been scraped. "And my dear son Morgan, of course," Idela said. "God grant that he comes back safe as well."

"We all keep him in our prayers, Highness. Always. And your daughter, too. Surely it is some comfort to have Princess Lillia with you."

"Lillia? Yes, certainly." But this seemed to distract her. "May I ask you a question, Brother? Do you know Lord Pasevalles well?"

"Well? I would not say so, Highness. I sometimes help him with some minor matters." But as he said it, Etan thought that sounded small and foolish, as though he were the sweeper of the Lord Chancellor's chambers. "I have some gift with numbers and letters. Lord Chamberlain Jeremias calls on me from time to time as well."

"I am certain he does. A man of learning is a jewel whose sparkle pleases many, even if he belongs only to God." She smiled, and this time it was full and broad. "Tell me a little about Pasevalles, though. He is always so busy; I have scarcely had a chance to speak with him in all the years I have been here. I'm told he is a very good man."

"Oh, yes, Highness. So everyone says, and so I have found it myself." He thought of the events of only an hour past, Pasevalles struggling to preserve the life of a woman that some would look on as a treacherous, uncanny danger, no matter the fondness the royal couple were said to have for the Sithi. "He is a good man."

"But his life, it has been hard, has it not? I have heard stories."

"I do not know the tales, Highness," he said with less than complete candor. Etan was beginning to feel as though something was going on that he did not understand, and he also realized that the wine had gone to his head, making everything in the room seem to bend toward him, including Princess Idela's fine green eyes, fixed attentively on his. Also, the dark-haired woman Begga was still dabbing soothing unguent on his face, a strange mixture of pain and pleasure which made Etan shiver. "Truly, my lady, I am a dull tool to discover the lord steward's history. I can claim no special knowledge, except of his kindness." He forced himself to sit straighter. Begga at last ended her ministrations, and at a signal from her mistress, packed up her jars and took her basket out of the room. "But it is op . . . opportune that you mention history." He swallowed the last of his wine without thinking, then suppressed a wince when the princess directed that it be filled again. Etan swore to himself he would drink no more, no matter how good it was. *God hates drunkards*, he reminded himself, *because they make themselves beasts in His eyes, rejecting His most precious gifts*. "Lord Pasevalles tells me that you have some books of your late husband's and seek some advice on their worth."

She looked amused by his attempt to rally himself. "Ah, you are a dutiful servant of your lords, both temporal and divine, Brother Etan."

While he picked his way through this compliment, she rose and, with a gesture he did not see, dismissed her maids from the room. "Come with me then, Brother. I see that you are one of those excellent, frustrating men who cannot rest while a task remains undone. No wonder you are one of God's chosen workers."

He wished it were entirely so, but he felt uncomfortably certain the faint sheen of perspiration on Princess Idela's breastbone and the sway of her walk as she led him into the next room would never so easily distract a soul whose only thought was to serve God.

Frailty, thou art Man, he told himself, quoting St. Agar. *Distraction, thou art*

Woman. To his dismay, he discovered he was still carrying his recently filled wine cup.

"In here, Brother," she said. "I had a few of the newer ones brought to me. In my husband's old chamber, his study, there are dozens more, many of them close to ruin simply from age, and I feared to move them. But I would also like to keep at least a few to remember my dear John Josua."

"Of course, Lady." He could not help noticing that none of the ladies-in-waiting had followed them into the intimate chamber, clearly the princess's dressing-room, as the one table held a standing mirror and an array of jewelry boxes. The room was paneled in velvet, so that it felt as though he was being cradled in soft gloves.

His face felt warm again. He started to take another sip, then thought better of it.

"There." She gestured to a chest set against the wall, with a woven Hernystiri blanket thrown over it, perhaps so it could be used as a seat. "Please see if any of them should be given to the great library Lord Tiamak is building in my husband's name. I know nothing of such things, and can read scarcely any of them. Most are in Nabbanai, but some are in writing such as I have never seen." She shuddered. "I told my dear John Josua he closed himself too much away in dark rooms with old words. But it was his joy, God preserve him."

"God preserve him," Etan echoed, then knelt down beside the chest. He was finding himself a bit clumsy; it took him long moments to fold the cloth neatly and set it aside, and his fumbling movements were made worse by the knowledge that the slender princess was standing behind him, watching. He worked the clasp open and lifted the lid.

The chest was indeed full of books, a dozen or more, although at first glance he saw nothing much older than perhaps a century or two, and most were much more recent, a random assembly of history and old romances from what he could see, Anitulles' *Battles*, *The Tales of Sir Emettin*, and others just as unexceptional. Etan himself owned a well-thumbed copy of *A True History of the Erkynlandish People*, and while it was nothing like this edition, bound in calfskin and its pages copiously illustrated, the words were no different. Thus the great truth first proposed by Vaxo of Harcha: *"Even the rich and noble cannot read words that have not been written, and the poor man who can read may sup on those that are written just as well as a prince . . ."*

Then Etan saw something at the bottom of the chest that made him pause. He moved the copy of Plesinnen that covered it, then lifted it out. Its binding was blackened and cracked with age. For a long moment, as he gently opened it, he did not believe, and his thoughts bounced wildly in his head like a spilled basket of hazelnuts.

I am drunk, he thought. *Surely I am drunk and seeing things that are not there.*

But there it was, written in careful script across the first page in archaic Nabbanai letters, *Tractit Eteris Vocinnen*—"A Treatise On The Aetheric Whispers." It had to be a mistake—no, a trick, some kind of counterfeit. Etan had only heard of one copy of Fortis' infamous book, and that was held deep in the bowels of the Sancellan Aedonitis, under the jealous eyes of the censor-priests. How could there be a copy here in the Hayholt, as if it were merely another courtly love-poem or a disquisition on the best use of arable land?

The fumes of wine fled him as if blown away by a sharp winter wind. Etan's hands were shaking; he did his best to hide it by closing the book. "This one is of some interest, Princess, and some of the rest may also be. I will confer with my superiors, if you will permit me to take this with me. Since it was your husband's, God rest him, I shall guard it with my life."

She waved her hand carelessly. The princess almost seemed disappointed, as if she had been hoping for more from his reaction. "As you see fit, Brother. It is all meaningless to me. Of course you may take it."

"Please take good care of them all, Highness." His heart was beating very fast. The book in his hands seemed as heavy as marble. "At least until I have a chance to talk to others who know old books better than I do. And perhaps it would be useful at some point to examine the rest of his collection as well."

"Of course. And if they are of some value, perhaps Lord Pasevalles would like to see them, too. Feel free to bring him with you next time."

"Thank you, Highness. It could be some of these will be a boon to the scholars who will one day flock to use your husband's library." The princess's pale skin and strong wine, her pretty, laughing ladies, the cool fingers on his cheek, none of them meant anything to Etan at this moment. He made his farewells as quickly and graciously as he could and left her, the book clutched against his chest.

As he hurried down the corridor, it felt almost as if he held a burning hot coal to his chest instead of an old book—this infamous, dark thing, banned by Mother Church and spoken of in hushed tones by scholars for hundreds of years, and now it was clutched in his own hand! Could it be true? Who could he tell? The archbishop? He would not dare bring such a thing to him—Gervis was a good, pious man who would order the whole chest full of books burned without further exploration, simply to protect the faithful. And Master Tiamak was still several sennights from returning to the castle. But could Etan keep it secret so long? Who else could be trusted?

More important, he wondered, would God Himself understand and forgive Etan's fascination? Or was he holding not just a book, but his own damnation?

16

A Layer of Fresh Snow

"Why should I?" Morgan couldn't look directly at her. When he was angry in front of her this way he felt like a child again, foolish and irresponsible, and that only made him more angry. "Grandfather doesn't want me there."

"Well, *I* want you there," the queen told him. "That should be enough." She blew on her fingers to warm them. Seeing his grandmother's red, cold hands, Morgan was unhappy with both her and himself, although he was not sure why.

After they had left Elvritshalla to begin their trip home, a spring blizzard had forced the royal progress off the road south, so for the moment they were guests at Blarbrekk Castle, the home of Jarl Halli and his family. The jarl was still in Elvritshalla because of Isgrimnur's funeral and Grimbrand's succession, but Halli's daughter and servants had welcomed the king and queen in their lord's absence. Lady Gerda was still apologizing for the lack of food and clean linen, but thanks to the able planning of Sir Jeremias, the royal progress carried enough of both to serve in most unexpected calamities.

"Don't sulk," the queen said. "Your grandfather *does* want you to attend the council."

"Oh, does he? You heard him, Grandmother—he was going to send me back to Erchester in disgrace. That's what he said. Because I'm irresponsible."

"And why did he say that, Morgan? Because you deliberately left your guards behind and went out into a strange city in the middle of the night. And onto a frozen lake!"

"Why does the king care so much? He's not the one who's got bruises from head to toe." Morgan knew this was not a very good argument, but even days later and leagues away from the scene of his embarrassment, he was still aching. "And why isn't Little Snenneq in trouble? It was his idea."

The queen shook her head, half amused, half appalled. "Saints defend us."

"What?" He realized he was getting loud, which was another useful way to humiliate himself. *Look, Prince Morgan is outside shouting at the queen. He's like a spoiled child, you know.* "Why is everyone always furious with me?"

"I said, don't *sulk*, young man." Queen Miriamele took her hands out of the sleeves of her robe long enough push a strand of wet, red-gold hair out of

Morgan's face, reminding him that to the aged king and queen he would probably never seem a grown man. "I can think of few less attractive traits in a
prince," the queen continued. "And your sister Lillia is beginning to do it, too.
Yes, your grandfather lost his temper with you, but with good reason. You are
the heir to the High Throne, Morgan. The lives of all the people in all the lands
we've traveled since the new year will depend on you. If you fall into a freezing
lake and drown, who will be our heir?"

"I *know*! I'm not stupid."

His grandmother sighed. "I do not have the strength for this, Your Highness. Come to the council or stay away as you wish. But a real prince must learn
to overcome his feelings for the good of his people."

"What does this council have to do with the good of anyone? A lot of
talking, a lot of tired old stories—"

His grandmother closed her eyes for a moment and took a deep breath.
"There is a grave difference between 'old stories' and 'history,' young man,
although sometimes it's hard to know which is which. Some stories seem old
but they never end, and they are just as important today as they were a century
ago. The Norns were here long before our Erkynland existed, and they still live
in their dreadful mountain up north, swarming in the dark like white beetles.
If they come out again, they will gladly kill every one of us, even your younger
sister. Is that nothing but an 'old story'?"

He looked down at his feet for a bit. Morgan understood that she was trying
to make peace, in a way, but something dark and raging had a grip on him, and
he couldn't shake it loose.

"If the Norns are so dreadful and terrible," he said at last, "then why didn't
you kill them all when you had the chance? Why didn't Grandfather do anything about them then, instead of staying home and sending that old Northman
Duke Isgrimnur to chase after them?" He felt a kind of sick satisfaction at seeing his grandmother's features go pale with fury.

"You do not know how lucky you are that I love you as much as I loved your
father, Morgan." The queen's words were carefully measured, colder than the
fluttering snow, "or I would slap your face for that. You speak of things you
know nothing about. No, look at me."

Morgan had not expected his flailing to result in an actual wound and did
not want to look at her. He was much more interested in his snow-flecked
boots.

"By Saint Rhiappa and the Holy Mother, boy, I said *look at me* and I meant it."

Morgan raised his eyes and wished he hadn't. The shocked anger on the queen's
face had become something more daunting, an expression that was no expression
at all, like the parade figure of a warrior-saint. He was not sure he'd ever seen her
so unhappy with him, and his stomach churned. "Very well," he said with what
he knew was poor grace, "I'm sorry. The duke was your friend—I know, I know.
He was a great man. I'm sorry and I'm a fool and I take it all back."

"You take it all back?" The queen leaned forward and dropped her voice.

"Listen to me well, child. Unless you manage to kill yourself with some stupid prank and break our hearts, you will be a king someday. You must learn to think not only before you act, but also *before you speak*. Among your family and our courtiers and servants, you might only hurt feelings, but with others you might begin a war—yes, a war—just by talking stupidly about people and situations you don't understand." She took a deep breath. "But I do not have the time to correct all your ignorance now. I am going inside. You have been invited to join us—which, I may remind you, is what is expected of a prince your age, and is not some irksome chore—but you may do as you please." She turned as if to go, but stopped in the doorway. "This is not the end. If you cannot manage to consider your words first, then I advise that you learn to speak less, young Prince Morgan. Much less."

Morgan knew he should follow her, but the unhappiness inside him wanted cold and suffering and solitude, so he lingered in the colonnade after she'd gone. Despite the quiet, he heard nothing until he felt the touch on his arm. "Holy Ransomer!" he cried, startled, but when he turned he saw, not a creeping Norn, but a figure like a fat child in a hooded jacket. "Snenneq, you startled me!"

"It is true," said the troll, grinning, "that I am silent like the *u'ituko* beast, who can cross snow without breaking even the crust."

Qina came up behind her betrothed. "Yes, silent," she said with a nod and a fond smile. *"Klomp, klomp! Crunch, crunch! Oh, no, rabbit run away!"*

"She teases only, friend Morgan," Snenneq assured him. "She knows that I have many gifts, but she likes to take fun of me. Women are not always having enough seriousness, do you agree?"

"Doubtless. Where have you two been?" Despite his irritation at the trouble that had come to him from the trolls' ice-sliding expedition, he was grateful for the company, or at least the distraction. It was quickly becoming clear that standing outside in the cold had not been one of his better ideas. "I looked for you earlier."

"The kitchen," said Snenneq promptly. "It was very instructing and full of nice smelling. The kitchen woman-lady has a name of great power and longness—she said it is, *'Erna But May God Save Me If They Ever Call Me Anything But Where's My Supper.'* We were being much impressed. Nobody in Yiqanuc has such a mouth full of name!"

"And I eat a dimple!" said Qina proudly.

"Dimple?"

"Dumple," explained Snenneq. "From the stew Erna Long-Name was at making."

"Ah," said Morgan. "Dumpling."

"I so much liked it," Qina said, her eyes a little dreamy. "Most fluffly."

Little Snenneq seemed concerned the conversation had wandered too far afield from his original purpose, so he gave his betrothed a meaningful look, then tried a new and more dignified tack. "Now, friend and prince Morgan, we have come in truth for asking, will you join out to the water with us? A trip to the lake?"

"No! In the name of all the saints, why would I?" Morgan wrapped his arms around himself and grimaced. "I still hurt all over from last time! And I was nearly sent home by my grandparents for sneaking out with you. Why would you want to go out on another lake, anyway? It's freezing cold!"

"To fish!" Little Snenneq said. "It is good the lake is freezing, so we can go out among the ice. We are cutting a hole in it, then we are lowering into it the string for the fish to take. With the . . . the . . ." He turned to Qina and made a shape with his finger.

"Hawk," she suggested.

"Hook?" tried Morgan.

Snenneq turned to the prince in delight. "That is being it! Yes! A hook on the string and the fish are coming. Hungry fish, down at the cold bottom. We will catch many!"

"I can't. I'm still in bad grace with my grandparents for going out to the lake in Elvritshalla."

Little Snenneq shook his head. "For my part, I am sorry. My father-in-law and mother-in-law, as they will one day be, were also upset with me. 'Snenneq,' they said, 'you are having no right for leading the prince into danger.' But we can go and find your guards or your swordsman friends to accompany our lake expedition."

Morgan didn't like that idea, either. Was he a child like his sister, in constant need of being watched? "Huh. If the old people had their way, we'd sit all day at their feet, waiting to be spoken to." He contemplated his wearisome lot in life. "Do you have any of that *kangkang* with you?"

Little Snenneq did indeed happen to be carrying a skin full of the tart, chest-warming beverage. Morgan accepted a long draught. "I don't need any guards," he said as he handed it back, "but my grandmother wants me to join her and the rest of them in the hall—the nobles and all. They're talking about the Norns and if there will be a war." In truth, he was still strongly considering avoiding the council meeting. He felt sure Astrian and Olveris would have found somewhere warm by now, a place to drink and tell lies without interference from Morgan's royal obligations.

"Ah," said Snenneq, impressed. "Then that is being something important and you must, of course, give them your counsel. You are having a good fortune, Prince Morgan!" And Qina nodded, agreeing.

"Good fortune?"

"That they are at recognizing your wisdom even with your young age. I have all my life been studying and practicing for importance in my tribe, but had scorning for my reward. It was only Qina's father, the so-wise Binbin-aqegabenik, who was recognizing my cleverness. All the rest of the older Qanuc were thinking me foolish—even a bragger." He frowned, then thumped his chest with his fist. "It was harming to even a heart of great bravery like Little

Snenneq's. But see, your people are more wisely thinking of you, Morgan Prince. They seek your counseling. They know your worthfulness!"

Morgan doubted that his grandparents and the rest truly did know his worthfulness—he wasn't exactly certain of it himself—but as he considered Snenneq's words he had to admit that he would also have been angry if the king and queen had not asked him to join them. Would they ask him again if he stayed away this time? They would surely call it 'sulking,' a word he loathed from the depths of his being. No, the more he thought about it, the more Morgan realized that it was the only sensible strategy. He would show up, and when they ignored him as they always did, his grandmother would have to admit he had been right.

"In any case, I suppose I had better be off," he said. "Good luck with your fishing. Don't fall in." It had been meant as a jest, but Morgan felt a pang of regret when he realized how sorry he would feel if anything bad happened to either of them, and he quickly made the sign of the Tree.

But Snenneq seemed immune to such superstitious doubts. "Oh ho! I will be giving it my closest attention. It is the fish who will be coming out, Morgan Prince, not Little Snenneq who will be falling in!"

"True," said Qina. "Because his leg holded will be. By me."

Morgan watched them walk away across the courtyard, two small shapes, hand in hand. When they had gone, he straightened his shoulders and headed inside to try to be a prince.

If there was one thing that age had taught Eolair of Nad Mullach, it was that the present instant was no more real than a layer of fresh snow. As he had seen this morning on a slow walk around the Blarbrekk Castle commons, the drifts might make everything look clean and new, but underneath waited the same old trees, stones, and earth. The older he got, the more he realized how unusual true change was.

These thoughts had been spurred by Prince Morgan's coming in from the cold to join them all at the table in the Earl's study, although why Morgan did so was a bit unclear, since the prince looked as though he expected to be scolded for something. It was funny, actually: Eolair had not known King Simon well until the young man took the throne of Erkynland, but he was certain he'd witnessed similar baffled, angry expressions on Simon's face during his first years of rule. And yet now, the same look from his grandson irritated the king to no end.

To be fair, Eolair had to admit that Morgan's unhappy expression irritated him a bit, too. He hoped the prince's appearance here was the beginning of a true change, not merely a new layer of snow. Morgan needed to take more interest in the affairs of the land, and not only because of a possible new threat from the north. Eolair was growing very dubious about King Hugh in Hernystir, the squabbling between the brothers in Nabban, and in fact the future of the High Ward. Decade after decade, it seemed, the old players shuffled off the scene, but those who followed them acted out the same parts, the same rituals of greed and foolishness.

But it's not entirely their fault, Eolair thought. *The young don't realize that they know almost nothing, or that nothing is ever new. That's their glory and their most dangerous flaw.*

"What we need most now is knowledge," King Simon declared, pulling Eolair's attention back to the council at hand as if he had guessed his secret thoughts and meant to share them. "Merciful Usires, how I miss Doctor Morgenes! Geloë, too, of course, bless her. Without their wisdom, and with no word from the Sithi, we can only guess at what the Norns might be doing."

"Yes, but we *are* without them," said Miriamele. "We must think about what we *do* know—and what we need to learn."

Prince Morgan stirred. "Morgenes—he was the one my father named me after, wasn't he? I never understood that, because everyone says they didn't even know each other."

"Your father never met him, but he read Morgenes' book about your great-grandfather, King John," Simon said. "That is how he knew him, and why he honored him—and you—with the name." He gave the prince a stern look. "And you should have read that book by now, too, as you kept promising you would. I managed when I was younger than you, and I scarcely knew how to read! You would have learned many lessons about kingship, and you would also know something about your father's namesake."

"Doctor Morgenes was indeed being very wise." Binabik now did what Eolair as Hand of the Throne usually had to do in such situations, namely, try to unpick quarrels before they began. Eolair was grateful to let someone else do it for a change. "But all wise people are not being gone from the world. Some of them are here now." The troll smiled. "I am not speaking of myself, with certainty, but instead our good Tiamak and Count Eolair, who between them have been seeing and reading so very many things. And, Majesties, you are wise ones yourselves. Few others have been at doing the things that you have."

"You rate yourself too modestly," Simon said with a brief smile. "But nobody here knows very much about the Norns, and that's what we need right now. The Sithi could help us, God knows, but they stay stubbornly silent. That's why I miss Morgenes and his wisdom so much right now. That's why I miss Geloë."

"Who is Geloë, anyway?" Morgan asked. "I've heard people saying her name."

"She was a *valada*," said Binabik. "What the Rimmersfolk call a wise woman."

"A *very* wise woman," said Miriamele.

"She was a shape-shifter," said Tiamak. "She could take the form of an owl. I saw her do it with my own eyes."

"She was a witch," Eolair said, then could not help smiling at the faces of the others as they turned toward him. "But of course she was! What else would you call her that would be more truthful? In Hernystir, where I was raised, the word is not quite so fearful as it is for you Aedonites. She could walk the Road of Dreams. By sweet Mircha's rains, Tiamak is right—she could even take the form of a bird!"

"She'd lived four hundred years or more," said Simon.

"Really?" said Tiamak. "How do you know that, Majesty?"

"Aditu told me."

"Ah-dee-too? Who is *that*?" asked Morgan, a touch plaintively.

"A woman of the Sithi," his grandmother said. "One of our closest allies."

"Four hundred years old," said Tiamak. "Amazing. When Geloë was dying, I heard Aditu call her 'Ruyan's Own.' Perhaps that was true—perhaps she really was a great-great-grandchild of the Navigator. The Tinukeda'ya nearly all live longer than men."

"This isn't fair," said Morgan. "I'm trying to pay attention, I swear I am, but who are all these people? Who's the Navigator, and what does he have to do with this Geloë? What's a Tinookidah or whatever you said? And what do any of these old stories have to do with someone finding dead Norns in a cow pasture in Rimmersgard last winter, which is what I thought you were all talking about?"

"Norns, yes, but Sithi as well," said Binabik. "That is the strangest thing we were hearing. But it is good that you have questions, Prince Morgan," Binabik said. "Perhaps, though, it is being too much for learning all in one day."

But Eolair saw a moment to educate the prince, a rare moment when the young man actually seemed to want to learn. "The Norns and the Sithi were once all one family, Highness—one race," he explained. "But not the Tinukeda'ya—Ruyan the Navigator's people. They were mostly slaves and servants, at least in the early days. Even their leader Ruyan, it is said, with all his skill and craft, was no more than a thrall to the immortals. Long, long ago, he and his people built a fleet of ships to carry the Sithi and Norns here from the place they call the Garden."

The king nodded. "My Sitha friend Jiriki said that, too—that the Sithi and Norns brought Ruyan's people here as slaves. I do not know where the Tinukeda'ya came from. Jiriki said their name means Ocean Children. And it's true that some of them live almost always on ships at sea. Miriamele met some."

"The Niskies," said the queen, nodding. "In fact one of them, Gan Itai, saved my life. The Niskies are the ones who protect the Nabbanai ships by singing the kilpa down."

"Ah," said Morgan, grasping at something he recognized. "Kilpa. I have heard of those things. Terrible, fishy creatures that steal sailors in the south from their ships and drown them."

"You are correct, Highness," Eolair said by way of encouragement. "And I have met Tinukeda'ya too, but from one of their other tribes," he said, remembering the frightened, big-eyed dwarrows of Mezutu'a. "You see, these Tinukeda'ya are a race of changelings that can be as different in form between themselves as a noble lady's lapdog is to a mastiff. These things matter to us now because all the creatures we are talking about, Sithi, Norns, Tinukeda'ya, live a long time."

"Some of them live damn near forever," said King Simon. "I'd guess the Norn Queen is still alive, even if she lost her power, as Aditu told us. Jiriki once said she was the oldest living thing in the world." He turned to the young prince. "That's why we want you to know these things, Morgan. Someday your grandmother and I will be gone—but the Norns won't be."

"But isn't there anyone now like this Geloë?" asked Morgan, who seemed finally to have grasped the seriousness of their concerns. "Somebody who knows about the Norns and what they might be doing?"

"There is being nobody like Geloë," said Binabik with a sad smile. "Not before, and not now that she is being gone. And there is also being nobody living today as knowledgeable about these things as your namesake Doctor Morgenes, Prince Morgan. No, it seems we will have to find the solving of this ourselves."

The troll was right, Eolair realized, even as the others began again to discuss the Norns and what Lady Alva's story might mean. There was no other like Geloë. Eolair had not known her well—he had only been in her presence for a few days, when he had visited Prince Josua's camp during the Storm King's War—but the memory of her bright, hunting-bird's eyes would never leave him. From a distance she had looked like many other peasant women, short but solid, with the cropped hair and unprepossessing clothes of someone who cared little what others might think of her. But to be in her presence, to be examined by that yellow stare, had been to feel her power—not the might of a conqueror or even a will in search of mastery over others, but the unselfconscious power of a stone standing in the middle of a mighty river—something which did not move but instead let everything else bend around it in a rush of pointless motion and noise.

And she had dirty fingernails, Eolair remembered—something else he had liked about her. Too busy doing what needed doing to waste any time being anything but herself. *Gods, yes,* he thought. *We would be immeasurably better off if all the Scrollbearers still lived—Geloë and Morgenes and Jarnauga and Father Dinivan—and if they were all here now to tell us what to do.* But Geloë had died at the hands of the Norns, as had Jarnauga, and the red priest Pryrates had murdered Father Dinivan in the Sancellan Aedonitis and burned Doctor Morgenes to death in his own chambers.

Eolair looked around the room. Here they all sat, the king and queen, the trolls from distant Yiqanuc, Tiamak who had been born in the marshy Wran, and young Morgan, confused and frustrated by all the things he did not understand. *But now we are the ones who must protect the realm,* he thought. *It is up to us to be those that others will speak of in some future time, the ones of whom they will say,*

"Thank the gods they were here." Because if we are not—if the tide of vengeance comes rolling down from the north again, and we fail to hold what others helped us keep at the last time of darkness—there may be nothing to say, and no one left to say it.

Miriamele had just sent her ladies ahead to prepare the bedchamber when she noticed Binabik waiting at the door of the jarl's study. The small man looked tired, but she thought she still might be unused to this aged version of a familiar face. She smiled at him. "It is so good to see you and Sisqi, Binabik. And your child, Qina—she's grown to be such a beauty! It all gives me heart."

He bumped his fist against his chest. "Heart is what we are all sometimes needing. As we say in Yiqanuc, *'Fear is the mother of wisdom, but every child must be leaving the home one day.'*"

Miriamele was still trying to work that out when Simon finished his conversation with Sir Kenrick about the disposition of the guards. Since they were staying in the house of a trusted ally, there had apparently been little to discuss.

Sir Kenrick paused in the doorway and bowed deeply to the queen, then looked down at the troll and made a curious half-bow, like an overbalanced nod: as with most of his fellows, the stocky captain marshal never quite knew how to treat the royal couple's odd friends. Matters of deference and title were often especially difficult. Just a fortnight past, Miriamele knew, Lord Chamberlain Jeremias had been almost in tears trying to decide what Binabik's rank, "Singing Man of Mintahoq Mountain," signified as far as precedence at table.

"He's my oldest and closest friend," Simon had told him, then hurriedly added, "after you, Jeremias, of course."

"One more question," Kenrick said now, "begging your Majesties' pardons. Perhaps if we make good time to Vestvennby we could give the men a day of freedom there. It would cheer them up after all this snow and short rations."

"I'm sure that can be arranged," said Simon.

"We will consider it, Sir Kenrick," the queen said with a meaningful glance at her husband.

"Why shouldn't they have a day in Vestvennby?" the king asked when the captain had departed.

"I didn't say they shouldn't, although we've lost time already with this storm. I just said *we* would consider it. Together. Before we make announcements."

"I didn't think you would disagree."

"You don't know unless you ask, husband."

He pursed his lips, but at last nodded. "I suppose that's true."

For a moment she wanted only to put her arms around him, only for the two of them to be alone somewhere without responsibilities, just a husband and wife. But that would not happen. That would never happen. She sighed and squeezed his hand. "Right, then. I think Binabik is waiting to speak with you."

"With both of you, to speak with exactness," said the troll, stepping forward. "But it is about something you were saying another day, friend Simon. When we were in Elvritshalla, you told that you have stopped dreaming. Was that a true saying?"

An expression crossed her husband's face that also reminded her of a younger Simon—a worried one. "It was," he said. "It is. You know I've always had strange dreams, Binabik, but especially in the Storm King years. I dreamed of the Uduntree, didn't I? Long before I saw it. The wheel, too, never knowing I'd be strapped to one! And I dreamed of Stormspike Mountain back in those days as well, and the Norn Queen, when I didn't know anything about her. In Geloë's house, when we walked the Dream Road—remember?"

Binabik nodded. "Of course I am remembering. And also what the great Sitha lady Amerasu told you—that you were perhaps one closer to the Road of Dreams than others. Has it changed in the years we have been apart?"

Simon shook his head. "Not truly. Sometimes it is less, but in the weeks before our son John Josua got ill, I dreamed of Pryrates every night. Miri can tell you."

"No, I can't. I don't want to remember." Sometimes it seemed like that terrible loss was everywhere around her, barely hidden, and to poke at anything, no matter how seemingly innocuous, was to risk revealing it. A moment before, she had been thinking of a thousand other things, but now it was back, the pain nearly as fresh as the moment they had lost their only child. "But yes," she said when she had composed herself, "Simon had terrible dreams in those days. Terrible."

"Once I dreamed that Pryrates was a cat, and that John Josua was a mouse, but he didn't know . . ."

"Enough!" said Miriamele, far more harshly than she had intended. When the two of them looked at her in surprise, she could only wave her hand. "I'm sorry, but I can't bear to hear it again."

Binabik frowned in sympathy. "I do not think the whole story must be told again, but I do have more questions for asking. Should I take your husband somewhere else to speak with him?"

"No. I'm well. If it's important I want to know too. Go ahead." She was a queen, she reminded herself—*the* queen. She would not hide from mere emotion, no matter how terrible its source or painful its visitation.

"Was it during a single night that this stopping happened, Simon?" Binabik asked him. "Or is it something that only later came to your notice?"

He thought about it. "When did I tell you about it? The night Sludig and his wife came, wasn't it? What saints' day was that?" He frowned and pulled on his beard. "Saint Vultinia, wasn't it?"

Binabik smiled. "I fear I do not know the Aedonite saints so well, except that they are many and their statue faces are mostly frowning."

"Can't blame them for that, with what happened to most of 'em," Simon said. "Lillia had a book her other grandfather gave her. Vultinia, yes, that was it—that one stuck with me. The Imperator's soldiers cut off all her fingers but she said she could still feel God's presence—isn't that right, Miri?"

Miriamele shuddered. "If you say so. It's a horrid book to give a child. Why are you asking about such a thing?"

"So I can know what day it was that I noticed about my dreams. St. Vultinia's Day is the third day of Avrel." He turned back to Binabik. "That means it must have been the end of Marris when I last had a dream I can remember. I went to bed late one night—the night of Isgrimnur's funeral, I guess it was— and had a very strange one. There was a black horse in a field, and it was foaling. But the foal wouldn't come out, and it was struggling, almost as though it was fighting not to be born. I don't know what it could signify." He shook his head, remembering. "And the black mare was screaming, screaming, and it was so terrible I woke up in a sweat. Do you remember, Miri?"

She shrugged. "I did not sleep well the night of Isgrimnur's funeral, either. That's all I remember."

"In any case," Simon said, "when I laid my head down again, I fell at once back into sleep, but it was like falling down a dark hole. Dark, dark, dark—but no dreams. And I swear I haven't dreamed since."

This sort of talk made Miriamele anxious. "Perhaps as you said, you simply don't remember them, Simon. Sometimes I don't remember my dreams either until someone mentions something that reminds me."

He shook his head emphatically. "No. This is different."

Binabik reached into his tunic and brought out a leather bag. "The last night of Marris-month. You call that Fools' Night, do you not?"

"That's right." Simon smiled. "I remember thinking during the funeral that good old Isgrimnur would have enjoyed a proper All Fools' celebration better, with drunken priests and masks and whatnot."

"Isgrimnur was indeed a man for merrymaking and loud singing. But I think Fools' Night is for more than merriment." Binabik was pouring the contents of the leather bag into his hands, a pile of small, polished bones. "In the mountains we are having something much like it at the leaving of winter, a moment of changing fortune. My master Ookekuq called it *so-hiq nammu ya*— a 'night of thin ice'. When the walls between this world and others are more easily crossed."

Simon was staring at the troll's knuckle bones with a mixture of fascination and concern. "I haven't seen those in a long time. I thought maybe you'd stopped using them."

"Stopped casting the bones? No. I have been teaching their use to Little Snenneq of late, though, and I do not like to tire them."

Miriamele almost smiled at the idea of tiring out a little pile of bones. "I always wondered about those," she admitted, "ever since I first met you in the forest. Whose bones are they?"

Binabik gave her a stern look. "Mine, of course." He turned to Simon. "Do you mind if I am casting them for you? Losing your way to the Road of Dreams is seeming strange to me, and on such a night of thin ice, even more."

Simon shook his head. "No. Of course not."

Binabik rolled the clicking bones in his hand and chanted quietly to himself, then crouched and spilled them from his palm onto the stone flags. He stared at them for long moments, then scooped them up and threw again. After he had thrown and considered for a third time, he looked up. "It is a strange casting, that is all I can say now, without much thought. First it was Black Crevice, then Slippery Snow. Now for the last I see Unexpected Visitor, which we also call No Shadow. All are signs of deceit and confusion."

"What does that mean?" Simon asked.

"Who can be saying without thought?" Binabik carefully picked up the tiny, yellowed shapes and returned them to the leather sack. He spoke a few more whispered words over it, then tucked it into his tunic. "I must consider. I will think of all that my wise master Ookekuq taught me. Unexpected Visitor I have not been seeing for many, many years. It is puzzling to me." He stood, levering himself up with a grunt and a brief grimace. Miri, who could remember when the troll had been as swift and spry as a squirrel—when they *all* had been so nimble—felt a moment's sadness. "I will also be at considering if there is something useful to be done for this not-dreaming that afflicts you, friend Simon."

"I'm not sure it's a kindness to give him back his bad dreams," Miri said.

"But in the days of the Storm King's War, there were things we could have been learning from Simon's dreams," Binabik told her. "Important things. Can we afford being ignorant now?"

"Not if ignorance is a risk to our people," Simon said. "They are what matters."

Binabik reached up and squeezed Miri's hand. "I was teasing you before," he said. "Just a small teasing. The knucklebones belong to me, but they are not from a person. They are the ankle bones of sheep." He showed her his familiar yellow smile. "Do you forgive my joking, queen and friend Miriamele?"

"Oh, without doubt," she told him, but the talk of Simon's bad dreams had not made a disturbing day any less so.

17

White Hand

Lord, I beseech You, make my arm strong and my aim true that I may smite Your enemies.

He killed the first one easily enough, putting his arrow through the Hikeda'ya's throat from a hundred paces downwind. By the time the white-clad figure crumpled to the snow Jarnulf was already gliding toward his second spot, keeping the wind in his face. He knew there would be a second scout, and a trained Sacrifice would be calculating the direction of the arrow even before reaching his comrade's body.

Jarnulf had already planned the site for his next shot and reached it in a few swift steps. The second of the Norns appeared below him, moving close to the uneven, white-drifted ground, eyes little more than black lines as he scanned the spot Jarnulf had just left. Thirty feet further up the rise, Jarnulf stood behind a row of aspens and drew his bow again. Even that tiny movement caught the Hikeda'ya's eye; Jarnulf had to hurry his shot because his target was already nocking an arrow. His shaft flew a little lower than he'd planned and caught his target in the belly, which might well kill him, but not quickly. The Norn spun and fell to his knees, then found the strength to scramble behind a mound of snow. From there he would only have a short distance to get into the cover of the forest.

Jarnulf cursed his clumsiness, then immediately regretted taking the Ransomer's name in vain even in the midst of peril. He knew he could not wait to see if the second scout was badly injured: if the creature had the strength to escape, he might make his way back to a larger body of Hikeda'ya, then Jarnulf himself would become the hunted one. But neither could he go straight after the wounded Sacrifice soldier, because if he lost the wind his victim would scent him coming and the wounded one still had a bow. Even badly wounded, the Hikeda'ya would only need one shot to end Jarnulf's career of vengeance against the immortals.

When he reached the next high place with a downward view, Jarnulf saw with relief that the injured Sacrifice was still crouching behind the sheltering hummock. Blood from his stomach wound was staining the snow around him . . . but not fast enough. The angle for a shot was bad, so instead of taking it and perhaps driving his enemy to cover, Jarnulf began a stealthy approach down the steep hillside. The rocks were slippery and there were points where he was completely exposed to a shot from below, but no shot came.

At the last, still some ten cubits above the valley floor, Jarnulf spotted the wounded one's legs behind the hummock. He could continue to circle down, but with the wind shifting direction he would spend long moments upwind and exposed, his scent blowing straight toward his enemy; it would simply be a matter of which of them got off the best shot. Jarnulf did not like the idea of trading arrows with even a wounded Hikeda'ya soldier. Instead, he moved to the edge of a stone outcropping, then dropped to the snowy ground below, only a short distance from the wounded Norn.

The snow was softer and deeper than he'd expected; instead of being able to land and leap forward, Jarnulf found himself floundering in a thigh-deep drift. He used his bow to help himself clamber out, but the scout had already heard him and turned, blood flecking his mouth and chin, red splashed over white like some kind of crude mask. Jarnulf didn't dare give the enemy time to lift his bow, but flung himself forward without even trying to draw his sword, instead pulling his long dagger as he half ran, half stumbled across slippery, snow-covered rocks to throw himself on his enemy.

For a moment it seemed he had succeeded: he struck the injured Hikeda'ya with his shoulder and his enemy's bow and nocked arrow danced uselessly away. But the Sacrifice was well trained and fast despite his wounds, and he had a blade of his own.

For long, near-silent moments they rolled across the snow, locked in an embrace as tight as any lovers', until Jarnulf managed to drive his blade up under his enemy's ribs close to the arrow wound. The stab did not kill the creature outright, but the blow was deep; now it was only a matter of time. His enemy's grip grew weaker. As he defended himself from Jarnulf's thrusts, his movements grew slower, heavier. At last, with blood spattered for several arm-spans on all sides, the Hikeda'ya scout slipped into a kind of moving half-sleep. Jarnulf wrestled him onto his back and thrust the long, thin blade through his eye and into his brain.

For a while he could only lay atop his enemy's body, gasping. Struggling hand-to-hand with even a wounded Sacrifice was like wrestling a large serpent, and all Jarnulf's muscles were trembling. He took deep breaths, fighting to get air back into his lungs, and if he had not heard a noise behind him between inhalation and exhalation, he would have died.

He only had time to roll to one side as the third Sacrifice leaped toward him; the spear-thrust meant to kill him went instead into the lifeless body of the dead Sacrifice. In a fury of self-disgust at having assumed there were only two soldiers on this wide patrol, Jarnulf grabbed at the spear and held on so it could not be withdrawn for another thrust. The Hikeda'ya leaned back, trying to pull the spear free, which gave Jarnulf an instant of safety. His enemy was too far back for him to strike at a vital organ, but close enough that he could stab down through the Sacrifice's booted foot. In the split-instant that the pale creature gasped (but did not scream—the Hikeda'ya were controlled even in agony) Jarnulf managed to reach the dead scout's bow. He swung it as hard as he could and shattered it across his attacker's face. As the white-clad soldier tried to shield his head from another blow, Jarnulf threw himself at him, pieces of the broken bow clutched in each hand, the bowstring still attached.

He managed to loop the bowstring over the Hikeda'ya's head, then let his momentum carry him past; a moment later he was behind his enemy, tightening the cord with all the strength he could muster, shoving his knee into the Hikeda'ya's back to keep the clawing fingers away from his head. The creature bloodied the backs of Jarnulf's hands with his nails as he struggled, but the bowstring had been made in Nakkiga and was nearly unbreakable, and Jarnulf outweighed his enemy. Despite the Hikeda'ya's probably greater strength, all Jarnulf had to do now was hold on.

It still took a long time—a horribly long time—but at last the white-skinned creature stopped struggling. Even so, Jarnulf held the cord tight until he could no longer keep his arms up, then let go and collapsed onto the snow beside the corpse. If there was a fourth Sacrifice nearby, Jarnulf knew he would soon be a dead man.

But there was no fourth member of the scouting party. Aching, scraped, wearier than he had been in weeks, Jarnulf staggered onto his feet to finish his sacred task, of which killing was only the first act. Corpses by themselves were meaningless. The *fear*—the fear was what mattered.

He dragged the three bodies to the trunk of a pine tree and set them against it. Next he took a palm full of blood from the gut-stabbed Norn, put his other hand down against the snow, and blew on the blood until it flew in spatters over his spread fingers. When he lifted it again, the clear outline of a white hand lay on the snow, limned in red blood, then he kneeled to pray.

"I dedicate the bodies of our enemies to you, O God. May they learn to fear Your wrath."

But unlike in earlier days, when he had finished he did not feel exultant or even satisfied. The sight of the dead Sacrifice scouts unsettled him in a way it hadn't before, the emptiness of their dark, dead eyes seeming to mirror his own hollowness. How could he simply go on doing what he had done for so many years when the corpse-giant's words had changed everything? If Queen Utuk'ku was awake and the Hikeda'ya were preparing for war, they were nothing like the spent force he had imagined and all his killing had accomplished nothing. Nothing but death and more death.

Jarnulf knew he could not linger near the bodies. He found his bow and retrieved his arrows. He cleaned his boots of blood so as not to make tracking too easy for any enemies that might be nearby, then climbed on shaking legs back up into the trees that crowned the hill. When he was well hidden from the spot where the dead Sacrifices lay motionless beneath the cold sky, Jarnulf fell to his knees, pressed together hands still tinctured with the blood of so-called immortals, and sent up another prayer, this one silent.

Father, my dear Father, wherever you are, in Heaven with the saints or a captive suffering in the enemy's dark stronghold, help me see my way.

And Almighty God, my other and truest Father, in the name of Your blessed Son Usires Aedon, my Ransomer, tell me what You would have your servant do. What good to punish mere slaves when their mistress the White Witch of Nakkiga still lives? I fear I have lost my way. Tell me what You require of me. Let Your servant know Your will.

He stood, but kept his head bowed for long moments.

I ask only this—send me a sign, O Lord. Send me a sign.

"You, Blackbird." Makho wiped a smear of grease from his chin and pointed to the white hares lying on the ground like a pile of blood-flecked snow. "Give those that remain to the giant."

Nezeru took up a brace in each hand. She counted herself lucky that she had been allowed a few handfuls of cooked meat herself, and wondered if Makho would have fed her at all if he did not think she was growing a child inside her. She was becoming used to the lowly role the Hand Chieftain had given her, not that she had any choice: it was clear Makho would have much rather left her at Bitter Moon Castle.

But it is better to be patient than to be noticed, Nezeru reminded herself. It was one of her father Viyeki's favorite sayings, although he himself was not always as retiring as he liked to pretend. But just now, when she was shamed, out-ranked, and with leagues between her and her family and clan, it seemed like good advice.

She crunched across the uneven snow toward the spot where the off-white bulk of the giant sat like a small mountain. As always, she stopped out of the creature's reach, then tossed the two strings of hares so that they landed near him. The great gray and white head lifted, and Nezeru froze in place despite herself. The wide nostrils flared.

"Ah." The giant's voice rumbled like a tunnel collapse in deep Nakkiga. "So Goh Gam Gar will not starve tonight." A leathery hand so brown it was nearly black reached out and enveloped the hares as though they were furry pea pods. "Sit and talk as I eat," he growled. His voice made her bones quiver. "Or are you feared of old Gar?"

Nezeru found her voice. "I fear only failure."

"An enemy you know well, I think. Sit."

Nezeru hesitated. She knew that the giant could not disobey the crystal goad that Makho held, and he would not let the giant harm her while he believed she carried a child. *In any case, I am still a Talon of the Queen,* she told herself. *Even my failure has not robbed me of that. Not yet.*

She found a fallen tree she judged to be just out of reach of the long arms, at least as long as the giant remained seated. The Hikeda'ya were camped beside the forest they had been skirting for several days, and trees were plentiful, but although he had permitted a cookfire, Makho had ordered her to build it small and to use only dry wood. She thought it was odd the chieftain showed so much caution here, in a place so empty of other living things.

The giant fixed her with a stare. His eyes were black, and should have been impossible to see beneath his bony brow-shelf, but a spark of pale green seemed to burn at the center of each. "You are female," the giant said abruptly. "You look like all the others, but I can smell your womb." He pinched one of the hares between thumb and forefingers as thick as Nezeru's arms, then sucked it in half, fur and all, before popping the rest into its mouth. She could hear the bones crunching as it chewed. "I hear you are going to whelp, but I do not smell that. Gar wonders why."

Nezeru felt a moment of trapped panic, but the creature had spoken almost conversationally; she decided to pretend she had not heard his last words. "Yes, I am female," she said at last. "How is it that you speak our tongue?"

"What tongue should I speak?" Goh Gam Gar smiled—at least she thought it was a sort of smile—showing a mouth full of broad yellow fangs. For a moment the giant looked almost like a person. Almost. "My kind do not speak among ourselves. We live far apart, and when two males meet they do not talk like your kind, they fight for the hunting territory. Much we must eat. We need a wide land to keep us fed." He bit the head off the second hare and sucked on it until the furry bag of skin had emptied, then rolled up the bloody hide and delicately consumed it.

"So how did you learn?"

"Many of us do, if we live long enough. Many of us have fought for your Queen Utuk'ku. We learn the words of command, of attack. But no one needs to teach us to kill." The toothy yellow grin appeared again. "But I speak best because I am the oldest. I am the greatest. Three hundred turns of the world or more Goh Gam Gar has been alive, and I have been the queen's captive for much of it. I fought for her in the southern lands, when the tower fell, and I alone of my people who went there came back to the mountains." The eyes narrowed. "Oh, yes, Gar has learned many of your words. Whips. Chains. Fire."

"Your loss in the south must have been great," she said carefully. "I know many giants died there."

"My mate. My whelps, some of them not full-grown." He gave her a shrewd look that made her drop her gaze.

"I am sorry to hear it." Nezeru was telling the truth, at least at that moment. Her own people had suffered so many losses over the years that no victory they might ever win would offset them all. Nezeru's people understood loss.

The giant was still staring at her. At first she almost hoped, fearful as it would be, that he was looking at her merely as a potential meal. But the longer she sat across from the monster, the more she believed something else was at work, perhaps even that he had worked out her secret.

Watching her did not stop Goh Gam Gar from throwing the last two hares in his mouth and swallowing them without chewing. It came to her that he would not have much more trouble doing the same to her.

"Come here, Blackbird," Makho called from the far side of the camp. The nickname came from the ancient story of a blackbird who had failed to deliver an important message because of cowardice. It was an old insult among the Hikeda'ya, and every time Makho used it, she felt it.

"Blackbird, is it?" A deep rumble came up through her feet and legs. The giant was laughing. "We have something in common, you and I. Your master Makho is also my master. He holds the queen's little gift. Did I refuse him or do something he did not like, he could make me lie on the ground howling in pain until my heart burst in my breast."

She got up and returned to the cookfire, which had been doused and was now only a thin trickle of smoke. The sun was vanishing behind the mountains to the west, and the whole valley was sunk in shadow. Soon night would come and they would be traveling again.

"See that the horses are saddled," said Makho before she even reached him. "Kemme has returned from scouting the way ahead. We will leave when the stars kindle."

The rocky valley narrowed into a defile. By the time the familiar stars had mounted into the sky above her head, Nezeru and the others were walking single file up a steep ridge, only the sureness of her footsteps preventing a tumble onto the jagged, snow-capped rocks below. Directly above the horizon the star called Mantis was following a dimmer light named Storm's Eye, which meant they had turned farther south than she would have guessed. Nezeru wondered why Makho had brought them so far into the lands of men when their destination lay so far to the east.

A ghost owl slid past just above her head, so close she could have touched it, a flash of silent white that appeared and disappeared in the space between heartbeats. A moment later Nezeru heard its barking call in the treetops below the ridge and a sudden, almost overwhelming desire for freedom struck her. It was such an unusual sensation that she could barely give it a name—to go where she wanted, to live as she chose . . . But of course that would only come with a betrayal of everyone and everything she knew. Nezeru could no more be free of her ordinal vow than she could put on wings and feathers like a Tinukeda'ya shape-shifter out of old legend and become a real blackbird. And without that vow, what was she, anyway? A halfblood. A coward and a liar. Only the success of their mission might change that, might give her a chance to make good again.

"The Mantis is bright tonight," said a voice just behind her. With the calm learned at the cost of countless beatings in her order-house days, Nezeru let the surprise wash over her without affecting her steps. White-robed Saomeji the Singer had come upon her, silent and unnoticed as an ermine, while she had been lost in thought. "That bodes well for our mission."

"Our lives are the queen's." It was the blandest of responses she could make.

He followed behind her in silence for a score of paces before saying quietly, "I would not have punished you as Makho did."

She thought that a very unusual remark. Makho and Kemme were far ahead of them both, and she could just see the top of Ibi-Khai's head past the next bend of the ridge-trail, so it was relatively safe to speak; but the *why* of it made no sense. Did he hope to catch her speaking some treason against the queen's chosen hand chieftain?

"I failed," she said. "I was punished as I deserved."

"Failure is usually as much a fault of the leader as of the follower who fails."

Nezeru could not make out what Saomeji wanted from her, and that worried her badly. The Singer had avoided her the last several days, but in that he was no different from any of the others—the stink of her crimes was on her like the rotted meat between the giant's teeth. Did he merely want to couple with her? That, at least, made some sense, but even if he had not been told about her being with child, she did not think the Singer would risk provoking their hand chieftain.

She took a breath. "Do you call Makho a failure, then?"

He laughed. She envied him the lightness she heard. "No, never. The queen and my master did well when they chose him. He is like a knife of finest blackstone, so sharp that he can cut the air itself and make it bleed."

"When you say your master, you mean Akhenabi." The Lord of Song's bottomless black eyes and wrinkled mask now lurked at the edges of many of her dreams. "Are you saying that he chose this Queen's Hand?"

He ignored her question. "The Lord of Song is more than my master. He will be the savior of our people." Saomeji spoke so flatly it almost sounded as though he didn't believe it, that he was speaking by rote, but there was a gleam in his alien golden eyes that she didn't recognize. "You interested him, handsister. I could tell."

His words touched something that had been disturbing her since Bitter Moon Castle. Emboldened by the distance between themselves and the rest of their comrades, she turned and asked him, "Why did your master let me go?"

The Singer's look was carefully blank. "This hand of Talons was ordered by the queen, and sworn to her and her alone. How could my master have interfered?"

This was ground far more dangerous than the slope they climbed, but now that she had started Nezeru felt a sort of heedless freedom, as though this night and this high place were both outside the bounds of what was ordinary. Another part of her was horrified by such risky behavior, but nothing had seemed quite the same since Makho had used the *hebi-kei* on her. "You surely know better than that, Singer Saomeji. Chieftain Makho was the queen's choice to lead this hand. Makho wished me sent back to Nakkiga for punishment. Why would Akhenabi thwart him of his will?"

Saomeji did not speak for a while, and they climbed in almost complete silence. For a Singer, he was well trained in stealth.

"Do you know anything of my master, hand-sister?" Saomeji said at last. "Beyond the stories children tell each other?"

"I know he is one of the very oldest," she said carefully. "One of the first Landborn, after our ships found their way here. I know that he has the queen's ear, and her trust. I know that he is feared in every land, by people who have never looked on his face or heard his voice." *And by me, too*, she thought. *How I wish I had never seen him so closely!*

Saomeji shook his head. "You know very little, then, young Nezeru. We are of an age, you and I, but I know more than you—much more." He looked straight ahead, as though describing a picture only he could see. "I have walked the deep places below Nakkiga, the ancient depths where our people no longer go, and I have seen things there that would send you into madness . . . but still I am as a child to Akhenabi and his closest kin. We all are. The old ones, the masked ones, are subtle beyond our understanding. What are we, who have lived but a few hundred turns of the seasons, to those who have passed a thousand winters—or ten thousand?" He opened his eyes, fixing her with his honey-yellow stare. "My master saw something in you. What that was I cannot say, nor even guess. As well might a snail try to understand the reasons of the foot that crushes him or spares him. Because we are *small*, Nezeru. We are small, you and I and even Makho, and our span is scarcely longer than that of the mortals who swarm the land and destroy our peace—a few centuries, then we are dust. The Queen does not die, and her chosen ones do not die either, although eventually all the rest of our kind find their ending. How can you and I judge the thoughts of those who have seen the very form of the world shift—seen mountains rise, seas dry?"

You like the sound of your own voice, Nezeru thought. *That is a failing most of your secretive order does not share.* But she only said, "So I cannot hope to understand the reason your master spared me because I have never seen a mountain grow?"

"If you like." Saomeji was amused again, and for some reason that frightened her. He could be no more privileged in his birth than she was—another half-blood, but with the added defect of the golden eyes of their traitorous Zida'ya cousins—so what gave this mongrel Singer such confidence? "It is not a failure of your youth but a failure of knowledge and imagination," he went on. "There are great matters in train, greater than you or I can know—or perhaps even guess at. But if Makho's anger has brought you despair, I bring you something that should melt that unhappiness like sun on shallow snow. And it is this—the most powerful of our folk see some purpose in you, Sacrifice Nezeru. Lord Akhenabi does not make mistakes." He walked a few more paces in silence, then said, "Look up."

The wind had risen as they neared the top of the ridge, and for a moment she thought she had misheard him above its noise. "Look up?"

"There. You see the stars hung in the sky like the lanterns above Black Water Field? My lord Akhenabi sees the very paths they travel, where they have been and where they will be. In my scant time in the Order of Song I have learned the way their movement pulls on those of us below, the way their light brings life to darkness, but my master even sees the darkness between them. Not the absence of their light, understand, but the darkness itself—he reads it like a book."

She looked up at the teeming stars. "I do not understand you."

She could hear the amusement in his voice. "I do not always understand myself, hand-sister. When I studied the Great Songs and the Lesser Songs in the order-house, it was as though a fire was lit in my thoughts. That fire still burns. Sometimes it warms me. Sometimes I feel it will consume me, blazing until I am only ash, floating up into those dark places where the stars do not hold sway."

Nezeru was beginning to think that this halfblood Singer was not merely subtle but actually mad, as damaged in his own way as she was by her own cowardice and failure. Was it true, then? Were all halfbloods corrupted by their birth?

Before either of them could speak again, Ibi-Khai appeared on the path ahead of them. "Dawn will be here soon," he announced. The Echo had pulled back his hood; his long black hair swirled around his narrow face. "Makho and Kemme have found a way down to the plain below." Ibi-Khai was clearly waiting for them to catch up, which meant no more unsettling private conversation with Saomeji. Nezeru felt relieved. "Make haste!" Ibi-Khai urged them. "We will stop there until the daystar is gone."

"The Queen watches over us," replied Saomeji.

"Our lives are hers," said Ibi-Khai, making the sign of fealty. "No praise of her is too great."

Jarnulf had rested as long as he dared. His injuries were minor—a few deep cuts, a long but shallow weal across his scalp, some scratches and scrapes. He had no idea if the three dead Norns had been a wide patrol out of Bitter Moon Castle or a scouting party for a larger force, but although this southern end of Moon's Reach Valley had been a good place for an improvised ambush, it was a bad spot for evading a determined hunting party of Sacrifices. Large troops of Hikeda'ya often brought the terrible white hounds from Nakkiga's kennels to guard the camp during the day, when the Cloud Children did not like to travel. With luck he might elude upright pursuers in the forested hills above the valley, but Jarnulf knew he had no such chance against a pack of Nakkiga hounds.

He also knew he could not make his way straight over the highest hills from where he stood now because of the icy, windscraped rocks of the steep crest. He would have more choices at the far end of the valley, including a pass low enough that he could climb it without suffering too badly, and if necessary could actually escape through into Hikeda'ya lands where it would be easier to hide, at least long enough to allow a wide troop to pass him on their way south. Normally Jarnulf would not have ventured so near to one of the border fortresses, but he could not rid his thoughts of the corpse-giant's dire words. If the creature had been truthful and the masked queen really was alive, then had it also spoken the truth about the Hikeda'ya planning to attack the lands of men once again? What would his solitary quest mean then—a dead Sacrifice here, a dead Sacrifice there—when thousands more of them marched south to kill mortal men and women?

It was the strangest war party that Jarnulf had ever seen. As he watched from a high, hidden place at the southern mouth of the pass, it was easy enough to see that the five human-sized shapes were all Hikeda'ya. Five of them traveling in the wild lands meant a "hand"—an assassination party or something like, since scouts tended to move in even smaller numbers. Like all their kind, this hand of hated Hikeda'ya traveled mostly by night and used fire sparingly. Nothing about them seemed exceptional. But instead of five, he was looking down on six travelers, and the sixth member of their party was monstrously huge. From where Jarnulf lurked, that one looked and moved like one of the Hunën, but if so, it was by far the biggest he had ever seen, and he had encountered more than a few. Also, the creature did not appear to be restrained in any way, which made no sense at all. The Hikeda'ya often used giants in battle, but each one required a small force of Sacrifices just to make sure the monsters attacked the Hikeda'ya's enemies and not the Hikeda'ya themselves. This giant actually appeared to be walking free—a companion instead of a slave, if such a thing could even be imagined.

Jarnulf needed to make a decision, and soon. Within half a day or less they would reach the spot where he had left the dead Norn scouts and signed the bloody work with his customary White Hand, so it was only good sense to keep as far away from these newcomers and their pet giant as possible. Still, there was something here he didn't understand, something that tugged at him and made him want to know more. Was this the sign he had asked God for? Or merely another strange event in this strangest of seasons?

And that is my weakness, he told himself. *At least some would say so. Father used to tell me, "Make curiosity your strength." But Master Xoka always said, "Wisdom seeks for nothing, because in time Death finds all, and then all lessons are learned." And still, all these years later, I swing back and forth like a weathercock between those two voices.*

At last, Father's way won out: Jarnulf began to move closer, but not too close, his movements parallel with the route of the strange traveling party. A Hunë could pick up a scent when even the sharp nose of a Hikeda'ya could not, and the last thing Jarnulf wanted was to become the quarry of a hunting giant.

The Talons found a place to rest that would be sheltered from the rising sun by a stone outcrop, but although Nezeru's legs were weary from the climb through the pass and the long descent, and an hour or two of sleep would be a useful thing, sleep would not come. The strange conversation with Saomeji had set her mind awhirl.

What *could* Akhenabi have seen in her? Ordinarily, to earn the notice of one of the high nobles of Nakkiga was a mark of pride, an invisible but very real badge that one would wear for an entire lifetime. And to be picked out by one of the Landborn was an honor so far beyond that as to be almost unknown. Why then did she feel as though a terrible weight now hung above her head?

Nezeru had always known she was different. She was always treated with careful distance by her father's family, friends, and servants, but other children had not been so circumspect. Every look and word of those lucky enough to have two Hikeda'ya parents reinforced Nezeru's knowledge that she was not like them, would never fully be one of them. She was a necessity caused by the failure of ordinary breeding, and thus a faintly embarrassing reminder of how far the Hikeda'ya had fallen from their years of glory.

There were no halfbloods in the Garden. She had been told that many times, in words and in other ways just as plain.

But she was nevertheless part of a group of successful recent births among the highest families, some of which had been barren for centuries, and whether she was fully accepted or not by those whose blood was entirely of the Garden, she was still noticed. In the year of her birth, only a few hundred children had been born to Nakkiga's noble families, and less than a quarter of those were full Hikeda'ya blood. Thus, when she proved superior to virtually all her fellows at the fighting games arranged between the youngest children; faster, smarter, and just as willing to hurt her own muddied, mongrel kind as she was to inflict pain on those who had scorned her for her birth, it did not escape the attention of the nobility. The Order of Sacrifice was always hungry for warriors in the years after their terrible defeat at old Asu'a. Like a drunkard trying to play a game of Thieves' Poetry, the odds had been against her from the first, and yet somehow she had overcome the shame of her blood to become a warrior. But that had not made the murmurs and the scornful faces that had surrounded her all her life any easier to ignore.

The crunching of snow and the smell of something spoiled came to her in the same moment, scattering her thoughts. Nezeru sat up, but it was only the giant, Goh Gam Gar, making his way across the snow in the last shadows of the dying night, headed away from the camp. Makho trailed a few paces behind the beast, his face an inscrutable mask.

"Lie down," the chieftain told her. "This is nothing to do with you."

She wanted no argument with Makho—at the moment she did not want his attention in any form—but although she eased herself back to the ground, she watched as the giant led him out from beneath the overhanging rock.

The giant wants to piss, she realized, *and our leader does not want him doing that too near our camp.* Someone without her training might have smiled at the idea, the leader of a Queen's Hand trailing his pet giant like a shepherd following his dog.

The two shapes, the small and the vast, were silhouetted for a brief moment against the purple sky and fading stars as she lay back down to rest. She had only just curled up and closed her eyes when the horses all began to shriek at once, and the ground beneath her heaved with a sharp, painful noise like a wedge splitting stone, followed immediately by the most terrifyingly deep roar of anger and surprise she had ever heard—a sound she could not have imagined being made by any living thing.

The ground was tipping and sliding, or that was how it seemed as Nezeru tried to struggle to her feet. Only a few paces away the dim field of white that had stretched beside them had become a huge, jagged circle of gray and black, and things—many *hundreds* of things—were streaming up out of the dark circle and onto the surface. She could still hear the giant bellowing, but his roars were muffled. Nezeru realized he must have fallen through a hole in the ice.

" '*Ware!*" shouted Kemme "*Furi'a!*" His sword rang as he tugged it from his scabbard. She struggled to find her own blade in the shards of ice at her feet. The first of the small black shapes came at them on all fours, scrambling like infant spiders, their eyes glinting in the half-light, their tiny faces twisted in eager fury. They had already pulled down one of the horses and, judging by the animal's panicked shrieks, were eating it alive.

Goblins, she realized, and her heart grew cold and heavy. *The giant has fallen through into one of their nests.* She heard Goh Gam Gar bellow again, but this time it was garbled, as though the great beast choked on his own blood.

He was gone from sight now, lost in the frozen earth, and the squeaking little manlike things the Hikeda'ya called Furi'a and mortals called "Diggers" were flooding up out of the broken ice like fire ants from a nest—already dozens had swarmed over Kemme and Ibi-Khai. She could not see or hear any sign of Makho, who had almost certainly gone down with the giant when the ice broke.

This is the end, then, Nezeru thought. *We will never escape so many.* Small, broken-nailed hands grabbed at her legs and squealing shapes began to climb her as though she were a tree. She did not even have time to sing her death song one last time before the creatures swarmed over her.

18

A Bad Book

Lillia had spent so much of her life staring at the painting of Saint Wiglaf behind the altar that she almost considered him a relative—the boring sort. Morning services were particularly hard. Lillia loved God as she should, but it was so difficult to sit still first thing in the day and listen to Father Nulles read from the Book of the Aedon about all the things God didn't want people to do.

At least it was an interesting painting: even as he was being hung from a tree for being an Aedonite, Saint Wiglaf was denouncing the Hernystiri usurper, King Tethtain. When she was little she had thought the martyr's name was Wiglamp because of the shining lines that surrounded his head in the painting, and she still thought of him that way, brave Wiglamp calling on God even as Tethtain's men tried to lift him from the ground, four of them straining against the rope as scowling, bearded Tethtain looked on. It had taken ten men to hang the single slender monk, which was a miracle, although Lillia had always thought it would have been a better miracle if they hadn't been able to hang him at all.

She tugged at Countess Rhona's hand, softly at first, then harder, trying to get her attention.

"Lillia, *what is it?*"

"I have to make water."

"Father is almost done. Hold yourself just a bit longer."

Lillia groaned, but quietly. Father Nulles was nice, in his rather pink-faced way, and she didn't want to upset him. She just didn't want to be in the chapel any longer.

At last Father finished listing the Great Sins and performed the blessing. Usually Rhona would speak with him for a little while afterward, but this time she just made Lillia curtsey, then pressed a silver coin into the priest's hand for the poor.

"I don't feel that well myself," the countess said as Lillia returned from the chapel privy and they made their way out into the long Walking Hall. "In fact, I think I need to lie down for a while."

"Lie down?" Lillia was horrified. "But I told you, there's a fair in the commons at Erchester today. They even have a bear who dances!"

"I'm sorry, honey-rabbit, but my courses are on me, and I only want to lay myself down."

Lillia made a face; it felt like an ugly one. "You said you'd take me. You're a liar!"

"Your manners are growing worse every day."

"You have to take me. You promised!"

Rhona frowned. "No, I don't, because I haven't the strength, whether I promised or not. What if I were dying—may the gods turn their ears away— what then? No, child, you'll have to stay home today."

"You can't make me. A princess is bigger than a countess, so you can't be the lord of me."

Her guardian sighed. "Mircha in her Cloak of Rains love you, girl, you're a great deal of work, and that's certain. But even you can't command this pain out of my innards, Your Fearsome Highness, so you'll have to entertain yourself in the residence today."

Lillia was so upset that for a moment she wanted to let go of the countess's hand and run away, but a look at Auntie Rhoner's pale face showed that she really wasn't well. Still, Lillia had been thinking about the dancing bear ever since one of the chambermaids told her about it the previous evening, and she wanted to see it more than, it seemed, she'd ever wanted anything. "If you feel better later, then can we go?"

"Child, I could feel ten times better and still not feel up to it. Perhaps to-morrow. Now, please, just let me lie down for a while."

But the countess must have felt a bit sorry for Lillia, because they took the longer way back, through the Hedge Garden. The recent rain had brought a flush of bright new greenery to the sculptured shapes, and since they hadn't been trimmed for a while, none of the animals were entirely recognizable at the moment, which Lillia liked very much. Was the old lion turning into a big rabbit? Was the noble horse becoming a dragon? She knew returning this way was a small gift from the countess, so she squeezed Rhona's hand in thanks.

When they got past the guards and into the residence, Rhona guided Lillia to her chamber. "Stay here, dear one. You've plenty to do, reading and sewing and your dolls. And if you're hungry before supper, ask one of your mother's ladies to find something for you. In fact, would you find one of them now and ask her to bring me a posset of treacle and nutmeg? My head is aching me fiercely."

Full of foul humors, Lillia sought out one of her mother's younger ladies-in-waiting and delivered Countess Rhona's charge, but declined the chance to wait and take the posset herself, something she had enjoyed doing when she was younger. Now that she was older she had more important things to do, and one of them was trying to think of a way she could get down to Erchester to see the dancing bear.

If she had been a boy, Lillia might have chanced sneaking out on her own. Her brother Morgan had done that more than a few times, she knew, and although he'd been punished, it had seemed to Lillia that the punishment had been a small matter indeed. But however lenient Queen Grandmother Miriamele might have been with Morgan, Lillia knew that things would not go so easily for her. Even in the heart of the Inner Bailey, she was not supposed to go off the grounds of the royal residence without a grown-up accompanying her, and often guards as well. Queen Grandmother might be away on a journey, but Lillia did not want to have to look into those fierce green eyes when she came back and admit she had flouted one of the very strictest rules.

But how else could she get to see the wonderful sights waiting for her in Erchester? The chambermaid had told her the bear had a sad face and was the most comical thing she'd ever seen, but she'd said there had also been jugglers and a fire-eater, and Hyrka dancers, and contests of wrestling and other sports. In another day or two it would be all over. What if Auntie Rho was really sick? Lillia would never get to see any of it!

The more she thought about it, the more she realized that she could not leave something this important to chance. If Uncle Timo or even King Grandfather Simon had been in the castle, she knew she could persuade one of them to take her, but they weren't, so she needed a plan.

She had wandered back into the walled Hedge Garden where she sat on a stone bench. As she swung her legs back and forth, she tore leaves into little pieces and dropped them spinning to the ground. The pile on the walkway had grown almost half a hand tall before the idea came to her. Thrilled, she wiped the sticky green juices on her dress, then charged back toward the residence.

As she approached the paneled door of her mother's chamber, Lillia could hear voices. One was her mother, of course, and the other was Grandfather Osric. She hoped that was a good sign. Her mother was usually at her kindest when there were other people around.

An experienced tactician, Lillia paused outside the door and tried to hear what they were saying. If they were having an argument, she knew it would be best to go away and come back later, because grown-ups, especially her mother, very seldom did anything nice for children if they were in a bad mood. She was glad to hear that their voices sounded fairly ordinary, although her mother did sound slightly grumpy about something.

". . . *It's not that simple,*" Mother was saying. "They don't want him to marry yet, although anyone can see it would be good for him. They don't think he's ready. Ready!" Her mother laughed, but she didn't sound very happy. "He's old enough to be chasing women up and down Main Row most nights."

"He's a young man," Lillia's grandfather said. "What do you expect?"

She was pretty sure they were talking about Morgan. Apparently her brother did little these days other than bothering ladies, from what Lillia kept hearing.

"Hah! I expect that if we wait long enough, the queen will have him married to some little pussycat of her own choosing, and then I will be pushed out the door! That's what I expect."

"You worry too much, daughter. Your son would never consent to such a thing—and neither would I. After all, I am Lord Constable as well as his grandfather. The throne needs me. They will not go out of their way to anger us."

"I wish it were that straightforward," her mother said.

Lillia waited for several long, silent moments before she knocked, so that it didn't seem as if she had been listening. One of her mother's maids opened the door and Lillia marched in. Her mother was sitting in her chair, embroidery hoop on her lap, and Grandfather Osric was standing in front of the window, frowning as he watched something going on below. Mother didn't look as if she'd actually started embroidering yet.

Lillia went right to her mother and curtseyed. "Good morning, Ma'am."

Her mother looked at her and smiled, but it was a tired smile. "Good morning, darling. Aren't you supposed to be with Countess Rhona today?"

Her grandfather turned. It was strange to see him without a hat, the top of his bare pink head exposed for everyone to see. Ever since she was a very small girl she had wanted to rub Grandfather Osric's head and see if it felt like the rest of his wrinkly, dry skin, but she had never been allowed to do it. *"He's a duke!"* everyone said, as though that had anything to do with what his head might feel like.

"Ah, there she is!" he said now. "My little princess!" But he looked weary too, and he didn't come over to pat her head as he sometimes did.

"Good morning, Grandfather." Lillia curtseyed again.

"You haven't answered my question, child," said her mother.

"Countess Rhona is unwell." Lillia looked at her grandfather, who had turned back to the window, and whispered loudly, *"She has her courses."*

Another weary smile. "Well, dear, I'm afraid I can't have you with me today. Your grandfather and I have many things to discuss and you'd just be in the way. You'll have to play by yourself."

"But there's a fair in Erchester! With a bear! A bear who dances—!"

"The countess can take you when her . . . when she's feeling better. Honestly, Lillia, I simply cannot find the time to watch over you today, let alone take you to a street fair."

"Can one of your ladies take me instead?"

"No. None of them watch you closely—and the servants are worse."

Was Lillia the only one in the whole castle who could see that outside the large window the sky was a bright, encouraging blue, and that the spring sun was shining as hard as it could? She scowled, although she knew it was her mother's least favorite expression. "There's no one else for me to go with."

"Then I suggest you read instead. What about that book that your grandfather gave you last time, the book about Saint Hildula? Have you finished that already? If you have, you can tell him all about it."

Her grandfather looked up, only half-interested, but Lillia recognized a trap when she saw one. Her mother knew very well that she hadn't read much more than the first page because it had been the dreariest thing she had ever seen, all about a good woman who had never done anything but be a nun until some Rimmersmen came and murdered her, except of course they barely talked about that interesting part at all—Lillia had skipped to the end to see—and instead the book was entirely about how very, very holy Hildula had been before that, and all the visions of Heaven she'd seen, and how much she had loved her lord Usires Aedon.

"I didn't quite finish it yet," Lillia admitted.

"Then go and do so. That's a much better way to use your day than going down into the city with all its foul vapors and dirty people." Her mother wrinkled her nose as though she could smell the filthy peasants at the fair all the way here in the Inner Keep.

Lillia saw that she had been outmaneuvered: her mother had gone immediately onto the attack while Lillia had still been hoping for a parley. "Yes, Ma'am." Not that she was actually going to read about Saint Hildula, who must have been about the most tedious saint ever, but she knew there was no sense in continuing the conversation. Mother never changed her mind. Never.

"Run along now, darling," her mother said. "I will see you at supper, I suppose. And say thank you to your grandfather for that book, since you like it so much. Go on, tell him."

"Thank you for the book, Grandfather Osric." Lillia hurried from the room before anyone asked her about the other books Osric had given her, all stories of very dutiful, very religious women. Her grandfather knew a lot about soldiers and armies, but Lillia thought he didn't have many ideas about presents for young girls.

With her grandparents and Uncle Timo traveling in the north, the only person Lillia could think of who might be able to help her now was nice Lord Pasevalles, but she couldn't find him anywhere. The grumpy old priest who worked for him said that he was in Erchester talking to some of the factors building her father's library. But the guard captain said that Pasevalles had come back, and was now in the Chancelry with the master of the mint, talking about boring old money. Where he was didn't matter so much to Lillia as the fact that he wasn't anywhere she looked, and she had all but given up on the idea of getting to see the lovely bear dance when one of the Chancelry servants mentioned that the Lord Chancellor sometimes went back to the residence to check on the very ill woman who was being tended there.

Lillia hadn't forgotten about the woman Pasevalles had brought into the castle, but Auntie Rhoner had worked hard to keep her away from the woman's bedside until Lillia had given up trying to see her. Was that where the Lord Chancellor was now? Lillia was torn between fear of whatever disease the ill woman had and a sudden desire to see what she looked like. Was she bony and weeping, like some of the beggar women in Erchester? The princess stood, hopping from one foot to the other as she tried to decide. Everybody said she should leave it to another day, but tomorrow was St. Savennin's Day, which meant the fair might soon be gone. That knowledge—and her curiosity, which never stayed quiet for long—finally pushed her up the stairs of the residence, past her family's chambers and up to the third floor.

The guard who was almost certainly supposed to be on duty at the top of the stairs was instead talking to a maid; the girl was laughing so hard at something the guard had said that she had turned a rather deep shade of red. It was not very difficult for Lillia to walk past the couple without being noticed.

When she reached the hallway it became fairly obvious that the maid she had seen was supposed to be watching over the ill woman, because the door to one of the rooms was wide open and there was no one inside except for a slender female shape stretched on the bed, her body covered by a thin blanket. As she approached, Lillia saw that the woman was tied down, which made her stop just inside the doorway, suddenly frightened. The sick woman must have heard her, because her head slowly turned until she could see Lillia.

Something truly was wrong with the woman—something frightening. Lillia wasn't sure exactly what it was, but it was more than just her tangled silvery hair and her hollow cheeks. Her eyes were strange, a bright, catlike yellow, and the shape of her face seemed wrong too.

Lillia gasped. She had never seen anyone like this. The woman only stared back, eyes not quite centered on Lillia's, as if she were only half awake. Then the strange woman's lips pursed, as if she would say something.

"P . . . p . . . p . . ." Nothing else came out of her, no word, only the soft popping noise. "Puh . . . puh . . ."

"Princess!" said someone behind her, startling Lillia so badly she squeaked and jumped. She turned around to find Brother Etan standing over her, his eyes wide, his face red and scary.

"I'm sorry!" she said. "I didn't know! I'm sorry!"

"You don't belong here, Princess," he said, but he sounded more worried than angry. A moment later, the maid who had been out on the landing came hurrying up behind him, flustered and clearly very frightened.

"I didn't mean to leave her! It's only that Tobiah the guard asked me a question, and she was sleeping, so we went out of the room. . . ."

Etan was standing beside the ill woman now. He put his fingers against her neck, then moved his hand to her forehead. The woman had stopped trying to talk and instead followed Brother Etan's hand with her wide, not-quite-human eyes. After a few moments, he turned his attention back to the maid.

"You." His words were clipped and abrupt. "Go back to your mistress and tell her I want another maid here. She and I will talk about this later."

"But I only—!"

He silenced her with a look. "Just go. I make no judgments, except that I want someone else here this morning."

The maid turned, face red and eyes wet with tears, and hurried away.

"As for you, Princess Lillia," Etan said, "I'm afraid this is not a good place for you to be, either."

"Is that lady sick?"

"After a fashion. Who is watching you today?"

Lillia knew when she was being treated like a child. She stood straight. "No one. I don't need someone to follow me around all the time. I'm not little."

"That's not . . ."

"She was trying to say something. She kept saying 'puh, puh,' but I don't know what that means. Was she trying to say 'princess'?"

"Possibly, but not likely, Highness. I doubt she knows who you are. At the moment, she doesn't know much of anything. She has a bad fever. Now, I beg pardon, but away with you, Princess Lillia. A sickroom is no place for a healthy girl like you."

"But I want to help!"

"The best help you can give me right now is to let me tend my patient." He looked at Lillia's face and his expression softened. "Perhaps you can help me another day, Princess. For right now, this woman needs rest and quiet. I'm going to leave too in just a moment."

"Well . . ." Lillia considered. "I'll go away if you tell me who she is. Why does she look like that? Is it 'cause she's ill?"

Brother Etan frowned, but Lillia could also see that she was going to get her way: She had a great deal of experience with the signs of defeated adulthood. "We don't know for certain who she is, Princess," the monk said, "but she is a Sitha."

"A Zither?" Even saying it was fearful and exciting. "You mean she's a real fairy?"

"Sitha. Yes. She was sent to our court as a messenger from her people. But someone attacked her."

Lillia felt a sudden chill. "Really?"

"Not here inside the castle," he said hurriedly. "A long way away. No one can hurt her here. And Lady Thelía and I are doing everything we can to make her better. So will you please let me get on with my task?"

Reluctantly, Lillia assented. "But I'll be back," she promised both Etan and the ill woman, who didn't seem to hear her. "I'll come back and help you take care of her."

Brother Etan rolled his eyes when he didn't think Lillia was looking, like that wouldn't be such a good thing.

As she went back down the corridor, she was sad. Nothing in the castle would be anywhere near as interesting as the Zither-woman—suddenly even a dancing bear didn't seem quite so fascinating. But she wasn't going to be allowed to help make this odd guest feel better.

"Nothing ever goes right around here," Lillia said, mostly to herself, but loud enough for anyone nearby to hear. "That is the horrible, unfair truth. Princesses don't get to do *anything* good."

As Etan was checking the Sitha-woman's wounds, she opened her eyes wide again. She tried to sit up, but her bonds prevented it. "Puh . . ." she said. "Puh . . ."

"Don't speak," he told her. "You must rest."

"Puh . . . *poison!*"

"Poison? What do you mean? I have given you nothing but good curatives, herbs to help your wounds . . ."

The maid sent as a replacement appeared in the doorway, but Etan waved her back into the hallway.

The Sitha-woman tried to say more, but could not. She licked her lips. He gave her water to drink. "I . . . feel it," she said at last in a voice like the rattle of dry grass. This was the first time Etan had heard her speak since he had helped Pasevalles hold her down and tie her limbs. "It rushes through me. I do not think I can fight it off . . ."

"Do you mean your wounds were poisoned?"

"The . . . arrows." She strained until she could turn her head enough to see his face. "Do you still have the . . . arrows?"

"By the Redeemer's Sacred Blood, I truly don't know. Lord Pasevalles and some soldiers brought you in. Most of the arrows were already broken off. I removed the arrowheads as best I could, but I don't know what became of them afterward." He couldn't tell if she was listening—her face had gone quite empty. "Can you understand me?"

She only nodded, as though her strength had left her.

"Are you certain you have been poisoned? The wounds themselves have mostly healed. I have simples I could try if there truly is poison in your blood, but it has been days since we brought you here . . ."

She only shook her head, loosely, as though her neck might be connected to her body by something less rigid than bones. "No." She managed to make her whispering voice forceful. *"Find . . . arrows . . ."* Her head sagged. Fearful, Etan climbed up onto the bed to measure her heartbeat, but was relieved to find that it seemed strong. He did not know enough about the Sitha—who did?—to be able to judge whether she was feverish or not.

Later, when the Sitha-woman was resting more peacefully, Brother Etan left her under the care of the second maid, a sensible young woman who calmly received the stern warnings that Etan knew might better have been given to her predecessor.

He could not find Pasevalles to tell him what the Sitha had said, but left a message with the Lord Chancellor's clerk before retreating to the only real privacy he had, the drawing office where the plans and models were being made for the new library. The chief architect, Seth of Woodsall, was visiting the marble quarry at Whitstan in southern Erkynland, but Etan often helped him with accounts, so his occasional presence drew little attention from the other engineers and builders.

Since Etan's own bed was in a dormitory hall in St. Sutrin's that was shared by dozens of other monks, the drawing office was also the only place he felt safe hiding the terrible, banned book from Prince John Josua's collection. Etan prayed daily that Lord Tiamak would come back before the chief architect returned so he could give the book to him instead of having to find another hiding spot. Tiamak's wife, Lady Thelía, had not accompanied her husband north, but although he respected her knowledge of herbs and medicaments more even than his own, he still did not feel he knew her well enough to trust her with the *Treatise on the Aetheric Whispers*. She was a clever and in many ways extremely broad-minded woman, but she had once been a nun.

The irony of his own position as a consecrated monk in one of God's holy orders did not escape him.

He closed the office door behind him, then went down on his knees to pray. At the end, he added a heartfelt request: *Please, O Lord, bring Lord Tiamak back to Erchester safe and soon!*

Etan had spent much of his life in a monastery, surrounded by his religious brothers, and he generally yearned for solitude. When he was on his own he could read and think without distraction, and sometimes—he felt sure—even hear the voice of God more clearly. Now, that had changed. His worries about the Sitha woman would have been enough to make him desperate for someone to share his burden, but his fear of discovery was greater. The forbidden book from the dead prince's collection haunted him every day.

Prayers finished, he pulled the book from the chest full of old parchments where he had hidden it. As always, when he actually held the *Treatise* in his hands, he was reluctant to open it, as though he stood on the threshold of some dark and ancient pagan temple.

But I cannot wait, he told himself. It was sickening just to know it existed, a book whose name was so black that even the library of the Sancellan Aedonitis kept it away from the rest of the collection, as though its pages carried some kind of disease.

A disease of bad ideas, Etan thought.

But did that mean that it had somehow caused Prince John Josua's death? All who had attended him had said that the prince's last days had been painful, terrible to endure both for the victim and those who cared for him. And even Tiamak, for all his experience and scholarship, had never been able to say what illness had killed the heir to the High Throne. A few had even whispered darkly of poison, though Tiamak had assured the king and queen he thought that highly unlikely, because the prince's illness followed no course he had ever encountered in his library of apothecarial writings.

Despite telling himself that the little Wrannaman was the best judge of such things, Etan still could not bring himself to open the book very often, although it was not the fear of envenomed pages that balked him. Like most educated men, he had heard countless rumors about the book, though all he knew of its author, Fortis the Recluse, was that he had been a bishop of the church who lived in the sixth century on the island of Warinsten, in those days still named

Gemmia and still part of Nabban's extensive empire. The book itself was written in an odd mixture of both old Nabbani and the tongue of Khandia, a land that even back in Fortis' time had been lost for centuries beneath the ocean waves. Nobody knew why Fortis had chosen that language, or where he had learned it, but church scholars had argued over the meaning of some of his most mysterious passages ever since.

What almost everyone agreed on, however, was that the wisdom contained in the *Treatise* was very dangerous. Just the headings at the beginning, in a later hand than that of the Recluse, showed the sort of subjects it contained: *Night-dwellers; Words of Power; History of Sin and Punishment; Gods of Nascadu and the Lost South*. But it was the title matter that had caused the book to be banned, a description of attempts to communicate with the demonic creatures who spoke through the aether, and whom Bishop Fortis swore he could hear using nothing more than a scrying stone and the wisdom he had learned in, as he put it, *"locations too disturbing to tell."*

Even Bishop Fortis himself might have regretted at the last gaining such wisdom. It was said that he had simply vanished one night. One of his clerks had helped him dress for bed, but just before dawn another clerk came to wake him and found him gone without trace. The tales suggested that certain sounds had been heard during the night of his disappearance—sounds his staff and servants had been too frightened to talk about with the lector's chief investigator, even under threat of excommunication. In any case, nothing more was ever heard from Fortis the Recluse, and the remaining copies of his book were put under ban by Lector Eogenis IV, collected, and supposedly all burned except for the censor's copy retained by the Sancellan Aedonitis.

A bad, dangerous, heretical book. Simply having it is sinful. Reason as you will, Brother, there is no getting around that.

Etan realized that he had been staring at the heavy black cover for a long time, so long that the candle was guttering, making shadows move fitfully along the walls. He took a breath, then another, then finally threw back the cover and began leafing through the fragile pages.

It had certainly been disturbing to find this infamous thing among Prince John Josua's possessions, and frightening to think what would happen to Etan himself if he was discovered, but neither of those things were what had him so worried, poised on the knife-edge between waiting for Lord Tiamak or going immediately to Lord Pasevalles, the only person of high rank, currently at the Hayholt, whom Etan really trusted. Because if it was a mystery how John Josua had obtained the book, it was no mystery who had owned it before the dead prince.

In one of the final chapters of Fortis' opus, titled *"Piercing the Veil,"* someone had written a note in the margin, commenting on one of the Khandian passages. It was a simple, if cryptic, note in Nabbanai script; Etan had discovered it the first time he leafed through the forbidden book after taking it from Princess Idela's chambers. It read, *"With the proper tools, this veil can be torn."*

The note seemed innocuous, but Etan had recognized the stark, impatient hand immediately, from long hours spent looking through the Hayholt's old chancelry records while on various errands for Lord Pasevalles. The man who had written this note had been dead for more than thirty years, but there was not a person in the royal household who did not know of him, and few would even speak his name aloud for fear of his vengeful ghost. After his death, all his possessions had been burned and his tower sealed shut, its doors and windows filled with quicklime *caimentos* and walled over. But somehow, the book had survived. It was without doubt a very, very bad book, but the most disturbing thing about it was the handwriting in the margin, because it unmistakably belonged to Pryrates, the Red Priest—the madman who had tried to bring the undead Storm King back to life.

19

The Moon's Token

King Simon was in a good mood, Eolair noted, and that was a
fine thing. The queen, too, was pleased that after months of travel, they were
finally on their way home to Erkynland. In fact, of all the royal party, only
Prince Morgan seemed off his feed—or off his drink, to be more precise, and
Eolair had been told why: Binabik's daughter and her man Little Snenneq had
apparently exacted a promise from Morgan not to drink too much, due to an
evening expedition they had planned. Unlike the illicit skating expedition, this
foray had been approved ahead of time, although Queen Miriamele's consent
had been reluctant. The king had only convinced her by saying, "A bit of exertion will be good for him. You don't want him to be a weakling king who
can lift nothing heavier than an ale-cup, do you?"

So as the Hand of the High Throne watched with qualified sympathy, the
prince drank nothing but watered wine that was more water than wine.

Outside the evening had finally grown quiet, although the wind had howled
and the snow flown all day. Yet another surprise spring storm had caught the
royal party in open land west of the Dimmerskog forest, forcing them off the
Vennweg and onto the unsuspecting hospitality of one Baron Narvi. Narvi was
an old knight of Rimmersgard blood, as attested by his name and the fair hair
of his youthful portrait in the outer hall, but he spoke the Westerling tongue
better than he spoke Rimmerspakk, and kept court at his tower house of Radfisk Foss in the spare, eastern Erkynlandish manner, with whitewashed walls
and little ornamentation. The latter might have been as much due to penury as
inclination—the Frostmarch borders were not rich territories at the best of
times, and the salmon, on which the baron's household made the largest part of
their living, had not yet begun the year's journey.

Thus nobody, least of all Baron Narvi himself, had expected the king and
queen to stop and take shelter at his modest castle just south of the forest,
above a steep river gorge where the Vestvenn River hurried down toward the
distant sea. But the beginning of Avrel had brought harsh weather instead of
sunshine, and although everybody in the royal party was now aching to get
back to the Hayholt—they had been traveling since Jonever and the turn of

the year—nobody wanted to risk trying to cross the wilderness of the eastern Frostmarch in the middle of a snowstorm.

Narvi, his lady wife, and his retainers were thrilled to entertain the royal couple, if somewhat ashamed of the meager fare they could offer, but as at Blarbrekk Castle, Jeremias supplemented the local supplies with stores from the High Throne's traveling household, ensuring everybody had plenty to eat and drink. Radfisk Foss was too poor a house to keep its own jugglers and musicians, so the landlords were delighted that the king and queen had brought entertainment of their own, including tumblers—one of whom could also juggle knives—and of course, a harper. Rinan found himself with the most eager audience he had met since leaving Erkynland. As the evening went along and the wine flowed, the young bard performed not just Erkynlandish songs but new ones he had learned in Hernystir and Rimmersgard during the journey. The queen even joined him, lending her unpolished but sweet voice to "She Is Ever Fair," earning herself and the harper a round of enthusiastic applause.

> *"Those shining lads and lasses will grow wan with age and care*
> *But She walks on through all the years, and She is ever fair . . ."*

At last, shortly before midnight, the baron and baroness excused themselves. "You have given us both honor and delight, Your Majesties," said Narvi, "but we are not used to such hours. Can we not persuade you to take our bed? It is not what you are used to, but it is the best in the house."

"Nonsense," said Simon, his tongue just the smallest bit fuzzy with drink. "You have treated us admirably, my good lord. Our men-at-arms are comfortable in the stables, and we shall sleep in the hall here."

Miriamele smiled and thanked them too, but she looked as though she might have preferred to take Narvi up on his offer of the best bed. Eolair, who seldom woke in the morning without some new aches apparently acquired in sleep, understood the queen's reluctance, but it was a pleasure to see Simon in a good mood, which was exactly what the wine and music and the roaring fire had given him.

Soon enough, King Simon, the trolls, and some of the others began trading old, largely true stories of the Storm King's War. The king much preferred that sort of tale, Eolair knew, especially those that painted Simon himself not as a hero but as the mooncalf boy he had once been. His pleasure in his own youthful foolishness seemed to grow with each cup of wine. "I was nothing when we started out—do you remember, Miri? I was a kitchen boy, green as grass. A kitchen boy!"

"Yes, Simon," said Miriamele, with a tiny smile for Binabik. "I think that is reasonably well known to all."

"But you were a kitchen boy of considerable bravery," said Binabik, "—like it or not. Not many would do the things you did, I am thinking." Sisqi murmured something to him and Binabik nodded. "My wife reminds me that you risked your life for me many times, even in our home on Mintahoq, when my own people had condemned me."

Simon made a face. "Tired of talking about me. Where's Morgan? Tell him about Isgrimnur. Tell him how Isgrimnur met me, first time. Tied over the back of a horse with my arse in the air!" He laughed. "There's glory, for you! There's glory." He peered around again. "Morgan should be hearing what a picture his grandfather made, riding upside down on Sludig's saddle . . ." He frowned. "But I don't see him."

"He has gone out," Miriamele said. "Marching around in the snow with Qina and her young man. Don't you remember?"

"Little Snenneq and Qina are at taking him to see some thing," said Binabik. "Mysterious, they were making it."

"Which is why I made him take guards," said the queen. "Do you truly not remember this, husband?"

"Gone out in this weather? To see what?" Simon finished his cup and bumped it against the table until one of the servants poured him some more. "What is better than hearing about how his grandfather was carried around the Frostmarch, draped over a saddle like a Hyrka bride!" He tried to demonstrate the position, but overtipped and would have fallen off the bench had not Sir Kenrick caught his arm.

"I think it may be time we all had some sleep," said Miriamele.

At first the king seemed inclined to argue, but a closer look at his wife's expression convinced him not to. "Very well," he said. "What is wrong with a few amusing stories, though, I'd like to know?"

As the king and Miriamele made their way across the hall to the sleeping spot prepared for them, and the rest of the courtiers and guards began to disperse, Binabik approached the royal couple and took Simon's elbow. The troll seemed to be holding something in his hand. Eolair was caught between curiosity and his wish to give the royal couple their privacy, but he could not shrug off his first impulse, which was to know all the High Throne's business.

"I have something for you, friend Simon," said Binabik. "Wear it close to you when you sleep."

Miriamele stared at the thing in Binabik's hand with obvious distaste. "What is it?"

"It is a talisman that I have been making. To help Simon find his dreams again—or to help the dreams find him."

Her husband reached for it, but she pulled his hand back. "No. It's ugly. It scares me."

The king's safety outweighing any kind of discretion, Eolair stepped forward for a closer look. The object nestled in Binabik's leathery palm was a bundle of bones, dried flowers, and black feathers, tied together with thread.

"I mean no offense, Binabik," said the count, "but I like this no more than the queen. Those are crow feathers, are they not? Remember, such things are sacred to Morriga, the Dark Mother. My people had to drive her worshippers out of our midst, and lately we have heard her evil name again in worrying circumstances."

The troll gave him a serious look. "Not the same at all, I am thinking, and we stand this night in Rimmersgard, not Hernystir. Things are being different in the north. Among my people, the crow is the messenger of all who are beyond the sky, Count Eolair, not just one cruel goddess. This is to help Simon's dreams find him once more."

"I don't care . . ." Miriamele began, but Simon pulled his hand from her grip and took the bundle of feathers and bones with exaggerated care, then stared at it with slightly cross-eyed intensity.

"I will wear it tonight," he said. "If there are answers for us on the Dream Road, as there were in the past, then I want to know them." He lifted his hand to forestall his wife and the lord steward. "No, no, don't scold me. Binabik is my friend, and I trust him. His cleverness has saved me many a time."

"Still, the queen is not wrong to fear, and neither is Count Eolair," the troll said. "Nothing is being simple where the Dream Road is in the matter. Let me come to you when you wake so you can tell me if you begin your dreaming once more."

Simon nodded and let his wife draw him away toward their makeshift bed-chamber, a frame of screens at the far end of the hall. Miriamele looked decidedly unhappy, and Eolair could not entirely blame her. Too many old stories and portents were in the wind, in a way not seen since the days of the Storm King's rise.

Yes, the new snow falls, but when it melts all that has been hidden comes back to the light, he thought. *Does nothing ever truly change?*

"If I may say so, Morgan—I mean, Highness," Sir Porto began, wheezing clouds of vapor like smoke from a hayfield fire, "and I mean no disrespect to the king's and queen's honorable troll friends, but—"

The first wave of the storm had passed just after sunset. The sky was clear but the hill path was almost obscured by fresh drifts. Morgan was laboring so hard to follow the two nimble trolls up the narrow, slippery way, and doing so by moonlight in addition to everything else, that he did not answer for some time. "What?" he said at last. "What? Out with it."

"I think this is a foolish adventure, Prince Morgan." The old knight seldom spoke so forcefully. "We are getting quite high up in the hills now. The guards have fallen a long distance behind us, and I am no longer the climber I was in my youth."

"You're doing well, though," Morgan said, secretly glad for the chance to catch his own breath.

"You are kind, Highness, but that misses my point. I don't know what these people from Yick-Nick plan for you, but I think we should go back."

Morgan sucked in enough air to make a derisive noise. "Nobody forced you to come, Porto. Even Astrian and Olveris had the good sense to stay inside where it's warm, and you can see how much my guards are worried about me, sitting on a rock down there somewhere. If you don't like it, go join them."

But even as he said it, Morgan was having his own second thoughts. He had supposed Snenneq and Qina simply meant to take him out walking, perhaps to look at another frozen lake—the young trolls had a strange love of being out of doors when more sensible people were sitting around a fire. Instead he found himself climbing up into the dark, slippery, stony hills for reasons they wouldn't yet explain to him. If his grandmother and grandfather knew he was endangering himself this way, they would doubtless be furious again. But somehow, for that very reason, he was determined not to turn back, not to give up and go home like a child who could not keep up with his elders.

"But I can't leave you," the old knight said with breathless indignation. "You are my liege!"

"That didn't stop the guards, did it? And I'm not your liege, anyway." Morgan looked up the path and saw Snenneq and Qina high on the slope above him now, little more than moving shadows against the stars and the black sky. "My grandmother and grandfather are your lieges—I'm only the heir. And if I fall off this damnable mountain and die, then it's even more certain I won't be anyone's liege."

"Highness!" Porto was horrified, and made the Tree sign with vigor. "Do not say such things, even in jest!"

"Very well. But I am going on, so if you are too, it's time to get on your feet."

They did not make it much farther up the mountainside before Sir Porto, weary and light-headed, lost his balance yet again and this time nearly fell down the long, steep slope. Qina, who by this point had circled back and was walking behind him, caught the old man's arm and steadied him until he could find a safe spot to sit down.

"It must be easier to be so small," said Porto as he watched Little Snenneq trotting back down the path toward them. "Every time I stand up I want to fall backward down the hill."

"This good place for old Porto Knight, I am thinking." Qina herself seemed quite fresh, her breathing even and not particularly deep as she shrugged off her pack and pulled out a woolen blanket. She had to stand on tiptoe to wrap it around the tall old man, even though Porto was sitting on a low slab of rock. "Now you have warm until we come back."

"But what will I tell the king and queen if something happens?" the old knight moaned.

"Nothing." Morgan was taking the opportunity to suck air deep into his lungs and shake snow out of his boots. "All will go well. The trolls will show me what they wish to show me, then we'll come back, and you and I will have a warming cup together. Or several, since I denied myself earlier."

"Now we must move again," said Snenneq, who seemed just as unwearied as Qina. The top of his head might only reach Morgan's chest when they stood side by side, but they were roughly the same size around the middle, and though his legs were short, his arms were almost as long as the prince's.

In fact he's made for climbing, Morgan thought. *Made for falling, me.*

"Come, friend Morgan," Snenneq said. "Follow us."

"Remind me again why I came with you?" he asked.

"Because I said I would show wonders to you," the troll told him.

"Ah. Yes. Of course." He patted Sir Porto on his blanketed shoulder, and said with a confidence he did not wholly feel, "Be brave, old campaigner. We'll be back very soon."

"Morgan Prince!" called Snenneq from somewhere above. "Almost we have reached a stopping place."

"Oh, praise the Aedon!" Morgan was feeling the cold badly now, and wishing he had drunk a great deal less water and a great deal more wine. "We're at the stopping place?"

"No," said Snenneq. "We are almost at *a* stopping place."

They scrambled up another bank of loose rock and then picked their way along a scarp that looked so narrow—though it was wider across than his shoulders—that Morgan sat down and inched along it like a child learning to crawl. He could see the lights of Radfisk Foss far below them now, obscured by the trees at the base of the slope and looking quite unreachably distant.

"Here is not for lingering," called Snenneq, despite the fact that he had just taken off his pack. "Our slowness makes me worry."

"Yes, well, I'm not all that happy myself," said Morgan. He was quite disinterested in the whole adventure now. If it had not been for the full moon, the four of them would have been climbing these perilous heights in darkness. He had been finding the company of Astrian and Olveris a bit flat of late—the knights seemed to be doing nothing more than waiting for the journey to end—but he was beginning to think it was not such a good idea to let the trolls call the dance either. "Snenneq, why are we here? In fact, where are we going?"

"It is not just a *where*," Little Snenneq said. "It is having more importance for *when*."

"Oh, God save me from mad trolls!" Morgan sat down on the broad ledge. "That is enough. We'll go back now."

"True it is only being a little more far," said Qina. "Do not be feared, Highness Prince."

"Prince Morgan. No, just 'Morgan.' Simpler. What is only a little more far?"

"The top," Snenneq explained. "But first you must be putting these on." He pulled an oilskinned bundle out of his pack and began to unwrap it. He set a pair of climbing irons before Morgan, then took the other for himself. Qina had already donned hers in what seemed less than a moment; it made Morgan feel dizzied. "Go to," Snenneq urged him. "You are remembering how, yes? But this time not for ice-sliding, only climbing." The troll laughed so loud he blew snow from the fur around his hood. "What did you call it—skatting? Skating? We will not be doing that tonight, I think." He paused, waiting for a response, grinning widely. At last he said, in a slightly injured tone, "That was a fine joke, you must admit."

"Do Singing Men have to be good at jokes?" Morgan asked, swearing silently as he knotted his cold fingers in a rawhide thong by accident.

"A Singing Man must be skilled in all things," Snenneq said with high seriousness. "Herding and hunting, making and finding, leaving and coming back again. He must travel so quietly the rabbits do not hear him pass. He must speak the languages of people and of animals and of storms—"

"He must speak when the moon is climbed too high," said Qina with a stern look.

"By the Mountain's Daughter, she is right!" Snenneq said. "You have kept me too long in conversing, Morgan Prince. Now we must go swiftly. Do not worry, Qina and myself will see you there safely."

"But where is *there*?" Morgan asked, getting cautiously onto his feet. At least this time the odd weight and protrusion of the climbing spikes felt almost familiar.

"I will tell you as we climb," Snenneq said. "Come."

If Morgan had feared some deathly scramble up a sheet of solid ice, he need not have feared. The path became steeper, and the spikes on his feet did help him not to slide, but even though they seemed to be climbing an endless slope he never felt he was in serious danger of a fall. Dying from a burst heart, though, seemed a definite possibility.

"Now hear me, Morgan Prince," Snenneq told him, slowing down just enough that Morgan could hear him if he worked hard to stay close. "Here is something I wish to be saying about your unhappiness."

"My . . . unhappiness? What unhappiness?"

Snenneq waved his hand. "I will one day be Singing Man of Mintahoq. Such things are clear to me as icy mountain water. Now, have you seen my ram that I ride? Big, is he not? He is called Falku, which in Qanuc speech means the tasty white fat. Not because I would eat him, but because he has much of it. Biggest of the rams, he always was."

Already Morgan had lost the troll's point, but he only had the strength to groan, which did not slow Snenneq at all. As far as Morgan knew, his only current unhappiness was that of being stuck in the breathless heights of the mountain with two tiny mad people who liked to climb icy slopes.

"But because my ram was biggest," Snenneq continued, now actually turned around so he could face Morgan and climb backward as he talked, "all the others must test their strength against him. Always, he was fighting. On his horns are the marks of many battles. So it always must be, I am thinking—the one who stands tallest cannot live the life of the small ones. Do you see some meaning there?"

Morgan had been scowling in discomfort so long his mouth was almost frozen into that shape. "The only meaning . . . I see . . . is that you . . . are meaning to kill me." He paused, trying to make sense of the troll's words. "Do you mean to say you hate me because I'm taller than you?"

"Ha!" Snenneq now added thigh-slapping to his backward maneuvers. "You see, you too can make jests almost as well as mine." He shook his head. "No, as *good* as mine. Almost."

"Snenneq-*henimaa*! Not so talk now!" Qina's firm tone surprised Morgan, who sometimes forgot she was only child-small, not an actual child. "Let Morgan Prince reach the top before you make more words."

Snenneq frowned, but turned around and resumed climbing, this time with what was clearly intended as quiet dignity.

A time passed in silence but for Morgan's noises of discomfort. Finally Little Snenneq called back, "We are now where we should be, and the time is still fresh—but we must hurry!"

Morgan did his best to pick up the pace, and at last, with an assist from Qina in the form of her small shoulder pushing against his hindquarters, he half-climbed, half-fell forward onto the hill's wide crest, nothing before or above him now but a sky bespattered with stars, and at its center, like a great wheel with which to steer the ship of the firmament, the pale, full moon. Morgan fell to his knees in relief, then quickly adjusted his position until he was not poking himself with his own spikes.

"Is that it?" he asked when he had regained his breath. Even with his scarf around his head his ears were so cold it was hard to keep his voice calm. "You brought me up here to look at the moon? I've *seen* the moon. We have the same moon in Erkynland, you know." He was so tired he almost felt like crying—not that he would have, especially in front of these small near-strangers.

Qina sat down beside him and Little Snenneq settled in on the other side, so that they all looked out together across the snow-shrouded foothills. To Morgan's right, the dark Dimmerskog stretched away like the rumpled pelt of an immense animal, the tips of its trees silvered by moonlight.

"It is fine to see all this, is it not?" asked Snenneq. "Others are wishing they could see so far, but only those who have climbed high can have this seeing."

Morgan huddled deeper in his cloak. "*Nobody* is wishing they could see so far, because nobody with any sense wants to be sitting on top of a mountain at night, freezing."

"Is so bad, for true?" asked Qina softly. "What you see, Highness Morgan?"

He swallowed a snappish reply. He had to admit that the moon looked astoundingly large from this vantage, and felt close enough to touch. All of creation seemed laid before him like one of the paintings on the chapel wall back home in the Hayholt. "No, it's not so bad, I suppose," he said. "But I still didn't need to climb so high just to see it."

"But you did, yes, with certainty," said Little Snenneq. "Not just to understand what others wish they could see, others who cannot climb so high as princes, but also because of what tonight is being."

Again Morgan bit back cross words. Something about the trolls was so different that he could not treat them as he did his other friends, whom he mocked and was mocked by in turn. *Well, except for Porto,* he thought, *who never mocks me.* This reminded him that the old soldier was still waiting for them down below, on the cold hillside. Whatever the trolls had planned, it would be cruel to the poor old fellow to drag it out any longer by arguing. "Very well. Tell me what is tonight being, Snenneq." He laughed despite his chattering teeth. "I mean, what is tonight?"

"Sedda's Token," the troll said promptly. "That is what we Qanuc name it. Sedda is being the moon, and if you see the biggest great-belly moon of springtime—what you call 'full moon'—from the top of a high, high place before it starts its journey down into the dark again, Sedda will give to you a token of the truth."

Morgan looked at him for a long moment. "Your pardon, but I didn't understand a word you just said."

"Here on this night, in this high place, we will cast the bones. You know how a Qanuc Singing Man casts the bones, do you not? Surely your grandfather has told you, after his long traveling with Qina's father, Binabik."

The idea sounded dimly familiar, but Morgan could not bear another long explanation with the cold scraping at his ears and nose and fingertips. "Yes," he said. "Casting the bones. Of course."

"Good." Snenneq produced a leather-wrapped bundle from of his heavy jacket, then brushed away the snow that lay before him on the rocky summit to make a bare patch. He tumbled several small, pale objects from the pouch into his hand. "The moon has a full belly and we are in a high place. We shall ask Sedda for a token for you."

"Why?"

"Because you are in need of guidance, I am thinking. Qina and her father agree."

Morgan bristled a little at the idea, but reminded himself that cold didn't care who thought what, and asked instead, "Why would this Sedda bother with someone who isn't a troll?"

"Because she is the Mother of All People, who wants only to keep her children safe."

While Snenneq began a whispered prayer in his own throaty tongue, Morgan thought briefly and a bit sourly about his own mother, whose desires seemed a great deal more complicated than those of Sedda the Moon-Mother.

After some moments, Snenneq tossed the bones as if they were a handful of dice, then squinted with keen interest at the way they fell. "Patience, my prince friend. Two more times must I cast them," he said.

When he had finished, Snenneq slowly gathered up the little bones and tipped them back into the leather pouch. "The Black Crevice and Clouds in the Pass, those were the first two. But the third was one I have not seen to fall before—I wonder if Qina's father has even cast it, though he taught it to me. Unnatural Birth, it is called."

Morgan was shivering again, despite the presence of small, solid people squeezed against him on either side. "Oh, that's charming. Are your bones calling me a bastard?"

The troll shook his head. "That is not what the words are meaning—or do you joke again? No, by what I have learned, they signify that something you expect, something you have long expected, will not come to you. Or will come, perhaps, but in much different form than you had been thinking." He frowned and weighed the sack of bones in his palm. "I think I should be speaking with Qina's father about this, because even I, clever as I certainly am, perhaps do not understand everything about this."

"Clever you am, yes," said Qina. "And full of humble."

Morgan heard the deep fondness beneath the gentle mockery and almost envied Snenneq such a forgiving love, but he was distracted by wondering what this whole adventure had been about. This was exactly why Father Nulles warned against fortune-telling, of course, that it was not only foreign and sinful, but never accurate. Because if the troll's words were true, something he had long expected would not come to him—and that could only mean the kingdom.

A prince and heir who does not become king, he thought. *Like my father, who died young.* "Are we finished, then?" he asked out loud, doing his best to keep his voice level. "Because I am so cold you may have to carry me down in a casket if we stay up here much longer."

The trolls were quiet on the long way back down to where Porto was waiting. That was fine with Morgan, who had nothing to say and no urge to hear anything more until he had poured a sufficiency of wine into his belly to thaw his frozen heart.

Despite his weariness and a great deal of drink, as well as the comfort of Baron Narvi's own bed, it took Simon a long time to fall asleep in the middle of the great hall with so many of his courtiers and servants sleeping around him. It had been long since he had slept like this, surrounded by many others, hearing so many taking breath, murmuring, even talking in the depths of dreams. As he lay in the dark clutching Binabik's talisman, the sounds they made plunged him back into memories of his youth, when he had slept piled in with the other scullions like so many loaves rising in the vast Hayholt kitchen.

Simon supposed that thinking of the past had somehow led him there, because soon he found himself roaming through the dark corridors and shaded grounds of that selfsame Hayholt, the great castle where he had grown up. To his surprise, the silent girl Leleth that he and Miriamele had known so long ago was with him, as if she and he had both been drawn to this lost place by some powerful call. He wanted to ask her what brought her back to the Hayholt, where she had once been Miriamele's handmaiden before the evil days descended on the castle, but the girl would not stay for him no matter how he called. Always she hurried just ahead, her skirts swaying as she moved in and out of shadows like a leaf caught on the breeze.

He followed Leleth down a long, covered passage that was a bit like the old tunnel between the stables and the outer keeps, but somehow was also a tree-canopied path through the woods around Da'ai Chikiza, the fairy city that had been swallowed by Aldheorte Forest centuries before Simon had been born. He and Miriamele and Binabik had floated through its dappled green tangle on a boat Valada Geloë had given them. Leleth had not been with them on that real journey, since she had been attacked by savage Norn hounds while fleeing the Hayholt, had nearly died from her wounds, and had never found her voice again. When Simon and the others left Geloë, who had given them all shelter and counsel, the little girl had stayed behind with the wise woman. In later days, Simon had sometimes seen Leleth again in dreams, both the waking and sleeping sort, so it was not too surprising to encounter her now, in this strange place full of shadows and half-ghosts. And only in dreams had Simon ever heard her voice, as he heard it again now.

"Beware the children," she called back to him. *"They are being called."*

"What children?" he asked, or thought he did, but his dream was full of voices and he was not sure if he had truly spoken. "What children?"

Leleth stepped through a gaping archway that Simon was sure had not been there a moment before, a dark space between two trees. All that remained was her voice.

"The children." It floated to him as though from the depths of a forgotten well. *"They are dead."* But even as those words chilled him, he thought he might be mistaken, that she might have called something else from the darkness—*"the children are death,"* or *"the children all dread."* "Leleth, where are you?" he cried. "What are you saying?" But the darkness between the trees was empty and silent.

Still moving in dreamy half-flight, as though only his eyes and ears were alive and connected to his teeming, confused thoughts, he followed her into the empty, dark place even as a part of him saw where he was going and tried desperately to stop him

It's a cave, he thought. *It's a hole. There's a monster inside it. It's a grave.*

Indeed, somehow he knew that what had at first seemed only a shadow between two tree trunks was something quite different—a passage lined with crumbling earth. Just when his terror became so great that he could not imagine going any farther, a line glowed into existence before him, a vertical stripe of light like a single sunbeam arrowing down to earth. His fear suddenly lessened, he found himself moving toward it, and as he did the light spread side to side, like great, radiant butterfly wings, but for one clot of black near the bottom.

A part of him understood that the glowing butterfly was made by doors opening in a dark room, allowing light to pour in, but at first it illuminated nothing. Then he saw that the clot of blackness was something standing in that light. After a moment Simon recognized it as a child's shape—a familiar child's shape.

"John Josua?" He moved closer. The boy stood motionless in the open doorway, arms spread to hold the doors open. Sleeping figures lay everywhere before the child's feet, and Simon was confused. Somehow he had found his way back to the old dormitory where the scullions slept. But what was John Josua doing here? He had never been a kitchen-worker like his father. In fact, it was strange that he could be a child at the same time that Simon himself was somehow a child. Had time itself been tipped sideways?

"Son?" He took a few steps closer, but John Josua seemed deep in thought. Simon did not look down—he was afraid to take his eyes off his son—but stepped as carefully as he could over the sleeping figures that lay between them. Some of the sleepers stirred and groaned, but none of them awoke.

Now he noticed another puzzle: for some reason, the floor of the great kitchen was covered with grass. It even seemed to be growing on top of the sleepers.

"Johnno? John Josua?" Simon drew nearer, and now could see the boy's head well enough to recognize the unforgettable swirl of his cowlick. He thought he would collapse under the weight of terror and joy. What had brought him back? And was he to be Simon's son again, or was Simon now to be his? John Josua had died, but Simon hadn't. Who was oldest?

The children are waking up, Leleth's voice called from somewhere, faint as a soft breeze through an unmown field. *They are being summoned back. Beware . . . !*

Some of the sleepers stirred, moving restlessly under the thick blanket of green that now covered them. Simon took one more step until he was close enough to touch the child-shape, and reached out to cup John Josua's chin in his hands, to look his lost son in the face.

But when he turned to his father, the child's eyes were black, the empty black of nothingness, of the end of all things.

Simon tried to scream, but couldn't. Suddenly the boy, his son, began to vanish, draining away into the ground like dark water from a leaking cistern. Only as Simon clutched at the vanishing essence did he finally discover his voice, crying his only child's name over and over even as John Josua became nothingness.

He was surrounded by lights, flickering, unsteady lights. The torches were all around him and more were coming, like fiery birds hastening to a shared meal. So bright! He blinked, and realized he was holding something in his hands. He looked and saw his fingers were clutching a scrap of white fabric.

"Simon!" It was Miriamele from somewhere behind him. The light was in his eyes, and he was confused, aching. John Josua! He had held him, had if only for a sliver of an instant touched his dead son again, and here was proof . . . !

"Simon," his wife cried, "wake up!"

She stood before him now, her familiar face the only ordinary thing in a mob of strangers. He was surrounded, and for a startled moment he felt like a beast at bay, crowded by the hunters who would take his life. Then he saw that one of them was a woman, her arms around a boy of no more than six or seven years, a slender child with something of John Josua's leanness but darker hair. The child was crying and his nightshirt was in tatters. Simon realized with growing horror that the child's gown was made of the same material as the torn scrap in his hand.

"What . . . ?" Simon looked around, saw Tiamak and a few others he recognized, found Miri again. "What happened here?"

His wife took his arm and led him away from the great double doors, back into the depths of the hall. "You had a dream, husband, a very bad dream."

"John Josua . . . I thought he was John Josua, come back. Leleth tried . . ." Simon could not remember all that had happened, but he was certain it was important. "It's the children. Leleth tried to tell me . . ."

"Leleth is more than two score and ten years gone," Miri said, and although she sounded angry, Simon could hear something else in her voice, too, something like fear, almost terror. "Never mind her. You scared that poor child to death. He was only coming into the hall to see if there was any food left from supper."

"Oh, sweet Usires," Simon said, his gut suddenly icy cold. "What did I do? Did I hurt him?"

"Just tore his nightclothes. He said you called him 'son.' That's how I knew." She helped him to lie back down on Baron Narvi's well-stuffed bed. "A bad dream. I am more angry with Binabik for giving you that thing than I am with you."

Simon shook his head. Part of him was relieved it hadn't been real, but part of him was not willing to let go. "It wasn't all a dream. I don't think it was. I think . . . what did Leleth say? *The children are dead.* I think that's what it was. Or was it, *the children are summoned* . . . ?"

"Sssshhhh." Miri put her hand against his lips. The fingers were cool and soothing, but her voice was less so. "No more talk, husband. You have frightened everyone quite enough."

"I will not sleep," he said. "How can I? That was no mere dream—"

"It was one of the baron's little grand-nephews," said the queen. "How could it have been anything else? Our John Josua is gone—by the Aedon's sweet mother, you know that, Simon! John Josua is in Heaven with Usires and God's angels. Why would he be roaming the earth? You know he is at rest." She reached for his hand, pried open his fingers. "Give that to me."

She took the talisman of feathers and flowers that Binabik had made him and threw it to the floor, then ground it beneath her heel, the small bones crunching like twigs. "I will burn it in the morning," she said.

Simon wanted to argue, but he felt as though he had fallen asleep in one country and awakened in another. "But I saw our son!"

"Demons can take familiar shapes. Enough. Go back to sleep."

Simon let his head fall back against the pallet and tried to concentrate on Miri's fingers stroking his brow. He could feel her fear and wondered why she was so frightened. *Just a dream, she says.* He was already feeling muddled in the dark behind his closed eyelids. *She's right. What else could it be . . . ?*

When he fell back into sleep, Simon did not dream again, or if he did, there was no trace of it in his memory when he woke.

20

His Bright Gem

The swarm of chittering, biting things seemed to have no ending. Nezeru cut them down like a slave mowing barley, but new Furi'a kept scrambling toward her across the tiny corpses of their fellows.

She had called out to Makho and her other companions a dozen times, even to the Singer Saomeji, but if any of them answered she could not hear it above the thin screeching of the goblins. The creatures seemed to be everywhere, boiling out of the ground like maggots from a rotting animal carcass, as if beneath its hard skin of snow and ice the earth itself was all putrefaction.

Where had they come from so suddenly? She remembered the giant Goh Gam Gar walking, then a moment later he had disappeared when the ground seemed to fall away beneath him. The earth beneath their feet must be riddled with Furi'a burrows, and the weight of the great beast had simply been too much.

She thought she heard Makho's shout, *"Here to me!"* but couldn't be certain where it came from. In any case, at that moment it was all she could do to keep the scuttling goblins from overwhelming her where she stood. Although dozens lay slaughtered around her feet, half a dozen of the hideous, manlike beasts were climbing her body, some with sharp stone blades in their tiny, malformed hands. Nezeru knew that if not for her jerkin and trews made of armored hide, the creatures would already be stabbing their crude knives into her flesh.

With a great shake, she managed to dislodge several of the things at once. "Makho!" she screamed. "Where are you? I am here!" But no one answered. The hand chieftain was either too busy defending himself or dead. The words of the first Queen's Stricture came to her, as if she were a child again.

Mother of All, give strength to your servant. My life is yours. My body is yours. My spirit is yours.

A desperate, blasphemous thought followed the prayer, as if someone else entirely had spoken in her mind. *But it was the queen who sent us here to die!* Even in the grip of fear, Nezeru was ashamed by this proof of her own cowardly mortal blood. Was she not a Queen's Talon, sworn and death-sung? If the Mother of All needed dragon's blood, then it was the Talons' holy task to provide it. If they died trying to do so—if Nezeru herself died here, overrun by these squeaking nightmares—what would that matter? Others would come to serve the queen. The Hikeda'ya would survive and the Garden would be remembered. Only the queen could promise that.

All this sped through her mind in a fraction of an instant, then Nezeru felt a pain sharp as fire—something was biting her wrist. She thrashed her arm but could not dislodge it. One of the Furi'a had managed to find a bare space between her glove and the sleeve of her jerkin, and now it hung there like a large rat that she could not shake loose. The rest of the goblins took advantage of her distraction to throw themselves at her, so Nezeru hammered the matted little head as hard as she could with the pommel of her sword until she felt the skull crunch. The digger dropped away from her now-bloody wrist, but another half dozen were already climbing up her legs; even as she pulled some off, others scrambled to reach her face. Every time she snatched one away, two more seemed to take its place, and the snowy ground all about was alive with Furi'a—more than she had ever seen, more than she had believed could exist in one place. Nezeru knew she was looking at her own death. Even an entire squadron of Sacrifices could not have prevailed against such vast numbers.

She began to chant her death-song, the one she had sung in the arena on the day she had become a Queen's Talon.

> *Hea-hai! Hea-hai!*
> *Yes, I live for the Garden,*
> *But I died when the blessed Garden died.*
> *Yes, I live for the Queen,*
> *But I died when her son the White Prince died . . .*

Suddenly, she saw a bright light sputter across the gray sky, then a burning ball of flame roared down into the center of the goblin swarm only a dozen paces from where she stood. Fire splashed over the swarming creatures as the arrow struck ground, in an instant changing their hungry chattering into shrieks of terror so high-pitched she could barely hear them. Another burning ball came hurtling down, striking closer to her this time. Nezeru threw herself to one side and began crawling. The digging creatures spattered by the fiery bolts shrieked and ran in all directions across the snow, blinded by pain and terror; a substantial number never moved again, but lay blackened and burning in the spots where the fire had struck them, their ugly little bodies twitching like the legs of dying insects. This was no ordinary fire, Nezeru recognized, but something thicker and hotter, a fire that clung where it fell and kept blazing.

As most of her enemies scattered, at least for the moment, she scraped with her knife at the clawing Furi'a that still clung to her, sawing loose some who would not release their grip, even in death. As she did, she saw a shape sliding down the nearby hill, a white figure against a white slope, carrying something that burned far brighter than the dim dawn skies. It was a flaming arrow, and even as the white-clad figure slid, the arrow flew from his bow like some mortal fable of an angry god flinging thunderbolts. The arrow splashed fire through the ranks of diggers still climbing from the hole in the ground. At first Nezeru thought this must be Saomeji wielding the powers of his order, but the figure did not have the Singer's compact size and, even in the weak light just before sunrise, his partially hooded face seemed oddly dark.

Nezeru felt the rumble beneath her feet a long moment before she heard it, then turned in time to see something huge erupt from beneath the snow like a mountain created in a single moment. It was Goh Gam Gar, roaring as he thrashed his way free of the broken ice, his fur matted all over with blood.

"To me!" someone shouted again, and Nezeru recognized the voice as Makho's. He was alive, although she still could not locate him. She *could* see the white-clad newcomer, who had a blazing arrow balanced on his bow and had almost reached the bottom of the slope; for a moment she could see the stranger's face clearly.

Their would-be savior was a mortal.

This mortal stopped a few long paces from the bottom of the slope and waved his arm urgently, then sent another streak of flame into the swarm of diggers where they were thickest, around the hole where the giant had first broken through. As the flames splashed them, the little creatures milled in screeching confusion, some still trying to climb out of the tunnels while others, many badly burned, fought to get back in. The din was terrible and shrill, like the piping of terrified bats. Nezeru saw now that the mortal carried a pot of flames in his hand, but had to set it down each time he wanted to draw his bow, which slowed him considerably on the steep slope.

Goh Gam Gar had dug his way out of the collapsed snow and out onto open ground with only one hand, because his other clutched the limp body of one of the Hikeda'ya as though it were a child's doll.

"Up here!" the mortal cried. "Up here, where it is only rock beneath. Their tunnels do not reach here!" To Nezeru's further astonishment, he said it in flawless *Hikeda'yasao*, the speech of Nakkiga.

Now that fire was no longer falling on them from the sky, the diggers were beginning to find their courage again. The terrified horde that had seemed about to disappear back into the earth only moments earlier now came rushing back out into the blue dawn. Nezeru knew she should wait for Makho to command them, but she could not see the hand chieftain at all and could barely hear his voice, so instead she scrambled over the bloody snow mounds toward the slope where the stranger waited, treading on tiny, burned bodies with almost every step.

A moment later Makho himself appeared at the opposite edge of the great hole. He was clearly exhausted and had taken many wounds—his arms, neck, and face were all dripping blood—but he found the strength to reach back down into the pit and help another red-smeared figure that Nezeru guessed must be Kemme, and then began dragging him up the hill. After a moment Kemme found the strength to stumble after Makho on his own. Even the giant had managed finally to clamber out of the hole, and was crawling up the icy slope on all fours, leaving broad streaks of red on the blue, dawn-brightened snow.

The stranger led Makho's Talons up the snowy hill until they reached a flat overhang of rock a hundred steps above the valley floor. Only when they were far enough beneath the overhang to feel stone both beneath their feet did they let themselves slump to the ground in exhaustion, gasping for breath. Nezeru's heart was beating even faster than it had in her fight to escape the island of the bones; she had been so certain death had come that it was hard for her to understand that she was still alive. Her very bones seemed to quiver within her. The smell of blood and burning goblin flesh was everywhere, fouler even than the stench of the giant at such close quarters.

For long moments no one spoke, then Makho stirred and sat up, glaring at their rescuer where he crouched a few yards away. For half a moment the golden color of the stranger's skin almost made Nezeru believe she had mis-identified him as a mortal, that he must really be a Zida'ya, the Hikeda'ya's untrustworthy cousins, but the bones of his face were nothing like theirs. It was only a long life in the sun that had given such strange color to his skin.

"Who are you?" Makho demanded of him. "How do you dare interfere in the great queen's business?"

The mortal, who wore clothing made of scraped white hides, gave Makho a look that Nezeru could only interpret as amused, as bizarre and dangerous as that seemed. He was tall and almost as slender as a Hikeda'ya, and his short, straight hair was colored a much lighter gold than his skin, so pale that it was almost white. "Ah, I beg pardon," he said to Makho. "Was it your business to die, then? Because otherwise, instead of interfering, I just saved your queen's hand from being eaten by goblins. I was taught that the Cloud People brought courtesy with them from the Garden as well as witchwood—"

Before the mortal had even finished, Makho lunged across the distance between them and pressed the tip of Cold Root, still festooned with the bloody hair and rags of dead Furi'a, against the stranger's throat, leaning so close that their faces were only a few handspans apart. "Why do you speak of witchwood, mortal?" Makho said in a serpent's hiss. "You are a spy."

The mortal only stared back at him, then said, "Look down."

Nezeru saw it at the same time as Makho himself did: even with the chieftain's sword at his throat, the stranger managed to draw his own long, thin blade in an instant. In a blink, its point was touching Makho's ribcage, poised just above his heart. Nezeru was stunned. Even Makho, for all his fierce scowl, seemed slightly unnerved, and no wonder: Who had ever heard of a mortal as swift as one of the Hikeda'ya?

"If I die, then you die in the same second," the stranger said with surprising mildness. "If you prefer another conclusion to this *ra'haishu*—" he used an old Hikeda'ya term that meant "tunnel meeting" and implied a mistake that could lead to sudden death—"then I suggest you take your blade (which by the way is in need of cleaning) away from my neck and we can begin again. I imagine this time you will begin by thanking me."

A low rumbling filled the shallow cave. It was Goh Gam Gar, crouched in a pool of his own blood, laughing. "I like it! This little ice rat has teeth!"

Makho pulled the crystal goad from his jerkin and pointed it toward the giant. His hand trembled, which was one of the more unexpected things Nezeru had seen in this long hour of surprises. "Open your mouth to me again, monster, and I will make you tear off your own head."

"I can see you must be a very popular leader," said the mortal.

"Makho," said Saomeji. "A moment . . ."

"Do not use my name, you fool."

"I am sorry, but I have words you must hear." The Singer held up his hands, which were stained with blood. Even his sleeves were drenched in red almost to the elbow. "Ibi-Khai is dead."

"What?" Makho turned from the stranger so quickly that Nezeru thought he might even have been grateful for the distraction. "Are you certain?"

Saomeji gestured to Ibi-Khai's motionless form, which the giant had set down on the ground a short distance away. "See for yourself. His throat has been torn out by the Furi'a. He was dead before we reached this spot."

"But how will we find our way through unknown lands?" Kemme demanded, as though angry at their dead comrade. "Only Ibi-Khai was told the way. Without another Echo to learn it from our masters, we are lost. We will never find . . ."

"Silence!" Makho had stepped back, his face rigid with fury, as well as something else Nezeru had never seen but which almost looked like fear. "Have you lost your wits, all of you? We will talk when we have decided what to do with this stranger—a stranger who very conveniently speaks our tongue." He glared at their mortal rescuer. "What is your name and business, creature, and how do you know the words of the Hikeda'ya?"

The stranger's long knife had disappeared again as suddenly as it had appeared; though he stared back at Makho without fear, he now showed empty hands. "My name is Jarnulf. I speak your tongue because I was raised beside the mountain, in Nakkiga-That-Was, before I became free."

"Liar," said Makho. "There are no free mortals in Nakkiga."

"I am not in Nakkiga, am I? But I was freed by my master, Denabi sey-Xoka."

Makho, Kemme, and Saomeji all stared at the stranger in surprise. Even Nezeru recognized the name.

"You lie." Makho held one hand poised near Cold Root's hilt. Violence filled the air like incense. "Anyone who speaks our tongue could claim to have belonged to the Weapons Master Denabi. His name is well known in all the lands of our people and any liar could learn it."

"I did not simply belong to him," Jarnulf said. "I was trained by the master's own hand." As with the long knife, the mortal's sword seemed almost to jump into his hand. "Do you wish to test me, Hand Chieftain?" the mortal asked. "It seems a poor idea to me, since you have already lost one of your company today."

Makho did not speak, but batted away the mortal's blade with his bare hand and then sprang into an astonishingly swift attack, Cold Root a silvery blur. Nezeru knew that for all her own speed, if she had been the target she would already be dead, but the mortal barely moved, tilting his wrist and sword just enough to divert Makho's lunge, pivoting easily on his heel to direct the force of the attack past him.

The hand chieftain did not let his obvious surprise at the skill of Jarnulf's defense end his attack. For a few brief moments both blades whirled and struck, struck again, then jumped apart. Neither had drawn blood, and the mortal did not look as if he had been seriously tested. Nezeru kept her expression carefully neutral, but inside she was amazed and disturbed. Their chieftain was known as one of the best blades in all the Order of Sacrifice. She herself would never have dared to cross swords with Makho, and yet here was a mortal, a former slave if he spoke the truth, who might be his equal.

"Chieftain Makho, I beg you stop," cried Saomeji. He stepped between the two of them, an act of bravery that impressed Nezeru almost as much as the fighting skill of the young mortal. "It is daylight now, which is the only thing that keeps the Furi'a from attacking us again. We must get farther from their nest, much farther, before the dark comes again. And we are already badly wearied."

"Speak for yourself," chortled the giant. "Goh Gam Gar has not had such sport since I ate one of the knights of old Asu'a during the Storm King's fall. Let the two of them fight on!"

Makho never turned his eyes from Jarnulf. "This creature is a spy. Everything he says is impossible. Trained by Denabi himself? A mortal slave with no collar?"

"I told you. Denabi-*z'hue* himself took the collar from my neck." Jarnulf looked at Makho again, then turned his gaze to the rest of the Hikeda'ya and deliberately set his blade point down against the snow, pushing it in until it stood on its own. "I will show you. You, the female—come and look." He untied the cords at the top of his hide jacket, folded back the collar, then tilted his head forward like a victim readied for sacrifice.

Nezeru didn't know what to do. Ibi-Khai lay dead, the rest were still listless from battle, and Makho only glared at the stranger like a wolf protecting its kill. She walked toward the stranger, waiting for her chieftain to order her to stop, but Makho said nothing.

The first surprise was that the mortal was only a little taller than she was. The second was his smell, a very strange mixture of scents she identified as typical of mortals, but strangely diminished, as well as a strong smell of pine sap. Nezeru leaned closer to examine him. A line of callused flesh ringed the base of his neck where it began to broaden into his shoulders, in exactly the place a slave-yoke would sit.

"He has a scar from the *kuwa*," she reported.

"Which proves only that he was a slave once," snapped Makho, "and perhaps still is, despite his fanciful tale of Denabi. How is it that a former slave roams free on the borders of Hikeda'ya lands?"

"Because I am Queen's Huntsman and a slave-taker," said Jarnulf, knotting his jacket closed again. "I capture those that try to flee the Queen's lands. If you still doubt me, I suggest you ask my former master."

"Denabi sey-Xoka went to wait for the Garden three circles of seasons ago," said Makho. "But I'm sure you knew that, since it makes your story more convenient."

A strange expression crossed the mortal's face, one Nezeru did not entirely recognize: there was sadness in it, but something else as well. "No. I did not know that my old master had died. I have not returned to Nakkiga in many years. I do my business with the border castles." Jarnulf's hand rose and sketched the Hikeda'ya sign for Hopeful Return. "So the Weapons Master travels back to the Garden. May his road be straight."

He had done it all so naturally, so much like any ordinary man of her people, that Nezeru could no longer doubt him. Even Makho had lost something of his usual certainty, but still stared at the newcomer as if he were some kind of wandering spirit or other dubious omen.

"Do you know the lands beyond our borders well, Queen's Huntsman?" Saomeji suddenly asked.

Jarnulf almost smiled, but it was not a friendly expression. "Of course. I travel far in search of traitors and the queen's other enemies. I know the lands beyond Nakkiga's old walls as well as I know my own skin, my own bones."

Saomeji turned to Makho. "Chieftain, perhaps this man does not bring us bad fortune but good. Ibi-Khai is dead. He was the only one told of our route—without him, we will not find our way to our destination. And if we turn back, it will take us at least a moon to return to Nakkiga and find another Echo."

"You have your Songs, little sorcerer," said Makho angrily. "All your precious secrets, your orders from your lord and master that you have not shared with me. *You* can lead us where we need to go."

Saomeji made a sign of regret. "My only real master is my duty to our queen—but no, Makho, I cannot lead us where we need to go. And unless you wish me to talk about it in front of this mortal you so distrust, the reasons will have to wait until you and I are alone."

Makho stared at him, eyes and face empty as a statue's. "So what are you saying?"

"This queen's huntsman knows these lands. We do not. Perhaps after what we have just suffered—and from which we still must escape—this is a stroke of good luck we should not ignore. Perhaps this one can help us find our way, so we do not have to go back to Nakkiga in defeat and failure." Nezeru heard a gentle increase of emphasis before "we." What he meant was "so *you* do not have to go back," and Makho knew it too.

"None of you has asked me whether I have any interest in leading you anywhere," pointed out Jarnulf. "To be honest, I am not sure I wish to spend so much time in your company, however exalted it might seem to an ex-slave like myself."

Makho glared at him before turning back to Saomeji. "Come to one side then and speak your mind to me, Singer. But, mortal, remember this: even if you are a freed slave, the shadow of the *kuwa* will be on your neck forever. Remain here until I decide what to do with you."

Jarnulf did not reply to this, but only smiled at him—smiled yet again at an angry chieftain of the Queen's Talons, as though he feared Makho not at all.

Nobody should ever be that brave—or that foolish, Nezeru thought. *What manner of odd creature has found us?*

More than twenty years in the heart of Stormspike had taught Tzoja caution, and most of that had been in quieter, safer times, when the queen still slept. Now Utuk'ku had returned, and Tzoja could almost feel Nakkiga shuddering into its old, dark wakefulness.

She opened the door of her small room and peered out into the corridor, the dark, silent corridor that sometimes made her feel she had arrived at the very end of the earth, so far from everything she had known as a child that even memories could no longer reach her. She saw no one, and what was more important, heard no one. Relieved, she ducked back inside.

She grabbed the frame of her bed, which despite not being very large took up much of the space in the room. She pulled it away from the wall, then felt for the sliding panel hidden behind it. When she found it she took the griefstone key that hung on a chain at her neck, turned it in the lock, and slid the panel open.

Inside were her most precious things—a straw doll, a colorful head scarf, a coin—all bits of her childhood and the free life she had led, although they were no longer the only secrets she kept there. She pushed them to one side and removed her candle and two carvings, one a soapstone statue of the Green Mother, Frayja, and the other a Holy Tree made of polished wood, with the upside-down body of tormented Usires upon it. Over the years, some had tried to convince her there was only one god, but Tzoja could not afford to limit the scope of her prayers.

"Please, great ones in the sky, keep my daughter Nezeru safe from harm. Do not let the shadow of death fall upon her. Do not let evil men whisper in her ear, or sing to her songs that will make her heart grow fearful.

"Reward a mother's devotion, Lady Fray. As no one may enter your sacred bower without your permission, let nothing that means Nezeru harm approach her." Finished, she kissed the little statue and moved on to the Tree.

"Reward a worshipper's devotion, Lord Usires. As you gave yourself to protect us all from your Father's wrath, protect my daughter from the wrathful ones that would harm her."

All prayers finished, she remained on her knees for some time watching the candle flame, which stood as steady in the breezeless room as if it were carved stone. She stared until she felt almost as though she could surround herself with that flame, could wrap it around her like a magical cloak and fly away from this place. Oh, if only that were true . . . !

Tzoja fought back pointless tears, then realized with a start that she had no idea how much time she had spent gazing at the candle. The noses of her captors were so sharp that the smell of it, small as it was, might be noticed by any Hikeda'ya who entered the corridor. She licked her fingers and snuffed it, then closed the sliding panel. She was just reaching for the goatskin bundle hidden at the very back, which was now her most precious possession, when the door rattled behind her. It was all Tzoja could do to stifle a cry of fear as she tried but failed to slide the panel closed and push the bed back before the door opened.

Her master stepped in. "My shining one, what are you doing?"

She was trembling all over, her relief unable to quiet her terror. She sank down onto her bed as the high magister closed the door behind him. "Oh, my lord Viyeki, you frightened me," she said. "I was only looking at my things, those few odds and ends you have kindly let me keep." She prayed he would not ask to see them: she had not been able to hide the goatskin bundle.

"You have lit a candle again," he said. "I can smell it. That is foolishness, Tzoja—dangerous foolishness." He knelt beside her, his heavy magister's cloak rustling. "You are shaking."

"Your arrival surprised me. I thought it was someone else . . . that I had been found out."

"Look at you! So terrified!" He sat on the low bed, gestured for her to come into his arms. "And yet again and again you risk your freedom—and mine, I should remind you—for a few superstitious trinkets."

"I am sorry, my lord," she said. "I am an ungrateful wretch, it's true—a fool. But it gives me happiness, to remember my life before coming here."

"Is your life as my mistress so unhappy, then?"

She pushed her head against the hardness of his narrow chest. He felt more like a slender youth than a grown man, this creature so many times her own age. Sometimes she felt his antiquity as a fatal chasm whose depths might destroy her but could never be known. He was as foreign to her as a horse or a bird, but she did not doubt his kindness. Sometimes she even loved him with the helpless, grateful love of a favored slave, but what else she felt for him she could not say: the emotions were too confusing, too strange. "No, my lord. You—and our child—are the great fortune of my life. If you had not found me

I would have died in the pens with the other breeding slaves. How could I be anything but grateful?"

Viyeki leaned back and looked her over carefully. "Grateful is not happy. A pampered slave is still a slave. I hate to see you troubled, my bright gem."

He was very clever, this immortal who had given her such extraordinary gifts of freedom, had granted her privileges far beyond what any of her kind had ever enjoyed among the Hikeda'ya. Tzoja reminded herself that whatever happened, she must always respect his intelligence. Many of his race were so steeped in the old traditions and hatreds that they could not see her kind as anything except animals, but Viyeki was different. He had thrived in the confusing years while the queen slept, discerning opportunities for useful change where others saw only destruction, failure, the end of everything.

"How can I be troubled now that you have come to see me?" she said, eager to change the subject. "Your company is a cure for all ailments."

Instead of smiling at such a fanciful notion, as she had hoped he would, Viyeki's thin mouth pulled into a tight line. "Ah. But I have news for you, and I do not think it will bring you that sort of happiness."

"What do you mean?" Her heart stuttered. Had she somehow been found out? "You have told me already of the queen's anger at slaves like me living in the houses of the nobility."

"I fear this is something different—something new."

She suddenly felt cold as the winds that swirled around Stormspike. "New?"

"It is not certain. But my cleric heard from his hearth brother, who is a commander of the Echoes, that I am to be given an important task by the Queen herself. A journey."

Now the cold that had seized her threatened to become something more, a deadly chill that would freeze her where she sat and stop her heart. "How can that be? How can anyone know it if you have not been told yourself?" She had already despaired of being ready to escape the house before Drukhi's Day. If the high magister was sent out of Nakkiga now, Tzoja knew she would not live to hear nine bells ring in the great temple.

Viyeki reached out and touched her face. "Are you weeping? How can this be? Such a task from the queen will be a great honor. It will bring great credit on my house and my child, too. Our child. You long for Nezeru to achieve honor—how much easier will that be if I bring a triumph back for the Mother of All?"

"I don't want my daughter to have honor! I want her to be happy, to be safe!" She looked at his uncomprehending face and the gap between them, the chasm, suddenly seemed not just impassable but incomprehensibly vast. "But it is not even Nezeru I fear for, it is for me. And for you!"

"I do not understand you, Tzoja."

She rubbed the tears from her eyes. She was furious with herself. The Norns, even the most decent among them like Viyeki, did not understand weeping over such things, no matter the depth of the sorrow, the span of the tragedy. To weep was to mark herself even more firmly as *other*, as little more than an animal. In her misery, she said something she knew she should not. "Are you really so foolish, my lord?"

He drew back, anger visible in the subtle movements of his face. "How dare you say that to me?"

"Because I care for you. As no one else does. And I am afraid."

He eyed her as though she might do something even more incomprehensible than crying, might sprout wings or begin barking like a hound. "Afraid? Of me?"

"No, Lord, of your enemies. Of *my* enemies."

"You fear the queen's words too much. You do not understand how things are with my people." The shift in his tone told her that he had decided that the animal was frightened by what it did not understand, that now he would soothe her. "You live in one of the greatest houses in all Nakkiga, and we have many slaves, mortal and Hikeda'ya. I am High Magister of the Builder's Order!"

"And that is why *you* have enemies." Sometimes Tzoja could not understand how Viyeki could be so canny about the treacherous world outside his house, but so oblivious to what passed within his own walls. "*My* enemies are right here in this great house. Your servants. Your wife."

"Khimabu?" Again, he was mystified. "She does not like you, it is true, but she would not dare harm you. You are the mother of my only child."

Tzoja could do nothing to contain her despair. "That is exactly why she would kill me if she had the chance, my lord. Can you really not see that?"

He shook his head, his expression grave. "If I leave, I will make certain that you are protected. You are accredited to our household list. All is in order and my will has been made clear. Nobody will dare to question it, even if I am absent on the queen's business. I promise you will be safe."

It was all she could do simply to find strength to answer him. "And who will keep *you* safe, my lord? If your enemies destroy you, what will your promises mean then? Great Ekimeniso promised to keep his people free—what did his promises mean after he was dead?"

"Do not quote my own race's history to me, Tzoja, especially in a way that treads close to the heretical. I allow you much liberty, but that is taking a step too far." Viyeki rearranged his robes and stood. "I wished only to tell you important news—glad news, in fact, at a time when all is uncertain among the nobles and magisters."

"No, don't leave," she said. "I'm sorry for speaking badly, my lord. Please, if you believe nothing else, believe that you, too, are in danger. Your enemies have been waiting for just such a moment."

"I will not hear such talk, Tzoja. You may not understand it, but you demean the honor of my entire household."

It was pointless. She bowed her head. "I am sorry, my lord."

"You will be safe. I promise you. And when I return, if this great task is indeed given to me, you will be as much the victor as I, because our daughter will also benefit." He moved to the door. "Do not light any more candles. If you are fearful, remember that your own mistakes can be your worst enemies."

And with that cold comfort, Viyeki slipped from her room. Like all his kind, he moved with the silent grace of a hunting beast.

But I think it is you, my lord, who does not understand. For all the centuries you have lived, you still do not understand that when great changes are afoot, the old certainties are no longer useful.

When she had given her lover enough time to depart the corridor, she set her bench to block the door and took the hide-wrapped bundle from its hiding place, then carefully spilled the contents onto her bed. A knife, some rope, the stubs of several candles, flint and firechalk, all the things she had hidden away so long ago, as well as the gloves she had bought at the last Animal Market. But she still needed more, much more, and instead of the weeks she had hoped for she now knew she had only days of safety left.

Even if her lover did not realize it, Tzoja knew that nothing in Nakkiga would ever be the same. The queen of the Norns had awakened after her long slumber, and her shadow had fallen upon her people again. In fact, shadows were thickening all across the ancient city

She slid the bundle back into its hiding place, and though she did not dare light the candle again, she still prayed one more time to gods old and new.

Jarnulf knew that in the end, he would have to swallow his hatred of their kind and agree to lead them. The Hikeda'ya scouts he had killed the day before still lay at the far end of the valley, propped against a tree, their destruction marked with the sign of the White Hand. He needed to make sure he kept these Talons from discovering the bodies. Their recent deaths and his own sudden presence would surely seem too much of a coincidence in lands as untraveled as these.

Hiding his vengeful acts was not the only reason he had decided to guide them: whether these Norns were a war party or a scouting party, they were also one of the strangest groups Jarnulf had yet encountered. Their leader Makho was nothing surprising, a cold, practical tactician, a hard-eyed killer armored in the Way of the Exiles. His second in command, Kemme, also seemed a familiar quantity, a soldier who would die happily as long as he could do it with his teeth sunk in an enemy's throat. But as Jarnulf watched the rest of them coming up the rocky scarp, the snow-covered plain where the diggers had attacked ever more distant below, he found he could not readily understand them. The other Talons, unusual though they might be, the halfblood Sacrifice Nezeru and the young, halfblood sorcerer Saomeji, were at least members of the usual Orders to be found making up a hand, as the dead Whisperer Ibi-Khai had also been. But the largest giant that Jarnulf had ever encountered trudged through the snow behind them, shaggy pelt curling and waving in the breeze, and the presence of Goh Gam Gar confounded him most of all.

"Up here," he called back to them. The sky was gray and lowering and even in mid-afternoon the light was beginning to fail. He did not want to face night on the ground, not so close to a nest of Furi'a. He also wanted to keep the Talons safe as well, at least until he understood their task, however much he might desire them all dead otherwise. Jarnulf had killed many warriors of their race over the years, but the presence of the giant told him that these five were something different; until he knew what made them so and what they were doing, he needed them alive.

When the Hikeda'ya reached the top of the rise Jarnulf pointed to a place where the horses could be tethered out of the wind and camp could be made. After Makho had given permission, Jarnulf tied up his own horse and began to build a fire in a long crevice of the rock face of their makeshift stable.

"We cannot show fire here, fool," Makho said when he saw. "We are no longer on the Queen's land."

"Trust me, there is no one within miles." Jarnulf kept working as he spoke, knowing that if he made eye contact he would be drawn into another confrontation. "Except the diggers, of course, but they hate flame. Which, I remind you, is why you are alive to complain at this moment. Feel free to thank me—I used the last of my pot of Perdruinese Fire saving you. It may be a year before I can get to a trading outpost and buy more."

"What of giants?" demanded Kemme. "Are we safe from them as well?"

"I doubt there are any about that are larger than your friend." He nodded toward Goh Gam Gar, who was digging himself a hole in the snow a short distance from the mouth of the crevice. Each of the giant's hands was nearly the size of a battle shield and he was making swift work of it. Jarnulf could not have missed the witchwood yoke around the giant's neck, a much bigger slave collar than the one he had once worn. It was clear the monster was being restrained, most likely by the red crystal Makho had been waving, and that was another interesting thing to consider.

"We Hikeda'ya are not like you sun-craving mortals," Makho said. "We do not hide during the dark hours. We travel. We do what our queen bids us."

"Which is? In truth, Chieftain Makho, it is hard to guide people who keep so many secrets."

Makho only glared at him. The giant laughed, a deep rumble like someone pushing a piece of heavy furniture across a wooden floor.

"Well, it does not matter," said Jarnulf. "You may well travel at night all that you wish—but not here. The goblins are fierce this spring, more lively than ever in my memory, and they attack everything that comes near. This whole valley is riddled with their tunnels, as you discovered, and there are other nests as large as the one you stumbled into. That is why I travel only along the rocks here, not down on the snow, where footfalls sound in those creatures' ears like the beating of a drum."

"Will you continue to guide us, then, stranger?" asked the one called Sao-meji. "Or at least tell us where we can find safe passage across these plains that are so near our enemies' lands?"

Like their Hikeda'ya masters, mortal slaves of Nakkiga learned early in life to fear the minions of Akhenabi's order, so Jarnulf would never trust this golden-eyed Norn, no matter how mildly he spoke: it was as much as he could do simply to hide his hatred of them all. But that did not stop him wondering why the halfblood Singer alone seemed to want good relations with a mortal stranger. Was he merely more practical than the rest of the stubborn Hikeda'ya? "Finding a route—such things are not done so easily in these lands," he answered at last. "I will lead you to a safer passage if I can, but I will have to know more to do so—where you are going, for instance. And I will do it for gold, of course, or some similarly useful reward."

"I should have known," said Makho. "A mortal can have no honor."

"What does honor have to do with this?" Jarnulf let his voice rise, mimicking pride and anger. "I have tasks of my own to perform, a trust that was placed in me just as yours was placed in you. While I am helping your hand toward whatever goal you have, it will be harder—if not impossible—to do what my masters demand of me, namely hunting down escaped slaves and others the queen wishes to see returned to Nakkiga's justice. And even if you are to feed me, I will still lose the bounties I might have had. That is the most of my living. Should I not be rewarded for that loss?" He put his hands on his hips, aping a stubborn merchant. "One silver drop for every day I lead you safely, to be paid when we part company." In truth, he had no use for silver drops—he would never be able to spend them unless he risked death by returning to Nakkiga itself—but if he did not ask for payment it would be as much as to announce he had some other purpose in wanting to accompany this puzzling collection.

"We are on more important business for the queen than merely capturing a few escaped slaves!" the one called Kemme said, so enraged that a touch of color climbed into his cheeks, a weakness the Hikeda'ya rarely displayed. Kemme might be a formidable warrior but he was no diplomat. "And you demand to be paid?" He seemed unaware of Makho's stony face beside him. "You have no idea of what we do, what honor the queen has given us! Instead of barking out insolent words, you should get on your miserable mortal knees in gratitude that we have left your misshapen head on your neck, because I can change that myself in an instant!" Kemme seemed ready to draw his blade, but this time Jarnulf did not have to engage in any dangerous demonstration, because in the moment of silence the chieftain Makho made a sound—just a small intake of air—and the soldier seemed to understand in an instant that he had said too much and too loudly. The almost invisible blush of fury drained from his cheek in the space of a heartbeat.

"Close your mouth and go attend to the horses, Sacrifice Kemme," Makho said in the coldest, deadest voice Jarnulf had yet heard him use. "Now. And take the Blackbird with you."

Kemme turned away from his master wearing a convincing mask of chastened obedience. He harshly ordered the female Sacrifice Nezeru to attend him, then walked off toward the horses, but Jarnulf guessed by a certain angle to his neck that Kemme's now-hidden features had gone rigid with disapproval and perhaps even resentment. Jarnulf knew that the tall Sacrifice would happily murder him, but he also wondered whether there might be some way to start driving a wedge between the leader and his second-in-command.

The chieftain now fixed Jarnulf with a look that reminded him of the violent stillness of a hawk just before it flew. Then the chieftain's face changed like the water beneath a swimmer abruptly turning dark and deep; another heartbeat and the expressionless mask was back in place. "Very well, Huntsman. What if I told you that we had a task far to the east—in the lands your people call Urmsheim? How would we reach it from here?"

Urmsheim! Jarnulf could not have guessed such a far-flung, largely empty place would have been their destination, and could not begin to guess why they wanted to visit that home of deadly beasts and deadlier storms. "That is a long distance away, through a fearful wilderness—yes, fearful even for the Hikeda'ya. Traveling there is not merely a question of directions, or of knowing what few roads lie beneath the snow, but of knowing how to avoid danger, which is everywhere there." He did his best to pretend that he had just reached his decision. "Very well. Pay my price before I raise it, as I am tempted to do, since I gave it before I knew your destination. If you treat with me fairly, I will lead you where you wish."

"Why should we need you to lead us the whole way?" the chieftain said, but this time the anger was gone from his voice. Now he was bargaining. It was one of the few things Hikeda'ya did that Jarnulf truly understood. "I know the direction—east, into the rising sun. You say to walk upon the high, rocky places. We can do that just as well without the company of a mortal."

Pressing made no sense. "Very well," he said. "I will leave you Queen's Talons, then, and be on my way, back to my pursuit of Nakkiga's fugitives. Remember, though, it is not only goblins you must avoid, but giants, *witiko'ya*, and *yukinva* as well, all plentiful in the eastern hills."

This time Makho looked to Saomeji and Jarnulf felt sure he saw something he had not seen from the chieftain previously, a cold, almost angry amusement. "Very well, Huntsman," said Makho. "You shall have what you ask, but not without limits. We shall let you choose the path for a few days before sealing the bargain, so that if you prove a foul guide we will not have been taken too far from our way. But know this—if you try to lead us astray, or in any way slow our progress, I will have Goh Gam Gar pull you to pieces and devour you while you still live. Understood?"

"It would be hard not to understand that." He made the two-handed sign for *Bargain Sealed* and Makho did the same.

I have set out on a strange path, Jarnulf thought. *I must serve the creatures who destroyed my family so that I can do the Redeemer's will.* He could not help marveling at the strangeness of God's plan. *This unexpected meeting may be the answer to all my prayers—that, or the death of me.*

Perhaps it will be both.

21

Crossroad

"Is that Vestvennby in the distance?" Miriamele shielded her eyes from the sun's glare. Out of sight far ahead, royal foot soldiers and local peasant farmers, happy to earn a few coppers, were doing their best to clear the way for the procession. Snow was banked high against the Royal North Road on either side, making a tunnel with white walls and gray sky for a roof, but she thought she could see a faint outline of towers. "Blessed Elysia, I pray it's so and that we are almost at the Erkynlandish border. I long to be home so badly—I don't think I've ever wished for it so much before."

"But why, Majesty?" Tiamak asked.

"Because I haven't ridden so much in years," she said. "To be entirely frank, my arse is sore."

Tiamak wasn't quite certain what to say, but the others in the royal party laughed, even Sisqi, although Tiamak was not certain the troll woman knew the word. At the moment, Tiamak was sharing a horse with Sisqi and Binabik so that they could converse more easily with the rest of the royal company on their tall steeds. Binabik's mighty white wolf Vaqana paced along beside them, watching her master and the strange creature on which he was riding with obvious concern and perhaps a hint of jealousy. Sisqi's riderless ram, tethered to the horse's saddle on a long rope, did not seem to care much one way or the other.

Simon frowned. "I'm not certain that's the kind of thing a queen should say, my dear."

"What should I say instead?" Miriamele demanded. "Should I call it my 'sit-upon,' as our well-bred daughter-in-law does?"

"I don't think you need be quite *that* proper," Simon said, amused. "Rachel and the chambermaids who raised me always said 'hindquarters' or 'rump' or just 'bottom.' But if you're in pain, my dear, why don't you ride in the carriage?"

"And miss everybody's talk, while you have all the pleasure?" She scowled at him. "Not likely, that."

"Yes, but if you did, then I could join you and claim I was doing it to give you company, instead of having to admit in front of all my soldiers that my arse hurts too."

Even the queen had to laugh at that, and for a while the talk was all lightness and good cheer. Tiamak was glad because his own mood had been dark of late—another reason he had decided to leave the carriage and share a horse with Binabik and his wife. But a saddle was not really meant to carry three passengers comfortably, he reflected, however small two of them might be.

Still, he thought, *it's nice for a change not to be the little one.* Usually he had to look up at almost everybody he dealt with, but now that the four trolls had joined the royal progress, he could finally enjoy the rare pleasure of being taller than someone else.

Eolair was seldom glad to be old, but as he watched from the doorway of his tent while the soldiers and servants set up camp for the night, he was at least grateful that his age and position allowed him to leave such tasks to others. He was feeling particularly ancient and full of aches tonight.

Too much time in the saddle, he thought. *There was a time I rode all day and then danced late into the evening.* He laughed quietly at his own complaints. *But who would want to dance with me now, a bundle of sticks dressed in courtier's clothes?*

A young guardsman trotted up. "Someone to see you, Count Eolair. He says his name is Sir Aelin and that you will know him."

"My nephew? Bagba's Herd, of course I do! Send him to me, please!"

Aelin was not his true nephew but the grandson of his sister—a grandnephew. Aelin had always been one of Eolair's favorites, and the count had been sad not to see him when they had passed through Hernystir back in Marris-month.

"Is that you?" he asked as the young man ducked through the tent flap a short time later. "By all the gods, it is! It is fine to see you, young man!"

Aelin bowed. "And you, Uncle."

Eolair looked his visitor up and down and was surprised at how much the youth had changed since he had last seen him. a full four or five years earlier when the young man had spent some time at the Hayholt. For one thing, Aelin was a youth no longer: he had filled out through the chest and had the full beard worn by many of the younger Hernystiri men at the Taig these days. His clothes, though, were rough and road-worn, the bottom of his cloak dripping, his boots smeared with mud. "You have ridden from Hernysadharc?" Eolair asked him.

"Yes, all the way across the New Frostmarch Road through the storms, with important messages for you and the High Throne—thank Mircha and the rest of the gods that the worst of the winter is over. My men and I have been riding for days, Uncle!"

"But why you as messenger, Aelin? I am very glad to see you, but—"

"In truth, I asked King Hugh to let me bring the letters, since I was at Nad Mullach when you came to the capitol." Aelin looked around, making certain the tent was empty. "One is from the dowager queen, and she asked me to make certain no one but you received it, my lord."

"From Inahwen? You may give that to me now." Eolair reached out and took the folded parchment, noting briefly Inahwen's wax seal before slipping it into the pouch on his belt. "And the others?"

"I did not look, Uncle. But I believe they are from Lord Pasevalles." He smiled. "I hope he has made your life easier. I hear he is a good man—perhaps even the next Hand of the Throne when you return to Nad Mullach?"

"He will be if I have my way. But I think Duke Osric, Prince Morgan's other grandfather, might think differently. He considers Pasevalles an upstart." Eolair called for a servant to bring wine. "But come, sit down. You have had a long, wearying ride."

"Long, yes, and more exciting than I'd like." Aelin took off his cloak, swung it out to show his uncle. "See how it is torn and tattered? I was pitched off my horse just north of Vestvennby."

"Praise the gods you weren't hurt! That was a piece of luck."

"Luckier than you might think. I was ahead of the others, and I fell out of the saddle because a giant nearly had me, except the unholy beast was as startled as I was. It stood in the middle of the road as I came around a bend."

"The Royal North Road? Here?" He felt something clutch in his chest. "Can it be true? They have never come so far south since the bad old days—the days of the Storm King. Are you sure it wasn't a bear or . . . or some wandering woodsman with even more beard than you?"

Aelin laughed at that, but his face was serious. "It was no bearded woodsman, Uncle. And no bear could swing a paw and nearly take my head off while I was standing up in my stirrups."

"Heavens save us." Eolair shook his head in distress. Too many strange events, too many fell signs! "Tell me what happened."

Aelin described the surprising encounter on the road, a mere few miles south of the royal encampment. "I did not look back for the monster, I simply limped after my horse as fast as I could and dragged myself back into the saddle. By the time I turned the giant was long gone, but the rest of my company saw its footprints."

The wine came, and after a few more questions Eolair turned the talk to other, less disturbing things, asking after his sister Elatha's health, and how life fared at Nad Mullach, the ancestral home that Eolair had not been able to visit this trip because of the demands of the royal progress. Talking about the place filled him with melancholy. More and more, the count was looking forward to the day when he could lay down his burdens and return there to spend his last years in peace—a gentleman farmer caring for his forefathers' land, the way he had always wished to be.

"Will you stay only this night, or can you stay and ride with us for a while on our way south?" he asked Aelin at last.

"I would love a more leisurely trip back," the younger man said, "and I'm fairly certain the presence of some hundreds of Erkynguards would keep any giants at bay, but Queen Inahwen said she hopes for an answer from you quickly. I fear that tomorrow, after you have had time to write back to her, my men and I must hurry back across the Frostmarch to Hernysadharc." Aelin was one of King Hugh's favorite young courtiers, known like his great-uncle as a man who could tread the measures of an intricate Dillathi ring dance or, with equal facility, the even more courtly steps of arguing preferment and royal favors. But what Eolair liked best about his young relative was Aelin's careful intelligence. The world was full of people quite certain they already knew the answer to every important question. The older Eolair got, the more he valued men—and women, too, most definitely—who thought for themselves, who asked questions, who were not satisfied with seemingly easy answers to difficult problems.

Some time later, when Aelin had gone to catch up with some of his friends among the Erkynlandish nobility, Eolair took up the letter from Inahwen, but not without trepidation. They had spoken so recently that it seemed strange she should send him a message, and even stranger she should go out of her way to send it with his own grand-nephew to keep it safe. What matter was so pressing that it could not wait until Eolair was back in the Hayholt?

> *My dearest Count,*
>
> *I hope you will forgive me for troubling you, especially with such a difficult request, when you have been so long traveling and away from Erkynland, where the high king and high queen depend so much upon you. But I am fearful, otherwise I would not trouble you, despite our long friendship.*
>
> *You will remember, I hope, that when you visited me in the Queen's Little House, we talked much about the Lady Tylleth and her influence upon King Hugh. I said something about her, and you asked me if that were really true, or only my dislike speaking.*

Inahwen had called the king's betrothed a witch, a bizarre word to come from the usually mild dowager queen. Eolair had certainly not forgotten.

> *I will leave it to you to decide whether I spoke harshly or not. You remember in the bad old days after my husband the king's death, when Skali of Rimmersgard and his army ruled our land and the remnants of the royal family hid in the mountains, what happened to my step-daughter Maegwin, may the gods preserve her spirit? Do you remember the place she found? She took you there, and you once told me that what she found in that place added to her sad state, perhaps even increased the madness that eventually overcame her.*
>
> *The Silverhome, it was called, that place under the mountains that the Sithi or their servants built, though poor Maegwin believed it the home of the gods. I confess I do not remember all you told me, and since at your suggestion we sealed those tunnels up years ago, I have not thought much upon it. Until now.*

The tunnels have been now opened again. Tylleth and certain of her followers, for lack of a better word, have convinced King Hugh to unblock the ways into the earth that Maegwin found, saying that the caverns are sacred to our people and should not be hidden from them.

I have never gone there myself, because I am too frail for such clambering, but I have heard from others that the king's mistress and her friends have made it into a sort of shrine (although not an Aedonite shrine, which would be bad enough) and that Tylleth and others conduct strange ceremonies there in the caverns under the Grianspog Mountains. They say they are merely restoring the worship of Cuamh the lord of the dark places underground (who, as you well know, the rest of us have never stopped venerating) but others say that the rituals are more serious than any mere worship of the Earthdog. In fact, I have heard tales from those I trust that they are worshipping someone else. I will not sully this letter with her foul name, for fear of her hearing it in her dark hall and bringing bad fortune upon us all, but you know the one I mean—she who was once called The Maker of Orphans and the Crow Mother.

Eolair sat back, rubbing his eyes. It was hard to read by candlelight these days, even if he held the parchment so close it nearly caught fire, but he did not want anyone else reading Inahwen's words to him—not even Aelin.

But here is the heart of the matter, my dear friend. It is not this alone that frightens me, although it does frighten me very much, nor even the reports that they have found some old scrying-stone of the Sithi and use it to beg favor from their grisly mistress. What is worst of all is the report that Tylleth has brought King Hugh himself down into this once-buried place, and that he joins her there in this ancient, dreadful worship.

I have no power in this court. Whatever loyalty Hugh once felt toward me is long gone, buried beneath the scorn of his betrothed and her courtiers. He is openly rude to me, cruel and cutting in front of all his subjects, although I give him no cause. Even were I to denounce these dreadful practices outright, I would be dismissed as a mad old woman, and anything I said would only be taken as proof that my wits have fled. You may be thinking that yourself, but I swear to you everything I say is true, and all that is hearsay comes to me from trustworthy sources, or is confirmed by many reports.

Please, Eolair, my friend and once-lover, I beg you to come back to the Taig. Bring Queen Miriamele and King Simon with you if you can. Only you and they can uproot this terrible madness before it rises up from the deeps like a noxious disease and overwhelms the Hernystir we both love.

Whatever you do, write to me back as quickly as you can, and send messages only through the most trusted sources, as I have trusted your own kinsman, Aelin. But please, do not dismiss what I say. Come to see for yourself. See the shared glances, the whispered secrets, and smell the foulness in the air. The unpleasantness that you saw here with King Simon and Queen Miriamele has only become worse, and now that I know the reason, I cannot sleep for fear of what is to come.

Despite the frightened words, her signature was as steady as Eolair had ever seen it.

He read the letter again, his stomach roiling within him. He did not want to believe it, of course—he did not want to believe any of it—but he knew Inahwen too well to doubt that she believed it herself, and her every word had the sound of someone still carefully testing her own reason, aware that what she said would sound impossible. Most would have scoffed, Eolair knew, but he had seen too many incredible things to dismiss Inahwen's fears. But it was a damnable time to ask him to come back to Hernysadharc, let alone bring the high queen and king, when they had all been away from Erkynland for months upon months.

Still, he knew he could not simply ignore Inahwen's need. He wondered whether Simon and Miriamele would allow him to postpone his own return to the Hayholt, if only for a fortnight or two, so that he could ride to Hernysadharc with Aelin and try to make some sense of what was going on there.

Eolair sighed and called his servant to pour him another cup of wine. It was past time for him to sleep, but he sensed it would not come easily this night. As he waited for the young man to finish pouring, a grim bit of poetry he had often heard in childhood seeped up from his memory, unbidden and unwanted—a song about the Morriga, the Mother of Crows.

I see the world of the dead
The world that is coming
Her world, all laid beneath her feet
Summer will have no flowers
Cows will give no milk
Women will lose all their modesty
And men all their valor
Fruitless forests
And empty seas
Great storms will rage
Around empty fortresses
Battles will be waged everywhere
And treacherous princelings
Will drape a shroud of sorrows
Over the world
Every man will be a betrayer
Every son a thief

The count sat up another hour waiting for Aelin to return, but decided at last that the young man was likely having too good a time with his fellows to rush back and sit with an aging great-uncle. At last Eolair went to his bed, oddly grateful for the distraction of his aching bones.

After their night on the moonlit hilltop and Snenneq's confusing ritual with the knuckle bones, not to mention the vaguely disheartening idea it had given Morgan about losing what he most expected, he had soured a little on the company of the trolls and had resumed spending time with his older friends.

"Have you heard the news?" he said as he pushed into their tent. "Count Eolair's nephew was attacked on the road by a giant! A real *Hüne!*"

The others looked up at him, Astrian already smiling as if at some jest, Olveris sharpening his sword, Porto bleary, as if just now roused from sleep, although it was long past the change of the evening watch. "Of course we have heard, Your Highness," Astrian said. "I thought by your excitement you brought something new—perhaps something from your grandfather's cupboard to soothe our throats, which are dry as Nascadu."

"And you think that is nothing?" Morgan shook his head in disgust. "A living giant! We are almost in Erkynland!"

"Erkynlanders are just as dull as the Rimmersgard folk. Why should I begrudge them a few giants of their own, to enliven their dreary days? And in truth, it is as well for the giant's sake it was not me he waylaid." Astrian patted his sheathed sword. "I would have poked a few holes in the beast and then we would have found out if it was truly as large as Sir Aelin claims."

Olveris smiled a sour smile at Astrian's boast and continued scraping stone against steel, but Porto sat up straight. "You are foolish to say such things," the old knight declared. "You do not know. Until you face one, you cannot know."

Olveris groaned and set his sword down. "Now it will be the giants of Nakkiga again. Porto killed dozens, he says."

"I have pretended to no such thing, sir, but I *have* faced a giant." The old knight was trying to retain his good temper, but only just managing. "Why must you always follow Astrian's lead in this dance, Olveris? Must all you Nabban-men scoff at what you do not know?"

"We know about you, old broomstick," Astrian said. "You would throw your sword in the air and take to your heels if you ever saw a living *orxis*."

Porto turned imploring eyes toward Morgan. "He speaks nonsense, Highness, I swear it. He knows nothing of the north or the days when I followed Duke Isgrimnur. On the mountain of Nakkiga, as the White Foxes call it, my fellow soldiers and I slew a great, fierce giant. By the Wounds of Saint Honora, the beast killed three of my companions. How could I forget?"

"No one says you forgot." Sir Astrian seated himself on a wooden chest and spread his bootheels wide on the tent's earth floor, then leaned toward the old knight. "We say that you have made it up. Please take note of the distinction."

"Enough, Astrian." Having spent much time of late with the kindhearted trolls, Morgan found it a little harder to countenance the younger knights' casual cruelties. "He is right—you do not know." He turned to Porto. "Did you really fight one? Was it as big as Aelin says this one was?"

"I do not know, my prince." Porto looked at his comrades with poorly hidden triumph on his face. "Because no man can think much about such things when one of those monsters stands before him, and if he says differently I call him a liar. I can only tell you the giant we fought was far, far bigger than me. I do not think I could have put my arms even halfway around its chest."

"And it grows with every year that passes," Astrian muttered, but he said it quietly and avoided Morgan's eye.

"It could grow no larger than it looked to me that first moment," Porto declared. "You would not believe how long its arms were, Prince Morgan. Like the trunks of grown birch trees, white and wide. But what I will never be able to forget—and I have tried, no matter what these two scapegraces might have you believe—is how it *looked* at me. Its eyes were like a man's. Yes, it had thought, I swear, and I think that was the worst of it." He made the sign of the Tree and looked at Morgan almost plaintively. "Why should our loving God spend the gift of reason on such a monster?"

"Back home, they say the kilpa that lurk in southern oceans are sailors who drowned," Olveris volunteered. It was so unusual of him to offer anything other than terse mockery that even Porto listened. "Mayhap the same is true for giants," he added. "Perhaps they are sinners cursed to roam the wilderness."

Morgan shuddered a little at the thought—to be so alone, so hated, but knowing you had once been a man! It was a horror he might even have enjoyed, like a particularly dreadful ghost tale, had Eolair's nephew Aelin encountered his giant fifty leagues away or years in the past, instead of this very day and just a short ride from where they sat.

The wind rattled the sides of the tent. None of them jumped, but even Astrian's grin looked a little forced as he said, "Ah! The monster is outside even now!"

"Stop," Porto spoke with a firmness Morgan had seldom heard. "Do not speak of devils, man, because devils listen. And do not mock God's monsters or He may show you your folly."

"Perhaps we should talk of other things," Morgan began, but Porto was telling his story again.

"It came upon us without noise—you cannot imagine that something so large can be so quiet." Porto's eyes were wide, as though he found himself back on the mountainside. "We did not guess it was there until it killed one of the other men and threw his headless body into the clearing where we stood. Then it came at us through the trees, pushing even the biggest trunks over and breaking the smaller ones like river reeds under its feet." He paused, shaking his head slowly as if, even after so many years, mere words could not explain it. "The fear came over me—it was like I had been thrown into an icy river. I could scarcely stand upright, my knees shook so. And then it roared, that mouth full of yellow teeth, that great, gaping mouth . . ."

"Well?" Morgan said after a few moments. "What happened? You have never told me so much of this tale before."

"Because nobody wanted to hear it," said Porto, full of wounded dignity. "Some were too busy mocking me for a liar." He glared at Astrian. "I would like to see you, Sir Dauntless, in such a moment. You may fear no human foe, but something so uncanny—it unmans you."

Astrian appeared ready to say something, but Morgan caught his eye. The knight bowed his head to the prince instead, as if to say, *"Very well, I will not interrupt this nonsense if it pleases Your Highness to hear it."*

"Did it wear armor, as they say the giants who fight for the White Foxes do?" Morgan asked.

"Not this one," Porto said. "Sludig, the duke's man, told me that most giants in the far north are wild, that only a few are kept always in the Norn Queen's service because the great brutes are dangerous even to their masters. This one went naked like any beast. That was one reason that what I saw in its eyes, that fearful, manlike cleverness, still disturbs my memory. But I thought little of any of this at the time. It was too big, too sudden. This was our death standing before us, tall as a tree and growling like an angry bear, none of us doubted that."

"How did you kill it?" Morgan had indeed heard Porto's stories of fighting giants and Norns many times, but had seldom paid much attention. He had never believed all that Astrian said, that they were only the tales an old drunkard concocted to make himself seem a hero, but he had never entirely believed the most lurid of Porto's recollections either. Now he was beginning to wonder, because everything Porto was saying had the feeling of real terror remembered.

"How? Luck," the knight said. "And God's grace. One of my comrades pierced its neck with a spear, another stabbed the creature in its leg near the cod, where the great vein of blood throbs. I struck it myself, but only in the back of the leg because I could reach nothing else. Still, that blow lamed it. We fought it a good while longer, but at last its blood was all out and it fell. My captain took its head."

"So you yourself did not *kill* a giant, precisely," said Astrian, all air and philosophy. "In truth, you hamstrung the monster. Were you lying down when that happened, perhaps pretending to be dead? Or was it so much higher than you that, as with the prince's little friend No-Neck the troll, you had to leap and leap to deal that deathly blow?"

But for once, Porto did not seem to mind the mockery, or even much notice it. "I make no claims to being a great hero like Tallistro. I fought because there was no other choice, except to die. But I do not apologize to you or anyone, Nabban-man. Few have faced those howling, hairy things and survived, fewer still have been in on the death of one."

The very matter-of-fact way he said it convinced Morgan. The prince sat back, examining Porto as though he had never really seen him before. He was still tall and must have been a formidable size in his youth. And Morgan knew that he had indeed been where he claimed, because when they were in Elvritshalla, the king's friend Jarl Sludig had told him at a gathering that he had caught sight of Porto in Morgan's company; Sludig did not remember the knight's name, but had recognized his long-boned face and frame from the days of the siege against the Norns. Morgan had even considered bringing Porto to meet the jarl, but the time in Elvritshalla had been hectic, with the Kopstade to explore and the sudden attentions of the trolls, and he had forgotten. Soon thereafter, they left Elvritshalla and Sludig behind. Morgan could not help feeling a twinge of regret now over his failure to bring the two men together.

"That truly is an astonishing tale, Sir Porto," he said, "and I believe you. You have memories, brave memories, that most men would envy."

"Thank you, Highness," said the old man, and made a slightly creaky imitation of a bow. "But to speak honestly, I wish I were in truth the liar that Astrian and Olveris find such joy in describing. My memories of those days give me no pleasure and still bring me ugly dreams."

The other two knights seemed to have run dry of insults. They all fell silent. The wind scrabbled at the tent cloth, and for that moment each man seemed to be thinking the same thing—of what might lurk outside in the darkness beyond those flimsy walls.

22

Death Songs

Makho deeply distrusted the mortal, but clearly he did not trust Nezeru much more. When the hand chieftain sent her out to scout the territory ahead, a role for which she had undergone careful training in the Order-house of Sacrifice, he sent Kemme with her.

Does he fear I will run away? Just thinking of it made her furious. *Does he think I hold my oath to our queen so lightly that I would desert my people simply because he whipped me—because I am in disgrace?* The weals on her back had mostly healed. They still ached fiercely in the cold, but that was as nothing compared to the pain of being thought untrustworthy. The fact that it was true—that she had already failed her hand-brothers twice—only made the pain worse.

"Why come so far south?" she asked Kemme as he followed her down a long, rocky slope, past drifts of snow and patches of yellow winter grass. "Not just deep into Rimmersgard, but almost to the edge of Erkynland?"

"Close your mouth, Blackbird. Do you know more than Makho?" He pushed his way through the long grasses, leaving a sinuous track like a snake. "The hare does not tell the fox where to hunt."

She knew she should be quiet, but his dismissiveness made her skin prickle. "The mortal Jarnulf said we should cross the great road miles farther north, closer to the mortal city of Kaldskryke."

"He did, did he? And how do we know what ambush he might be leading us to if we do not scout all this country?" Kemme's face was full of unhidden anger. "Who are you? I was nobody—a Sacrifice from an indifferent family, stuck in a backwater league of our order under a lazy, self-serving commander. But my lord Makho remembered me—he asked for me to join him. Now I am a Queen's Talon. Do you think I care what you or some mortal have to say? Enough of your pointless questions, Blackbird." In fact, this was the first time Nezeru had spoken in a very long time, but he made it seem as if she had been prattling ceaselessly.

The sky was lightening now, but they were still a good distance from their camp, which added to Nezeru's unhappiness. She did not like these bare, open lands away from the forested hilltops, and she especially did not like moving so close to the mortal road. It was largely deserted this time of the year, with storms still coming down from the mountains and across the Frostmarch, but that was no proof against being seen by enemies. The only fast way to travel east to Urmsheim was to pass between the Dimmerskog Forest and great Drorshullven Lake. Jarnulf had suggested they cross the mortal road just past Kaldskryke, skirting the southern edge of the forest before heading east into the wilderness, but Makho had dismissed the idea, apparently leery of some trap. *So now we are here, exposed, practically in daylight, almost begging to be seen,* Nezeru thought. Was secrecy no longer a part of their task? Why had they not simply crossed the road nearer to the forest instead of risking the much more populated lands near Vestvennby?

She could think of no answer that made sense, and that troubled her.

After a long time on open ground Nezeru and Kemme started to climb up into the hills that bordered the road. She was reluctantly impressed by how swiftly and quietly he traveled. She knew he had fought at Asu'a during the failed War of Return, and had also defended the Nakkiga Gate against invading mortals. She did not underestimate his strength or his bravery. But his loyalty to Makho made it impossible for him to hear any question about strategy except as an attack on their chieftain.

They crested the hill, and Kemme led them until they reached a little grove of pine trees at the top of a slope whose steep drop to the valley floor was broken only by clumps of trees and a few large stones. On the near edge of the valley ran the ancient track the mortals called the North Road until it vanished where the valley curved at its southern end. Most of the widest part of the valley lay on the other side of the old road, where stands of tall green grass rippled in the wind. The grasses had come with the season, springing up amid the patches of melting snow, and the valley floor seemed a tapestry woven in a wide variety of greens and whites. Here and there Nezeru could make out the dull silver sheen of running water from a tangle of streams snaking across the valley floor that later in the spring would overspill their low banks, join together, and become a single rushing flood beside the North Road. Such an abundance of water and new growth made Nezeru slightly dizzy, accustomed as she was to the hard, dark soil of Hikeda'ya lands, so it was a moment before she saw what Kemme had already seen: something upright was moving in the distance.

Far out across the valley and a bit north of where the two Hikeda'ya stood was a host of two-legged shapes busy at some task, bent, arms swinging. They were too far away for Nezeru to make out clearly what they were doing— mortal eyes would not have discerned them at all—but Kemme gave her a contemptuous look, as though their presence proved some point her stubborn ignorance had denied. He signaled her to follow him northward along the slope above the road so they could get a better view, and Nezeru did as she was told.

As they drew a little nearer to the distant figures the morning sun finally breached the eastern hills and began its climb into the sky, so they turned farther up the hillside in search of cover. Following Kemme silently through the trees, Nezeru was again troubled by what seemed like clear tactical mistakes, first by Makho and now by Kemme. If their goal was to cross the mortals' great road safely and vanish into the waste, far from spying mortal eyes, why had they come so far south in the first place before crossing, and why bother now to approach what almost certainly would turn out to be the mortal inhabitants of some nearby village? Even the stealth of trained Sacrifices could be betrayed by accidents, by unexpected noises or the appearance of unforeseen others. What could be learned here that was worth taking such a risk?

Finally they drew close enough to see that the people on the far side of the road were indeed mortals, about two or three score of them, all garbed like peasants. Most were cutting grass with sickles, but some seemed to be uprooting it with their bare hands. Moments later Nezeru saw that the mowers seemed to be protected—or perhaps prevented from escaping—by a handful of other mortals who watched them from horseback.

The two Sacrifices spent a long, silent time watching, and after a while Nezeru had to fight against impatience. The longer they crouched here staring, the higher the sun rose, and the growing brightness of the landscape was threatening to turn her discomfort into something more like fear, for all her training. Was she the truly mad one? Why was Kemme putting them—and perhaps even their mission from the Mother of All—at risk simply to watch a group of farm slaves?

Kemme seemed especially fixed on the three riders watching over the workers, though so far they had mostly sat in their saddles observing their charges from a distance. Occasionally one rode a little way in one direction or another toward where a knot of mowers had gathered, and each time a horseman approached, the workers quickly dispersed and returned to their labor. Then, as one of the riders wheeled, Nezeru spotted a glint of metal and realized the distant figure was wearing armor, which seemed strange to her. What mortal peasants could afford men-at-arms to watch over them while they toiled? And what mortal knights would give their time to such an unexceptional endeavor? No, she decided, these workers must certainly be slaves under guard. She also thought the mortal overseers must be impressively brutal to use so few guards to watch over so many.

One of the other riders abruptly turned his horse away from the group and came riding across the valley toward the North Road, heading straight toward the Hikeda'ya's hiding spot. Nezeru knew he could not have possibly seen them from that distance, but Kemme was already climbing down the slope toward better cover. When he reached it, he began to move toward the spot where the rider was headed. Nezeru followed carefully, hoping that he would soon tire of watching the mortals so they could go back to their hidden camp.

Then things began to happen very quickly.

The armored rider reached the road and crossed it, then spurred his mount up the slope, only a few hundred paces below Kemme. Moving in swift silence,

Kemme hurried along through the trees above the mortal and his horse until he reached a spot just above them, but out of the rider's sight

The knight dismounted a little way up the slope and tied his mount to a tree branch, then took a wine-sack from his saddle and had a long drink. When he finished, he took off his helmet and hung it on the pommel of his saddle. He had a brown beard and the boiled reddish skin of his kind, and surveyed the landscape with the unhurried air of someone trying to remember whether or not he had ever seen this place before.

Kemme had risen almost before Nezeru sensed his movement, his bow already drawn. His arrow flew buzzing like a deadly wasp and struck the rider in the chest, piercing the mortal's mail-coat with such force that the impact tumbled him down the slope. He lay there in a sprawl and did not move. Kemme sprang down the hill and crouched over the body, staring at the dead face as if at a long-sought enemy.

"No ambush, the mortal claims?" he hissed as Nezeru reached him. "No ambush? Then why is this man in armor? That rabble cutting grass are no mere farmers, they are foragers for an army."

Nezeru bent and looked the dead man up and down. He wore a green surcoat over his armor that bore the stitched insignia of a pair of dragons supporting a shield, one worm red, the other white. "I have been told of this mark," she said. "I think it is—"

Kemme turned and slapped her across the face so hard that she stumbled backward several steps.

"I said, I am tired of hearing you speak." He stared at her as at an animal, his violet eyes empty. "Makho told me I cannot kill you because of the child you carry, but you do not need both your hands to give birth. If you make another sound I will remove one." He yanked his knife from his belt to cut a piece of the surcoat from the dead mortal's body.

Nezeru sank into a half-crouch. Her face ached, but that was nothing compared to her sudden alarm. It was not the blow that surprised her—harsh discipline was common in the Order of Sacrifice—but Kemme's obvious hatred, only barely kept in check. Again, she was struck with the depth and breadth of her failures.

And if he or the chieftain ever discovers that there is no child? She did not want to think about what would happen then.

She was so distracted, and Kemme so busy wrestling with the heavy, armored body as he searched it, that the other mortal rider had approached to less than a bowshot away before either of them noticed.

The approaching horseman could not clearly make out what they were doing because of the patchy undergrowth, but it was obvious that he could see the dead knight's riderless horse and the fallen man's legs with Kemme bent over them, because he abruptly reined up and then turned and galloped away. Kemme cursed and leaped to his feet, drawing his bow as he sprinted after the fleeing rider. The mortal lifted a horn to his mouth and blew three long, shrill bursts before Kemme's arrow lifted him from the saddle and dashed him to the ground. His horse plunged on across the road and out into the valley.

The last remaining rider, far away with the foragers, had heard the call and now turned to see the riderless horse. He lifted his own horn to his lips. The alarm call echoed down the valley, then a few moments' later was answered by other horns farther to the north.

Nezeru felt she was caught in a waking dream. All her fears of discovery had come true.

Kemme ripped the last of the surcoat loose, then kicked the dead man down the slope with such fury that the corpse uprooted a few saplings and carried them with it. The older Sacrifice turned and began running up the hillside, back toward their camp.

Nezeru sprinted after him, using her hands for support as she bent close to the slope, following his path of broken branches. One of them at least must survive to warn the others, and she no longer trusted Kemme's impulsiveness. She had not created this particular folly, and although she might have failed her earlier charge, she was still a Sacrifice, one of the queen's chosen Talons. She could not let another failure bring disgrace to her family and clan.

The hillside had been alive with the crying of horns for long moments, but now she heard something else—a low rumble sweeping through the valley, as if the earth itself had begun to roll and twitch in anger. As they topped the ridgeline, Nezeru looked back through the trees and saw a great force of armed, mounted men thundering along the ancient road from the northern end of the valley, an ocean wave of green surcoats befoamed with silvery helmets and lances glittering in the morning sun—a force of a hundred armored men or more. Some of the riders were already peeling off from the main troop, steering their mounts up the very slope on which she and Kemme were climbing, getting closer with each harsh but measured breath she took. Nezeru could feel the drumming of their hooves through her feet.

We have served our queen badly, was all she could think. *Hea-hai! We all will die as failures.*

The camp was full of frantic activity, like an ant's nest exposed by the blade of a plow. "Where is the king?" Miriamele demanded.

"He is in the arming tent, Majesty," said Eolair, turning away from a group of soldiers.

"The arming tent? We have an arming tent?"

"I am afraid so," he said. "At least since word of the Norn attack came to us."

She was about to scold him for letting the king play at soldiers, but Eolair looked frail, as if he had been ill. *My God*, she thought, *he looks nearly as old as my grandfather did when he died. Poor Eolair. Do we put too much upon him?* "Just tell me where it is, Lord Steward, if you please."

"Let me take you there, Majesty."

"I think you would be better employed with the soldiers—or perhaps separating truth from rumor. I have been told several times already that five hundred Norns are in the hills, sent from Stormspike to assassinate us. A force of five hundred so far south, traveling in daylight, and this is the first we have heard? That seems unlikely to me."

"And to me, my queen." Eolair shook his head. "But do not doubt there are Norns, whatever the numbers. Sir Irwyn saw them before they fled into the trees on the hilltop, and Irwyn is a trustworthy man. He was at the defense of Asu'a, so he knows them of old. And I told you of my nephew's encounter with a giant. The danger is nothing to scoff at, mistress, if you will pardon me for saying so."

She tried to calm herself a little. Eolair was right, as he often was, even if it did not suit her mood. "I have no complaint with sending soldiers to track down these killers. And if they are Norns, they are some fifty leagues beyond their own borders, which is also something worth worrying about—in fact, I have been worrying since we heard Lady Alva's story in Elvritshalla. But I can make no sense out of why my husband feels he has any need to involve himself. That is why we brought all these soldiers and knights, is it not?"

"Of course, Majesty."

"I'm glad we agree. Point me toward this 'arming tent'."

But for the array of candles standing on a chest, the tent was so dark that at first Miriamele could see nothing but shadows and hear nothing but the murmur of a quiet voice reciting the ancient prayer, the Soldier's Cantis.

> *Though I stand in a furrow of the field, one among many*
> *And though I know not whether I shall be mown*
> *Or left to wither beneath the sun*
> *I know that my Redeemer promised to be my guide and my teacher*
> *That in his care I will grow again some day in the Lord's garden,*
> *Which is Heaven,*
> *Among green things and by clear waters . . .*

"Simon?" she called. "Are you here?"

"Yes, my dear. You need not rise for Her Majesty, Jeremias, because you'll tip me over."

As her vision improved she made out her husband standing with one foot on a weapons chest while Sir Jeremias knelt at his feet, fastening the buckles of a greave. Simon was mostly armored, but his chest plate, the one Miriamele had thought was only for public show, still leaned against the tent wall. Two squires stood at wide-eyed near-attention behind the king, and Bishop Putnam, senior of the priests traveling with the royal party, was kneeling not far from Jeremias so that he could use the light of the candles to read from the Book of Aedon. "What, precisely, are you doing, husband?" the queen asked in what she hoped was a measured voice "And you, Lord Chamberlain?"

Jeremias looked up at her, and for a moment he might have been the guilty boy she had first met. "If the Lord Chamberlain is p-present," he said with the hint of a stutter, "it is his duty to dress the king."

> And His angels sing in sweet voices
> Of the goodness of our God.
> And the song they sing is this,
> 'Because you have heard the Redeemer's voice,
> You need fear no foreigner, no barbarian, no beast
> Who flee the Lord's sight and carry evil in their hearts.
> You need fear no storm, no thunderbolt, no wrack of earth
> Because that which is in you is His, and He knows you always
> Be you surrounded by enemies, be you ever outnumbered.'

"Just so," Simon said. "And dressing the king ought to include armor, don't you think?"

She could now make out the high color in his cheeks, as though he had been drinking. "It's only another sort of thing to wear," her husband said. "And it seems good sense when there may be fighting."

"It's more than that, Majesty." Jeremias spoke with such emphasis that the bishop hesitated in his recitation. "The king's armor is a sacred thing. A *holy* thing."

After a pause, His Eminence Putnam continued.

> Because you have set your love on Him, therefore will He deliver you.
> He is enthroned on high that He can see your heart, and that by the hand
> Of His redeeming Son it has been cleansed,
> And you will hear His mighty call when it comes,
> That will on some day, perhaps this day,
> Summon you home.

Putnam's droning irritated her. She wanted to speak to her husband, but what could be worse than interrupting a prayer at a time like this? But this *cantis* was a prayer she had never liked because it made death in battle seem somehow a victory. Miriamele had seen too many dead, especially too many she had loved, for the thought of Heaven's mercy to soothe her much. Those who fell might find a holy welcome with their Father and His son, but that did not make it easier for those left behind. Those who would have to go on alone.

"It may *be* a holy thing," she said, moving closer to her husband so she could lower her voice. "I do not pretend to such wisdom. But it is certainly a foolish

thing. Simon, you cannot take such a risk. There may be nothing like the rumored five hundred, but Irwyn says these Norns killed Sir Jubal with an arrow
from a great distance. If you fight, you will be their chief target."

"I don't intend to fight, Miri," the king told her, but the way he looked away
told her it was at least half a lie.

That is the way men speak when they think we don't understand their cursed pride,
Miri thought, but this time the ancient frustration frightened her more than it
angered her. "Then what are you going to do, husband?"

To the Lord all praise! the bishop intoned loudly, as if to cover the sounds of
royal discord.

> *To His son all praise!*
> *To the garden that is Heaven where you shall live,*
> *All praise!*

Putnam then repeated the words in Nabbanai to complete the *cantis*, but did
not immediately rise, as though he continued with silent prayer of his own.

Jeremias carefully fastened Simon's other greave, then did the same with the
poleyns that would protect the king's knees. "Most of our men have never
fought against the White Foxes," Simon said as he watched. "Now they must
face them, perhaps within the hour. They are afraid—superstitious and afraid."

"As they should be. You and I know all too well what those monsters can do."

"Just so, Miri. But the men know that I have faced them, as has Eolair. We
can show them not to fear just by being there with them."

"Just by being in bowshot for some Norn assassin to strike you down, you
should say. Just by risking your life needlessly. You are the king, Simon!"

"And you are the queen." He smiled. His bottom half was now covered in
plate, and he lifted his arms so Jeremias and the two young squires could buckle
the two sides of his cuirass into place. Simon's arming shirt was embroidered,
lovingly if not skillfully, with the Holy Tree—Miriamele remembered stitch-
ing it years before, in a time when she had reason to hope it would never be
worn in an actual battle. Seeing it now brought a pang. For a moment the gleam
of Simon's broad white forelock, the streak the dragon's blood had burned in
his graying hair, stood out as though it shone with its own light. She caught her
breath. Her heart was beating swiftly.

Oh, Simon, she thought—*don't throw your magic away on trifles!* She was not
exactly sure what the thought meant, but a grim foreboding had clutched her.
"I wish you wouldn't do this," she said. "I am afraid."

"You? The bravest woman who ever drew breath?" He smiled at her, and
for a moment was nothing more than her jolly, maddening husband, the one
she had loved for so long and through so much. "Come, now. I will not let
anything harm me. I would not dare, my lady."

She knew she could not stop him without a furious argument, and she also
knew that the demands of Man's Pride might seem foolish and dangerous to her

but were real and important among men, especially for a king. "Promise me at least that you will stay in the back, then," she said at last. "Promise me you will not ride up to the front where one of those demons can see you and shoot at you."

He gave her a look—the always-love, but with a hint of grievance. "If you insist."

"I do. Even if there are hundreds of Norns up there, it will not be worth your being killed. Remember the things we have still to do, Simon. Remember your promises to Isgrimnur."

He nodded briskly. "I know. Don't shame me, Miri. I remember. I remember all of it."

She went to him then and kissed his cheek, felt the tangle of his beard scratching against her cheek. Just the smell of him, of his neck and hair, made her ache with desire. "So do I, husband. Every bit of our story. And I want to share the rest of it with you, not mourning you."

He watched her leave the tent. She had known him so long that she knew exactly what his gaze felt like, even from behind.

Nezeru brought Saomeji water. He let her pour it into his mouth without a word or even meeting her eyes, as though he were a dying animal.

"By your skills you have saved us, Singer," she told him, and her gratitude was not feigned. Saomeji did not answer but only lay back against the stone, breathing regularly but shallowly.

Their hiding place had at first seemed like no hiding place at all, a great split stone the size of a barn that sat near the top of the hill, broken in two halves like a dropped melon. The massive sections stood several paces apart, and anything between the two halves should have been visible from a long distance. But the Singer had used a skill that he called "stonesinging," and now Nezeru's entire company, including the mortal Jarnulf, their horses, and even monstrous Goh Gam Gar, sheltered between the rough hemispheres, apparently invisible to all searching eyes—at least those of mortals. Nezeru had watched a company of armed men search for them less than a bowshot away, oblivious to their hiding place, although Nezeru could see the mortals clearly, as if through no more than a faint mist.

"What do they see?" Jarnulf asked quietly as another trio of mortal soldiers blundered past, clearly unable to understand how the Norns had managed to vanish on a surrounded hilltop. Late afternoon was now fading into twilight; the growing darkness turned the mortals into clumsy children, stumbling and bumping into each other, unable to find safe footing in their heavy armor, even as their quarry sat observing them from only a few paces away.

"They see only stone," said Saomeji, still laboring for breath. His eyes were as reddened as if he had just stepped out of a violent windstorm. "Just as they hear us no better than were we surrounded by the stone they imagine is there. But you still must keep your voices low."

"You tried to lead us into a trap, slave," Kemme hissed at Jarnulf.

"I will not bear that burden," the mortal said. "I would have taken you across the road several leagues north of here. You know that is true."

Kemme darted a look at Makho, but the chieftain's face showed no liking for the dispute, so Kemme turned away again. He had seated himself at the edge of the stone, the boundary of Saomeji's song-of-unseeing, and now he glared at the mortal searchers like a hungry animal. He raised his bow as if to aim. "Look at the vermin. I could spit all three of them with one shaft."

"And then the rest would come running," Makho said in a quiet but blade-sharp voice. "And they would all wonder how a Hikeda'ya arrow leaped out of a solid stone. Do not be so impatient, hand-brother. You will get your chance soon enough." He turned to Jarnulf, and all outward emotion vanished from his face—Nezeru found it more chilling than his earlier angers. "You say you did not want this, but I am not sure. Give me answers or I will kill you myself, mortal, no matter the noise." Everyone else had fallen silent, watching them. The chieftain held up the piece of torn green surcoat stitched with the twin dragon symbol. "This is the emblem of the Erkynguard, the soldiers who kill for the royal household that now rules in our old capital of Asu'a. Many hundreds of them surround this hill. What are they doing so far north of their own lands? Did you plan to meet them and exchange messages, or simply to lead us to them so that we Hikeda'ya would be killed, and you could claim bounty from the mortals?"

Saomeji stirred beside her, and Nezeru wondered what the Singer would do if it came to a fight. She had clearly underestimated his skills—few of even the most accomplished songmasters could manage what the halfblood had done to hide them.

Jarnulf met Makho's stare, his face as empty of expression as the chieftain's. Nezeru felt even more certain the mortal was Hikeda'ya-bred—surely no ordinary man of his race could hide his feelings so completely. Or did he think he was invincible? She knew Makho could not be defeated the same way twice; next time the chieftain would be prepared for the stranger's surprising speed.

"I told you that the king and queen of the High Throne were journeying to the great city in Rimmersgard the northmen call Elvritshalla," Jarnulf said. "Every mortal in these lands must have known it—don't blame me because you chose to ignore it." He made the gesture *Defense Against Falsehood*. "The royal party should have been long past us on their way back—the weather must have delayed their return—but remember, I said we should cross the North Road two days ago near the forest and strike east. *You* are the one who would not trust me and insisted we find another spot. No, Makho of the Talons, I think it is *your* suspicions that will kill *me*."

"He is too insolent," Kemme said. "Give him the death he expects, then we do not have to hear his lies. He is a spy who has led us into a trap."

Jarnulf smiled grimly. "Of course I have. And what better way for me to make certain of that than to die in the same trap? Do you think that when it is dark, and we try to break free, these short-sighted Erkynguards will be looking to see which of us are Hikeda'ya and which of us are the Hikeda'ya's mortal slaves—slaves whom they despise even more than you?" He shook his head. "Kill me if you will—or at least you may try." He let his hand drop to his blade. "It might not be so easy as you imagine. But if you do not wish to test me now while enemies surround us, then tend to your own affairs, and I will tend to mine."

Jarnulf bent and took a short, charred stick from the fire, then walked back down the narrow space between the split stone to his pack, which was farther along the crevasse, near the giant Goh Gam Gar.

"What are you doing, mortal?" Makho demanded.

He did not look back. "Writing out my death song."

Kemme, Makho, and Saomeji, who was fast regaining his strength, huddled in urgent talk, plotting a path they could take when the blue-gray evening had gone fully dark. Already dozens of the mortals' torches had bloomed at the bottom of the hill.

Nezeru understood the situation, though she had been excluded from the discussion: Saomeji had said that he could not long maintain the protective illusion in daylight, and it was clear the mortal soldiers would wait sensibly for morning, as if the hilltop were a besieged castle, instead of hunting for the Hikeda'ya in the dark. That meant the best time to try to break out would be in the last hours before the sun returned, when the mortals were at their weakest and most timid. But even with the aid of darkness and a little surprise, she did not think their queen's hand would survive—not all of them, at least. The queen's Hikeda'ya were so few, and the mortals were so many—!

Mother of All, give strength to your servant. My life is yours. My body is yours. My spirit is yours. Nezeru calmed herself with the familiar, soothing litanies of duty she had been taught long before her first woman's blood. *Better to die fighting to escape,* she told herself, *than to die hiding like lowly animals. We live for the queen so we must die for her as well, without complaint. Otherwise our oaths are meaningless.*

Halfway down the hidden space between the great stones, past the giant's hairy bulk, she saw the pale-haired mortal scratching away with his burnt branch on a dry, scraped goathide he had taken from his pack and unrolled across his lap. Makho had risen once to look at what he was writing, but had walked back shaking his head. Nezeru was curious, and her body ached for something to do, even just to rise and walk a few steps.

As she passed the giant, who had looked asleep, Goh Gam Gar opened one of his blood-tinged eyes. As always, she found it hard to meet that only partially animal stare. The creature's voice was a deep rumble. "Death is coming, little Blackbird."

Nezeru hesitated. "Of course it is. Death comes for all—except the Queen of the Mountain. But death is only a door, and the Garden is on the far side."

"Nicely said." Goh Gam Gar scratched his hairy belly with a clawed finger as wide as Nezeru's wrist. "For someone who has never died."

As she clambered over his mighty legs, almost sickened by the bristling fur scratching against her ankles, Nezeru felt the deep rumble of the monster's laughter.

The mortal had make crude symbols all over the hide, lines and branching forks and simple shapes. She thought it looked artless, and was almost saddened for him, that his death should be celebrated with such an indistinguished scrawl. As she watched, he finished the final row and held it at a little distance to examine his work. She thought the charcoal-scratchings looked like something a child would make on his first day learning from the Chroniclers.

"Does it say something?" she asked. "What kind of marks are those?"

"Those marks are the old runes of my people, from the time before we became your people's slaves," he said without looking up. "It is my death song. You should understand that. Sacrifices make them too—especially you Talons."

For a moment she was almost pleased he understood the difference, knew something of the sweat and blood and suffering it had cost her to become not just any Sacrifice, but a Talon of the Queen. "But we do not write our songs on skins." Nezeru still had not decided what to make of the mortal, but this was something she could understand. "We sing them after we have taken our sacred oath." She remembered the ageless cavern where the ceremony had taken place, the crack in the floor that had spilled heady, sweet fumes that rose from the holy Well, and the inhuman voices that had sung so softly and sweetly in the dark deeps. "Little more than a circle of seasons has passed since that day—I remember it as clearly as if no time had passed."

"You are fortunate, then, Sacrifice Nezeru, that yours is safely sung. My people do it differently so I am not so lucky." He gave her a keen look that she could not decipher. "Go and ask the giant to come here."

Uncertain, but also wondering what the mortal planned, Nezeru crept back up the crevasse to where Goh Gam Gar lay, big as a toppled haywain. He did not open his eyes until she told him that Jarnulf wanted him, then he grunted and rolled over. He did not stand, but crawled on hands and knees the several paces to the end where the Rimmersman sat, blocking most of the width of the crevice as he went, forcing Nezeru back to Jarnulf's side.

"Do you wish me to crush your skull?" Goh Gam Gar asked the mortal with what sounded like honest curiosity. "I did not take you for a coward, little man, but perhaps you would prefer to die on your own terms?"

Jarnulf's smile was icy. "When I die, I aim to take as many with me as I can, Jarl Hunë. I suspect you would be a rough partner for such an enterprise." His pale blue eyes looked a blank gray in the gathering dark. "I do not think you love Chieftain Makho, the one who gives you pain."

"No. I do not love him."

"Then help me play a small trick. I am not death-sung like these Hikeda'ya.

My last song must fly high and far, so that the old gods of my people can see it from Himnhalla—from the starry heavens."

"Do you wish me to throw it?" The giant watched as Jarnulf wrapped the hide around the arrow shaft, the ashy symbols now hidden. "I fear I will crush it instead."

"I can send it farther and higher with my bow than you can, even with those great thews of yours," Jarnulf said. "All I need you to do is to remain where you are and block the space between the two stones, so that Makho and his angry friend Kemme cannot see what I do."

"And what will you do in return? A slave like me is too poor to do favors, especially for doomed mortals, and I already helped you once."

Nezeru did not understand what the giant meant. Helped the mortal how? When?

"The doomed part is not up to you, Goh Gam Gar," Jarnulf replied. "As for my repayment, that will be for you to decide one day. Tell me, do we have a bargain?"

The giant laughed and stole a casual glance over his massive shoulder. At the far end of the crevice, beyond the horses, Makho and the other two Hikeda'ya were still planning either escape or brave death. "It would be a good joke, I think, but when the time comes for you to repay me, the jest may no longer be so much to your liking."

"We have both worn collars," said Jarnulf. "They do not take away a man's honor—or a giant's, is my guess. I will live by my bargain."

"Very well." Goh Gam Gar tilted himself so that he blocked all view across the passage from the far end. "Talk to your old gods. You might ask them why they hate giants so much that their servants have always tried to slay us."

"If I meet them tonight, I promise I will ask." Jarnulf rose to a crouch, arrow in one hand, and took up his bow. "Ah," he said, "I nearly forgot the last touch to my death song. There will be plenty of blood later, I think, but I need a little now to make the words powerful enough for the gods to hear." He drew the point of his arrow across the muscle of his leg, freeing a stripe of blood. He then rolled the hide in it, smearing it with a red that looked almost black in the twilight. "I will go only a short distance," he said to Nezeru. "You will be able to watch me."

"What do you mean?" she demanded. "I thought you only meant to loose an arrow. You can't leave this place! You will give us away."

"There is no one nearby. Ask Goh Gam Gar."

The giant flared his immense nostrils. "He speaks the truth. The men with armor have all gone down to the bottom of the hill to wait."

"You have your own bow, do you not, Sacrifice Nezeru?" Jarnulf fixed his pale eyes on hers but she could not guess at his thought. "If I do anything more than what I have said, feel free to put an arrow in my back. Can you see? There is no cover in this direction for a long distance. I know the skills of those trained by the Order of Sacrifice. You will be able to kill me easily."

"I cannot let you disobey our chieftain," she said. "If you go beyond this stone, I have no choice but to put an arrow in you."

"And I am going, arrow or no," he told her. "But here is something else for you to consider while you ponder whether to hasten my death by a few short hours. Why did your Singer and Makho sneak off in secret earlier to meet with a mortal?"

"What?" She was so surprised it was all she could do to keep her voice low. "What nonsense is this?"

"When you and Kemme were sent to scout the land ahead. Your chieftain told the giant to watch me, but Goh Gam Gar was lax, and I slipped off to follow them."

"Slipped off? I'll wager the beast let you go." At least now she knew the earlier favor that Goh Gam Gar had mentioned. But she still could not make sense of what Jarnulf had said. "Why do you say Makho met with a mortal? How could that be?"

"Because I saw it. It happened in the last hours of darkness, before you two brought the whole of the Erkynlandish army down upon our heads. Saomeji and your chieftain met with a rider who came up the great road from the south."

"A messenger from Nakkiga—" she began.

"Do you think after spending much of my life among both kinds that I do not know the difference between the scent of your folk and that of mortals like myself? If you had seen them, even from a distance as I did, you would not have mistaken the stranger for anything but one of my race, either. Face to face with the Singer and Makho, he was like a short-legged dog among buck deer. Your comrades showed no surprise at his arrival, and talked with him for some little time, then the mortal got back onto his horse and rode away toward the south."

"Not toward the army that surrounds us? Because they were behind us, coming from the north." She shook her head. "That only makes your lie more obvious, Huntsman. Where would he come from in this wilderness, if not out of the numbers of this mortal army?"

"That I cannot say, unless he was a wide-ranging scout, but he wore no insignia I could see, only an old cloak, as though he did not wish his identity to be too obvious. In any case, why would your chieftain have a secret meeting with a member of the army that hunts us?" He stood. "Now, I must send my song to the gods—and *you* must decide whether to feather my back or not, Sacrifice Nezeru, because the others will be done with their talking soon."

She watched in near disbelief as he turned his back on her and edged to the end of the space protected by the cleft boulder and Saomeji's song. She nocked an arrow and drew her bow, but as with the child on the island of the bones, she could not find the conviction to let fly. At last she lowered it again.

"Go, then and be quick," she whispered. "But if you take a step beyond that fallen log I promise I will kill you. Your gods will never know your name, but the ravens will pick your bones long before the sun has found its way back into the sky."

"Very fair." Jarnulf got down on hands and knees, then crawled out of the crevasse, waiting until he had gone several paces down the slope before rising.

Nezeru watched, uncomfortably aware of the massive creature behind her whose bulk sealed her off from the rest of the Talons, but even more miserably conscious of her fellow Hikeda'ya on the giant's far side.

Once he was away from the great, cloven stone, Jarnulf made his way swiftly and quietly down the slope and stopped just before the fallen log, looking back to make certain Nezeru saw him. Then, his mouth moving as if he sang or chanted something she could not hear, he drew his bow and pointed the arrow up and out toward the south, away from the mortal soldiers waiting at the bottom of the hill. When he released the string the arrow leaped into the air, carrying his red-smeared parchment silently across the violet sky, dwindling as it rose until at last it spent its strength and began to curve down into the trees.

Jarnulf scrambled back to the great halved stone even more quickly than he had gone, still blocked from the view of the others by the immensity of Goh Gam Gar. He had only just taken his place again when Nezeru heard the horses snort restlessly as someone came toward them from the far end.

"What have you done here?" demanded Saomeji, his voice a quiet snarl, his yellow eyes wild. It was the first time she had ever heard the Singer sound angry. "Someone has broken the line of my song!" He stood behind the giant on tip-toe, unwilling to get too close to the monster but struggling to see past him. "Was it you, mortal? What have you done?"

"Done?" Jarnulf laughed. "Have we not enough to worry about? I wanted a piss and the Hunë didn't want to move, so I stepped out and did it on the hill, just there." He shook his head. "I did not know that joining your company meant I could only piss when and where you said, Singer. If you'd told me, I might have chosen different traveling companions."

Makho came up behind Saomeji, his face cold. "You do *nothing* without asking me first, mortal." He looked at Nezeru. "What did he do?"

Another crossroad had come. "Only what he said, Hand Chieftain." Lies to her superior now rolled from her tongue as though she had practiced the crime for years. She was troubled by that, but also impressed with her own unexpected facility. "He did it before I knew what he planned, but came back promptly, so I did not slay him."

"You are far too patient for my liking, Blackbird." Makho turned to the mortal once more. "Stay there and do not move again until the moon sets or I will have the giant pull off your skin. I cannot deal with you now when there is planning yet unfinished, but I will not forget."

Nezeru knew better than to question Makho when he was angry, but he turned toward her as though she had voiced some doubt. "When real darkness comes, we will make these mortals fear us." He shook his head. "I swear by the Garden left behind, you and the Shu'do-tkzayha are both more trouble than you are worth."

"I can only speak for myself," said Jarnulf, so lightly that he almost sounded cheerful. "But I am a tool, and a very useful one. A good leader should know how to use me."

Makho did not rise to the bait. "I will use you until you break, if I so please," he told the mortal in a flat, dead voice. "Like any slave. Then I will toss you aside and never think of you again. Never doubt that."

"It is just that you do not seem to have enough warriors at your command to carelessly destroy one as skilled as I am," Jarnulf said cheerfully.

Was he trying to provoke the chieftain? Nezeru could not understand such recklessness, but Makho seemed to have decided to let him live, at least for the present. She realized that if Makho and the Singer had indeed met in secret with a mortal, if that tale was not merely mischief-making by Jarnulf, she no longer understood anything about what the Hikeda'ya were doing in this strange land.

Help me, Mother of All, she thought, half prayer, half lament. *I want only to do your will. Help me see my path.*

"Do not worry for me," Makho told Jarnulf. "I have all that I need. My blood flows for the queen, and I was given this task from her holy hand. I swear by my Talon oath and my ancestor's fabled sword that the mortal scum below will not take us, alive or dead. And by the time the sun rises again, they will weep over their own fallen." The chieftain now turned toward Nezeru, his eyes as dark as onyx beads in the white mask of his face. "Others have doubted me or misjudged me before this—Hikeda'ya and mortals alike. They are all dead." He slapped at his sword hilt. "As I said, we wait only until the moon sets. Then the blood of the animals who stole our land will be spilled across this hillside. A great, red river of the foul stuff."

23

Testament of the White Hand

Farewell, O my children! Farewell, O my wife!
I am called to defend what I love more than life
For no man who is true hides when battle horns blow
And the fields of his fathers are befouled by the foe
We shall push back this trespass or we'll die where we stand,
But we'll give not an inch of our fair Erkynland!

The young harper Rinan was doing his best. It was a spirited rendition of "Fair Erkynland," and his clear voice floated sweetly through the chill evening air, though he sang to a group of foot soldiers who would not look at him. If anything, they seemed to huddle closer to the fire as he approached, and many of their faces were tight with anger.

Farewell to my family! My neighbors, farewell!
I cannot turn back from the war's sounding knell
I am called to the battle, so must rush to the field
And there make a stand, and to no stranger yield
We shall push back this trespass or we'll die where we stand
But we'll give not an inch of our fair Erkynland!

The king rode a little nearer. The first soldiers to recognize him scrambled to their feet and then fell to their knees, chain mail clinking; others quickly followed suit. Rinan stopped singing as he turned to see what had caused the disruption, his harp ringing on for the length of a heart's beat before he, too, took a knee and bowed, his face pale as death.

As Simon looked down at the tops of all those bent heads, he felt a pang in his heart unrelated to his fears about the upcoming struggle. *What happens when everyone who knew me before is gone?* he wondered. *All that will be left is a world full of people who only know me as the king.* "Oh, saints preserve us," he said at last, "do get up, men. You don't want to get your breeks wet just before a battle. You'll have reason enough to wet them later on."

Some of the fighting men merely goggled at this, but a few laughed as if against their will, and soon many of the others were smiling as well: the Commoner King as many called him was well-liked by his soldiers. Simon passed a few words with them, naming a couple that he recognized, letting them know in all ways he could find that they were his men, that he valued their lives.

"Remember," he told them, "it's harder to go slow. It's harder to keep up your courage without running and shouting. But that's what you'll need to do. The Norns are clever, but here is a good joke—we Erkynlanders are too stupid to care! We'll have them boxed like a hare, boys, you'll see." He turned to Rinan, who was still kneeling. "Do me a kindness, will you, harper? Give me a little company as I go around the camp."

"I—I have no horse, sire."

Simon climbed down from the saddle. "Nothing to worry. I'll lead mine."

They walked for a while in silence, boots crunching through the occasional patch of snow. Every fifty paces or so a fire burned, mostly small, the pits dug in haste. Each had its contingent of soldiers, with others loitering between the campfire stations. They made something above eight hundred men all together, all the troops Sir Kenrick could spare without leaving vulnerable the camp back up the road.

"They don't really like songs about blood and killing and such," he said at last.

"Majesty?" the harper asked. "I mean—I beg your pardon, Majesty?"

"Not just before it's actually going to happen. Nobody wants to hear about men dying when men are about to die."

"Do you mean the song I was singing, sire?"

"No, I tell a lie. The Rimmersmen do. They're mad for it. The night before a battle they drink until they can barely stand, then they sing songs about hacking off people's heads and the death of the gods. Giants killing snakes! And they're not even pagans anymore." He laughed. "God save me, you should have seen them. Duke Isgrímnur, dear old Isgrimnur, he was usually the loudest."

The harper smiled, but it lacked conviction.

"No, you must think of some songs that will make the men merry instead," Simon said. "A little teary-eyed? That's well enough, too. Songs about girls always go down well. And home. Almost everyone likes those. Do you see what I mean?"

"I . . . I think I do, Majesty."

"Good. We're all on this road together, young Rinan. We all want to get back home, so we all do what we can to get us there safely. You have an important part to play, young man, just like the rest."

The harper was still walking beside him as Simon made his way toward the largest group of men, clumped at the eastern base of the steep hill. He had already had one visit from Eolair and two from Captain Marshal Kenrick. Jeremias had even come to inspect the king's armor, and had sworn he would return with a better tasset that would not hang askew.

"Aren't you tired, Majesty?" Rinan asked. "It is past the middle watches of night."

"My men are all awake—or most of them, at least. Never underestimate a soldier's ability to steal some sleep. In the Thrithings war all those years ago I saw men sleep standing up, waiting for the trumpet to blow." He nodded. "But sleeping or not, while they wait, I wait with them." The king looked over his army. "Do you wonder that most of our forces are set on this side of the hill?"

The weary harper tried to be attentive. By the last of the moon's light, his face had a sickly look. "Sire?"

"It's because the other side of the hill is steep. Too steep even for Norns, I'd say, and Eolair and the soldiers agree. No way off until most of the way down. So we have set only a few scouts there to watch. But we have many pickets up there above us—" he started to point up the slope, then remembered he might be observed, even in the near-dark, "—who'll let us know if the Norns are coming. Then, you see, the rest of the men can be up the hill here and coming around from the sides as well. We even have fowling nets to keep those sly creatures from slipping past us." Simon was rather proud of the nets, which had been his idea. He would never forget the stories he'd heard from Josua and the others, so long ago now, of being hunted by the White Foxes through the Aldheorte Forest, how the pale devils moved quickly and silently as cats. "And speaking of those pale devils, there may not be more than a few of them," he said suddenly. "We only know for certain that there are at least two, because Sir Irwyn saw them. Irwyn's a sensible man."

Rinan nodded. He was wide-eyed now—mostly from fear, was Simon's guess—and kept peering nervously up at the forested hillside.

Simon chuckled. "You're like my Miri. The queen. She thinks I'm going to go charging up there like when I was a young man—well, in truth I was a mere boy for much of the fighting during the Storm King's War. I was older when we fought the Thrithings-men. But it's always fearful, just before. Always." He shook his head sadly. "How many years do you have, lad?"

"Fifteen years, your Majesty. But my saint's day is near."

"Hah. I was much the same age as you when . . . well, when I saw the first of all this sort of thing." He waved to indicate the hidden enemy, the waiting soldiers. "Not by choice, of course. See, that's what I was trying to tell you the other day. Do you remember? When I lost my temper and grumbled at you a bit?"

Now Rinan's gaze was fixed on the king and only the king. "Yes, sire. I remember, sire."

"It's because you were singing a song about me, but the song wasn't really true." Simon scratched vigorously at his chin. The strap of his helmet had given him an itch, and he wasn't even wearing it any more. "And the truth is important, because . . . because, well, it just is." Simon was frustrated: For a moment, he thought he had a grasp on something important, the kind of thing Doctor Morgenes would have said. "You see, lad, there's the world in songs and stories, and then there's the world that actually happens to you. And they're not the same. Even the songs that are about real things—songs that are mostly true, I mean—they're about people thinking about those things afterward. Do you see what I'm trying to say?"

"I think so, Majesty."

"Because in a song, someone's riding off to slay a dragon, and his heart is full of noble ideas and fair maidens that need saving and all that. But in the world that we truly live in, someone rides off to save his own life, and then he's wandering around and strange things are happening to him that don't make good sense. And it's not that he's going to slay a dragon, it's that suddenly a dragon is coming at him, and he's trying not to die. And if he's lucky—or very good, and I wasn't that, I promise you, I was very, very lucky—he doesn't die. And then they make a song about him. Do you see?"

Rinan actually managed to smile. "I do, sire. I believe I do."

Simon felt relieved. "I'm glad. Because sometimes when I try to explain things to people they look at me like I'm a bit mad, but because I'm the *king* part of the high king and high queen, they don't say it."

"That was a very good explanation, in truth, Your Majesty."

"I suppose that's the main thing I was trying to get at, then," said the king. "What I learned from everything that happened to me. That you don't ever think you're in a song, if you know what I mean—"

A sound had begun as Simon was speaking, faint at first, but now rising like a storm wind—people shouting, some actually screaming—and he forgot what he had been saying. Torches moved up the hill, wavering like fireflies as soldiers broke rank and charged up to help the scouts on the hillside above.

Simon turned, hoping to spot Eolair or Kenrick, but could not locate them in the scramble. He knew he had to find trustworthy soldiers quickly so he could get the young harper back to the safety of the camp. Then his horse reared, and Simon had to struggle to hold onto the reins and keep the animal from bolting. When he turned, he found that young Rinan was down on his knees, as if praying. A moment later he saw the terrible shape of an arrow quivering high in the side of the young man's chest, just under his arm. Then the harper slumped face forward into the black dirt.

"Continue with my armor," Morgan told his squire. Melkin only stared at him, then glanced toward the massive Erkynguard soldier at the front door as if for permission. That made Morgan angry enough to feel he could spew smoke like an oven. "Why do you look to him? Is he your prince or am I?" He turned to the guard. "Am I permitted to put my armor on, guardsman, in case we are overrun?"

The soldier gave an uncomfortable shrug. He was a bulky, blue-jawed man with eyes so narrow they could scarcely be seen in the shadowed slot of his helmet. "Of course, your Highness, that is sensible. I was told only that you were to stay here, not, God save me, to tell your Highness what to do in your own tent."

"Stay here, my grandmother says. *Stay here!*" Morgan waggled his arm until Melkin began buckling on the pieces of his vambrace once more. "Sir Astrian is not staying here. Sir Olveris is not here. Even Porto, that tottering, ancient drunkard, is not expected to stay here with the women."

"I am not a woman, your Highness," said Melkin with a certain wavering dignity. "And neither is the guard. It's just us here."

"Well, then, we are expected to stay *near* the women." Morgan felt curiously light-headed, his stomach empty and his face hot. The thought of the battle he could now dimly hear was truthfully more frightening than exciting, but the idea of everyone knowing that he, the prince, had been kept from it seemed far, far worse. "God's curse on this, I am a man's age! I could be doing something!" He whirled to point at the guard, almost knocking Melkin onto his backside. "Those men out there need help!"

The guard stared back at him, and for a moment it seemed he would stay silent. Then he said, slowly and carefully, "They do, your Highness. I'd like to help them myself, and with good fortune I might even do nearly as much as your Highness. With good fortune, as I said." His words were slow but hard, like the crunch-crunch-crunch of marching feet. "But instead I'm to stay here with you—near the women, as you say—because that is the order my queen gave to me."

For a moment Morgan felt so hot all over that he could not tell if he was about to laugh or cry or shout until he burst like a bubble. But the disgusted look he thought he saw on the soldier's face, and Melkin's cowering posture on the ground, as though Morgan might hit him, made him feel as childish as his sister Lillia at her stubborn worst. *More disgrace.* He swallowed, then forced himself to swallow again, letting the rest of the angry words drain back into his depths, unspoken. Then, with princely calm belied by tight-clenched fists and palm-scoring nails, he nodded courteously to the guard before sinking onto a stool to make it easier for Melkin to finish dressing him.

Simon's heart felt pierced, as though the arrow had struck him instead of Rinan. He got down on one knee, fighting the weight of his own armor, and tried to turn the boy over. Another arrow whistled past.

Exposed. God spite me, I'm a damned fool!

He held onto his horse's reins with one hand and got as firm a grip as he could on the harper's collar, then grabbed at the back of his belt instead. He dragged the limp, surprisingly heavy body toward the front of the hill and the largest number of his soldiers, trying to let his armored horse serve as protection for both of them. The cries from higher up the hillside had grown in volume and pitch; now the king could hear men screeching in terror and pain. He looked up to see the irregular line of torches run against some invisible wall, many falling away as others continued upward until, having gone a little higher up the slope, they fell too.

How many Norns are on the hilltop? Have we been tricked? Is it some sort of ambush?

As he reached the greatest concentration of his own men, a milling, confused mass of shouting shadows, he found Kenrick the captain marshal standing in his stirrups, trying to form the nearest soldiers into a more orderly troop. Arrows were whizzing past, not in great volume, but with terrible accuracy. A man fell just a few feet from Simon, then Kenrick's horse shrieked, reared, and toppled with a clash of armor, flattening the undergrowth so that Simon lost sight of Kenrick entirely in the chaos of the horse's flailing legs and terrified sounds. Men were running both toward the hill and away from it, but far too many soldiers already lay arrow-pierced and limb-tangled on the ground, like dolls strewn by an angry child. Only a few of them were still moving.

"Simon? Simon!"

To his horror, he recognized his wife's voice. "Miri!" he shouted. "Away! Get back to the camp." He couldn't see her, but he could hear that she was far too close. Everything around him seemed to be falling apart. "Back to the camp!"

He had to go and find her, get her out of harm's way, but he couldn't leave the wounded harper lying helpless on the ground in the middle of this madness where he might be crushed by one of the horses, many of which were riderless and half-mad with fear. Staring about in desperation, Simon spotted a bit of bright cloth, then saw Jeremias crouching behind a wagon wheel some twenty paces away, his fine clothes in muddy tatters, his hat half-covering his face.

"Help me!" Simon shouted. "Jeremias, help me! It's young Rinan—he's been shot!"

Jeremias's round face turned toward them, and what Simon could see of his friend's features looked as bloodless as a split apple. Simon dragged Rinan in the chamberlain's direction, but before he could cross the distance a group of strange, small riders leaped past him, almost knocking him sprawling, then went bounding up the hill—riders not on horses, but on bounding, long-legged sheep.

Something nudged the back of his neck. Simon spun, almost letting go of the wounded harper. A nightmarish, grinning beast face leered at him out of the darkness. The king had a moment of terror before he recognized the white wolf.

"Friend Simon!" Binabik bent down from his perch atop Vaqana. "Daughter of the Mountains, I am so happy you are still being alive! I feared for you!"

"This young man has been shot with a Norn arrow."

Binabik slid down the wolf's back and dropped to his knees beside Rinan.

The harper's face was so pale and slack that Simon was certain he was beyond hope, but Binabik pressed his head to the youth's chest, then probed with his fingers at the wound around the arrow's shaft.

"He has breath still," the troll said, but before he could say more a ram came leaping back down the hillside and skidded to a stop beside him. Binabik's daughter Qina had her hood pulled low over her face and a spear in her hand.

"Ninit-e, Afa!" she cried.

"A moment, daughter." Binabik turned to Simon. "She is fearing for her mother and Little Snenneq, who are already up the hill and at helping your men." The troll said something brisk and guttural to Qina in their own tongue. She scowled horribly, but turned her ram away from the hill and rode swiftly through the mêlée of soldiers pulling back from the slope. "She is now going to find you help. She is not happy with this. Like her mother she is fierce as windblown ice. Now, I go to help my wife and Little Snenneq. Be safe, friend Simon! Wait for Qina!"

He and Vaqana bounded away; within a matter of two or three heartbeats the troll and his mount had become only a fast moving shadow in the under-growth.

The torches that still burned on the hillside had re-formed into a shaky noose of light that was slowly moving toward the summit. It had only reached the halfway point, yet there seemed less than half as many torches now. Simon wondered how many of his men had already fallen, and how strong the enemy truly was. He and Kenrick and the others had been too careless, and he cursed himself for it. What if they had bearded an entire Norn army?

Still, why would they be here if not to attack us? he told himself. *Better we found them before we were surprised.*

"Simon? Majesty? Are you still there?"

"Jeremias? Yes, I'm still here, with the harper. Come and help me."

"I'm trying—my cloak is caught under the wheel of this wagon." Jeremias's voice was shrill, as if he had been plunged straight back into the horrors of his youth. Simon had suffered terribly in the Storm King's War, but so had Jeremias, without the same measure of glory that had come for his friend.

Something had slowed the Erkynguards' stumbling retreat from the center of the line; Simon heard shouting and cursing as voices from the darkness behind him tried to drive the soldiers back into place. But just as he was about to call to Jeremias again, another chorus of ragged cries rose from the hillside above, then a single, dreadful shriek split the thickening night. It was nothing so terribly ordinary as a soldier's death cry, a thing made of pain and finality, it was the helpless screeching of a man seeing something in waking life that had previously been locked in the vaults of nightmare.

The scream lifted, grew ragged, and then was swallowed by a roar so loud and thunderously deep it might have come from the mountain itself; a moment later the hillside erupted in terrified cries accompanied by the drum-cracks of breaking trees. Even in a dark night lit only by torches, Simon could see a broad ripple moving down the hill as great trees fell, singly and in clumps, and as the ripple sped downward as a wave of screams raced before it. Simon could only imagine that somehow the entire crest of the hill had broken loose and was rolling or sliding down the tree-covered slope, sweeping all before it. He bent to pick up the wounded harper, hoping to drag him at least a little farther away from danger, then remembered his friend Jeremias, only a short distance away and just as helpless.

Simon didn't see the shadow fly down from the hillside until it struck the ground before him. It was only luck that it landed well short of where he cradled the unmoving Rinan, because whatever it was seemed as big as a man. The great projectile, flung out of the darkness toward him like a sling stone, skidded with an odd, flailing motion until it stopped just before him. Simon saw a dim gleam of chain armor and a white hand thrust out at an illogical angle. It was man-sized because it had been a man.

The dead Erkynguardsman had been hit so hard that he had nearly broken in half; the body was folded on itself so that soldier's legs were above the place where his head had once been—a head that was now only a bloody knob of raw skin, bone, and broken teeth. At the sight of it, for a long moment, Simon could pull no air into his lungs.

The sound of snapping trees grew even louder, and with it rose that deep, rumbling roar again: Simon felt it shaking his legs and arms and teeth, and thought it would turn his insides to jelly. This was not the first time he had heard such a sound so close by, and it terrified him.

Most of the torches were now gone from the hill above, the remaining few wildly scattered and moving erratically. Simon had just managed to lift the wounded youth off the muddy ground when something huge came tearing through the trees only a hundred cubits away from him, smashing its way through full-grown ashes and even oaks like a madman kicking through a pile of kindling.

Rinan's unmoving form dropped from Simon's suddenly nerveless fingers as the vast, manlike shape broke out from the edge of the forest, trunks splintering and leaping before it as if shot from bombards. For a moment the world seemed to spin, and he was plunged back into that terrible moment in the past, lost in the hills behind Naglimund, with Binabik dying and Simon and Miriamele caught between a desperate, wounded giant and its escape. It was as though time had turned and devoured its own tail.

Blessed Aedon, take care of Miri and be with me now, was all he had time to think.

The giant crashing down the slope toward him was the biggest one Simon had ever seen, a vast gray shadow that seemed taller than a house, its fanged jaws open and bellowing. It held an uprooted tree in one hand as a club, and when it saw Simon standing over the harper's body it turned and lurched toward him. Its legs were stumpy and thick, but each was nearly as long as Simon was tall, and the rest of the creature towered above it, the muscles of its huge chest and arms knotting beneath pale fur as it lifted the trunk to smash Simon like a fly.

Then another shape came stumbling into the open space between Simon and the giant, an Erkynlandish soldier so dazed and bloody he did not even see the monster, but stopped, swaying, to peer at Simon as though he recognized him. Simon did not even have a chance to shout a warning before the giant swung the great tree, obliterating the upper half of the soldier in a wet burst of blood and flesh.

Simon placed himself between the monster and the wounded harper and lifted his sword. The blade trembled like a mariner's compass too close to a lodestone, but that did not matter: Simon knew that no sword was going to stop such a thing, or even slow it. The giant thundered toward him, each flat-footed step making the ground shake so that Simon could barely stand. The sounds of terrified men, the many small fires blossoming on the wooded hillside, even the great, bone-shaking roars of the thing itself all faded away until he could hear nothing and see only the great shadow bearing down on him.

Like the dragon. His thoughts were swirls of dust, blown feathers. *Like the dragon all over again. Again and again fighting, and never to rest . . . !*

He lifted his sword. Better to die fighting, that was all—he and his blade would make no other difference. Everything that was him, that was Simon, would fly into bits before he could even pink the creature.

The great trunk swung toward him, a storm cloud, a whistling darkness. Simon was thrown sideways, and instead of a blow that would knock his bones to powder, felt only the blast of great wind. He fell down, down.

Is this what it feels like to die? Am I dead?

He was lying on something that was neither soft nor hard. He opened his eyes, and saw that he had tumbled across the body of Rinan. Although he still had no idea what had happened, he tried to scramble back so that he did not crush the harper. Something was holding his legs. Something . . .

Another thundering noise, that of hoofbeats this time, and then a flurry of pale shapes burst out of the darkness of the hillside and galloped past him, swift and unexpected. He rolled onto his side to watch the white horses as they rushed away, following in the track of the giant. The creature's great back was toward Simon now as it led the Norns toward the road. The White Foxes galloped after him, their hair whipping like pennants as they sped toward freedom, toward escape. Simon was stunned to count no more than half a dozen Norn riders—so few to cause so much horror, so few—!

"But I'm . . . I'm not dead." He realized he had said it out loud. He could not understand how the giant had failed to kill him. He tried to move his legs again, but couldn't. A panicky moment ended when he saw that someone was clinging to him.

"Jeremias?" he asked. Jeremias had his arms wrapped tight around Simon's knees. It seemed so unlikely—like another part of the dream: the king's oldest friend had grabbed him and dragged him down so that the giant's blow had missed. "God's Blood, Jeremias! You saved my life."

His friend stared back at him for a moment, his bloodless, shocked face covered in dirt and ashes, then Jeremias Chandler, Lord Chamberlain of the Hayholt, burst into helpless tears.

Count Eolair knew that the gods had gifted him with life and vitality beyond many, and he was grateful for that. At an age when most men were dead or doddering, he still moved among the greatest and the most powerful of all lands, and had responsibilities that any ambitious man would envy. Instead of sitting in the sun or playing with grandchildren before the hearth, he spent his days in the saddle with the young men, and worried at night about the fate of entire kingdoms. But in this hour he felt truly old—older than he had ever felt. It was as though the previous night had hollowed him out, leaving nothing but a fragile shell, as if any sharp blow or even a hard breeze might crumble him into flakes and powder.

"Just tell us the worst of it." Queen Miriamele was composed, the only sign of her misery in the redness of her eyes. For an instant, he thought he saw in that sharp, stubborn face what her father Elias might have been had he not been lured by the priest Pryrates, had he not fallen into madness and shadows. "How many dead?"

"It makes my heart ache to tell you, Majesty. Twenty-three men dead, but with several others not likely to last the day. Twice that number hurt. Colfer will lose his arm, but he was lucky—the man beside him was crushed like a rotten fruit—" Eolair shook his head. "Forgive me, Majesties. You do not need to know all the horrors this day has seen."

"Of course we do," she said. "In fact, I will go visiting with you when we have finished here. The king has been wounded, so he can wait to go among them until tomorrow."

"That's foolish. I'm scarcely hurt, Miri," Simon said, but to Eolair he seemed worse than hurt. If the queen looked like she had been crying, Simon looked like someone who could not even remember how to cry, as though something important inside him had collapsed and might never be rebuilt. He could certainly understand why the queen didn't want Simon going out among the men yet. Still, there was no way he could tell that to the king.

"Rest and let the queen visit the men, sire," he said. "I will bring your commanders here, and you can take stock with them."

"Take stock? What is there to discuss? A handful of White Foxes just killed two dozen of our people, one of them right in front of me. Right in front of me." Simon took a long time before speaking again. "An innocent, God save us all."

"We must discuss whether we send a troop of men after the enemy, for one thing," Eolair said.

"Pointless." The king shook his head. "They would be hard enough to catch on foot, but on those tireless Stormspike horses . . . there is no sense in even following. Believe me, if I thought otherwise, I'd be leading the way myself."

"No you wouldn't," his wife said. "Do not even speak that way."

"Why?" The king grimaced and rolled into a more comfortable position on the cot. "I took no real injuries." Simon pointed at Tiamak, who was rolling his cutting instruments back into their oilcloth wrapping, preparing to go out among the wounded again. "Ask him."

Tiamak turned and nodded wearily. "The king is bruised and scraped and his ribs are tender—but, yes, his Majesty is largely correct." He shared a quick glance with Eolair before turning to the king. "Still, you are terribly weary, Simon."

"I've already slept. The rest of you haven't." The king had been all but tricked into an hour's worth of rest around dawn after Tiamak—at Eolair's quiet suggestion—had insisted that the shocked, heartsick monarch down a cup of strong Perdruinese brandy. "I can't lie around any longer when the men are hurt and frightened, and many are dead. You already stopped me from going among them once."

"They didn't need to see you like that, husband," the queen said. "You would have brought them no comfort. Bleeding and filthy—you looked like some monster yourself."

The king was now almost sulking. "Only because Jeremias pulled me down into the muck. When he saved me, of course—saved my life! I don't want to sound ungrateful. Bless him and keep him, I couldn't believe it when I looked down and—" Simon trailed off and looked around. Eolair politely waited for him to catch up. "Your pardon," he said. "What else is there? Why were those creatures here, so far south?"

Eolair could only shake his head. "At this point we can but guess, Majesty. No, I do not think we are even ready to do that."

"And has anyone found evidence of how many of the evil things there were?" Miriamele asked. "Did we kill any?"

"If we did," said Tiamak, quietly as was his usual way, but with unusual firmness, "I would very much like to see the body."

"None." Eolair spread his hands. "We found no fallen but our own. Apparently the five we saw—and the giant, of course—were all."

"They are terrible, fierce fighters," said Simon. "Cold and difficult to kill as snakes. I'd truly hoped we would never have to face them again."

A herald appeared in the doorway of the tent and announced Sir Kenrick, the burly, bearded young captain marshal, who held one hand close to his side. Eolair stirred, wondering if the captain was injured. The way he kept the hand out of sight made Eolair anxious, and he took a few steps closer to Kenrick and let his hand fall discreetly to his sword hilt, wondering if he still had enough of his old speed should something be badly amiss. "Captain, what do you have there for us?" he asked.

"Any sign of the bastards?" the king called from his cot.

"Gone, sire," said Kenrick. "Melted into the open lands on the other side of the road. You'd think the Hunë would leave an easy track to follow, but there are a lot of rocky stretches in the grassland here—I'd warrant they're on their way back to Stormspike, heading due north." He raised his hand to his chest. "But, I beg your pardon, Majesties, as the lord steward noticed, I have something else to show you. I sent men sweeping both ways up and down the road, looking for other enemies. I told them especially to look for any sign of recent activity, something that might suggest another ambush. They saw nothing of that, but they did come across this a short way down the road to the south, sticking right out of the mud—the man who found it said it looked at first like a spring flower." He carefully offered the thing he had been cradling to the queen.

It was an arrow, but not one of the Norns' black shafts. It looked like mortal work, and made in haste at that, the rawhide cord irregular where it wrapped the arrowhead, as though a broadhead from one arrow had been used to repair a different one. But what was most unusual about it was the roll of blood-smeared parchment wrapped around the shaft and tied tightly with another rawhide thong.

Miriamele looked it over. "You said this was found close by, in the road? It certainly doesn't look to be one of ours."

"No, Majesty," said Kenrick.

"It looks like the arrow of someone who has been living rough," said Eolair. "And it isn't the first. We found several more like this one on the hill this morning—but only sticking in trees. As far as we could discover, not a one of these hit any of our soldiers. All those who had been shot, it was Norn arrows that pierced them."

"Unpeel that bloody hide," said Simon. "What is it?"

Eolair took his knife and handed it to the queen. She cut the thread and unwound it, then unfurled the hide so carefully and gently that Simon groaned at how slowly she did it. This was the first thing that had happened since the previous day that even came close to making Eolair smile, but he still did not feel solid enough for that: whatever was holding him together seemed more fragile than even that slender rawhide cord.

"What kind of letters are those?" the queen asked, holding up the latticed hide. Untidy rows of strange characters filled it, drawn in black. "Eolair, can you read this? Tiamak?"

Eolair had seen things like it, but could not remember where. He shook his head.

"I can, Majesty," Tiamak said. "Or at least I think I can."

"Is it Wrannaman writing, then?" Simon asked in surprise. "That would be a strange turn!"

"No, sire." Tiamak took the hide from the queen, then squinted as he tilted it toward the nearest torch. "These are the runes that Rimmersmen once used."

Simon squinted and frowned. "That doesn't look like Rimmerspakk."

"It is, but the runes are different. I said 'once used'. These are the old signs, the ones they brought from their former land, across the sea of icebergs. Only the Black Rimmersmen still use them in Osten Ard now. The Norns' slaves."

"But why would four or five Norns have a slave?" Eolair asked. "So far from their border? It makes little sense, unless one of the White Foxes was some kind of royalty?" He turned to Tiamak. "Can you read what it says?"

"As I said, this language is old Rimmerspakk, the ancient version of what I learned. I will try to make what I can of it."

It took him a little while. As Tiamak puzzled through possible meanings, Binabik came in from the cold morning to say that the last of their rams had been found, which meant that even the four-legged members of the troll's own small party had survived. When he saw what the Wrannaman was doing, he leaned close to look over his shoulder.

"It is not being much like the Rimmerspakk I can read," the troll admitted.

"I think I have the sense of it now," said Tiamak, looking down to the translation he had written on a parchment: "'I travel with the Hikeda'ya,' it says. 'I am not one of them, but I will stay with them. This is what I must do. They travel on a mission to Urmsheim. I do not know why, but the mission is important to Nakkiga. The queen of the Hikeda'ya has awakened from her long sleep. The North is full of rumor and preparation for war. I heard one of this company say that the queen seeks the witchwood crown. I do not know what that means, but it is important to them. What I do know is that the queen of the north lives again, and while she lives, she plans our deaths.'" Tiamak cleared his throat. "It is signed 'Jarnulf of the White Hand'."

Eolair suddenly felt as if something was shifting beneath him, not a fixed, solid thing like rocks and earth, but a tangle of plans and assumptions that had seemed strong enough to bear them up only a few short hours before.

Queen Miriamele looked as troubled as Eolair felt. "Strange . . . and frightening. Do you know who this Jarnulf is, Count Eolair? Kenrick? Have any of you heard of him or this White Hand?"

As heads were shaking, Sir Kenrick held out his hand again. "Also we found this, which was lying near the arrow. It seems to have fallen loose when the arrow struck the ground. My man said he thought by the angle it had stuck in the mud that the arrow must have been fired from high up on the hillside." The captain opened his hand, exposing a shiny something on a slither of silver chain.

"He Who Always Steps On Sand!" Tiamak cried, an oath Eolair had only heard the little man use when he was badly surprised. Coming forward to look more closely, the count saw it was a circle of silver dangling from a silver chain. A silver feather was laid across the circle, along with another shape Eolair could not quite make out. "This is the sign of the League of the Scroll," Tiamak said hoarsely. "But ours are gold, not silver—and there has never been any Jarnulf in the League!"

King Simon stared at the silver charm, then swung his feet off the cot and turned to the Hand of the Throne. Eolair sighed, foreseeing what was to come.

"Old friend," Simon told him, "this attack, all of this—well, it changes things."

Eolair felt no surprise, only a small sadness. "Yes, sire. Of course it does. I will tell my great-nephew Aelin that I cannot go back with him to Hernysadharc. Give me time only to write a letter to Queen Inahwen."

"Of course, of course." But something in the king's face said that even this morning's discoveries, strange and ominous as they were, had not disturbed him like the death of the young harper, nor could much distract him from it. "Yes, I'm sorry, but that's it, old friend. We can't do without you—not now."

"Of course, sire. I understand." And in that moment, Eolair was not really certain that any such ordinary plans or frustrations mattered. It seemed the shift of balance he had sensed earlier had been just a hint of something even larger, a great and heavy pivot that would change the world so much that, no matter what they did, its full force would soon be upon them.

PART TWO

Orphans

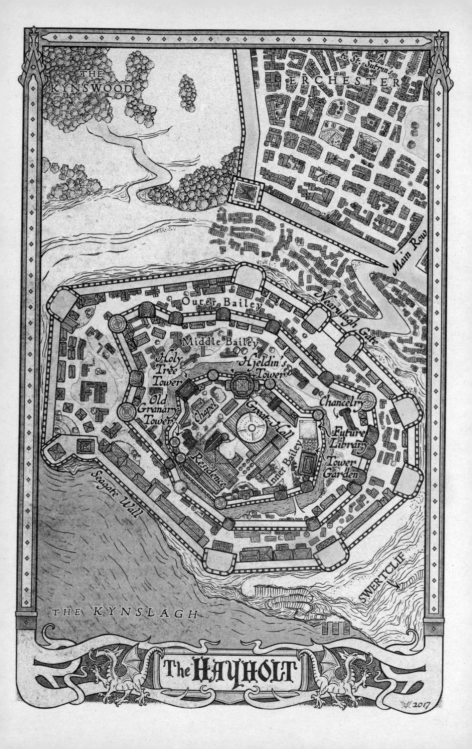

THE
KYNSWOOD

ERCHESTER

St. Sutrin's

Main Row

Outer Bailey

Nearulagh Gate

Middle Bailey

Holy
Tree
Tower

Hjeldin's
Tower

Chancelry

Old
Granary
Tower

Chapel

Great Hall

Future
Library

Inner Bailey

Tower
Garden

Residence

Seagate Wall

SWERTCLIF

THE KYNSLAGH

The HAYHOLT

2017

Heaven took my wife. Now it
Has also taken my son.
My eyes are not allowed a
Dry season. It is too much
For my heart. I long for death.
When the rain falls and enters
The earth, when a pearl drops into
The depths of the sea, you can
Dive in the sea and find the
Pearl, you can dig in the earth
And find the water. But no one
Has ever come back from the
Underground Springs. Once gone, life
Is over for good. My chest
Tightens against me. I have
No one to turn to. Nothing,
Not even a shadow in a mirror.

—MEI YAO CH'EN

24

Terrible Flame

In the wild lands north of Kwanitupul, the swamp called
the Varn stretched in a broad tongue of wet lowland all the way to the shores
of the Unhav, the wide lake that the city people of Nabban called by a name in
their own language, Eadne. The grasslander riders knew this northernmost part
of the Varn well: In spring and summer the people of the Thrithings hunted
here for birds and fish and otters (whose pelts the stone-dwellers prized and paid
for handsomely), so the grasslanders had learned the safe ways through this
treacherous, trackless landscape while they had still been children.

"Why do the city men even come to live here?" Fremur asked. "They are
not like us or even the Varnamen. They will be eaten by crocodiles or ghants.
They will stumble off the safe tracks and drown."

"Only a few of them," said Unver. "Then the rest will drain the Varn and
build farms."

Fremur hoped that wasn't true, but he had learned long ago not to argue
with Unver. The tall, quiet man did not say much, but what he said was usually
correct.

"Impossible," said Odrig, Fremur's brother, who was the thane of their clan
even though their father still lived. "Only a coward would believe that stone-
dwellers could take our land. We will push them into the ocean."

"Only a coward or a fool," said Drojan, looking to Odrig for approval.

Unver did not say anything, and his hawk-nosed face remained impassive,
but Fremur could almost feel the man's anger tighten, like the stretching of a
bowstring. Unver thumped his heels against his horse's ribs and rode a little way
ahead, picking his way through the tufts of reeds and the muddy pools on ancient tracks that would disappear again with the first rains of autumn.

"Fool," said Drojan again, but not as loudly as he might have. Like Odrig,
Drojan was barrel-chested and strong, but though Odrig might be as tall as
Unver, Drojan was a head shorter and a great deal slower. If Drojan had not
been Thane Odrig's friend and lackey since childhood, Fremur felt sure he
would not be insulting Unver so freely.

Odrig laughed. "No need to pick fights," he said. "There will be blood to
spill soon enough."

Fremur was not entirely certain himself how he felt about Unver. The tall man was no one's friend, and he had made it clear many times that he thought Fremur little more admirable than his elder brother Odrig. Still, there was something about pale-skinned Unver that Fremur could not ignore, some quality of purposeful reserve, of unusual thoughts unshared. Old beyond his three decades, uninterested in boasts or contests or drinking until he staggered, Unver was simply not like the other Thrithings-men.

If Fremur was uncertain of his feelings about Unver, he was in no doubt how he felt about his brother Odrig, the thane: he hated him. Odrig was one of the largest, fiercest men in the Crane Clan. He had acted like its leader since he was a youth, but when their father Hurvalt had been god-struck seven summers earlier, Odrig had inherited the clan's bones and banner in fact as well as in his own estimation. Hurvalt still lived, but the old thane was now little more than a simpleton. Odrig had ruled the family since that moment, and had made that hard old man, their father, seem like a soft, soft woman. Fremur was no coward, and in a different clan he might have thrived, but his older brother treated him like a child.

No, he thought. *Not like a child. Like a dog. Kick me when he pleases and throw me a bone if it suits him. If he were not my brother and my thane, if he were simply another clansman, I would have put a knife in him years ago.*

Sometimes Fremur thought of simply leaving the Crane Clan for another—the Fitches or Kestrels, or even the Antelopes up in the Meadow Thrithing, whom he had seen once at a gathering and admired for their tall, handsome women. Sometimes he even thought it would be better to wander unhomed and without a clan than to continue putting up with Odrig's abuse, but he could not leave their sister Kulva to suffer alone.

It seemed strange to hate his own flesh and blood so, but time and again Odrig Stonefist had proved himself worth hating.

They rode swiftly through the hills that hemmed the marshy lowlands, but paused before descending into the wide valley. The settlement stretching before them was mostly dark, but here and there a torch burned along the wooden stockade, and Fremur thought he could see movement above the gate. Unver, as usual, rode a little way apart from the others, bent low over the saddle and wrapped in his long, dark cloak so that it was hard to tell by moonlight where horse ended and rider began.

Odrig reined up and scanned the wall. Inside lay the paddocks where the settlers' cattle and sheep were kept, along with the greatest prize of all, their horses. The stone-dweller's beasts might not compare to Thrithings-steeds, but they were still useful for crossbreeding, and even more useful for selling to Varnamen and others who could not afford the prices at Nabbanai horse markets.

Odrig stood high in his stirrups, scanning the darkness. Much as he loathed him, Fremur had to admit his brother had the look of a proper grasslands thane. Odrig had taken a wife, as a thane should, and had long ago grown out his man's beard. Unver and Drojan, despite being more or less the same age, still had the long mustaches and smooth chins of unmarried men, while Fremur's own mustaches did not even reach the bottom of his jaw.

"Where are Tunzdan and his damned cousins?" Odrig growled, but a moment later a nightjar's call echoed three times from the nearest hill. "There. Good." He bared his teeth in a grin. "Now we wait for Bordelm to start the celebration." He looked to Unver. "If this plan of yours doesn't work, be sure I'll leave you behind to be skinned by the city-men."

Unver only stared back at him as though the thane hadn't said anything worth hearing.

For long, tense moments the Crane-men sat and waited, motionless as stones. Then, along the far edge of the settlement, a great fire blossomed on the palisade. Suddenly the night was full of cries, both the shouts of Bordelm's clansmen and the cries of startled sentries at the tall wooden gates. Torches bounced along the top of the gate as the other guards rushed back and forth, trying to make out what was happening on the far end of the settlement.

Odrig now lifted his horn to his lips and blew three short blasts, then dug in his spurs and set off down the hillside at a gallop with Drojan and Unver just behind him. Fremur clapped heels into his horse's ribcage and followed them. A larger force of mounted men were sweeping down from one of the other hillsides—their cousin Tunzdan and his own sprawling family-clan, more than a dozen Cranes with a taste for plunder and violence.

At Unver's suggestion, Bordelm and the others had brought buckets of pitch to smear along the palisade logs before setting the fire, and the scheme had clearly worked: as Fremur and the others neared the settlement, the moonlight was outshone by the unsteady orange glare of the burning wall. Fremur heard shouts and screams from inside the settlement as the stonedwellers woke to discover that something terrible was happening. Every now and then an arrow would fly from inside the walls, gleaming red for a moment in the firelight, but the Crane clansmen had arrows of their own, wrapped in pitchy rags; within moments, dozens of flaming missiles were being shot back over the wall, starting fires in roof thatch all over the settlement.

The clansmen quickly reached the gate in the high wall. The guards had deserted it to run toward the fire on the far side of the settlement. Unver climbed on top of his saddle, balancing with his arms spread. The moment his horse was close enough, he leaped up and caught the top of the gate, curling his fingers around two of the sharpened posts, then pulled himself over. A moment later the bolt slid back and the gate opened.

Odrig laughed. "See, they are inviting us in, my blood-drinkers! Let us not shame their hospitality by refusing!"

Fremur caught at the reins of Unver's black horse and led it through the gate. The tall man took it back without a word and vaulted back into his saddle, then spurred forward. Fremur stayed close behind him.

Inside, the settlement was ablaze. People were running all directions in disorganized terror, but it was easy enough to tell the mounted Thrithings-men from the Nabbanai settlers, who wore flapping night-shirts or were barely half-dressed. Some of the guards had never made it across to the burning wall on the far side of the settlement, and turned now to stand against Odrig and his raiders. As the smoke swirled and the shrieks of women and children and the death cries of men rose into the night sky, these guards became the center of knots of resistance.

The Cranes did not care—they did not intend to wipe out a settlement of many hundreds, not with less than half a hundred men of their own. Their goal was the fenced paddock at the center of the village where the animals were kept.

Fremur had been on raids before, but never against such a large target. Before tonight the men of the Crane Clan had confined their attacks to isolated farmsteads or the lands of absent Nabbanai lords who seldom had enough men to protect their holdings from determined assaults. But this was a very different kind of strike, and Fremur could not help wondering how Odrig would deal with the obvious success of Unver's idea. Odrig already disliked the tall, quiet man, who alone among the Cranes did not treat Fremur's brother as his lord and master.

Most of the clansmen were already headed toward the paddocks at the center of the settlement, but Odrig stopped to take on a Nabbanai settler who was intent on defending his village with a billhook. The settler had no armor and wore only a long shirt, but Odrig seemed to be enjoying the sport, slashing at the man's hands where he held his makeshift weapon and blocking the man's return swipes, laughing all the while.

His brother laughed frequently, but Fremur had learned early in his life that when Odrig was laughing, someone else was usually bleeding.

Odrig now began inflicting cuts on the settler, slashing his face and arms so that the man's nightshirt was ribboned with blood. Fires had started in many other places throughout the settlement now and smoke was spreading everywhere.

"Come, Mouse!" Odrig shouted to Fremur. "Take an ear or his nose for your own—a trophy!"

Fremur had always hated the name his brother gave him, little more than another way of calling him a weakling and coward, and he did not want to watch Odrig toying with the settler, who was now weeping and stumbling in the mud as Odrig inflicted cut after cut on him. Instead he spurred away toward the center of the village.

Much of the palisade was aflame now, and scores of roofs had caught as well. Fremur could hear the awful cries of those trapped in the burning houses, men, women, and children, but he felt no pity.

This is our land—our fathers' and their fathers'. The Nabban-men should go back to their stone houses or die.

As he neared the center of the village, where the chaos of animal noises and human screams was at its loudest, Fremur saw that a handful of his Crane clansmen had blundered down a passage between houses and now were trapped against the inner wall of the palisade by a dozen or so settlers wielding billhooks and hayforks, as well as two or three armored settlement guards with long spears. It was impossible to make out the clansmen's faces in the smoky, inconstant light, but by the ribbons wrapping their horses' tails he guessed they might be some of Tunzdan's men. The Cranes were fighting desperately but they were hemmed in, and the long spears of the guards were forcing them farther and farther back toward the wall.

Fremur hesitated for a moment. He owed nothing to Tunzdan, one of Odrig's chief allies, but these were still his clansmen: how could he hold his head up as a man if he abandoned them to these land-stealing farmers? He spurred toward the angry mob. Before he could reach them, though, a great shadow swept past him like the Grass Thunderer himself.

It was Unver on his black horse Deofol, the curve of his sword a red crescent against the sky. The tall man crashed into the rear of the settlers and several of them collapsed immediately, shoulders or necks fountaining blood. Others shouted in terrified surprise as their hunt of the clansmen fell into fatal disorder. It all happened so quickly that Fremur slowed to watch as the cornered Cranes, heartened by their enemies' confusion, now plunged forward into the mass of settlers. The first to fall were the armored guards, and moments later the rest of the settlers were fleeing for their lives while the Thrithings-men, changed from quarry back to hunters in mere moments, shouted and sang with joy at their rescue and rode the stragglers down.

Unver stood in his stirrups and pointed with his sword toward the center of the town. "There!" he shouted at the clansmen. "Find your brothers there!"

And in that moment, with the leaping red blaze silhouetting him against the night sky, illuminating Unver's sharp features and flapping cloak so that he seemed half-man, half-raven, Fremur felt something squeeze at his heart, a strange mix of admiration and terror. Surely this wasn't Unver any longer, but Tasdar the Anvil Smasher himself, one of the powerful spirits worshipped by all the grassland clans.

"What are you staring at, you fool?" the godlike figure shouted at him. "It is almost time to ride home."

Fremur realized with a start that Unver was right—even Odrig would not wait much longer before retreating, not when they were so greatly outnumbered by the settlers. After all, this was not a killing mission but a plundering mission. He also realized with a sinking heart that he was going to be returning from the raid empty-handed. He knew what Odrig and his cronies would say about that, and it would not be kind.

Fremur followed Unver as they rode toward the middle of the settlement, passing other clansmen driving the settlement's animals in small groups toward the gate—here a Crane with a half dozen bleating sheep, there a pair of Cranes with several eye-rolling cattle. One of Bordelm's cousins clutched the harnesses of two heavy plow-horses, which would never do as war-beasts but would serve admirably to pull a Thrithings wagon.

As Unver and Fremur burst into the open center of the village, through screeching, heedless settlers and clansmen now eager to escape with their prizes, Fremur saw that the paddock fences had been thrown down, broken into splinters in places, and that all but a few of the valuable animals were already gone. As he spurred after a squawking goose, which hurried just ahead of him with its wings spread, he saw Unver dismount and then vanish into the shadowy doorway of a burning barn. He came out leading a huge bull, a magnificent creature with a rope hanging from its ringed nose. Unver's usually grim face wore a lopsided smile.

"Even late to the feast, look what I've found!" the tall man said. "And he was just about to overcook, too!"

Fremur had never seen Unver look outright happy—not that he could remember. It was a strange sight, but even as he wondered at it, an arrow whizzed past his head and buried itself in a timber of the blazing barn. Some of the settlers still meant to fight back.

Unver swung his long body back into the saddle in an instant, then he and Fremur led the bull toward the front gate. Many of the settlers were fighting back in earnest now with stones and the occasional bow and arrow, emboldened by the Thrithings-men's retreat and hoping to pick off a few as they rode by. Fremur and Unver were not struck, but Fremur saw one of Tunzdan's riders fall from his horse just a short distance away, an arrow in his leg; before he could regain his saddle he was dragged away into the shadows between houses by a mob of settlers.

"Don't," Unver said as Fremur hesitated. "It's too late for him. Ride now."

Fremur didn't have to be told twice. He and Unver were among the last to flee the settlement; any moment now the gates would close and they would be trapped inside. Clansmen captured on raids were usually burned to death, and sometimes that was the most merciful part of their treatment. Fremur laid his head against his horse's neck to offer a smaller target to any bowmen.

Finally he saw the sagging gate before them. They went through at a trot, slowed by the trailing bull, and within moments the settlement began to fall away behind them, the smoke and flames and screams growing fainter with each hoofbeat, like a dream disappearing with morning light.

"A good evening's work," said Unver, hunched low in his saddle, one hand still clutching the rope. The captive bull was being forced along at a pace far faster than it liked, lowing and snorting with discomfort. Unver was grinning, and again Fremur was struck by the strangeness of seeing the man happy. "A good evening!"

They had reached the first rise, the walls of the settlement only a stone's-throw behind them, when something struck Fremur in the head like a lightning bolt. For a moment he had no idea of what up was or down, or of anything except that the night was full of bursting white stars, then something like a giant hand stretched out and slapped him so hard the blazing white turned to solid black.

When Fremur could think again, he was lying on his back and could still see the flaming walls. His horse was gone, Unver was gone, and he was helpless. He tried to roll onto his stomach, but could only get halfway there. Blood—it must be blood, he thought, because it was wet and dark—dripped from his scalp, pooling on his hands and making the dark grass even darker. He lifted his head, which felt as though someone was beating it like a drum, and saw three figures running toward him from the settlement gate.

They shot me, was all he could think. *They shot me in the head with an arrow.* He reached back. His helmet was gone somewhere, but although the back of his head was slick with blood and complicated with tattered, stinging flesh, he could not find the arrow he had been certain must be sticking into his skull.

The settlers were getting closer, half-running in their excitement at having brought down one of the hated raiders. Fremur could see they were Nabban-men, their upper lips shaved, their eyes bright with the excitement of revenge. One was already nocking a new arrow, while the other two carried billhooks.

They're going to cut me up like a spring lamb, Fremur thought, and it was almost funny, except that his head hurt so badly. *But I'm not a lamb, I'm a man.*

Then something dark leaped over him, all but flicking his face as it went, with a rumble and roar of air like a thundercloud punishing the earth. It was a horse, rider low on its neck, but now the rider rose in his stirrups and lifted his curved blade, bright and deadly as a lightning-flash.

Then it all faded and Fremur could no longer see anything, though he could hear men's voices, shouting, some screams. Darkness was returning. Was he dying? Had some of the other clansmen come to help him? Fremur didn't know, but he could not imagine that any of it mattered very much.

For a long time after the sun rose he couldn't get off his bedroll. Instead he lay with eyes closed and listened to the strange sounds of the living world, the living world that he seemed still to be a part of. Birds—so many birds! Warbling, whistling, chirping, fluting, their noise seemed deafening. Had it always been this way? Why had he never noticed?

Something touched his arm. Fremur flinched and tried to roll over, but the sudden movement made his head hurt so badly that he groaned and gave up.

Another touch, then a light stroke across his forehead.

"Fre? Are you awake?" The voice was like a breeze, cooling him.

"Kulva?" He opened his eyes, but just a little. The light was fierce, like knives.

"I brought you water," his sister said. "How is your head?"

"Like a broken pot. I thought I was a dead man."

"Don't say that! The spirits who saved you will be angry."

The light was a little less sharp now, so he decided to sit up—very slowly. "It wasn't the spirits who saved me, it was Unver Long Legs." He could see it now, Unver and Deofol leaping over him where he lay wounded, sweeping down on the settlers to savage them like a wolf among chickens. "It was Unver. He must have given up his bull to come back for me." Fremur managed to prop himself on his elbows, which was as far as he could get before a wave of pain sloshed through his skull. Kulva's worried face hung over him like a midday moon.

"Unver is a good man, but you still should not tempt any spirits," his sister said, frowning. "Here, drink." She helped him put the cup to his lips and poured a little water in his mouth. He lifted his hand to take it from her but she pushed it away. "Just let me tend you. Always so proud!"

"I'm a man of the Crane Clan. I was only wounded in a fight. I can take care of myself." He knew he sounded like a child. "In any case, if the spirits want me to get better, they'll make me better."

The beginnings of a smile twisted her lips, but she fought it down. "Oh, yes. Men on men's business. Forgive me for trying to help you while you lay on the ground, moaning. Everyone else has been up for hours."

"By the Stone Holder!" He groaned as he sat fully upright. "Why did no one tell me? Is Odrig angry?"

"He laughed." Kulva clearly did not approve. "He laughed, then he went off to the lake with Drojan to hunt."

That was a relief. Fremur pulled himself up so he could sit cross-legged, which helped his balance. His head felt like a swollen bladder—if it got any more full, he thought, he would begin to piss out his ears.

"What are you laughing about, Fre?"

"I don't know. My head hurts. Is there something to eat?"

"I brought you bread." She reached into her apron and pulled out a leaf-wrapped bundle.

Fremur unwrapped the bannock and took a bite. Chewing seemed to make his entire head feel odd, like a precariously balanced rock that might roll away with a push. He took several bites, then suddenly found he did not want any more. Even with food in his stomach, he still felt strange. The colors around him, like the voices of the birds, seemed too strong—surely the world had never been so bright! The wagons of the clan seemed to gleam like jewels, and the colorful ribbons that decorated them were searing streaks of light. But when he closed his eyes, instead of darkness he saw Unver standing atop the wall of the settlement, made into a giant by firelight, the Anvil Smasher come to life. In that moment, the tall clansman had seemed to be touched by divine fire like a great thane—or like something even greater.

"He saved me," he said quietly. "Saved many."

"What did you say? Here, drink more water." Kulva handed him the cup again. As Fremur drank, the colors began to seem less painful, less striking, but his sister was still a brightness hovering before him. She was not beautiful, not as the clanfolk reckoned beauty—she was thin, for one thing, and her hair was an indistinguished shade of brown too fair to be striking. Her skin was also freckled beyond any ordinary notions of comeliness, but Fremur thought her kindness and the honest steadiness of her eyes made her beautiful. When their mother had named her Kulva, which meant dove, their father had said, "Well, then she's a bony, speckled dove, fit only for the stew-pot." But when their mother died in his fourth or fifth year of life, Kulva had taken on the role of Fremur's protector. Now he could scarcely remember their mother's face without thinking of Kulva's instead.

Their father Hurvalt had never been kind, but he had never gone out of his way to inflict pain. Fremur thought Odrig had inherited the worst of the old man, but without Hurvalt's love for his people, and although she would never say anything against the eldest brother who headed the family and the clan, Fremur knew Kulva felt the same way.

"I have to get up," he said.

"Why? You should rest."

"I will speak to Unver." A part of him was annoyed that a woman, even his dear sister, should question him. Men of the clans were not questioned, at least not by their sisters or wives. "I owe him my life."

"Unver will still be at his father's wagon when you are fit to walk."

"No." He got his legs under him, then rose to his feet, shaky as a newborn colt. "I am fit to walk now. I am a man of the Crane Clan."

Kulva sighed. "Of course you are."

Zhakar, stepfather of Unver Long Legs, was sitting on the steps of his wagon, smoking his pipe and scowling at the clouds overhead, which was more or less what Fremur had expected. Zhakar was too old and lame now to be a threat to a grown man, but being unable to enforce his will with a fist or a strap had, if anything, only made his outlook on life more unpleasant. He had been a strong, handsome man once, at least so others in the clan said, but now he was little more than bone and sinew covered with wrinkled brown skin, like a hide left out in the sun and rain too long.

"What do you want, boy?" the old man said. "Did your brother send you?" Thane Odrig was one of the few people Zhakar respected, which Fremur knew meant "feared."

"I've come to speak to Unver."

The old man took out his pipe and spat. "Speak to Unver? That clod scarcely has two words for anyone, and the spirits know he's no use elseways. Went out on a raid and came back with nothing."

"He saved my life. That's why he didn't bring anything back."

For a moment Fremur thought the old man would get up, hobble toward him, and try to strike him, his scowl was so fierce. "Saved your life? By my wheels and whip, that makes him even more the fool. Your father should have drowned you at birth like a kitten, scrawny whelp that you are. As I should have done when mine was given to me, too."

"Where is he?" Fremur did not want to trade words with Zhakar any longer than he had to. His head still hurt, and the walk across the camp had made it worse. He was imagining what it would be like to shove a knife into the old bastard's throat, and considering it just made him want to do it even more. No wonder Unver hardly ever spoke, if this was all he had to speak with.

The old man spat again. "Tinkering with that useless pile of sticks of his. Which will never be anything but a pile of old sticks, cluttering up my paddock."

Fremur let his eyes rove slowly across the collection of broken pots, stew bones, and other rubbish strewn on the ground around the wagon. "That's a shame."

Now Zhakar did start to rise, his face reddening, but thought better of it after a moment. "Don't loose your tongue at me, boy. I'll have it out of your mouth. I'm not so old I can't teach a pup like you some respect. I still have my whip!"

"May it give you much pleasure, then."

Fremur headed for the paddock out behind the ramshackle wagon. Unver's big horse Deofol and the others were cropping grass at the near end. Unver was on the far side of the paddock, just outside the fence, hammering ashwood spokes into a wheel hub to replace one that had cracked as it was being mounted. The rest of the unfinished wagon stood nearby in the shade of a paltry copse of aspens, axle-end propped on a stone while Unver made the new wheel. The wagon was still far from complete—once the wheels were all on, a season's worth of careful ornamenting, polishing, and painting would still remain.

Unver looked up from his pounding as Fremur approached, but did not speak. The younger man could not think of anything to say at first, so he stood and watched until words came to him.

"Last night, Unver. You saved me."

The tall man took one hand off the maul and swept straight dark hair from his eyes. He had taken off his shirt and hung it from a branch, and his chest and long arms gleamed with sweat. He stared at Fremur for a moment, then shrugged. "I saw no purpose in letting you die."

"But you lost your plunder because of me. In fact, you came back with nothing."

Unver made a sour face. "You must have talked to my stepfather."

"You didn't need to do it, but you helped me. And those others. Why?"

"What is the point of leaving men to die?" Unver took up the maul and began pounding at a spoke with precise but powerful blows. "Are we clansfolk so many, then, and the stone-dwellers so few, that we should leave many dead behind just to steal a few horses and cattle? *Nabban* horses?"

"But you could have sold that bull. That would have paid for all the paint and fittings you're going to want." No Thrithings-man could expect to set himself up as a true man of importance, to get married and be respected, without his own wagon. It was odd that Unver had waited so long to build one, but he had always been a strange fellow, private, even secretive.

"Why do you care?" Unver demanded. "What does it matter to you, Fremur Hurvalt's son?"

"It's my fault. You lost your prize because of me. You could have had all the paint and brass you wanted."

"It's true that is all I need," said Unver. For the first time in a while, Fremur saw the anger that Unver hid underneath his silences. The cords of his arms bunched as he rammed another spoke into the next open slot, but he was scowling as though it did not fit at all. "I have the horses already. One day soon I will travel as a man should travel." Something in his eyes changed; for a moment, something long hidden looked out instead. "One day I will go where I want. Do as I please. And no one . . ." He trailed off.

"So why did you come back to help me?"

"Because it needed doing. Because . . ." Unver gave the spoke a couple of more heavy blows, then abruptly dropped the maul. "I am tired of answering your questions. Your head must still be broken, to make you ask so many. You should go and lie down."

Fremur knew when he was being dismissed, and he also knew that it would be no wiser to anger Unver than it was to anger Odrig. Unver would not beat him as his brother would, but he would stay angry for days or even weeks, and Fremur didn't want that. "Enough, then," he said. "Thank you for not leaving me behind."

"It is better to be alive than dead," said Unver, which was probably the closest he would ever come to replying in kind.

As Fremur walked away he thought he could feel Unver's fury beating out from where he stood like the heat of a bonfire, but somehow Fremur didn't think that it was him or even Unver's poisonous stepfather that made the tall man so angry.

He burns, Fremur realized. *Sometimes the embers are low, but they never go out. And some day he will burst into flame.* Fremur thought again of how he had seen Unver the night before, stretched against the billowing flames and dark sky, and he trembled, just as he had when his mother had told him stories of the vengeful spirits of air and grass that surrounded them.

A terrible flame.

25

Example of a Dead Hedgehog

Something was wrong. *The air was heavyhot, the sky thick with mist. Even the clear waters of Sumiyu Shisa had turned dark, and bubbled like boiling soup. Tanahaya stumbled along the banks of this counterfeit place that should have been her home, her heart, the vale of Shisae'ron she knew so well. She headed toward Willow Hall and the place of her birth, but found it difficult to walk. The ground was muddy, almost boiling, and the steamy air choked her. Again and again she found herself slipping backward, as though she were trying to climb a long, steep slope.*

At last she reached the riverside glen where her family home stood, but this too had changed beyond recognition.

Fallow. Unharvested. The waste—!

Even the front stairway, a graceful construction of carefully arranged white stones, had become a thing of mud and rubbish. The hall, roofed only by the great willow trees themselves, was now a fleshpicked rib cage of leaning posts slowly declining into the ooze.

"Mother?" she called, but only silence was at home.

Fearful now, Tanahaya tried to find her way into her childhood refuge, but as if her own memory rejected her, the drooping willow branches were slimy and the leaves came loose in her hands like hair from the head of a corpse. The deeper she went into the house the less she recognized, and the harder it was to fight through the choking heat and sinking floor. Every way she turned some fallen trunk blocked her way, or a jumbled nonsense that should have been a patterned stone floor mocked her. All that kept her moving was the fixed idea that she had some reason to be here, that she had returned for something important, although she could no longer remember what that might be.

A section of ground dissolved beneath her feet and she almost tumbled down into a tangle of muddy roots that waited for her like some sea creature. Pitched forward onto her hands and knees, she kept crawling toward the center of the house, the place where her mother had tended the fire and sang her sweetling soothe-songs, but the roots of the willows squirmed beneath her, coiling and writhing like snakes, and it was all she could do to inch forward, her hands and arms now slick with black mud, her eyes full of hot, stinging mist.

"Mother?" At last she could see the hearth, and to her joy she saw that it was whole,

the only part of the house not chewed by decay and collapse. All was as her mother had made it and wished it, the fire pit of orderly white stones, the ritual objects set on their low table of carved wood, jars and bowls and bundles of grassy calmcares and other simples Tanahaya had seen all through her childhood, objects so familiar that even to view their shapes again was to feel a fierce longing for days that were gone. But in the center of the table, as though her mother had only put it down an instant before, sat something Tanahaya had never seen before—an egg made of gleaming, polished witchwood, its pearly gray marbled with a dozen other colors amost too subtle to make out. Just to see that beautiful ovoid made her want to take it up and protect it. Why had her mother left it behind? What was Tanahaya supposed to do? Everything she knew was changed—changed and ruined—and yet this puzzle remained.

She heard a noise behind her then—not a footfall, but a long, sucking, slither of a sound. Before she could see what was there, the ground beneath her gave way again and dropped her into hot, sticky darkness. All else—the house of her childhood, the gleaming witchwood egg, even the thing that was Tanahaya-I-myself—vanished back into smothering oblivion.

She was fighting a war, a terrible struggle against a powerful enemy, and so far she had lost every skirmish. But Tanahaya could not retreat because the battle was taking place inside her own body.

In her moments of clear thought she knew that it was some kind of poison that was destroying her, not the wounds. Like all of her people, Tanahaya had deep reserves of strength for fighting illness and injury, but each day she was growing weaker. She could feel the filth inside her trying to make its way through her blood to her heart, like savage raiders rowing their warships upriver to attack a great city. She knew that before much longer the corruption would overwhelm her.

But this poison that smeared those arrows and crawls now through my veins must be the creation of mortals. If it had been crafted by our cousins the Hikeda'ya, I would have lost the battle long ago.

It still made scant sense: what mortals would go out of their way to destroy her? If it had been ordinary arrows that had struck her down she could believe it had been merely the fearful response of a human poacher seeing something strange—the mortals, the Sunset Children, tended to attack that which they did not understand, as all the Zida'ya knew. But the venom coursing through her was something no poacher would use, since it would poison any game it struck down. What sense for a hungry man to risk death or imprisonment to shoot something that couldn't be eaten?

No, the venom on the arrows had been meant to kill, and only a child of her sturdy, ancient race would have survived this long. Tanahaya could imagine an enemy who might not want her to reach this place and its king and queen, a mortal who hated Tanahaya's people and meant to keep her away at all costs, but how could such a person have known she was coming? It reminded her of Sijandi and his still unknown fate. Surely in such dangerous times Lord Jiriki and Lady Aditu would never have told anyone about her mission but those they trusted most. But even if one of Tanahaya's own kind wanted her dead for some incomprehensible reason, why would they give that task to mortals?

During her moments of respite from the arrow-fever, thoughts like these swam through her head like startled fish; but those interludes of sense were growing less frequent. Tanahaya knew if something did not change soon, she would lose this fight.

When she thrashed her way up from the darkness the next time, it was to find a face hanging over her, a young mortal woman, features pinched tight with fear and her hands pulled tight against her breast for fear she might accidentally touch the sick creature lying in the bed.

"Get . . . healer . . ." was all Tanahaya could say. "Need . . . healer . . ."

The woman stared at her in horrified fascination for a moment. Tanahaya realized she had spoken in her own tongue, not in the common speech of mortals. She tried again. "Bring . . . the healer."

That was all the strength she had. The dark, the heat, and the rot reached out and dragged her back down into boiling black depths.

"Why do you put water on plants, Aunt Tia-Lia? Why don't they drown? I saw a mouse drown in the moat once. I couldn't reach him, and Grandfather Osric wouldn't help me get him out. He swam for a long time, but then he died."

"You drink water, little Lillia, and yet *you* don't drown. A little water is good for living things—in fact, it is necessary. Too much, though, is bad. Now hold that candle a little closer, please."

The princess thought about this. "How much is too much?"

Aunt Tia-Lia was still looking at the plants, not at Lillia. "There is no single answer to that question."

Lillia loved Tia-Lia, but she didn't always like the answers she gave. "Can a plant drown?"

"If you give them too much water, yes. Now, please, my darling, let me finish this, then you can help me draw pictures of those flowers I told you about."

Princess Lillia's next question was forestalled by the noisy arrival of a young serving maid at the door of the forcing shed. The maid seemed to have run a long way, because her face was red and she was gasping. "Oh, Lady Thelía, are you in there?" she cried, leaning on the gate. "Merciful Rhiap, I didn't know what to do. Brother Etan is gone down to the city, and she's in a terrible way and I just don't know! She says to bring a healer, but I don't know anything about that!"

"Calm down, girl, I can't understand you. Who needs a healer?"

"The strange woman. The one upstairs in the Residence that Brother Etan helps you tend! She was moaning and carrying on, and I went to see what was wrong, and then her eyes opened up—just like that! Scared me witless! And she kept saying she wanted a healer, a healer. But Brother is gone down to the city."

Thelía looked up to the heavens. "Not even one day to tend my garden?" she asked, then set down her watering can. "Calm yourself, girl. I will come. Let me just wash my hands."

Lillia didn't really understand why Uncle Timo and Aunt Tia-Lia were married, because they were so different. For one thing, Aunt Tia-Lia was much taller than her husband, which struck Lillia as very strange. Also, Uncle Timo's skin was brown, but his wife's skin was pale, except on her hands and the back of her neck where the sun had darkened her. Uncle Timo was quiet and shy and had a limp, but Aunt Tia-Lia wasn't ever shy about anything, and she walked so fast that Lillia could barely keep up with her—like now, as they made their way swiftly across the Inner Bailey.

She had once asked her mother why people married each other. "Because God sends you someone, then you have children together," had been her mother's answer, but that didn't explain Uncle Timo and his bride either, because they didn't have any children of their own. Lillia's own father was dead, but he and Mother had still had children, Lillia and her big brother Morgan. "Are there other reasons people marry each other?" she had asked, but Mother had only told her, "I can't imagine any," and Lillia had recognized from the tone of her mother's words that it also meant, "I'm tired of talking."

Now, as she hurried to keep up with Aunt Tia-Lia, she was wondering about it again. "Why do people get married?" she asked.

"Lots of reasons, I suppose." She turned to look past Lillia to the maid. "Hurry yourself, girl. I understand why you had to leave her alone, but that doesn't mean we should dawdle."

"I am hurrying, Lady Thelía," said the maid. "It just doesn't look like it, because my legs aren't so long as yours. I wouldn't have left her alone, but Brother Etan said that Martha wasn't to watch over her anymore, so there's just me . . ."

Aunt Tia-Lia made a face. "Enough explaining, dear, just keep a good pace, will you? As to *your* question, Princess Lillia, sometimes people marry because their parents want them to. Other times they marry because they want companionship—don't frown, that's a very unbecoming face. 'Companionship' means having a friend to keep you company. Do you understand?"

Lillia nodded. "And what about lovers, like in the stories? Do they get married?"

"Oh, yes. And sometimes they stay in love, but sometimes they don't. I would say it's one of the more untrustworthy reasons for marriage."

"Why . . . ?" Lillia was feeling out of breath. "Why did you marry Uncle Timo?"

Aunt Tia-Lia looked a little surprised by the question. "Why? I suppose . . . well, companionship, certainly. But mostly because I had never met a kind man—a *good* man—who also asked so many questions, who was more interested in simply finding things out than in telling other people how things were or how they should be."

"I don't understand."

Her aunt (who was not really her aunt, just as Uncle Timo was not really her uncle—Lillia called them that because that's how they felt to her) shook her head, but with a little smile to soften it. "I really think we will have to talk about this another time, dear. We're almost there and you are all red in the face. Now save your breath for climbing."

Lillia could hear the groans of the maid as she struggled up the stairs behind them, but she did her best to stay right behind Aunt Tia-Lia. "I saw the lady before," she said as they reached the landing. "The one who's ill. I think she's a witch."

"What do you mean?"

"She doesn't look right. She's scary."

Aunt Tia-Lia didn't say anything, but pushed open the door. The lady on the bed wasn't tied down as she had been the last time Lillia had seen her. She looked much sicker than before, the golden color of her skin beginning to turn a bluish-gray, her face covered in drops of sweat. "Is she going to die?" Lillia asked in what she thought was an appropriately quiet voice. "Brother Etan said she was a Zither."

"A what?" Her sort-of aunt stood beside the bed, staring down at the woman. "No, she is a *Sitha*. The people some call fairies." She carefully seated herself on the bed and began to touch the woman in different places, on her face, her neck. She even leaned forward to put her head against the woman's chest, which made Lillia a little anxious. She still didn't know what either a Zither (or a Sither) was, so she was by no means sure you couldn't be one of those and a witch, too. The woman's eyes opened just enough that Lillia could see the whites, then closed again. Then the fairy opened her mouth and let out a long, shuddering breath but nothing more.

"She is burning up with fever!" Aunt Tia-Lia said. "Tabata, you should be bathing her face and forehead with cool water—wrists, too. I see no water here at all."

"There was some, yesterday . . ."

"Oh, for the love . . . ! Go and get some more, quickly. A bucket from the well, and a clean cloth. Now!"

The maid scurried out. She did not seem sad to have been given an errand, which seemed odd, because Lillia would have been furious to be sent away.

Aunt Tia-Lia found a bowl that still had a bit of water in it and used her own sleeve to dab it on the woman's brow. The eyes came the rest of the way open, and for a moment the strange golden stare locked with Aunt Tia-Lia's lovely, ordinary brown one. Then the woman licked her lips and said, in a whispery voice, *"P-p-poison—"* Her slender fingers closed on Aunt Tia-Lia's hand and she spoke again, in a voice so tiny that even Lillia, for all her worry about this strange person, leaned closer to hear. *"Need . . . !"*

"What do you need, dear?" Tia-Lia leaned forward too. "Tell me . . ."

But the woman only shook her head—slowly, as if it were a great weight to move. Then she lifted her hand and held it trembling in the air.

"She wants the bowl of water," said Lillia.

"I think you're right." The bowl was moved closer, and the Sither-woman lowered her hand into it, then lifted it out, the whole operation so achingly slow that it was all Lillia could do not to help her. Then the long fingers reached out toward the stool beside the bed. Slowly she traced a shape on the seat, the water gleaming in the late-afternoon sunlight. As Lillia and Aunt Tia-Lia stared at it, the door opened.

"Do you have the water?" her auntie asked without looking.

"I beg your pardon, Lady Thelía—I did not know water was wanted."

Tia-Lia looked up in surprise. "Brother Etan! I was told you were gone down to the city."

"I was, Lady Thelía. I was searching for a few herbs that might prove useful. Last time I came here, she told me she was poisoned—that was very clear. I have brought back Harchan dittany and some refined oil of rue."

"I do not think either of those will help, I'm sorry to say. Look, she has drawn something with her finger, the poor creature," said Aunt Tia-Lia. "It was all she could manage." The Sither woman's eyes had fallen closed again, and her hand had drooped, her arm now hanging off the edge of the bed, even that very small effort an exhausting one. "I looked in on her last night and she seemed to be sleeping peacefully."

Etan moved around the bed so he could examine the seat of the wooden stool. "What she's drawn—is it a heart?"

"I don't know what else it could be. Perhaps she wishes us to find a herb with heart-shaped leaves?" Thelía pursed her lips. "I must think. Perhaps there is something in one of my husband's books—"

The maid Tabata now reappeared, weighed down by a sloshing bucket that she had to carry with both hands, which had clearly made it awkward to climb the stairs, because she was all a-sweat. "I think I might be about to have a fit," she announced in a mournful voice. "I banged my leg terribly on the way up."

Tia-Lia nodded in an offhand way. "Bless you, how sad. Leave that bucket here—yes, and the cloth—and you may go sit and nurse your wounds. If you have a fit, be sure to let me know."

When the maid had gone off—rather happily and briskly for someone with a banged knee, Lillia thought—her aunt and the monk mopped the Sither-woman's brow and limbs. When they had finished the task and arranged the blankets over her slender body once more, Thelía said, "Brother Etan, will you go to our rooms and get my husband's book, the *Sovran Remedies*—oh, and now that I think of it, also my copy of Patillan. We may find our heart-shaped herb there."

"But how do we know she is even right about poison, Lady Thelía? This morning she was raving about mountains walking!"

"We don't even know why she is here, Etan," Aunt Tia-Lia said—Lillia thought she sounded a bit cross. "Why balk at anything which might be of help? We must try our best to save her."

"Of course—she is one of God's creatures, I am sure, regardless of what some think."

"Not just that, you silly man." Now her aunt turned, and her expression seemed a mixture of amusement and irritation. "Can you imagine what my husband will think if we let a living Sitha die before he has even had a chance to see her? Tiamak will be broken-hearted. You recall what happened with the hedgehog, do you not? And that beast was ancient, snappish, and only had three legs. Still, when it perished he was miserable from St. Tunath's Day all the way to the following spring." She made a wry face. "Not that I am saying that this is the same. Poor woman."

"You make a good point, my lady." Brother Etan stood. "I will go and fetch the books."

He gave Lillia a worried smile as he squeezed past her in the doorway. Lillia thought the monk might be a little frightened of Aunt Tia-Lia.

The Lord Chancellor had far too many things that needed his attention to be idling at the window in this fashion, but it was hard to pull himself away. Below him, fishing boats dotted the Kynslagh like water-beetles, and when the wind changed direction he could hear the fishermen calling—not their words, but just the soft rasp of their voices as they shouted to each other, boat to boat. The sun was still two hours or more from noon, but clouds had rolled across the sky and the water was shiny gray, like a pewter plate.

Pasevalles stifled a brief tug of selfishness: he would regret having to give this view back to Eolair when the Lord Steward returned. The window in his own chamber was largely blocked by the bulk of Holy Tree Tower. He liked to stand on top of the tower, but being so close to its walls left only a confining, prisoning view that made his heart heavy, a scene as dark as judgment, as punishment.

Do not be distracted, he scolded himself. *Froye needs an answer.*

He turned from the window with regret, but returned to the desk and the latest letter from his informant at the Nabbanai court and began to read it a second time.

My dear sir, you cannot know how it pains me to say so, but I would not be performing my duty to your kindness if I did not inform you that things are very dangerous right now in this country.

The duke's brother Drusis, as you know, has made the grasslanders' attacks on Nabbanai settlements into a cause of reproach. He rails against his brother's laxity at every meeting of the Dominate. The conflict has caused great unrest, not only in the mansions of the nobles, but even down in the streets among the merchants, workers, and the poor, so that it sometimes seems people here can talk of nothing else.

And Drusis is not entirely wrong, good my lord, to warn of the dangers of this enemy. The folk of Nabban have always feared and detested the Thrithings-men, who have no fixed homes, no villages or farms, and are little better than savages. And it is true that horsemen have increased their raids of late. In the last half a year they have struck several times, burning crops and villages and attacking the tenants of the lords who own great houses along the border. This is nothing new, although the murderousness of the raids seems to be increasing. God grant we have no war with them, because the Thrithings-men are many and they are fearsome fighters, although ill-organized. They fight as a disorderly rabble, fierce when they are winning, but prone to dispersal and retreat when they suffer a setback, which is why, for all their numbers, that Nabban and Erkynland have been able to keep them penned on the grasslands all these years.

Yet although they remain a great threat, it is not the horsemen that provoke my letter to you, but rather the duke's brother. Drusis, despite the backing of several of the eastern and northern lords in the Dominate, has been balked to this point in his struggle with Duke Saluceris by his lack of support among the nobles whose holdings are far from the Thrithings borderlands. His attempts to force his brother into action have therefore always failed.

Of late this has changed. Drusis has recently made a powerful ally, linking his fortune to the Ingadarine House, who, as you know, have long been the second most powerful family in Nabban after the Duke's own Benidrivine House. Drusis and Dallo Ingadaris have met many times, and it is whispered that soon Earl Dallo will announce that Drusis will marry his daughter.

I express no disapproval of House Ingadaris, of course. I know our High Queen Miriamele traces half her blood to that family, and Saluceris himself carries their blood in his veins as well. But those were days when the two houses were closely linked, which is no longer true. More and more over the last years, they have found themselves at odds, and it is no secret that Dallo Ingadaris wishes the Dominiate, where he is strong, to have a greater say over Nabban's government. That can only happen if Duke Saluceris is weakened, and that is the reason, of course, that Dallo has shown favor to Drusis by offering him his daughter Turia . . .

Pasevalles didn't bother to reread the rest, the small bits of other business he had asked Froye to undertake for him, most of which concerned the ongoing struggle between Osten Ard's two greatest trading powers, the Sindigato Perdruine and the upstart Northern Alliance. But none of the rest of Count Froye's news had the import of Drusis's marrying Dallo Ingadarine's daughter, which would add a huge complication to an already intricate, dangerous situation that Pasevalles had been worrying over for months. Drusis was growing in power too quickly, and Duke Saluceris seemed unconcerned, or perhaps was actually helpless to fight back. To Pasevalles it all smelled of disaster. Sometimes it was hard not to wonder whether he had been helping the wrong brother.

What could be done? King Simon and Queen Miriamele were still a fortnight away from the Hayholt. Pasevalles had heard rumors from merchants, whose ships had recently returned from the south, that conflict between the two rival Nabbanai houses had grown loud and occasionally violent, with drunken street brawls and a near-riot at the Circus of Larexes after the chariot races. House Ingadaris had long resented the power King John had given to House Benidrivis, and now the Ingadarine supporters, who wore the Albatross badge of the house and called themselves "Stormbirds," were brawling in public with the duke's Kingfisher loyalists.

It's like an overturned lantern, he thought. *How quickly do I have to put out this fire before it catches and grows beyond control?* But Nabban was also the most populous nation of the High Ward, its leaders historically prideful and stubborn. What could he do to keep the fire from spreading too fast?

I can do nothing, he realized. *Only the king and queen can do what needs to be done. And they are not here.*

His brooding was interrupted by a knock. The guard announced Brother Etan, so Pasevalles folded the letter and put it into his purse.

"Forgive me for bothering you, my lord."

"Nonsense, Brother. I welcome a distraction. What news?"

The young monk seemed uneasy. "Lady Thelía and I have been with the Sitha woman. When she's been able to speak, she says she has been poisoned, and it certainly seems there might be some truth to that. Nearly a month has passed since she was struck down, and still she suffers terrible fevers."

"What poison could have effects that would last so long and still not kill?"

"I couldn't say, Lord. My experience does not lie that way, and please remember that the patient is . . . unusual."

Pasevalles smiled despite himself. "That's so. But you still have not told me how she fares at the moment."

"She has mostly slept since Lady Thelía began to give her physic. Her rest seems a little more peaceful now, but it is hard to say. She is very weak. Her breathing is so soft it is hard to see her breast lift and fall sometimes."

"I will pray for her, as I'm sure you do." Pasevalles did his best to disperse the swarm of other worries that had beset him like buzzing flies. "Will you take some wine, Brother?"

"No. No, thank you, my lord. I am needed back at St. Sutrin's for Nonamansa, and I would not have His Eminence Archbishop Gervis smell it on my breath."

"Well, by the Bowl of Saint Pelippa, what would he have you drink instead? Nothing but well water? It would be a short, sad, and sickly life for you then, wouldn't it?"

Etan smiled, but his heart did not seem to be in it. "I suppose it would, my lord. But there is something else I wish to talk to you about. It concerns the princess. Dowager Princess Idela, that is."

"Ah." Pasevalles did his best to keep a cheerful expression on his face. "Of course. I asked you to help her with those books of her husband's. Did you know the prince, Etan?"

"Prince John Josua? No, Lord Chancellor. I was still at the abbey of St. Cuthman's in Meremund when he was taken from us. I know the prince was a much-loved young man, a great scholar." There was still something odd in Etan's expression, but Pasevalles could not unpuzzle it.

"Yes, he was a very fine man, Brother. But God did not give him a strong body, and he was often sickly. That is one reason, I think, that he grew so bookish. The volumes he collected could take him to many places that his frail body could not."

Pasevalles wished he could return to the matter of Froye's letter. "And were the volumes worthy of being preserved in the new library? Of course, simply having belonged to the prince would give them value, I think, since the library is being created in his honor."

"Yes, lord. Most of them were interesting but not unusual. However . . ."

Etan trailed off. Pasevalles could hear it too, the noise of a scuffle just outside the door. His hand dropped to the dagger at his waist, but a moment later he recognized one of the voices—a small but distinctly high-pitched voice.

The door popped open and Princess Lillia spilled into the room, followed closely by a flustered Erkynguardsman, who might as well have been trying to capture an oiled serpent. "Pasevalles!" the child shouted. "Lord Pasevalles! Have you heard the news?"

"I'm sorry, my lord," the red-faced guard said. "I was afraid I might hurt her if I grabbed too hard . . ."

Pasevalles waved him out, but before the guard could retreat, another face appeared in the door behind the princess.

"Oh, you wicked child!" said Countess Rhona. "Mircha love you, you are quick as a cat! I'm sorry, Lord Pasevalles, she simply outran me."

"Have you heard?" said Lillia, jumping up and down in excitement. "Have you heard? Grandma and Grandpa are coming!"

Pasevalles tried to make sense of the sudden eruption. "Have I heard what? Yes, they are coming soon. A fortnight, perhaps . . ."

Lillia stopped and her eyes grew wide at the importance of her message and at Pasevalles' amazing, wonderful ignorance. "No! They're *here!*"

He turned helplessly to the countess. "What is she talking about?"

"She's telling the truth, actually, Lord Pasevalles. The messenger just arrived. They're not *here*, Lillia, you silly girl, but they are very close. The messenger says they stayed last night at Dalchester, but are already on the road for home today."

"Dalchester? But they will be here by tomorrow night! Why are they so early?"

Countess Rhona shook her head. "The messenger from the king and queen would not say—not to me, anyway. He's waiting for you down in the post hall. Will you go to him?"

"Of course." Pasevalles stood. "This is excellent news! Brother Etan, we will continue our conversation some other time, yes?"

"Yes, my lord." The monk looked a bit grim, but Pasevalles supposed it was the memory of dealing with the dowager princess that made him so.

He is a little unhappy with me for using him as a shield against Princess Idela, perhaps. Still, no matter. Etan's discontent, whatever caused it, could wait. The king and queen were returning—early, yes, but not a moment too soon as far as Pasevalles was concerned. Many things had to be made ready to welcome them home as they deserved.

26

The Inner Council

The Avrel gusts were so strong they made the banners on tower tops jump and snap—"a wind so hard you could hang your clothes on it," as old Rachel the Dragon, the mistress of chambermaids during Simon's youth, used to say. Simon even saw a few green and gold pennants whisked from people's hands and thrown up into the sky to race with the clouds. Market Square was filled with cheering people, thousands of them, along with hundreds of merchants busily selling them beer and food, as well as at least a few other folk, Simon felt sure, intent on picking their pockets. All of Erchester, it seemed, had come out to welcome home their queen and their king.

"Can you believe it?" he asked his wife.

Miriamele was smiling, but it was the smile she wore when her days holding court ran long, when she was worried and tired. "Believe what?"

"This." People in the crowd were actually calling out his name, familiar as old friends. He could never quite make her understand how strange it seemed to him. His wife had been looked at all her life, praised and scorned by folk she had never met, her clothes and appearance and even her facial expressions discussed by strangers as comfortably as if she were a member of their household. "All right, me. They all came out to see me—a kitchen boy. Because someone else decided I'm a king, so they all said, 'Well, that's all right then. Hooray for King Simon!'"

Like Rinan, he thought, and the memory of the boy's pale, slack face came back to him, as it had for days. The harper hadn't seen someone who had once been a confused, frightened youth like himself, he'd seen only a grown man. He'd only seen the king. And he'd done what his king had told him to do. *Now that boy is dead*, Simon thought, *buried with two dozen more men in a field by the side of the Frostmarch Road. Because he believed—*

"You hear cheers only for the king?" Miriamele asked him.

"I didn't mean it that way, dear one," he told her. "I meant because you're used to this." He looked at the children leaning perilously out of the upper windows as they left Market Square and entered Main Row, took a deep breath, and did his best to stop thinking about the harper. "I'm not. I never will be. What do they *see?*"

"They see the king—and the queen. They see us and they know that things are as they should be, that God is still watching over them." She looked out across the field of faces. "They see that the seasons will come and go as they should, that the rain will fall and the crops will grow. They see that someone is here to protect them from the evil things they fear."

"You don't sound as if you believe any of that."

"Oh, Simon, what does it matter?" Miri looked at him, but only for a moment, then turned back to the crowds, her queenly smile once more in place. "It's all a pageant, like St. Tunath's Day. We pretend to take care of them and they pretend to love us."

"But they do love us," Simon said. "Don't they?"

"As long as the seasons turn and the rain falls and the barley sprouts, yes. Not that you and I have much to do with any of that. And if we go to war and their brothers and sons die, they'll blame us."

He looked at her face, her wise, familiar, beloved face. "You're frightened by what happened on the road—aren't you? And that White Hand fellow's message?"

"Of course I'm frightened, and you should be too. Because you were almost killed, Simon. Because we thought we had pushed those pale-skinned things back into the mountains for good. And now it's going to start all over again. The war with the Norns almost killed us when we were young and strong, and we are neither of those things now."

"I was frightened for you as well," he said, not certain what he was defending, but still feeling a need. "I heard your voice just before they charged. I didn't know where you were!"

Miri reached across to touch his hand but said nothing more for a while.

They rode through the widest streets and into St. Sutrin's Square. Here the crowds were making festival in front of the great church; they cheered loudly as the royal procession made its way past. Musicians were playing and those who had room to dance were dancing. Simon and Miriamele stopped to exchange greetings with Archbishop Gervis and the mayor of Erchester, Thomas Oystercatcher, a fat, shrewd man who made sure everyone saw him bow to the king and queen—but not *too* low—and be acknowledged in turn. The merchants and city government of Erchester always fiercely protected their independence, even on a day of celebration. After his bows, the mayor straightened and waved his cap to the crowd as though he were the one being celebrated.

"Squeezing every last drop out of the teat, Lord Mayor?" the queen asked him, but quietly, so that only the mayor, the king, and the archbishop heard her.

The tall buildings on either side of Main Row now blocked the sun, and the returning royal party rode down a long corridor of shadow, horses' hooves squelching in the mud. The soldiers in front of them had taken off their helmets to show their faces as they waved to the crowds on either side, many of them friends and loved ones who had not seen them since the beginning of winter.

"Look at them all," Miriamele said. For a moment Simon thought she was talking about the unhelmeted soldiers, but then realized she meant the cheering residents of Erchester. Main Row had opened up into the wide thoroughfare just before the Nearulagh Gate and the entrance to the Hayholt. "Half of them have never known anything else but peace. Or you and I as their monarchs."

"But surely that is good." His own mood had been sorrowful all day, but his wife's thoughts seemed even darker, grim enough to worry him. "That's what we worked for. To give them peace and help keep them fed. That's *good*, Miri."

"It has been. Perhaps it won't be from now on."

He pursed his lips and kept silent. Simon had learned early in his marriage that there were times when he could only make things worse. *She's never forgotten what her father did to these people and this land,* he thought. *She's never forgotten her father at all, more's the pity.*

For a moment he thought of King Elias back in his brief heyday, riding through this same gate on the way to his coronation, beneath these same wonderful, detailed carvings of Prester John's century-old victory over Adrivis, the last imperator of Nabban. The decline of the ancient southern empire had begun long before, but after John's victory, Nabban, once the master of the world, had become merely a part of John's own empire—a domain stretching from the islands in the warm southern ocean to the freezing northlands of Rimmersgard. And when John had died at last in great old age, and Miriamele's father, the king's handsome, brave son Elias had taken the throne in peaceful succession, it had briefly seemed a great empire in truth, an empire of peace and plenty—and permanence.

But only a scant year later Erchester had become a haunted place, with men and women scuttling like beetles from one place of dubious shelter to another, houses collapsed under the weight of snow and neglect, and strange shadows walking the empty streets by night. The Hayholt and its proud towers had become something even more frightening, a warren of whispered secrets and heart-rending screams that could not be ignored but were never investigated, as the castle's dwindling population hid behind locked doors after sundown.

In the end, Miriamele had been forced to kill her own father. It was to save him as much as to stop him, and had quite possibly saved them all, but she never spoke of it, and Simon tried never to mention it.

But it will never be that way again—we won't let it. Miri must know that. Yes, bad things will still happen—that's the lot of mortal man—but Miri and I, we are meant to be the happily-afterward.

The king found himself unconvincing.

If Erchester was a broil of banners and cheering throngs, the royal company found a slightly more reserved greeting in the castle itself, although the courtiers and servants were clearly delighted to see their monarchs returned. Simon, Miriamele, and the other nobles dismounted in the Outer Bailey and most of the troops dispersed from there to the barracks, although the royal guard still surrounded the king and queen. Simon did his best to look pleased and grateful as functionary after functionary came forward to greet the royal couple and welcome them home.

The last of them, holding the Hayholt's ceremonial keys, was Lord Chancellor Pasevalles himself. He knelt before them and presented the box and its shiny contents, but did not immediately rise. His straw-colored hair still showed no gray, Simon noted with a touch of envy, since Pasevalles was only a few years younger.

"I fear we have much to discuss," he told them now. "I know Your Majesties are both weary—"

"No, you are right, Lord Chancellor," Simon said, and Miri nodded. "There are things you must know immediately as well. In fact, once we eat and take a short rest, the queen and I will need you in the Great Hall when the clock strikes two. Count Eolair and Duke Osric and the others of the Inner Council will be wanted as well. Oh, and make sure Prince Morgan is there too, please."

"Of course, Majesty." But Pasevalles looked ill-at-ease.

"What's wrong, Lord Chancellor?" Miri asked.

"Just . . . many things have happened in your absence." He leaned forward and spoke quietly, although the nearest of the courtiers stood some distance away. "We have received what seems to be an envoy from the Sithi."

"From Jiriki and Aditu? We have?" Simon was astonished, and his heart seemed to swell in his chest—this was good news indeed. "Excellent! Where is he? Miri, did you hear?"

"I heard." But the queen was looking at the Lord Chancellor's face, and saw there what Simon had not noticed. "But there is more, is there not? You said 'seems'."

Pasevalles nodded. "Yes, Your Majesty. The envoy is not a *he*, but a *she*. And somebody tried to kill her. Whether they succeeded still remains to be seen, but she is in grim condition."

With the return of the royal party, the stables hosted a bustling, noisy throng of horses, grooms, stable boys, muckers, and of course several dozen squires, each watching jealously over his master's or mistress's prize mount. The returning animals blew and nickered loudly as they were led to their stalls, as though greeting all the friends and relatives they had left behind.

In other circumstances, especially after the morning's long ride, Morgan would have happily let his own squire Melkin take charge of Cavan, but the gelding had begun to limp during the last part of the journey through Erchester, and Morgan wanted to make sure that he would be looked after properly. He saw one of the older grooms and beckoned him over.

"Yes, Highness? And welcome back home, Prince Morgan."

"Here now, Cavan, settle." Morgan patted the horse's neck. "He's favoring his right front foot. I think there might be a small stone under his shoe, but I couldn't find it."

"I'll have the farrier see to him directly, Your Highness," the groom said, bowing and taking the reins. "And we've got plenty of good, sweet summer grass for him as well, don't you worry."

As Morgan watched the groom lead his palfrey off through the surge of bandy-legged men, scurrying boys, and snorting horses, something struck him on the back of the legs so hard that his knees almost buckled, and a pair of arms snaked around his waist and squeezed. A brief instant of surprised panic vanished at the sound of a familiar voice.

"I'm so angry at you! You said you would write me letters, and you didn't!"

He tried to reach back to pry his sister loose, but she was already scrambling around to the front and had begun clutching at his tunic and stamping on his feet as though she meant to climb him like a tree.

"Hold, hold!" he laughed. "I did write to you." He bent down and picked her up and embraced her. "You're heavier. Have you been sneaking sweetmeats out of the kitchen? Wasn't anyone watching over you?" He held her away from him, although her vigorous wriggling made it difficult to keep his grip. It was more than a little shocking to see that she looked older, too, her face clearly longer and thinner, even as she stretched it in a grimace. "And you've lost a tooth, Lil! You look like an old beggar woman!"

She tried to slap his head but he avoided the blow. "You wrote one letter, Morgan," she said, "and that was so long ago—in Feyever-month! I know because I got it just after Candlemansa. Grandma and Grandpa sent me lots of letters in the royal post, and Uncle Timo too, but you only sent that one!" Lillia stared at him with the fiercest of scowls, then suddenly she brightened. "Did you know there's a Sither here in the castle? She's nearly dead but Aunt Tia-Lia said she's a real fairy."

He had no idea what his sister was talking about, and could not help laughing. "I missed you too. I'm sorry I didn't write more." He embraced her and kissed her cheek, but she still struggled. "Now I need something to eat, and badly. Can you help me with that?"

"Silly." She gave him a look that contained as much disgust as love, and in that instant Morgan felt himself to be truly home. "You don't need help. Someone will get it for you. You're a prince."

"Ah, you're right. I forgot. Very well, then I command you to go and find me something so I can break my fast."

She shook her head. "That's silly, too. I'm a princess. I don't have to."

"Then I suppose I will have to kidnap you and force you to do my bidding!" He bent suddenly and grabbed her around the waist, then lifted her up and dumped her over his shoulder. "Captured by a fierce giant! Princess Pigling is surely doomed!"

She stopped kicking and squealing for a moment. "A giant! I forgot! One of the soldiers told us there was a giant where you were, and the knights all fought with it! Is that true, Morgan? Did you really fight with a giant?"

Something like a shadow swept across his thoughts, darkening the moment of happiness into something more complicated. He carefully set her down on the hay-strewn floor. "Nothing to worry about," he told her. "I never saw any giant."

"We missed you so! You must be delighted to be home, Your Majesty. Back where things can be done properly." Smelling of orris root and ever so slightly of perspiration (because the day had turned warm) Lady Tamar, wife of the Baron of Aynsberry, bent and began lacing up Miriamele's corset. A young woman of fragile health, Tamar had not traveled north.

"Oh, yes. Delighted." But after the comparative freedom of months of travel, of many days' riding for every day spent on the heavy, public business of state, Miriamele was in no hurry to return to more formal attire for this Inner Council meeting. She had never liked wearing a corset at the best of times, but now it felt like being nailed into a coffin.

In quick order, the women arranged her jewelry and pinned her heavy headdress into place. Lady Tamar, who had discovered she was with child just when the royal progress had set out for Rimmersgard, was now very distinctly rounded. "You are so beautiful, my queen," Tamar said as she viewed the ladies' handiwork. "How proud your husband will be!"

Miriamele only sighed. She felt like a saint's statue being prepared for a feast day.

Lady Shulamit leaned in. "By your leave, Majesty, may I paint your face? Forgive me for saying so, but your skin has been much reddened by the sun."

"Oh, very well." Miriamele hated this too, but suffered it for high occasions—times when she felt she must look the part of the perfect queen. She wrinkled her nose at the vinegary smell of the whitener, but let the young noblewoman apply it. She could feel it drying her already dry skin when Lady Tamar passed her a mirror. It was difficult to lift the glass to a position where she could see her reflection with three women leaning over her and another one bumping uncomfortably against her shins while she put Miriamele's shoes on. When the queen finally caught a glimpse of herself, smeared white as a phantom, she nearly dropped the mirror.

"No!" she said. "No. Take it off."

"What? Take what off, Majesty?"

"The face paint. I will not look like this. Not today." What had stared back from the mirror was not her own familiar, aging features but something like the hideous apparitions she had seen rushing toward her out of the blackness beside the North Road, the corpse faces of the escaping Norns. "Now, Shulamit. It makes me look like one of the White Foxes."

The ladies were surprised enough that they barely hid their startled looks, but Lady Shulamit dutifully began to scrub away the lead and vinegar whitener with a damp cloth.

Miriamele's hands were shaking so badly that she had to clasp them together in her lap. She knew her ladies must be confused. How could they know what she had seen, what she had felt? Those who had accompanied her to Elvritshalla had been in the tents and under guard when the Norns fought their way down the steep hill, whereas Miriamele had been out in the darkness, in the crush of men and animals, looking for her husband. The ladies had seen nothing but each others' worried faces as they huddled together in the royal tent, waiting for the whole frightening thing to end. But their queen had seen that huge monster crash through the trees toward them like an ogre from the earliest hours of time, when God's misfit creatures still roamed the land, and men could only hide from them and pray for salvation.

The giant had been bad enough, but these women could not even dream of what it had been like as the Norns had swept down in the monster's wake, lying close against their dark horses, their faces appearing out of the night like funeral masks, shrieking and laughing as they plunged through ten times their number of armed men and vanished into the grasslands beyond the road, leaving behind only the bodies of those who had been unable to get out of their way.

No, Miriamele decided. *I will not go to council looking like one of those horrid demons.*

"Go to, scrub it all off," she said. "Better I should be as sun-pinched as any peasant. And I will not wear the black mantle, either. Bring me the blue one, with the stars, the one like an evening sky. Yes, we continue to mourn Duke Isgrimnur, but today I must wear something different."

Her ladies, not entirely understanding the queen's strange mood, hurried to obey.

To Miri's surprise, her husband was waiting for her outside the throne room.

"Where are the others?" she asked. "Why haven't you gone in?"

"Because I wished to go in with my wife—my queen." He smiled, but she could tell he was as troubled as she was. "I went to see the Sitha messenger."

"Did she speak to you?"

He shook his head. "Thelía has done all she can for her, and she rests peacefully, but she scarcely moves. They say she seems to be slipping farther away each day."

"Is there nothing to do for her?"

"Yes—or at least I think there might be. We must send her back to her people, Miri. They have healers that know more than even Tiamak or his lady, especially about healing their own folk."

Now it was Miriamele's turn to shake her head. "Sweet Elysia! I had hoped we would have a few days to take our rest, to think and talk and take council about this attack by the Norns and the message on the arrow. But I should have known better."

"Yes, my dear one, you probably should have."

She sighed. "Did you see our granddaughter?"

"I did, but only for a moment. I swear Lillia has grown a handspan since we left. She scolded me for going straightaway to a council meeting, so I've promised to watch her ride her pony later." He crooked his elbow. "Shall we go in, my dear? The others are waiting for us."

The great throne room had been cleaned and the banners carefully dusted for the return of the High King and High Queen, but the months away made it seem almost unfamiliar, Miriamele thought. The vast chair of dragon's bones, Prester John's famous throne, sat on the daïs at one end of the hall, soaked in sunlight that arrowed down from the high windows, its back shadowed by the lowering, monstrous skull of the dragon Shurakai. The beast had been the centerpiece of a great and momentous lie, its death claimed by King John when, in fact, it had been killed by Simon's ancestor Ealhstan the Fisher King. For that and other reasons, Simon had never much liked the object, and for a while had even banished it from the throne room entirely: for a year or more after they had been crowned the great chair languished in the courtyard outside, exposed to the elements. But though Simon disliked it, the people of Erkynland felt very differently, and eventually he had given in and allowed it to be moved back into a position of honor in the hall. Still, neither he nor his wife would sit in it. Miriamele understood that it meant continuity to the common people, but she hated it for the memory of her father's last mad years.

In any case, she reminded herself, *we are two, not one—a king and a queen, ruling together, even if some of the nobles seem to forget that sometimes. A single throne would not do for us both.* And suddenly she felt a flush of gratitude for the man at her left, the kitchen boy she had married.

I tried to keep him out of my heart, she thought. *The saints know that I tried! I did not wish this life for him. I was raised for this duty that never ends—he should have had something better. But thank God I have him!*

She gave Simon's arm a squeeze. He could not have guessed what she was thinking, but he squeezed back.

The Pellarine Table sat at the base of the daïs. The long table had been in the castle for centuries, a gift from the Nabbanai imperator Pellaris to King Tethtain, the Hernystiri conqueror who had briefly added Erkynland to his domains, and who in his last few years of life had even used the Hayholt as one of his royal residences. Seated around it, attended by a number of serving-folk, waited over a dozen people in a surprising assortment of shapes and sizes, the greatest gathering of the Inner Council since Miriamele and Simon had begun to put their own more cautious stamp on the government of Erkynland and the High Ward.

To the left of Simon's empty chair sat Count Eolair in his post as Hand of the Throne, so deeply caught up with a pile of correspondence that at first he did not realize the king and queen had entered the throne room. To his right was Pasevalles, the Lord Chancellor, carrying his own wooden box full of letters. On the other side, next to Miriamele's chair, pride of place went to Lord Constable Osric, Duke of Falshire and Wentmouth as well as father of John Josua's widow Idela. Miriamele did not much like her son's widow, but she had better feelings about Osric himself, a careful, sensible land-owner who had distinguished himself in the Second Thrithings War before his daughter had been born.

Ranged on either side of them sat several more friends and court notables: Tiamak; Sir Kenrick and his commander, Sir Zakiel, prominent officers of the Erkynguard; and His Eminence, Archbishop Gervis of St. Sutrin's, the highest religious authority in Erkynland, a generally benevolent and occasionally useful fellow who also served as the Royal Almoner. Gathered at the table as well were Lord Feran, Master of Horse and marshal of the castle; and Earl Rowson of Glenwick, whom Simon and Miriamele referred to privately as "Rowson the Inevitable." Because he was head of one of Erkynland's most powerful families—some of old King John's earliest supporters—Rowson had to be included in even the most intimate gatherings of power, despite being one of the stubbornest and least inquiring people in Erchester. Simon had a slightly more optimistic view of him, which was another of the many reasons Miriamele felt that her husband was as lucky to be married to her as she to him: she was his only defense against his abiding flaw of too much kindness. Simon found it hard to say no to even the scruffiest and laziest ne'er-do-wells.

At the far end of the long table, looking even smaller because of the distance, sat Binabik and Sisqi, who were receiving curious stares from those who had not traveled north with the royal couple. Beside them sat Tiamak, but his wife was absent, tending the wounded Sitha. Miriamele was also pleased and relieved to see her good friend Countess Rhona seated nearby. Both she and Simon valued the countess's common sense, and the things to be discussed today would require level heads. Also, as Miriamele knew well, the countess noticed things that many of the male courtiers did not, and often understood currents in the life of the castle that the men did not even know existed.

The queen was much less pleased to see that her grandson was again absent, and hoped her husband had not noticed. He was already angry with Morgan over his many transgressions during their northern travels.

Simon gave his wife a significant look, and at first she thought he had guessed what she was thinking, but she realized her misunderstanding a moment later when he turned to Count Eolair. "I know your heart is elsewhere, old friend," Simon said quietly. "But we need you now. The queen and I ask you to lead the Inner Council today."

The lord steward nodded. "Of course, Majesty."

Miriamele could not help feeling a pang of sorrow for him. She could guess what it had cost him to refuse Queen Inahwen's request for his help. Thirty years and more Eolair had served the High Throne—a man who refused all titles and rewards, a man who could have and perhaps should have taken

Hernystir's throne for himself after the Storm King's War, or at least so Miriamele had always thought, and she knew Simon agreed. Surely no man more
politic and more useful lived anywhere beneath the High Ward.

And that is his one true failing, she thought. *If Simon is too kind, Eolair is too
dutiful. He has never been selfish enough.* It had been her idea to have him lead the
council meeting. She knew the count was pained at the thought of having failed
Queen Inahwen, and Miri had learned from her grandfather and father that the
best way to recapture the attention of a useful man was to give him an important task. If only her father had not strayed from the wisdom his own father had
taught him!

"Hear me, all!" announced the royal herald at Miriamele's signal, and
stamped his staff on the stone flags, checking the quiet conversations along the
table. "His Majesty the king and Her Majesty the queen command you to audience!"

When the room was silent, Simon said, "We thank the good Lord for bringing us safely back to you all. It is good to be in Erkynland once more. We wish
it could be in happier times, but this coming week will be a busy one for all of
us. Drorsday next will see a memorial mansa for Duke Isgrimnur, our dear
friend." For a moment the ghost of a smile flitted across his face. "Appropriate,
I think. As good an Aedonite as Isgrimnur was, he could never lose the habit
of swearing by the old gods in moments of upset."

A few who had known the duke laughed, and others nodded. News of Isgrimnur's death had arrived with royal dispatches from Elvritshalla a fortnight
or more earlier, so the king's words came as no surprise.

"After the memorial service, Freyday next will see a meeting of the Great
Council, at which there will be much to discuss. Many of you have heard some
stories of the attack we suffered as we left Rimmersgard. Events in Nabban, as
Lord Pasevalles has made clear, also call for our attention, and there is the
strange matter of the Sithi envoy, too."

At this, Sir Kenrick and some of the others who been traveling with the king
and queen looked confused. "Please, Majesty," the guard captain asked, "have
we had some message from the Sithi people, after all these years?"

"As I said, we will discuss it in the Great Council," the king said. "Today we
have a more pressing matter. Lord Steward, now is your moment." Simon gestured for Eolair. "Tell everyone all of what has happened, and together we will
try to puzzle out what it means. Understand, though, that you people gathered
here are the closest to the throne, our dearest friends and closest allies. Until
the queen and I say otherwise, this news is not to leave this room."

"But the attack by the whiteskins has already been trumpeted around
Erchester, Majesty," said Count Rowson with the air of someone who would
soon put everything right.

"The attack, yes," said Miriamele, nettled as she often was by the man's
presumption. Simply being the scion of one of the oldest families in Erkynland
did not give anyone the right to freely interrupt her husband. "But there are

details known only to a few—important details. Surely you would like to learn those details, Count, so that your always-excellent counsel can be fully informed . . . ?"

Rowson could seldom tell when she was employing irony, one of the things she disliked most about him. He sat a little taller in his chair and stroked his beard in a way he clearly thought bespoke wisdom. "Of course, Majesty. My only goal is to serve the High Throne."

"Then let me tell you the facts we know, my lords," said Eolair.

As always, Eolair spoke concisely and carefully, laying out what was known, not what was supposed. Still, despite Eolair's passion for the truth, he did not relate Lady Alva's story of Norn and Sithi corpses in far-off Engby. Simon and Miriamele had agreed it was too soon to make it generally known because some of the nobles might decide that the only conflict was between two clans of immortals and then refuse to heed the other signs of danger. Most of them had never completely understood or trusted their rulers' friendship with the Fair Ones, as they called them.

"Those of us who were on the North Road are agreed that we have never seen a giant of such a size," Eolair finished. "Fully twice the height of a man and perhaps ten times the weight."

"Have the fairies bred them so big, then?" Duke Osric asked. "That would be grim indeed. I've been told that in past battles we lost a dozen men or more for every one of those things we killed."

"We do not know the answer to that, Your Grace," said Eolair. "But even if the White Foxes now breed those monsters as though they were hounds or horses, it is still not the greatest of our problems." He unrolled the blood-smirched piece of parchment. "After the Norns escaped us—fleeing east, we discovered—one of Sir Kenrick's soldiers found this in the road. Archbishop, do you recognize this writing?"

Gervis rose and came closer to inspect it, leaning against Eolair's chair for support. "Those are Rimmersgard runes!" he said. "Why should the Norns write in such a way?"

"Because as Lord Tiamak explained, Your Grace," Eolair answered him, "the message itself—and it *is* a message—claims that the writer is not one of the Norns, but only one who travels with them, perhaps as a prisoner or slave. Tiamak?"

The Wrannaman came slowly forward. His limp, acquired in the days Miriamele had first met him, had grown worse with the passing years. He explained the ancient source of the runes to the Inner Council, then read the message out loud. When he had finished, the throne room was silent for no little time.

"It is a trick," said Earl Rowson at last. "Some damnable bit of trickery by the whiteskins, to put us off our guard."

"That is possible, my lord," said Tiamak mildly. "But if they would cozen us somehow, why concoct a story designed, not to make us think them harmless, but to put us on our guard? And why go to such strange lengths to pass it to us instead of just leaving it behind in an abandoned camp to be found?"

"The name Jarnulf means nothing to me, but I have heard rumors of something called the White Hand," Duke Osric said. "It's a tale told in the northern lands that sometimes makes its way south, a tribe of bandits by that name who prey on the Norns, killing them whenever they cross the border into mortal lands. But I thought it most likely only the memory of some ancient hero and his band, like Jack Mundwode."

"That could be true," the king said. "Or it could be an old name taken by someone new—someone with a grudge against the Norns. Tiamak, show them what else was with the message."

Tiamak nodded and drew something shiny from the inner folds of his loose mantle, then set it out on the table. All of the council who had not seen it before leaned closer to look.

"But what is it?" Osric asked. "I do not recognize this badge."

"I am not surprised," Tiamak said. "For we keep our membership and our business quiet."

"*We?*" asked Archbishop Gervis. "Do you mean you are somehow connected to this person, Lord Tiamak? The one who sent this message?"

Tiamak turned to Simon and Miriamele. "How much of the story do I tell, Majesties? For it is a long one."

"As much as you need to," Miriamele said. "Enough to show the members of the Inner Council why we must take this seriously."

Tiamak nodded, and ran a hand through his dark, thinning hair. "First, my noble lords and ladies, you do not realize it but you have already met more than one member of the group that uses this symbol—the League of the Scroll." He pointed to the end of the table. "Like me, Binabik of Yiqanuc is part of the League, and has been since his master gave him an emblem much like this one, back in the early days of the Storm King's War."

Binabik reached into the collar of his homespun shirt and pulled out a shining object, then held it up in his small, thick fingers. "And I have been wearing it with proudness ever since," he said. "The League has done much for protecting peace and wisdom from those who are valuing neither one."

"Your pardon, Lord Tiamak," said Archbishop Gervis, "but I find this somewhat alarming. Do you mean that all the time you have been acting as advisor to the High Throne you have been also part of a secret guild? Are all your members foreigners?"

Tiamak shook his head. "If by 'foreigners' you mean those who look different from yourself, Your Excellency, then the answer is no. In fact, for many years before he disappeared, Prince Josua himself, King John's younger son, was one of our number. And if Josua still lives, as Heaven grant, he may still be wearing the same token." He smiled politely. "But this secret guild, as you name it, comes closer to home than that. My friend Father Strangyeard was also a part of it. You remember him, I trust?"

"Strangyeard? The royal chaplain?" Now Gervis looked openly baffled. "Of course I remember him, and still mourn his passing. A fine man, a godly man. What do you mean? What is this mysterious society?"

"With their Majesties' leave, I will explain," Tiamak told him. "The members of the League of the Scroll are scholars, bound by oath to preserve wisdom. It is a great honor, but also an onerous and sometimes fatal duty, since sometimes the only way to preserve wisdom is by fighting against those who would drag the world back into darkness. Several of our members died in the Storm King's War. But dangerous as it may be, that duty cannot be asked for, as a man might ask for a royal favor. A position in the League must instead be granted by a current Scrollbearer—that is what we call ourselves—often when that member thinks his or her own time is short. If possible, the shiny emblem you see here, or at least one much like it, is given as well. You have seen Binabik's, the gift of his master. I received mine from another good Aedonite, Father Dinivan of Nabban, when he fell defending the lector himself from Pryrates the red priest."

"Father Dinivan? Lector Ranessin's secretary?" Gervis seemed astonished to find another churchman involved. "I remember him, too!"

"Yes, Dinivan. And Strangyeard received his from Jarnauga of Tungoldyr when that good, wise man stayed behind, giving his life to enable Josua and his people to escape from Naglimund when all seemed lost."

"Hold a moment," said Duke Osric. "You say 'Jarnauga'? But this fellow with the arrow is named Jarnulf, and obviously he is a Rimmersman too. Could he be some relative of the fellow you knew?"

Tiamak shook his head. "I never knew Jarnauga myself, because I was not at Josua's castle, Naglimund, when Jarnauga came there. But Strangyeard thought very highly of him, especially considering the short time they had together. As to your question, it has occurred to Binabik and to me as well. But we have no answer. If Jarnauga had kin, no record of their names survive. Strangyeard never mentioned them, and Jarnauga's own scroll and quill pendant is on my neck at this moment." Tiamak reached into his mantle and produced another pendant, then carefully removed it and put it on the table beside the first. "By the form of his writing, though, this Jarnulf is from the tribe of Rimmersmen enslaved long ago by the Norns. Jarnauga of Tungoldyr was of the free Rimmersfolk, our allies under the dukes of Elvritshalla and the High Ward."

"So if this Jarnulf is a member of your group of scholars," Osric asked, "who made him so? Who gave him this?"

"I beg your pardon, my lord, but you move forward too swiftly. There are other things that are strange here. See how the League symbols of the honorable troll and myself are made of gold? This one is not. In truth, I have never heard of the League making such things in silver, not even in the earliest days of our company. But that is not all that puzzles us," Tiamak said. "Binabik and I have examined this token carefully and made an interesting discovery." He picked up his own chain and the necklace that had accompanied Jarnulf's message, then handed them both to the duke. "Look closely. Tell me what you see."

Osric held them close, squinting. "I see nothing. Perhaps this new one is a little less finely made."

"You are right, my lord. Now turn it over."

Osric raised an eyebrow, but did as the little man asked. "I see nothing of import."

"Exactly. Now look at mine. Turn it over as you did the other."

The duke stared for a moment, then his brow lifted in surprise. "There is writing on yours, but it is too damnable small for me to read."

"There is writing because a Scrollbearer pendant must have it," Tiamak said. "Those tiny letters, 'POQM,' signify the Nabbanai words, *'Podos orbiem, quil meminit'*—'He who remembers can make the world anew.'"

"But it's not on the pendant this Jarnulf fellow sent, and his is silver, not gold. What does all that mean?" asked Simon.

"That we are fearing this letter found on the Frostmarch Road is likely not being from a true Scrollbearer, Duke Osric," Binabik explained. "Or at least that the pendant itself is not being a genuine thing."

"The motto goes back to King Simon's ancestor, Ealhstan the Fisher King," Tiamak said. "The one who founded the League. It is our credo, and you will find those letters scribed minutely on Binabik's pendant as well, and Josua's wherever he may be, and that of Lady Faiera of Perdruin. Together we are the last of the Scrollbearers."

"The last?" asked Archbishop Gervis. He sounded as if that might almost be a relief.

"We have lost many of our wisest, and those of us who are still loyal to the League have been searching for new candidates equal to the responsibility. I confess that we Scrollbearers have let ourselves be distracted by other things in these years of relative peace. But now . . . well, suffice it to say that it seems there is need for the League once more."

"But why?" Count Rowson demanded. "I can't keep all this straight, but surely an attack by a dozen or so bloody White Foxes and a single giant doesn't signify the end of the world. Why do you all look like the sky is about to tumble on our heads? Why all this nonsense about leagues and scrollbringers and such?"

"Because of what the message from this Jarnulf says, my lord." Count Eolair had been quiet for a long time, and even Miri found his sudden words a bit startling. "The man claims connection to the League, or implies it, and says that the queen of the Norns is awake and seeking vengeance against us. But we are dealing with far more than words! Here is something else we have not told you yet—something important we heard from an old friend and his wife." A few murmured conversations faltered and fell into silence. Eolair looked to the king and queen for permission. The royal pair conferred with silent glances, then Miriamele nodded. "Thank you, Majesties," Eolair said, then turned back to the council. "Our old ally Sludig of Engby and his wife discovered that the White Foxes are again crossing their land in eastern Rimmersgard after decades of absence, and that the Norns also seem to be at war with their Sithi kin. Now, consider that the Norns also attacked soldiers of the High Ward—the king's and queen's own soldiers!—only a short distance from the borders of Erkynland itself, when they could easily have hidden from us instead. This is not one small exception to the ordinary, but two great ones, and they have come at much the same time. Are these not reasons to be concerned, my lord?" It was rare to see Eolair angry, but the lord steward was not hiding his unhappiness very success-fully. "The king and queen both fought against the Norns in the Storm King's War. So did I. We saw at first hand what they can do—and what they almost did. King Seoman and Queen Miriamele saw this very castle ablaze with unreal fire and cast back hundreds of years into the past. Is that not true, Majesties?"

Simon nodded. "Dear God, yes. It sounds like a song or a tale but it's all true. We saw it."

"And *that* is why we are concerned, good Lord Rowson," Eolair finished. "If we had been only a small bit less fortunate in our other struggles with the Norns, we would none of us be here today to have this council meeting."

Even Rowson's bluster was stilled by Eolair's hard tone. Miriamele guessed that some of the count's unhappiness came from the terrible timing, this new threat that had pulled him away from the country of his birth and of his heart, Hernystir.

"What then are we to do?" Duke Osric asked. "Even if everything you fear is true, Lord Steward, how are we to act on such vague warnings? If the fairies come against us in the open we can fight them, but unless that happens they can hide inside their mountain until doomsday, and we cannot reach them, as Isgrimnur found out all those years ago."

Eolair looked to the king and queen. Simon was lost in thought, so Miri-amele nodded and said, "We do not plan to act on anything yet, except to ac-knowledge that we need to know more, and that these are troubling signs. Certainly with most of the trouble so far confined to the north, it seems too early to call for more soldiers, although it would be wise to make certain those soldiers will be ready when we need them." She paused, considering. "Tiamak—and Binabik, too, if he will be so kind while he is our guest—should do their best to discover more about this Black Rimmersman Jarnulf. Perhaps more importantly, they will see if they can find the meaning of his words about 'witchwood crown.' We know too well what witchwood is—the Norns use it in their swords and armor—but we have never heard of any 'crown' made from it. Still, whatever it might be, if Utuk'ku wants it, it almost certainly means nothing good for us. And that must be all for now, I think, because the rest of us have much to do simply dealing with the problems that already beset us, especially since the king and I have been absent from the Hayholt for long months." She turned to Simon. "Is there anything else to be said?"

Simon started. "Sorry, my love. I was just thinking about Geloë and Morgenes. God in His heaven, what I would not give to have those two wise ones with us now—" He trailed off.

"We do not know these people, my king," Archbishop Gervis said after waiting a long moment for Simon to finish.

"No," he said, and Miriamele could hear the sadness in Simon's voice that he did not let his face show. "No, you don't."

He felt things deep in his bones, her husband.

27

Noontide at
The Quarely Maid

It was a relief for Morgan to be back in his favorite place again, the seat of his empire, the secure heart of his principality; still, and for reasons that he couldn't quite understand, he was not enjoying it the way he had imagined he would.

The window by the door was open. It was a matter for the philosophers whether the stink of the hot day was drifting into the tavern or the stink of the tavern was drifting out. All Morgan knew was that it was hideously warm, and that after months on the road, mostly in open wilderness, the odor of civilization was hard to ignore. The street outside was still littered with the remnants of yesterday's procession, when he had ridden in with his grandparents and the rest of the royal company. The people had cheered for him, but not in the same way they cheered for the king and queen.

I'll wager they're already telling tales about me, he thought. *Saying that I hid in the camp back on the Frostmarch while others fought the Norns—even my old grandfather fought! As if I didn't try to join the soldiers. Grandmother even posted a guard to keep me from helping.*

"If you are feeling glum, Highness," Sir Astrian remarked, "—as the sour look on your face suggests—then I recommend you dedicate yourself to a life of service to others, thus redeeming yourself. And another stoup of ale for all would be a fine first step in your new life."

"I wouldn't mind a little more ale, either," said Sir Porto. "But it hardly seems proper to send the prince after it." He frowned and considered. "Olveris, you go."

Sir Olveris only raised one eyebrow and stared at Porto down his long, thin nose.

"Since no one here has the initiative to do what must be done," said Astrian, "*I* will essay the labor that the rest of you shirk." He turned toward the far side of the room, where the taverner was berating the potboy. "Hatcher! Another pot for the prince's table!"

The landlord looked at him for a moment, appearing something less than delighted, then returned to saying things about the potboy's ancestry that seemed clearly fanciful even to Morgan in his only slightly inebriated state.

"Is he going to bring some?" Porto asked at last.

"To deny service to the heir-apparent is to flout the High Ward itself," said Astrian. "Society itself would founder and Erkynland would soon be overrun by barbarian hordes. And barbarian hordes are notably unwilling to pay tavern owners for ale that they can take more easily by force of arms. Of course Hatcher will bring some."

"When we were in the north," said Olveris, "I kept hoping Astrian would freeze. I was curious to see if, when he finally thawed, he'd just continue on with whatever he'd been saying."

"Listen to you, Olveris." Astrian gave him a look of disgust. "Everything I say glitters with wisdom—the more I speak, the brighter the day for everyone. You, you speak ten words in two years and none of them are worth waiting for."

Morgan was only half listening; something was gnawing at him, like a mouse in the wall of a house.

It's those damned trolls, he thought. *Before Snenneq dragged me up onto that mountain in the middle of the night, I was splendid. Everything was splendid. Now, I feel like I was in love and the girl ran off with another man.*

"What troubles you, Highness?" said Astrian. "Honesty compels me to say that you have the face of a constipated martyr."

Morgan did not want to be poked just now, although most times he welcomed it. But something had changed and he felt he had to puzzle out what it was. It was ruining his appreciation of a day's drinking, for one thing. "Nothing. Nothing troubles me."

"Bravely said and bravely lied, my prince. Come, you must tell us. What more sympathetic ears could you find than mine and Olveris's, although his are rather high, and he will be forced to bend down to hear you."

"What of me?" Porto sounded as querulous as a child in need of a nap. "Are my ears not sympathetic?"

"Only the Lord God himself could guess what those great flaps are meant for," said Astrian. "Listening? No, more likely to capture the wind and sail to Harcha."

"I grow my hair long to hide them," said Porto sadly. "It's true, they are large."

"Large? You might as well call the great, rolling ocean 'slightly wet.' You might as well call a lion a stray cat!"

Hatcher, the taverner, appeared, bowing to Morgan. He held a filthy cloth in his hands and wrung it continually in his fingers as he spoke, like a pious man telling his station beads.

"I beg your pardon, Highness," he said. "As always, I welcome your custom here at *The Quarely Maid*—"

"As you should," Astrian said. "What other middling low establishment—

forgive me, I am being frank—can claim such an exclusive clientele? Now go away and bring us that ale."

"Here, now." Hatcher was a husky, hairy man, but at the moment he looked as though he might weep. "No call for that. What's that you're sitting on? A bench, and a good one. And what do you call this?" He leaned forward and rapped his knuckle against the wood. "A table. The first place in Badger Street or anywhere near Market Square with a real, true table, this is. I'm not asking His Highness to sit on the floor. I'm not asking him to balance his bowl on his lap. This is quality, this place of mine."

Morgan looked at the rest of the drinkers, who were seated around trestles made of planks balanced on barrelheads. The rest of the drinkers looked back, pleased by any diversion, as always. "Quality," Morgan repeated.

"Yes, Your Highness. And, begging your pardon, my prince, but you'll notice that every leg on this table is the same length. No broken, tipping-over trash in here."

"Except Porto," said Astrian.

Morgan could not help laughing. The old man sat up—it was true, he had been leaning a bit precariously—and tried to look indignant.

"But all this quality is costing me," said Hatcher, determined not to be distracted. "So we come to a delicate matter, Your Highness, if I may be so bold."

"As if we could stop you," said Astrian. "You are clearly determined to bore us all until we must find another wayside oasis in which to soothe our nerves."

"Don't joke, Sir Astrian. You've been good to me—the prince has been good to me—and his custom is always welcome here. Speaking of quality, the Lady Strange herself came in just the other night."

"Liza? Ah, I miss the girl," said Astrian. "What is she doing these days? Have those red bumps gone away?"

"Just so," said the publican, ignoring him. "Liza Strange herself, and you know she's quality, too. Won't even bed a man who doesn't have an income and a house." Hatcher appeared to have muddled himself a bit, and stopped to get his bearings. "Anyroad, as I said, I'm grateful for your custom, Highness," he told Morgan, "but there is the matter, begging your pardon, of some unpaid bills."

Morgan sighed. "Oh, for God's bloody sake, just send them to Lord Jeremias the royal chamberlain. He'll make it all right."

"But that's just the thing," said Hatcher. "Before you left for the north, the lord chamberlain sent me a letter, a very stiff letter, and said the household wouldn't no longer be responsible for your tavern bills. That's what he said. And that I should stop dunning him. That you would take care of it yourself from now on."

A minor annoyance was swiftly becoming a rather large source of alarm. "It's a mistake," Morgan said. "I'm sure it's a mistake. Write to him again."

"Three times already. The last time was the time he answered." Hatcher looked quite cruelly caught between the urge to toady and the urge not to lose his establishment. "And the thing of it is, Highness, what you owe——" He bent forward and put his bearded face close to Morgan's ear. "Two gold pieces already, and a handful of silver. And that is without the door that came off last Decander. I had to replace that, hinges and all."

"So what you're saying is that I'm not welcome here?" Morgan asked, doing his best to put the chill of outraged nobility in his voice.

"Oh, by all the saints, no!" Hatcher, having taken his brave stand, quickly retreated. "But you see, Highness, I can't keep extending credit forever. It doesn't signify, you see that. And now that you're back, well, I thought we should have this talk. So that I don't have to take other measures."

"Other measures?" Astrian leaned over the table. "Are you threatening us, potsman?"

Morgan saw the genuine fear in Hatcher's face and intervened. "Enough, Astrian. Nobody is threatening anyone." *Except my mood*, he thought, because a chance to drink himself into a better frame of mind had now been kicked to pieces. He stood up. This dark building smelling of hops and sweat suddenly felt like the last place he wanted to be. "You will have your money, Hatcher. I swear on my honor as a prince of Erkynland."

"There," said the publican, smiling and wiping sweat from his square, red face. "There. As nicely and courteously said as anyone could want. Your companions could take a lesson from you, Your Highness. That's how the nobility behaves, honest and open-handed." His eyes narrowed just a bit. "Might I ask when, if it's not too impolite, sire? Because I owe money to the brewer myself, you see, and he's been making noises that I have to say I don't like much."

"I'll let you know, Hatcher. Come on, you lot." Morgan stood and waited for his friends to get up. Porto had a bit of a sway, like a tall tree with shallow roots. Astrian and Olveris seemed almost completely sober, but Morgan knew that wasn't so. They both built slowly to drunkenness; sometimes it wasn't possible to tell until Astrian lost his temper or Olveris fell asleep sitting up, which he did almost as regularly as old Porto. In fact, Morgan wasn't certain either of them was ever completely sober.

Now what will I do today? He had hoped to avoid thinking of such things, had wanted only to drift quietly and forget the trip to Elvritshalla, the humiliation of being kept out of the fight with the Norns, and that strange night on the mountain beneath the mocking moon. *What will I do ever again?* At the moment, he could think of nothing that appealed, nothing that would change his grim, strange mood.

Why did those terrible trolls take me up on top of that cliff? I haven't had a peaceful or happy moment since.

He almost wished he had fallen.

Lady Thelía, Brother Etan could not help thinking, was both the most ladylike and the most *un*ladylike noblewoman he had ever encountered. In some ways she was the ideal lady: she never lost her temper in public, as far as he could tell, and she dealt with everyone, whether maid or Lord Constable, with the same evenhandedness. But unlike most of the women in the court, Lady Thelía also had no problem getting her hands dirty. She was completely undisturbed by blood or anything else that was a natural part of life, and she seemed to revel in situations that would send most of her peers running or fainting.

Of course, in one sense those sort of ladies were not her peers at all: Lady Thelía came from a fairly ordinary merchant family, one that had not even tried to purchase a title, despite more than middling success and a better than modest villa in the hills of Nabban. And before she met and married Tiamak, himself among the most unlikely lords in all of Aedondom, she had been a nun.

It's clear she wasn't raised to be a delicate bloom, Etan thought as she examined the Sitha woman, this time with her husband watching.

"She has not spoken for days, and as you see, her breathing remains rapid and shallow." Thelía lifted the woman's eyelid and examined the eyeball beneath with no more trepidation than if it were a coin or a stone. Anyone who had not spent several days in her company, as Brother Etan had in the last fortnight, would have thought her disinterested, even callous, but he had seen her deep frustration at not being able to help this stranger.

"I am very willing to believe she has been poisoned," Tiamak said. He turned to Etan. "And nobody can find the arrowheads dug from the wounds?"

Etan shook his head. "No. They were here one day and gone another. I remember at first they were lying on a white cloth, smeared with blood. Lord Pasevalles does not know what happened to them, either."

Tiamak nodded. "Can you describe them to me?"

"I can try." The monk closed his eyes, trying to recall that day, when he had found the Sitha fighting an armed guard to a standstill with her bare hands. "What remained of the shafts was very, very dark, I think, as though they had been rubbed with ink."

"Like Norn arrows. But I am not convinced by that. If you think of anything else, Brother, please don't hesitate to tell me." He turned to his wife. "Black arrows. Could they have come from the Norns, do you think?"

She made a face. "Don't ask me about arrows. You know more of such things than I do—all those years in the swamp hunting for food. And what difference would it make?"

"Because it is uncommon to see black arrows in this part of the world except those used by the Norns," the small man said. "But I think I have seen such black shafts rubbed with lampblack in the south, when I was growing up."

"Are you saying that they might have been Wrannaman arrows?" Etan asked.

"No! Goodness, no, although there are clans who do use poison. But our arrows are much too small to make such holes as you say she had when she was brought in from the Kynswood, and our bows would never have penetrated her flesh so deeply—they are for close-up work, birds and snakes and other small animals. Those wounds were made with war arrows."

Thelía had finished examining the patient's wounds, which had largely healed, though the fever still would not release her. "And poisoned, too, perhaps. Does any other tribe or people that you know use such things on their arrows?"

"Poison? I cannot speak for this Sitha's own people or their cousins the Norns," said Tiamak. "And that is a problem not easily overcome—we have so little knowledge of her race in their ordinary state of being. But there are others in the lands below Nabban where mortals once used poison on their arrows when they went to war—or when they carried out a killing and wished to make certain the victim did not survive. He frowned. "In fact, now that I think on it, there are clans in the Thrithings, especially in the Lake Thrithings, who used to make a poison just to smear on arrowheads. They called it Demon's Helmet—you know it as wolfsbane. But I did not think it was still in use."

Etan felt suddenly queasy. "If this is wolfsbane that has poisoned her, there is no cure!"

"We knew already that she was beyond our physicking," said Lady Thelía.

"I am sad to say that my good wife is correct." Tiamak shook his head. "But there might be some value in a very, very small amount of foxglove being given to her."

"Foxglove? You mean that thing the children call Fairy Houses? But that is a poison, too."

"As you know, Brother, many things are poisonous in one measure but helpful in another," said Tiamak. "And in any case, I am sadly certain it will not cure her, but perhaps it will give her a bit more life and even bring her back enough that she can speak to us a little before the end." He shrugged. "I can think of nothing else. Wife, can you?"

"No," she said. "I will prepare the foxglove for you—I have a little in the herb garden." So, after pulling the covers back over the pallid, motionless Sitha, Lady Thelía went out.

"My wife and her garden could kill me five times at a single breakfast, if she so chose," said Tiamak with a smile that surprised Etan—it did not seem like a light matter. "It is a capital reason to be a good husband, did I not have enough reasons already." He felt the Sitha woman's forehead once more, then turned away. "And you said there was something else you wished to speak to me about, Brother?"

Etan had been waiting with as much patience as he could muster to tell him about the book he had found in Prince John Josua's effects. "Yes, my lord. While you were gone, Lord Chancellor Pasevalles asked me if I would go to look at some books of the late Prince John Josua's. Princess Idela wondered if we might want them for the library."

"That was kind of her," said Tiamak. "But I thought we had all of John Josua's books."

"Apparently not, my lord. She has at least one chest you haven't seen before. Of that I am sure, because of what I found there."

As Etan described the discovery of *A Treatise on the Aetheric Whispers* and what he knew of its author, Fortis the Recluse, Tiamak listened with an unusual, remote expression. Etan could not help wondering if he had got things wrong somehow, if the book was not, in fact, the infamous object he had been so certain about.

". . . And so I have it now, my lord, hidden in the engineers' drawing room," he concluded, "though I do not like to leave it there. I have gone back to examine Prince John Josua's possessions again, and although I did not find anything that made me fearful like the *Treatise*, I must confess there are several other volumes that I didn't recognize, and many of which I cannot even identify the language in which they're written. Did I do wrong?"

Tiamak was silent for a while and Etan grew ever more certain that he had made some mistake.

"Have you told anyone else about this book?" the little man finally asked. "Did you say anything of it to Princess Idela?"

"No. I did not want her worried. I meant to tell Lord Pasevalles, but we were interrupted."

Tiamak nodded. "I would like to see it. I have heard of it, although I have heard very little. I did not know that the church considered it such a dreadful thing."

"It has been on the proscribed list for two centuries, my lord." Etan made the sign of the Holy Tree. "Even having it . . . I fear that I endanger my soul."

To Etan's great relief, Tiamak did not laugh or even smile. "You have clearly been under much strain of late. I can see it in your face, Brother."

"It frightens me," he confessed. "Just knowing it is in the castle frightens me, but it is worse having possession of it myself."

Tiamak nodded. "I understand, but of course I cannot tell you whether you are right to fear. It was very difficult for me, in my old life, to get much news of the things other scholars did. I only heard what my friends in the League of the Scroll told me and what I could learn from the few wise folk I could find in Kwanitupul. I do not know if the Church is right or wrong to be so concerned with the bishop's book, but as I said, I would certainly like to see it. Can you bring it to me later tonight?"

"I'm afraid I will not be free until after evening prayers at the cathedral, my lord."

Now Tiamak did smile. "Until this evening, then. In the meantime, I must help my wife do what we can for this poor woman, and then I have business with the king and queen."

Etan sensed that he had been released, or even dismissed, but he could not help lingering. "One more question, Lord Tiamak?"

"Yes, of course."

"Did you see the Norns that attacked the royal company? The ones the northerners call White Foxes? Are they as fearsome as legend makes them?"

"I did not see them this time, no. He Who Always Steps On Sand was watching out for me that evening, and I was far from the fighting. But I have seen them before—seen them in this very castle, in the last days of the Storm King's War. I do not know about the book you found, Brother Etan, and its apparently black history, but I can promise you that the stories about the Norns *are* true—they are fierce, they are clever, and they hate us. Yes, the White Foxes are to be feared. May the heavens grant we never see them in our lands again."

Suddenly wishing he had not asked, Etan made the sign of the Tree again before he went out.

"I'm sorry everything is still in such a muddle," Jeremias said. "It's been very . . . things have been . . ."

"Things have been a muddle for all of us," Simon told him. "Don't worry."

"It's just that . . ." Jeremias broke off, his eye caught by Miriamele, who was being helped out of her dress behind a screen by two of her ladies in waiting. She saw him and gave him a look, which made him redden.

"Master of the Bedchamber is a title of honor, Jeremias," she said, her gown halfway down her shoulders. She wore only a shift underneath. "You don't actually have to stay with us."

Jeremias turned an even deeper shade of pink. "I beg your pardon, Majesty."

"Yes, it truly has been a long day," Simon said, wondering why Jeremias would not take the hint. "Everyone is tired."

"I just wanted to thank you. For including me in the Inner Council."

Simon waved his hand. "You have always been a good friend, Jeremias, and you saved my life on the Frostmarch Road. I intend to give you more honor—and responsiblities, too, never fear. But I notice you didn't say much."

The Lord Chamberlain shrugged and would not look up at him. At times, he seemed little more than the awkward youth of Simon's own childhood, somehow transported into the thickening body of a middle-aged man. "What would I have to say? I keep track of food and linens. I don't know anything about making war."

"Please, Jeremias," said Miriamele, her voice a little impatient. "Nobody is going to make war, at least we hope not. We simply have to be prepared for what may happen. Just like you with your linens and food."

Jeremias was looking at the floor, but squared his shoulders. "Still, you have been good to me, Simon. You both have."

Simon could tell he wanted to say something else, but the king had been listening to people all day long and he was dizzy with talk. "You're my friend and always will be, Jem. Now, would you please accompany the queen's ladies to the outer room? We'd like to go to bed."

Jeremias looked stricken. "Of course! I'm sorry, it's late. I wasn't thinking."

"The servants can go too," Simon said. "Miri and I would like a little time to talk alone."

"Of course, Majesties." He straightened, whatever was troubling him put aside by the reminder of his duties. Simon hated treating Jeremias like just another underling, but he had reached the point where he was about ready to pick the lord chamberlain up by the scruff and drag him, along with the ladies-in-waiting, the servants, and the squires, straight out of the bedchamber.

When the little caravan had at last departed, Simon pulled off his clothes and climbed under the coverlet. Miriamele put her jewelry back into the box and sat down to brush her hair.

"What do you think all that was about?" he asked.

"What? Jeremias?"

"I was beginning to wonder if he was ever going to leave. I thought he was going to insist on putting my slippers on." He scowled. "I hate it when he acts like that, like a faithful hound. He's known me since we were both grasshoppers."

"You've treated him well, Simon. A chandler's apprentice who became Lord Chamberlain of the High Throne—he doesn't have much to complain about."

Simon knew her tone. "In other words, stop worrying so much."

She caught his eye in the mirror and showed him a weary smile. "Precisely."

Simon sat higher against the headboard so he could watch her more easily. "I suppose you're right. It's not like we don't have enough to deal with. You heard what Tiamak said about the Sitha woman."

"He and Thelía and that nice Brother Etan have done all that could be done, Simon. Don't take every trouble on yourself."

"But why did they send someone after all this time? And what are we going to do?"

"What can we do?" Miriamele asked. "She is dying. We must try to find out who shot her, I suppose, although it was probably poachers."

"With poisoned arrows?" Simon shook his head. "Beside, that's not what I mean. What are we going to do about *her*? She'll die if we don't get her back to her people."

Miriamele rose from her mirror and came and sat at the end of the bed. "Even if we knew how to find Jiriki and the rest, we don't know that they could do anything for her. She's dying, Simon. Any mortal would have been dead before we returned. When the Sithi don't hear from her, they will send another envoy, or a message."

"But we can't just wait!" Simon would have been shocked at her callousness, but long experience had taught him that a tired Miriamele was a rather heartless Miriamele. He took a breath and started again. "We can't *afford* to wait, Miri. Do you think it's just chance that the Sithi were sending her to us now, after years of nothing, at the very moment when the Norns are stirring again—when they're crossing our borders and that silver-faced bitch, their queen, is hunting for something called the Witchwood Crown?"

"We may be putting too much trust in that bizarre message."

"But why go to the trouble of sending us any message at all?"

"Perhaps this Jarnalf thought he would be captured."

"Jarn*ulf*, wasn't it?" Simon put his hands behind his head and watched his wife looking at herself in the glass. "No, that doesn't make sense, either. And don't you see, Miri, even if the Sithi hadn't sent this messenger or whatever she is, it would still be time to try to reach out to them. Jiriki may know what's happening with the Norns, but if he doesn't, he should be told all that we've heard." He sighed. "And I want to see him again so badly."

"His sister, you mean."

"Aditu? Yes, her, too."

"Yes, her, too." His wife was suddenly distant. "It must be nice to live forever like the Sithi," she said, staring into the mirror. "To stay young and lovely while everyone else is getting old."

Simon laughed. "Would you really like that? To stay the young girl I first met while I grew old, old, old beside you? While everyone else around us grew old too? I like your wrinkles and your gray hairs, wife. They remind me of the life we've had together."

She put her hairbrush down with exaggerated care, as if what she truly wanted to do was throw it at him. "So you are telling me that if Aditu were here now, slinking around with her flimsy garb and her charming, mysterious ways, you wouldn't be following her like a dog smelling raw meat?"

"What is this? Are you jealous? Of Aditu? Dearest, I haven't seen her for years and years! Not to mention that there was never anything between us. Oh, and that she's at least a couple of centuries older than either of us." He tried to be amused, but it was more difficult than he expected. "I thought you cared for Jiriki and Aditu as I did, Miri."

"You lived with them. I didn't." Miriamele sighed. "Oh, I don't know. I do care about them. I was as excited as you when I thought things would change between their people and ours. But they've always been secretive. They prefer to stay hidden, to stay out of our affairs."

"The Sithi prefer to remain hidden because our people kept trying to kill them, my dear. I hoped—we both hoped—we could change that. But even more important, they know the Norns far better than we do. Now, come to bed. I want to talk to you about something else."

"I'm very tired, Simon."

"Not that. But here—climb in beside me. You'll catch cold, sitting out like that in your nightdress." He held the coverlet up for her and she slid close, so that he could feel the cool of her skin through the thin cloth she wore.

"I'm here. What did you want to talk about?"

Simon took a breath. "I think we should take the Sitha woman back to her people in Aldheorte Forest. And I think I should go with her. It's time for us to talk to Jiriki and the rest of the Sithi—to find out why they have been silent so long."

Miriamele stiffened against his side. "Absolutely not."

"But why? Miri, you saw those creatures we fought—that giant! What if we must go to war against the Norns again? I would not think of doing it without advice from the Sithi. And I don't think we can stand by and simply let their envoy die, either. Not when her own people may be able to heal her."

The queen spoke quietly but she was not happy. "Some of that makes sense, and I need to think about it. But whatever happens, *you* are not going, Simon. Between that trip to Meremund and then traveling to Elvritshalla for poor Isgrimnur, our people here have scarcely seen you in the last half-year. You tell me there could be a war, but then the first thing you propose is to go charging off across the countryside again like you did when you were young, on some noble, jolly quest to find the Sithi?"

"You are bending my words until I don't even recognize them." He hated when she talked to him as if all he wanted to do was be young and without responsibilities again. Of course, there was a secret part of him that sometimes wished for just that—but who did not have such a peevish, childlike voice inside them, urging them to throw off the coils of maturity? "And I am not speaking as the boy you once met, or even as your husband. I am speaking as the king of all the High Ward."

"And I am speaking as the queen. And the queen says that the king cannot afford to go sailing off on an adventure in the midst of all that we have to deal with. Did you forget Hernystir and the tales of Hugh's devil-worship? Did you not hear Pasevalles tell us Nabban is a boiling cauldron that could spill over at any moment?"

He kept his mouth closed a long time, waiting until he no longer felt like grinding his teeth together in frustration. "Then what should we do, Miriamele? I won't simply wait for this woman to die and hope that Jiriki sends someone else."

She turned her back to him, but stayed close enough to benefit from the heat of his body. "Send Eolair if you must send someone. He is Hand of the Throne. Such duties are his, and he knows the Sithi almost as well as we do."

"Eolair is so worried about Hernystir he can barely keep his mind on what is in front of him."

"All the more reason to send him. Give him something important to occupy him until we know better whether Hugh is truly becoming a problem. Send Eolair, or send someone else. But *you* are not going, Simon."

He lay silently for a while, thinking.

"Miri?"

She didn't answer immediately. "What?"

"Are you angry at me?"

"For suggesting you should go riding off to find the Sithi when there are a hundred things here that require your attention? Why should I be?"

"You're angry."

She rolled over, put her head upon his chest. "Yes, a bit. It will pass, though. It always does."

28

Cradle Songs of Red Pig Lagoon

It was a long walk across the camp to the edge of the meadow where Unver and his stepfather kept their wagons, but several days had passed since Fremur had last seen the tall man. Everybody else was spreading the news, but he wondered if Unver had heard anything at all.

Fremur did not like walking, but when his horse had eventually wandered back after the raid on the stone-dweller settlement his brother Odrig had claimed it, saying, "Any man who cannot keep his horse does not deserve one."

Everyone in the Crane Clan seemed to know about this, so there was no shortage of mockery as Fremur trudged between the wagons and out toward Birch Meadow. He kept his head down and bit his lip to prevent himself from shouting back. Odrig himself had made it clear that he approved of the insults: *"Until you grow a man's tough skin, you are useless to me or anyone else,"* he had said only the previous night. *"You are like a warrior made of cheese."* Odrig's way of toughening a man's skin seemed to be frequent beatings and humiliation in front of the other clansfolk.

Fremur did not think the skin of his body had toughened much since child-hood, but there were times when he felt certain his heart had shrunken and hardened like wet leather left in the sun. He often thought of himself that way, as if his insides were a rawhide knot, something that would only grow tighter the harder it was pulled. He sensed something like that in Unver as well, al-though whatever was drawn tight inside Unver was under much greater strain, like the huge ropes used to tug the standing stones at the Clan Ground back upright after an earth tremor had felled them. The ropes had creaked with every pull against the stones' unimaginable weight, until it seemed like the great cords and the muscles of the men who pulled on them were at war with the earth itself. Unver was like that, but his cords never slackened. The other men of the Crane Clan disliked him but they feared him too, his height and long arms and his hard, blank face, as unchanging as one of those stones, stand-ing against all wind and weather.

He is too fierce, and he does not bend his neck to my brother. Someday Odrig will kill him or drive him out of the clan.

Nobody in the clan, except perhaps for the tall man's stepfather Zhakar, could even remember Unver's real name. When he had first come to the clan as a gangly boy, someone had asked him who he was. *"Unver,"* he had replied, staring at Odrig and the other boys like a bear surrounded by baying dogs—it meant *"nobody"*— and that was what the clan had called him ever since. Even Fremur's sister Kulva still called him that, and she was one of the few folk who treated the tall man with kindness. To the rest, he was only a strange, unfriendly clansman who lived with his drunken stepfather on the outskirts of the camp—a good horseman and fierce fighter, but otherwise to be avoided.

As Fremur reached the edge of the meadow he saw old Zhakar sitting on the steps of his wagon, sharpening a knife with long, screeching strokes. Fremur wanted nothing to do with the sour old man, so he took a path through the trees, around behind Zhakar's ill-maintained wagon and into the grove of birches where, as expected, he found Unver, who was using stones to smooth the wood of his unfinished wagon while his big, dark horse Deofol nipped listlessly at the grass. The green was thick on the plains at this time of the year, and all the horses were growing fat. It was a time of celebration, at least for most of the clan.

"Ho, rider," Fremur called. "May your hooves always find the path."

Unver looked up. "I can't say the same for you. Where is your horse?"

Fremur didn't really want to talk about it. Instead, he nodded toward Unver's wagon, which looked as though it was nearly finished, an altogether finer piece of work than his stepfather Zhakar's rickety cart. The wagon was not yet painted, but every joint showed careful attention, and every spoke of the wheels had been rubbed as smooth as glass. "How does it go?"

"Well enough." Unver held out the wineskin.

"I would help you to finish, if you want," Fremur said, taking a sip of the sour red stuff. "Your wagon, I mean, not your wine. Since I have no horse, there is little else for me to do."

Unver raised an eyebrow but did not ask the obvious question. "There is more polishing to do before the paint. You could help with that—but the Grass Thunderer save you if you put a nick in the wood, Mouse."

He did not know why he said what he said next, but he said it. "I have never liked that name."

Unver watched him take a long swallow, then took the wine back and had a drink himself before wiping the residue from his long mustaches. He was not so dark as most of the clan, whose skin the sun and dust of the plains usually turned the color of cherry wood. Unver's flesh was lighter, like the rounded tan stones in the bottom of riverbeds. His prominent nose was sharp and thin, his cheekbones high, but the strangest thing about him were his eyes, gray as rainclouds.

Fremur waited, but Unver did not ask him to explain what he had said about his nickname. Instead, the tall man watched as a pair of clansmen rode by on the far side of the meadow, a long bowshot away. The squinting, storm-colored eyes followed them until they were gone, as though Unver were a hunting animal and they were prey.

Fremur was growing frustrated by the other man's silence. He had come here with a yearning for comradeship, looking for someone else who knew what it meant to be an outsider in his own clan. "What do you think of my sister Kulva?" he said, then immediately regretted it. He had come to give news. This was not the best way to deliver it, but he had been stung by Unver's seeming disinterest.

The other man looked at him carefully, as though the words might be some kind of trap. "She is a woman." He seemed to realize this was inadequate. "She is a good woman."

"You care about her." Fremur said it as a statement, not a question.

Unver's expression grew more remote, as if a cold wind had brought frost. "She is nothing particular to me. And it is nothing to you, either."

"I have seen you walking together."

Unver's hand dropped to the knife at his belt and his face hardened into something fearsome. "You have been spying for Odrig—"

"No! No, but I have seen you together twice, walking and talking, when I was looking for her. And I know my sister. She would not be so easy with you if you had not spoken together that way many times."

Still the gray eyes fixed him, but at last Unver let his hand fall away from the knife. "Why do you say these things to me, Fremur? Do you plan to defend her honor yourself? If you insist it will be so, but you will die for nothing and her reputation will be ruined. I have not dishonored her in any way. We merely spoke away from wagging tongues." He narrowed his eyes. "Or are tongues wagging already? Is that what you have come to tell me?"

Fremur was about to answer him, but Unver leaped to his feet suddenly and strode toward the unpainted wagon. "You must think me a fool, as all the rest of the clan does. Would I try to steal the sister of the thane? I would be hunted forever." He stopped and spread his arms. "No! This is what I have built with my own hands—the finest wagon in the Crane Clan. I have gone on every raid, I have taken every task anyone would give me. Look!" He threw open the door of the wagon and pulled out an oilcloth bundle. He unwrapped it as Fremur stared, revealing a tumble of bright objects. "Real gold for the horses' traces and reins. Silver for the hinges and fittings, specially made by the finest smith in the Lynx Clan. When I show this wagon to your brother, he and those other fools, their eyes will pop out! He will have no choice but to give Kulva to me." Unver was breathing hard as he rolled the oilcloth again, as though he had run a long way. He shook the bundle at Fremur and the fittings clinked. "She will ride like a queen of the lakelands!"

Fremur now felt sick at his stomach. He had only wanted to make bad blood between Unver and his hated brother. He had not understood . . .

"But that is not . . . !"

"Not enough?" He was angry and would not look at Fremur. "Then I will get enough. I will bring your brother a dowry of fine horses. Not all my gold has gone to buy fittings!"

"Unver, no." Fremur shook his head. He did not know where to begin. "That is not what . . . I only came to tell you . . ."

His eyes almost seemed mad. "*What*? Tell me what?"

"That my sister Kulva . . ." Fremur swallowed. It was not easy, because the lump in his throat seemed big enough to choke him. "My brother has promised her to Drojan. They will set out the marriage stones at the clan gathering, when the moon is full."

Unver did not say a word for long moments. He only looked at Fremur as though he had suddenly sprouted feathers and flown into the air. "A lie," he said at last, but his voice was hollow.

"It is no lie. I hadn't seen you for days, and I didn't know if you'd heard." He was suddenly frightened, and tried to find words that would change the frighteningly animal look in the man's eyes. "I didn't know that she meant so much to you, Unver—that is truth. But you must have known Odrig would never give her to you! You are . . ." He could not think of how to say it, because he was the same way himself. Like a fish in a stream, how could he find a word for the water that was everywhere, that they both breathed and swam in? "You are unworthy. That is what Odrig thinks. Drojan is his friend. Drojan does everything that Odrig says."

The oilcloth bundle dropped from Unver's fingers to the ground and his face went pale as dry grass. For a stretching moment, Fremur was certain Unver would pull the knife from his belt and kill him, and he knew there was nothing he could do to prevent it. Expressions flickered across the tall man's face so swiftly that Fremur could not make sense of any of them. Then Unver found his voice.

"Go!" he roared. "Get away from me! You and your cursed family! What are you but the crow who brings bad tidings, screeching and preening on a tree branch? Your sister is as false as a stone-dweller's bargain!"

"It's not her doing . . ."

"Go!" And with this last cry of rage, Unver turned his back on Fremur and strode back toward the wagon he had worked on so long and carefully. He put his hands against the side of it and pushed until the muscles of his neck bulged. The wood creaked and the wagon tottered, but it did not tip: it was too large for any single man to push it over, or so Fremur thought. Then Unver bent his legs beneath him, leaned his entire body into the side of the wagon, and, with a wordless cry of rage, managed to topple it. It fell slowly, as in a dream, and hit the hard ground with a crash like thunder, splintering into pieces.

Fremur turned and ran.

Jesa carefully swaddled Serasina and brought her to her mother, who was sitting near the window with three of her ladies-in-waiting, taking advantage of the afternoon light to work at their sewing.

"Ah, there she is, the little coney, the little fur-rabbit," said the duchess. She set down her sewing and took the baby from Jesa, who stood by patiently. It was time for little Serasina to nap, and this was how it was done. Jesa did not entirely understand why a woman who loved her daughter as much as Duchess Canthia spent so little time holding her. In the Wran, where Jesa had been born, a child was put in a sling against her mother's belly as soon as she could hold her head up, and rode that way all day. Drylander children, at least those Jesa had known here in Nabban, were treated more like beautiful jewelry or clothing, to be taken out by their mothers and admired, then soon put back again.

It was puzzling, but Jesa had given up trying to understand. Things were just different here among the drylanders, and Jesa had to believe that She Who Birthed Mankind had made them that way for some good reason. But as she took the baby back from the duchess and set her in her huge, painted cradle, it was hard to imagine what that reason could be.

Despite the tight swaddling, little Serasina fussed and wriggled. To quiet her, Jesa sank into a crouch beside the cradle and began to rock it. Duchess Canthia was a kind woman, and would not have begrudged her a stool to sit on, but Jesa was never entirely comfortable perched on such a thing. Some of the furniture the drylanders used felt to her as untrustworthy as ill-made boats, as if any moment they might tip and throw her down. She had been squatting on her heels since she had been only a few months older than little Serasina, and she was comfortable that way.

The duchess and her ladies talked quietly among themselves, but Jesa could tell from the way they glanced over their shoulders toward the cradle that Serasina's crying was irritating some of them, so she began to sing one of the songs her own mother had sung to her, long ago in their house on stilts in Red Pig Lagoon.

> Come moon, come sweet moon
> Come across the marsh, bring an armful of mallows
> Come in a pole boat, bring a handful of hyacinths
> Come across the stream, bring a comb of honey
> Come on a carry-chair, bring milk and curd
> Come on walking feet, bring a basket of bilberries
> Now listen to me and hold them tight
> Keep them here for baby's delight

As Jesa sang and rocked the cradle, she wondered if she would ever hold a baby of her own. She had not been much more than a child herself when she first came to Nabban, purchased as a companion and servant for the duchess when they were both young girls. Canthia had been fond of her, so when she grew up and began to have children of her own, first her son Blasis and now the new baby, the duchess had kept Jesa on as nurse for the children. Jesa missed her home sometimes, of course, and would never entirely get used to going days at a time without feeling soil or water beneath her feet. But when Jesa thought of her own mother and all that woman's backbreaking work, gathering and pounding roots all day long, mending nets, and tending children as well, or when she considered the many other Wran-folk she saw here in Nabban whose daily work seemed so hard and dangerous, she thought that even with no child of her own, she must still be one of the luckiest people in the world.

Jesa had just begun a new cradle song when someone knocked at the door. One of the duchess' ladies-in-waiting rose to open it. It was the duke himself, and when Saluceris made it clear he wanted to talk to his wife in private, the highborn ladies gathered themselves up and went out, chatting happily about visiting the Sancellan's courtyard garden as though they would have been headed there even had the duchess's husband not arrived.

Duke Saluceris glanced briefly at Jesa where she crouched beside the cradle, but his gaze slid from her face as though she were made of polished stone. That was one of the strangest things about the drylanders, Jesa had always thought: if they were not speaking to a servant face to face, they pretended that servant did not exist, as if their maids and nurses were only furniture.

As the duke approached, Duchess Canthia smiled and lifted her cheek. Saluceris bent and gave his wife a kiss. "I'm sorry to send your companions away," he told her, "but Tersian Vullis is pressing me for an answer and I can't delay it much longer."

"An answer to what?"

"The betrothal. Surely you remember! I've been patient because of your condition, but Vullis has been waiting a long time."

Canthia frowned very slightly, and Jesa thought it was like a cloud crossing the sun, bringing a moment of shadow to a beautiful day. "You say *the* betrothal, my husband, but surely I remember you speaking of *a* betrothal, or at least a suggestion of one by the margrave. Yes, that's right, I remember you said Vullis wished to wed his daughter to our Blasis. And I also remember saying that we would speak of it after the baby came." She smiled. "And surely before we speak of it any more, you should go and look at *your* beautiful daughter, who is sleeping like the angelic gift that she is."

The duke sighed. "Don't be difficult. Of course I want to see my daughter."

Jesa stopped rocking as Saluceris approached the cradle. Since he still did not look at her, only at tiny Serasina in her blanket, Jesa could examine the duke. She seldom saw him from so close, despite her long connection with Duchess Canthia, and it always surprised her to see how very ordinary he was, this man with pale, fishbelly skin and a neat, sandy beard. He was tall and handsome enough in the bony-faced, drylander way, but he was in no way surprising. How could it be that after the High King and High Queen, those far away people who Jesa knew only from stories—mythic figures like They Who Watch And Shape—Duke Saluceris was perhaps the most important person in all the world?

The thought dizzied her a bit, as it often did, and with him standing so close she was terrified at the thought she might suddenly tip and fall out of her squat.

Only now that she was a woman herself had Jesa begun to understand how the drylander world worked, and what a small, disregarded part of things her birthplace, the Wran, truly was. The realization had come to her just a few years before, when she learned that her mistress (who was also in many ways her closest friend from childhood on) was going to marry not just another lord, but the Duke of Nabban himself, master of the biggest, most populous nation in all of the world. The thought had been so frightening that for many sleepless nights Jesa had thought about running away back to the swamp, back to her familiar lagoon. A girl like her had no business in the houses of such people. She could barely read, and what little she knew she had taught herself from watching Canthia and her tutors, but always from a distance.

One night, shortly before the marriage, she had huddled all night at the foot of Canthia's bed, miserable at the idea of going to live in the Sancellan Mahistrevis, the great palace at the top of one of Nabban's highest hills, where hundreds of servants already lived, each one fiercely envious of her position, no doubt. Here in this strange country, Jesa knew, even monarchs had been killed; the other servants would probably do away with her in her bed the first night. They would beat the young Wrannawoman and throw her off the Sancellan's wall, and she would plummet all the way down to lie broken in the market at St. Galdin's Square.

Don't be a fool, Jesa, she had told herself over and over again throughout that long night. *Jesa Green Honeybird, the elders named you. Green Honeybird didn't run home to her nest when Tree Python chased her, she turned around and blinded him with her beak! Don't shame your namesake by acting like a coward.*

And as if her spirit bird had come to her then, in that dark night and in such a daunting, foreign place, Jesa had felt something whisper past her face and weave itself into a crown of air around her head. Then it was gone. But after that moment she had not been as frightened, and when she entered the Sancellan Mahistrevis for the first time a fortnight later, following her mistress, she had been astonished and gratified to find she had lost her fear. From Red Pig Lagoon to this strange place—what a journey she was on!

After he had stroked his infant daughter's face with a careful forefinger, Duke Saluceris abandoned the cradle, and within a few moments had begun pacing back and forth in front of the large window that looked out over the harbor.

"It's really very difficult to see anything but you just now, my lord," said the duchess, "and you won't stay in one place long enough for me to look at you properly, either. It's not very restful."

"I said, don't be difficult, Canthia. I need Vullis, little as I like to admit it.

The Dominiate is meeting next month and Dallo Ingadaris is introducing some damnable notion of a tariff on wool for no other reason than to push me into a fight with the High Throne. But if I have Vullis, he will pull all our northern and western lords to my side."

The duchess smiled sadly. "My poor husband. You work so hard! Surely you do not have to convince people to listen to you—you are the duke! The king and queen themselves chose you."

"My brother hates me for it. And those cursed Ingadarines are going to do everything they can to use him as a weapon against me."

Little Serasina woke up then and began to fuss, and soon Jesa lost track of what the duchess and her husband were talking about. She had heard so much of this sort of thing that at first she had been frightened all the time—Thrithingsmen were raiding! Nabban's houses were at war with each other!—but now she knew that the world was bigger than she had understood, that things which seemed close when her mistress and others spoke of them were actually far away and unlikely ever to trouble the duke directly, let alone harm Jesa herself.

But some things, she had also learned, were actually closer than they seemed to be. This was proved true again just as Jesa finished patting and rocking the baby into quiet once more and put her back in her cradle. A guard knocked on the door and announced the duke's brother Drusis, Earl of Trevinta and Eadne.

"How can this be?" Saluceris looked startled, almost fearful. "He was at his place in the east." He stood up. "Never mind. I will meet him downstairs, dear, to spare you . . ."

But even before he had finished the sentence, the doors swung inward, and Drusis strode in. "Forgive me," the duke's brother half-shouted, as if to a crowd. "I am filthy from the road, and I intrude on you even in your own chamber, dear sister-in-law!"

Jesa, who could be timid at the best of times, leaped in surprise at the newcomer's loud voice: she had never been in a small room with Earl Drusis before, though she had seen him at court functions, and he was always the subject of much conversation. Taller than his brother the duke and impressively muscular, Drusis was also daunting in other ways, with a handsome, full-lipped face and thick, curly hair, brown with a brassy shine. He wore the armor of a cavalry general, although technically he was neither, or at least that was what Jesa had heard Saluceris complain many times. He also seemed to seethe with strength and youth, although he was but a single, slim hour younger than his brother. It was almost impossible not to stare at him, though Jesa was terrified at the idea of meeting his eyes.

"You are welcome any time, good Drusis, of course," said Duchess Canthia, holding out her hand to him. "This house is yours, also, and always will be."

"You are too kind, sister-in-law." He bowed and then kissed her hand.

"Of course you are welcome," echoed Saluceris, but after the thunder of his brother's entrance, his words were spoken quietly, even reluctantly. "We are merely surprised to see you, brother. We thought you were at Chasu Orientis."

"And so I was. But I wasted no time getting back. I could not bear to think of you and your young family sitting here in the Sancellan, oblivious to the dangers that threaten."

"Dangers? What dangers?" the duke demanded. Jesa thought he seemed split between genuine worry and annoyance at his brother's sudden, loud presence.

"The horse-eaters. They have attacked us! They have attacked Chasu Orientis!"

Duchess Canthia put her sewing down. "That is terrible, Drusis. When did this happen?"

"Just a sennight ago." Drusis walked to the window, looked down on the harbor and all the sails bobbling there like resting gulls.

"I cannot believe the Thrithings-men would be so mad, to attack your home. What did they do?"

"Oh, they did not besiege the castle itself," said Drusis, waving his hand as if to swat away a troublesome fly. "But they attacked Drinas Novis, a town within a few miles of the castle, on the edge of my land."

"A settlement."

"Yes, I suppose. What does the name we give it matter? The barbarians killed a score of our people, wounded three times that many, and burned half the houses to the ground. Nearly twenty people dead, Saluceris—men, women, and children! Does it matter that their town is new?"

Saluceris shook his head. "Of course not. But it matters to the Thrithings-men that we are building towns on what was once their land."

Drusis shook his head in outrage. "Are you defending these murderers, brother? What kind of thing is that for the duke of Nabban to do, when our own people are being killed by savages?"

"It is terrible," said Canthia, looking to her husband. "Surely there is something we can do for them?"

Jesa thought Saluceris looked like a man who had just discovered that the widow he was marrying already had eight fat, hungry children. "Of course we can help, wife. But you, brother, I don't understand what you want. Do you not have two score knights or more at Chasu Orientis, and pikemen a-plenty?"

When Drusis scowled, his entire face changed, the strong, handsome features becoming almost a mummer's mask of sullen anger. "Do you think this is the only thing that has happened of late? Lesta Hermis had his land raided three times in Feyever. Last Novander the cursed Thrithings-men attacked the party of Escritor Raelis on his way to Kwanitupul. How long must we wait before we do something? Until they have set fire to the Mahistrevan Hill, murdered our children, and raped our women in their own homes?" His dark face had grown even darker with anger, but his eyes caught Duchess Canthia's and it seemed to fluster him. "I beg your pardon for my harsh speech, my lady. I am upset and careless because of it." He turned back to his brother. "Do not think because you wear the ducal ring by a fluke of birth, Saluceris, that I will stand back and see our land overrun by savages, our villages burned, our people slaughtered."

"You grow hot too quickly, Drusis," said the duke. As his brother had grown darker, Saluceris had grown paler, so that they seemed opposites rather than the product of a single womb. "Stand back and see our land overrun? I have said nothing of the sort—those words are all yours." He took a breath, and even Jesa could see the duke was fighting for control. When he lifted a hand up to stroke his beard, his fingers were trembling. "No, we will discuss the problem and deal with it as we always have, in council with our fellow nobles in the Dominiate. Now, you have had a long ride, I doubt not, and little in the way of rest or refreshment—the dust of the road is still on you." Saluceris clapped his hands and within a moment two servants had stepped through the door. "Take my brother to his accustomed chamber and see that he has everything he needs," the duke told them. "We will speak again later, Drusis."

Jesa saw that the earl's face was still red with anger, but thought she saw something else too, a gleam in Drusis' eye like a hunter whose prey had finally broken cover. "Very well. But I will not hide my feelings in front of Ingadaris, Albias, Claves and the rest. If you will not help me to stamp out these grassland vermin, brother, I will do it myself!"

With that, he turned and strode out of the chamber, the two male servants scurrying to keep up with him.

Little Serasina was crying again, and this time the duchess came and took her from Jesa, pressing her daughter close against her and giving her a finger to suck until the baby's hitching sobs had quieted. "Fetch the wet-nurse," she told Jesa. "Too much shouting. The child will need feeding before she'll sleep again."

As Jesa was on her way out, she heard her mistress tell the duke, "I would forgive your brother much if I thought he was truly angry."

"What?" The duke sounded confused. "What are you saying, Canthia?"

"That I think it is an imposture. That he wears that angry face and those stormy sentiments like a mask."

"You do not understand Drusis, wife. He has always been strong-headed since he was a child, hot as fire. He has always leaped first and looked afterward."

"Oh, I think he looks exactly where he is going to leap," Canthia said, and it was surprising for Jesa to hear the harsh undercurrent in the duchess' sweet voice. "I think he looks very carefully."

The door fell closed behind her and Jesa did not hear any more.

29

Brown Bones and Black Statues

"What difference should it make that I didn't come to the Inner Council meeting?" Morgan demanded. He and his grandfather were alone in the throne room, or as alone as a king and prince could be in chamber where so many Erkynguards stood at silent attention. "You've never cared about that before."

Simon let out a weary sigh and waited to compose himself before replying. "That's not true, Morgan. We haven't argued with you every time you have chosen to ignore us about councils or many other things, but that doesn't mean your grandmother and I don't care." He was angry, of course, but as always, he found it hard to look at the prince without seeing his lost son. The same heavy, scowling brows, the same handsome features—at least, when they were not twisted in a childlike pout, as they were now. Morgan was not as tall and thin as his father had grown to be, but he had John Josua's sharp features; Simon sometimes felt as if he were chastising poor, dead Johnno when he scolded his grandson. "But things are different, now, Morgan. It is time for you to step up, to take some responsibility, not disappear with your friends into the stews of Erchester when all the rest of us are worrying about going to war."

"Responsibility, oh, of course," said the prince bitterly. "I'm supposed to act like a man because I am the heir—yes, yes, I know. But you refused to let me fight when we were attacked by the Norns."

At least this was a complaint Simon could understand. "That was not by my choice. The queen was worried for you. We did not know the strength of the enemy—"

"No one else was kept away from the fighting! Even Grandmother was out among the soldiers. The queen!"

Simon had to fight back another frustrated sigh. He wished Miriamele had been able to talk to him that night before making her decision. It was one thing to protect the prince, another to do it in such a way that the lad felt unmanned and humiliated.

"What's done is done," he said at last. "But what will come is still up to you, lad."

Morgan stared at him, and for a moment Simon thought he saw a fearful hint of Miri's mad father in the boy's bright, furious stare. "Let me *do* something," the prince pleaded. "I can wield a sword perfectly well. Astrian taught me—"

"Astrian has taught you tricks," said Simon. "I have seen it. Yes, the Nabban-man is an able fighter, but he has shown you clever stratagems for knife-fights, for tavern brawls. Fighting in a real battle—in full armor, in hot sun—it is the strongest man who has the best chance to survive. A battle is not a tournament. You will not be able to rest between bouts and measure each opponent." His voice got louder as he warmed to the subject. "No! Arrows will be flying at you! Enemies will attack you from behind even as you fight with someone else."

"I *am* strong," Morgan said. "How could you know? You don't care, you don't ask. The only time you talk to me is to tell me what a fool I am—how I always embarrass the High Throne."

Simon knew he had lost control of his feelings, but at the moment he could only see his grandson following his son into early death, no matter how different their paths. "God's Bloody Tree, boy," he cried, "do you not hear me? A warrior who prepares for battle in a tavern will likely not live long enough to see that tavern again. Is that why you do not pay the folk who sell you and your friends all that ale? Do you plan a martyr's death to clear your bills? Then you are not just a fool, but a heartless fool, because you will cause grief to all you leave behind. Have your grandmother and I not suffered enough?"

Morgan opened his mouth, and for a moment Simon thought that the prince might say something that neither of them could ignore nor forget, and he knew it would be in large part his own fault. To the relief of the king's more reasonable self, which was still fighting against his fury for mastery of his feelings, his grandson said nothing, only turned and walked out without asking permission or bowing. Simon watched him go, biting back the angry words he knew would only make things worse.

"Well," he said to the air, to the chair of bones and the ancient banners hanging from the ceiling, "what other cheerful things will this day bring me?"

"At least one, I am hoping," said a voice from the doorway.

Simon looked up to see Binabik. These days the troll dressed not for the cold of his homeland, but in soft linens. Simon thought it made him look a little like one of Tiamak's folk. "Has the noon hour struck already, then?"

"It still lacks a quarter-hour or such, is my thought," Binabik said. "But I wished to be speaking to you first, just us two, because I know the queen does not like the matter. I was waiting for you to be finishing to speak with your grandson, then I saw him go by with a face like a Mintahoq blizzard, so it seemed the conversation was ending."

"It never ends. It's always the same."

"Ah, the stubbornness of the young. Nearly as difficult it is being as the stubbornness of the old."

Simon raised an eyebrow. "What do you mean by *that*?"

Binabik might have smiled, but it was hard to know because it was gone in an instant. "It is having no importance, my old friend. An old Qanuc saying, only. No, I came now because of wishing to ask you something. Are you still having no dreams?"

Simon decided he did not mind a change of subject. "None at all, and I cannot tell you how strange that feels. Not even of my poor, dead harper, though I see his face when I am awake all the time. What do you think has happened to me?"

"I have no way of saying, Simon-friend. It could be nothing—since, as Miriamele was suggesting, for many people it is always being that way. But to me it has the feeling of a different thing. Still, I can be offering no wisdom, and neither Tiamak nor his lady wife have any knowing of it either, though we have searched most strenuously in their books when they were not tending the Sitha."

"Ah, yes." The king sighed. Another missed opportunity. "Does she show any sign of getting better?"

The troll shook his head. "No—she grows slowly worse, if I am any of a judge. But sometimes she is speaking in her fever. Her name is *Tanahaya*, it seems. Have you heard such a name before, perhaps during your living in Jao é-Tinukai'i? It might shine some light on why the Sithi were sending her to you."

"No. But I met so many Sithi there, and very few told me their names. Most of them didn't think much of mortals."

Binabik looked up at the Dragonbone Chair on the daïs behind Simon, squatting above the king's and queen's more modest thrones like a gargoyle perched on a cathedral wall. "I see King John's seat of bones is still being here. What of all the times you told me of your wish for hiding it away?"

"Miri won't let me. But I hate it. Every time I look at it, I think of the lying stories about Prester John all over again. I wish I'd never found out."

"About who really was killing the dragon? Would you have been preferring to keep your ignorance than to know your ancestor's great deed and of King John taking the credit?"

"No, of course not. But leaving the cursed thing out this way for everyone to see seems like . . . like saying that the truth doesn't matter."

Binabik nodded gravely. "Perhaps. But sometimes, I am thinking, a lie is only the truth that is believed at that time. Nobody meant to teach you something that was wrong, I am thinking."

Miriamele appeared from the chapel, trailed by Sisqi and Qina, looking like a mother bear with two cubs. "Ah, yes, the old throne," she said. "We kept it outside for a while, but the common people hated that. They loved my grandfather Prester John—they love him still—and they'll always think of it as his throne. So at last I convinced my husband to put it back here, in the Great Hall."

"Convinced?" Simon let out a snort. "More like ordered."

"Decisions between wife and husband have sometimes complication," Sisqi suggested with a smile. "Some things I am thinking must be explained by one to the other."

"Yes, very often," Miri agreed. "Especially to husbands."

"If everyone is finished amusing each other with how stupid and stubborn I am," Simon said darkly, "perhaps we could go outside and talk there. I'm tired of dust and statues and old bones. And also old stories that aren't true."

"We can't go out until Eolair arrives," said Miriamele. "He is coming to meet us here."

Simon scowled, but knew there was nothing to be done. He got out of his chair and lowered himself onto the top step of the daïs, pointedly ignoring his wife's frown. She disliked his habit of doing unkingly things, even when only friends were around to see. "Morgan is not going to join us," he told Miri, but did not explain farther. "Who else are we waiting for?"

"Ah, here you all are," called Eolair as he entered through the ornate throne room door.

"And now we are going outside." Simon clambered to his feet. The most important thing about leading, he had learned, whether the thing being led was a kingdom or a small group of friends, was simply to take initiative, then others would follow. Miriamele knew this too, of course. Sometimes it became a race between the two of them to see who would get to implement a decision first.

A dozen Erkynguards followed the company out of the throne room, trailing the king and queen as always, like a pack of helmeted hounds in green livery. Simon sometimes said trying to go anywhere without them was like trying to sneak through the kennel yard with a handful of meat scraps.

"We may be grateful for that, one day," was Miriamele's usual reply.

Outside, as the sun climbed high in the sky, Simon led his friends toward the Tower Garden, as it was called, because it was built beside the spot where Green Angel Tower had once stood. The garden had high walls and, after all these years, tall trees, along with a complicated braid of pathways marked by hedges. They left the guards outside, except for a pair inside the only gate. The largest remaining piece of the angel herself, the statue's head, sat on a plinth of stone at the center of the garden. A group of servants had just finished setting out a noontide meal of cold meat, fruit, cheese and bread on the shady grass; Simon thanked them and dismissed them. He was determined that at least this once, he and his friends could pour their own wine. "We need only wait for Tiamak," he said. "He has some business to attend to, but he said he should be here by the time the bells ring noon. Pasevalles, too."

"You planned all this, didn't you?" his wife said.

"I told you I didn't want to be inside. Look, Miri, it's a lovely Avrel day. Why shouldn't we be out in the sun with our friends?"

She laughed. "Why shouldn't we, indeed? I think it's a very fine idea, husband."

*   *   *

Tiamak arrived a short while later, but Pasevalles sent a message begging forgiveness: a small crisis in the counting house was going to prevent him joining
them, so they toasted him in his absence. But despite the warmth of the afternoon and the extreme pleasure of the company, Simon drank very moderately,
and saw that Miri did the same. Without discussing it, they kept the conversation to pleasant subjects. Qina and her father sang a Qanuc song about a clever
snow rabbit outwitting a fox, and the girl acted out the part of the rabbit with
such shrewd charm that everyone laughed.

When they had finished eating, Sisqi rose and signaled her daughter to come
with her.

"The meal was good," Sisqi said. "Now we go, but first we say our thanking."

"Where are you off to?" Miri asked.

"They are off to find Little Snenneq," Binabik said. "Qina is convinced that
her young man is not receiving enough nourishment, and she wishes to take
him some of what we ate for our luncheon."

Simon, thinking of the stout young troll, who despite his short stature was
wider than the king himself, could only chuckle. "Very sensible," was all he
said out loud, but Binabik saw his look and smiled.

"You will be understanding the pity we show him," said his friend, "in
memory of another young man lost in strange lands who also was being always
hungry."

"I still sometimes dream of those pigeons you roasted for me when we first
met in the woods," Simon admitted. "I think those were the finest things I've
ever eaten."

"No better sauce there is being than hunger."

When mother and daughter had gone, Miri and Simon looked at each other,
then at the three who remained, Binabik, Eolair, and Tiamak.

"You are not just our oldest friends," Simon said. "But more important, you
were with us in the Storm King's War. You all know we've seen many strange
signs of late—Lady Alva's Norn and Sithi corpses, the Norns and their tame
giant far to the south of their usual haunts. And an envoy to us from the Sithi,
after all these years, ambushed in our own Kynswood."

"Don't forget the message from this Jarnulf man traveling with the Norns,"
his wife said. "He says the Norn Queen is awake, and that she seeks a witchwood crown."

"I think we all take the threat of trouble from the Norns seriously, Majesties," said Eolair. "But remember, Isgrimnur said he thought very few of them
were left when he besieged Nakkiga, and they are slow to breed, like the Sithi.
Still, I have dispatched messages to our allies to prepare against the possibility
of war—but quietly, for now. It is the border forts that are most important, to
protect us, but even more importantly, to let us know of any attack from the
north as quickly as possible."

They discussed how to get more soldiers into the Frostmarch forts without causing an alarm, and about establishing a more trustworthy system of sending and receiving messages.

"I will inform Sir Zakiel, Majesties," Eolair said when they had done. "The arrangements can be underway by tomorrow."

"Good," said Simon. "Then, Tiamak, perhaps you can tell us whether you have learned anything new about the message on the arrow. Do you know yet whether this Jarnulf fellow is in fact some relative of Jarnauga's, or what he means by the Witchwood Crown?"

Tiamak shook his head. "About Jarnulf we have nothing to tell you. Binabik and I have studied everything we can find here in the Hayholt, and he is mentioned in no Scrollbearer's letters. There is also no mention in letters or books of any witchwood crown. The nobleman Cais Sterna of Nabban, who visited old Asu'a in the days the Sithi still ruled there, said that the fairy rulers wore crowns that, though beautifully carved, were made of ordinary birchwood."

"Is there anyone else who might know?" Simon asked. "Mother Church must have lots of books. And you mentioned Scrollbearers. Is there still a League?"

"Of sorts," said Tiamak, frowning. "Binabik and I, of course, and Josua—if he yet lives. Geloë once was offered a place, but she suggested we give it instead to Faiera of Perdruin. Geloë never much liked to tie herself down to the things of men and women. She was happier in the forest, with her animals and birds."

"Then what of this Lady Faiera?" asked Miriamele. "Now that you say her name I remember it, but I have not heard you speak of her in years."

"She fell silent at much the same time as Josua disappeared," Tiamak said. "I sent her many letters, but never had reply. There was plague in Ansis Pellipé at the time, and also a bad fire in the quarter of the city where she lived, so it is all too sadly possible that she is dead." He paused as Simon and Miriamele both made the sign of the Tree. "I am sorry to have so little hopeful news to tell you, Majesties. So many things have taken my attention. Also, since we have been at peace for most of the last twenty years I did not feel it as urgently as I might have. In fact, I confess that after we failed in our search for Josua, I several times put off restoring the League, saying to myself, 'There is too much to do here, and we may yet hear from Josua. Even so, when spring comes, I will take a trip to Nabban and begin the search for more Scrollbearers,' or 'When the king and queen return from Meremund, I will begin the task in earnest.'" He was morose. "Thus do years slip by and so do our chances to do what we know we should."

"You are hardly the only one who can claim that, Tiamak," said Miriamele. Simon knew, despite her tone, that she had a soft spot for the Wrannaman after all they had survived together with Isgrimnur and Camaris in the south.

"So it is only the Sithi who might tell us something," the king said. "But their envoy seems to be dying."

"Poisoned, she told us when she could still speak," said Tiamak. "Certainly something is stealing away her strength even so long after she was attacked."

"Which may be the end of any chance of help from the Sithi." Simon looked pointedly at the queen.

She nodded. "Yes, you need not worry—I was just going to speak of it." She turned back to the others. "The king and I have decided to send the Sitha-woman back to her people. We hope they can heal her. At the very least, though, we must find out if they know what the Norns are planning, and tell them what we've learned. Whatever shadow has fallen between our races, the Sithi were our allies in the last war, and they know more of the Norns and their dreadful, evil queen than anyone else."

Miriamele paused, then looked to Count Eolair. She seemed almost shame-faced. "The king and I are sorry to have to call on you again, old friend, but because we do not know why the Sithi have shunned us, or why they have changed toward us, we need to send someone with their wounded envoy who has had dealings with the Sithi before, someone who can also speak for the king and myself. You are by far the best choice."

Simon was watching Eolair closely, and was certain he saw a slight, almost imperceptible flinch.

"Of course, Majesty." It was hidden again an instant later, and Eolair was all duty. "I will do as you and the king say. But I do have one concern. It will be a long journey, and I am old now. What if something should happen to me on the way?"

Miri frowned. "Do you think it would be too much for you?" She was clearly disappointed.

"No, Majesty. But it is foolish to pretend that I am still a young man. At my age, the gods might call me back at any time. If this mission is as important as we all believe, then perhaps I should have a companion who could deliver the Sitha woman and be your ambassador if something happened to me."

"Of course, you may choose to bring someone appropriate with you," Miri-amele said. "But we have confidence in you and your strength, dear Count."

"Thank you." He smiled. "I hope the gods agree with you. But may I make a suggestion?" he said. "Perhaps it would be good for Prince Morgan to accom-pany me as another envoy."

"That seems an excellent idea!" said Simon quickly, and earned himself a glare from his wife.

"Absolutely not! The king and I have already discussed this. Our grandson is too young, and the journey is too dangerous—we're not even certain where the Sithi can be found. And Morgan is the heir to the throne!"

"An heir who has never done anything but waste time in taverns and other low places . . ." Simon began, but did not get far.

"No. It is impossible." She spoke with such harsh finality that Binabik, Eolair, and Tiamak all stirred uneasily and tried to find something worth looking at.

"Well," said Count Eolair at last, "then it seems I must consider who else might accompany me. Also, I suppose I should begin making arrangements for the journey itself. Binabik, Tiamak, where do you think we should search for the Fair Ones? It seems a difficult task to find a people so famously skilled at hiding from mortals."

"They will be somewhere in the southern reach of Aldheorte Forest, I am thinking," Binabik said. "What I have learned from my master, and from Simon himself, tells me their woodland city of Jao é-Tinukai'i is somewhere there, but they range far on all sides of it. I am guessing that if you follow the Forest Road eastward and stop with frequency to announce yourself, the Sithi will hear of your approach."

"Thank you, good Sir Troll. You would make a very good Hand of the Throne." Eolair's smile was weary now. "I will consult what maps we have of that part of the world, then. When would Your Majesties like me to set out?"

"As soon as possible, I'm afraid." Miriamele had regained her composure. She leaned forward and put her hand on Eolair's. "And you must take a company of Erkynguards with you, of course. We want you back safe, noble Eolair. We could not do for long without you."

"Of course, Majesty." Eolair began to climb to his feet, somewhat more slowly than he once would have. "Binabik, Tiamak, if you would come along and give me the loan of more of your good counsel as I begin to plan the journey, I would be grateful."

As the three got up to leave the garden, Simon asked Tiamak to stay.

"They can wait for you," he said. "We have another need, I'm afraid. All this talk of the past has reminded me that I made a promise to Isgrimnur—that I owe something to that good old man's memory."

"Simon, what are you talking about?" the queen demanded.

"You know, my dear. Your Uncle Josua's children. The royal family who would have had the high throne had Prince Josua been willing to rule."

"Not now, Simon. There is too much else that needs our attention."

"Just so. And that's why I'm asking Tiamak." He turned back to the counselor, who was leaning on his stick to rest his lame leg. "You recall that Isgrimnur and his wife Gutrun were the godparents to Josua and Vorzheva's two children, the twins Derra and Deornoth. On his deathbed, Isgrimnur told us his greatest regret was that he did not know what had happened to them."

Tiamak raised an eyebrow. "They have been missing a long time, Majesty—many, many years."

"Nearly a score, I think. When did the League last hear from Josua?"

"I believe it was in the Founding Year 1176, the tenth of your Majesties' reign. So, yes, well beyond twenty years. The trail must be very cold." Tiamak gave them a look that Simon thought had more than a little dread in it. "What is it that you wish of me?"

"Well, to find them, of course. All of them, if possible, but I promised Duke Isgrimnur that we would discover what happened to Josua's and Vorzheva's children." He considered for a moment. "Blessed Rhiap, they might have children of their own by now!"

"If they lived, yes."

Miriamele had finally heard enough. "Simon, this is . . . well, it is not fool-ishness. We do owe Isgrimnur this. But now is not the time. Nabban is in open conflict, the Thrithings-men are raiding its cities, and now this news of the Norns . . . how can we think of adding another problem to solve?"

"And if we do not honor Isgrimnur's wish now, then when do we?" Simon could be just as stubborn as his wife when he wanted to. "What if there is war in the grasslands? What if Nabban truly does fall into chaos? Then the trail that Tiamak says is already cold will only grow colder—if it remains at all! Josua and Vorzheva and their children are the last of your father's family besides us. Doesn't that mean anything?"

"That is unfair," his wife said, her face grim. "Most unfair."

"Just tell me what you need from me," Tiamak said after a long silence. "I can gather all of the letters from Josua—I still have all mine, and of course Strangyeard had many from him as well."

"You said they were all examined and puzzled over long ago," Simon said. "You had Miri's and mine from him as well, as I recall, and they did not tell us where he had gone or what had happened. No, you must go there—to Kwan-itupul, where he and Vorzheva lived, and to wherever the trail leads you. We must finally discover what happened to them all, especially the children. We owe that to Isgrimnur. We would probably none of us be here today if not for the duke. And if not for Prince Josua too, of course."

The look on Tiamak's face was strange to Simon. It took him a moment to realize it was something he had not seen very often since he had taken the throne—the expression of someone who dearly wanted to say "no" to him.

"I am not sure it is a good idea," Tiamak said at last.

"All thanks to our blessed Redeemer," Miriamele said. "Someone is finally speaking sense."

"What? What do you mean, Tiamak? Josua is—or was—the prince of Erkynland, and he has simply vanished! Uncle of the queen! We argued of this in the past and nobody wished to hear me say it, but may God defend against it, should something happen to us and ours, Josua's family would be the only remaining blood of old King John. And even if Morgan takes the throne, as the queen and I hope, how can we ignore Isgrimnur's dying wish?" Simon felt heat in his face and knew he was getting red. "Come, Tiamak, Isgrimnur was your friend, too!"

Now it was the Wrannaman who gave him a grim look. "That is not it, Majesty . . . Simon." Tiamak lifted his cane and gestured to his bad leg. "It is that I do not walk well these days. I cannot even ride in a wagon without pain."

"You just rode in one all the way to Elvritshalla."

"And I will be honest, my old friend—I suffered the whole way. But do not misunderstand me. It is not the pain I fear now, but the slowness. Who knows how far this trail will lead? I would have to stop frequently and rest, there is no getting around that. The most willing heart can only force a crippled body so far. It would take me a very long time, and—begging your pardon for what must sound very proud—I fear you will miss my counsel in the dangerous months ahead if I am not here. Binabik will be leaving soon with his family. You are sending Eolair away, too."

Simon scowled. "I am sorry for your hurts, of course—of course!—but I think you fear mostly to leave the library behind. You love that task more than anything else."

"Not true." For a moment Simon was surprised to see something else he hadn't encountered before—his quiet counselor showing anger, though of the most careful and controlled sort. "Not true and also not fair. It is my wife I would most hate to leave, but even so, if it were the best solution I would do so. Of course I would. I am sworn to the High Throne and to you two. You know that, and you wrong me to suggest otherwise."

Simon felt like a scolded child, but he also knew Tiamak was right—he had been unfair to him. "Enough. I apologize again for my foolish words. But what are we to do if you don't go? As you pointed out, there is no one else to send, since Eolair is going to look for the Sithi. Must we postpone this yet again, and risk never finding what happened to them?"

"Perhaps not." Tiamak's unhappiness seemed to have passed. "There is one who might be able to do this, I think—and, strangely, I was beginning to wonder what I might do to help him."

"Who are you talking about?"

"Brother Etan. You know him."

Simon waggled his hand impatiently. "Yes, the young monk with the startled look."

Tiamak smiled. "Now that you say it, I can see it. Yes, the one with the startled look. You do not know Etan well, but I do, and I have been impressed by him since the archbishop first sent him to us. He has a keen mind, a depth of curiosity I seldom see, and a good heart."

"But still, something so important . . ." Simon did not like the idea of sending someone he barely knew. It felt like a slight to Isgrimnur's memory.

"Let me tell you one thing about Etan," Tiamak said. "You may remember that when Father Strangyeard died—my dear old friend Strangyeard, how I miss him now!—his scroll was never passed along."

Miriamele nodded. "Because it happened so quickly. The fever took so many that summer."

Simon remembered. He had not guessed how much he would miss the old archivist until it was too late and he was gone. "God preserve us, it was a terrible time."

"He asked me, in his final hours, to keep the scroll until I found someone worthy of it. I have begun to think that Brother Etan is that person—that he should be invited to join the League of the Scroll. That should tell you what I think of him."

"Well, I suppose that is a strong recommendation indeed. Are you certain he's up to it?"

"The task itself? Yes. He is young and in good health. Also, he has the scholar's way of never trusting easy answers. I can think of no better candidate. But even more importantly, I think it would be good for him."

"How so?"

"He has been much troubled since our return from Rimmersgard by . . . by a certain matter."

Simon could tell that Tiamak had chosen to give the bare minimum of information, and for a moment he was irritated. "A certain matter?"

"Nothing that either of you should worry about, Majesties—a thing important only to scholars like Etan and myself—but it has unsettled him. He has not been sleeping well, and like many of his sort of contemplative, religious folk, he has taken it much to heart. I think it might be a good thing for him to have something new on which to bring his thoughts to bear, and other sights beside the familiar castle and cathedral life."

Simon held up his hand. "If you can swear he is up to it, that is good enough for me. Miriamele?"

"Of course we would rather have you here, Tiamak," she said. "As you may guess, I am not pleased we should be doing this now." She darted a look at her husband. "But if we can send your . . . League apprentice, I suppose we could call him, then I will not fight it."

"Let it be so, then." Simon nodded. "And I would like to talk to this Etan before he goes. Let him know the importance of this."

"Of course, Majesty." But Tiamak showed that odd flicker again, a hint of resistance.

Simon decided to ignore it. "And you will make sure he has all that he needs to search for Josua and Vorzheva and their children? To search for the truth?"

"I swear by my village, Majesties. I swear by my oath to the High Ward."

After Tiamak was gone, Simon avoided meeting Miriamele's eye. He knew she would have complaints, and he was not in the mood to defend himself. Instead he looked at the food and empty cups left behind on the grass.

"Shall we carry all this in? It will be just like my scullion days," he said.

"We will send servants," Miriamele said crisply, and gathered her skirts beneath her as she rose. "I was never a scullion, if you remember."

Simon watched her go. She was angry at him again, but with so many possible reasons, he wasn't entirely sure why. *How can I lose arguments I don't even know I'm having?* he wondered.

Irritated, he kicked over a cup and watched the wine bleed out onto the grass, then followed his wife back into the residence.

When Tiamak reached his chambers, he discovered that Thelía was already there and looking rather annoyed, although what had upset her was not immediately clear.

"I give you good day, my dearest," he said. "How is your patient?"

"The Sitha? No better, but God be thanked, no worse. Still, there is something that is eluding me—eluding all of us—and I cannot put my hand upon it."

Tiamak sighed. "I feel much the same, both with her and several other matters. I have felt this way for weeks now. It is like watching the surface of a stream back home, in my younger days. There are ripples I do not understand. It might be only rocks beneath the water, or it might be something moving."

"What troubles you?"

"Oh, everything and nothing. Too much to tell just now."

"Then I will leave you to think in silence, if you will only do me one kindness."

"And that is?"

"Pour me a cup of the yellow dock cordial, will you? I am so weary today, and my head is aching."

"A whole cup?"

"Very well, a half a cup. I will drink it slowly." She frowned at him, but it was meant to be playful. "You are too cautious with me, Timo. We drylander women are sturdy too, you know."

"Oh, that I know." He uncorked the small jug and poured a generous measure into one of their precious glass cups, then held it up to the afternoon sun spilling through the window. It was a large window, and the primary reason Tiamak had chosen these rooms, which were otherwise less than grand, but he missed the light of his previous existence more than anything else. He gave the cup a shake and watched the cloudy liquid swirl like an unsettled sky.

"Thank you, husband," Thelía said as she took it.

He left her with her drink and went to the table. What he was about to do had been in his head since Etan had first shown him the forbidden book. Tiamak had realized immediately upon seeing the *Aetheric Whispers* that he would need advice from another scholar, but the League was nothing like what it had been—only three Scrollbearers left, and that was if Faiera lived! He had been considering Etan as a new Scrollbearer because of the young monk's active mind and good heart, but he was someone to be trained into the League and groomed as a scholar, not someone who could immediately step in and help. And help was what Tiamak truly needed just now.

His wife was reading Sarchoun's *On The Movement of Blood And Pneuma* as she sipped her cordial, which suggested she was still worrying over the dying Sitha. Thelía seemed to think of little else since his return from the royal progress, and came back to their rooms most days only to use one of their books of physick or to sleep. Tiamak was not the most demanding husband, but he was beginning to feel a bit jealous toward the poisoned woman who was getting all his wife's attention.

No good brooding, he told himself. *Instead, I should thank He Who Always Steps On Sand that Thelía is alive and well, and that we are both here together. And my energies could be better used, too.*

He took a sheet of parchment out of the writing box, cut a quill for use, and began writing.

My dear friend Aengas, he began, then worried briefly that it was too informal. He decided he would leave it as it was.

I send you this letter because I have a need for your knowledge that outweighs the shame of distracting you from your life and work. A most unusual book has come into my possession, a book that neither you nor I have ever seen, but only heard of, a thing of great infamy.

That said, I would not trouble you even so, except that I fear its contents may have bearing on other important matters. The book is mostly written in old Nabbanai, which is straightforward enough, but as a kind of code, the author—I will not use his name here, but you will know it, as you will know of the book—uses Khandian words in place of most of the important names and processes. I know little of the language of Khandia. You do, however. I trust you can see the shape of my dilemma.

This book cannot be sent unless I were to carry it myself, which is impossible just now as my duties here in Erchester prevent it. I do not ask you to come—I know it is too much to ask anyone in your condition—but I have no other ideas. Do you know anyone else who could help me, old friend? Are there scholars outside the Aedonite church who know something of the Khand's ancient tongue? If you have guessed the name of this book, you have also guessed why I cannot go to the Sancellan Aedonitis for help, and why I cannot say more in a letter which must be entrusted to a messenger, even a royal messenger.

I hope this finds you as well as can be, and that your work goes well. Whatever your answer to this query, I will look forward to your writings on Warinsten and the ruins of Kementari.

Your brother in spirit,
Tiamak of the Village Grove, now of Erchester

He read it over, then blotted it and folded it before applying his seal. He would put it in the next southbound post himself, to make certain it stayed secret. It would likely come to nothing—Aengas was notoriously uninterested in other people's work—but Tiamak felt the need to do something, anything. Since the day that fearful premonition had swept over as they journeyed across the Frostmarch, he had been haunted by an inexplicable feeling that his time was now short, that something was about to disrupt everything that had been ordinary in his and Thelía's lives, like a large rock dropped into a small pond.

May the Elders grant that I am as poor at seeing the future as I am at reading

Khandian, he prayed. But it provoked a sudden, worrying thought. *What am I sending Brother Etan into? Should I go myself instead?*

Such questions had no simple answers, of course—none that any but the gods could know.

Tiamak kissed his wife on the top of her head as he headed toward the door, then saw that the cordial glass was almost dropping from her fingers; she had fallen asleep with Sarchoun still open on her lap. He removed the book and then took the glass, which fortunately was all but empty, and set both on the table before he left.

"Sleep well, dearest wife," he whispered as he closed the door. "Sleep safe."

30

The Slow Game

They rode northeast over the wide plain the Rimmersmen called Osterdyr, forest to the north and the lake, wide as the sea, stretching for miles beside them on the south, making their way out of the southern springtime and into snows that would not melt until much later in the year. Makho was pleased by their escape from what he called "the mortals' trap," but when Kemme said, for the second time in as many hours, "Four Talons and a Giant, but we killed dozens of their best!" the chieftain stared at him in displeasure.

"The queen would expect no less, Sacrifice," was all he said, but Kemme did not speak of it again afterward.

Still, Makho was pleased by what had happened, and during those long days of riding he did not go out of his way to make Nezeru's life any more miserable than he had before, though he still treated her with contempt.

Storm after storm blew through the gap, but bad weather was never much of a discouragement to the Hikeda'ya, and because this bleak part of the northern world was almost uninhabited, the queen's hand could ride toward the distant peak called Jinyaha-yu'a in daylight as well as darkness. But Makho had not lost all caution: the mortal Jarnulf knew the territory better than did any of the Hikeda'ya, and was consulted frequently, but he was never allowed to lead the hand or even ride at the front. Makho took that place himself, behind only the giant Goh Gam Gar, whose task it was to clear the way when the snow lay piled too deep for their horses to pass. Kemme and Saomeji rode with the chieftain and were close in his counsels as well. Thus it was that Nezeru and the mortal became the endmost riders of the small company.

Jarnulf slowed his horse in a way that Nezeru knew she was not supposed to notice. She guessed that he sought to speak with her because she was in disgrace, and would try to draw her out with the idea of making her an ally. The other Hikeda'ya all suspected the mortal's motives, and in this at least Nezeru agreed with them. Queen's Huntsmen were known to be solitary and cruel, as well as murderously proud of their freedom when the rest of their brethren were collared slaves. It seemed hard to believe one of the huntsmen would so lightly join his fortune with a party of Talons.

"So, Sacrifice Nezeru," Jarnulf said abruptly. "How do you come here?"

It still seemed strange that someone who looked so alien could speak her mother tongue so flawlessly. He even made the secondary "k" sound as well as the Hikeda'ya themselves, on the inward breath instead of the outward. And his grasp of the subtleties was good too, asking her "how" she had come instead of "why," which had the sound of interrogation.

"The queen sent me. How do *you* come here, Freedman Jarnulf?" she asked.

He smiled, recognizing, as she had, that it was to be a long, slow game, one that could last for days. In this land of endless, snowy plains, of gray-white skies and stunted forests of dark, gnarled trees, nobody was in a hurry.

"I come out of the slave pens of Nakkiga, of course," he said. "Nakkiga-That-Was to be more precise, the old city outside the mountain. I was born in White Snail Castle at the foot of Stormspike, and I was taught from the time I could draw breath to fear the queen. So in that way, no different from you."

"Except I wore no slave collar. And I was taught not to fear her but to love her."

"It comes to much the same." His look was mocking. "And I knew you were not born in the slave pens, Sacrifice. That is obvious in your every movement."

"What do you mean?"

"The hue of your skin and the shape of your face tell me you are a halfblood, but you move like one raised among Nakkiga's nobility. Am I right?"

"You are," she said, nettled by the accuracy of his guess. "Is there more that you can see of my past merely by looking, Queen's Huntsman?"

He showed the hint of another self-satisfied smile. Mortals, even this one, were so over-generous with their thoughts, Nezeru thought: their faces were like books, with everything written there. "It is not only your proud posture that tells me you were raised in a noble house before you joined your order," he said. "You clearly learned the *Hao sa-Rashi*—the Way of the Exiles that is taught to children of the higher clans. And the stiffness with which you still perform some of the gestures tell me it is not long since you left the house of your childhood."

"How so?"

"As your people grow older, their performance of the ancient gestures grows smoother and less careful. Among the eldest—in the queen's Landborn advisers, for instance—it is impossible to tell that they have ever expressed themselves or moved in any other way."

Nezeru was a bit taken aback: whatever else he might be, this mortal was no fool. But she was also beginning to enjoy the game. "Let me tell you something about yourself, then," she said. "You had a teacher, the sort that slaves do not usually have. You learned the fighting arts and even horsemanship before you left the slave life. And you have tried to *unlearn* the same sort of rote gestures you mock in me, at least enough to pass for an ordinary Rimmersman among your own kind." She was gratified by a slight shift at the edge of his mouth—a strike! "Now why would you do such a thing, try to disguise how you were raised?"

"I give you honor, Sacrifice Nezeru. Your eye is keen, although I had spoken of my teacher Xoka before. But the reason I had to unlearn the gestures taught me as a child slave should be obvious. As one of the queen's huntsmen, I range the whole of these lands from the border of her domain down into Rimmersgard—and occasionally, as this time, all the way into the northern reaches of Erkynland. I must deal with other mortals that I meet in my travels, and I often trade in their villages. What do you think I would receive instead of jerked meat and grain if they knew I was one of Queen Utuk'ku's slave-catchers?"

"A noose, perhaps. And an iron cage for your bones." Now she smiled, with the conscious desire to show him how pleasant it would be to see him thus. "I hear that the bodies of traitors are often hung along the borders of the mortal lands, to show what the rest of your kind think of those who take the Norn queen's silver, as they say."

"Exactly."

They rode in silence for a while. Far ahead, Nezeru could see the humped silhouette of the giant, like a moving snowdrift. Behind him, Makho spoke with Saomeji, with Kemme following a little way behind. More and more in these last days the chieftain and the Singer seemed to be in deep conversation, often arguing, and Nezeru wished she knew why. She also wondered why Saomeji's master Akhenabi had allowed her to remain with this hand when Makho had wanted her sent back to Nakkiga for punishment. Their mission was important, of course, but surely the Lord of Song could have picked any one of dozens to replace her from his own entourage of Singers and Sacrifice-trained guards. And Akhenabi, in the plundering of her thoughts, could not have failed to learn that she had lied about being with child. Why had that also been ignored? Certainly the arch-Singer had not informed Makho, who clearly still believed her lie.

"If I am right, as I think I am, that you are young for your kind," Jarnulf said abruptly, as if he had been listening to her thoughts, "how have *you* come to join this grave undertaking—whatever it may be?"

"I was top of my file in the Order of Sacrifice." She could hear the tightness in her own voice, and was unhappy with herself. Was it so obvious that she, too, had wondered at the same thing? "I killed six armed slaves with my bare hands. I crippled two rival Sacrifices in the Games. I can fight as well as any male and better than most."

"Oh, I am certain," he said. "But still, files pass through the Order of Sacrifice every few years, don't they? There must have been dozens of other warriors who reached equally high rank in their own time, and who have been blooded since in actual battle.

"Because you have not been in real battle before our fight with the Erkynlanders, have you?"

She was surprised by how that stung her. "A bad guess, mortal. I have been in many fights, many struggles," she said almost too quickly, thinking of the islanders she had slaughtered, but also of the one she had let escape.

"Ah." Irritatingly, he acted as though she had agreed with him. "So who are your parents, Sacrifice? They must be powerful indeed to secure such an important posting for their daughter while she is still so young."

"My youth means nothing."

"Really? It certainly means something to me. Your people live to be a hundred times as old as mine—and yet I would wager that despite your high position and honors, I have lived longer than you have in this world, beneath these stars." He spread his fingers toward the night sky. "I have seen twenty-eight summers. How many have you seen?"

"Meaningless." She kept her face immobile, but now she wanted to kill him and silence his mockery. "You jab at me so you do not have to answer any questions of your own."

The pale blue eyes surveyed her. "Then I apologize. I suppose, in a way, I am a guest, and should be better behaved. Question away, Sacrifice. Is there something about me that warrants your interest?"

"Interest? Perhaps." Nezeru knew she had lost her calm. She silently repeated the Prayer of Loyal Servants until she could think with her customary clarity. "Your arrows are different than ours," she said at last.

He raised his eyebrows in feigned surprise. "Well, *that* is certainly cause for concern."

"Not in and of itself, no. But yours are fletched with hawk or eagle feathers. We Sacrifices use feathers from the black goose."

"Do you want a contest, then, to see whose arrows fly most truly? I may not be Hikeda'ya, but nobody yet has complained of my skill with a bow."

"I do not seek a contest—although it might be interesting to have such a thing one day, you and I." Now she allowed herself to smile, just a little. It felt like power, like lifting her cloak to display a sharp blade. "But I followed you down the hill that night we escaped the mortal army and I saw many arrows with that fletching. They were all sticking into trees."

For a moment he rode in silence. "I'm afraid I don't understand you, Sacrifice."

"Oh, I think you do, Freedman. For someone who professes to be a skilled archer, you seem to have hit very few mortal targets."

He dismissed it with a shake of his head. "The hills were full of mortals that night. They were all around us before we broke for freedom. Surely I am not responsible for every arrow that was not feathered with black goose."

"No. But few of our mortal enemies would have been shooting from behind us, so I still have trouble understanding how so many arrows in the line of our downhill charge would have missed their target—unless the trees *were* the target."

The mortal's face was a mask, as blank at that of any Hikeda'ya at his or her duty. "Do you have a point, Sacrifice?"

"Call me Nezeru, please. I think we have passed that stage of formality, don't you? After all, we have fought together, killed mortals together, and now we ride together. And I will call you 'Jarnulf'. Or is that not your true name?"

"As true as any." He looked at her with what she gauged to be a little more respect than previously. "But you still have not answered my question. Who gave you your mortal blood?"

She considered for a moment. "My mother. She is of Rimmersgard, like you."

"A slave also, like me and the rest of my family?"

"Not exactly." And that was true—there really was no precedent for the relationship between Nezeru's noble father and her outlander mother. "But I think she would recognize much of your life."

"I hope not, Lady Nezeru. Because I would not wish my life on anyone." Suddenly, surprisingly, he spurred his horse ahead and did not slow until he had reached a position halfway between Nezeru and leaders of the company.

Yes, she thought, not without pleasure. *It will be a long, slow game with this one.*

His earliest memories were of the cold, of huddling in the slave barracks with the other children. The winds that descended from the Nornfells and swirled around great Stormspike seemed always to be in motion, always searching for a way into the crude buildings, and their whistling song haunted his childhood. Even crushed in with other shivering children, thin bodies pressed together like mouslings in a nest of rags, Jarnulf was never warm.

He remembered the cold, and of course the hunger. The Hikeda'ya did not consider children fit for any but the lightest of labors until they had reached a certain size, usually at about ten years of age, so they did not concern themselves overmuch with feeding the slaves' offspring. Those who showed themselves strong enough to survive would be worth keeping, but those that did not were a waste of good grain, so children were given just enough thin gruel to keep them alive. If some of the larger took food from the smaller, it only proved the stronger were more worthy of life and would bring their owners more value. The sickly were left to die. For centuries, that had been the way among the Hikeda'ya with their own children—why should the spawn of mortal slaves be treated any differently?

Jarnulf had known his mother Ragna for only a few years of his young life, and although he felt certain he still remembered her face, he could never be quite sure. What he did remember was her voice, one of the few gentle things of his childhood, lovely, soft, and sweet as birdsong. Her quiet words, as they huddled together at night trying not to wake the others, were his only memories of comfort. She told him stories of her family and of his people, and even taught him the rudiments of reading and writing in the old runes their ancestors had brought across the ocean to Osten Ard. But when he was only eight years old—his brother Jarngrimnur a year younger, and his sister Gret barely four years of age—another female slave died, and their mother was moved into the castle to replace her. Jarnulf and his brother and sister never saw her again.

For the younger ones, Jarnulf did his best to take her place, especially for little Gret, wrapping the child in his arms as the long nights crept past and the wind tugged and probed at the cracks in the cold stone buildings the Hikeda'ya called the "slave barns." Some nights Gret shivered for hours, even in her sleep. His brother suffered too, and in the first winter after their mother left, Jarngrimnur died of the sweating sickness and his body was carted away to the Field of the Nameless to be burned.

The slave barns and the slaves themselves belonged to White Snail Castle, one of the last great estates still remaining in Nakkiga-That-Was, the city outside the mountain, which had once spread far beyond the base of great Stormspike. The old city had been a miracle of fluted stone and wide causeways, of great stone houses and walls, but now it was largely fallen into ruin. Still, a few of the older families had refused to withdraw inside the mountain; they kept to the old ways, living in the ancient gyrfalcon castles perched on the mountainside, supervising their own slaves and Bound farmers instead of leaving the work to overseers who were slaves themselves. The masters of White Snail Castle and the other outside estates raised sheep and cattle and horses on the terraced hillsides of Stormspike's eastern foothills, living the way their ancestors had when they first came to this land of exile they called *Do'sae né-Sogeyu*—the Shadow Garden.

Jarnulf had gained more from his mother and his long-lost father than merely his slender, strong build, his height, and his knowledge of the old runes. His mother had also taught him to watch and to think, had showed him that the way to defeat strength was not always simply to be stronger.

"Do not mistake me," she had told him more than once. "We are strong too, even though we are slaves. Remember, we come of the Jarn clan—the Iron clan—and the fairies have always hated iron and feared its power." Again and again Ragna had insisted he learn to keep his temper, reminded him that there were other ways to fight, even to win. "Cleverness can save you where strength or size cannot," she had told him, illustrating it with the story of how the fire god Loken once tricked the king of the ogres. "Patience can do it, too, because Time can do what men cannot."

Jarnulf had liked that story in particular because he knew about giants. He often saw the massive creatures at work—the Hikeda'ya called them *Raoni*—moving heavy rocks and beams for their masters, because the giants were slaves just like Jarnulf. Seeing them, he had realized that there were some enemies he would never be strong enough to fight, and it was a lesson he would not forget. Thus, when their mother was taken away to be a house slave, instead of attacking the Hikeda'ya overseers who came for her, young Jarnulf had held in his anger until he felt scorched inside, but had said and done nothing.

Cleverness can do it, he had told himself over and over, though his blood seemed to boil inside him. *Patience can also do it,* he had thought, clutching the favorite saying of Ragna's even as she was led away, not even allowed to look back, *because Time can do what men cannot.* But it had been a bitter day and the wound had never healed.

As he had grown older he had begun to be chosen for the sort of jobs that the Hikeda'ya gave to young slaves, cutting black barley on the steep hillsides until his skin itched all over, and carrying water to the harvesters, rubbish to the midden, and nightsoil to the fields. In this way he began to come into contact with the children of his Hikeda'ya masters. The estate that surrounded White Snail Castle was like a little city, and housed many kinds of people. The giants and the changeling creatures called Pengi seemed little more than animals, and were considered lower even than Jarnulf and his mortal kind, but several castes of Hikeda'ya lived in the castle as well—the Bound, the Pledged, and the Recognized. The Bound were the farmers, who had only a little more freedom than the slaves, but were still Hikeda'ya: even the meanest and lowest of them had life or death power over any mortal. The Pledged were the master's soldiers and other important servants and functionaries. And of course the master and his family were of the Recognized, the caste of those who had been confirmed in the ranks of nobility by the queen herself.

Jarnulf hardly ever saw the children of the Recognized, who were raised and educated in the castle's great keep, but the young sons and daughters of the Pledged came every day to a fallow field near the slave barns, a place put aside for the purpose of training them in the arts of war, since all Hikeda'ya except the Bound were taught to fight.

At first Jarnulf only watched them when he could snatch a moment of freedom. He was especially fascinated by the old, sharp-faced Hikeda'ya who supervised them. It was hard to guess the years of Jarnulf's masters, who did not age as mortals did, but this teacher moved with a certain lack of hurry that suggested experience, and he did not leave his hair white as most of the other men did, but colored it a shade of witchwood gray that had fallen from fashion long before Jarnulf or even his grandparents had been born.

He learned that the old man was a famous swordsman and one-time Sacrifice commander named Denabi sey-Xoka. None of the other slaves knew much more than that about him, but everyone on the estate could hear his piercing voice as he shouted at, directed, and mocked his students, Hikeda'ya youth only a little older and bigger than Jarnulf himself. The young slave was grateful for that voice, which he could hear even at a distance, and which allowed him to memorize most of what the old warrior was telling his charges.

Soon Jarnulf had begun hurrying through whatever work he was given so that he could steal a few moments near the edge of the training field, watching the young Hikeda'ya learn to wield sword and spear and shoot a bow. After a while, frustrated by having no weapon of his own, Jarnulf sat up nights after his sister had fallen asleep and made himself a wooden sword from scraps, tying stones to it with stolen twine to give it enough weight for proper practice. He kept it hidden in a stand of birch trees near the training ground, and would lurk in their shade, blocked (as he thought) from the view of the young warriors at work, and imitate what they were being taught.

When the keen-eyed Hikeda'ya students finally noticed him, as had been more or less inevitable, retribution was swift and painful. A half dozen of them broke away from the main group and ran toward him. Before Jarnulf could get away, they vaulted the fence and surrounded him. For a few moments he held them at bay, whirling his wooden blade and dodging their first attacks, but before long they moved in close and overwhelmed him with numbers. They beat him with the flats of their swords until he fell to the ground, then beat him some more, and ended by kicking his limp form until he thought he would die from pain and lack of breath. At last they lost interest. After breaking his wooden sword and scattering the pieces over him like funeral flowers, the children of his masters wandered back to their practice.

Jarnulf lay for a long time with his belly against the ground and his face in the cold, wet dirt, wanting to get up, or at least to crawl off and hide his shame, but his ribs were aching so badly he could not push himself upright. He felt the sun move across the sky, and knew that if he could not climb to his feet he would lie out all night, and that would mean death. But every movement seemed to grind something broken inside of him against something else equally damaged. He wept silently as the wind began to increase.

"By the Garden, what is lying here?" The voice was cheerful but mocking. "Is it a little mouse that the cat has played with? Poor mouse. Happy cat."

Jarnulf tried to roll over to see who was talking, but the pain was too great.

"Or is it a fish that has climbed out of Lake Rumiya and tried to walk like an animal? How strange, to find a fish so far from water."

It was maddening. Jarnulf pulled his knees underneath himself, letting out a gasp of agony as he felt all the bruised places, the cracked places. He choked down a cry—it came out as a gurgle from behind his clenched teeth—and at last managed to push himself up to where he could see who was talking. It was Xoka himself, the old warrior who trained the Pledged, staring down at him with an amused look. Older Hikeda'ya had much the same appearance as younger, but the effect of centuries of sun and wind showed up at last even on their near-ageless faces. Xoka was less fine-featured than younger male Hikeda'ya, as though his face had been carved with blunt, crude tools.

Jarnulf crouched on his hands and knees. It was hard to hold his head up.

"Do you have a name, little mouse, little fish?" the weapons master asked. "Or are you a dog? You look like a dog, down on all fours that way."

Why should this important fellow go out of his way to mock a dying slave? Jarnulf kept his mouth closed.

"But your tail is not wagging," said Xoka. "I will call you *San'nakuno*—Sad Little Dog." He walked closer. The swordsman wore the loose black garb of a soldier, but with no signs of rank, and his white feet were bare. One of his slender, callused hands probed along Jarnulf's side, feeling the damage where the students had kicked him over and over again. "I like dogs," Xoka said, "especially dogs with spirit. I will offer you a bargain. If you can get yourself back to the slave quarters tonight, and come to me tomorrow after your work is finished, I will teach you how to bite the way a dog should. Would you like that?"

Jarnulf did not understand him—*bite*? He kept silent.

"Or you may stay here. Nobody else will help you, as you should know—here strays are left to die." And so saying, the old Hikeda'ya turned and walked back toward the practice field.

The sun was long gone behind the great mountain by the time Jarnulf finally managed to get onto his feet and began staggering back to the slave barracks. He shivered through the night, the cold so fierce that when he finally slept he dreamed that he had died, that he lay beside his brother Jarngrimnur on a burning funeral boat like their ancient ancestors. But the next day he dragged himself up from bed when the summoning bell rang and limped out to his work.

Z'ue Xoka was waiting for him as he'd said he would be. The old master said nothing, only threw Jarnulf a practice sword and commanded, "Show me the twelve starting positions, San'nakuno."

From that hour forward Jarnulf had a teacher. The lessons were only when the old swordsman was in the mood, and did not happen every day, at least at first, but often enough that Jarnulf always had something new to practice at night when the other slaves were asleep. He again took to sneaking from the barracks so he could practice his movements with the wooden sword he hid in the trees near the slave barn. Even the coldest weather would find him out of doors working through the silent dance of attack and defense, his feet and hands turning blue from the chill. Some nights he barely made it back into his bed before the bell rang, summoning him out to work once more.

Xoka never said so, but he seemed impressed by the boy's capacity to learn and the diligence with which he worked. Still, he treated Jarnulf at least as roughly as he did the children of the masters: he hardly ever spoke, and made most of his corrections with the flat of his own blade, swift, painful blows to Jarnulf's exposed wrist or undefended skull, but he gave fewer and fewer of these as time passed.

As he grew out of childhood and toward manhood, Jarnulf felt himself to be living two lives, the dream life of his working hours and his true life, those hours spent defending himself against Xoka with Shadow Form and Water Form, then countering with one of the intricacies of attack. When he did well enough that the master would retreat from him with a slight smile, Jarnulf felt that he had found his true purpose in the world.

What he only understood later was that Denabi sey-Xoka had not taken an interest in him as a person, but as an object to be trained. The old Hikeda'ya found great satisfaction in knowing that he could train even a mongrel pup—a mortal!—to fight as well as the highborn children of his race. In a way, Jarnulf eventually came to realize, he was no more real to the weapons-master than a chunk of soapstone that a bored man whose great days had passed might carve into a fetish of a god or a likeness of a beloved hound. Jarnulf was not a person to Xoka, he was a pastime.

But Jarnulf did not know it for a long while, and several years passed before he understood it—years that were the best of his young life.

Then one day the soldiers of the Hamakha came and took his sister Gret away.

"You have been silent a long time," Nezeru said.

Jarnulf blinked his eyes. He had been staring at the way ahead without really seeing it, the great broad track the giant had made, the snow lifted on either side like a frozen ocean wave. "I was . . . remembering something."

"That, I guessed."

She truly was a strange one, this Sacrifice. She had all but told him that she knew he had not tried to kill the Erkynlander soldiers during their escape. He suspected that she had doubts about the arrow he had shot from the hillside as well. But at the same time, she seemed more curious about him than mistrustful. Hikeda'ya as young as she was hardly ever reached the frontier beyond Nakkiga's inner borders, but the few that he had met were usually full of unshakeable belief, not only in the Queen and the Holy Garden, but in the disgusting, animal lowliness of mortals. What made this one different?

She was part mortal herself, of course, but he had lived with halfbloods in the slave barracks, and if anything they had been more hateful to the other mortals than the pureblood overseers had been. The Hikeda'ya had bred with humans all Jarnulf's life. It was not as common among the highest noble clans, and was virtually unheard of among the few oldest, Landborn families, but it was not unusual. What *was* rare was that a halfblood like Nezeru should reach such a position of trust at such a young age. Even mortal youths in mortal lands were seldom so honored.

No, there was a mystery there, but without knowing more about her father and his place in the ranks of the queen's servitors, Jarnulf could only speculate. And speculation, he had learned, was often the enemy of action.

All that is important is how she may best be used. Because I am sworn to a holy duty, and I will not fail You, my God.

"Do you not sometimes wonder at the tricks fate plays?" he said aloud.

Her face at first seemed to hold only contempt, but he thought there might be a glimmer of something else there as well. Unease?

"There is no fate," she said. "There are no tricks. I do what the queen bids me to do. That is the only path, and if I stay on the path, there is no confusion— no tricks, as you would call it."

"I speak of one thing, you speak of another," he said, then looked to make sure they were still well behind the others before he continued. "I speak of unlikeliness, you call it confusion, as if the world conspired against you. I will try a different path. How likely is it that you should be given such an honor, Sacrifice Nezeru, to serve as a Queen's Talon, when hundreds upon hundreds of other Sacrifices, older and more experienced, were passed over?"

"You asked this before. I answered you. I earned my place."

"But if you are so valuable, so rare, why is it that your chieftain has punished you so savagely?"

She darted him a look that was little short of hateful. "You know nothing of me, mortal. Of any of us."

"I have seen your back, the scars you bear. They are not all completely healed. Do not fear I was spying on you—the sight came by accident. You are very modest for one of your race. Most of your folk treat nakedness as nothing, perhaps because unlike we poor mortals, you feel little cold. But you are different, Sacrifice Nezeru, careful—or perhaps only shy of displaying your wounds. Still, I saw them."

Her face had gone quite pale. He thought she looked as lifeless as carved marble. "I earned that punishment. I failed my duty."

"Still. Still. You spoke once of your father as we rode a few days ago. He is always very busy now that the queen is awake, you said. I guess that he is an important noble in high office. Am I right?"

She looked now as though she wished to get away from him. She truly was young, he thought: for all her bland exterior, for all the Hikeda'ya reserve, she had not entirely learned to hide her feelings. Jarnulf had long been a hunter, and Norns had long been his quarry—his prey. He could see her thoughts moving uncomfortably behind her rigid expression.

"Who are you to ask me questions?" she said. "Why do you not go and ask Makho about *his* father?"

"Because then I would have to fight him, and one of us would die. Either way, it would diminish our chances in the dangerous lands ahead. But you are different than Hand Chieftain Makho. He knows nothing but what he has been taught, and he is content with that. You are not, although such confusion—that was your word, wasn't it? Confusion?—such confusion frightens you. That is plain. But why?"

"Your questions are pointless and unwanted, mortal. In fact, I think more than ever that you mean some harm to this hand and its mission."

"Nothing could be further from the truth. I want this mission to succeed." And Jarnulf did not have to worry about hiding his actual feelings this time, because he was not lying.

Despite the similarity of their faces and shapes to those of mortals, or even to that of the Hikeda'ya themselves, Viyeki could never quite make himself believe that the Pengi, the Tinukeda'ya changelings, were much more than animals. The oldest Builders in his order claimed to recall a time when even the lowest of them could talk, but it was hard to believe that now. And when he looked into the empty, cowlike eyes of the Carry-men currently standing beside the great capstan as they waited for a command from their overseer, Viyeki found the whole idea even more incomprehensible.

"Step into the cart, please, High Magister," said a voice behind him. "We have a long journey still to go."

Viyeki turned to the tall soldier in the silvery dragon mask. "Tell me your name again, officer, so that I may know who to blame if this adventure goes wrong."

The guard inclined his head. "I am Hamakha First Armiger S'yessu. I am commissioned by the queen herself for special service."

Viyeki looked at the soldier's surcoat, at the simple maze he wore as an insignia. "But you wear only the Hamakha helm, not the Hamakha crest."

"That is why I am called an armiger, High Magister."

"Then who do you serve? Not Queen Utuk'ku."

"We all serve the queen, High Magister."

"Just tell me who has sent for me, rousing me from my home in my hour of rest. If it is the palace, why we are not going there?"

The guard's voice did not change. "I am forbidden to tell more than I have, High Magister. But you will learn all soon enough if you will simply step into the cart."

Whatever his summoners planned, it was clearly not meant to be secret. Nearly everyone in his household, his wife Khimabu, his secretary, and many of his servants, had seen the soldier and his labyrinth token waiting at the front door, the token that usually symbolized a summons to the Omei'yo Palace. But the messenger had stated in front of all of them that they were bound for somewhere other than the Maze, and that none of High Magister Viyeki's retinue could attend him. Khimabu had balked at this, of course, insisting her husband wait until more comprehensible orders were sent, but Viyeki had weathered the deadly court politics of Nakkiga for a long time; he was even a bit intrigued by such an unusual summons.

Still, he did not like the wide, steaming vent that now confronted him here, below the city, or the ancient cart and capstan waiting to lower him even farther into the deeps of the great mountain.

"I cannot believe that the queen would wish to meet me in such a place," he said.

"The queen is not here, High Magister," the guard said. "That at least I can tell you."

"His lordship Akhenabi? High Celebrant Zuniyabe?"

The guard shook his head. "Please, High Magister. The cart awaits us."

After a long moment's consideration, Viyeki stepped into the mine cart. The dragon-helmed guard entered behind him and closed the barred door, then gave a signal to the overseer of the Carry-men. The huge creatures, only slightly smaller than wild giants, began to crank the capstan.

The massive ropes creaked as the cart shuddered down into the depths, past level after level, each a dark doorway into the roots of the mountain, where Carry-men and other slaves dug for sulfur and gold. As the cart bumped and shook, Viyeki felt the air grow warmer and ever closer, until it pressed at his ears. There was something else pushing at him too, a discomfort he could queasily detect just at the edge of his senses, but could not identify.

At last the cart groaned to a halt, and the guard in the serpent mask pushed the door open. "Go forward, High Magister."

The queasy feeling had grown stronger. For the first time, he felt real reluctance. "What about you?"

"I have a passenger to carry back, then I will return for you." The guard sounded impatient at Viyeki's hesitation. "You must not fear, High Magister."

Viyeki got out and walked down the low passage. His trained eye told him it had been cut through the mountain long, long ago, or at least with stone tools, not metal or witchwood as used in more recent eras. The strange discomfort inside him grew stronger, as though he stood in the bow of a pitching ship; the heat of the place brought out sweat on his skin. He slowed, but that did not stem the sensation, so he silently said the Prayer for the Queen's Strength and continued forward.

The corridor turned and bent, then suddenly opened out into a great cavern, this one untouched by tools of any kind, or so it looked to his practiced eye. Shifting red and yellow light turned the entire cavern the color of fire, and in its center a large crevasse belched steam and smoke, as though he were in some smaller version of the Chamber of the Well. From time to time flames darted upward from the cleft in the stone like the tongue of a hungry dragon. Other than that movement, the rocky chamber seemed empty, though the sensations of heat and oppression had grown even more powerful. He no longer felt only a sickness in his guts, but something stronger, a kind of growing terror that clutched at his chest and dried his mouth and throat.

What place is this? A cavern so far below the excavation levels? No Builder had a hand in this, not in my lifetime.

Viyeki stared for long moments into the shifting light and clouds at the center of the chamber before he realized that a mote of darkness drifting high in the clouds of steam above the crevasse was something more. In fact, it had arms and legs and wore a billowing cloak. The tightening of his chest increased. His heart sped.

Have they hung someone there? he thought in sudden shock. *Is this a place of execution? May the Garden defend me, was my family right to fear? Is that why I've been brought to this hidden place?* He stopped, unwilling to go closer to the pit and the slowly moving shadow that dangled high above it.

"I wonder how long he would fall if I pushed him in," someone said just beside his ear. "Would he cook on the way down?"

Even Viyeki, veteran of centuries in the conspiratorial darkness of Nakkiga, nearly cried out in horrified surprise. He whirled, his hand dropping to the knife on his belt.

Jijibo the Dreamer stood behind him, Utuk'ku's strange, many-times-great-grandnephew, his narrow face bobbing up and down.

"Lord Jijibo, you startled me." Viyeki's eyes turned helplessly back to the figure hanging so high above them in the wavering haze and orange light. "Who is that? Why was I brought here?"

"Does he truly not know?" the queen's kinsman said. "I did not think him such a fool. Does he not remember that I told him his family had been noticed?" And then, a moment later, without change of tone: "Yes, I *would* like to have a dried salmon for my meal today." Now Jijibo pointed a bony finger toward the dark shape floating high in the plume of steam: "Only look, Magister Viyeki. The answer to both your questions waits there."

Viyeki stared at the figure. "You mean, that's not a prisoner?"

"Oh, a prisoner, yes, most definitely," said the Dreamer. "But not of the sort you mean. Hmmm, hmmm, yes, I do wonder what it would be like to flay all your skin from your body."

In his previous encounters with Jijibo, Viyeki had learned that it was best to pretend most of the things the mad one said had not been spoken aloud, no matter how dire or shocking. "I still do not understand you, Lord Dreamer. *Who* has summoned me?"

"I cannot stay to talk, noble Lord Viyeki," Jijibo said with a touch of impatience. "One day when we are dead, we will all smell like this, did you know? The snake in the apple cart is waiting to take me back to my chambers, you see." He grinned. The Dreamer looked like something poorly made, his skin pulled a little too tight over his bones, his eyes a little too wide. Even his teeth were crooked. "Look at him frown!" he said. "And he has not even met the whisperer yet. How I would love to have that halfblood daughter of his! I would not take her skin off, no, no. Too crude. How would I learn anything?"

Finished with words, Jijibo then made a huge, exaggerated bow and strode off in the direction from which Viyeki had come, presumably to the waiting mine cart. Viyeki watched him go, confused and disturbed by what Jijibo had said about his daughter. Only a moment later did he hear the other thing that the Dreamer had said.

Whisperer, he thought. *Does he truly mean—?*

Our time is short, a voice said, and the shock of it made his skin crawl. This time the words were not spoken into his ear but seemed to form directly in his thoughts. It was not the queen's voice in his head this time, but something more strained and distant, as though it drifted to him down a long, long tunnel. *Ignore the holy fool,* the voice continued on, and the words felt harsh and dry as bits of drifting ash. *He is not part of what you must do.*

Viyeki spun, heart racing even faster, but whoever had spoken was not behind him, nor anywhere in sight. Then a movement at the edge of his vision tugged his gaze upward once more. The dark figure in the billowing cloak was being lowered from the heights, spinning down slowly through the steam and flickering firelight of the great vent.

No, not lowered, Viyeki saw a moment later. There were no wires, no ropes, no noose. He had never seen anything like it, not from the great sorcerer Akhenabi, not from Queen Utuk'ku herself.

"What do you want of me?" he cried, and was shamed by the frightened quaver in his own voice.

As the robed figure drifted down to float just above the crevice, he saw that the face peering from the hood was featureless, covered in bandages, not even eyes or mouth left uncovered. Viyeki shuddered. He knew now who had summoned him, but the knowledge did not slow his pounding heart. The shape stopped, drifting slightly in the hot air rising from the fiery crevice. A terrible aura of death washed over the magister—not a scent, but something deeper, something beyond his physical senses, a terror that made his mind quail in disgust and fear.

I am one of the queen's high nobles, he told himself, although he could scarcely think. He measured his breaths until he could summon the strength to speak. "Lady Ommu, the Whisperer," he said, and even the name in his mouth was fearsome. "Great mistress, was it you who summoned this humble servant of the queen?"

For a long moment the faceless thing did not reply, and he was certain it must be listening to the terrified thundering of his blood. Even the queen herself had never filled him with such dread.

Magister Viyeki, I have watched you. The thoughts came in whispering fragments, as if carried on an inconstant wind, and scratched at his thoughts like the claws of rats. *From the wasteland of death, I have seen things even the queen could not see as she drifted in the* yi'indra *through the land of dreams and endings. I have seen your bloodline, like a shining road, leading to this moment and to all that will come after.*

Everything in him urged him to turn, to run, but Viyeki forced himself to stand instead and answer that terrible whisper with the steadiest voice he could manage.

"I cannot believe I am anything to you, great mistress. Not to one of the Red Hand. Not to one who has twice returned from the other side of death."

You are much to me . . . because of the web of circumstance. Beyond death . . . I could see many things. Each word seemed to echo slowly through Viyeki's head. *You are part of the great perhaps. Soon the queen will give you a task, but your blood tells me that you have an even greater task to come . . . that of saving the Hikeda'ya race. Do you understand, little magister? Vast things . . . are now in motion.*

He bowed his head, not in piety, but because it was impossible to look for long at the unnatural light seeping from between Ommu's bandages where a face should be. "Two tasks, but only one of them from the Mother of All? I do not understand you, Mistress."

No, you do not, said the Whisperer, her voice like a wind from the loneliest place that ever existed. *You cannot. Remember this only. I have come from beyond death itself—from the shores of Unbeing. I can tell only truth. And I say that to complete that greater task, a moment will come when you will have to choose.*

"What . . . what do you mean, Mistress?"

To save what you love, you will be forced to kill that which you love even more. If you fail, all will fall to pieces. Your people—and they are my people, too—will die and vanish from the world.

Viyeki felt suddenly helpless, sickened. "But why me, Mistress? My blood is as nothing compared to the greatest of our people!"

The voice came at last, as thin as if it had blown to him from beyond the moon and stars. *You might as well ask why up is not down . . . or dark is not light. It is ordered so. And I cannot tell anything but truth. Now leave me. I wish to bathe in the blood of the earth. I am cold here in your world, you see . . . so cold!*

Ommu abruptly turned her back on him, the hooded robe swirling more slowly than seemed right. She drifted upward once more until she was only a spot of darkness high in the wafting flames, like a spider waiting inconspicuously at the edge of its web.

Viyeki did not bow, but stumbled out of the cavern as fast as he could, hurrying toward the mine cart and the long shaft that would carry him back to a place that made better sense. His skin was cold as ice, his heart a loose stone rattling in his chest. The chief Builder, who had spent countless years in the deep places of the earth, had never in his life wanted so badly to smell fresh air, and maybe even see a glimpse of light from the true sky.

31

A High, Dark Place

"There will be wine," Astrian promised. "Good wine. Captain Kenrick has promised to roll out several casks of Perdruin claret. That's worth an earful of boring soldier's talk, isn't it?"

Because Morgan had not yet been able to pay Hatcher the publican, they were ensconced in *The Jackdaw* this evening instead of *The Quarely Maid*, their usual port of call.

"Nothing is worth that sort of boredom," said Olveris, ending his most recent silence. "That's why I'm starting to get drunk now. So I can stand it until the Perdruin is opened."

"You make light of it, but Sir Zakiel deserves this honor," said Porto, frowning at them. "The Order of the Red Drake is not one of your cheapjack trinkets, given to anyone who can bow deep enough to impress the court. It is a warrior's honor!"

"Will you truly not come, Highness?" Astrian asked Morgan. "It should be an amusing time."

The prince shook his head. "My grandfather will be there. Hell's hammers, *both* my grandfathers will be there. They will drink too much and spend the night telling old war stories. And they will both glare at me because I haven't been in any wars."

"That is nothing to be ashamed of," said Porto seriously. "Rather, it is something to inspire gratitude."

"Easy for you to say, man. You've been to war. You've all been to war. That's the first thing anyone thinks when they see any one of you—'Oh, there's a soldier.' What's the first thing they think of when they see me? 'Ah, the prince. He's quite spoiled, you know. Just drinks all day and dices.'"

"Yes, but you drink and dice with us, the brave soldiers," Astrian said, smiling. "That has to count for something."

Morgan was not in the mood to be amused. The hard words he had heard from the king still echoed in his thoughts. "No, I'm not going. The last thing I want to do is hear how the Erkynguard protected me from danger when the Norns attacked. I would have fought! It's not my fault I was forbidden to come out by the queen."

"It's not your fault," Astrian said. "Nor are you the only one who missed out. I was on the mountainside, but only dodged a few arrows. I never even saw any of the fairies."

"But you've been in fights and battles a-plenty. Nobody's going to think you're a coward."

"Nobody thinks you're a coward, Highness," Porto said.

"Hah! Everybody does. The nobles at court and the people in Erchester. Did you hear them when we rode in? Half of them were calling me Tosspot and Prince More-Wine. I heard them."

"And the other half were cheering you," Astrian said. "It is a known truth that the people are fickle, my prince. They are like children who do not know what they want. Offer them milk, they cry. Take the milk away, they cry even harder."

"Or piss all over you," said Olveris.

"Just so." Astrian poured Morgan another cup. "Go on, take this and warm your blood enough to come with us. You'll enjoy the evening."

"No." Morgan pushed himself upright, then got to his feet, although not without a few adjustments; he did not actually feel very well, and hadn't all morning. Waking up with an aching head was not as appealing a sign of maturity as it had been a year earlier, when he had first begun drinking steadily with Astrian and the others. "I'm going to find something else to do. I wish you well, gentlemen. I hope Kenrick's Perdruin is as fine as everyone has said."

He got up and started toward the door as steadily as he could, then remembered the royal guards who would be waiting for him in front of the inn. He turned back across the tavern toward the back door and the privy yard.

"Our young prince is troubled these days," he heard old Porto say as he passed near his friends' table. Sir Astrian's reply was lost in the noises of a drunken argument outside as Morgan pushed the door open, but he did hear the others laugh.

Morgan realized long before he reached the residence that the last thing he wanted to do was go to bed, but he had left himself with very little chance for company or diversion. Most of the Erkynguard were either at the Red Drake banquet or on duty. The keep's several guardrooms were empty except for a few old veterans nursing their bones in front of the fire, and he already owed money to the participants of the one dice game he found going on at the Nearulagh Gate guardhouse.

As a strategist, I'm a complete failure, he thought to himself. *Trying to avoid my grandparents, I have maneuvered myself into a night of boredom and loneliness.*

Even as he crossed into the castle's Middle Bailey he could hear the festivities down at the town hall in Erchester. From the shouts and laughter and off-key songs floating on the wind, Sir Zakiel's comrades in arms were swiftly working their way through the claret. Most of the Hayholt must be with them, Morgan thought, because they certainly were not to be seen anywhere here. All around him the shops and houses were shuttered for the night.

Morgan was still in the grip of a prickly anger that even the cool evening had not soothed, and for some reason the silence of the nighttime castle was nettling him more than the sounds of distant merriment from Main Row. For the third or fourth time since entering the Hayholt he considered returning to Erchester, not to attend the banquet at the town hall but to go in search of some less public entertainments, but though he knew the gate guards would be perfectly happy to let him out again despite the late hour, he also knew word of it would eventually get back to his grandparents.

A memory from his childhood poked at him as he made his way through the quiet, narrow streets, of an evening like this when everybody seemed to be somewhere else, a night when Morgan had found himself all alone—a Midsummer's Eve in the time just before his father had fallen ill and died. Young Morgan, seven years old, had been recovering from warmwater fever after spending more than a sennight in bed. His mother was ill with the same complaint, but where Morgan's only bedside companion was an old nurse named Cloda, Princess Idela, in her own chambers, was surrounded by ladies-in-waiting and attended by frequent visitors.

On that night, with his health mostly returned, the prince had found himself bored and in a bad temper, so he waited until Cloda had fallen asleep in a chair beside the bed, then dressed and made his way to his mother's rooms. She had been horrified to see him, certain that although he had just gone through the same fever, he would make himself ill all over again, and so Idela had made her ladies send him away. At a loss, Morgan wandered through the residence, desperate for distraction. Because he had been in bed so long, he did not remember it was Midsummer's Eve, and was puzzled and even a little worried to find everybody gone.

At last, he had left the residence and made his way across the innermost keep to his father's chambers in the Old Granary Tower—a bit less of a tower than the name indicated, really more of a roundhouse built against the wall of the Inner Keep and had turned out to be too damp to use as an actual granary. Prince John Josua kept the door firmly locked, and Morgan often had to bang on it over and over until his father finally heard him and came down, distracted and irritated. In truth, despite what he had told Porto, there had only been one time his father truly had not recognized him, and in his last year John Josua had always seemed so impatient to get back to his studies that Morgan had truly felt he might as well be some faceless servant.

But on that night, in that strange, seemingly uninhabited version of the Hayholt, his father never came, though Morgan thumped on the heavy timbers until his knuckles were sore. At last, more out of annoyance than anything else, he had yanked on the door and—to his astonishment—it swung open.

With no sign of guards and no response to any of his calls, Morgan was caught between excitement at what was suddenly being presented to him after so many years of curiosity and the knowledge that his father—who never let anyone into his private chambers in the tower—would certainly disapprove.

But something about the oddness of the evening and his enforced and overlong bed rest had made him feel more adventurous than usual, and so he had climbed the tower stairs by the flickering light of the torches ensconced at each landing, all the way to his father's chambers at the top.

That door was also unlocked, which somehow confirmed in Morgan's mind the idea that he was meant by some superior power to keep exploring, so he slipped inside. A lantern was burning on one of the tables, as though his father had only just stepped out. After so many years of wondering what his father did up there, it had turned out to be a bit disappointing. Except for its great size, the chamber did not look much different than his father's retiring room back in the residence. Several tables and benches stood around the room, and every surface was piled high with heavy old books and musty, ancient scrolls. And almost all of them seemed to be in use, propped open to a certain page or partly unrolled and then weighted by a smooth stone or another heavy book.

None of the volumes seemed to be the kind that interested Morgan, like tales of knightly adventure or histories of war and other exciting subjects, and very few were even in a language he could read, so after a certain amount of perfunctory exploration he went out again. If there was nothing worth looking at in his father's chambers, it was clearly not in his best interest to be caught and punished for the incursion.

On the ground floor he had paused, distracted slightly by a certain clamminess to the air, unusual for summer, and also by the presence of an odor he could not identify but seemed quite unlike anything he had smelled outside or on the upper floors. To his surprise, he now saw another set of stairs that led down below the ground floor. He had missed them when he came in, because they were tucked behind the stone spiral of the stairs he had just descended. A kind of wooden frame had been set across them, not to keep people out, Morgan guessed, so much as to prevent someone's stumbling into the dark stairwell by accident. He leaned over and breathed deeply. What came to him was not just damp, he realized, but something stranger, something that smelled . . . old. He did not know precisely what that meant, but his curiosity had been seized and he was just about to lift the wooden slats out of the way when the main tower door grated open, and he looked up in surprise to see his father's tall, angular form looming in the doorway.

Prince John Josua had made a strange spectacle, swaying unsteadily, eyes wide with shock. "Morgan?" he had said, and his words were slurred. "By God, boy, is that you? What are you doing here?" A scattering of rose petals were strewen in John Josua's disordered, dark hair and on his shoulders, and Morgan remembered that it was Midsummer's Eve, that the castle was doubtless so quiet because most of the inhabitants were out celebrating at the bonfires along the Hayclif.

Before Morgan could say anything, John Josua saw that the boy was leaning with his hands on the wooden gateway laid over the descending stairs. Before Morgan could speak, John Josua's eyes narrowed, and his expression changed.

"What are you doing? You are never to come in here, and you are never, never to go anywhere near those stairs! You could fall and be killed!"

Morgan had tried to protest, but before he could say anything his father had grabbed him and yanked him away from the stairwell so forcefully that Morgan had lost his footing and tumbled to the floor. John Josua, all beard and hair and wild eyes like a madman in the street, had then yanked Morgan up onto to his feet.

"Never come in here again!" his father had shouted. He smelled of wine and bonfire smoke. "It is too perilous for a child! Where are the guards? I'll have their heads for this. Is everybody around me a fool?"

Then, with no further words, he had carried Morgan to the front door of the roundhouse tower and set him down on the porch, then slammed the heavy door shut behind him.

The two of them never spoke of that night, and by the time Midsummer came again his father was gone and Morgan would never speak to him again about anything, at least not in this world.

He had almost forgotten where he was, wandering lost in memories toward the gate to the Inner Bailey, when someone spoke behind him.

"Look! Qina, it is our friend Morgan!"

He turned to see Little Snenneq and his betrothed hurrying after him across the commons. Snenneq had spread his arms wide. "We were about to go back to our beds, but here you are! Did Binabik, my father-in-law to-be, send you to find us?"

Morgan sighed. "No. I was just out walking."

Snenneq smiled broadly. "I did not think your people ever did this, unless it was necessary for them."

"Walking?"

"Going out of doors. Your people are seeming to hate it. It is the one thing I least understand. Qina has said the same, is that not right?"

"Perhaps because of smelling," she suggested.

"Smelling?" As usual, Morgan had been with the trolls only a short time and already he was confused, but in his unhappy, half-drunken mood it did not charm him the way it usually did.

"Because your people throw their *amaq* and *kukaq* right outside their homes," Snenneq explained.

"Yes," Qina said, nodding. "Into the . . . land river."

Morgan could only squint, completely lost. "Land river?"

Snenneq and Qina conferred briefly but vigorously in Qanuc. "In the street, she is meaning. The foulness is thrown into the street."

Morgan shrugged. "It's a city. That's how it is in cities."

Snenneq nodded. "And those who have wealth are making others to clean it away, so their own house does not have such the *kukaq* smell. But in other places, it is piling high!"

"I don't really want to talk about . . . *kukaq*," Morgan said. "I don't really want to talk about anything. I was on my way back to the residence. To bed."

"As we were, but this is a lucky meeting, I think." Snenneq smiled his broad, yellow smile. One thing Morgan had to admit about trolls, they seemed to have all their teeth. "Because I had questions that I had hoped for answering."

Morgan felt a strong need to silence his unhappy thoughts. "I will answer any questions if you have some *kangkang*. Do you?"

Snenneq showed the yellow grin again and pulled a drinking skin from inside his hooded jacket. Morgan took it and allowed himself a long but still cautious swallow. He had learned to drink the stuff, but it tasted like tar water, and too long a drought would send him to his knees, coughing and spluttering. However, it had the sovereign benefit of working swiftly; as he wiped his lips, he could already feel the warm *kangkang* glow in his stomach, working its way back up toward his head.

He sucked in a breath, felt the inside of his mouth tingling. "Questions?" he asked.

"Qina's father Binabik has been very busy," said Little Snenneq. "Not much time he has given to showing us your . . . what is the word? Village? Town?"

"*City*. Yes, Erchester is a city. Almost the biggest in all of Osten Ard, in fact." Most of the time he might be heartily sick of what Erchester had to offer, but he did not want it compared unfavorably to some trollish campground in the freezing mountains.

"City. Just so." Snenneq nodded. "And so we have questions. The first one is, why does everyone here go inside at night? Even in Mintahoq where the cold winds blow, people visit each other's caves."

Morgan didn't have an easy answer for that. "Tonight, many of the guards and nobles are at a celebration in Erchester City. But the rest of the time . . . well, that's just the way people do things here. Because the streets are dark. I mean, it's not so much that they're dangerous, especially not here in the castle, but people here don't . . ."

"Ah! Because streets are covered in *amaq*!" said Snenneq, clearly pleased to have the answer at last. "Your people are not visiting after dark because they do not want to walk in the filth. With certainty. Now another questioning, if you are so kind."

Morgan didn't bother to correct him. Streets were just empty at night, that was all. "More kangkang," he said instead. As the oily, burning liquid ran down his throat, he found himself growing less concerned with the ruin of his evening. Perhaps there were still ways it could be salvaged.

"Snenneq, ask Morgan Highness of the big basket," urged Qina. "What it is?"

Morgan could only goggle until Snenneq pointed past the gate of the Inner Bailey, between the close-leaning buildings. Morgan squinted until he could make out what the troll was indicating: the gray bulk of Hjeldin's Tower where it loomed above the rooftops, nestled against the keep's northern wall.

"Basket?" asked Morgan. "Do you mean the tower?"

"Yes, tower!" said Snenneq. "We have baskets that shape at home in Yiqa-nuc. We use them to cook roots. Tower. Why does no one go in or out of it? We stood before it today, and the doors are all locked and chained."

First the Granary, now this. It seemed to be a night for thinking about pro-hibited buildings, for some reason, and Morgan felt a superstitious pang. "That's called Hjeldin's Tower." *Kangkang* was spreading through his limbs now, bright and warm as sunshine, or so it felt, and the pang quickly subsided. "Nobody goes in because it's haunted."

Snenneq shook his head. "I do not know this word."

"Someone tries to kill it?" volunteered Qina, but she didn't sound too certain.

Morgan puzzled for a moment, then smiled. "Not *hunted*—haunted. When ghosts and evil spirits and demons are somewhere, that's called haunted."

Snenneq made a gesture with his closed fist. "*Kikkasut!* But if demons live there, why do your people let it remain like an honored uncle? Each day we are here I see people pulling down other stone buildings and making new ones."

"Demons don't live there anymore." Morgan was quite certain of that now, although as a child, he (along with many of the castle's other residents) had been less sure. The prince and his playmates had often dared each other to mount the stairs and touch the tower's great oak doors, or climb on the guardhouse that protected them. He could still remember the terrifying thrill of approaching that frightening, forbidden place. Now, it gave him the beginning of an idea. "Do you not know about Pryrates? I'd have thought Qina's father would have told you all about him. By all the saints, the others here never stop talking about the Red Priest." He snorted. "You'd think he still lived there. Some fools think he does." He reached out for the skin of *kangkang* and had another healthy gulp.

"We are knowing the name Pryrates, yes," said Snenneq, making the fist gesture again. "He was a priest who did terrible things in the Storm King's war, for the queen's father Elias when he was being king."

"Yes, but he wasn't just some boring priest," Morgan said. "He commanded demons. He was the one who tried to bring back the Storm King."

"Then why his . . . tower . . . now standing?" Qina asked.

"Yes," said Snenneq, "this is puzzling me, too. On Mintahoq, if a man does such things, we would be burning the inside of his cave to clean it, then fill it with dirt and rocks, but that is because a mountain cannot be broken up and pulled down."

Morgan held out his hand for the skin, then realized he was still holding it. He set out through the gate in the general direction of the tower's squat shadow, waving for the trolls to follow him. "They used to talk about it so much I stopped listening. Who wants to hear old things all the time? But I think my grandparents said there were tunnels all down in the ground underneath the castle. Underneath our feet now, even!" That reminded him of something—a clammy smell, flower petals, wide, angry eyes—but he pushed it away again. "And there were things inside the tower too, dangerous things . . ." He trailed off, uncertain now whether he was repeating things his elders had told him, or merely the exciting stories he had traded with other children. "Poison, and . . . and other bad things. So they chained the doors and boarded over the windows. Where the top opens they poured in rocks to fill the upper story, so nobody could get in."

Snenneq's eyes opened wide. "The top opens?"

"Part of it. The bad priest used to watch the stars. That's what I was told. He had . . . machines up there, too. Special mirrors and scrying glasses, I think. Things." Morgan waved his hand—the specifics were far away, and the spreading warmth of *kangkang* was here with him right now, making everything less worrisome. "It's true. I've been on the roof. You can look inside and see all the stones."

"You have been on it, the tower?" Snenneq asked. "But you were saying it is forbidden."

"Huh." Morgan waved his hand again. "Do you always do what your elders tell you? It's not dangerous—not if you can climb, anyway. When I was just a boy I climbed every wall in this castle, every tower." Which was a bit of an exaggeration, but after a humbling night with the trolls on the frozen lake, then another in the high cold hills of the Grianspog, he wanted them to know that he was not without skills and experience of his own.

Hjeldin's Tower loomed only a short distance ahead. The crescent moon floated beside the tower's shoulder like an angel of the Lord whispering to Usires in an old painting. Looking at it now, truly looking at it for the first time in a long while, Morgan was struck again by how different it was from the structures nearby; little surprise the trolls had wondered about it. Even before they were boarded up, the tower's windows had been weirdly narrow, like squinted eyes. The only large openings, the top-floor windows that had once been filled with leaded red glass, were now just holes dark as the sockets of a skull. Other than those and a few chimneys, the tower was featureless, and its squat, cylindrical form did make it look a bit like—perhaps not a basket, as the trolls had thought, but one of the great tureens from the castle kitchen.

And what happens when you leave the lid on the boiling pot too long? Morgan wondered, then shook his head, trying to free himself from such a strange, unsettling thought. "But you could see for yourself about the stones on top of the tower," he told the trolls. "I mean, if you wanted to. But probably you wouldn't. Because of the things people say about it."

"I do not understand you, friend Morgan," said Snenneq. "See for myself? How can I? It is night time and we are on the ground." He looked around. "Do you mean we could climb that other tower tomorrow?" He pointed at the shadowy spire of Holy Tree Tower on the far side of the chapel and of the residence. "And look down on it?"

"No, I meant you could see what's up there by climbing it," said Morgan in his most carefully careless voice. "I thought you trolls were good at that."

"There are none better," said Snenneq. "Anyone can be telling the truth of that, whether they have been to Yiqanuc or not. Do you not have a saying in your speech, *'Nimble as a troll on a mountain track'*?"

"Yes, but people say lots of things that other people tell them are true, without ever seeing if those people are right." Morgan felt a momentary twinge; Snenneq meant well, and he was very good at delivering the *kangkang,* but Morgan had felt an itch all evening, and though he still could not identify it, he was beginning to see a way to scratch it. "I'm not certain I could climb it myself any more, of course. Some of the handholds are fragile, and I'm a bit too heavy now." He patted his waistline. "I suppose you're too big for it too, Snenneq."

The troll gave him a look, half irritation, half suspicion. "What do you mean? It is forbidden by your king and queen to go onto it. That is what you were yourself saying."

"Oh, yes." Morgan laughed. "There are rules against it. Don't want to break any rules."

Qina said something in the troll language. It sounded brief and to the point. Morgan thought it was like the noise an unhappy pigeon might make. "She says you are sounding like you *do* want to break rules," Snenneq explained.

"Never mind," said Morgan. "It would be too hard, in any case. It's not the kind of climbing you're used to."

Little Snenneq looked up at the smooth bulk of the tower, his face as round as a second moon. "If it were not forbidden," he said after a moment, "I could be doing it."

Qina said something else, her voice even sharper this time. Snenneq did not translate it, but looked at Morgan. He shucked off his pack and dropped it on the ground, then began to dig in it. Qina spoke to him again in the troll tongue, but this time Snenneq ignored her. After a moment, he pulled a coil of slender cord from the pack and dropped it on the ground.

"You carry rope with you?" said Morgan, surprised.

"With certainness." He pulled off his jacket. Underneath he wore a shirt of some simple, homespun cloth that left his thick, dark arms bare. "I carry many things. That is because one day I will be a Singing Man, and such a man must be always preparing for what will happen. But the rope is not for me. If I am climbing up, then when I get to the top, I will let down the rope. Then you can be climbing too, Morgan Prince, and we will discover who is right and who is not."

Qina had clearly lost her patience for the whole enterprise. She turned her back on them both and began walking back toward the center of the keep.

"Qinananamookta!" Snenneq called, but she did not look around.

Morgan was beginning to feel the smallest bit concerned with how things were going until Little Snenneq threw him the drinking skin. "Only enough to be taking for courage," the troll warned. "Even with a rope, I am thinking you will not find it an easy climb."

Morgan wiped his mouth, enjoying the fire in his throat and belly. "You're really going to climb up the tower?"

Snenneq gave him a look of mixed amusement and disgust. "Words may be things of air, but once they are spoken, they are also things that exist. Do you believe a troll of Yiqanuc is without honor or pride?" He bent down to lace his rawhide boots more tightly, then walked to the base of the tower near the gate-house and began studying the close-fitting stones.

One more quick draught of *kangkang* helped to banish the last of Morgan's reservations. What was there to worry about, after all? Trolls were famous climbers. The king had bragged often enough about his time in the mountains with Binabik and his people. And although Morgan had been a bit more seden-tary of late than in his adventurous childhood days—well, what of it? With a rope, he could easily make it. Hadn't he been the best climber of all his friends?

Qina had disappeared from sight by the time Snenneq began to clamber up the wall, and that gave Morgan another moment of concern: What if she went straight back and reported what they were doing?

No, what Little Snenneq's doing, he corrected himself. *Nobody says I have to follow him up his silly rope.* In fact, he thought, what would be just about perfect would be if a party of rescuers arrived just as Snenneq reached the top. Snenneq would be the one to take the blame, and Morgan would be able to honorably avoid climbing.

He took another swallow of *kangkang* to convince himself. The molten liq-uid ran down the center of him and into his stomach, filling him with cheerful unconcern. Anyway, what would it signify if they did get into trouble? He was already in so much trouble now that it hardly mattered. What mattered was that the evening had been boring but now it was not.

To Morgan's surprise, Snenneq did not choose the easy path up onto the wall where Hjeldin's Tower was set, an assembly of hoary old stones with broad spaces between them to make things easier, but instead began climbing the tower itself just beside the gatehouse. Within a few moments he had lifted himself above the level of the gatehouse roof and was clinging to the tower's belly like a crawling fly.

Morgan could not help being impressed by the sureness with which Snenneq made his way. The moon was up and the light was good, but he also seemed to have an uncanny ability to guess at which cracks would work best. Once Snen-neq placed a foot or a hand, he seldom lifted it until it was time to let go and move up. Still, even a troll could only go so swiftly up a smooth, vertical wall. Once or twice the facing stones proved unequal to the chore, cracking loose to expose the darker bricks beneath. Once, Little Snenneq even hung by just his hands for long moments, struggling to find a place to stick in his toe, and Mor-gan grew so anxious watching him that he had to have another long drink.

Within a short time Snenneq reached the second floor windows, little more than arrow slits that had been filled in with stone shards when the tower was sealed. The troll scooped some of the stones out, letting them clatter onto the cobbled roadway below, then stuck both his feet into the hollow he'd made and rested there for a short while.

"A good night for climbing, this is," he called down. "I can see much of the village from here."

"City," Morgan called back, suddenly conscious of how loud they must be. "You know, I've been thinking that maybe this is not such a good idea after all."

"I cannot hear you speaking, Morgan Prince. Not one word."

Down at St. Sutrin's in the city, the bell tolled for compline. Morgan started to lift the drinking skin again, then thought better of it. The best part of his mood was beginning to curl a bit at the edges. If Little Snenneq reached the top, Morgan knew he would have to climb, too, or he would never be able to look him in the face again. What if Astrian and the rest heard that Morgan had challenged Snenneq and then turned coward himself? They would never let him hear the end of it. Astrian would make a dozen new names for him, each more humiliating than the last. It would be worse than the night of battle on the North Road, stuck in the camp with the women and old men, knowing that only a few hundred steps away Erkynlandish soldiers were fighting and dying.

He tossed the drinking skin onto Snenneq's pack. No more tonight, he told himself—or at least not until the climbing was finished. Still, he found himself praying in a most un-Morgan-like way that Snenneq would give up and come back down.

But nothing like that happened. As the prince watched, stomach growing more and more knotted, the little man made his deliberate way higher and higher, past the arrow-slits of the third story and up the moon-silvered facing of the fourth. Sometimes he hunted long moments for his next handhold—once he even dangled himself by his fingers alone until he could find a place to lodge his foot a cubit or more to one side—but no challenge seemed to hold him back for long. In the middle of his own growing concern, Morgan couldn't help admiring the troll's skill. Snenneq might look broad across the middle, even a bit fat, but the husky little fellow was strong, too, and matched his strength with a good eye and soft touch.

Morgan swallowed. It had become obvious to him some time earlier that Snenneq was a much better climber than he had ever been. Now it was becoming just as clear that unless something terrible happened, Snenneq was going to reach the top. Morgan's palms were damp despite the cool of the night.

You're a fool, Morgan Prince, he told himself. *You're a drunkard and a fool. Everything your grandparents say is right.*

At the highest floor, Snenneq veered a little farther from his course than Morgan expected. The prince realized that the little man was using the stone sills of the black, empty windows to begin the last part of his climb. For a moment, as he crabwalked along the lower part of the window, his fingers digging into the stone facing above, something seemed to reach out of the dark space near his legs and grab at him. Morgan gasped, his heart speeding, but it was only a strange shadow caused by the unevenness of the stones filling the window.

Fool, he scolded himself. *This is bad enough without making ghosts up out of the thin air.*

Still, it was hard to forget all the childhood stories about Pryrates, about the

Red Priest's hairless head and cruel face and the sound of his boots as he walked through the keep at night. Pryrates' father had been a demon, some of the stories claimed. He could speak to the dead.

Snenneq had reached the edge of the roof, nothing above him but the shallow dome that covered the top of the tower. The troll pulled himself over the edge—for a moment his legs kicked in the air, like a frog jumping into the water—and then vanished. Morgan stood and stared upward, his heart beating fast again.

Snenneq's head appeared a few instants later along the edge of the roof, a dark knot silhouetted by moonlight. "I have been tying the rope!" he called down, voice muffled by distance. A moment later Morgan saw a flash of silvery-gray as the coils spun down. The end bounced, swung, and stopped to hang just about the height of the wall. Snenneq called down something else, but this time Morgan could not make it out before the troll disappeared behind the edge of the tower roof.

What had he said? For Morgan to climb up and join him? Or could it have been something else? Perhaps he had said, *"It's not safe. Stay there. I'm coming down."* But if that was the case, where was he?

Morgan waited. And waited. And waited.

The moon slipped into a nest of clouds and hid itself. The *kangkang* skin, so near, seemed to call to him with a voice of sweet solace. A few more drinks, and he wouldn't care about any of it. He could stay down here and have a little nap, and eventually someone else would come and take care of things. Snenneq would climb back down, or Qina would return with the guards, or with her father.

Or with my grandparents . . .

He began to pace, and the night seemed to suck much of the drunkenness from his veins, leaving only a sickened chill. How could he sit waiting for someone else to come? He had given his word, the promise of a prince. He had goaded—yes, goaded—the troll into climbing the dangerous tower. Perhaps even now Snenneq was lying there, having slipped or tripped in the dark and hurt himself badly. And what if little Qina had got herself lost in the complicated maze of passageways and alleys at the heart of the ancient keep? Then nobody would be coming, and nobody was going to do anything except Morgan himself. He would have to climb.

Is that what Snenneq's fortune-telling bones meant, his Black Crevice and his Unnatural Birth? That I'll never be king because I'm going to fall off a tower and die?

The rope hung down in the moonlight, a line of silver against the dark stone, swaying in an occasional breeze.

Morgan wiped his hands on his clothing, then bent and got some dirt on his palms from between the cobbles and rubbed them until they were mostly dry. It was going to be hard enough to climb without sweaty hands.

Getting to the place where the rope dangled was not as bad as Morgan had feared. The wall had not been refaced in years and the spaces between its stones were wide. Once or twice he had to pull his knife from his belt and scrape out some of the old mortar so that he could dig his fingers or toes in deep enough, but it was not until he reached the top of the wall that he began to understand how much trouble he was in.

The rope hung just a few inches beyond his grasp, but in such a way that he would have to jump slightly outward from the base of the wall to reach it. That meant that if he failed to hang on, he would go straight down to the cobbles below. He was only at the tower's second story, which was probably not far enough to kill him, but from where he clung beside the tower, the distance looked quite enough to break a leg or an arm or even a pair of each.

Morgan was now deeply regretting the whole foolish adventure. The first part of the climb, easy as it had been, had burned all the jolly *kangkang* out of his head. That was how it felt, in any case, although when he looked down and the cobbles below him wavered and swam like stones at the bottom of a rippling stream, he wasn't quite so certain.

At last he found a foothold on the tower itself and swung out on one foot and one handhold as far as he could, so that the rope was only a handspan beyond his reach. He dried his hands, said a prayer to Saint Rhiappa, another to Saint Sutrin, then added one last prayer to Elysia, the mother of the Aedon, wanting all the sympathetic help he could get. Before he could think about it too much, he dug in his toe for leverage, then sprang up and out, grabbing for the rope.

He caught it and held on, but just as his heart thrilled with relief, the rope swung back from where his leap had carried it, Morgan dangling at the end of it like a plumb bob, and smashed him hard against the tower's stony side. It was all he could do not to let go, and for moments he just hung on the rope like a sick ape clinging to a tree branch.

After a bit, his grip began to loosen, so he scrabbled with his feet until he found a place to put his toes in the cracks between facing blocks. He had some purchase with his feet now, but was hanging at an angle away from the tower wall with nearly all his weight on his arms. He did his best to inch up that way, a little bit at a time, and at first felt a small renewal of confidence as he managed to spider his way up the outside of the second story, bracing with his feet when he had to change his grip to a higher part of the rope. When he missed a foothold he swung out alarmingly, but managed to find a grip in the cracks of the wall on his backswing, then to cling there until he found his breath.

Within a short while he had climbed high enough that he felt sure he would not survive a fall. He also began to believe that he was not going to be able to use the rope all the way to the top, since his shoulders were already burning with the strain and his fingers were beginning to cramp. He cursed himself, a silent string of panicky epithets that would have made his tutors' eyes bulge in shock and sent them scurrying to chapel.

Only one thing to do, he realized at last. *Have to do it like the troll*. That meant giving up the rope, but at least then his legs would take an equal share of the load. *Sweet Aedon preserve me, if I die, what will people think? They'll think I was an idiot. Of course they will. And they'll be right.*

But he had no other choice, except perhaps to shout for help, and much as his arms ached, he was even more frightened by the thought of bringing the whole of the Inner Bailey here to see his wretched foolishness. He tied the rope around his waist in case he missed his target entirely, then gently swung himself back and forth until he dared to take one hand off and reach for the wall. The first time he failed to find purchase, but the second time he found a crack, and when he wedged his fingers into it his swinging stopped. He searched with his toes until he found places to dig in his feet, but already his knot was loosening around his waist and he was beginning to sag farther from the wall.

He sent another prayer to Elysia, thinking of the Mother of God's kind, forgiving face, the kind of face that would even find mercy for drunken young idiots, then as he swung again toward the tower, he let go of the rope completely and jabbed his aching fingers into the nearest crevice in the stone facing. The knot unwound and the rope slithered off, swinging back to hang out of his reach behind him. Morgan's gut went cold. Now he could only move up or down by clinging to the wall as Snenneq had done.

What followed was a waking nightmare. Morgan did not remember much of it afterward, but every single movement, every release, every risk, every move from one crumbling handhold to another seemed to take hours. He knew it would haunt his dreams for the rest of his life, if he was lucky enough to survive. He did his best to ignore the pain and inch upward, impossibly slowly, crawling the vertical face of the tower like a caterpillar, so tired and agonizingly sore that he did not remember what it felt like to do anything else. The third floor passed, and the fourth went by too, as wretchedly slow as waiting for snow to melt. Morgan could think of nothing except the need to find a handhold, find a foothold, to move up. The weight of his own body began to feel like somebody else's weight, as if another entire person was dangling from his ankles or plucking at his arms, trying to yank him backward into emptiness and death.

The fourth floor edged past him, then he was onto the fifth. He could see only what was above him, could do nothing except push his body close to the tower wall and search with his fingers for the next place to grab. One of his shoes fell off but he hardly noticed the difference. Up and up he climbed, except that now it had become something both more and less than climbing. For long moments he imagined himself crawling over a flat surface, belly down, while a great wind tried to blow him away. Later, he thought he was clambering through a tunnel into another country, a land of warmth and rest. But no matter what he thought, or dreamed, always something kept pulling at him, trying to fling him into empty space, some horrible enemy that wanted to smash him to death against the stones.

Morgan came out of another season of darkness to realize he could not find a handhold because there were no more—his free hand was groping in empty space. He looked up for the first time in a long while and saw that he had reached the top. The sight so astonished him that he almost lost his grip, but the quickening of his heart and his blood pushed his thoughts back to the night and the tower again.

Pulling himself up over the top seemed like the most difficult thing he had ever done. At one point, as he tried to lift his knee high enough to get it up onto the tower roof, he burst into tears. No one came to help him. He called out Snenneq's name, or thought he did, but no one responded.

At last he levered the heaviest part of his body over the edge so he could collapse onto the curved, dome-shaped roof, then he scrabbled forward until he felt it beneath his legs as well. He rolled onto his back, gasping, his sinews throbbing with fiery pain. Whether he slept then or merely stopped thinking, he could not tell, but for a while he lay in darkness. When at last he opened his eyes again he saw nothing above him except the stars.

I don't know their names, he thought. *Someone—Sir Porto? Grandfather?—tried to teach me once, but I didn't pay attention.*

If these were truly his own stars. If he had not climbed so high he had reached some other world, some land in the sky.

At last he rolled over and dragged himself up on all fours. There was no sign at all of Snenneq on the roof, although Morgan should have been able to see him. The shallow slope of the dome curved gently upward before him, mounting only a few cubits in height between its edge and its center. It wasn't a dome of windows and light such as stood above Saint Sutrin's cathedral, but a dome as solid, stony, and secretive as the rest of Hjeldin's Tower. Near the top of it the builders had made four great hatchways, one facing each quadrant of the sky. The hatch doors had been chained shut when the tower was abandoned, but now one of the hatches was open and the lid thrown back, the square black opening gaping at the sky like a hungry mouth.

"Snenneq?" Morgan tested the dome, which felt more solid than the walls themselves. It still held some of the day's heat, even in the dark. He began to climb toward the open hatch. Why would the troll break it open and go inside the infamous tower? Did Snenneq really have so little fear of other peoples' phantoms?

What if he didn't open it? Morgan thought suddenly. *What if someone else did? What if he was just standing there, and it opened behind him like the lid of a spider's den . . . and then something came out and took him?*

The picture in his head was too horrifying to be endured. Morgan crept forward in unwitting imitation of his climb up, stomach dragging on the lead roof, until he reached the open hatch. But he truly, truly did not want to look inside.

He's here because of you, a voice told him, almost as if someone else spoke straight into his ear—someone honorable. Someone different. *He's here because of you. If he's in there, you have to find him.*

But Morgan did not want to look inside the hatch, let alone go in. Who knew what a dangerous shambles it must be, closed up for twenty years or more, empty for all this time?

But what if it isn't empty? Again he imagined the hatch opening silently behind the troll, the shadowy shape emerging . . .

He pushed his head out beyond the edge of the hatch. The top chamber of the tower was full of large, loose rocks as he had expected, but there were dark places among them that almost looked like some monstrously huge mole or rat had been tunneling between the piled stones. Morgan was wishing harder than he had ever wished in his life that he had a torch—no, that he had a torch and a sword and three or four stout friends—when he saw something move. Something was alive in the chamber below him, down in the darkness of the tower's top floor, down in the shadows.

"Snenneq?" he called quietly, but his blood was drumming and the cracked voice that came from his lips scarcely sounded like his own. Then the shape turned to look up at him. Morgan had only an instant to see the hairless face catch the moonlight, the empty black eyes, the rags of a hood that might once have been red, then the hammerblows of his own heartbeats filled his head as he gasped and pushed himself away from the hatch. Trying to scramble to his feet, Morgan missed his footing and fell forward instead, cracking his jaw against the edge of the hatch. A sudden, bright shouting of stars overwhelmed him for an instant, then the black swallowed him up.

32

Rosewater and Balsam

The Chancelry was part of a long building in the Middle Bailey that in King John's day had been the castle mews. They had been destroyed in the fall of Green Angel Tower and the new stables erected in the outermost ring of the keep. It was not so much a sign that horses and royal carriages had become less important, Pasevalles reflected, as that counting and keeping money had grown even more so.

The Chancelry building had the shape of a long bone, something that two dogs might fight over, pulling at each end. This was appropriate, because while one end belonged to Pasevalles as Lord Chancellor, the other end belonged to Archbishop Gervis, the Lord Treasurer, and Pasevalles had to admit the relationship between the two occasionally came down to something like the contendings of a couple of mastiffs under the royal supper table.

Still, it was a relief for the Lord Chancellor to be able to sink back into his own labors without having to do Count Eolair's most important work as well. Many of the issues closest to his heart had been all but ignored while the royal couple were traveling, and he was anxious to catch up.

Clerks hurried back and forth down the long hall like bees in clover, bearing piles of documents—ledger rolls, pleading letters, and tax records, each with its own complicated history. Pasevalles could not help being sourly amused by the misunderstanding most of the kingdom's subjects had about power—that the king and queen merely sat on their thrones and decided what should be done next, then their eager minions hurried out and turned these whims into fact. In truth, ruling anything, let alone the largest kingdom in the history of Osten Ard, was a process of learning about and reacting to hundreds upon hundreds of small problems, some of which would quickly become larger problems if left unsolved, and then persisting with them until they had been solved or at least reduced from crisis to mere irritation. And standing between a ruler and these solutions was not a horde of loyal subjects waiting only to be told what to do, but thousands of individuals, each with his own plans and wants, most of them quite willing to break the rules if they could get away with it, and yet each of them also furious at any idea their own rights might be somehow abrogated. And of these plaintiffs, the nobles were the worst, prickly and full of righteous demands.

Pasevalles had been born the nephew of an important Nabbanai border lord, Baron Seriddan of Metessa, and his childhood in the baron's castle had also been the last time he was satisfied with his lot in life. Though his own father, Brindalles, had been a quiet and scholarly sort, young Pasevalles had always had his own eye set on a life of valor. He had even taken it upon himself to care for the family collection of arms and armor, because no one else in Metessa seemed to care about the greatness of the past—at least not the way Pasevalles did. All the years of his childhood the great armor hall and the foundry where armor was built and repaired had been his true homes; he had been nearly a stranger to his father's study. He had learned to read and write and do sums, of course, as any young man in a noble family was expected to do, but had considered every hour spent beneath his tutors' watchful gazes to be an hour wasted, time when he could have been out watching the men at arms practicing or performing the tasks he had allotted to himself in the armor hall, preserving the glory of his ancestors' warlike ways and dreaming that a similar glory would one day be his.

But dreams change, he told himself. *Especially those of children.*

Pasevalles's dreams had changed for good on the day that Prince Josua, brother of King Elias and son of Prester John, had arrived in Metessa seeking help in his struggle against his brother and his brother's terrifying ally, Ineluki the Storm King. Pasevalles had been too young to understand all of it, of course—he was a mere eight years old—but he had been thrilled to learn that the legendary Sir Camaris, greatest warrior of his age, was alive and fighting for Josua. And when Josua's siege of the Hayholt began, Pasevalles would have been even more thrilled that his own scholar father had joined the fighting, going so far as to volunteer for a masquerade, pretending to be Josua while the prince led a group of men and Sithi into the castle by other means.

But Pasevalles had not been there. He did not see the glory of his father's charge, riding the prince's horse in through the very gates of the Hayholt. Neither was he there to see the terrible ending when King Elias' trap was revealed, and his father was cut down and hacked to pieces by defenders in the castle courtyard.

Pasevalles had instead found all this out when the messengers had reached Metessa a fortnight later, just a day ahead of the bodies of Pasevalles' father and his uncle Seriddan, who had died of his wounds a few days after the battle.

The weeks and months after hardly existed in his memory now, a black vortex of time, days and nights in seemingly endless succession where all he felt was pain and disbelief. It was not until his aunt decided to remarry a year later that Pasevalles had begun to take notice of his surroundings again.

None of that went well, either. His mother died from one of the fevers that scourged Nabban after the Storm King's Wars. His aunt, who had married the widower who owned the adjoining barony, also died from that same fever. And his aunt's new husband had promptly turned Pasevalles out, sending him to live with poor relatives along Nabban's northern coast in a house so cold and damp that he might as well have been living in the marshes themselves. Bitter, chilly days . . .

No. Anger is a distraction, he reminded himself. *Anger is the enemy of success.* He had plans, he had a purpose, he had responsibilities and should not let himself be weighed down by bad, old memories. At this very moment he had a huge pile of bills waiting to be approved and taken to the king and queen, as well as dozens of other payments waiting to be examined one last time before being dispersed to the crown's various creditors, because rebuilding castles was expensive work. All these years later, the Erkynland was still paying for the Storm King's War. And, just to make the need to avoid wallowing in the past even more obvious, here came Father Wibert with another pile of petitions.

"Where does your Lordship want these?" his secretary asked. "On the floor? In your lap?" Wibert was not a young man, but age had made him thinner rather than heavier. He had something like a sense of humor, but that was all it was—something like it. In fact, the most interesting thing about Wibert was his complete disinterest in anything other than himself. Pasevalles found him extremely useful, but nobody in the castle thought of him as a charming companion.

"On the floor, I suppose." Pasevalles noticed something that did not look like the other documents. "What's that on the top?"

"A letter from Princess Idela," said Wibert with a mirthless grin. "Scented. She wants a favor, I'm betting." He set down the tipping pile of documents, gave them a cursory straightening, then plucked the folded sheet off the top and handed it to Pasevalles. "The good Lord grant us all patience. Why He thought of women is more than I can understand."

I don't doubt that's true, Pasevalles thought. People in the Hayholt sometimes suggested Wibert had been born a priest. Pasevalles knew it was nearly true: Wibert had arrived from St. Sutrin's orphanage when he was still a young boy, to work as an acolyte in the cathedral. Pasevalles doubted the monk had ever had a moment in his life free of Mother Church looking over his shoulder.

"Are you going to open it?"

Pasevalles felt an unpleasant remark rise to his but did not indulge himself. Wibert had all the social grace of a plowhorse let loose in the royal chapel, but he was a useful man, hard-working, incurious, and, best of all, absolutely predictable.

"I will look at it later, thank you. Just set it there on the table."

Father Wibert hung about for a few moments, clearly hoping that the Lord Chancellor would change his mind and open the princess dowager's letter—like so many of the clergy, Pasevalles had found, Wibert lived for gossip—but eventually he gave up and went out. Pasevalles thought that with his bony elbows and knees, his secretary looked more like a string-puppet than a man of God.

And that is my curse, he thought to himself. *To see what truly is instead of what others would prefer me to see.* It was a curse, beyond doubt, but he sometimes thought it was also a glory, to be less blind than others, who hid themselves from that which they did not want to know.

He picked up the letter from the princess with a certain caution, as if the folded paper itself might have a blade-sharp edge. That was what he thought of sometimes when he saw the princess—a knife, something that could lie unused and unnoticed for a long time, and then suddenly emerge to change everything in a dreadful moment. He wondered if it were actually true of Prince John Josua's widow or if, for once, he was fooling himself. In any case, he feared the complications she could bring, but he was also not blind to the advantages her friendship could gain him. He sniffed the letter. Scented, as Wibert had noted— rosewater and balsam, the profane and the sacred mixed, earth and spirit. A message? Or just her ordinary scent? Pasevalles studied the seal, and when he was certain it was unbroken, he opened and unfolded the letter.

My dearest Lord,

I know that the absence of our beloved king and queen kept you most busy in recent months. In truth, we all are in debt to you for your hard, selfless work. I am certain that some day your value to this kingdom will be noticed and you will be rewarded as you deserve.

Subtle as a slaughterer's hammer, he thought. *Come now, my lady, you can do better.*

Still, I must chide you just a little, dear Pasevalles. It was most kind of you to send that sweet Brother Etan to examine poor John Josua's books, but I must be honest and say that I had hoped you would do the job yourself, not simply because I trust your eye and your discretion, but because I had selfishly hoped to spend some time in your company.

"Dear Pasevalles," too. The princess was not bothering to work up to her point slowly. He wondered why she was so determined to make him an ally. Had something happened on the royal trip north, something that Pasevalles himself had not heard, that caused her to worry about her position at court? It was hard to imagine anything that could change her situation. She was the widow of the prince and mother of the heir-apparent. Surely nothing could undo either of those two facts.

To that end, perhaps you and I could put aside an evening after supper when you might lay aside the heavy cares of your high station and come join me for a glass of Comis wine. My ladies will be present, so you need not fear for your reputation or mine.

He could not help smiling at that. She was a sly woman, the princess. Quite different from her bluff, practical father.

There is much I would like to discuss with you, most certainly including the library that will bear my husband's name and the books of his still in my possession. Perhaps we could meet after the church service St. Dinan's day. Say you will come.

Of course, a mere Lord Chancellor could not refuse such a request, and Pasevalles had no idea of doing so. He had avoided the princess as long as he could while he dealt with more pressing matters, because he was certain that one way or another what she wanted most from him was his time and attention. Still, he was beginning to be intrigued by the steadfastness of her pursuit. What could she be seeking? Surely it could be nothing so obvious as a widowed woman seeking attention from an unmarried man? He had always supposed Princess Idela more subtle than that.

Pasevalles wrote a suitably fulsome reply, then blotted and folded it before affixing his seal—his own seal, not the Seal of the High Throne he was permitted to use as Lord Chancellor when he wrote in the king's and queen's names. If Idela wanted something from him, he was going to work very carefully to keep it separate from his hard-won position as long as possible. Because unlike those who had been born into their high station in life, or married into it, Pasevalles had fought his way into a position of importance purely by hard work and clever choices. But that also meant that without family or titled spouse, he had little to protect what he had gained. Fortune was a wheel, as Pasevalles knew better than most, and the Wheel of Fortune could spin again without warning, raising some and throwing others into the dust.

The bees, who had been driven away by the young monk's work among the rosemary plants, now began to settle back into contented browsing, but Brother Etan was less happy. He looked, Tiamak thought, as though he had awakened one morning to find the sky below him and the earth above him. "You are so pale," he said. "Are you well, Brother? You seem unwell. Is this not good news that I bring?"

"Good news?" Etan stared as though he could not understand what the other man was saying. "I pray forgiveness, Lord—but how could it be good news? I am to give up my home and my work here and go out into the world—into foreign lands and among barbarians! And my task is to look for children who have been missing twenty years and more. Surely this is a fruitless engagement."

Tiamak pursed his lips, unhappy with himself. "Oh, dear. I see. He Who Always Steps On Sand forgive me, I have not followed a careful path." He reached out and put his slender hand on Etan's sleeve. "Come, sit with me here and let me explain."

Etan allowed himself to be led out of the cathedral's herb garden to a bench on the path beside it. The monk absentmindedly wiped his hands against his cassock, but instead of the rosemary oils on his hands being wiped away, the fluff from his garment simply stuck to his palms and fingers instead.

"I was born in the swamp, you know," Tiamak told him. "As a child in the Wran, I could hardly grasp that there were other places, let alone how different they were. I did not know anyone who had ever worn shoes! But that was all I knew. When I left the first time and went up the water to Kwanitupul, I was astonished that such a place could exist. So many people! And nobody ever touched land, or so it seemed. Kwanitupul is almost entirely built on platforms, you see."

"I know something of Kwanitupul, Lord Tiamak. You have told me about it before."

He smiled. "Yes, but I am not talking about Kwanitupul. I am talking about traveling away from one's home and familiar surroundings. Because Kwanitupul was only the most magnificent, terrifying thing I had ever seen for a very brief while. Then I went on to Perdruin, an island that seemed to me as large as the Wran, and most of it one big and bustling city. And then I saw Nabban itself . . . !" Tiamak shook his head. "I am glad I did not see that first after I left the swamp, because I think such size and noise and bustle would have stopped my heart."

"But I am not, if you will forgive me, Lord, a Wrannaman," Etan said. "I live in one of the Osten Ard's largest cities. I have met people from all over the world here. It is not quite the same as living in . . . well, a swamp."

"No, of course it isn't. But the point I am trying to make is that there is nothing that grows one's thoughts so much as seeing new things." *Slowly*, Tiamak told himself. *Slowly, so as only to dazzle, not blind.* "You are a very wise young man, Etan, but you have been sheltered. This is your chance to see parts of the world even Archbishop Gervis has never seen and never will see."

"But why? That is my question? Why me? And why this strange task now, when there seem to be so many other things I could turn my hand to?"

"Because I think you would be the best choice for the task, first of all." Tiamak let himself become a little firmer. "I have some experience of the people, and some little experience of wisdom, and I do not often say, 'There is a man who is already wise, but who can become wiser still, a true and rare thinker'. But I believe you are such a person."

Now Etan was clearly confused again. "But could not anyone do this better than me, my lord? Some knight, or better still some nobleman who could compel people to answer his questions?"

"Anybody can lie, Brother. People tell the powerful folk what they think those folk want to hear. That, or they deem power too dangerous and so they do not tell them anything at all. If we send a large royal mission, with Sir Zakiel or Count Eolair in charge, people will line up to tell them half-truths and honest rumors in the hope of currying favor. That is not the way to learn something truly useful—and it is certainly no way to keep what you want to learn a secret."

"This is to be secret?"

"How else? Should we, in a time when another war with the Norns seems all too frighteningly possible, trumpet the news that King John's only surviving son, who most think died in the last battle with the Storm King, is actually alive but we have lost track of him, along with his wife and two royal children? It would take years to unravel the true and false stories that would follow such a revelation, not to mention it would doubtless spawn pretenders to the throne as well, all claiming to be one of Josua's vanished children. And do you not think the news of this disappearance would also be keenly appreciated under Stormspike? Then we would find ourselves not just looking for Josua, but quite possibly in a competition to find him against the Norns themselves."

"I suppose I see some sense in what you say." Etan frowned, thinking it over. "But why now? As you say, we might soon be at war—although I confess I had not realized the situation was so dire. Why dig up a matter that has lain undisturbed for twenty years or more?"

Tiamak could not repress a sigh. "Because it has not lain undisturbed for twenty years. No, we have tried on several occasions to find out the truth of Josua's disappearance and always failed. But two things make this a current problem. One is that our king and queen made a promise to Duke Isgrimnur on his deathbed to renew the search for Josua's children—Isgrimnur's god-children. Solace to the soul of that good old man would be reason enough, trust me. But there is another reason, one even the king and queen have not yet entirely realized. No, don't ask me yet," he said, forestalling Etan's questions. "Each thing in its own time. Let us go to my chambers. My wife is caring for the poisoned Sithi-woman, so we will have some privacy for a little while that we cannot have anywhere else in this busy city or even the castle. Come."

Brother Etan was clearly still troubled. Tiamak sympathized—it was a great deal to take in all at once. "How did you come to work in the castle?" he asked, pouring them each a cup of wine.

"*In* the castle? Because Lord Pasevalles asked for me, my lord, and the Archbishop said I might go and help him in the Chancelry."

Tiamak could not help smiling. "No, in fact, that is not quite how you came to work in the castle. I had been watching you, and when Pasevalles was looking for help I suggested he ask for you. Obviously, he found my suggestion useful. And I have been selfish enough to employ you for a few tasks myself, as you know. But that is not precisely the question that should interest you. Why do you think *I* noticed you?"

Etan lifted his hands in frustration. "I have no idea, Lord Tiamak, and in truth I am a bit weary answering, because it seems everything I know is wrong."

"Very good. I like that you stand up for yourself. A man of philosophy must trust his own thoughts, at least enough to follow them and see where they lead. I noticed you because you were ambitious." He held up his hand. "No, no, I do not mean it in any bad way. You were not seeking fame, or reward. But you have what I would call a restless mind. It is not content to do things the old way simply because that is how they have always been done. You look at a problem as something to be solved, rather than something to be avoided. That is a form of ambition. And you have *ideas*. That is ambition, too. Do you remember when you told Pasevalles that hanging baskets on a loop of rope would be faster for moving things back and forth between the Treasury and the Chancelry than using messengers?"

"I recall it now that you say it," said Etan. "But how do *you* know about it?"

"Because I have made it my business to know about you, Brother. I am interested in people who think for themselves, who value knowledge as knowledge, but also for what good it may do their fellow men." Tiamak sipped a little of his own wine. "This is not very good, I'm afraid. Neither Lady Thelía nor I drink spirits often, so we never know what to keep on hand for other people."

Etan waved his hand to show that it did not matter.

"Very well," Tiamak said. "Listen carefully, because much of what I will tell you now will bear directly on your task—a task, as I should have made clear at the beginning, that you are free to refuse."

The monk's look of surprise grew more exaggerated. "I am? I confess, I did not know that."

"Of course. Unless it were an obvious matter of life or death, I would not send someone away against his will—away from, as you said, his home and his work. But I suspect by the time I've finished talking to you here, you will see the benefits of this opportunity and will not hesitate to accept it."

A certain interest crept into Etan's face. "Truly? Is that a wager, my lord?"

"Of sorts. Let's say this—if you do not see the clear advantages to you in taking this task, and ask for it to be given to you, I will apologize and we will never speak of it again. You will bear no stain or discredit for refusing. Is that fair?"

"More than fair."

"Good. Then listen while I begin with the story of Ealhstan— the Fisher King as many of the people call him—the first true Erkynlandish king. He was also, by the way, King Simon's ancestor."

"I have heard something about that."

"Not much, I wager. The king is oddly ashamed of his own blood—no, not his blood, but the right to rule that was granted him because of it. But that is common to much of what we are going to talk about now—the fact that in some ways, great men and women are just as foolishly complicated as the rest of us."

"Very well." Etan added water to his third cup of wine, since he was thirsty but did not want his wits to be muddled. "I will give it back to you such as I understand it." As the afternoon had stretched on, the parade of names and events had become more than slightly dizzying, despite Lord Tiamak's patient willingness to explain things over and over. "The League of the Scroll was founded by King Ealhstan here in the Hayholt, to protect and increase knowledge. Over the years there have been many members, usually seven at a time, but in recent years the numbers have dwindled."

"Not so much dwindled," Tiamak said. "We never fully replaced the original members who died during the war or . . . well, you know what happened to Pryrates."

Etan nodded. The red priest was not spoken of by Mother Church in any official way, but men of God were quite willing to tell tales in private when they had the chance, and Pryrates was a demon-figure who still horrified and fascinated. "I understand. But Prince Josua was a Scrollbearer! I never knew that."

"After the tower fell and the war was over, yes," Tiamak said. "It seemed like an ideal role for someone like Josua, who had an active, useful mind and, while he cared very much about his father's kingdom, he did not wish to rule it. The sad part is that we had him in the League only a few years before he disappeared."

"Leaving his children with their mother . . . what was her name? Vorsava?"

"Vorzheva, daughter of a Thrithings clan-leader. Yes, their twin children, Derra and Deornoth. But whether he disappeared and left his wife alone we really don't know."

"Because after Josua's last letters, nobody heard from any of them."

"Yes, and later I will show you those letters, because they are the starting point for any search. But don't misunderstand, Brother. The king and queen did not ignore this matter—Josua was the queen's uncle. He knighted Simon when the king was only a kitchen boy. They both loved him very much."

"I understand. Now, forgive me if I have the order wrong, my lord, but Duke Isgrimnur and Count Eolair both made trips south to Kwanitupul to search for them. And you went with them."

"I went with Eolair, which was the first time we searched for them." Tiamak smiled. "I had not known the count well before. I am grateful we were able to journey together."

"But you said you found nothing. The inn that Josua owned had been sold, and the new owners said they did not know where the family had gone. Who sold it? Josua or Vorzheva?"

"The money was paid to a dark-haired woman who might have been Vorzheva," Tiamak replied. "The price was not high, which suggests that, for whatever reason, she did not want to hold out for a better one."

"So did Vor-shay-vah go back to her home?" Etan asked, pleased that he could finally wrap his mouth around the unfamiliar name. "You said she was from the High Thrithings."

"She hated the grasslands, and she hated her father, who was a clan-chief. That is all I know for certain. If she did go back, Eolair could find nobody among the Thrithings-folk who knew anything about it. We did not speak to her father, but someone else did on our behalf, and told us he said that if she had come back with Josua's children, he would have killed them all."

"Barbarian monster."

"Yes, but such men are not limited to the grasslands and the swamps of Osten Ard. You may find them everywhere. Even in the Church."

Etan bridled a bit, but did his best not to be distracted. Lord Tiamak might have his pagan prejudices but he was a good man who meant well. That was all that mattered. "So, no sign of them to be found, and no sign of where they went. And did any of the other Scrollbearers hear anything from him before he vanished? What about the woman in Perdruin?"

"Lady Faiera. We know nothing for certain, because she disappeared at much the same time, or at least stopped answering letters from other Scrollbearers."

"Could the disappearances be connected?" Etan asked. "I hope I am not being disrespectful, but is it not possible that Prince Josua and this woman . . . well . . ."

"Ran away together? You may ask any question without fear, Brother. I'm glad you asked that one because of course it occurred to us as well. Eolair and I searched for her. Did I not tell you what we found?"

"No. Unless I missed it in all the other names and such."

Tiamak smiled. "Possibly so, but more likely I forgot. Eolair and I went to Perdruin to seek her out and see what she could tell us, because Josua had mentioned in one of his last letters that he, himself, had questions for her—important questions, he said." Tiamak shook his head. "Imagine then, when we discovered that not only was she gone, her house had burned."

"Burned? How? Was she not a noblewoman?"

"By blood, yes, but not by circumstances. She lived in a house in one of the most crowded parts of Perdruin, in a district called the Cauldron down by the docks in the oldest part of the city. Her house was one of a row, the houses as old and tumbledown as the rest of the district. It looks more like Kwanitupul there than it does like Perdruin. Ah, but you have not been to Kwanitupul, either. Well, in any case, a year before we arrived, sometime near Josua's disappearance, a fire had begun in that row of houses. All those in the middle of the street had been gutted, and several others in adjoining streets had burned as well. Many died, but all that was left behind were charred bones. We do not know if she was there. We do not know if Josua was there."

"Could that be the end, then? A terrible accident, and the prince and this Lady Faiera killed in a fire?"

"That might be the reason we never saw either of them again, of course. But even so, it does not tell us where Vorzheva went with the children, and that is our true quest." He patted the monk on the arm. "Where did the children go?"

Etan sat back. He felt quite overwhelmed. "It is a great deal to take in, my lord. Why do you think I will want to undertake such a difficult if not hopeless task, twenty years too late? You said you thought I would agree."

"Because not only is it an important task to the king and queen—for them it is about loyalty to one's friends and keeping promises—but it is an opportunity you might never have again. A wonderful opportunity."

"To look for people twenty years lost?"

The little Wrannaman reached out and squeezed Etan's hand. "I told you I wanted you to accept this charge of your own free will, Brother, and I meant it. But consider this last, important reason." Tiamak lowered his voice a little. "You are a man in whom, whether he knows it completely or not, the love of learning runs very deep. What better chance will you ever have to see something of the world than as an envoy of the High Throne, with all the privileges of the position, sent to travel the south in the search for truth? Have you never wanted to see the Sancellan Aedonitis, the seat of your religion? Have you never longed to see the ruins of the ancient cities that once covered the southern islands? And what of Perdruin, whose every breeze is scented with the smell of goods from all over Osten Ard? How could you say no to that opportunity, especially when you know that it would bring you gratitude from the king and queen?"

Etan felt like Saint Sutrin being tempted by the disguised angel. "You make a strong case, my lord. Is it truly up to me to decide?"

"Yes, of course. And if you say you will undertake it, I will give you such letters from Josua as I have. From Lady Faiera, too. You will have knowledge about the League of the Scroll that none but Scrollbearers have possessed. What say you, Brother? Do you need time to think?"

Before he could answer, they heard the clatter of hurrying footsteps in the passageway outside his chambers. Etan looked up in alarm, so surfeited with secrets he half-expected someone to break in and arrest him.

Tiamak did not wait, but limped across the chamber before the knocking even began and opened the door to reveal a stout priest there, Tiamak's secretary, all gasps and dripping sweat.

"Father Avner!" said Tiamak. "Is something wrong?"

"Lord Tiamak, your wife Lady Thelía bids you come swiftly! To the royal chapel! She says you must come now!"

"Take a breath, Father," said Tiamak. Etan thought he sounded much calmer than he could truly be. "Take as many of them as you need to tell the story straight. Of course I'll come. What's amiss? Is it the Sitha woman?"

Father Avner wagged his shaven head in confusion. "Sitha? I don't know about that, Lord. But the prince has fallen off the tower."

Shocked, Brother Etan made the sign of the Tree. "God preserve him!" he said. "And us!"

"Is Prince Morgan badly hurt?" Tiamak demanded. "Dead?"

"I don't know—she only told me to fetch you," said Avner. "But they say he fell off Hjeldin's Tower, and that is very, very tall . . ."

Tiamak hurried toward the door. Etan leaped to his feet and went after him. The messenger, his task accomplished, now bent over and put his hands on his knees, struggling to get his breath back.

33

Secrets and Promises

Every time the queen tried to get close to Morgan on his make-shift bed, hastily set up in the royal chapel, Lady Thelía frowned at her and politely asked her to move back again. Miriamele bristled at being waved away like a child, but did her best to keep her temper.

Thelía finally straightened up. "Now, Majesty, you may have your turn. The tidings are good—he merely fell while at the top of the tower, not off it, thank our merciful Lord. Other than a quite impressive lump on his jaw and a bloody foot, I have found nothing worse than some cuts and scrapes and bruises."

"Blessed Elysia be praised!" Miri kneeled down and dabbed at Morgan's forehead with a damp cloth. "Thanks to Almighty God you are not worse hurt. Poor lad!"

"Poor lad?" The king was pale, and his voice was hoarse, although Miriamele knew that was as much because of fear as anger. "Climbing on Hjeldin's Tower! Climbing that evil, forbidden thing!"

Morgan groaned and opened his eyes. The royal couple and the others in the chapel—servants, a pair of vergers, and the chaplain, Father Nulles—all murmured their relief. "Where is Snenneq?" the prince asked after he had looked around for a few groggy moments. His eyes widened in fear. "Is he all right? Did he fall?"

"No, he didn't fall," his grandfather said. "He's well, and thank the Lord and all His angels for that. Snenneq climbed down and found help. Binabik was already looking for you two after his daughter came back." The king took a deep breath before speaking, but his voice still quavered with anger. "Boy, what were you thinking? Were you thinking at all?"

"Don't shout at him now," Miriamele said, dabbing Morgan's brow. She had been so terrified when the servants came for her. The time it took her to get from her chambers to the chapel where the guards had brought her grandson seemed like a nightmare. In fact, it had been very much like the nightmares that had tormented her nearly every night in the first year after John Josua's death—always hurrying, knowing he needed her, but always too late. Every one of those dreams had ended in a closed door, or an empty bed, or footprints in a grassy field, but no other sign of her lost, beloved son. She could only thank God over and over that this ending had been different.

"I need to talk to Snenneq," said Morgan, who still looked frightened. "Can someone bring him here?"

"No, you need to sleep, Highness," said Lady Thelía. "That is what you need. Sleep is the sovereign cure for almost any hurt that does not kill you. And Usires be praised, your fall, however unfortunate, does not seem to have done you any lasting damage."

Tiamak and young Brother Etan appeared in the doorway of the chapel, their faces suggesting they had not yet heard that the prince had not actually fallen off the tower and was not too badly hurt. Miriamele watched as the chaplain went to speak to them.

"Oh, my heart is beating so fast," she told her husband. "I was so worried."

"Our grandson doesn't seem to bring us much else," Simon said. "But this is the worst."

"Don't you dare shout at him—not in front of all these people." Miri kept her voice low. "You can wait until he's in his own room again."

"And that will happen soon enough," Simon declared. "We are not going to leave him here in the chapel. He's not lying in state, he's just given his foolish chin a good thump. We'll carry him upstairs that way, in the same blanket he's lying on." And before Miriamele could object, he began giving orders to the servants.

"Carefully, please!" said Thelía as two male servants and two Erkynguard took a corner each and lifted Morgan. "We do not know for certain that he has not cracked a rib."

"All of them," Morgan moaned as he was bumped a little in the process of lifting him off the steps in front of the altar. "Every damnable one is cracked, I'm sure."

"And serves you right, you young . . . mooncalf," the king said, but quietly, so that only Miriamele heard him. She was too weary with fright to smile, but she remembered how many times a younger Simon had been called that himself.

Lillia had heard the news, and was waiting breathlessly to see her brother. She was allowed to speak to him for a moment before he was carried out, just so she could see that Morgan was not badly hurt. The little girl scolded him so severely that Miriamele could not help feeling a little sorry for her grandson, much as he deserved it.

Lord Chancellor Pasevalles had arrived too, as pale with surprise and worry as everyone else. "How is he, Majesty?" Pasevalles asked after the procession had passed and he could step through the doorway. "I just heard. Pray God he is not badly hurt . . . ?"

"Took a thump on the jaw, that's all," growled Simon, although it was Miriamele that Pasevalles had addressed. "Hope it teaches him a lesson. God knows what everybody will think—everyone knows that tower is forbidden!" Simon shook his head, more of a shudder than a negation. "Why would anyone want to go near that cursed place? I've warned him about it enough times."

"Too many times," said Miriamele. "It's just a story to him, like one of your Jack Mundwode tales."

"Praise God, I am much relieved, Majesties," said the Lord Chancellor, smiling. "So he will be well?"

"Only bruised and scraped, says Lady Thelía." Miriamele's own hands were still trembling. "And with a fine purple lump on his chin. Thanks be to our blessed Mother it was not worse." She quickly explained what had happened, or at least what she had learned: that Little Snenneq had gone and found help, that several workmen with tools and harnesses had mounted to the roof of Hjeldin's Tower, and then managed to lower the insensible Morgan to the ground.

"But he did not go *inside* the tower, I hope," Pasevalles said.

"Apparently not," said Simon. "Just slipped on the roof and hit his head. We have that to be grateful for, at least. Horrible, poisonous place. I was in it myself, you know. During the war. I still have dreams . . ." The king broke off, staring at nothing.

"If you will pardon me, then, Majesties, I will return to the Chancelry," Pasevalles said. "I was in the middle of something most important, but of course the moment I heard I hurried straight here."

"Why not?" said the king. "No reason everybody's day should be wasted because our grandson doesn't have the good sense to—"

"Yes, go, Pasevalles," Miri told him, interrupting her husband. "Say a prayer for his speedy recovery, please."

"I will light a candle this evening at mansa."

Tiamak and his wife and Brother Etan had all joined Morgan's blanket-progress back to his bed upstairs. After Pasevalles had left the chapel, only the servants, Father Nulles, and the chapel folk remained. Nulles offered his sincere sorrow at what had happened, and Miri did her best to be gracious, but what she really wanted to do was go and tend her grandson. Even Simon's anger seemed beside the point to her. The accident had already happened. There was no sense stewing over it, fuming and cursing. But when she told Simon they should go to see that the prince was comfortable in his rooms, he balked.

"You go if you want. I can't even look at him just now."

Miri felt a flare of anger. "You did worse when you were his age."

"That's different, Miri. I was not the heir to the throne. I wasn't a prince, I was just a kitchen boy. Nobody would have cared if I lived or died."

"Some would," she said, softened by a memory. "I always thought you looked interesting."

"Hah." Simon loosened enough to laugh a little. "Interesting. Yes, I'm sure you looked at a gawky, red-haired scullion tripping over his own feet and thought, 'I'd like to have a long chat with *that* likely fellow.'"

"No, that isn't what I thought." She could suddenly recall the very day she had first seen Simon running across the Inner Keep like a clumsy young colt trying its first gallop, limbs going everywhere except where they should. "I thought, 'He looks so free! Like he hasn't a care in the world. I wonder what that feels like?' That's what I thought."

"Well, at least you don't pretend you were caught by my handsome face."

"I spent my life among handsome faces, first in Meremund, then here," she said. "But I'd never seen anyone who looked less like he cared what other people were thinking than you did."

Now Simon laughed again, this time finding something more like his natural humor. "It wasn't that I didn't care at all about what people thought, I just kept forgetting, my dear one. Rachel always said that—'It's not that you're purely foolish, boy, it's that you don't remember to be clever unless you're trying to get out of a punishment.'"

"I know you miss her," Miri said. "But she scared me. Always glaring at me like she knew I'd left a mess somewhere that she'd have to clean up."

"Rachel the Dragon—the chambermaid who glared at messy princesses." Simon nodded. "Yes, that's how she would have liked to be remembered."

"Are you going to come with me to see Morgan?"

Simon shook his head. "I've seen him. I'll let you treat with him for a bit. But you and I are going to have a talk about this—you do know that, don't you?"

Miriamele sighed. "Yes, I do, and I agree he deserves punishment, but I won't let you bully him."

"It's not punishment he needs, Miri. It's something different. He has to start acting like a man, not a child."

"Don't scowl like that. It makes you look like a child yourself. No, it makes you look like Morgan." It was true, she realized—except for the hair color and the prince's lack of freckles, the resemblance was quite remarkable, especially when she remembered Simon at the same age. No wonder she had trouble staying angry at their feckless grandson.

They parted in front of the royal chapel, the king to return to scheduling the assizes with Count Eolair. Before she left, Simon squeezed her hand to reassure her, a little message between the two of them, a way to be alone together even when the whole court surrounded them.

The guards and servants had carried Morgan out of the chapel and across the courtyard to reach the wider set of stairs, because Morgan had already complained several times about the pain of being jostled, but even on the wider steps it was difficult for the men at the top end of the blanket to walk upstairs backward while lifting the weight of the man-sized prince.

As Pasevalles watched, a pair of prisoners emerged from the guardroom near the base of the stairs, two men in irons accompanied by several Erkynguards. When they saw the fuss on the stairs, the two prisoners pushed their way toward it, ignoring the complaints from their guards, who seemed rather half-hearted about the exercise of their duty. The Lord Chancellor understood a moment later when he recognized the prisoners.

"Ho, there!" he called to the sergeant of the guards. "I see you have our friends Sir Astrian and Sir Olveris."

"And hello to you, Lord Pasevalles!" Astrian called out cheerfully. "Yes, we have been taken up for the terrible crime of enjoying a few drinks, and now we're on our way to listen to Lord Zakiel scold us."

"But first we wanted to give the prince our best wishes for a swift recovery," said Olveris. With his dour, serious voice, he almost made it sound true.

"Did you hear, fellows? I fell off Hjeldin's Tower!" called Morgan from the depth of the carrying-blanket. "Thumped my jaw, cracked all my ribs! I'm in terrible pain!" But he was laughing a little breathlessly, as if it truly did hurt. "Tell Porto I shall be as feeble as he is after this."

The prisoners shouted cheerfully after him as he was carried up the next set of stairs and then through a door into the Residence.

"All right, you," said the sergeant. "You've paid your respects to the prince. What do you say we get moving?"

"Just a moment, Sergeant," said Pasevalles.

"Yes, Lord Chancellor?" The guardsman looked down at himself quickly, perhaps checking for splotches of food or anything else that Pasevalles might deem an offense against his position.

"I will take these men. I have business with them."

"But Lord Zakiel wants them brought to him."

"I understand. Tell Zakiel I will release this pair of criminals to his justice when I've finished, but first I have a pressing matter to discuss with them both."

The guard captain hesitated, plainly unhappy about relinquishing his prisoners, but even more unhappy with the idea of flouting the lord chancellor, one of the kingdom's most powerful men. Self-preservation won out over strict application of the rules. "Very well, my lord. If it's you who's taking responsibility, my lord."

"I am. And you may tell Zakiel I said so. If he needs me to give him my seal on it, send someone over to my office in the Chancelry and my secretary Wibert will give it. I will make sure the prisoners are returned to your leader just as they are now—still a bit drunk and very stupid—and he may do what he likes then. Hang them if he pleases."

"Oh, I don't think they'll hang, my lord."

"No, probably not, more's the pity."

"Are you going to give us a treat, then?" Astrian demanded. "Take us to the market and buy us each a meat pie?"

"You will be lucky if I do not have you both made *into* meat pies," said Pasevalles as the guard captain handed over his charges. "Now, march to the Chancelry. And don't dawdle."

"Aren't you going to take these fetters off?" asked Astrian.

"You must be jesting," said Pasevalles. "I wish they were heavier."

In the Chancelry, Pasevalles banished Father Wibert and his other secretaries and clerics to the outer chambers so he could be alone with the two soldiers. He had known Astrian for a long time, since his days in Nabban, and had known Olveris almost as long. He had seen them at their best and worst. He had never been so angry at either.

"What in the name of Saint Cornellis and all the other saints do you think you were doing?" He could barely keep his voice low to avoid sharing his anger with everyone in the great Chancelry building. "You know you are not to leave Morgan alone, and especially not when he's getting into this kind of madness. He could have been killed! It is only by the grace of God that he was not!"

Astrian looked a little chastened, but not much. "You told us he was drinking too much, my lord. We tried to get him to come with us to Zakiel's ceremony, but when he wouldn't . . ." He shrugged. "Welladay, what were we to do?"

"What were you to do? Go with him! Stay with him! And when he said, 'I'm going to climb that God-damned forbidden tower and fall off,' you were to say, 'No, you're not, Your Highness. You're to stay with us.' *That's* what you were supposed to do. What do you think I pay you lummocks for?"

"He's stubborn," offered Olveris.

"Stubborn? Of course he's stubborn. He's a spoiled boy barely into manhood, whose boon companions are drunken idiots. Young men his age do stupid things. It is your job to prevent him from doing them."

"We *try*—" began Astrian in a put-upon tone.

"Don't. Don't even start to make excuses." Pasevalles paced back and forth beside the table where months of accumulated work waited for him while he dealt with nonsense like this. "Do you not understand how important that boy is? He is the heir to Prester John's kingdom—the whole of the High Ward. After the king and queen, he is the most important person in this world—more important than His Sacredness, the Lector of Mother Church!" He glared, daring either one of them to reply. Having caught the drift of the conversation, neither one did. "What do you think would happen if the Lector's Horsemen's Guard let the old man go climbing around on the roof of the Sancellan Aedonitis at night and *fall off*? Do you think they'd keep their posts? Or do you think they might be drawn and quartered in Galdin's Square in front of a shrieking mob? Well? What do you think?"

"He didn't really fall *off* the tower," Astrian said quietly. "Not all the way off. Nothing around it but cobblestones. He'd have burst like a dropped egg."

"So, is that your idea of successfully protecting the heir-apparent? He only smashed his ribs and nearly broke his jaw, but he didn't burst like an egg?"

"That's not what I mean," murmured Astrian.

"We understand why you're angry, my lord," said Olveris.

"No, I don't think you do," said Pasevalles. "Because you seem to think you're the only men I trust with this work. Believe me, I can find hundreds of men who could do a better job of it than you've managed. Do you really think I couldn't find someone better in the short time it would take me to have you both taken to the headsman's block?"

Olveris, at least, looked a little pale, and a faint sheen of sweat dotted his olive skin. "No, Lord."

"No, Lord," echoed Astrian. "But—"

"*Enough*. I am going to send you back to Zakiel. Wibert will take you, because I am sick to my guts at the sight of you. And if you give either one of them any trouble, or even speak rudely, I will insist that Lord Zakiel put you in the deepest prison hole beneath the castle, behind the biggest lock he can find, and leave you there until you have rotted. Am I understood?"

"Yes, Lord," said Astrian.

"Yes, Lord," said Olveris.

Pasevalles walked to the outer chamber and called for his chief secretary. "Go now," he said when he returned with the cleric. "And whatever punishment Zakiel gives you, you will thank him and apologize. No, don't bother to say anything. I am sick of the sound of you both."

After the other hangers-on had dispersed, after Lady Thelía and Tiamak were convinced that they had done all they could and none of his injuries were serious, Morgan was left alone with only his squire, Melkin, a pair of servants, and his grandmother.

"I will never understand why you would do such a thing, Morgan." The queen was not just disappointed but downright angry. As she had become more certain he was not badly hurt, her sympathies had dissipated. It had been a bit like watching a pot slowly boiling. Morgan could not even imagine what his grandfather was going to say, and was wondering how long he could avoid hearing it. "What were you thinking? Talk to me!"

"I don't know." He tried to roll over onto his side so he wouldn't have to look at her flushed, unhappy face, but his ribs hurt too much. "I don't know. I just . . . it just happened."

"We will talk about this. Tomorrow, after you have had a night's sleep."

"It's not even afternoon yet."

"Then after you have had an afternoon's *and* a night's sleep. Your grandfather is very, very unhappy."

"Well, *that's* a surprise."

"Don't be rude, Morgan, and do *not* try to be humorous. It's really not a good idea at this moment." She put her hand on the side of his bed to steady herself as she stood. Sometimes the prince forgot that his grandmother was more than fifty years old, because she was quick to smile and almost girlish in her laughter. He knew he should feel bad for making her worry, but for some reason seeing how slowly she stood after a long time sitting just made him feel even worse. Even stranger, it made him as angry as if she thumped him in the jaw herself. Sometimes it seemed like people only cared about him so they would have an excuse to be unhappy with him. "Are you going now, Grandmother?"

"Yes. The life of the castle and the capital must go on, no matter what." She shook her head. "I pray someday you will learn that truth, Morgan—how everyone else must labor to preserve the kingdom you take for granted. To preserve your birthright."

"I don't take it for granted." But in fact, he could think of nothing worse than having to spend his days like his grandmother and grandfather did, listening to bishops and merchants and nobles, everyone with their complaints and requests for favors, all of them bad-tempered and selfish. He thought he would rather be the meanest peasant in Erkynland, mowing grass in the sweat of his brow all day. At least then he wouldn't have to talk to fools. At least he wouldn't have to do favors for ungrateful people. But that was what his grandparents and his mother wanted for him, and then they wondered why he wasn't more pleased about it.

"Where is your mother?" said the queen as she paused in the doorway. "Why isn't she here? Is it possible she hasn't heard?"

Morgan knew the question wasn't directed at him—he generally knew less about his mother's whereabouts than anyone else in the Hayholt—so he didn't even bother to shrug.

"Well, she should be here." His grandmother sent one of the servants to the dowager princess to make sure she knew what had happened, then paused in the doorway again, this time because a small, stout figure was waiting just outside.

"I have come to see the prince," said Little Snenneq. "I am wondering about his healthiness. If he is well."

"He is, thanks to you," Morgan's grandmother said. "Although I'm sure the king and I would like to hear from you at some point what you were doing up there with him."

"I am being as sad and angry as can be at myself." The troll had an extremely serious expression on his round face. "You may ask me any questioning you wish, Queen Majesty. Ask and ask and ask, and still I will answer more."

"Well, not now," the queen said, slightly flustered, and went out.

Morgan sent Melkin and the remaining servants to wait outside. "What did you tell them?" he demanded of Snenneq when they were alone.

"I could not say nothing had happened, friend Morgan! You were blooding from your chin and elsewhere. I had to say you slipped and fell down, striking your head most painfully."

"That was true. But they must have seen that door, that hatch, was open."

Snenneq shook his head. "I closed it before I went for help."

Morgan let himself fall back, and only then realized that he had been clenching all his muscles for so long he could not remember when he started. "Thank God! Oh, brave, clever Snenneq! They would have had me in the dungeon if they found out I even thought about going inside the tower. But what happened to you? I couldn't find you when I got to the top. Where were you?" A sudden memory jabbed him, dark and cold as a rusted spearpoint. "Did you see the man in red?"

Snenneq shook his head once more, his face puzzled. "I did not see anyone. When I found the doorway open leading down into the tower—"

"So you weren't the one who opened it?"

"No. With certainty, no. I would not have. I saw that it was open, though, and I was having much interest to take a quick look inside, so I was . . . climbing down into the piles of rocks. It was foolish, because I was not careful to make certain climbing out would also have such easiness. But then, when I was inside, my thoughts began to grow strange."

"I think that happened to me, too. Do you think it was magic? From the red priest?"

"Another question whose answer I am not knowing. For me, it was like dreaming. I thought I heard your voice, but so far away. And I . . . I saw things. Confusing. Without clearness. Also like dreams—bad dreams . . ." Snenneq shook his head yet again, but this time as if to clear away bad thoughts. "Then I realized I was back beneath the doorway in the roof again and you were lying there above me, with blooding . . ."

"Bleeding."

"With bleeding from your face. I climbed out and closed the doorway in the roof, then hurried down the rope and went to find others, because I was knowing I could not carry you myself." Snenneq sighed. "I am sorry if I have brought you trouble. It was not my intending."

Morgan thought for a moment. "You call me 'Friend Morgan.' Do you truly want to be my friend?"

"I *am* your friend. I am meant to help you find your destiny. It is only your knowing it that we are waiting for," said Snenneq with a crooked smile.

Morgan couldn't quite puzzle this out, but he had other concerns. "Then listen carefully. Whatever you do, *don't tell anyone that hatch was open or that you went in!* It's going to be bad enough as things are. Only Heaven knows what punishment they're going to give me, but if you tell them you went inside Hjeldin's Tower it's going to be ten times as bad. Do you understand?"

Snenneq was frowning. "But I was thinking it would be good at least to tell Qina's father, Binabik. He is having much wiseness about such things, and what happened was very strange."

"No!" Morgan realized he was almost shouting. "No," he said more quietly. "Don't. If you're my friend, you won't tell anyone about it. Just keep saying what you said—that we were on the roof, and I slipped and fell and hit my head. Do you understand? Say you understand."

"Of course I am understanding . . ."

"You're my friend, aren't you? You say you're my friend."

"That is not being the point, Morgan Prince."

"Just 'Morgan'—friends don't call each other 'prince.' You'll do what I ask, won't you? After all, there was no harm done." He gave the troll a look he hoped was sincere. "Please? Please tell me you won't say anything to anyone."

Little Snenneq took a deep breath. His face was troubled, his shoulders rounded. At last, he said, "If that is your wish."

"It is," said Morgan, relieved. "Oh, it most certainly, definitely, absolutely is. Not a word to anyone." He raised himself up a little again, despite his painful ribs. "Did you really not see him?"

"I heard you speaking about it when I found you—you too were sounding like someone dreaming. But no, I saw no one but you and myself. Perhaps because you gave your head a hit, you were dreaming."

"No. *I saw him*—and it was before I fell. It was horrible," said Morgan. "*He* was horrible. Face all shriveled, eyes all black. I think it was the red priest himself, or his ghost. I think it was Pryrates."

"Then should not someone know of that—your great-parents, or Binabik?"

"No." Morgan had no doubt about it whatsoever. "No, that would be the worst thing that could happen. The very worst thing."

34

Feeding the Familiar

They met on Black Water Field, the great square at the edge of the mists, where the mighty waters of Kigarasku the Tearfall, crashed down the broad basalt face of the Heartwall before disappearing into the mountain's un-plumbed depths. No crowd had gathered there, just Viyeki, his troop of Build-ers, and their escort of Sacrifices. And no cheering throng lined the broad Glinting Passage as they made their way through the city and toward the gates of the mountain. Only war parties marched out openly before the people of Nakkiga, and this was not one of those, but Viyeki was less certain about what kind of company it truly was, and the silence of their departure only made his unease stronger. He had never before led a work party that required such a heavy military guard. His workers and engineers numbered more than a hun-dred, but twice that many stony-faced Sacrifices accompanied them. Where in the queen's northern lands would Builders need so much protection, even with their high magister as part of the company?

It was all so strange, so unprecedented, and since his last journey into the depths, the haunting words of Ommu the Whisperer would not leave his thoughts: *"To save what you love, you will be forced to kill that which you love even more."* What could that mean? Would he have to murder Tzoja or even his beloved only child Nezeru to save his people? He could not even imagine such a thing without feeling ill. If anyone else had said it he would have thought it nonsense, but Ommu had come back from outside of life itself; he could not easily convince himself she was mistaken.

I am the head of my clan and the high magister of a great order, he told himself. *If the life of the Hikeda'ya is truly in my hands, I will have to harden myself to any deed that will save our race . . .*

"Your pardon, great master," said Riugo. Chief of Viyeki's household guards, he had never before had to deal with quite so many soldiers from the Order of Sacrifice and was having trouble hiding his unease. "Forgive my for-wardness, but when are we to know our destination? I ask not from undue curiosity, but only so that I may perform my duty and make certain your august personage will be safe."

"You will know soon after I know," Viyeki told him. He could not miss a flicker of eye-white here and there among the other guards as they traded glances, disturbed by such vagueness. Hikeda'ya liked order, and none of them liked it better than Celebrants and Sacrifices.

Rivgo finally seemed to have conquered his troublesome feelings. "Thank you, great master," he said, face expressionless, then let his horse fall back into line.

Viyeki did not know where they were bound or exactly what they were doing, because that was the way the queen wanted it, but that did not mean he was content in his ignorance. Nobody could hold a position like his without giving at least some thought to precisely what they were told not to think about. But such illicit considerations of course could not be shared, not even with other magisters. To be one of the queen's chief servitors was in many ways to lead a very lonely life.

Perhaps this solitude is the Garden's way of keeping me strong for my queen. After all, the Mother of the People has no contemporaries, and there are few who can even remember the early days in this land. It must be far more difficult for her than for any mere minion. How much strength she shows, to put up with such loneliness for all our sakes!

The soldiers at the great front gates of the city stood in respectful silence as Viyeki's company filed past them and out of the mountain. It was strange to think what a short time had passed since the mountain had collapsed, sealing Nakkiga inside and saving them from destruction at the hands of vengeful mortals. Many seasons had passed before the Builders could dig out the entrances to the city, but for the long-lived Hikeda'ya, that had been the merest moment.

Viyeki did not like to think about the mountain's fall, though. He still carried secrets from that time—deadly, dangerous secrets.

They crossed the trampled plain that had once been the Field of Banners, then continued down the old Royal Way through the ruins of the old city outside the gates, past dry canals and fallen bridges, until they reached the bank of the Iceflame. Instead of crossing it, they turned to follow the river's banks toward the crumbled remnants of the walls that had once defended Nakkiga-That-Was, following the river east. Despite the rebuilding of large parts of the old city during the queen's sleep, this outer section was still largely empty, inhabited only by animals and a few broken slaves, too useless to drag back to the fields or to their masters' manors. These escapees lived like pigeons, peering down from the roofs at Viyeki's company, darting in and out of unlocked upper stories. They believed they were avoiding recapture by their own cleverness, but Viyeki knew they were simply not worth the time or effort from the queen's soldiers that it would take to round them up. It reminded him of a poem from Shun'y'asu's forbidden book,

> *We believe that our actions thwart fate, that we extend our lives each day*
> *By guile and brave struggle.*
> *But the minions of mortality are only overwhelmed by this busy season*
> *And swiftly enough they will catch up their work again.*

Buyo, the commander of the Sacrifice league meant to guard Viyeki's Builders, slowed his horse until the magister caught up. Beside Viyeki, Riugo
straightened in his saddle, but the commander showed no interest in him, instead addressing Viyeki directly, albeit with proper deference. "Your pardon,
High Magister, but we approach the outer gates."

It was hard to miss the immense, tumbled ruins of the outer walls that
loomed before them, but Viyeki only inclined his head in acknowledgment. "I
see them, Commander Buyo."

The Sacrifice touched his chest. "Forgive me for my terrible rudeness, Magister Viyeki, but I am directed to say that once we pass out of Nakkiga-That-
Was, and until we reach the borders of our land where you will be given the
queen's orders, you and your men must do only what I say. Your safety is my
utmost concern."

"Heard and accepted, Commander."

Buyo nodded again and made a stiff gesture of respect. "Thank you, High
Magister. Soon, I am sure, all will be clear to you, and then you will direct me
once more as befits your station."

On the far side of the gates, instead of the open, empty land that Viyeki had
expected, he was surprised to see an entire company waiting for them. For an
unnerving instant he thought it might be a Northman ambush, but he soon saw
that those waiting were all Hikeda'ya, armored Sacrifices as well as some from
other orders. Was there to be yet another ceremony? Had the near-endless ritual pledges and prayers at Black Water Field not been enough for one day?

Two figures stood apart from the soldiers; as he examined them, Viyeki's
unease grew. One was tall and imposing, with ornamented black armor that
showed him to be a high-ranking Sacrifice. The other, smaller figure was
clearly from the House of Song—the arrogant posture gave it away as surely as
the hooded robe. Who could this odd pair be, Viyeki wondered, and why did
they wait for him? Did they bring some bad news that had missed him at home?
Had something happened to his daughter Nezeru, or had Viyeki himself been
undone by some unexpected treachery from Akhenabi? But why would the
Lord of Song wait until such a late moment? Viyeki reined up and did his best
to wait patiently, hiding all feeling behind the mask of his position.

"High Master Viyeki, we have been waiting for you!" said the small, slender
one, executing a shallow bow. The voice was female. "I give you greetings from
my master Lord Akhenabi. I am Host Singer Sogeyu." She then indicated her
tall, sharp-featured companion. "And this is General Kikiti of the Order of
Sacrifice." The general inclined his head. Viyeki knew Kikiti, as did most of
Nakkiga, from his vigorous suppression of dissent during the Northmen's siege
of their mountain. Some people claimed as many had died at the hands of Kikiti's warriors as had been killed by the mortals.

"And why are you here?" Viyeki asked.

"To accompany you," said Sogeyu, as though it were the most obvious thing
in the world. She drew back her hood to reveal a shaved head like an acolyte's

and an unmasked face, but Viyeki could tell from her spare, thin-skinned features that the host singer was by no means young. "In fact, I carry your orders from the Mother of All, which I will give you when the time comes."

"My orders?" Viyeki was caught by surprise. "But I thought that Commander Buyo was going to give them to me."

Sogeyu showed the closest thing to a smile that Singers generally revealed, a slight thinning of the lips to denote amusement, though her eyes remained as hard and lifeless as blackstone. "Oh, no, Magister. Your mission is too important to be entrusted to mere league commanders. Our all-knowing queen and my master wish to be sure these important directives are given directly to you—at the proper moment."

Without leaving the hands of the Order of Song, you mean, Viyeki thought, caught between deep unease at all that was strange here and anger at how he was being manipulated. "Does this mean you two will accompany me to the edge of our lands?"

"Oh, and beyond, great magister." Again, the tiniest stretching of the mouth, but the host singer was not being so openly expressive by accident, Viyeki knew. A message was being sent.

But what does she mean by 'beyond'? Where are we bound?

The additional troop of Singers and Sacrifices fell in behind them. As Viyeki's troop marched out past the last of the ruined walls and into the wilderness around the derelict outer city, the magister did his best to recover some kind of equanimity.

I do not understand what is happening here, he thought, *but for you, Great Mother, I will go anywhere, do anything. May the memory of the Garden preserve you and all the People.*

And so Viyeki sey-Enduya, lord of the Builders' Order, rode out of Nakkiga and into the wide world, a world that he knew hated him and all his kind.

He is gone, Tzoja kept thinking over and over. *He is gone, and I am alone and helpless in a house full of enemies.*

She was ashamed of herself for thinking such weak thoughts, and she knew Viyeki would have been disgusted, but that was just the problem: for all his wisdom, the one she loved did not understand his own household, his own people, in the same way that she did. How could he? Magister Viyeki was a noble of an old noble family and he was male. He did not notice the silent hatred that slaves felt for even the kindest masters. He could not grasp the murderousness of a spurned wife.

Still, though, despite her worries, she was surprised when the knock on her door came less than a bell after the High Magister had departed. She opened it cautiously and was relieved to discover that it was only one of the serving girls.

Tzoja did not even have a chance open her mouth before the servant spoke, as emotionless as a cat yawning.

"My mistress sends to know if you will join her for the evening meal, now that the master is gone."

So the bitch Khimabu was ready to begin hostilities before Viyeki had even reached the outskirts of Nakkiga-That-Was. Tzoja was caught off balance, and was furious with herself for not being ready. She had expected a respite of a day or so before Viyeki's wife began her campaign in earnest, but obviously that was not to be.

The easiest thing to do would be to refuse, of course, to claim she didn't feel well. That was probably what Lady Khimabu expected. In fact, that might very well be the excuse Viyeki's wife would use to take Tzoja into her own care, and then to make sure that the mortal woman's health took a sudden and surprising turn for the worse. Good sense dictated she should go nowhere near Khimabu's end of the residence.

"Tell your mistress that I offer her many thanks and will come at the appointed hour."

The servant gave no sign of surprise except for a very slight hesitation before bowing and retreating, but Tzoja knew she had managed an unexpected maneuver. She could only hope that either it would intrigue Khimabu enough to convince her to hold off a little longer, or that the dinner was only meant to be an exploratory gambit anyway, the opening of a cat-and-mouse game that could keep the lady of the house cheerfully occupied during the early days of her husband's absence.

Still, Tzoja knew it was a very dangerous gamble on her own part. She was not entirely helpless: She had a poison-stone to protect her, one she had brought with her from her days in the household of Valada Roskva, so many long years ago—or so many to Tzoja, at any rate. But poison was only one of many ways the mistress of the house could remove Tzoja as a rival.

All the centuries the Norns have lived in this dark mountain, she thought. *How can a people live this way—hiding from the sunshine, barely sipping at the light as though it were some dangerously potent liquor?* But it was no good to yearn after sunlight, however much she missed it now. This mountain was where Tzoja would have to make her stand if she was to survive. And the most dangerous skirmish yet was only hours away.

She began to take garments from the cedar wood chest. Dressing to confront a rival was a difficult chore in any situation, but dressing for a rival who embodied a race with a history and outlook so different from hers, a rival who also wanted her dead, made the choices even more complicated.

As she held up and considered two possible gowns, Tzoja wondered if she dared to carry her poison-stone with her. If she did, she would need a place to hide it, a billowing sleeve or something similar where she could reach it quickly when the situation presented itself, and then hide it away again just as swiftly.

She lifted it from the secret box where she kept the few mementos of her previous life and held it up to the flickering light of her lamp so she could see its tiny holes, delicate as Perdruinese lace. She was certain it had saved her at least once, when she had first arrived in the household, and she certainly would feel much safer with it somewhere near her hand tonight. But to be caught with such a thing would be a mortal insult; if it were discovered, Khimabu would not need to destroy her in secret, but could claim that Tzoja was carrying it because she herself had put something poisonous in the meal. At the very least, Khimabu could send Tzoja back to the slave barracks without Viyeki's protection, making her available to any Hikeda'ya male who wished to claim her. She did not doubt that in such a situation, Lady Khimabu would be happy to send a few suitors Tzoja's way, the rough sort who might have an accident with a fragile mortal woman.

Reluctantly, she set the poison-stone back in the small box and hid it once more behind the panel. If she truly was to dine at Khimabu's table, it would be without protection. She would be staking everything on one throw of the dice. Still, what chance did she have otherwise? The lady of the house, especially a lady as well born and well connected as Khimabu, always had all the power. Tzoja, as usual, would only have her wits.

Such an uneven contest, she thought. *But is life itself any different? That is a game nobody wins. Even the Hikeda'ya eventually must die.*

Except for the queen, of course, Tzoja reminded herself. In any country, in any time, the Norn Queen remained the exception to all rules.

"I give you greetings in the name of the Queen and the Garden." Lady Khimabu did not rise from her low couch. Her pet ermine poked its head out of her voluminous sleeve and gave Tzoja a brief, critical appraisal before disappearing once more.

"As do I, great lady," Tzoja replied. "I thank you for inviting one such as me to your table. The honor is above me." She waited to be asked to sit, although since there were only two couches set out, it was fairly obvious where her place was to be.

Khimabu did not seem in a great hurry to indulge her. "No need for false modesty, dear younger sister Tzoja. All know the great service you have performed for our master's house. But I see you have dressed with a modesty that befits your humility."

Tzoja bowed. She had put on her finest gown, of course, an intricate weave of flowing, faintly shimmering spinsilk beaded with tiny pearls. This was just Khimabu's way of poking at her, reminding her of her low station in the household. The gown was not showy, it was true, but no auxiliary wife, still less a mortal one, would make the mistake of outdressing the mistress of the household. Khimabu wore a beautiful, billowing swirl of pale green with gold tones that glowed beneath the outer fabric, the whole garment covered with an elaborate fretwork of knotted cords in darker green. Donning such a gown was the work of several servants over a goodly amount of time. Khimabu's beauteous swirl of dark hair and her peerless face had also been brought to perfection with the help of many trained hands.

"Come, sit, Tzoja," she said. "There is no need for such formality with me. The sort of intimacy we share makes us family!" Khimabu spread her long fingers just below her chin, an ancient formal gesture called "the fan" that indicated a kind of pleasure at the speaker's own daring.

As Tzoja lowered herself onto the couch with as much grace as she could manage—none of the half-dozen servants came forward to help her—the ermine poked its head out of Khimabu's sleeve again. Its eyes were like black stones set into the white fur of the face. It abruptly slithered across its mistress and vanished into her other sleeve. The creature's brief reappearance gave Tzoja the beginning of an idea.

"You are most kind, my lady," she said out loud. "It is an honor to join you. I have always thought this was one of the most beautiful rooms in this beautiful house."

In truth, the dining salon was quite striking, a room many times as high as it was wide, not uncommon among the Hikeda'ya, whose greatest sign of wealth and privilege was access to the light wells that stretched across the northern and southern faces of Do'Nakkiga—the mountain Tzoja had once called Stormspike. Never in her childhood had she ever dreamed that she would one day be living in such a terrifying, infamous place.

The salon's stone walls were softened ever so slightly by long hangings decorated with what Tzoja had come to understand was a sort of poetry, bits of old tales about the Garden or praise of the Queen, painted in ways Viyeki's people found pleasing to the eye. The few pieces of furniture in the room were spare, made from polished black and gray stone, another habit of the Hikeda'ya, who largely shunned color in their homes, though not always on their persons: the green gown her enemy wore would be considered a very daring thing to wear outside of this house.

Khimabu *was* beautiful. There was no doubting it. Tzoja had grown up among people who thought the Norns demons and monsters, but if they could see Khimabu's sculpted features, her long, regal nose, her splendid high cheekbones and large, liquid black eyes, they would have had to admit she was a lovely demon indeed.

"You stare at me," Khimabu said, and made the fan sign again, but this time with a small twist at the end that suggested a certain impatience. "Has it really been so long since we have spent time together, dear younger sister, that you have forgotten how I look? I know that time seems to pass more swiftly for your people." A glint in the eye, the meaning quite clear. "Forgive me if I have been forgetful."

"No, Lady. I am, as always, astonished to find your beauty is even greater in life than it was in my memory."

Khimabu laid one finger beside her cheek, a gesture Tzoja did not immediately recognize. "You flatter me, my dear one. You have charms of your own, as you well know."

In other words: My husband liked you well enough to bed you. And if you hadn't borne a child, you would have been back in the slave pens long ago, or worse. Tzoja spread her hands in what she knew was a clumsy version of a Hikeda'ya gesture, but whose meaning was too clear to mistake: *How can anyone guess what males will do?* "I am grateful," is what she said out loud.

Khimabu made a tiny gesture. One of the Bound servants left his position against the wall and was at his mistress' side so quickly he seemed almost to dissolve and reform. "You may serve," she told him.

The ermine was out again and watching Tzoja, whiskers twitching. She had never liked Khimabu's pet. Its eyes were too bright, too . . . intrusive. It felt like she was being watched by an unpleasant child. But for once, as she watched it frisking in and out of Khimabu's sleeves and around the low couch, she was grateful for its presence.

The servants brought dishes to the table, roasted glacier waxwings and the bitter *puju* bread made from the barley grown in the cold valleys below Storm-spike's eastern flank, cooked in the ashes of a fire until it was as crisp and hard as wood. The Hikeda'ya had a great fondness for it, but Tzoja had never learned to like it. All she ever tasted was the ashes.

As she made appropriate sounds about the arrangement and quality of the food, she took a morsel of *puju* in her hand and broke off a piece, then pretended to take a bite, rolling it between thumb and fingers until she had made it into a stiff ball. She then dropped it onto the floor as surreptitiously as she could, and kicked it with equal caution toward Khimabu's couch.

"And the birds look especially delicious," she said out loud, doing her best not to make it obvious she was also watching the floor. As was the custom, the waxwings were served all but whole, feathers scorched away but feet and heads still attached, the beaks like black thorns, the eyes like burned currants.

The ermine had noticed the morsel of bread, and now balanced on the edge of the couch, nose twitching. It looked up at her with a nasty twinkle, as if it knew what she was doing, but after a moment, as Tzoja pretended to take another bite, it leaped down and snapped up the small tidbit, then slithered back onto the couch.

"As you know, our generous lord, High Magister Viyeki, has been given a great honor by the Mother of All," said Khimabu. "All blessings upon her, the queen has put fortyfold soldiers at his command to watch over and guard his engineers and laborers."

"It's quite wonderful how the queen recognizes my master's worth," said Tzoja dutifully. Judging by the still-twitching nose and malicious little bead eyes, the ermine was not suffering from his taste of *puju*. This time Tzoja took an actual bite, doing her best to hide her dislike of its harsh flavor. "Do you know where he is bound?"

"By the Garden, no!" Khimabu made another graceful gesture, this one signifying that it was beyond her powers to know the counsels of the wise. "He goes at the queen's bidding and is sworn to secrecy. It is clearly a mission of some importance, though, so we must bear the burden of his absence bravely." She spread her hands in a double fan. She was changing the subject. "But you have already had to bear the sadness of your daughter's absence, although that brings high honor to our house as well. Imagine—despite her . . . drawbacks, she is a Queen's Talon!"

"She was very lucky to be chosen, but of course the queen is never wrong."

"Never. And Nezeru so young!"

Tzoja had flicked a couple of shreds of the roasted waxwing into the ermine's hunting range while concentrating on her *puju*. She did her best to watch without seeming to as the little creature approached, sniffed, and then gobbled them down. Another few moments, then if the animal survived, she could move on to eating some of the bird as well, which to this point she had only pushed around on her platter. "You have been very kind to Nezeru, Lady Khimabu. You have treated her with the kindness you would show your own daughter." That was a dreadful exaggeration—Khimabu had never been anything other than coldly correct to her husband's child by another woman—but neither of the two women were paying much attention to what the other appeared to be saying.

"Oh, it is only right to do so. Is she not my husband's child? Have you not gifted us—gifted our entire household—with her birth?" The bland look on Khimabu's face was indistinguishable from murderous rage, but that was usually true with the Hikeda'ya. "But you must fear for her, so far away."

"I do, but I trust in the queen's wisdom." As Tzoja watched, the ermine coiled itself on Khimabu's shoulder and almost seemed to be paying attention to the conversation. The animal did not appear to have been poisoned, though, so Tzoja began picking at her own bird with the scraping-fork the Hikeda'ya preferred to use on cooked meat, taking it in only in small quantities. "My Lord Viyeki once told me that part of the reason for our daughter's swift advancement was your own family's support of her, my lady. That was very generous of you."

Khimabu's gesture was a strange one, *water on flat rock*, which usually meant that all would be revealed in the fullness of time. The magister's wife seemed to notice this herself only after beginning, because she quickly turned it into a more ordinary sign, one that represented a carefully prescribed amount of social gratitude. "That which helps my husband helps me and all my family. Not that my relatives are themselves overlooked or unappreciated. The queen has often been kind enough to take notice of them."

"Your uncle is high in one of the orders, I've been told, but I have never known the details." Tzoja had always assumed it must be the Order of Sacrifice, since that was the order that had taken Nezeru and awarded her with great responsibility. For once the conversation and her actual curiosity had dovetailed in an acceptable way. "Is it permitted to ask which?"

Khimabu's eyes positively glittered with what looked to Tzoja like malicious amusement, although her face showed nothing that was not correct. "Of course it is permissible to ask, dear little sister. We share so much already. My uncle Inyakki is one of the chief clerics in the employ of Akhenabi, Lord of the Order of Song."

A sudden chill ran up Tzoja's spine. A Singer? Why had she not known that? Why had Viyeki never told her?

As she sat, temporarily dumbfounded, the ermine abruptly scrambled from Khimabu's shoulder, down the lady's sleeve and onto the pale leather of the couch beside her. A moment later, it made a little *urp* noise and began to vomit, spewing out a tiny pile of gristle and sludge and pale liquid.

Tzoja could only stare in horrified fascination, the meat in her own mouth suddenly unchewable because her tongue had gone dry as dust.

"Ah, my little companion seems to have had a bit too much of this rich food," said Khimabu, a smile in her voice if not on her face. "Have you been stealing from our plates, tiny villain? Have you been making free with everyone's supper?" She turned her masklike face toward Tzoja. "He is terrible, you know. He will eat anything and everything, without caution—he would poison himself if I did not constantly watch him! Why, what is wrong, Tzoja? You look quite pale for one of your complexion. Please don't worry for him. He will be fine, soon. I'll have a servant clean up right now if it puts you off your meal."

"Actually, I'm afraid I *am* feeling a bit unwell," Tzoja said. "I think like your pet, the food is a bit rich for me."

"Familiar," said Khimabu.

"What?"

"That is what we always called such animals growing up. Not pets but familiars. They are so much more than mere pets." And as if to demonstrate the truth of this, the ermine looked up from its own pool of sick and stared right at Tzoja. She could almost have sworn it was amused.

She got up, her legs shaky. The bitch Khimabu had been toying with her all along—she must have seen everything. *What a fool, what a failure I must appear to this beautiful, heartless creature,* Tzoja thought—a cheap, shabby copy that some craftsman had thrown aside half-finished. "Please forgive me, Lady Khimabu. Your hospitality has been most kind, your conversation most enlightening."

"But you are not unwell, are you? How sad!" She made the spread-hands sign of sorrowful condolence, exaggerated to make clear its insincerity, Tzoja felt sure. "We were just beginning to talk!"

"I do apologize. I think I need to lie down."

"But of course. We will continue this at supper tomorrow night, then, if you are well enough. Now that my husband is absent, this is my chance to get to know you properly. I would not let anything interfere with that."

Once she had backed out of the dining salon, Tzoja hurried back across the great house to her own chamber on shaking legs, her heart booming in her chest so that it seemed everyone behind the closed doors of the silent hall must hear it.

She will kill me. But she'll play with me first, because she enjoys it. Tzoja could barely breathe as she fumbled with the latch of her door. *I cannot stay here, but there is nowhere safe for me in this haunted country, or any way to leave it.*

She closed the door behind her, locked it with latch and bolt, then forced herself to vomit the few scraps she'd eaten into her chamber pot before tumbling onto her bed, breathless with despair.

35

The Man with the Odd Smile

"**Hurry up,** child! The Duchess is waiting for you!" Even though Duke Saluceris was not present, his ancient valet Oren still considered himself chief among the servants of the Domos Bendriyan, the family palace built by the first Benidrivis some two hundred years earlier. Jesa sometimes thought stiff old Oren might actually have been there since the first stones were laid. He certainly acted like it.

"Her Lady said to clean and swaddle the baby, Master Oren," she said, trying to keep the irritation from her voice but not succeeding. "And that is what I am doing." She would not have dared speak back to a superior servant in her first years with the Duchess, but Jesa knew her place now, and also knew that it would take a fairly serious breach of courtesy for Duchess Canthia to turn against her.

"Her *Ladyship*, you swamp brat, not 'Her Lady'. How can a servant in a great house not be able to speak correctly?"

"It is not even your tongue," Jesa replied, somewhat daringly. "It is old King John's tongue, and you do not speak it so goodly, either." She was not satisfied with the swaddling, so she unwrapped little Serasina and began again. "And I am here for caring for the baby, not for making your ears happy."

Oren shook his head. "This," he said grimly. "This is just what I have said—even servants these days are insolent."

"Not insolent," Jesa said. "Just busy. Much busy." Ah, if Oren only understood the Wrannaman tongue, how she would put him in his place! The language of her birth had many, many ways for a woman to correct a man who had set himself too highly.

After a moment's consideration, she decided a translation might still carry the meaning: "Now, if you have nothing to do but hang from a branch, you might as well go back to your nest and make spit bubbles." It didn't quite carry the same weight as the original, which likened an unwanted commentator to one of the ghants, horrid, murderous creatures that infested the back ways of the marshy Wran, but conveyed her general meaning.

"Disrespectful beast," said Oren. "Talk sense." But he seemed to lose interest in scolding her further and wandered off, presumably to bark at the grooms or the coachman about something.

Jesa finished little Serasina's swaddling, testing it with her finger to make sure the blanket was not wrapped either too loosely or too tightly. The baby made a pop-eyed face and let out a minuscule belch. Jesa laughed and picked her up, then carried her as carefully out to the stairs and down to the front doors as if she were her own baby.

The coach, a great rectangular chamber on wheels, was waiting for them on the cobbled forecourt. Jesa made a curtsy, then handed little Serasina up to her mother before climbing the steps.

"Will she be warm enough?" the duchess asked, frowning in concern.

If anyone found Nabban chilly, it was Jesa, child of the humid swamps, but the day was lovely, a near-perfect Avril morning with only a small hint of a breeze and the morning fog long since scoured from the hills on which the Domos Benidriyan perched. "It is a good day, Your Grace. I believe she is warm enough."

"Are you sure? Oh, I worry so. Just sennight last I heard a terrible story of fever in Purta Falessis."

"She is very strong, your little one. Look, see her look around! She is not cold and sick. She likes the air!"

"I hope so." The duchess squeezed her daughter tightly for a moment, then handed her back to Jesa. "But you are right—it's a lovely day to be out." She knocked on the carriage roof. As the driver snapped the reins and the team of horses began to pull, Canthia nodded and smiled at the servants lined up to see them off, more than two dozen of the household staff all together, maids and grooms and valets.

As the carriage rolled across the grounds and through the palace gates, all the hills of Nabban were laid out before them. The Domos Benidriyan stood above the vineyards and other palaces of one of the great hills, the Antigine, and had a fine view of the other two tallest crests, the Redenturine, home of the Sancellan Aedonitis, the heart of Mother Church, and the steep Mahistrevine that rose above the harbor with the ducal palace at its peak, like a figurehead on the bow of a ship.

Because of her humble beginnings in the Wran, Jesa had never got used to the idea of riding in the ducal carriage—there were only four or five such carriages in all Nabban (one belonged to the Lector himself!) and fewer than a dozen in all the known world, her mistress had once told her. It was also a painful ride. Even on smooth dirt the carriage jounced, and on cobblestones, at speed, she felt like she was sitting on a branch in a high wind, struggling to hold on while it whipped up and down. But just now the driver was in no hurry and the horses were all pulling strongly and evenly. Little Serasina had been fed by the wet nurse before being changed, and had already dropped into the sleep of innocence.

As they made their way down the steeply winding road, people came out to look and sometimes to wave or cheer, and the duchess looked out on her subjects with a fixed smile. As some children leaped up and down, shouting in excitement, Canthia smiled more broadly and waved back, but except for that brief moment, the duchess seemed almost sad.

"Is everything right, Your Grace?"

The duchess nodded. "All is well, Jesa. I just cannot help worrying about my husband. He should have come here to the hill with Serasina and me, but I could not convince him. He works so hard! I fear he will make himself ill."

"He is strong, your husband," said Jesa.

"In some ways." Duchess Canthia smiled. "But in some ways, he is like all men—strong without bending. And things that do not bend . . . well, sometimes they break."

Jesa did not understand this. From everything she understood, many of the people in Nabban who were angry with the Duke thought he was too forgiving, that he was allowing his brother and the Albatross people—what were their names?—too much freedom to complain and make trouble. *Ingadarine House*, she remembered then: the Albatross was House Ingadaris, just as the Kingfisher was House Benidrivis. The rival families of Nabban were harder to keep track of than even the village squabbles she had grown up with and their complicated old stories about which fishing spot belonged to which family. Having money and carriages and stone houses did not seem to keep drylanders from fighting with each other just as much as marsh-folk.

After a while, as the carriage descended from the hill into the close-cramped neighborhoods of the poor, fewer people gathered to cheer the ducal carriage, although many still stood to watch them pass. Looking at the faces, Jesa could not help feeling a shiver of worry at the scowls many of them wore. But when the road swung out and followed the course of the Great Canal, she began to have an idea why so many of them looked angry. A great swath of buildings along the canal had been burned; some of them still leaked plumes of smoke into the gray sky. At the turn of a bend, she could see that a broad cloud of smoke hung over the near side of the city as well, just inside the walls. Now she remembered a messenger telling her mistress the previous night that there had been a riot in the warehouse district. But surely that had happened two or three days ago, or so the messenger had said—why were some of the buildings still burning?

It was well into the afternoon by the time they reached the city walls. The chief gatewarden came out in full regalia to speak to them when the carriage stopped in front of the huge iron and timber North Gate. He stood on the carriage steps, and had to take off his broad hat to get his head in at the window on the door.

"Why are the gates closed, Warden?" asked Canthia. "It is the middle of the day!"

"Your Grace, there is trouble in Tellis Narassi." That was a poor neighborhood on the other side of the gates, Jesa knew, inhabited primarily by immigrants from the southern islands. She also knew that it was close to the Patorine Hill where Dallo Ingadaris kept his townhouse. She wondered if Duke Saluceris' rival had something to do with the disturbance.

Jesa might wonder, but Duchess Canthia had no doubts. "A curse on Count Dallo," she said. "He should have cleared this rabble from the streets himself. Is there a better way around?"

"Your Grace can have her driver continue around to the Port Gate," the chief warder said. "If you go that way, you can come up Harbor Way to the Mahistrevine Road."

"That will take hours more," the duchess said. "I have a hungry child in my carriage." She looked over at Jesa as if contemplating the strength of her own forces.

"Please, Mistress," Jesa said quietly. "Let us do what this good man says. Let us go around."

"No one will harm the Duke's child," Canthia declared. "And no one will harm the Duchess. This is Nabban, not some backwater. There is a sacred law of safe passage inside the city."

Jesa knew nothing about such a law, but she did know that people were not supposed to set roofs on fire either, and yet a cloud of black smoke hung just a short distance away over the city wall. Once people broke one rule, they did not usually wait long before breaking another. "No, Mistress, I beg you! Think of your child!"

"It is my child I am thinking of," said the duchess. "I will not let my husband's brother and his bullies forbid the duke's family the use of our own streets!" She turned to the gatewarden. "Open them up, Captain. We will drive through."

The warden's reluctance showed in his face, but he waved to the guards in the gatehouse and they turned the great windlass. The gates slowly swung open, and the driver urged the horses through, with the warden still standing on the carriage step.

"Merchants Road is blocked just up ahead, Your Grace," the warden said. "You cannot go that way. If you insist, you must go by Sailmakers Road, but even so I cannot let you go with no more than a driver and two guards. I will give you eight of my riders to clear your way."

"Do you not need them to protect the gate?" asked the duchess.

He gave her a look of helplessness. "Please, Your Grace. It is a bad day for you to be abroad in the city. Let me help as I can."

"Very well. We will go up Sailmakers Road." She looked down at her baby, still cradled in Jesa's arms. "I thank you for your thoughtfulness, Warden."

"It is my duty, Your Grace. I wish I could do more. But I wish even more that you would reconsider." He darted a look at Jesa, so worried that he was willing to seek an ally even in a Wrannawoman nursemaid. "I wish in truth you would turn your carriage around and return to your house in the hills."

"That cannot be, Warden." Duchess Canthia's tone made the end of the conversation quite clear.

Eight petty-knights with lances formed up in front of the carriage before they started forward again. Following the gate-warden's suggestion, the driver turned the wide carriage into Sailmakers Road, which ran along the Great Canal in the shadow of the walls. But after they had left that broad thorough-fare they found themselves in a series of narrow back streets where their progress slowed to a walking man's pace. Once they had to stop and change the hitching of the horses to get around a tight corner, setting the tired beasts in three rows so that they could make their way through the tight space between the looming buildings. None of those who watched in curiosity as this lengthy trick was performed seemed anything other than interested to see Duchess Canthia at such close range, but Jesa did not like the way they crowded up to peer in the windows while the carriage was stopped. She put her back to the nearest window, trying to protect baby Serasina from staring eyes.

They finally reached the wider Harbor Road, which mounted toward the Mahistrevine Hill and the Sancellan from the west. With the sun now at their backs but still high in the sky, Jesa felt her heart beating more easily. Then the vast carriage rattled to a stop again.

"We cannot go further this way, Your Grace," called the driver.

"Whyever not?" the duchess asked.

One of the petty-knights brought his horse close to the carriage. "There is an ostler's wagon overturned at the far side of St. Lavennin's Square, Your Grace. The square is full, and they are breaking open the casks." He was look-ing at something neither the duchess or Jesa could see. "Oh, Merciful Elysia," he said quietly.

"What? What is it?"

"Someone has lit the cart on fire, Your Grace." He stood in his stirrups and shouted to the driver. "Hurry, man! You must turn this carriage around! We will be trapped here."

The mounted knights moved in beside the carriage as the driver began to pull the horses around, but already the crowd in the square was pushing in close, most of the people simply curious, a few conspicuously drunk. Jesa moved in toward the middle of her seat as the faces of those who managed to wriggle forward between the mounted guards leered in from both sides.

"I cannot turn it around without unhitching the horses!" the driver called. "But I do not.—"

Duchess Canthia waited for a long moment. Outside, the crush of people was actually making the carriage shake. It was all Jesa could do not to scream in fear, but she did not want to upset baby Serasina, who had just awakened and was goggling her eyes, trying to decide whether to cry or not.

"Driver?" the duchess called. "Driver?"

The crush was so great now that the carriage swayed continuously. Jesa caught a glimpse of a face she had not seen before, a strange-looking, disheveled man with an even stranger smile, who seemed content to stand a short distance back from the carriage peering in at them.

One of the petty-knights appeared at the window. "Your Grace, someone has pulled the driver off the carriage! You are in danger if you remain here. Come with me onto my horse. We will have to cut our way out!"

But before the duchess could reply, the knight suddenly toppled from his saddle and was swallowed up by the sea of people. His horse high-stepped away into the crowd, knocking people down while making a squealing noise that Jesa had never heard an animal make before. Together with the shrieks of those the beast trod upon, the din grew so piercingly loud that Jesa thought she was losing her mind.

"Duchess," she cried, "we have to run! We must get out and run!" The dark-haired man with the odd grin was back near the carriage window again, staring as though he watched an enjoyable performance, even as others rocked the vehicle from side to side. There was something strange about the man's face besides the fixed smile, something rough and odd and unusual about his skin. Jesa could also see more than a few red Albatross badges scattered through the crowd, and nary a Kingfisher. "It's a trap!" she cried. "They'll murder us!"

"Nonsense," said Canthia, but her eyes said she did not entirely believe what she was saying. "My husband's crest is on the carriage! They will never dare to harm their duchess or their duke's child!"

Now the vehicle swayed even more violently, so that Jesa slid from her seat and into the duchess. It was only luck that little Serasina was not crushed between them.

"Get out, get out!" Jesa shouted, but she could barely hear herself above the shouts from the surrounding crowd. She reached for the door beside the duchess but the press of people outside was too thick and the door would not open. Suddenly the whole carriage tipped sideways. Jesa turned to her own side and saw the man with the odd smile again, but now he was climbing in through the window.

"She is calling me," the man said. His grin was fixed like a stone carving, and he spoke as calmly as if he continued a conversation he and Jesa had begun earlier. He first worked his shoulders through the carriage window, then his arms. Duchess Canthia had fallen forward as the carriage tipped, and could not get up from where she was wedged between the seat and the floor. The intruder reached toward the baby in Jesa's arms, and she saw that he had a sharpened wooden stake in one hand. "I am summoned by the Whisperer—I must go to her," the smiling man said, so offhandedly he might have been talking to himself. "But it is such a long way! So I will bring her a gift—something warm . . ."

Jesa managed to get her foot up and kick the intruder full in the face, but he only fell back a short way, and managed to gouge her leg with his stake, drawing blood, before she could pull it back. He began to climb again until he had forced his entire upper body into the carriage. Jesa gave the baby to Duchess

Canthia and did her best to shield the tiny body with her own, kicking and hitting out at the intruder, but this time he blocked the blows with his free arm and continued to clamber in, still grinning.

The last thing I will ever see . . . that terrible face . . . Jesa thought, then suddenly the man's demented grin contracted in puzzlement; a moment later he was jerked backward out of the carriage. Jesa did not see what happened, but heard a whistling cry that began as rage and ended as nothing. A lacy spray of blood splashed the carriage window frame.

The noise outside abruptly changed. The cacophony of voices grew louder and more shrill, but now Jesa also heard the thunder of shod hooves on cobblestone, then screams and other dreadful noises that, if less human, might have come from a butcher's yard. The carriage stopped swaying.

Another face appeared in the window. To Jesa's surprise, the newcomer's skin was as dark as her own, but he wore shiny armor. He had taken off his helmet, and his broad, handsome face was full of worry.

"Your Grace, do you live?" he asked, trying to sort out who was who in the muddle into which Jesa, the duchess, and the baby had fallen.

"Yes, I live," the duchess said from beneath Jesa. "And thanks to our beloved Ransomer, the Aedon, my baby also lives. Who are you?"

"Viscount Matreu of Spenit, Your Grace. We have met before, but it was long ago. Thanks be to God that my men and I were riding this way! We have put the rabble to flight. Are you injured?"

"Not as far as I can tell," Canthia said. "Will you get off me now, Jesa, so I can speak to our rescuer? Thank you." The duchess worriedly examined little Serasina, but the baby seemed to be no worse than startled by the events. "What do we do now? Can we drive on?"

"I fear your driver is dead, and so are several of your guards," said Matreu. "And both of the wide roads out of this square are blocked. We will have to take you and your child and your servant onto our horses."

Jesa thought she had never seen a man so admirable, in part because she felt sure that without his intervention, she and her mistress and innocent little Serasina would all be dead. In that moment, if someone had told her the dark-skinned count was one of the Aedonite God's angels, she would have seriously considered turning her back on He Who Always Steps On Sand to embrace a new faith. But her joy and wonder were short-lived: as she was helped out of the carriage and saw the way it had been defaced and damaged, and then caught sight of all the bodies lying on the ground, she swooned and stumbled and would have fallen had not one of Count Matreu's soldiers leaned down from his saddle and caught her arm.

Jesa felt as though she dreamed: things that had happened and things that were happening were now swirled together, with little to tell them apart. She would remember little of the ride to the Sancellan Mahistrevis except the smoke in the air and the puzzled, sometimes hostile looks of the citizens they passed. As they made their slow way up the hill Duchess Canthia rode in front of the count, carrying her baby, while Jesa clung to the back of one of the other knights. She had never been on a horse before, and the experience was only slightly less frightening than what had happened in the carriage.

The one thing she definitely saw, and would wish ever afterward that she hadn't, was beside the carriage when she first stepped down. The smiling man's head was no longer attached to his body. Both parts of him lay on the cobbles just a short distance away, each surrounded by a pool of shiny blood, and the severed head still wore the same strange grin.

"It is an outrage!" said Duke Saluceris. "God preserve us, they tried to murder my wife and child! I will have my brother's head for this—and Dallo the Ingadarine's as well!"

"We should move on him now, before he can leave the city." This was Idexes Claves, Lord Chancellor and one of the duke's closest allies.

"But what of your brother?" demanded Rillian Albias, the Solicitor General. Like the other nobles crowded into the parlor, the leader of the Albian house was armed for war. "We cannot take up Dallo and leave Drusis loose. The Stormbirds all but count your brother as their leader already—they know who holds the power."

The Duchess, who had been stroking Serasina's face as she fell asleep in her basket, now stood. "Stay with her," she told Jesa before going to join the men. She left the door open, doubtless to listen in case little Serasina should cry, but it allowed Jesa to hear and see what was going on. She was still fascinated by the viscount. Since she had come to Nabban she had seen almost no one who looked like herself who was not a servant or something lower.

"Gentlemen," the duchess said, "I am as disturbed by this as any of you, but we cannot allow ourselves to be driven to illegal action."

"I beg your pardon, Your Grace," Idexes said, "but legalities will do us no good when our enemies murder us in our beds." His tone was respectful, but his thin face looked as though he had bitten a lemon by accident.

"I doubt my husband feels the same—do you, Saluceris?"

Jesa winced, and was glad no one could see her in the darkened room where the baby was sleeping. The duchess was generally sweet-tempered, but Canthia did not like Idexes at all: if the duke did not take her side, there would be trouble later.

"It is more complicated than that, my dear wife," said Saluceris; Jesa could almost feel the look she felt sure the duchess must be giving him.

"Of course it is, my dear husband. That is the point I am making. Do you think that if you round up the leaders of the mob they will admit that Drusis and the Ingadarines urged them to riot?"

"They will tell the truth under torture," insisted Rillian Albias.

"They will say anything their torturers suggest," said the duchess. "And their families will hate us forever, and other houses will take their sides who are now neutral, and Lector Vidian himself will denounce us—do not forget that he became lector largely because of Dallo Ingadaris' father. And I have not even pointed out that the High Queen in Erkynland is Ingadarine by blood. How much sympathy will we have from the High Throne if we execute the queen's cousin on the evidence of a few tortured peasants?"

Jesa could hear Idexes struggling to remain courteous. "And what does Her Grace suggest? That we allow this attack to go unpunished? That we pretend it never happened? Do you know, they burned three of my warehouses? Nine hundred gold imperators worth of goods lost!"

"For all your talk of murder," the duchess said, "your concern seems to be more with your money."

"That is unfair. Your Grace, must I have my motives impugned?" Idexes was clearly talking to the duke now—Jesa saw him clink past the opening of the door, his armor jingling. "We are your staunchest allies, Duke Saluceris. Must we suffer for it?"

"Enough, enough." Saluceris sounded tired and frustrated, his anger now turned on something more inward. "Yes, Idexes, you are my ally. I do not forget that. And I'm sure the duchess does not forget it, either. Do you, my lady?"

"Of course not, my lord." But Canthia did not sound very contrite.

"May *I* say something, Your Grace?"

Jesa straightened a little, recognizing the voice of Viscount Matreu, her rescuer.

"Why is this man here?" Rillian Albias asked suddenly. "Those of us gathered here have been with you all along, Your Grace. Who is this man and how does he gain a place among us?"

"You know me perfectly well, Count Rillian," said Matreu.

"This man saved my life, and the life of the Duke's child," said the duchess. "Have you something to say against him? Because I will be interested to hear what that might be, that would keep the one man who actually did something useful out of this discussion."

"Please, my dear. Rillian did not know all that happened, as he has just arrived." But the duke's voice was indeed a little sharper as he addressed the count of Albias. "Matreu has done a heroic thing, for which you should all thank him a thousand times. Of course he may speak."

"Thank you, Your Grace. I only wished to point out that the riot did not begin this evening. It began last night, when three men wearing the Ingadarine albatross were found dead on the steps of Sacred Redeemer's Church in Tellis Narassi. The rumor is that it was another brawl between Kingfishers and Stormbirds, as they more and more call themselves. But this one went further than most and ended in murder. To put things plainly, it was not difficult for your enemies to find angry folk in that neighborhood this morning. If my counsel means anything, I suggest that an even-handed approach might be more useful. Find all who engaged in the brawl, no matter which side they were on, and punish the survivors."

"Are you mad?" said Idexes shrilly. "Punish our own men for defending themselves? Your Grace, the Ingadarines swagger all over the north side of the city as though one of their own sits here in the Sancellan Mahistrevis. They pick fights with our armed soldiers when they can find them, and when they cannot, they find innocents who happen to be wearing some token of support for *your* throne and then beat them half to death. Apparently a few of these villains ran into someone who fought back against their mischief. You cannot make an example of your own supporters!"

"I disagree," said Matreu. "That is exactly what you must do if you wish to keep the peace, Duke Saluceris. Punish all who engage in illegal brawling, regardless of what badge they wear or to what house they bear allegiance. Only that way will you convince the rest of Nabban that you want peace and justice."

"Peace and justice," snorted Rillian. "It sounds to me as though you wish to take the sword from the duke's hand and replace it with a justice's staff. Do you confront your own enemies with a book of laws?"

"Sometimes it is not so easy to know who your enemies are, Count Rillian. And sometimes those who act with foolish swiftness make more enemies than they dispatch."

Jesa had to restrain the urge to cry out in pleasure at this sally, as if she were watching a game of feather-float between her brothers back home in Red Pig Lagoon. She knew that if she made a noise she would certainly be sent away, so she moved a little farther back into the shadows and sat with her hand over her mouth. Still, she was delighted to know that someone who looked so much like herself could stand and trade words with some of the mightiest men in Nabban.

"Your Grace," said a new voice with the gravelly scrape of age. "I think we waste our time in argument between ourselves that makes more smoke than heat. This is your decision and yours alone."

"That I know, Uncle," the duke said. "And as always, I value your calm words. But I would still know *your* mind."

Now Jesa knew it was old Envalles who had spoken, the brother of Duke Saluceris' late mother. Jesa had not heard him come in, but it made sense he would be present, since he was one of the duke's chief counselors. She liked Envalles, who was one of the few members of the household beside the duchess herself who ever spoke to Jesa. Sometimes he even brought her apples from his estate outside the city.

"As it happens, Your Grace, I agree with Count Idexes and Count Rillian that this assault on your wife and child cannot be ignored. But I also think there is merit in what Viscount Matreu says. Surely the people of Nabban will be as angered at this dreadful affront as we all are. Never forget, the real danger here is your brother. Without Drusis, Dallo Ingadaris is only a fat nobleman with money."

"A fat nobleman with more money than God himself and five hundred armed men inside the city walls!" protested Idexes.

"Nevertheless, it is not solely Ingadarine gold that creates this rebellion,"

Envalles said. "Some of the concerns they speak for are genuine, even if their motives are not."

"Such as?" asked Saluceris.

"We have talked of it several times in the past sennight already," said his uncle. "The Thrithings-folk continue to raid the easternmost counties, burning settlements, stealing cattle and sheep, killing those who oppose them. Much of Count Dallo's influence comes from the border nobles. They are frightened, and they are right to be so. The men of the grasslands are numerous. If they ever cease fighting among themselves—if anyone ever unites them—Nabban itself will be in danger. All the civilized lands will be."

"I respect your uncle's wisdom," said Rialles in a way that made it sound to Jesa as if he spoke through clenched teeth, "but I think in this case he is being foolish."

"Dangerous words," said the duchess, but she was not as loud as she could have been.

"Why foolish?" asked Saluceris.

"Because any movement against the grasslanders will rebound against us," Rillian said. "Shall we send Drusis to fight them? Or Dallo, or Tiyanis Sulis? Because the Sulian lands are threatened as well. Should one of them defeat the grassmen but die in battle, then yes, all would be well. But if he pacifies the Thrithings and brings prisoners and booty back to Nabban like one of the old Imperators? What then? And if that victorious general is your brother Drusis, the very people who support you most would step aside to let him be put on the ducal throne."

"What you say makes sense, but does that mean we cannot strike the grasslanders at all?" demanded the duke. "I have no heir to send. My son Blasis is scarcely three years old—a bit too young to carry my standard into battle."

"Do not jest, husband, please." Canthia sounded genuinely pained at the thought.

"Send me, Your Grace," said Idexes suddenly. "Let me lead a force against the Thrithings-men. I will make those mud-men fear the Kingfisher again!"

"But it must not be only your allies who do this," said old Envalles. "Nobles of the houses whose lands have been raided must also be allowed to satisfy their honor—and their greed for glory and plunder."

"What plunder could the grasslanders have?" Rillian snorted. "Wagons? Sheep?"

"Horses," came Matreu's prompt reply. "The finest horses in all the world. Several thousand Thrithings steeds would be prize enough for any campaign, and their bloodlines would enrich our stables for centuries. More importantly, though, it would draw the attention of the common folk, who already talk about the grass-men as though they were unstoppable demons. But do not forget justice for this riot, too, Your Grace. An even-handed punishment, not unduly severe except for those who actually incited or committed murder, will also help to pour water on Dallo Ingadarine and your brother, where they would rather set a fire."

Either the room fell silent then or the voices of those discussing these high, frightening matters fell too low for Jesa to hear. She did not know what to think, although she was prejudiced toward all Viscount Matreu had said. She wished she knew more about him, this unlikely man who had suddenly thrust his way into the very innermost circles of the duke's household.

She curled up beside Serasina's cradle, but still felt unsettled. Such terrible things! War, murder, torture, all discussed in a single room in a great stone house.

How can men rule other men? she wondered. *How do they know they are right and not wrong? How can you know enough to take someone's life? Is that the difference between the drylanders' God and He Who Always Steps On Sand?* Did their God, the one they worshipped in their high stone churches, direct the hands of men, so that no man was killed who did not deserve it? She wished she could believe that.

After a while she took little Serasina out of her cradle and hugged her to her breast for comfort. The baby wiggled a bit, gurgled, and then was silent. Together she and Jesa fell asleep in the dark.

36

A Foolish Dream

After riding for several days and nights across the Osterdyr plain, across thawing mud, newborn streams, and swelling rivers that had been covered in ice only a short time ago, Makho's Talons now crossed back into the lands the snow seldom left, league upon league of empty tundra. Nezeru had never seen such a desolate, empty place. But for a few marks of wagon or sledge preserved in frozen mud, or the occasional view of a distant village (never more than a few high-peaked roofs, chimneys leaking smoke into the cold, gray air) this might have been some country that neither mortal nor immortal had ever discovered. But Osterdyr was not as empty as it appeared.

"Someone or something is following us," Makho announced as they ate a sparse meal one morning. "When the wind is right, I can smell animal fat and animal skins and the stink of mortals."

"No mortal would be fool enough to let us catch him," said Kemme, then looked at Jarnulf with a grin that was nothing more than bared teeth.

"Surely even the Hikeda'ya are not foolish enough to think themselves unkillable," Jarnulf said. "It might be a good idea to learn who is following us."

"It is not one, it is many," said Goh Gam Gar. As usual, the giant sat at a distance from the rest of them—Makho, as master of the collar that kept the monster docile, was always careful to stay beyond the reach of those long arms. Goh Gam Gar was eating the carcass of a frozen elk he'd found, tearing the icy mass into pieces and devouring it bones and all with, Nezeru thought, the righteous pleasure of a Hikeda'ya nobleman eating slices from a still-wriggling Lake Rumiya salmon. The giant largely foraged for himself, devouring huge quantities of berries and leafy plants when he couldn't get meat. But when he did have the chance to hunt, he nearly always succeeded: Nezeru had seen him snatch a live squirrel off a branch and throw it into his mouth with a single motion, then swallow it in one gulp, like a fur-covered berry.

"Many?" Nezeru asked. "Many what?"

"Many mortals. They are too far away to count their numbers, but their stink has been with us for a while." Goh Gam Gar let out a deep, rumbling laugh. "I doubt they are fewer than this company, however. What small party of mortals would follow the Hikeda'ya?"

"But who could it be?" Nezeru asked.

"These lands are mostly empty of settlements," Jarnulf said. "But there are bandits who prey on travelers and merchant convoys all the way down to the Erkynlandish border. They find these empty lands a convenient base. There is also the Skalijar."

Nezeru heard *Skolli-yar*, a word she did not know. "And who or what is that?"

"Bandits, but of a different sort. They came from the remnants of the Rimmersgarders who fought for you Hikeda'ya in the war, although they did not understand that was what they did. They were crushed by your Zida'ya cousins in Hernystir and their leader, a man named Skali, was killed. After that, many of the survivors turned their backs on their own people and the newer Aedonite faith, returning to the gods of their forefathers. But do not think them allies. They believe both the Hikeda'ya and the Zida'ya to be demons and will kill them when they can."

Makho was staring out at the northern horizon, where the snows still covered the meadows and the distant hills. "It is interesting that you chose to bring us this way, and now we are followed, mortal. It is also interesting you know so much about these outlaw Rimmersmen."

"I helped you escape from goblins, Hand Chieftain Makho, when otherwise you all would have died. I brought you safely through the Springmarsh and found river fords for you. And also I led you through the edges of the Dimmerskog without harm, where there are creatures uglier and more unpleasant to meet even than our friend Goh Gam Gar. Still you treat me with distrust, though you have traveled twice as fast as you would have without me."

"Yes. Just as we traveled swiftly toward the mortal ruler and his mortal army not so long ago."

Jarnulf's face remained cold, his eyes unblinking. "That mistake was not mine, as you well know. I grow tired of hearing that foolish accusation."

Now Saomeji, who had been looking east, contemplating the foothills of Urmsheim, said, "It still is not clear to me why you *do* help us, mortal. You have had many opportunities to escape."

"Escape?" Jarnulf laughed. "Why should I escape? I am no Rimmersman, whatever I look like. I was raised among the Hikeda'ya. You made me what I am. If I am not one of the most important servants of the Mother of All, I am still one of her huntsmen. Why should I not do what I can to aid her Talons?"

"You make a fair point," said Saomeji, lacing his fingers together and performing a bow that even Jarnulf must have recognized as mocking. "We Hikeda'ya are a suspicious race, of course, having so often found ourselves betrayed by mortals. Forgive me for questioning your motives, Huntsman."

For a moment, as he turned from the Singer in disgust, Jarnulf's icy blue eyes met Nezeru's. She had no idea what the mortal was thinking, and that by itself was intriguing—in her small experience of his race, they were guileless as cattle.

She did not fully believe him about his motives, but for some reason she could not quite name, she also did not believe he meant to betray them.

I have never met a creature I understood less, Nezeru thought. *Not even the giant.*

Within days they reached the foothills the Northmen called Urmsbakkir, and began the slow ascent toward Urmsheim itself, which jutted like a wolf's fang above the smaller peaks on either side. Farther south the world enjoyed the full coming of spring: Nezeru knew that despite the snow on the ground, the slaves and Bound workers outside Nakkiga would be crawling out of their hovels to spend as much time as they could in the sun. But here at the northern edge of the world it was still winter, as it almost always was.

As the cold mists rose, the slopes became steeper; climbing became steadily more difficult. The Hikeda'ya were more and more often forced to lead their horses. Sometimes the giant had to lift the terrified animals over an obstacle; Nezeru found it almost painful to watch the usually stolid Nakkiga steeds' eye-rolling panic at the monster's touch. Other tracks were too narrow for Goh Gam Gar himself, forcing him to find a different way up. Makho would always keep him in sight, the crystal goad clutched firmly in his hand until the giant had rejoined the procession.

Unless he was giving orders, Makho hardly talked with any of the company but the Singer Saomeji during these days which made Nezeru uneasy. She did not understand exactly what had happened at Bitter Moon Castle, but it was clear Akhenabi's intervention had changed things profoundly, and even Makho himself seemed uneasy with their new mission.

They were near the base of Urmsheim itself, working their way up a difficult hill when the attack came.

The slope was scree spotted with drifts of snow—an accumulation of loose rock and boulders that the horses, if led, could just manage to climb. Because of the danger to whoever was below, they took the horses up one at a time.

Kemme had already reached the crest, and Saomeji had climbed it behind him. Nezeru watched from the bottom of the hill as Jarnulf led his own horse up over the loose rock. The mortal was almost as light and precise of foot as the Hikeda'ya, but that did not prevent both man and mount nearly tumbling when an errant hoof started a small avalanche beneath them. Nezeru moved quickly to the side to avoid stones as big as her head tumbling toward her. Jarnulf spread his arms for a moment before regaining his balance. He examined his horse, which had toppled onto its side, then urged the shaken beast onto its feet again and began to lead it up the last few steps to the crest.

It had become clear earlier that the giant would not be able to make it up this loose slope without causing a much larger rockfall, so the great beast and Makho were taking a longer but less steep way, a gully strewn with boulders so large that the giant often had to put Makho's horse under his arm and carry it, like a Nakkiga noblewoman with a pet lynx. The horse occasionally wriggled and kicked in fear at being held by the monster, but it had been raised in the stables deep beneath the mountain and stayed silent.

As Nezeru stood, poised to begin her own climb as soon as Jarnulf was off the dangerous slope, she saw Makho turn abruptly, as though someone had shouted to him. A moment later he staggered. Nezeru thought the usually sure-footed Makho had simply put a foot wrong until she saw the arrow quivering in his shoulder. Then the chieftain slipped from the tall rock and tumbled out of her sight.

A moment later loud, hoarse cries tore the air as a troop of bearded men came swarming across the hilltop toward Kemme and Saomeji from both sides, loosing arrows. The first flights missed, which gave the two Hikeda'ya a chance to find shelter behind an outcropping near the brow of the hill, but it was clear that in moments they would be surrounded and cut down. Nezeru counted something near two dozen attackers, all mortal men in ragged clothing. Only a few had drawn their bows; the rest hurried forward with axes and swords raised.

There was no time to force her horse to climb the slope. She scrambled upward as quickly as she could, using her hands almost as frequently as her feet. Arrows began to snap past her head: the enemies atop the hill had seen her.

Trying to move swiftly over the loose stones was like a bad dream but Nezeru knew she had no choice, since the slope offered nowhere to hide. An arrow ripped through her hood where it lay against her back, but she kept scrambling upward on all fours. An instant later, just as she reached the top, another shaft broke against a stone not an arm's-length from her face. She threw herself down and lay with half her body still on the slope until she spotted her shaggy mortal attacker hurrying forward to finish her. Her bow was caught beneath her, so she pulled her knife and, after a split-instant to locate the balance, threw it with as much strength as she could muster. The blade whirled end over end, and though she did not manage to lodge it in his throat, the pommel broke the man's nose, dropping him face-first to the ground with blood sheeting down his face.

Safe for a moment, Nezeru turned to where Kemme and Saomeji still huddled against the tall stone on the crest even as a half dozen or more of the bearded men drew closer with every heartbeat. The Northmen's excited shouts were as incomprehensible to her ears as the barking of hounds. She scrambled off the slope onto a snowy patch of dirty snow and dead grasses, then took her bow from her shoulder. Her first arrow missed, but her second took one of the attackers in the thigh. He stumbled and fell, then got to his feet to pluck the arrow from his leg. As he did, Nezeru nocked another arrow and sent it whistling through his chain mail and into his chest.

The rest of the attackers were nearly on top of Saomeji and Kemme, and some now split off from the main group to charge downhill toward Nezeru and

Jarnulf, who stood only a little distance above her. She thought the mortals made an ugly collection, bearded men much bigger than herself wearing ill-matched armor, slavering and howling like wild dogs.

Jarnulf had thrown down his bow and pulled out his sword, and now he waded into the first pair to reach him, his blade so swift it seemed almost ghostly in the misty air. As Nezeru climbed back to her feet she saw three more attackers sprinting toward her. She managed to knock one down with an arrow to the body, but couldn't tell whether the shot had been fatal. Then, as the other two rushed at her, one with sword drawn and the other swinging a heavy two-handed ax, she threw herself forward, swinging her bow, and hit the ax-wielder in the face with it. He stumbled and fell to his knees, bleeding from the nose and eyes, but she had won only a momentary respite because his companion was still coming.

Nezeru threw down the bow and drew her sword from its belt ring in time to guide the weight of the man's swinging blade to one side, but the bearded mortal was strong and the point of his blade still hit her shoulder. Her witch-wood armor took most of the force, but her arm went numb and for a moment she could only hold her sword with the other hand as her attacker turned, teeth bared and eyes wild, and rushed at her once more, blade swinging for her head. Behind him, the ax-wielding man whose nose she had broken was climbing to his feet. She had only moments before he came to help the swordsman.

Rock Serpent retreat, she told herself. *Grass Blade to take the force. A kick to keep him going.*

She parried. Her opponent stumbled past as she whirled away and then helped him along with her foot. But even as he staggered and lost his footing, stopping himself only by putting his sword hand and blade flat on the snowy ground, the ax-man was on her, his face streaming with blood, the whites of his eyes staring out of the scarlet smear as bright as candleflames. He had clearly decided that she was no easy victim, and began to move her backward with swift but skillful swings of his ax. She dared not try to take the blows on her sword: the blade might survive the clash, but her shoulder was still tingling from the swordsman's strike and she was afraid she might lose all sense in it if it was hit hard again. But she could hear the man with the sword getting up behind her, his boots scuffling in loose stones. She located Jarnulf, barely visible in the mist and still occupied with his own attackers. She could not even guess what Kemme and the Singer were doing.

The Dance! she reminded herself. *Think only of the Dance of Sacrifice.*

Nezeru had spent hour after hour in the Blood Yards as her teachers sent armed men and women against her, some of them already trained Sacrifices, but far more often criminals and slaves who had tried to escape and were now forced into the role of unwilling soldiers, with no hope of living out the day unless they killed her. In just one of the grueling sessions at the Yards she had fought from the third hour of the clock until the ninth, facing twenty-two opponents in all. The last, as Nezeru was staggering with weariness, had been a trained killer named Summer Ice, one of the Order of Sacrifice's most deadly graduates but under sentence of death for being found drunk on duty.

I beat him, she reminded herself, *though I was half-dead when I fought him. I killed them all. That is why I am here.*

"I stand for the Queen!" she shouted. Her enemies could not understand her, of course, but the swordsman shouted something back and charged her.

The first surprise of the attack over, she reminded herself what her sword-mentors had taught her and began to take control, planning ahead as if she were playing *shent* with her father. She angled herself so that she could retreat toward the spot where Jarnulf fought, then did her best to even the odds by not letting her opponents get onto either side of her.

She was startled by a sudden loud crack like thunder, then another, but although she could see flashes of light at the corner of her eye, she dared not look. *The Dance,* she told herself. *Only the Dance.* But that did not mean she could not pretend to look. At the next loud thundercrack from nearby, she swiveled her eyes for an instant; the swordsman took the bait, swinging for her neck. She dropped to her knees and gutted him with a swift, two-handed thrust of her own blade, then was back up again before her other foe could take advantage.

Now she could hear the noises of sword on sword very close behind her. "Mortal, I am here!" she called.

"I can see you, queenswoman," Jarnulf said. "Stay where you are—I have a little trick I've been saving."

Her own moment came as he was speaking. Her opponent swung his heavy ax again, but though she had to move quickly to avoid it, she could see he was tired and starting to slow, so as he pulled it back again she leaped toward him and stabbed downward, shoving her light, narrow blade through his foot so that he shrieked and stumbled backward. She held onto her blade, widened her stance, bent and yanked hard. The man went over on his back in a puff of snow, losing his ax as he fell. She tried to free her sword to finish him, but the blade would not come completely free of his boot, so she scooped up the man's own ax and crashed it through his forehead before he could do more than rise onto his elbows. He fell back, his already unlovely, broken-nosed face now a scarlet ruin.

She turned in time to see the end of Jarnulf's "trick." He was whirling his sword above his head with only one hand on the hilt—Nezeru could not tell whether it was to be attack or defense. The lone mortal facing him could not understand it either, and with a shout of frustration, threw himself forward just as Jarnulf let go of the sword, which flew well over the man's head and disappeared behind him. As the man gaped at this bizarre ploy, Jarnulf ducked under the man's swinging cut, then seemed to clutch at the bearded fighter's waist. A moment later they both went down in a confusing roil of furs and limbs.

Jarnulf was the one who stood up, however, his unusually long knife gripped in his hand. Not even Nezeru had seen him draw it, but it was bloodied almost to the guard.

"You fight like a Sacrifice," she said.

"I told you. The great Xoka himself taught me."

The mist was streaming past them now, caught by a sudden wind from the heights. Nezeru found she could see across the hillcrest, which was littered with the bodies of their enemies. Makho had been knocked to the ground by a huge man with an eyepatch, who stood over the chieftain, ready to finish him. She scrambled up the slope, but knew she would never reach them in time.

The one-eyed man brought his sword up to stab Makho, but just before the killing blow fell, the mortal looked in Nezeru's direction and his lone eye opened wide with surprise, as if she were a long-lost daughter, some child he had thought never to see again.

"You . . . ?" was all he said, then an arrow sprouted from his chest, shivering among his furs like the branch of a leafless tree. His mouth gaped in his thick, dark beard, and Nezeru saw blood run down his chest like a black river, then another arrow took him in the forehead and threw him backward to the ground.

Only then did Nezeru turn to see Jarnulf, who had scrambled back to his discarded bow. Only then did she realize that it must have been him, not her, who had so surprised the one-eyed man.

Nezeru's legs were still moving, but now without purpose. She stumbled to a stop. Nothing else stirred except Jarnulf as he crunched across the snowy gravel toward her.

"He was a big one," he said, but she thought she heard something beneath his words, something that gave the lie to his offhand tone. "But still I think Makho will not thank me."

"The mortal seemed to recognize you," Nezeru said, then immediately wished she hadn't spoken. *Never give what you know away until it is useful to reveal it.* That was what her father had taught her, and her mother too, both in their own ways, and it had been the root of many of her teachers' lessons in the Order of Sacrifice.

Jarnulf gave her a look. "Not likely," he said, but again she thought she detected something more beneath the words. "I've never seen the ugly bastard before." He looked around. "I don't see anyone else coming. I think that was all of them."

She held her tongue as they reached Makho, who lay on his stomach, struggling to rise. The arrow that had struck him earlier was gone, although the wound was obvious and bloody. Nezeru had no doubt he had pulled it out with his own hands, eager to join the fighting.

A short distance away, beside the big stone, they found Kemme and Saomeji in the middle of a circle of bearded corpses. Kemme was wounded in a dozen places but was already sitting up, tightening his belt around his arm to staunch the blood from the worst of his wounds. The Singer lay motionless a short distance away. He seemed unharmed as far as Nezeru could see, and even when she turned him over she could find no blood, but he was utterly insensible and limp as a rag, as though he had fallen asleep in the middle of the life and death struggle.

"What happened here?" she wondered aloud. "What did these mortals want?"

Jarnulf bent over one of the corpses and cut something free, then held it up—a wedge-shaped piece of iron dangling on a leather cord. "Do you see this?" He shook the heavy medallion. "Hovnir, the Ax of Udun Rimmer, the old god of my people. These are Skalijar, as I guessed."

"But why should they hunt us?"

Jarnulf shrugged. "We are bound for Urmsheim. There is a place there called the Uduntree, sacred to the old gods of the Rimmersfolk. I told you, they think your people demons. They wanted to keep us off their sacred ground."

"A foolish reason to die." She turned back to examining Saomeji.

"Do you know any better ones?" Jarnulf asked, but before she could even wonder what such a strange thing meant, he let out a low whistle of surprise. When she turned to see what had startled him, she saw he had lifted up another corpse. It was really only half a corpse, though, since everything from the shoulders up was gone, leaving only a smoking tatter of burnt furs and blackened flesh pierced by jagged bits of bone. "By God, what happened to this one?" Jarnulf said, his eyes wide. For the first time since the fighting had begun, she saw real fear on his face.

"The Singer did that," said Kemme, getting unevenly to his feet. "A pretty trick of his I did not have much chance to watch. Something to do with stones. He killed several that way before he fell down like that."

"We must get him and Makho to shelter," said Nezeru.

Kemme stared at her, blood smeared across his hawklike face. "Until Makho can speak for himself, only I give orders, halfblood." He pointed at Saomeji. "You two take the Singer, I will carry Makho."

Jarnulf was looking around. "Where is the giant? I don't see him."

Kemme's mouth began to curl into a sneer until he grasped the meaning of what Jarnulf had said. Then, with a snarl of frustration, he fell to his knees and plucked at Makho's belt until he found the pouch that held the crystal rod. He stood up, holding it, and cupped one hand to his mouth.

"Giant! Where are you? Come to me now, or I will choke you and roast your heart. Do you feel your collar?" He held the rod near his lips, whispered something—Nezeru thought she heard a low murmur of song. An instant later, a terrible bellow of pain and fury rose from the slope below.

"*Curse you!*" came Goh Gam Gar's booming voice. "*I am trapped under stones down here! If you do that to me again, I will dig through the very mountain itself to rip your head off!*"

Kemme laughed harshly. He whispered to the rod again, and was rewarded with another ground-shaking bellow from the giant. "Well, I suppose we should dig him out," he said at last. "Then he can carry the other two to shelter."

*　　*　　*

It was strange to sit around a fire as mortals did, but when Saomeji had recovered enough to speak he had begged them to light one. Now he huddled beside it, as weak as if he had just survived a terrible fever. The smoke drifted up and out of the shallow cavern to be shredded by the mounting wind.

"A trick, of sorts," he said when Jarnulf asked him about the burned corpses. "It was a piece of luck we were surrounded by the right kind of stones. Most will not hold so much heat long enough."

"Long enough for what?"

"Long enough to throw them before they burst." He shook his head and inched a bit closer to the flames. "I sang fire into them until they grew hot, then threw them." He lifted his right hand. The skin was terribly red and blistered. "But it is hard to bring so much force to bear so quickly. I am exhausted. I am sure I will sleep as if I were a child again."

Later, while they were out gathering more wood, a task that Nezeru had never performed before, she found herself near Jarnulf while Kemme, the other member of the expedition, was a good distance away.

"So those were Skalijar," she said. "Will we meet more of them?"

Jarnulf banged a log against a tree, knocking snow from it. "I doubt it. They waited until they felt it was the best time to attack, when the giant was not with us. That was more than two score men that we killed. If there had been more, they would have already made themselves known."

"But why? Why would they attack us? You said they believe us demons. Why would they take such a risk?"

"You do not understand mortals, Sacrifice, even if you are half a mortal yourself. We do not always do what makes sense. Especially when we are driven by fear or rage."

"They were so afraid of us that they attacked us?"

"They were afraid of us doing what we are going to do—climb Urmsheim, their sacred mountain. And they believed they could prevent us because their gods wanted it so—that with the gods' help, they could defeat demons. That is their story. That is the tale that gives their lives sense."

"So you are saying that they were foolish, like children."

Jarnulf added a new log to his pile, then stepped back and looked at her squarely. "I am saying that all living things that think have a story, something that makes sense out of the howling chaos into which they are born. You should know, Nezeru of the Order of Sacrifice. Your people would have curled up and died long ago if you did not cling to the story of the Garden and of your undying queen. You believe that she will lead you back to happiness again, just as in those long-ago days, and so you endure terrible hardships, dreadful wars. You do not even protest the fact that you will likely not be alive to see that happiness if it ever comes."

For a moment, Nezeru could not understand him. "But you know that is not a mere story. The Garden, the queen—it is all true!"

Jarnulf's face was again carefully emotionless. "If you say so."

"But she is your queen, too! Are you not her huntsman—her slave-taker? Do you not labor in her service?" Frightened that they had reached such strange territory of thought, she looked around for Kemme, but he was still high up the slope.

"I have my own story. Being a servant of the Queen of the Hikeda'ya does not command my thoughts as well. Even you could think differently if you chose."

"That is treason!"

"If you say so."

"How do you know I will not go to Kemme or Makho and tell them what you say?"

"I don't. Is that part of your story? That when somebody's words make you frightened, you must see that one destroyed?"

Nezeru had never experienced anything like this and did not know how to think about it. His ideas were worse than treasonous, they were terrifying. They turned the world upside down. But at the same time, as though she had been pushed from a great height, she also felt a moment of wild freedom simply contemplating such things. It frightened her, but she was not ready to flee from it. "You are a very strange, very dangerous man."

"You could not even guess."

She watched him as he continued his search for wood, as calm as if he had not just called the Mother of All a liar and the Garden a foolish dream. "How can you live without a story, mortal? How could anyone live that way?"

"You'd be surprised. And I never said I didn't have a story of my own. When you meet someone who has lost his story, then you will see someone who is *truly* dangerous." He surveyed his stack of logs and broken branches. "Perhaps it is time for us to go back. I cannot carry more than this."

But now Nezeru wanted to talk. She knew so many things that proved him wrong, but why should she even argue with him? Surely it would be better to denounce him and have done with it. She knew that any feeling of confusion as strong as this must be a sort of dark magic. But all she could think of were more questions.

"You know a lot about the Skalijar," she said. "Why is that?"

He gave her an irritated look. "I told you all. I have moved through this part of the world for years. I have also been farther to the south than you can even imagine—well into the lands of mortals. I have been in their cities."

"You have? How?"

The edge of his mouth curled—was he fighting a smile? "Well, do not forget, Sacrifice Nezeru, I *am* a mortal. Nobody was likely to be very surprised to see another Rimmersman."

More questions fought for release, but even she was surprised at the first one that escaped. "What are they like? The mortal cities?"

He shrugged. "Loud. Dirty—in fact, you would think them filthy. People build higgledy-piggledy, wherever they choose. People do what they want, and when they get in each others' way, they argue."

Nezeru could not imagine this. "How can such a thing be? It must be dreadful! Why would their rulers let them behave so?"

"Two possibilities, Sacrifice. One is that their rulers are not as strong and clever as ours. Another is that they do not fear freedom as much as ours do."

"You make a joke. That is not freedom, to fight with other people, to do what you wish! That is chaos."

"Well, perhaps that is the difference, then. Mortals feel more comfortable with the freedom of chaos than the freedom of obedience."

Now she felt certain that he was inventing things that could not be true, and it made her angry. "You knew that man," she said suddenly. "He knew you."

Jarnulf showed her a blank face. "What man are you talking about?"

"The one-eyed man of the Skalijar who tried to kill Makho. He saw you, and he recognized you."

"I doubt that. But if he did, it is no mystery. I have been traveling the borderlands for years. I have had encounters with such people before. I have killed some of them, but others no doubt lived to remember me."

Nezeru shook her head. "I do not believe you, mortal. That was not the look he gave you. That was not what was in his face—the sight of an old enemy. He was surprised to see you, but he recognized you."

"None of that disproves what I have said."

From high up the slope, Kemme turned and began to make his way back toward them, a huge pile of logs cradled in an improvised sling over his back.

"Just tell me the truth," Nezeru said, and was aware of a kind of desperation in her need to know, although she could not say why. "Did you know that one-eyed man?"

He turned to look at her as he shouldered his burden of wood, and to her astonishment, he smiled broadly, like a man who had just been given high praise or rich reward. "I never saw him before this day."

He was lying, of course, and not only that, he knew that *she* knew he was lying—he had as much as told her so with that easy, self-satisfied grin. It should have sent her running to Makho, but it did not. Instead, it filled her with a curious agitation she had never known, so unexpected and so unusual that for long moments she could not even make sense of what it was. Only as she followed his lean form back toward the cave where Makho and Saomeji waited, did she begin to understand it.

This man—this mortal man, she thought wonderingly. *No, this traitor. Why does he fascinate me so?*

37

Two Bedroom Conversations

It was a warm night. The upper floors of the Hayholt's royal residence were full of hot damp air that had the sparking feel of imminent thunder. The servants had been dismissed to the outer room and now the queen sat naked at her mirror, brushing her hair.

"God reminds us that these bodies are only loaned to us, to clothe our spirits while we walk the sinful earth," she said suddenly.

Simon was huddled in the bed already, wearing a night shirt despite the heat. He had been thinking about Urmsheim again (perhaps because these days it no longer came to him in dreams), thinking on those long ago days when he and Jiriki and Binabik and the others had climbed to the Uduntree. Beneath it all lay the deeper memory of the dragon's icy blue stare, the agonizing splash of its hot, black blood. Thinking of it again, he shivered. "I'm sorry. What are you talking about, wife?"

"This," she said, cupping her breasts with her hands. "This fading, falling body."

"I think you are beautiful," he said.

"You are kind to say so."

"What do you mean, kind? Do you call me a liar, woman?" He laughed. "I loved you from the first moment I saw you. Do you think me that shallow, now that I am old too? Come to bed."

"Not yet." She continued brushing. Miriamele kept her hair long now, but a part of Simon missed the days when she had been less careful, less formal, when she had cut her hair short to hide her identity, like someone out of a story.

God's Blood, have we truly become old? he wondered. *I do not feel old. I feel the same, but . . . weathered. Like a ship that has plowed the same waves for many years. The rigging is slack, the sails have holes, but the bottom is still seaworthy.* He laughed again.

"What is funny?" Her voice had the brittle sound he knew too well.

"Just . . . I just thought that I am glad our bottoms are still seaworthy."

Miriamele gave him a sharp look over her shoulder, then glanced down at her own pale, vulnerable body. "Do you mock me, husband?"

"Never. Oh, dear one, not in a thousand, thousand years. Come to bed."

"I will. But do not think you will paw me tonight and paddle my cheek and make me forgive you. I am angry, Simon."

He sighed. "Still?"

"What do you mean, still? You act as if this were a lark, a game. We are sending our only heir—our only grandson!—away into the wild woods. Into danger."

"We are all sent into danger," he said, and was quite pleased with himself for the idea. "And we will all fail in the end. That is God's will. It does no good to struggle against it."

"You are punishing your grandson because I will not let you go marching off to look for the Sithi." She stared directly at her own reflection. She would not meet his eye. "I thought we were equals, husband. I have learned the truth."

"What? What nonsense is this? You know as well as I do that the boy needs seasoning. He has lived only for himself."

"And getting him killed will improve that?"

Simon slapped his hands on the bedclothes in frustration. "I do not wish to see him harmed, may God preserve us, I wish to see him *grown*. What will happen when we die if he does not change? The whole of the High Ward in the hands of a selfish boy—a boy who does not want to be a man, except when it comes to drinking and wenching. For the love of the Aedon, Miriamele, he climbed Hjeldin's Tower on a drunken wager! What if he had fallen and dashed out his brains on the cobblestones? Would you still say he was better off here than going out into the world?"

"Do not invent things to try to shame me, Simon. You have never been kind to him."

Simon closed his eyes, fighting against the weary anger that he had thought was behind them tonight. "Come to bed. You will take ill, sitting uncovered like that."

"Perhaps you had better send me off on some dangerous task. That would be a more certain way of silencing me."

"Damn me, do you think I want him to go because I want him harmed, Miri? Are you mad? It is you who wants to keep him home because . . . because you cannot forgive yourself for John Josua." Even as he said it, Simon knew he had opened a door that was better left closed. Her silence seemed to confirm it.

When that silence had stretched a while, he said, "Miri? Dear wife? That was wrong of me. That is a pain that should be left out of our disagreements."

"No," she said. "No, there is some truth in what you say. But how can you not feel that, too? After losing our only son, how can you so blithely send your grandson out into the perils of the wild world?"

"Because he is to be a king, Miri. A king cannot be shielded from consequences, or he will become a king who does not understand what ruling means."

"Is this about my father, then? His madness?"

"No, no, no." He took a deep breath, trying to think of words that would carry his meaning when he did not entirely understand it himself. "This is a far bigger matter than you make it. I said to you once, let me go to the Sithi. They are our allies, but they have fallen away from us. But you would not let me go. If we ever needed their counsel, we need it now. So someone must go to them."

"Then Eolair is the right choice. We do not need to send our heir as well."

"But it is not about what we need, it is about what Morgan needs." He lifted the coverlet. "Come here. I promise not to paw you. Come here and talk to me. It makes my bones ache just watching you sitting there in the cold."

"It is not cold, it is summer-warm though spring has barely ended. Are you having the dreams again?" Something changed in her voice, just a little. "Is it the mountain?"

"No dreams still. But I remember the mountain, of course. That is not all that is in my mind, though. Come here. Come to bed."

As if to remind him that she was no servant to hurry at his command, the queen slid the brush through her hair a few more times. At last, she put down the mirror and the brush and came to the bed and slipped quickly under the coverlet that Simon held.

"Are you hiding your charms from me?" he said, half-amused. "Are you afraid I will be overcome with base lust? S'Tree, now that I think of it, I might be." He reached for her, felt the cool, silky flesh of her hip beneath his fingers. "Come here and find out."

"No! Stop! You gave me a promise!" She pushed his hand away, but wiggled closer so that he could press himself against her. "You are in a good mood because you have won the argument and will have your way about our grandson. But I am not going to share your mood. Go to sleep."

He let his head fall back against the pillow and stared up at the canopy, blue cloth studded with stars, like a map of the firmament. "Why do you think that I wanted so badly to go to the Sithi?" he said at last.

Miriamele stirred. "Because we need their wisdom. And you are right about that, Simon . . ."

"No. I wanted to go to the Sithi because I miss my friends."

"You have many friends. Binabik is right here with you!"

"Not for much longer, Miri. How long has it been since we saw him last, before now? Years. And how long since we have seen any Sithi-folk except their poisoned messenger? Ten years? More, I think." He pushed himself up a little so that he could cradle her head in the crook of his arm. It was hard for Simon to understand, when they were close like this, how such a small person as his wife should be so powerful, should be able to reach into his heart at will and squeeze it, leaving no wound on his flesh but making his soul ache. "I miss them, Miri. I miss the days we traveled together. Not because I miss being young—although that's there, of course—but because I miss having true friends."

She turned a little to look at him. "You have many true friends."

"Friends at court are not true friends. There are a few, like Jeremias and Eolair, who knew me before we were put on the throne . . ."

"I was not *put on* the throne, remember. I was the king's daughter."

"Unbend a little, my sweetheart. There was never a more unpopular monarch than your father since Crexis the Goat killed the Redeemer. The truth is, neither of us should have ruled. It should have been your father's brother Josua, who led the fight against him, but Josua passed the throne to us instead." He reached over and carefully began to stroke her hair. "But all this is neither here or there. I want to see the Sithi again. I cannot say why, but I will never feel complete again if I do not. The world we knew in our youth is gone, but the Sithi are not. You never saw Jao é-Tinukai'i, but there is nothing like it in the world. Even the greatest cities the Sithi once built can't compare. It was like a song, a story . . ." He could not find the words and fell silent.

"What does that have to do with Morgan? *He* doesn't know the Sithi, and will probably not feel anything like the same thing as you if he meets them. He will complain that they don't know any funny songs and the women are too old." She laughed suddenly in spite of herself. "I imagine he will be less successful seducing women who have lived a thousand years."

"I imagine so." Simon closed his eyes. The stars on the canopy were beginning to dizzy him. He had not realized until this moment that he was tired. "God gives us one short life, Miriamele. I was lucky to have wise teachers— Binabik, Geloë, Aditu, Jiriki, and most of all Morgenes. They taught me to see beyond the obvious. I try to remember that. Morgan has had no such teacher."

"Then *be that teacher*, Simon. Do not send him away. The Sithi are not as they were. They are not going to take him in and tutor him."

"But that is just the point, Miri. You're right. The Sithi are different than they were to me, or at least they seem to have changed. The world is different than it was when we were young. We have tried to teach him, but Morgan has never wanted to learn anything from us, so he has to learn for himself. So far, he has only had a little patch of the world to explore, and he has known it only as a prince. No wonder he sees little beyond the bottom of a tankard!"

"You can't make him be like you, Simon."

"I don't want to. I want him to learn things on his own. Not completely alone, of course. Eolair is one of the kindest, wisest men I know. And don't forget, Morgan will also have the trolls as companions for much of the trip. I know Binabik and Sisqi won't let him come to harm if it can be avoided or escaped."

"Don't, Simon. Don't be so trusting. God didn't save John Josua, for all our prayers."

"I trust nothing as true except what I have seen, Miri. That's why Morgan needs something different. He will grow. He will see something of the world, a part of it that does not know to bow down to him, to indulge him, to pardon him when he behaves badly. What if you had never left Meremund? What if you had spent the whole of the Storm King's war living in a castle, hearing news only from servants who didn't want to upset you? What if you had never tested your own courage?"

"Many would have been happier if I hadn't," she said with some bitterness. "They called me mannish. They called me a witch for cutting my hair and wearing men's garb."

"Not me," said Simon, but could not keep the yawn inside him any longer. "I called you perfect. I called you my love."

She slid her head up a little higher, so that her mouth was close to his ear. Even after so many years, the feeling of her warm breath there still made him shudder a little. "Go to sleep," she said. "You are tired and tomorrow will be a difficult day." She kissed him. "But do not think you have cured all my unhappiness or curbed all my anger."

"Wouldn't dream of it." Sleep was tugging at him, and for once he was glad he had stopped dreaming. He didn't want to see that deadly blue eye again. He didn't want to feel that ancient, unforgotten cold.

He was knocking, knocking so loud the entire castle must hear it, but still the heavy door remained shut, a solid rectangle of dark wood. He pounded until his knuckles were sore, but still no one answered him.

"Father!" His voice was high and quavering because he was close to tears, but knew that if he let them flow he would be mocked—princes do not weep. "Father, are you there? Why won't you answer?"

Just when he was about to turn away, as he had so many other times, the door silently swung open, then stopped, exposing a black gap of barely a hand's breadth. He stared. His heart seemed to be thumping as loud as his knuckles had against the ancient wood, as though someone was still knocking. Somehow he knew that his father stood on just the other side, waiting and listening. His father had finally opened the door. He was waiting for his son.

But he's dead, *Morgan realized, and his stomach clenched in sudden terror. The door began to swing inward again, the dark gap growing larger but revealing nothing but black-ness beyond.* No, my father's dead. He's been dead for years—I don't want to see him that way—!

He sat up, damp with sweat, tangled in a blanket atop a vaguely familiar bed with a warm, slender body stretched next to him. The pounding continued.

"Your Highness!" someone called from the other side of the door, and he recognized the voice of Melkin, his squire. "Please, your Highness, open up! I have a message for you!"

"God's bloody Tree!" Morgan cursed, trying to still his speeding heart. What good was strong drink if it didn't keep away bad dreams? Especially that one, the old one that had plagued him so long. The worst one. "In the name of the Aedon, go away!" he shouted, then groaned and rolled on his side. He tried to pull the covers over his head, but the young Rimmerswoman beside him complained at being stifled and tugged them off her face. This ordinary sound and movement pushed back the darkness tangling the prince's thoughts.

What was the girl's name again? *Svana*. The swan. Not a bad name for her, actually. Her hair had been so fair it was almost white, her limbs long and graceful. At least, that was what he had thought when he had been drunk. He wasn't so certain he wanted to look too closely in the harsh daylight.

The rapping at the door resumed. "Highness, please, don't go back to sleep! The king and queen have summoned you!"

Morgan groaned. His jaw still throbbed from the blow he had suffered on the tower roof, and his brains felt so foul from too much wine the night before that he would have welcomed his own beheading in Market Square. Instead, he was to be hauled out of his warm sickbed—although in all honesty he had to admit that he was the one who had deliberately made himself sick with drink—to be scolded, doubtless in front of the whole court, for the disaster of Hjeldin's Tower.

"I said go away, Melkin. Come back when the sun is higher. Tell them I climbed a mountain and flew away." Oh, sweet Usires, but it would be wonderful to be able to float away on the warm wind. "What time is it?"

"Nearly twelve of the clock, Highness."

"Then come back when the sun is lower instead." He unsquinted his eyes for a moment. Even with the windows shuttered, the light leaking past the edges tortured him. "Below the horizon would be best."

"But Highness! The king and queen . . . !"

"The king and queen can wait. It'll give them more time to think of things to scold me for. They'll thank me, you'll see."

"But Prince Morgan . . ."

"Go piss in your ear, Melkin."

Just as he was settling back into the sticky clutches of sleep, the door to the room banged open. Startled, Morgan rolled onto his side, but when he peered through slitted eyes at the doorway, instead of his squire's lanky form he was surprised to see what looked like one of the mountain trolls standing there waving something at him.

"Get up, Highness!" the stumpy figure announced. "I have good news for you."

Squinting against the hateful light, he saw at last that it was no troll but only Mistress Buttercup, the extremely short, largely round proprietress of the house. He groaned again. "Good news?"

"Your debt is paid, Prince Morgan." She shook the sack in her hand, which clinked substantively. "The Lord Chamberlain has sent gold on your behalf, at the orders of the king and queen."

"What?" He pulled himself up to a sitting position, which required him to remove Svana's elbow from his chest. "Then why are you waking me?"

"Because this substantial sum was given to me on the understanding that there would be no more coming. Which means that as of this moment, you are detaining my little frost-princess there without pecuniary return to me, and occupying one of my expensive beds as well." She put her hands on her hips, grinning broadly. "Neither did your benefactors pay for breakfast, so get on with you, Your Highness. Up you go and out."

"But you've been paid!" Which made no sense. Why would his grandparents do such a thing when they were angry with him? "Why are you brawling and shouting at my door when the sun is barely in the sky?"

"Barely touching noon, you mean. Up, up, young princeling, or I will have to get the Ox brothers to help you out of bed." She waddled to the side of the bed and poked at him with the spoon she often carried. "Your family has paid your debt, for which I give all thanks to a merciful God—and so should you, because you had all but bought this place if it had waited any longer—but it was with the understanding I reject your custom from here forward. Consider your custom rejected, Highness, but of course with my many thanks for your patronage." Buttercup smiled. Through the throbbing of his head, Morgan thought she looked a bit spiteful. "Up with you. Or have you suddenly become shy?"

He pulled on his breeks slowly and then went looking for the rest of his clothes, trying to make sense of what had just happened, while Mistress Buttercup helped him out by pointing with her spoon. "Over there, I think I detect a sleeve. Under Svana, yes. And your shoes, I see them peeking from under the bed like a pair of frightened puppies. Ah, and there is your jerkin, noble Highness, hanging from the window shutter. How *did* it get there?"

Dressed at last, and with a trailing ceremonial procession made up of Buttercup, the two thick-headed Ox brothers, and pale Svana still wrapped in the coverlet they had shared, he let his squire Melkin lead him out the door and into the hideous, scalding light of the sun.

"On behalf of my girls and my purse, Prince Morgan, I thank you!" called Buttercup. "I cannot say come again, because I have law from the High Throne itself saying I may not, so I will not. But I can say, 'Good journey!'"

"Good journey? It is scarcely a moment's walk back to the Hayholt," Morgan grumbled to Melkin. "What in the name of all the saints is going on today?"

"I couldn't guess, Your Highness," Melkin said, but Morgan thought his squire looked a bit shifty around the eyes. He couldn't consider it too deeply, though, because it took all his concentration simply to wade through the blazing sunshine.

Miriamele thought that summoning Morgan to the throne room was a bit much, but she had promised to let Simon do what he thought best.

The queen was among the few that had good memories of the lofty chamber. As a small child she had watched her grandfather enthroned here beneath the centuried banners, dispensing justice from the Dragonbone Chair. Later she had watched her father playing the same role in this same hall, although the good days had not lasted long that time. The hall had always reminded her of a great cave, the banners of the king's subject countries and peoples hanging down like dripstones, and at the center of the mock-cavern, the dragon itself. Of course, this dragon was only bones, a skeleton throne the color of yellow ocher which neither she nor Simon wanted to use.

"Morgan, prince of the land and heir to the High Throne, you have been chosen for a great task," Simon said, using his Important Things To Say voice that Miriamele found slightly annoying.

The prince looked as though he had come from a rough night. Miriamele would have felt more sorry for him as he blinked and shrugged and shook his head if he had managed to wash and dress himself first. Instead, he looked as though he had been dragged straight in from some Erchester gutter. Many of the courtiers present, and there were more than a few, whispered behind their hands at his condition, but they knew better than to openly mock the prince in front of his grandparents. She wished her husband had chosen to speak to the prince in private, but Simon had lost his patience over the hours it had taken to find him, and no longer seemed interested in sparing Morgan's feelings.

As Simon explained the nature of the great task, a vital mission to the court of the Sithi coupled with the need to get the poisoned Sithi envoy back to her own healers, Morgan only listened with mouth open. When Simon announced that Count Eolair and Morgan himself would be the ambassadors, the prince stared at him with a look of such incomprehension that Miriamele momentarily lost all her sympathy and in fact wanted to slap him.

"Me? Why should *I* go?" Morgan demanded.

Simon was cold. Too cold, Miriamele thought, but still she kept her promise and held her tongue. "The first and best reason, young man, is because your king and your queen have told you to do so. There are other reasons which I will gladly share with you in private."

"But I don't know anything about the Sithi!"

"And they know nothing about you. Let us hope they don't regret the loss of that innocence after they meet you." Simon looked like a thunderstorm, but he was struggling to find gentler words, Miriamele could see. "You will be traveling with Count Eolair. The lord steward knows them as well as almost any man alive. But what is more important, you are traveling to see them as a prince of the High Ward, and as the heir to the throne. That is something important, boy, very important. Do you see that? Tell me you do, I pray you."

Morgan only stared sullenly, so Simon took a breath, then laid out the rest of the charge he and Miriamele were putting upon them. Mounted knights and a foot troop of Erkynguard would accompany the envoys, and the trolls would ride with them until the groups went their separate way and Binabik's family continued back to Yiqanuc.

The prince listened for a while, then stirred. "And who can I take with me to fill the long days? Melkin is a rather poor conversationalist." He stared at his squire, who tried to make himself look even smaller.

"If you do not think that Eolair and Binabik, two of the cleverest, wisest men in all of Osten Ard are company enough," Simon said with a sour face, "I suppose we can permit you to take one of your companions—I'm not certain I would call them friends—with you on the journey."

"Praise the saints and angels," said Morgan, for the first time showing something other than resentment. "I shall hate to leave the others behind, but Astrian is a good man with a jest as well as a sword—"

"Ho, lad, ho!" said Simon. "I didn't say you could *pick* one of your friends, I said you could *take* one of your friends. You may bring Sir Porto. He has carried a sword on behalf of the throne, at least, and proved himself a good man, even if that was long ago. We plan to surround you with wisdom and experience, Morgan—not accomplices."

"Porto! But he is a hundred years old! A thousand!" Morgan stood up now, his face white and his hands shaking from the prior night's indulgence as much as from anger. "This is all meant to punish me, isn't it? All because I won't do what you want from me. You hope they will lose me in the forest or in the eastern mountains somewhere and I will never embarrass you again."

"By merciful Rhiap!" Simon hunched forward, his beard spreading against his breastbone, and for a moment Miriamele saw something in her so-familiar husband that looked more like one of the ancient prophets than the kind man she knew. "Do you think that I would risk a mission this important, risk my best counselors and soldiers, just to punish you? Boy, you make me angry indeed. *Very* angry."

"Majesty . . . husband . . ." Miriamele said, putting aside her resolve for a moment. "Let us remember what we do here."

Simon darted her a cross look, but saw that Binabik and Count Eolair were watching him worriedly as well. He took a moment to recover his calm before speaking again. "I will tell you once more, Prince, that this is a task very close to my heart, and to your grandmother's heart as well. We send you, not to see you punished, but to see you succeed. We send you because we need you to do good for the throne. That throne will be yours someday." He looked at Morgan, who had folded his arms across his chest and was clearly not going to kneel again. "You may go and see to your preparations now. St. Callistan's Day is in three days, and you will leave then."

Morgan's face was wan with outrage, and he clearly considered further argument, but for the first time he looked to his grandmother. She shook her head, slowly but firmly. Some of his color returned. He bowed his head.

"As Your Majesties wish," was all he said, then bowed with careful correctness, turned, and walked out of the throne hall. His squire scuttled after him, trying to keep up without turning his back on the king and queen, something that made him walk an uneven, awkward path.

"Binabik and I will take good care of your grandson, Majesties, never fear," Count Eolair said. "And he will be a credit to you when all is done. Prince Morgan is a good young man, never doubt it."

"Yes, he will be well and growing to a fine man, I am thinking, Simon." Binabik spoke so quietly that none in the great hall could hear him but the count, the king, and the queen. "I have been reminded by him sometimes of another young man I once knew, confused and angry."

"If you're talking about me, I pray he doesn't have to go through what I did," said Simon. "But now I am cross with myself for losing my temper. I didn't mean to send him off yet. There is one important thing still to do." He sat up straight, raising his voice to silence the murmuring courtiers. "One more thing do we send with these brave envoys, to help them on their way. An object of great veneration. Tiamak, do you have it?"

Tiamak limped forward with a large wooden chest, which he handed to Simon. When the king opened it and lifted up what was inside, a stir went through the room, although few could have guessed exactly what it was he held.

"Here is the horn Ti-tuno." Simon held it up to the light streaming through the windows and the silver chasing glinted. "This belonged to Camaris the Great, Prester John's finest and most godly knight. It was found broken on the field of battle here at the Hayholt, where the war against the Storm King ended."

"May God rest that brave old man's soul," said Miriamele, remembering the sadness of bringing Camaris out of the contentment of madness and back to cruel sanity.

"The story has long been told that this horn is of Sithi make, carved from a tooth of one of the great worms," Simon continued, then waited until another wave of whispered conversation broke and fell back. "If you wind it at each stopping place when you reach Aldheorte Forest, I feel sure the Sithi will know you are there." He lowered the horn back into the box, then signaled the lord steward to step forward. "Take it with our blessing, Count Eolair, and our love. May it bring you success in your mission, and then lead you safe home again as well."

Eolair took the box. "I pray it is so, Majesty."

"We all do," said Miriamele. "We will pray for your safety every day until you and Prince Morgan come home to us." Her eyes felt warm and suddenly wet. "Every day."

38

The Factor's Ship

Eolair knew he should have sent one of his underlings to deal with the royal kitchens. On the best of days the heat there was overwhelming, and what might be a cozy refuge in deep winter would be sweating agony on a hot day like this. But he knew Benamin the royal butler well, and knew that the man's pride made him difficult on those with a less important position than himself. Sometimes Eolair wondered if Benamin realized that the Hand of the Throne actually outranked him, but at least he was respectful.

Several months' worth of supplies finally arranged for the trip to Aldheorte Forest and the eastern lands along the Thrithings border, Eolair was heading back toward his chambers when he saw a small man kneeling on the floor just outside the pantry door. The man was shaking, and for a moment Eolair drew back, fearful of disease, but the little man looked up toward the ceiling and cried out, *"Och, cawer lim!"* in the count's own Hernystiri tongue—*"Help me!"*—and began to weep. His wide-eyed face showed no taint of disease, only despair, and Eolair's heart was touched to hear such a piteous cry from a countryman.

"What is it, fellow?" he asked in their shared tongue. *"What afflicts you?"*

"The summons!" the man said. *"Do you hear? She calls us all! She calls us! Help me go home!"*

Eolair recognized him now—a kitchen worker, one he had seen but never spoken with before. He had not known the man was Hernystiri, but the fellow's obvious misery made the count wish he had found it out sooner. Homesickness was a terrible thing, especially at the end of a long life in a strange land. But Eolair also knew there was nothing he could do, not when his own journey was so close at hand. *"Surely this is your home, too,"* Eolair said, still in the Hernystiri tongue. *"You have friends here, do you not?"*

The man stared at him for a long moment, as though seeing him for the first time. *"Help me,"* he said again, more firmly this time. *"I must go. She calls me."*

"Who calls you?"

"I said, help me! You must!" The weeping man had stopped weeping, and now he reached up and grabbed at Eolair's wrist with surprising strength, so much so that it felt like he was squeezing the bones together.

"*Let go!*" The count yanked his arm free. "*That is no way to treat a country-man.*"

He was so busy rubbing his sore wrist that he did not see the change in the man's face, the way the bulging eyes grew narrow and heavy-lidded. Neither did he see the carving knife the man had drawn from his ragged shirt; but then Eolair felt a burning pain in his chest and a harsh thump as blade hit bone, and looked down in amazement to see blood seeping through his doublet just below his shoulder. The kitchen worker, with a desperate grimace on his face, was lifting the knife to strike again. Eolair knew he should reach out to stop him, but for some reason could not. A coldness began to steal over him and his thoughts drifted like ashes on a hot wind. The room was quickly growing dark, filling with shadows that murmured as they surrounded him.

"*Why have you . . . done this?*" Eolair asked, but his own voice sounded far away.

"*They will not stop me!*" the man with the knife shouted, even as the shadows began to clutch at him, too. "*I hear you, Summoner, and I am coming! Your servant hears you!*"

The royal packet ship was called *The Princess,* a small, handsome cog bobbing at anchor just inside the Kynslagh breakwater, the dragons of the High Throne entwined in bright colors across its square sail.

Tiamak and Brother Etan descended the long, steep stairway toward the quay behind the Hayholt's seagate, where the longboat waited that would take Etan out to the *Princess.* The smell of hot tar made him wrinkle his nose, and the gulls knifing past his head with their high-pitched cries made him fear for his balance on the damp stone steps. Tiamak had to go slowly, always leading with his stronger leg, and his halting pace made the monk even more anxious.

"You did not need to come down to see me off," said Etan. "I hate to see you give yourself pain on my account."

"How could I send you off into the world without even a proper farewell, my young friend?" Tiamak smiled. "That is how I left my home in Village Grove the first time, without even a niece or nephew waving to me. Such loneliness! Besides, there is someone I wish you to meet."

This surprised Etan, who could only guess that Lord Tiamak meant the captain of the royal packet, but before he could ask him, the little man slipped on a wet stone and would have tumbled down to the nearest landing if Etan had not grabbed his arm.

"Now I am really worried," the monk said as he helped Tiamak back to safe footing. "How are you going to climb back up?"

"More slowly than I am climbing down, for one thing," said Tiamak with a slightly breathless chuckle. "It is easier going up—at least with stairs."

Etan didn't understand Tiamak's remark, but they were on the last leg of the staircase now and the steps were slippery with spray from the waters splashing in through the sea gate. The seawall loomed high above them, blocking the morning sun and casting the stone stairs into shadow. Only a few ships and boats floated in the small harbor behind the seawall, but most of them contained goods for the castle, so the docks were alive with sailors and workmen.

As they reached the bottom, Etan saw a man waiting for them. The stranger was small and thin, and because his skin was darker than most of the Erkynlanders unloading cargo, at first Etan thought the man might be another of Lord Tiamak's folk. Only as they stepped off onto the quay could he see that the man's face was longer and bonier than any Wrannaman's, and his skin a bit more pale; also unlike the royal counselor, he had dark whiskers all over his face, a short growth that looked as if it had been shaved a sennight earlier and not touched since.

"Ah, glory to the Aedon!" the stranger said, showing a wide smile full of black gaps. "There you are, Lord Tiamak, our darling. But it is good to see you safe and well!"

Tiamak gave a little snort. "Save your congratulations until I've reached the top again." He turned to Brother Etan. "This is Madi. He will be your guide on your journey."

Etan was startled. This was the first he had heard of anyone accompanying him. "Your pardon, Lord, but I do not understand."

"Bless him, of course he doesn't," the stranger said. "He's never been nowhere, you see? He doesn't understand about the wide world."

"And *you* still don't understand anything about staying quiet until it's your turn," said Tiamak sternly. "Don't fear, Brother. Madi's a good man, even if his tongue wags a bit too much. He's been to Kwanitupul and Nabban and all over the South. And he's also very, very good with horses."

"I can find 'em by smell, I can train 'em from colts, and I can make 'em dance if someone plays the music. That's my Hyrka blood."

"You're a Hyrka?" All Etan knew about Hyrkas was what everyone knew, that they were wild folk who moved around. He had only ever seen them at local markets, where they sold inexpensive trinkets and mended pots and pans. He had heard that they also had a magical way with horses, and certainly those animals he had seen attached to Hyrka carts had looked healthy enough.

"Aye, my lovely man, that I am. Our wheels never rest."

Etan turned in confusion to Tiamak. "Do I really need a guide?"

"You are on royal business, Brother, do not forget. What if something happens to you? What if you fall and hit your head—who will tend you? Who will tell us where you are? The men of some monkish orders may travel as solitaries, but that is not the way to conduct the business of the king and queen."

"Then it seems to make more sense to send a larger party. What if we are attacked by bandits?"

Tiamak wagged his finger. "Do not try to teach an old uncle how to dig for turtle eggs. There is a balance in this, as in all things. Too many people traveling and everyone will be curious about your business. People will find you just to sell information, and that is likely to be only what the seller thinks you want to hear. And those who do not want you to discover the answers you seek will also know of your coming. It is like a long journey through the swamp by boat. One person may disappear without trace. Too many will sink the canoe. No, there is a balance, and Madi will perform many useful tasks for the amount I am paying him."

"For the *pittance* you are paying me, my sweet little lord," the Hyrka said loudly, laughing. "Surely that's what you mean."

"Silence, Madi." Tiamak turned to Etan. "That is a phrase you will find very useful, by the by. I suggest you memorize it."

Etan just stood. He understood Tiamak's logic, but the idea of having a companion, especially one who seemed so unlike himself, was daunting. Where would he find the quiet hours to pray?

Madi was grinning. "Here, you've scared the poor fellow to death, Lord Tiamak. Don't fear, Brother. I won't rob you and leave you dead by the road. I like priests. And I like Lord Tiamak. Lovely fellow for a mud man."

"Considering you're not getting paid more than what your food and expenses will cost until you finish the job to my satisfaction," Tiamak told him, "I suggest you find a more respectful name to call me than 'mud man.'"

"Begging your pardon, Lord," said Madi. "You are right, so right." But he did not seem particularly chastened.

Tiamak handed the purse to Etan. "This must last you until you reach Kwanitupul. Do not let this reprobate use it to buy drink, whatever he tells you. He is a good man, I swear that he is, but he is a worthless devil when he's been drinking."

"Ah, but I have truly given it up, my lord," said Madi. "The poison will not pass my lips again. I am a changed man. Did you know, dear one, I've even married my wife!"

"What does that mean?" Etan asked, interested despite himself.

"He can tell you later," Tiamak said. "I am sure it is a story that will take up many hours of travel between here and Meremund, where you will take ship for Nabban. But right now the packet is waiting for you both, and I still have more to say." Tiamak drew a bundle wrapped in oilcloth from under his robe. "I myself copied these for you so you could take them with you. They are letters from Prince Josua and other Scrollbearers, from the year before he vanished. They may help you in your quest. At the least, they will give you some idea of the kind of man that Prince Josua was, why he was so loved and why his loss has been felt so keenly."

"I will read them all, my lord," said Etan, taking the package.

"You may write to me as well. In the bundle you will find a list of places where you can find someone to carry letters safely back here to the Hayholt. I hope you share any news you find as quickly as is possible. The king and queen are most anxious to learn about the prince and his children."

"Of course. I will write as often as I can."

"Don't worry too much about how often," said Tiamak with a smile. "Write when you have something important to tell me or something important to ask. I suspect this task will keep you quite busy, and you will be traveling as well."

Somebody on the ship's boat was ringing a bell.

"That means they are waiting for you," said Tiamak. "Have you been on boat or ship before?"

"Boats? Only as a boy. Only on the shallow bits of the Ymstrecca."

"Well, as you will see, the Gleniwent is different from any stream, and the ocean is more different still. Do not fear. *The Princess* is a fine ship and its captain is one of Erkynland's best. He will have you in Meremund in a day or so, and then I have bought you passage on a respectable merchant ship around the Horn of Nabban and into Firannos Bay. It will be fine weather for traveling, and I'm sure you will be in Kwanitupul before the Day of the Sister Saints."

Etan's heart sank at the thought of a month on pitching, rolling ships, but he had promised both his God and his monarchs that he would perform this task, so he gave Tiamak a sickly smile and clasped his hand. "Thank you, my lord. I will do my best."

"You will do splendidly, I know." He looked over the monk's shoulder. "You had better hurry, now, Brother. Madi is already taking your bag onto the landing boat."

Etan turned to see that the scrawny Hyrkaman was indeed dragging his precious possessions up the gangplank and onto the boat, which was piled so high with jars and sacks that the brackish water of the castle harbor almost reached the rails.

Several of the oarsmen made the sign of the Tree as Etan passed. For a moment, as he squeezed himself into a spot in the center of the boat between two sacks of grain, that cheered him. Then Madi came and squatted beside him. "Don't take it to heart, Brother, sir."

"What?"

"Sailors always hate having a priest on board. Bad luck, they say. In the old days, sometimes they'd push one overboard in a bad storm or when the kilpa-beasts were particular bad, just to see if it helped." He noticed Etan's expression. "Oh, but they don't do that no more, sir. Not this close to shore, anyway."

Etan closed his eyes and began to pray as the lines were loosed and the little boat steered toward the sea gate and the Kynslagh beyond.

Pasevalles found Sir Porto in the guard barracks, where the old soldier still had a bed, despite having passed beyond his years of useful service. Unlike many of the other knights, Porto was not descended from landed gentry—his knighthood had been bestowed for deeds of honor in the long-ago war against the Norns—so without his place in the barracks the ancient soldier would have had nowhere to go. That, along with the pittance soldiers were paid, even when they were too old or injured to fight, had been one of King Simon's cleverest ideas, Pasevalles had long thought, and it had helped to cement the loyalty of his guardsmen.

"You have heard the news, I'm sure," said Pasevalles.

Porto was sitting on his cot, a pile of meager belongings lying beside him, but he rose to bend an ancient knee. "I am to go east, Lord Chancellor, with the prince. We are in search of the fairies, I am told."

"You sound as if that were a punishment, not an honor," Pasevalles said.

Porto gestured helplessly. "I have only just returned from the north. I am old, m'lord, and tired."

"You are old, yes, but presumably age has brought you some wisdom as well. Did you know you were picked out of all other companions by the king himself?"

Porto brightened a little. "Is that true? The messenger said something like it, but I did not believe it. I thought it just a bit of honey glaze on a tough hock of beef."

"Yes, it's true. It is as much to gain wisdom as anything else that the prince is being sent. Have you any wisdom you haven't used up yet?"

"I hope so, my lord." Porto's shoulders sagged again. "But I have only one horse, and he is near as old as I am. I fear he will not survive a second long journey so soon."

"Then rejoice, because I have arranged a new mount for you. A handsome, strong young charger from the Stanshire grasslands, out of my own stable. You may come see him, if you wish."

"Truly? My lord, you are too good." Porto looked a bit more hopeful. "I only hope I can prove deserving of such kindness."

"You will, if you listen to me now." Pasevalles crouched so that his eyes were level with Porto's, a strange and seemingly ignoble thing for a noble of his importance to do. "Prince Morgan must come home again. He must return hale and hearty."

"Well, to be sure, m'lord."

"Listen to me, Porto. I have allowed you and Astrian and your tall, silent friend Olveris to lead the prince down all sorts of dangerous alleys, because I knew that the two Nabban-men were uncommon swordsmen and could deal with almost any problem that would arise. But this time they will not be with you. The safety of the prince will depend on you alone."

"Me alone?" Porto looked not just startled but almost horrified. "Surely there will be a troop of guards with him, Lord Pasevalles. What can an old man like me do that all those swords and brave hearts could not?"

"You can pay attention. You can keep an eye on him. That is my trust. Here." He handed the old man a purse, which Porto took with shaking hands.

"What is it?"

"Look, if you please."

Porto unknotted the string and tipped out a shiny handful of coins. "Five silver towers!" he said. "For me?"

"And that is but a portion of what you will receive if Prince Morgan comes back safely. I will give you twenty more of those if the prince comes back to the castle sound in mind and body. Also, you will keep the horse I have given you and have twenty-five more silver pieces just like these every year of your life."

Porto's mouth gaped. For a long moment he did not speak, but tears trembled on his lower eyelids. "My lord, I cannot think what to say . . ."

"Say nothing, then. Do what I ask and all will be yours. Protect Prince Morgan at all costs. He is vitally important to this kingdom and all of Osten Ard, as everyone knows. Give him your wisdom, but more importantly, give him your attention. Aldheorte Forest and the country that runs beside it is treacherous, with the High Thrithings barbarians on one side of it and only our merciful God knows what lurking in the forest itself. Even the Sithi can be unpredictable, if you do find them. They have killed men before now."

Porto slowly lowered himself to the floor, creaking like a drawbridge, and prostrated himself at Pasevalles' feet. "I will serve you so faithfully, Lord, that our prince could have no better companion. For I do love the boy well, you know. He is a good lad, for all that people say about him. He has a good heart in his chest."

"Well, then, we are agreed. And keeping all of his parts where they belong is my greatest concern, so see that you do watch over him. Not too much drink, either—not for either of you. Am I understood?"

"Like Saint Sutrin himself, preaching to the islanders."

"Good. When you wish to see your new horse, go to the stables and ask the head groom."

Porto shook his head in wonderment as he clambered onto his cot again. "All that silver! I had forgotten about the horse. And he will be mine to keep?" At Pasevalles' nod, the old knight's weathered face again split in a wide smile. "I will be a rich man when I return. I will be able to hire a squire to tend me. Perhaps I will even seek a wife."

"All these dreams are nothing if aught happens to the young prince," Pasevalles said. "Mind what I've told you. Recite it to yourself with your morning prayers."

When the Lord Chancellor took his leave, Porto was still pouring his little fortune in silver coins back and forth from one hand to the other, murmuring happily to himself.

After a long and wearisome climb back up the steps of the seawall, Tiamak had just reached the top when he saw a new ship approaching Erchester's harbor, just a short distance from the entrance. It was quite a bold, swift-looking vessel, a trading cog by its shape, the castle higher than was usual. Its appointments were painted in bright blues and reds, and it bore a green insignia on its mast that Tiamak thought he recognized, although it seemed unlikely in the extreme that it should be here.

"Ho, there!" he called down to a young harborman cleaning the hinges on the sea gate below him. "Can you make out that ship?"

The fellow turned and squinted out to the Kynslagh. "I do not know her device, my lord!" he called back.

"What is it?"

"A green branch with berries, it looks. Nicely fitted out, too, my lord. A rich merchantman, I'd wager."

"Gods of my fathers! I cannot believe it." Tiamak began to make his way across the top of the seawall. After so many steps already, he was not up to climbing back down to the harbor. He would ask to borrow the royal carriage instead and take the roundabout road to the port. If the ship carried the passenger he suspected, he would need the carriage anyway.

By the time Tiamak reached the harbor the *Yew Tree* had docked and its passenger was being carried down the unusually wide gangplank on a litter. Tiamak watched as four burly sailors struggled beneath the weight of one man, doing their best to keep the litter level, until they could set it down on the dockside stones. He could hardly believe his eyes. He had not expected ever to see this particular passenger again, let alone see him here in Erchester, seventy or eighty leagues from his Abaingeat home.

Tiamak hurried forward. "Viscount Aengas! What a surprise! What are you doing here?"

The Viscount looked up from his conversation with a slender young man who had followed behind the sailors. "Ah, it's you! But I am a viscount no longer, my friend. I gave the title up—did you not hear, or is Abaingeat too far away for you to care? My younger brother holds the title now, may it give him more joy than it gave me. I am merely Aengas of Ban Farrig again. Well, I suppose I am a baron, so I must be called Lord. You cannot snub me, Tiamak, even in my lessened state! And of course, I remain a factor for the Northern Alliance, which helps to pay for honey and wine." He turned to the young man at his side. "Give me water, will you, good Brannan?"

"He's not just a factor," Brannan said as he produced a drinking skin, then upended it and squirted water into the big man's mouth. "He's the most important one." The youth said it in almost an accusing way, as if his employer's modesty annoyed him. Tiamak guessed that Aengas might be a difficult master. He had been thrown from a horse some years earlier, taking a terrible fall. Afterwards, his legs were useless and his arms not much better—he could use them, but without much strength or dexterity. But he had retained his sharp wits and sharper tongue. Even before his injury, though, he had not been one of the world's most patient men.

"But I am still amazed to see you," Tiamak said. "What brings you here? I just sent you a letter, less than a fortnight ago."

"Of course you did, man. That's why I'm here. If you truly have a copy of you-know-what," he mimed opening a book, "then I really must see it for myself. It is unprecedented!"

Tiamak could only shake his head. "I didn't expect . . . I never thought you would come."

Aengas grinned. "Of course you didn't. Everybody thinks that because a man cannot walk, he is helpless. But you see, my fine Lord Tiamak, that is precisely what gold is for! Those who can pay will achieve startling results! Now, take me to this prodigy, this forgotten tome, this terrifying compendium! I am as hungry to see it as I am hungry in the ordinary way—and trust me, I am mightily hungry in the ordinary way. Is your cook any good?"

"*My* cook?" Tiamak laughed. "There is no such person. But our castle kitchen is not to be scoffed at. His Majesty, the king, does like his meals. I don't think you will suffer too terribly while you are here."

"That," said Aengas, "does not sound particularly reassuring. It's a good thing that Brother Brannan here can cook."

"Brother Brannan? He is a monk . . . ?"

"No longer, my rabbit. He left St. Agar's Order some years ago, but he learned his way around a refectory and a herb garden first, I'm pleased to say. If he can find a few ways to spice up your infamously bland Erkynlandish fodder, I may survive the next few months."

"Months? You are staying so long?"

"Of course! It is not just the you-know-what I am here to see, but everything in your late prince's collection, not to mention all the other volumes you have gathered for the library. It will be most exciting! If I don't die of starvation first, of course. That is a serious possibility if we stand here working the hinges of our jaws much longer."

Tiamak shook his head. Generally quiet and soft-spoken himself, he had always found Aengas a little overwhelming. Still, there were few scholars in all of Osten Ard who could touch him for knowledge of ancient books and writing.

"Well?" Aengas demanded. "Shall I have my men shove me into your carriage, or must they carry me all the way up to the castle?"

"The carriage, of course." Tiamak stood to one side while the brawny sailors lifted Aengas from his litter and installed him on a seat. "I saw your sail in the harbor—that's why I brought it. I said to myself, 'That's the *Yew Tree*!' I could scarcely believe you were here in Erchester."

"They say that old Camaris used to come down on his enemies like a bolt from the sky." Aengas chuckled. "So it is with me, except it is my friends that I fall upon like the wrath of God Almighty, sudden and surprising." His expression grew more serious. "I couldn't help it, you know. When you wrote me about the . . . well, I was so excited that I could scarcely sleep."

"Truly? I know so little about it, or about the author."

"You will know more when we can speak in private. Truly, it is strange that it should come to light now." He shook his head as if to clear cobwebs and grinned again. "No mind. We will not cloud the air with secrets and speculations here in the open. On to the Hayholt, my brave and precious Tiamak! And on, I devoutly hope, to an early supper as well!"

Tiamak, Aengas, and his helper Brannan rode the long way back up from the docks by the Harbor Road and into Erchester. The only parts of Aengas that still moved with complete freedom were his head and his neck, both of which he employed freely as they made their way up Main Row.

"Look at that!" he said. "Is that new? I swear, it has only been a few years since I was last here, but you have been building like madmen!"

"The merchants, mostly. It has been a good time for trade."

"Thanks to our shipping confederation, in large part. The Northern Alliance has helped make the waters between here and Nabban safer than they have been in a century or more, since the Sea Emperors ruled."

"Last I heard from you, shipping was being deviled by pirates in the seas off the southern islands."

"There are not so many pirates making bold in the south now—we caught and hanged that devil Braxas, the worst of them, and the rest are now less bold—but other problems have replaced them. The kilpa, for one. In recent months they are as bad as I've ever known them—worse, I think."

Tiamak was glad, suddenly and selfishly, that it was Brother Etan and not himself currently traveling by ship to the south. The kilpa were nightmarish things that lived in the sea. They looked a little like men, which made them worse to Tiamak than even larger, fiercer creatures. "Bad? How so?"

"Stirred up, somehow. More sightings, more attacks. They have even come ashore in some places, something I have never known them to do."

"Ashore?" That sounded disturbing indeed. "What do you mean, ashore?"

"What do you think I mean, my dear fellow? Ashore, flopping and dragging and sticking their loathsome heads into houses where decent people live—if you can call the Nabbanai or the Perdruinese decent folk." Aengas laughed, but it was more old habit than genuine mirth. "Something has roused the nasty creatures for the first time in a generation. It is worrying."

"For the first time since the Storm King's War," Tiamak said. "That seems an evil sign. What of the Niskies? Are they still capable of—how do they call it?—singing the kilpa down?"

"Yes, when they are minding their ships as they are used to. But even the Niskie-people have grown strange, our captains say. There are days when they will not go to sea, and even when they do, sometimes they seem as confused and lethargic as fever victims. Most odd, all of it. But I should not bore you with the Alliance's concerns. How is your clever wife? And the king and queen?"

"All are well, and you will see them all. Except your countryman, Count Eolair, who may be occupied preparing for a long journey of his own."

"Ah, too bad—he is a good and very clean man, that Eolair," said Aengas. "I remember when I was young, my mother would hold him up as a model to emulate—'Think of noble Eolair!' she would say. 'He never squabbled with his brother over the last pie!' For years, I hated him for a prim ne'er-do-wrong, 'til I met him and realized it was not his fault that my mother worshipped him—that he was a perfectly decent fellow, and that he might even have squabbled over a pie or two in his own childhood, whatever Mother claimed. He was always a handsome fellow, too, even when I saw him last, and he had grown old." He shook his head. "Growing old is most inconvenient for us all. Still, I have the advantage over most of my peers, having lost most of my faculties already!"

Tiamak smiled. "You have not lost your tongue. Were any of your ancestors bards? Certainly there must be at least a little poetry in your blood."

"If there is, I have done my damnedest to kill it with wine and the cold winds of Abaingeat. I can't abide poets. They interrupt those of us who prefer conversation to be a sport shared between several players, not the work of a single performer who must be silently admired."

Now Tiamak laughed. "Somehow, I cannot see you silently admiring anyone."

"Not for their use of words, no."

As they wound through the southern districts of Erchester, Lord Aengas noticed many things that had changed since his last visit and commented on all of them at length. The carriage passed shabby old St. Wiglaf's Minster, which had survived the Storm King's War and looked as though it might have been around since the Sithi fled the Hayholt all those centuries ago. They turned into Fish Way, where the last of the morning's catch lay waiting for late buyers in the strengthening sun.

"Not exactly the perfumed nights of lost Khand," said Aengas, wrinkling his nose.

"If you had let me know you were coming," Tiamak told him, "I might perhaps have arranged a nicer route to the castle."

"If I had let you know I was coming then my enemies would have heard too, and rushed to defraud me while I was sailing up the Gleniwent."

Tiamak was taken aback. "Are you suggesting that I cannot keep a secret?"

"Not you, my dear swamp man. The Hayholt leaks like an ancient cog. I don't even have to bribe anyone here to learn what the High Throne is doing—your servants are uncommonly gossipy, and the court's nobles are generally in such a hurry to take advantage of their superior knowledge that they do not bother to hide their tracks. I have spies in half a dozen of their houses—no, I shall not tell you which, so do not moon those sad brown Wran eyes at me. I generally know what the High Throne plans to do within a day of the king and queen knowing it themselves." He paused, and his superior smile curled into annoyance. "Tiamak, my limping love, are you even listening to me?"

"I am sorry, Aengas, but there is something strange going on." He squinted. "There are soldiers in front of the Nearulagh Gate."

"It seems to me that it would be very wicked of Lord Constable Osric and his men if there were *not* soldiers at the gate."

"No, I mean many soldiers." Tiamak leaned his head out of the carriage window. "Many, *many* soldiers."

Even as he spoke, three guards from the double-phalanx stepped forward, pikes at the ready, to block the carriage from going any farther.

"What goes on here?" Tiamak asked the nearest Erkynguard. "I am Lord Tiamak, Counselor to the High Throne."

"Of course, my lord," said the sergeant who led them. "As to what's in the air, I fear we couldn't tell you. Order came down, triple the guard on the gate. Don't let anyone out."

"Well, we wish to come in. Is that a problem?"

"No, my lord. Just let us have a look." Tiamak moved back so the sergeant could lean in to inspect the inside of the carriage. "Do you vouch for this gentleman, Lord Tiamak?" the sergeant said.

Aengas slowly swiveled his head to stare back. "It is scarcely necessary to vouch for the loyalty of Aengas ec-Carpilbin. I am First Factor of Abaingeat."

The guard-sergeant tightened his lips. "Then I am sorry for the inconvenience, Lord Factor, but our orders were not given lightly. I do not know you, much to my shame, I'm certain. Do you vouch for him, Lord Tiamak?"

"Yes, yes, of course. Lord Aengas is an old friend of the High Throne—and of myself."

"Then you may continue." The sergeant turned and signaled to the guardhouse. A moment later the portcullis began to creak upward.

"What in Brynioch's name has happened?" Aengas wondered as they drove through.

"We shall know soon enough." Tiamak's heart was pounding.

It seemed to take a very long time for the carriage to make its way through the gates of the two inner baileys, but as they approached the front of the royal residence, Tiamak saw even more guards posted outside. To his slight relief, he also saw Pasevalles in urgent conversation with Zakiel, the guard captain.

"Lord Chancellor!" Tiamak called as the carriage rolled to a halt on the broad drive before the residence, and a half dozen Erkynguard moved forward to surround it. "What happens here?"

"Praise be to Elysia and her saints," Pasevalles said as he approached. His face was pale and his hair was wet, as if he had been called directly from his bath. "I'm glad to see you are well, Lord Tiamak. The king and queen were most concerned when we could not find you."

"I have been at the docks, saying goodbye to one friend and discovering, quite to my surprise, that another has arrived. Lord Pasevalles, this is Aengas, former Viscount of Carpilbin, now First Factor of Abaingeat."

"I have heard of you, my lord."

"Forgive me for not bowing," Aengas replied.

"But what is going on here?" Tiamak asked. "You said the king and queen—they are both well?"

"In fact," said Pasevalles, "everybody is well, except for the poor fool who tried to kill Count Eolair. And even he is not too badly hurt." His expression belied his casual words. Tiamak had never seen the stolid Lord Chancellor so upset: his anger was obvious, fierce, and also new to Tiamak. He was glad he was not its target.

"*What*?" Tiamak could only stare. Suddenly Pasevalles' pale features and disheveled appearance made sense. "Was Eolair harmed?"

"A stab wound near his shoulder that struck bone or it would have been worse. Some cuts to his hands," said the Lord Chancellor. "We are fortunate his attacker was no soldier. He seems to have been a madman—he has worked here in the castle for more than a year. A Hernystirman."

It sank in after a moment, and seemed to settle in Tiamak's guts. "A Hernystirman? Did he work in the kitchen? Is his name . . . oh, what was it? Is his name Riggan?"

"Yes, I think that's what someone said. Do you know him?"

"I know of him. My wife tended him once." He was in no hurry to tell the rest of the story, of the man babbling about the Morriga, the Mother of Crows.

"Has he been questioned?"

"Yes, but he speaks no sense," said Pasevalles. "You may see him later if you wish. I would be pleased to have your thoughts."

"But who was he?"

"Come inside and you will have answers to all your questions," Pasevalles told him. "The king and queen will want to know you have been found alive and hale." He waved, signaling to the guards that the carriage's occupants were welcome inside the residence. At Tiamak's request, Captain Zakiel picked out four strong soldiers to carry Aengas's litter into the throne hall.

As he limped after the litter, ignoring the murmurs of the soldiers as they struggled beneath Lord Aengas' considerable weight, Tiamak found his thoughts swirling like a flock of marsh teal startled into flight. On the one hand, the attack had apparently been the work of some kind of lunatic, one of Eolair's own countrymen with who knew what kind of mad, festering grudge—likely a meaningless, and fortunately bootless, crime. But it also felt like the vision of disaster that had come to him on the plains of the Frostmarch, showing its true form at last.

Evil times, he thought helplessly, almost as if someone else spoke in his head. *With so many strange signs, how can I doubt that evil times are truly upon us? He Who Always Steps On Sand, please guide me now, because I feel the ground turning treacherous all around me.*

39

A Grassland Wedding

It was hot again, very hot for the Third Green Moon. The air seemed to crackle, as if someone had rubbed a dry fleece across it, and when Fremur looked through the wagon's small window he could see no clouds anywhere. He felt as though some fell creature breathed on his neck, but he knew he could not delay going out to join the clan any longer. His sister was being married to Drojan and his brother Odrig was giving the feast.

He untangled the ribbons of his best shirt one last time. Before the day was ended, he knew, the full-sleeved white garment would be dripping with his sweat and muddy from the hands of others, from being clapped on the back and dragged into unwanted wrestling matches with drunken guests. His aunt would have to sew on new ribbons, because half of them would be torn off during the festivities.

It would all feel different, he thought, *if Drojan was not such a pig.*

Fremur saw nothing wrong with a woman, even his sister Kulva, being given away in marriage to a man chosen by the head of the family, especially when the head of the family was also the clan's thane. That was how it had always been done. But when their father Hurvalt had been thane, before he had been struck dumb and crippled by the gods, he would have balked at giving one of his daughters to a swaggering fool like Drojan, whose only accomplishment was that of being Odrig's crony. And in fact Hurvalt had given their oldest sister to a man she cared for, although he could have chosen a richer suitor.

"The clan's happiness is more important to a thane than it is to any other clansman," his father had told him once. *"A thane must always think with two minds, both his own and the wisdom of his ancestors. And the ancestors care only that the clan survives."*

His father was one of the first people Fremur saw when he stepped down from the wagon onto the grass of the paddock where the wedding feast was to take place. Hurvalt sat on a bench in the scant shade of the wagon, wrapped in blankets despite the heat, his body as curled and useless as a fallen leaf.

Fremur knelt at his father's feet. "May the Sky Piercer watch over you. And may he bring you joy on your daughter's wedding day."

His father rolled his eyes in Fremur's direction, but otherwise gave no sign of having heard. He had not spoken for seven summers, but he had always been a strong man, and even though he could not speak or feed himself and could not walk without two men supporting him, he lived on. Fremur wondered what the Sky Piercer, the clan's guardian, meant by the terrible exercise of letting Hurvalt go on breathing long after he had lost his manhood.

We are Crane Clan, he reminded himself. *We do not question the Sky Piercer.*

The expanse of grass, with Odrig's herd of horses fenced at one end, was surrounded by wagons of all sizes. Every member of Clan Kragni was there— no, Fremur corrected himself, *almost* every member—as well as important folk from neighboring clans like the Dragonfly, Adder, and White Spot Deer, with whom the Cranes often intermarried. Fremur's family, at least the women and his many nieces and nephews, had already taken their places near Thane Odrig's wagon. As usual, the younger boys were playing at men's work, straddling the wooden paddock fence as though it were a horse's saddle, smacking at each other with long sticks, and of course ignoring all warnings from their female relatives. Several of Fremur's aunts and cousins whistled to him as he walked past. He nodded, but did not stop, even when some of the boys begged him to.

Most of the rest of the clanfolk had gathered in the center of the paddock, where a tent had been erected for the bride to wait, and where food and drink were laid out on colorful blankets and covered with fairy-nets to keep the flies away. Although Odrig had not stinted, buying several barrels of stone-dweller beer to swell the happiness of the feast, those barrels had not been breached. That did not mean that the day's drinking had not begun: many of the clansmen had brought their own *yerut*, the fermented mare's milk that the Thrithings-folk had drunk since time before time. The number of snoring, bearded men scattered across the grass, along with the sour smell of vomit, told Fremur all that he needed to know.

Odrig stood near the tent with Drojan and several others, passing a skin of *yerut* and playing a knife-throwing game directed at the paddock's nearest fencepost a few dozen paces away. Fremur knew he should stop and speak the Blessing of the Sky Piercer to his brother the thane, but at that moment he did not want to talk to Odrig, still less Drojan, whose charms were not improved by the crimson flush of drunkenness or the gap-toothed bray of his laughter. Fremur made a wider circuit out into the paddock so he could reach the tent from the other side without having to talk to the thane and his closest supporters. He was not particularly successful.

"Hoy, there, little brother!" Odrig shouted. "Where are you going? Not to the bride's tent to sit with the women, I hope!"

"He wants you to choose him a husband, Thane!" bellowed Drojan.

Odrig enjoyed this jest, and grabbed Drojan's scarred face and squeezed it as if it was a child's. "Mark your new brother, Mouse!" he said. "Come and drink his health, or must I start looking, as Drojan says, for a strong man to take care of you? I do not think I could get many horses for you, though, scrawny thing that you are."

"That's what a veil is for," suggested another of his brother's friends, and they all laughed.

It was no use trying to avoid them completely; ignoring Odrig only made him more determined. And, in truth, Fremur himself was not entirely certain what it was that filled him with such unease and disgust today. Drojan was a pig, but as Odrig's friend he would prosper and their sister would be well-kept, with thick blankets and a fine wagon. Kulva might not like him, but that was often the case among Thrithings brides, and more often than not the wife learned in time to care about her husband as well as care for him.

"I will join you in a moment," he told Odrig. "I wish to give our sister a blessing."

"I will give her something more than that tonight!" crowed Drojan. "Like the rabbit who married a bear, she will be limping tomorrow morning!"

Odrig seemed to find this even funnier than the others did. Again he gripped Drojan's face with drunken fondness, wiggling his friend's head from side to side like a father with a beloved child. "Unless the bear drinks too much," Odrig said, "and can only offer his bride a limp willow branch as his wedding gift!"

More hilarity. Fremur waved, doing his best to smile, and continued on his way.

The wedding tent was a precious thing made of true Khandian silk, or so his mother had once told him. She had awaited her own marriage in it, as had her mother and grandmother before her. The outside walls were stitched in an ornamental pattern of blue rivers and lakes and green grass, a sort of map of their family's history in the land the stone-dwellers called the Lake Thrithings. A red pennant festooned with crane feathers and daubed with the symbol of the Sky Piercer waved at the top of the conical tent, and ribbons fluttered from every corner and all around the doorway.

Two men called Bride Guards, clothed in leather armor and holding long spears, waited outside the tent on either side of the doorway. One of them tried to stop Fremur as he approached, but the other said, "He can go in. He is the bride's brother, and the shaman is already there." Fremur had guessed as much. Because the shaman was male, the women's sanctuary of the tent had been pierced and legitimate male visitors were now allowed. Still, he stopped before the doorway and wiped the sweat from his face, then murmured his apologies to the Mother of the Green for entering her territory before lifting the flap to step inside.

It was dark within the tent, and hotter inside than out. In the moments it took his eyes to make peace with the darkness, he thought he saw a hunched, two-headed figure wearing a face out of nightmare. His heart sped for a moment before he realized it was only the shapes of his sister and old Burtan the shaman as he bent over her to perform the ritual purification with ash and salt. It was strange that Burtan, whom Fremur had known his whole life, should become such a fearsome figure with only the donning of a headdress and leather mask, but so it was. When he saw the priest look up at him, Fremur felt a moment of superstitious terror, though he knew that the old shaman only stared because he was nearly blind.

"The blessings of the skies upon you, Grandfather," he said, as was expected, and pulled a small silver coin from his pocket he had brought for just this moment. "I would speak with the bride. I am her brother."

"I know you, Fremur," said Burtan, his voice reedy but his annoyance plain. "Do not think me so old, so foolish . . ." Only at that moment, as it came close to his face, did he notice the coin in Fremur's fingers. "Ah, so. Of course. But do not take long. The horns will sound at sun-high, and that is not long now."

How the old man knew that after sitting in a darkened tent all morning, Fremur was not sure. "You are wise, Grandfather," was all he said. Even an old shaman with milky eyes should never be mocked or angered. In fact, as his sister had once pointed out, the older ones were closer to death and thus closer to the gods, and so should be humored whenever possible. Both gods and shamans could easily bring down bad luck on those who displeased them.

The shaman whispered something to Fremur's aunt, who laughed quietly. She sat beside Kulva in place of their mother, who had died in the Year of the Autumn Floods, two winters before Odrig first became leader of the Crane Clan. Five other female relatives were also crowded into the small tent, which smelled of sweat and the scented oils burning in small clay lamps. The lamps were not meant to provide light—the top of the wedding tent where the poles came together was open to the bright sky—but to entice the spirit of the Sky Piercer to swoop low to smell their sweet odor and bless the coming marriage.

"Are you well, Kulva?" Fremur asked his sister.

She stirred to life only slowly, as if she had been thinking of something or someone quite different than her surroundings. She wore the full curved head-dress and veil, so that only her eyes were visible. Again, Fremur felt a quiver of superstitious discomfort: In her white blanket and white veil, his sister looked like a ghost. He thought she also looked bleary, as though she had been drink-ing, too. It was not impossible to imagine her female relatives giving her a few sips of *yerut* for courage on this important day.

"Is that you, Fremur?" she said at last. "How is our father? Is he happy?"

It seemed an odd question, all else considered. "I saw him. He appears no different than he did yesterday, or will tomorrow."

"I was wondering what he would think. To see me married to Drojan."

"He would be happy to see you given to a man with a brave future in the clan, I'm sure."

"Would he?" She sounded weary, distant. "Perhaps. It must be nearly time."

"The shaman will call you when the sun is at the top of the sky."

"So little time left," she said. "So little time!"

"Because you are married does not mean you will be a different person. You will still be Kulva, still gentle as the dove for which you were named."

"And doves are often shot by men with bows. Brought home in a sack to the cookfire. Given out to the thane's favorites."

"Do not speak that way." Despite the fact that her disquiet echoed his own, Fremur turned to his aunt and the other women. "Why do you let her go on like this? Isn't it your job to prepare her for her wedding day, to bring her to her husband in good cheer?"

One of his female relatives made a noise in the back of her throat. "Oh, yes. Like a lamb to the sacrificial stone."

"Quiet, you," said Fremur's aunt. "She will be well, Nephew. She will bring the family honor. Crane women are strong."

"Strong," said Kulva, and began to laugh quietly.

Fremur was taken aback. He had hoped in part that seeing his sister dressed in the old manner, in the company of women who had themselves been readied for their own weddings, would make him feel steadier, might even puncture the grim mood that hovered over him like a thundercloud. Instead it had made things worse, or at least it had revealed to him things he had not wanted to know.

"Are you unhappy, sister? But what you do is blessed. The Sky Piercer wants you to be fruitful. The Sky Piercer wants you to enlarge the clan. Are these such terrible things for a woman to do?"

"Oh, no," she said. "Does not every woman wish to be married? Does not every woman want a husband, who can tell her what to do after she leaves her father's house?"

"Girl, you walk on treacherous ground," one of the women said.

"Leave us now, Fremur." His aunt's face seemed to show both amusement and concern. For a moment, and it was only a moment, Fremur had a vision of a world he had never quite imagined before, the world of women when no men were present. It felt as though a familiar path had suddenly turned to slip-sand beneath his feet.

He again asked for the Blessing of the Crane, although his sister was still laughing quietly to herself, and he felt sure she did not hear him. Then he went out into the strong, bold light of the sun again. No clouds hung in the sky, but he could still feel his own cloud hovering close.

Standing at the paddock's gate, which was festooned in ribbons and draped with a fine carpet, the three callers lifted horns to their lips and blew—three short bursts then three long. They repeated the call, which hung over the paddock like something tangible, as if the hot air was too thick to allow the sounds to disperse entirely. Drojan and Odrig, who had gone out of the gate only moments before, now returned, Fremur's brother dressed in the full finery of a thane, with a fur cape over his shoulders and the ancient signet of the Crane Clan hanging on a thong around his neck. Drojan, his mustaches extravagantly oiled, was wearing a bridegroom's decorated shirt and a wide sash around his waist that were already rumpled and stained.

"We come for a bride," said Drojan, slurring his words a little. "Are we welcome?"

"You are welcome in this camp," said the chief of the callers, and then the three hornblowers led the groom and the thane toward the tent. They stopped under the canopy that had been erected in front of the tent door. Fremur envied them even that small patch of shade.

The shaman appeared from the tent so quickly and noiselessly that it was hard to believe he had lived almost eighty summers. He still wore his leather mask. Other than his eyes, the hanging mask revealed only the bottom of his almost toothless mouth.

"Who comes to this place?" the old man asked in a voice that seemed to have grown considerably stronger since the last time Fremur had heard him speak.

"A bridegroom, seeking his bride," said Drojan. He whispered something to Odrig, but the thane did not respond, looking out across the gathered clansfolk as if searching for something or someone.

"And has the bride-price been paid?" asked Burtan.

"Seven fine horses," Drojan said. "Damn fine horses, isn't that right?"

Again, Odrig seemed not to be paying attention, but he nodded.

The old shaman began to chant in a tongue that none of the other clansfolk understood, a tongue that some said had been given to the first clansmen when the First Spirit had made them. As he did, Kulva was led from the tent by the women, out under the canopy. They were singing, a counterpoint to the shaman's chant, with words that women had sung at grassland weddings since the sun was young.

> May you have a son in front of you
> May you have a daughter beside you,
> May your hand be dipped in oil
> May your hand be dipped in flour
> May you hold your tongue
> May you not blame your husband's mother,
> May you respect your clan elders
> May you yield to younger ones in time
> May you be modest and keep your wagon clean.

As the shaman finished, a breeze came up, the first one Fremur had felt all day, making the canopy and the walls of the tent flutter. Guests turned to each other with smiles at this sign of the spirits' favor, and even Fremur felt himself relax a little as the shaman sprinkled more salt and ash in a circle around the canopy.

Drojan pushed himself in beside Kulva, jostling one of her older female relatives as he passed and earning a look that would have curled the hair of anyone less oblivious. "Is it not time yet to get to the binding, old man?" the groom asked loudly. "The day is hot, and I am waiting for my beer . . . and my bed."

A few of the guests laughed, although enough looked on with flat expressions that it was clear Drojan was not the most beloved member of Clan Kragni. But before the irritated shaman could answer him, another voice spoke up.

"You do not need a bed, Drojan the Foul—you need a sty!"

Even as Drojan peered out into the surrounding crowd of guests in reddening fury, Fremur's heart sank from behind his ribs down into his gut, then lay there heavy as an ancestor stone. He knew the voice. It was Unver's, and worse, Unver sounded very drunk.

The tall man stepped out of the throng, the wedding guests parting before him. Unver's garments were muddy and ragged, as if he had slept several days out of doors; but, as if in some horrible jest, he wore over them the long, spotlessly clean vest of a suitor, covered with bright stitchery of birds and flowers. Fremur was relieved to see that at least Unver's long, curved sword still hung in its scabbard on his belt.

"What do you want?" Drojan cried, sounding genuinely surprised in his drunkenness. "You have no place here, halfbreed. Go away. This is my wedding day."

Odrig laughed loudly. "There! You heard the bridegroom. You are not wanted at this feast, no matter how hungry you are."

"I am hungry for what is mine," Unver said, peering out from underneath an oily tangle of black hair. "It is you, Odrig, who must answer."

Odrig put on a look of mock-astonishment. "Me? You blame me? For what?"

"You did not call the *vitmaers*—did not proclaim the betrothal to the clans," said Unver in a deep, cold voice, although he stumbled a little in his words. "That is against our law!"

"Against our law?" Odrig laughed again. "You, outsider, would tell me about our law? Begone, before I make an example of you."

"I too have the horses! I have seven horses for Kulva's bride-price."

"Offal!" shouted Drojan, and lurched forward to grab Unver by the collar. Unver dealt him a blow to the head that sent Drojan stumbling and reeling. The groom tripped and fell to the ground, muddying his garments. A few watchers laughed, and Fremur saw that the crowd was not entirely against Unver.

"You have seven horses?" said Odrig, watching Drojan struggling to regain his feet. "That is amusing, since your stepfather Zhakar also had seven fine horses which he traded to me only yesterday for several cows and my second-best wagon. He is quite a wealthy man now, your stepfather!"

For a moment Unver only stood, for the first time seeming to realize that something was happening here beyond a drunken argument. "Those . . . no, those horses are mine. He had no right . . ."

"Take it up with the old man, not me," Odrig began, but even as he spoke Fremur saw that Drojan had regained his feet, eyes and face both red with rage. He stumbled toward Unver with a long dagger in his hand. Fremur opened his mouth to call a warning, but someone else spoke first.

"Unver!" cried Kulva. "'Ware!"

The sound of her voice startled him, but he turned in time to catch Drojan's arm, then twisted it so hard the bridegroom cried out in pain as Unver threw him to the ground. Drojan was shorter but powerfully muscled, and not such a coward that he would only strike from behind; within a moment he climbed back onto his feet and lunged toward his enemy once more. Unver still had not drawn his own sword or dagger, and this time Drojan almost managed to drive the blade into his guts before he could stop him. They wrestled, first on their feet like two shambling bears, the knife pressing against the birds stitched on Unver's breast, then their feet went out from under them and they rolled together on the ground.

"No! Stop them!" Kulva tried to run forward, but Odrig caught her and yanked her back, knocking her tall headdress askew. She hung helpless in his powerful grip, her feet barely touching the ground.

"Let them settle it, woman," growled Odrig. "Let your husband finish with your lover. If Drojan is willing to take you spoiled, then vengeance is his right."

At first it seemed vengeance might be swift in coming: on the ground, Unver's greater height was no advantage, and Drojan had the knife. Also, Fremur could almost believe that Unver was not fighting as hard as he could, as if somehow death were merely one more way the day might end for him. Then Drojan found a momentary opening and tried to stab at Unver's face, swiping the blade along his cheek and jaw, opening a terrible cut that immediately began sheeting blood down the tall man's face and neck.

A strange sound arose then, a low rumble that for a panicky moment Fremur thought might be the gods themselves shaking the ground in rage at this sacrilegious display. Then he realized it was no tremor, but Unver growling deep in his chest as he fought with bare hands to keep Drojan's knife away from his body.

As the crowd leaned forward to watch, some shouting, many more in silent fear, Unver wrapped one hand around the wrist of Drojan's knife-hand, then put his other hand under the bridegroom's chin and pushed until Drojan's head tipped back at a painful angle. Unver then brought a knee up and threw the other man over onto his side. Mud and torn grass were flung in all directions as they struggled together, then a strained, gurgling cry rose from the confused tangle of limbs. A moment later both men fell back and lay still.

Before anyone dared to move closer, Unver slid himself out of his enemy's grasp. Drojan did not move, but lay face down as his lifeblood pooled beneath him, painting the bright grass. But it was not Drojan for whom the bride cried out.

"Unver!" she cried. "Oh, Unver, why . . . ?"

"Dead on . . . his own . . . cursed blade." Unver sat up, his once spotless vest now smeared and spattered with blood, his face a red mask, then slowly got to his feet, tottering a little and struggling for breath. "You saw," he said to the wide-eyed onlookers. "I fought only to defend myself."

Odrig had gone as pale as the frost that dusted the long grass in winter. He grabbed his sister around the waist and lifted her off her feet, holding her against his chest as easily as if she were a child, though she struggled to get free. *"You!"* he shouted at Unver, his voice hoarse with fury. "Do you think you can come onto the thane's land, into my own paddock, kill my friend and bondsman, and be suffered to live?"

"Give me Kulva." Unver's outstretched arms were wet with blood to the elbows. "I seek no other quarrel. We will go away. The Crane Clan will not see us again."

"The Crane Clan will not see you because you will be buried beneath the pen where the pigs shit," said Odrig. "Do you think I would give my sister to you even if you had paid the bride-price? You, a castoff of the Stallion Clan, the whelp of a coward and a whore? My father was a fool to take you in."

"Your father . . . was a good man before he lost his wits," said Unver. He let his hand stray to his own sword and its muddied hilt. "You are nothing like him."

Odrig pulled Kulva close, clenched his hand in her hair and pulled tight, so that the bridal headdress tore free and fell to the ground in a tumble of ribbons and bright pins. "She will never be yours, outsider. I would see her dead first. I *will* see her dead first." And then, in a swift, terrible instant, Odrig's knife was out and in his hand. He dragged it across Kulva's throat below the chin, freeing a leaping spray of red. Women and even some men shouted out in horror. Kulva's hands came up as if to close the dreadful wound, but then the thane released her and she dropped to all fours, blood gurgling out onto the ground.

Fremur felt himself grow faint. The world darkened to a great tunnel around that cataract of red. His sister. Their sister. Odrig had killed their sister.

Unver yanked at his sword so hard that he half-pulled the scabbard from his belt, then leaped toward the thane with a bellow of helpless, furious pain. Odrig drew his own blade, calm as a man sitting down to eat supper, and stepped over dying Kulva as though she were nothing but a rock or a tuft of grass. The two swords clashed and rebounded. Guests screamed and cursed as they threw themselves back from the fighters.

Unver's struggle with Drojan had been a thing of dirt and grunting silence, two drunken, angry men rolling on the ground, fighting over a single knife. This was something entirely different, a flicker of shining blades, a dance of clanging metal. Within moments the grass around the pair had been torn away or stamped down into the black mud. Unver, Fremur could see, was still slowed by drunkenness, but his eyes blazed with a fury Fremur had never seen, even in battle against the men of the cities. Odrig was even larger than Unver, the biggest man in the clan, but he recognized the power of his opponent's anger and did not waste any more breath on taunts or curses.

Fremur could no more prevent this fight than catch lightning in his hands. He knew it would only end when someone died, and Fremur could not make himself believe that Unver might win. He ran to Kulva's side and kneeled beside her, but the blood was running out of her too fast to be stanched. He tried to hold the wound closed, but blood pulsed out between his fingers. It all seemed like a terrible dream—his own helplessness, the clanfolk's shouts and shocked faces, his sister's dying noises.

Odrig and Unver circled each other, and their curved swords flew back and forth like the beaks of birds, neither man able to get past the other's guard, neither foolish enough to engage too closely too soon. Unver, still hot with rage, took a swipe at Odrig's face; then, when the thane blocked him with his blade, he tried to score Odrig's face with his sword's point. He missed by the length of a fingernail, but Odrig's eyes widened and he redoubled his efforts, hammering away with blow after clanging blow so that Unver could do nothing but defend himself and slowly give ground. The circle of trampled grass and pitted mud widened beneath them, wedding guests now stumbling over each other in their hurry to get out of the way.

The sun was high in the sky. Both men were sweating heavily, and Unver Long Legs was covered with blood, much of it his own. He lost his grip on his sword for a moment and Odrig almost flicked the weapon out of his hand, but although he had to throw himself to the ground and roll away to avoid Odrig's slashing attack, he managed to hang on to his weapon and direct away another strike that had been intended as a killing blow, but this time the sharp edge of Odrig's sword bit into his left shoulder before he could knock it away.

Now that his enemy was bleeding from his shoulder as well, Odrig backed off a step and took a slower, more deliberate approach, fighting mostly to keep Unver moving and the blood flowing from his wound until it exhausted him. It seemed like a strategy that could not fail, and indeed, after several more rattling flurries of blows, it became apparent that Unver was slowing down. He ceased making attacks, concentrating instead on keeping Odrig's long, probing blade away. Odrig responded by changing his tactics to slash at Unver's legs and exposed arms whenever possible, and by doing this gave him several more small, but bloody wounds.

Unver misstepped, barely avoided a blow to his head, then stumbled again, his free hand clutching his belly. It seemed plain that the fight was nearly over. Sickened, Fremur turned Kulva closer to his chest, as if to shield her from the sight of Unver's imminent death, but could not look at her face for more than an instant: Her eyes were open, as if she looked at him in accusation.

"I did nothing," he said quietly, but a black, hopeless rage boiled inside him. "I could do nothing."

At the sound of several loud clangs in succession he looked up. Unver was in a half-crouch, doing his best to slip Odrig's heavy strokes. Clearly, the thane meant to end this. The sun beat down, and the grass sparkled with wet scarlet: Unver had several more wounds, so many that it was hard to count them in the general mire of his bloodied clothing.

Then, just as Odrig drew back for a better killing angle, Unver leaped up at him with what must have been his final strength and swung at his head. Odrig guided the blow away easily with his own blade and then turned his sword over, trapping Unver's weapon, but the sound of their two weapons striking each other seemed so odd and muffled that even Odrig, the path of his death-stroke now open, hesitated for a moment to glance at the blade he had turned aside.

It was not Unver's sword that had swung toward the thane's head, and was now imprisoned by the grip of Odrig's own blade. It was Unver's scabbard, torn loose from his belt. His sword was still in his other hand.

Odrig had only a moment to gape; then, even as the realization of what he was seeing drained the blood from his face, Unver plunged his own curved blade into Odrig's belly so hard that its point tented the back of his feast-day garment.

The ending came so suddenly and so surprisingly that none of the guests even cried out. Odrig's knees went limp. He collapsed onto Unver, who held him up for a moment, his own legs shaking, then stepped out of the way and let the thane fall into the mud.

Unver, bloody and silent, walked toward Fremur. The guests between them nearly flew in their hurry to get out of his way, but the tall man did not seem to see them, as though he passed living through the Land of Shadows. When he reached Fremur he said nothing, but only bent and lifted Kulva's body out of her brother's grasp. Unver was exhausted, and the dead weight of her made him stagger, but he managed to put her over his shoulder. Then, still without a word, he turned and walked across the paddock, two bodies left lying in the grass behind him and the clan guests shrinking back as from a leper. He walked unsteadily toward the gate that led out of the paddock, Kulva bouncing on his shoulder, her hair unbound now and waving behind him like a horse's tail. For long moments, no one around the wedding tent said anything, but only watched Unver's diminishing figure.

"Don't let him go!" someone shouted at last. "He killed the thane!"

"Murderer!" someone else cried, and there was a general roar of agreement, mostly from the men.

A few guests near Fremur drew their swords to go after Unver, startling Fremur as though from a sudden dream. The anger that had bubbled inside him was still hot, but now felt hard as stone. He pulled his own blade and slapped the nearest man on the arm with it, hard enough to make him drop his weapon.

"What are you doing?" the man snarled. It was Gezdahn Baldhead, one of the friends who had been drinking with Drojan and Odrig only an hour before, his face bright pink with astonishment and thwarted anger. "We must catch the halfblood before he gets to his horse!"

"No." Fremur held his sword out sideways in front of Gezdahn and the others, like a paddock gate. He felt curiously clear-headed, as if he alone had stood soberly by while everyone else had drunk themselves into madness.

"Get out of my way, Fremur-mouse," Gezdahn snarled, "or you'll get the same thing."

Fremur placed the point of his own curved sword against the man's chest. "You will do nothing. Odrig is dead. My *brother* the thane is dead. That means

I am thane of the Crane Clan until we choose another at the next clan moot. Do you deny the law?"

Gezdahn stared at him, anger fighting surprise as if the Fremur he knew had disappeared and been replaced by some strange demon from another world. "*You?*"

"I am eldest male of Odrig's house. That means I am thane."

"But he stole your sister's body!" cried another man. "He will shame her."

"He will not shame her. He will mourn her, you fool, and then he will bury her. We have time enough to think about what Unver has done. Put up your swords. If you want to bury someone, you have two corpses right here."

"You do not know what you are doing," Gezdahn said, but after staring at Fremur for a moment he slid his blade back into the sheath. Fremur felt as if his own face must be shining, he felt so hot beneath his skin.

"No. But neither do you. Nor do any of the rest of us." A vision had come to him even as he had drawn his sword—the fires of the stone dweller settlement biting at the sky, and Unver looming above it all like some great hunting bird sent down from Heaven to scourge the people's enemies. "Do you not see? The gods have spoken to us today. The Sky Piercer has given us a great message and we must understand it before we act."

And although he saw nothing but anger from his brother's friends, he saw something else on the faces of many gathered there—not merely confusion and horror, but also a kind of awe. Even old Burtan the shaman seemed chastened, as though he had witnessed, not just something horrible, but something that was important as well. Fremur was glad to see the old man understood. The others might understand in time. Some never would, perhaps. That was what happened, his father had once told him, when the gods spoke to men.

40

Watching Like God

There once was a woman who lived in the sky,
Lived in the sky, lived in the sky . . .

Something small but surprisingly heavy was bouncing on Morgan's chest, an
evil fairy by the sound of its piping voice.

There once was a woman who lived in the sky,
And her name was Grandmother Sun.

He groaned and tried to push it off, but it clung like a burr.

She rode upon a cloudy horse
A cloudy horse, a cloudy horse
She rode upon a cloudy horse
And her name was Grandmother Sun!

"God's hell," he said, "what are you?"

"You said a cursing word against God," the fairy pointed out with obvious
relish. "I'm going to tell Archbishop Gervis, and he'll mixcommunicate you."

"Go away. Sleeping."

"You have to get up, because you're going away today, Morgan. And I'm
angry at you because you didn't come and say goodbye."

He opened one eye. The light in his room was not sufficient to illuminate
the shape perched atop him, but he had already identified the noxious spirit as
his sister. "How could I come and say goodbye when I haven't left yet?"

"You were going to. You were going to go away without even coming to
say goodbye."

He rolled Lillia off his chest and then draped an arm across her, pinning her
down. "I came to your room last night to do that because I thought we were
leaving early, but you weren't there. How is that my fault?"

"Because I had a bad dream. I went and got in bed with Auntie Rhoner."
His younger sister had learned several years ago that her grandmother's friend

was named "Countess Rhona," but as with many other matters, Lillia showed no interest in changing her ways to please others. Morgan had a stubborn streak of his own, but he was a mere journeyman of self-interest compared to his little sister's mastery of the craft.

"And I was supposed to know that? Besides, I don't think Auntie Rhoner would have wanted me climbing into bed with her too, Lil."

"No, because you're too big. And you smell bad."

"Liar."

"You do. You smell like Brother Olov." He had tutored the children for a year, until his habit of pilfering small objects for drinking money became too hard to overlook, and he was returned to St. Sutrin's Abbey. During his tutoring days he had hidden jugs of wine in unlikely places around the residence so he could sneak out for a drink between lessons.

Morgan rolled over, turning his back on his young sister. "Go away, Pigling. I'm trying to sleep."

"Get up! It's time to get up and you have to say goodbye to me."

"Goodbye."

"No, proper. You have to get up and say it proper. Otherwise it doesn't work."

"What doesn't work?"

"I said a special prayer this morning. It was a special one so that God would remember you were going away and He would promise you'd come back safe."

Morgan grunted. "Did He?"

"Did He what?"

"Did God promise you?"

"I don't know. Don't be mean!" She wasn't just half-cross, the way she usually was when he was pretending to be difficult—or actually being difficult, which also happened fairly frequently. Morgan thought she sounded quite upset, close to tears.

He groaned again and rolled onto his back, still pinning her as best he could so she didn't climb back on top of him. His young sister had a habit of straddling his chest and pretending he was a horse—a very frolicsome horse, to judge by her jouncing rides—but that felt worse than usual this morning, with his stomach still full of the previous night's cheap wine. In fact, Morgan hadn't stayed out terribly late or drunk terribly much, because he had thought the company would be leaving at dawn; when he had returned to the residence after supper he had learned about Count Eolair and their delayed departure. But he still didn't want Lillia thumping on his belly, hobbledy-hoy.

"I suppose when I'm gone, Your Bouncy Highness will have to put that pony out to pasture and get a real horse." His jest was met with silence. He looked over to where she lay, now nestled against his rib cage. Tears were spilling over and running down her cheeks. "Why are you crying, Pigling?"

"You know why! You know."

"Because I'm going away."

"Yes. Again! After you just came back!"

"It's not my idea."

"I don't care if you never grow to a man. I don't want you to go."

"Grow to a man?"

"That's what Auntie Rhoner said. 'He has to go out into the world and learn to be a man.' That's what she said."

Morgan frowned and began to lever himself into a sitting position, which entailed disentangling himself from an unhappy seven-year-old. Rhona's words angered him, much as he liked the Hernystiri noblewoman. Why did everyone think he was such a failure at manhood? He could fight with a sword, ride a horse, drink with the best of them, and he had also had his share of doings with women as well. At the same age his grandfather had been scouring bowls and pots in the castle kitchen. Was it Morgan's fault that there was no Storm King to force him to war, no mad King Elias, no red priest Pryrates?

Thinking of the red priest, he suddenly remembered what he thought he had seen in the tower; it came swift and strong enough for Lillia to notice. "If you're cold, get back under the blanket," she said. "We'll make a tent."

"No, no tent, Pigling. I really do have to get up and get ready." At least so he assumed. "What time is it?"

"Eleven of the clock."

"Damnation!"

"You said another word against God!"

"I did not. Come on, off me, give me room to swing my legs." He put his feet down on the cold floor, swallowed another and even more florid curse. "You're sure it's eleven? Not ten? Where's Melkin?"

"He's gone to make certain all your gear is ready. That's what he said. He's the one who told me what time it was."

Which meant it was true. Melkin was not the most gifted squire, but he nearly always knew the time. His life's great dream, he had once admitted to his lord, the prince, was to have a clock of his own to tend. Morgan could imagine nothing more boring in all the lands of Osten Ard than spending one's days up a tower, tending a clock.

"Go and get me something to eat, will you?" he asked his sister. "I'll wash and put on some clean clothes. I'm supposed to go see Mother—oh, and Grandfather and Grandmother too before I leave, no doubt so they can tell me again what an idle devil I am, and how this ride into the empty wilderness in search of fairies is going to put me right."

Lillia gave him a searching stare. "Are you *really* going to visit the real, true fairies?"

"I suppose." It was much easier to sit up in bed when you hadn't been drinking all night. He had almost forgotten that. "If we ever find them. But they're not exactly fairies. You saw the woman upstairs, didn't you? Did you think she was a real, true fairy?"

"I did, Morgan. Her eyes were like a cat. And she was so very, very thin!"

"Well, we're taking her back to her people, so they can try to make her better."

"She should pray to God. That's what Father Nulles says. God can make her better. But fairies don't pray to God. They don't even believe in God."

"Well, then God probably won't cure her, so someone else will have to. You don't want her to die, do you?"

Lillia's eyes got big. "Oh, no! That would be too bad."

"That's why we're taking her back to her people, see? To get her some fairy medicine. And speaking of magical things that make people feel better, what about some food?"

"Grandfather said if you wanted something to eat before your journey, you should have come down to eat when everyone else was having theirs."

"Grandfather would say that, yes." He scowled, then saw Lillia's offended expression. "But I'm sure he didn't mean nobody could go to the kitchen and see if anything was . . . lying about. Just going to waste, if you see what I mean."

She gave him another disapproving look. "That would be stealing."

Morgan sighed. "Someday, I am going to be the ruler of this place, and you will be a most important lady. All this will belong to us."

She stared, sensing a trick of some kind. "So?"

"So if you find some food for me in the kitchen, it won't be stealing. I'll just be borrowing it from myself. You see that, don't you?"

Her brow wrinkled, but at last she got up. "You won't lock the door like you always do while I'm gone, will you?"

"No, but if you take too long, I'll be downstairs having an audience with Grandfather and Grandmother. So hurry!"

Lillia looked at him carefully, not quite sure he was telling the truth, but at last she turned and headed for the door. "You promise, remember. Don't lock the door."

"I won't. But hurry yourself, Pigling. I'm famished!"

For long moments after she had gone out, Morgan just sat on the edge of the bed enjoying the quiet, but something was tugging at his heart. He was going to miss his sister, he realized, and the thought gave his heart a painful squeeze. He hadn't thought about it until now, but it was true. He was going to miss the castle and the city too, of course, miss his friends and his favorite haunts, and even his mother and his grandparents, no matter what they thought of him. But most of all, he was going to miss that small and difficult girl.

His mother Princess Idela was in her chambers with her circle of ladies, sewing and gossiping. Even before noon it was another hot day, and one of the younger chambermaids walked around them with a large fan, cooling them.

Morgan kneeled and took Idela's cool hand, pressed it to his lips. "I give you good morning, Mother."

"I am devastated," she announced, although she did not truly sound as if it were so. "I do not know what to say, except that I will not rest until you've returned again, my dearest son."

"It should not be too long. At least I hope not. Count Eolair said we should be back before the end of summer."

"Oh, and what a terrible thing that was! To think someone would try to harm him. That poor old man! How is the dear count this morning?"

Morgan clenched his teeth, but smiled. "I don't know, Mother. I have not been downstairs yet. I came to say goodbye to you first."

"What a good son." She turned, smiling to her circle. "Can anyone wonder I will miss him so?"

The ladies all nodded and murmured and smiled back at him. Some of the noblewomen who surrounded his mother were scarcely older than Morgan himself, but although many of them were pretty, they seemed oddly beyond his reach or even his understanding, as though they belonged to an alien race, like the Sitha woman he and Eolair were taking home.

"I am as you have raised me, Mother."

"Ah, ah!" she said. "I cannot take the blame for everything. Some of your adventures have more to do with the rough company you keep than anything I taught you."

He tried to smile. "Perhaps. In any case, the others will be waiting for me downstairs—we are to leave soon if we are to make Woodsall by dark."

His mother shook her head. "Oh, I hate to think of you traveling in the Aldheorte, or even near it. That is a place of evil repute. Promise to say your prayers at morning and nightfall, no matter what happens, and keep the Holy Tree around your neck always. Promise!"

"I promise."

"Good. Because even in these days of peace, the Devil is at work in the world. Here, I have a gift for you to take with you." She bent and felt carefully through the items in her sewing basket until she found it. It was a Book of the Aedon, small but beautifully bound. "This was my own mother's," she said. "She gave it to me when she knew I would go away to Erchester to be married. She thought the city was a hive of sin, with robbers in every alley."

"She wasn't far wrong."

His mother let out a most surprising giggle. "I was never allowed to find out. You don't suppose a young bride-to-be like myself was permitted to roam the city, do you? Especially a duke's daughter. Not without guards and chaperones, at least." She sounded almost wistful. "It might have been exciting . . ." She recovered the thread of her thought. "In any case, you must keep this with you at all times. It was made by the monks of St. Yistrin's and it will keep you safe. And you must promise me to read a little from it each day, when you have finished your riding. Promise!"

Morgan was beginning to lose track of all the things he was promising the women of his family. "Of course, Mother." He took the book, then leaned forward. When she lifted her cheek to him, he kissed it. "Thank you. I will think of you whenever I see it."

"Don't just look at it! Read it!" She said it with a curiously powerful emphasis that he did not understand.

"As I said, of course. I will." He straightened up. "I really must go."

"Tell Count Eolair he must take good care of you. You are precious, and not just because you are the heir. You are precious to *me*."

Morgan nodded, but he knew there was no threat in the world, not even a fire-breathing dragon or a company of Norns, that could ever make him tell Count Eolair to take good care of him because he was precious to his mother.

He bowed to the ladies, who smiled and said quiet, gracious things, then he kissed his mother's hand once more and went out.

"Every morning, every night!" she called after him.

"I will!" he called back. When he finally reached the sanctuary of the hall he tucked the Book of Aedon into his shirt, under his jerkin. His grandmother's holy book. Was there some kind of a conspiracy among the women to make him a proper man? Or to keep him from becoming one? Morgan couldn't guess.

He found his grandfather in the throne hall, seated in his chair instead of on the royal throne, something Morgan always found confusing and irritating. What point was there to having a throne in the first place, let alone a legendary one made from the bones of an actual dragon, if you never used it?

When I am king, I will never sit in anything else. A dark thought flitted across Morgan's mind. *If it comes to be, that is. If the troll's fortune-telling was mistaken.*

Thinking of Snenneq brought back the night atop Hjeldin's Tower. A part of him wanted to confess everything to his grandparents, the open hatch, the hairless specter in red, but it was all beginning to seem unreal, like a bad dream. Had he seen the phantom before he hit his head, or after he had stunned himself? And if he told the tale, he knew his grandfather would be even angrier. He would send men up the tower to open it up, and when they found nothing the Hayholt would be full of laughing tales of "Prince Morgan's ghost." In the light of day, he now felt more and more certain that the specter must only have been bad air from the long-sealed tower and the disorder of his own rattled brains. Still, a part of him wondered whether he should tell someone.

His grandfather was talking to Eolair, who sat beside him in the queen's seat, a dispensation obviously given him because of the bandaged wound just beneath his collarbone. The great hall was otherwise empty except for a few guards in the shadows, a strange emptiness for a room that was usually as active as a small city.

"Ah, good, you're here," said the king when he saw him. "No, don't kneel, lad, come here and join us." He turned back to the count. "And Tiamak and his lady are certain?"

Eolair smiled wearily. He was a bit wan, but looked otherwise hale. "Yes, they are certain. No one of the blows was more than a cut. Bloody, but mostly harmless."

"Harmless? Not from that puddle of blood I saw in the forehall. A child could swim in it. You are lucky it happened here, where your wounds could be tended."

"Beg pardon, Majesty, Count Eolair," said Morgan, "but I have heard only a little of what happened. I'm glad to see you well, though, my lord. Are you truly well enough to ride?"

"It was only a shallow wound, praise the gods. It startled me more than anything, and the struggling had already made me light-headed. Today's and tomorrow's travel will be on good royal roads. I will be well."

"What madman did this to you?"

Eolair carefully shook his head. "A Hernystirman who had been working for some time in the castle bake house. He was quiet and kept to himself. Nobody heard him say anything against me or anyone else. He was in distress, and I tried to help him. I do not even know if it was only me he wished to harm—he could not have known when I would be coming."

"Praise God you were spared," said Morgan. He would have liked an excuse to call off the journey, but not at the expense of a good old man like the lord steward. "Did you kill the man?"

Eolair's laugh was rueful. "As I said, I was light-headed. It was all I could do to hold onto him and keep him from a vital blow until others heard me and came to help."

"Well, I'm glad you're safe and that it wasn't worse."

"As are we all," said his grandfather. "Pasevalles has been trying to find out what the fellow wanted, or whether he is simply moon-mad and that's an end on it, but without luck."

"I cannot believe it was anything planned," said Eolair. "Too slapdash. Just a madman, babbling about being 'summoned.' Perhaps he followed me here from our country with some insane grudge, perhaps he simply fixed on me because I spoke Hernystiri to him." The count rose slowly from the chair. "With your permission, Majesty, I will leave you and the prince to say your goodbyes while I see to the last of the details." He turned to Morgan. "When the noon bells ring, Highness?"

"I will be there." But Morgan was worrying now. What if Eolair was too weak to command the mission? Or what if he died along the way? He was quite old, after all. Then even more responsibility would fall on Morgan's own shoulders. And no doubt, if things went wrong, the blame would fall on him as well.

"So, lad," said the king. "Here we are. No, here *you* are, about to undertake a mission for the High Throne. How does it feel?"

Morgan knew what his grandfather wanted to hear, although he felt like a Hyrka's dancing dog for giving it to him. "It feels like a great honor, Your Majesty."

Any idea of telling the king what he thought he had seen on Hjeldin's Tower now sifted away like sand in an hourglass. If they did not even want him around, why would they care what he thought he saw?

King Simon smelled the insincerity, catching Morgan by surprise. "Come, would you try to peddle me a branch of the Aedon's Execution Tree? I asked you how it felt, not what you thought you should say."

"Very well." Morgan didn't like being pulled up short, even by the king. "It feels as though you want to be rid of me. Your Majesty."

His grandfather looked at him with surprise and hurt. "Do you really think that? Merciful Rhiap, Morgan, do you truly think that?"

"Why shouldn't I? You have done nothing but disapprove of me for longer than I can remember." He glanced around the nearly empty throne room. "Where is the queen?"

"What?"

"Where is my grandmother? Is she too ashamed to say goodbye to me? Or is she angry because you forced her into going along with the idea?"

For a moment the king's face reddened, and the prince, full of righteous anger himself, braced himself for the bellowing to come. Instead—and now it was Morgan's turn to be surprised—the king forced a laugh and leaned back in his seat. "I had that coming, didn't I? No, the queen's not avoiding you. Your grandmother will be out to see you off. I just wanted to speak to you myself."

"Well, then, you have. May I go?"

The king's long face now clouded like a sky preparing to rain. "God's Holy Tree, boy, do you really think that of me? That I dislike you so?"

"I didn't say that, but I think it's probably true. I said you disapproved of me, and you have said that yourself enough times. Do you take it back?"

"No, damn it! But I don't disapprove of *you*, lad, I disapprove of what you've been doing. Tournaments, gambling, drinking, in and out of bawdy-houses, your only real friends men twice your age but half your wit! Let alone climbing around on that God-cursed tower in the middle of the night. Do you have any idea, young man, of the evil that's buried there? Any idea at all?"

A chill squeezed Morgan's heart at the memory of a spectral, hairless head, but he was determined not to show it. "I've heard all the stories, sire. Gossips' tales, to frighten children." He did not truly believe that after what he had seen, but admitting it in front of his grandfather would be like conceding that the old man was right about everything.

"Gossips' tales, is it?" The king glowered. "Shall I tell you of what *I* saw the night I fled this castle, when I was no older than you? A man sacrificed, a high noble of this kingdom, his throat slit by White Foxes and his blood used to seal a pact between King Elias and the Storm King himself. And do you know who arranged that bargain? It was Pryrates, the man whose tower you so stupidly climbed."

Morgan flinched. The thing was, the king was right—he *had* been stupid. But that didn't make hearing it any easier. "And what should I have feared?" he demanded. "Norns crawling out of the shadows with white, clawed hands to drag me to Hell? The ghost of a mad priest? Or perhaps just a few rats? Old buildings have plenty of rats, they say, and their scratching is commonly mistaken for ghosts."

His grandfather shook his head. "I was in that tower, boy, when Pryrates was still alive. If you had seen a quarter of what I saw, you would never dare make such a jest. Rats! If only . . . ! Blessed Elysia, please forgive this fool of a boy, because he doesn't know any better."

"If that's all you have to say to me, Your Majesty, then I might as well be on my way. With your permission, of course."

For a moment they stayed that way, Morgan on one knee but poised to rise, his grandfather leaning forward on the second-best throne, pawing at his beard in frustration. "Well, then," the king said at last. "Be on your way. But the day will come—I pray it will, anyway—when you will look back and realize that all your grandmother and I wanted was what was best for you."

"And on that day, I'll thank you, I'm sure." Morgan stood, barely able to hide the way his body was quivering with anger and sorrow and other feelings that had no names. "But now it seems to me that what you really want is me gone—gone where I can't embarrass you any longer with my bad behavior and my dubious friends. In truth, none of you ever cared for me very much anyway. Not you, or my blessed mother, or even my father."

His grandfather's face twisted into an expression that Morgan felt certain was fury, but he didn't care. Should he make the old man feel good for forcing him off on some bootless, fool's errand?

"Has a devil got into you, boy?" The king's hand trembled as he raised it, as if he tried to protect himself from something. "Bad enough you say such cruel things about the rest of us who have cared for you so long, but your *father*? By the sacred blood of the Ransomer, your poor father loved you!"

"Yes, I'm certain he did. For a time." He bowed stiffly. "I go now at your order, Majesty." He turned and marched toward the door, waiting for King Simon to say something else, but he had fallen silent—doubtless too enraged to speak. It did not matter: his grandfather had won the argument simply by being the more powerful.

There is no victory when you fight a king, Morgan thought, and did not look back as he left the throne room. *Kings always win.*

But someday I will *be the king.*

Lord Chancellor Pasevalles watched from the highest window of Holy Tree Tower as the prince's procession set out. He had planned to see Prince Morgan and the Hand of the Throne off on their journey, but when the time came, and to his surprise, he found himself awash in painful memories. It had been a bright, warm day when his own father and uncle had set out for Nabban, having cast their lots with Prince Josua, Camaris, and the rest in the great war. That long-ago day had been like this one in other ways, too, especially the mixture of pride, hope, and fear the crowd had felt as loved ones set out into the unknown. As a child he had cheered without reservation, thrilled that his uncle Baron Seriddan and his father Brindalles were off to do a splendid thing on behalf of splendid people. After all, if Sir Camaris himself, the greatest warrior of his age or perhaps any age, had turned up after all hope was past, then how could their cause fail?

And it had not failed. In fact right here in the Hayholt they had sent the undead Storm King back to hell and defeated his mortal lackeys, King Elias and his warlock-priest, Pryrates. But that did not mean that all those who fought against them had survived to enjoy the victory: Pasevalles's father and uncle would never see their home again, and with them gone, the fabric of his life had begun to fall apart.

All his childhood Pasevalles had devoured stories of heroism and knightly ideals, but after his father's death, those stories no longer made sense. It was not only people that had died in the Storm King's War.

Pasevalles stared down at the tide of men on foot and horseback preparing to make their way out of the Middle Bailey and down to the castle gates. From high above, the small army looked almost like a single creature, one of the weird little monstrosities that lived in pools along the shores of the Kynslagh, something with no guiding thought that nevertheless reached for and grasped and consumed what it needed. What were the Sithi going to make of this party of armed mortals? Would they welcome them in, as the king and queen hoped, or would they avoid them as unwanted intruders? Worse still, would they see them as something more dangerous? Pasevalles was not happy that Prince Morgan, the heir-apparent, was being sent on such a mission. Everything he had fought for since becoming Lord Chancellor, every piece of hard work and subtle negotiation, would come to nothing if the prince was lost. And yet King Simon and Queen Miriamele insisted on sending him away. It seemed so careless to Pasevalles, so foolish, that he was just as glad he had exiled himself to this high perch in the castle's tallest tower.

Do they not understand how close they are to loss at every moment? Do they not understand how suddenly Fate can take their loved ones—just sweep them away, like crumbs brushed from a tablecloth?

He saw a flash of dull gold below—the prince's hair: Morgan had pulled back his hood to kiss his grandmother's cheek. Pasevalles felt like a thief or spy, watching their private moment from above.

Is that how God feels sometimes? When He watches but does nothing? Like a spy?

It was a strange, disturbing thought, and Pasevalles shook it off. He walked to the next window, then leaned out until he located Count Eolair, who was talking with the commander of the Erkynguards platoon that would accompany them. Pasevalles knew he would miss Eolair: The lord steward was someone Pasevalles understood, someone who had experienced tragedy in his life and been chastened by it. Like Pasevalles, Eolair recognized the power of

Heaven to knock down anything that a man could create, to make a mockery of all hopes and plans. And yet there was Bishop Gervis, only a few yards from Eolair, waving his censer and reciting prayers as though his reedy voice might make God Himself sit up and take notice.

I am angry today, Pasevalles told himself. *I must be careful. That is no mood in which to make decisions.*

But some days the old wounds simply ached, and there was nothing he could do to soothe them except to take himself away from other people.

He looked up at the sky. That, at least, augured well. A few clouds blew past overhead like sheep who had lost their flock, carried on a wind from the Thrithings, but otherwise the sky was a serious, solemn blue.

A single trumpet's blare wafted up from below, then several more. He watched the procession, led by the prince and Eolair, as it made its way toward the Nearulagh Gate and the journey down Main Row through Erchester. How small they were already becoming! How distant! From this height, he could still make out Prince Morgan, but like all the rest of the company, when he turned to look back at his home, the prince had no face. He was nothing more than an actor in all this, as they all were.

As we all of us are, Pasevalles thought. *Taking whatever role God gives us and being grateful for it, without ever knowing if we are to be the hero of the story or the butt of the jest.*

Too much bitterness, Pasevalles told himself—in fact, too much thinking. He had work to do.

The lord chancellor turned away from the window. He did not watch as the prince, the count, and their company passed through the Hayholt gates and out into the wide, dangerous world.

PART THREE

Exiles

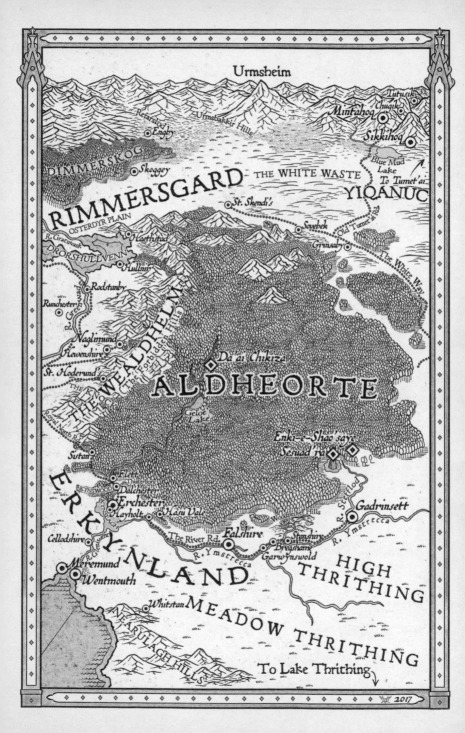

. . . Bring the lute—I will sing,
Fashioning a song of the Desolate City.
The song says:
Border winds hurrying
Above the castle cold.
Well and pathway gone from sight,
Hill and grave mound crumbling.
A thousand years,
Ten thousand ages,
All end thus—
What is there to say?

—PAO CHAO

Inhale, exhale
Forward, back
Living, dying
Arrows, let flown each to each
Meet midway and slice
The void in aimless flight—
Thus I return to the source.

—GESSHU SOKO

This final scene I'll not see
to the end—my dream
is fraying.

—CHOKO

41

Hern's Horde

A **spring storm** was rushing across the Frostmarch. The horizon was black and full of swirling movement, the mountains invisible, as if someone had dumped a bucket of pitch across the northern world. Aelin thought the great wavefront of clouds looked like something alive.

"That'll be on us soon, sir," said one of the soldiers as he caught up with Aelin on the hillcrest. "Long before we reach Carn Inbarh."

"Can't be helped." Like the others, Aelin had pulled his hood up against the growing wind. Just in the last hour the day had gone from ordinary to stormy and dark as ink. "We need to reach the earl with my uncle Eolair's message, and we need to do it swiftly. We'll just have to ride faster and stay ahead of the worst of the weather."

His squire Jarreth shook his head. "Not Brynioch in his silver chariot could stay ahead of that, sir. It will bring darkness within the hour, I warrant. The meadows are still wet and muddy from the winter, and full of holes. The horses' will break their ankles or we will break our necks."

"Bagba's Belt!" Aelin reined up, turned to look directly at the northern sky. Jarreth was right, of course—the storm looked more like an avalanche than any ordinary weather, something that would roll over them and not just soak them, but crush them. Still, his great-uncle Eolair had been very firm that his letter must reach Earl Murdo as quickly as possible. Aelin only wished he knew what was in it, so that he could judge how much risk was necessary, but Count Eolair had been very firm: no one but Murdo was to open it, and if it seemed likely to fall into anyone else's hands it was to be destroyed first. Sir Aelin did not know what the message contained, but he felt certain it had something to do with King Hugh, and Hugh had already shown himself not to be the forgiving sort, so Aelin had kept its existence secret even from his own men. But hanging onto that secret would do no good if they lost their way in the dark, or tumbled into a ravine. And outlaws also roamed this part of the southern Frostmarch. Aelin's band of well-armed men would discourage ordinary cutpurses but not an organized troop of brigands like Flann's Crows or even the Skalijar, who did sometimes range this far south.

One of the younger soldiers, a fellow who'd grown up in this outlying part of Hernystir, cleared his throat and said, "Sir?"

"What is it, Evan?"

"We are not so far from Dunath Tower."

"The border station? How near are we?"

The young man lifted his visor and squinted across the glen. "Unless I miss my guess, that is the valley of the Inniscrich just beyond these hills."

"The Inniscrich? So near?"

"We have been riding fast, Sir Aelin." He said it almost as an apology.

"Well, by old One-Arm, I believe you're right." He almost thought he could make the tower out, but knew it must be a trick of the storm: in truth, it had to be too far away to see. Still, they could be there in only an hour or so of hard riding. They would get wet, but they would have somewhere to dry off and stay the night while they waited for the storm to pass. Important as the message to Earl Murdo must be, it could wait until the next day, surely. What other choice did they have?

Aelin turned to the others. "Let us thank the gods that we have Evan with us, who has the sense to know where in the world he is. And while we're at it, let us pray that Mircha will hold back the worst of her downpour until we've reached the border station."

Jarreth pulled his cloak tighter. "And let us pray also that they have their cookfires burning and a spigot in the ale cask. We'll need a lot of warming by the time we get there."

Aelin smiled, but shook his head. "I'm afraid you will be building your own fires, my friend. The tower will be empty. King Hugh recalled the Dunath Tower garrison, and I doubt the replacements from Rimmersgard will reach it until the roads are dry up north. Except for a few bats and an owl or two, we'll have the place to ourselves."

"Don't say that, Sir Aelin." Young Evan looked unexpectedly pale. "There are things . . ." He could not find the words he wanted, and only shook his head. "I grew up here. There are things in these hills, bad things. Not all of them are natural."

"Natural or not, they will have several good men of Hernystir to deal with if they prove themselves awkward," Aelin said, with more cheer than he felt. He was angry at Evan for sharing his peasant superstitions with the others, undercutting what should be a moment of relief. "And if your bad things try to keep any of us from getting warm and dry, well, they will spend the night on the Frostmarch themselves, and wonder how it happened!"

The main part of the storm was almost upon them now, its outrider clouds running before the wind, flinging down cold rain as Sir Aelin's band climbed through the hills. As they made their way up the slope, through the thrashing, wind-rattled trees, Aelin heard a thin, continuous roaring from ahead of them, like the rumbling snores of some monstrous sleeping bear. When they reached the crown of the hill they could all see what made it—the mighty Inniscrich, its swollen waters dull pewter in the stormlight, busy with white wave caps as the wind made its surface froth and dance.

At the far end of the valley, still a good ride away, Dunath Tower loomed over the river, a rectangular mass of dark stone that seemed to have shrugged its way loose from the surrounding trees to take a better look. Once, long ago in the days of Tethtain's empire, it had served as a nobleman's house at an important boundary between the king's land and that of the hostile northmen. Now there was peace between those two onetime enemies, but the north still offered a threat; Dunath Tower was a boundary fort now, a watchtower against the White Foxes of the Nornfell Mountains, alternately staffed by small garrisons from Hernystir and Rimmersgard.

The rain was punching down hard; the weight of the water thumping on Aelin's hood felt more like a fall of hailstones. "One last ride, men," he cried, "and then we will be under a roof!"

He spurred his horse, which slid a little as it found its footing, but then leaped away along the ridge of the hill. His men followed, the sound of hoofbeats on the muddy ground briefly louder than either the river or the storm.

As they drew closer to the fortress, following the course of the swollen river from a healthy distance up the hillside, Aelin was astonished to see lights burning in the tower windows. The wind and rain were too fierce to even rein up and consider, but he had seen the previous garrison return to Hernysadharc with his own eyes before he departed with Count Eolair's message. He could only guess that the Rimmersmen had arrived earlier than he had thought they could.

The men were cheered, of course, to see signs of life in the midst of so much cold, damp, and darkness, but they were less pleased to discover the tower's gate firmly shut and nobody answering their hale. Aelin could not guess how long they stood beside the narrow spot in the river, wrapped in the storm's darkness, splashed not just by rain but also the floating white foam thrown up by the river's force far below them, cold and soaked to the bone as they thumped away at the gate.

"Can no one hear me?" Aelin shouted, beating the iron-bound wood with the butt of his spear until it seemed louder in his ears than the thunder. "I am Aelin, knight of King Hugh, from Hernysadharc. Let us in, for the love of great Brynioch!"

At last a face appeared on the roof atop the guard tower.

"Ho, there! You say you are Hernystiri?"

Aelin was relieved but puzzled to recognize a countryman's voice. "Yes. Sir Aelin, come from Hernysadharc. Will you let us in?"

The head withdrew without enlightening him.

"Are these people mad?" his squire Jarreth muttered. "They can see we are Hernystirmen like they are. Why don't they let us in?"

At last, when it seemed as if they would be left on the desolate road outside the fort until the storm blew them away or froze them to the spot, the gate creaked open, spilling torchlight into their faces.

Aelin received another surprise when he and his men rode through into the tower's courtyard. The armed men who surrounded them wore no insignia, not that of the Hernystiri borderers or the Rimmersmen meant to replace them, and for a moment Aelin feared they had let themselves be taken by bandits. "Who are you?" he demanded. "Who is your leader here?"

A man with a thin, weather-beaten face and a nose like the beak of a hunting bird stepped forward. "That would be me, Sir Aelin," he said in perfect Herynsytiri.

"How do you know my name?"

"Easier to explain inside, under cover. You and your men are soaked."

Aelin and his troop let themselves be led out of the courtyard and into the tower itself. The tower's bottom floor was the stable; their horses joined the more than a dozen already tied up there. Then they climbed to the main hall, where a fire was burning in the great hearth and several more men waited. Here the light was better, so that Aelin could finally make out the insignia on the brooch that held the spokesman's cloak.

"You are Silver Stags!" he said, surprised.

"Every man of us," said the hawk-faced one. "I am Samreas, the lieutenant of this company. I recognized you from the court, Sir Aelin."

"But what are the royal guards doing here?" Aelin thought he saw a few smirks among the waiting soldiers, which seemed a strange response to an obvious question. The Stags were King Hugh's handpicked troop, most of them hardened veterans of the second Thrithings War. It was even said that some had remained behind in the grasslands when the rest returned to Hernystir, working as hired swords for various of the local thanes.

"The king's business, of course. Sit down by the fire and warm yourselves. I will tell the captain you're here."

Aelin could only stare as Sir Samreas made his way up the stairs. Aelin's men were already pulling off their soaking cloaks and pushing toward the fire, but their leader was disturbed. What would soldiers of the king's elite guard be doing in such a remote place? Was the king also here? Surely Hugh would never travel with such a small force: judging by what he had seen, Aelin thought less than half an ordinary company were in the tower.

A few moments later Samreas returned with a burly, middle-aged man who wore his mustaches and sidewhiskers long in the grasslands tradition that many Hernystiri soldiers had brought back from the Second Thrithings War. Aelin recognized the man, but did not know him well.

"Baron Curudan," he said. "Brynioch's blessings for this roof and this fire. You command these men, then?"

"For my many sins, yes." The baron grinned and stretched out his hand.

"Welcome, Sir Aelin. I fought with your great-uncle at the Stefflod. How is he? Is he well?"

Aelin clasped his hand. The baron had a strong grip. "Count Eolair goes on like a man half his age. He has only recently returned from one long journey and now is off on another, all on behalf of the High Throne."

"Ah, yes. I saw him at Hernysadharc only a month ago."

"I beg your pardon, Baron, but what are the Silver Stags doing here?"

Curudan waved his large hand. "I might ask you something similar, sir— what brings kin of the famous count to this remote spot? Let us drink together and talk. I imagine we can find something to feed your men, as well as to wet their throats, eh, Samreas?"

"I think so, Baron," said the hawk-nosed man.

"Well, see to Sir Aelin's folk, then. Aelin, you come with me."

Thunder rattled the skies outside as Curudan led him up the stairs to a wide chamber with a table and several well-made chairs. A few moments later one of the baron's soldiers appeared with a platter of bread, cold meat, and cheese, and a beaker for Aelin already poured. The man refilled the baron's own beaker from a pitcher, then set it down on the table before departing. Aelin had inherited more than blood from his great-uncle Eolair—he had taken some of his caution, too. In a strange situation like this, he did not like drinking something unless he knew he shared it with his host, so he only pretended to sip from his own wine as Curudan spoke.

"We are here because the king has heard rumor that someone might take advantage of the garrison being withdrawn," the baron told him. "He wants to make certain it is handed over to the Rimmersman as the High Ward dictates."

"Then why did he withdraw the garrison at all? Why not just wait for the northerners to get here?"

"Perhaps because King Hugh did not hear the rumor until after our troops had left." Curudan shrugged. "You have many questions, sir. Why are *you* here? It seems strange that the illustrious Eolair's nephew should arrive just when the tower was thought to be empty."

Aelin had to struggle to keep anger from his voice. "I promise you, we had no intention of stopping here until a few hours ago. The storm overtook us on the road. We are headed for Carn Inbarh—I have messages for Earl Murdo. I can show them to you."

"Murdo, eh?" Curudan cocked an eyebrow. "Well, the seals will show me who they're from." He threw back his head and took a long swallow of his wine, then refilled his glass from the pitcher.

"Do not make yourself too free with my communications, Baron." Aelin did not like the offhand power Curudan was flaunting. "They are from Count Eolair, and he is not a man to be trifled with, even by the Silver Stags."

"Huh." Curudan wiped his mouth. "Because he is the Hand of the Throne, yes. Because he is an important servant of our masters in Erkynland."

Aelin now felt sure he did not want to drink from his own beaker. He rose and carried it to the shuttered window. "Yes, my great-uncle is an important, powerful man. And he has earned that distinction. Do you think otherwise?" As he spoke, he hid the cup with his body and poured the wine into the crack between the window and the wooden shutter, letting it run down the rain-splashed wall outside.

"No, no," Curudan said, laughing. "You misunderstand me. Come and have something to eat—you must be hungry after your long ride." But Curudan did not explain how the young knight had misunderstood.

Aelin poured himself wine from the pitcher that the baron had been using, and for the rest of the conversation, which Curudan carefully kept to uncontroversial subjects, he ate only what foods the baron had already eaten.

"You must be tired, Sir Aelin," said his host at last, sliding back his chair. "You and your men can have a safe, dry night's sleep here. Then on the morning you can set out refreshed for Murdo's lands."

"Thank you, Baron." Aelin did his best to smile and look grateful, but he was more unsettled than ever. Not even a word about "When the storm breaks," but instead the plain suggestion that they would not be welcome more than this one night.

Downstairs, his men were yawning and curling up on their now dry cloaks, making themselves comfortable close to the fire as it burned down to coals. The plates and cups scattered about the room showed that they too had been given food and drink. Only young Evan, the local lad, seemed alert. Aelin made himself a place to lie down near him.

"Did you drink the wine?" Aelin asked quietly.

Evan looked around to see if anyone was watching, then gave a small, discreet shake of his head. "I do not drink wine, sir," he whispered. "I am an Aedonite. I hope that does not give you offense."

"No offense at all," said Aelin. "But it is the first I have heard that Aedonites drink no wine."

"My family belongs to a very severe sect." They were both whispering now. A few of the baron's men looked over at them, but without curiosity. "Water— Aedon's Ale, as we call it—is our only drink."

"Good news, that. We will take turns watching, then. I have an ill feeling about what goes on here."

"Something is strange," Evan agreed. "One of them said they are the protectors of this tower until the Rimmersmen come, but I have never seen such a lax garrison." He looked around the room. "They act as if they are waiting for something."

"You are right." Aelin's heart beat faster. Until now, he had not been able to give his uneasy feeling a name, but the young soldier had done it. The baron's men seemed to be expecting something . . . or someone. "I will take first watch. Sleep now. I drank very little wine myself, and only from the baron's own jug."

"Do not let them know you are awake, Sir Aelin," the young man whispered. "I think they expect us all to sleep soundly tonight."

"I could not sleep now if I had to," Aelin told him. "Rest while you can."

He lay back and closed his eyes, feigning sleep, but his heart was rabbiting and his thoughts were chaotic. Outside, the storm bellowed and hissed like some monster that the gods might have fought at the dawning of the world.

In his dream a forest had grown over him as he slept. He could feel the clutching roots, ancient and cold, as they tangled his limbs and dragged him ever deeper into the ground.

"*Ours,*" the trees whispered, though he could barely hear them because he was surrounded by dark, damp earth, which crept not only into his ears but his mouth and nose and, somehow, even beneath his skin. He was becoming soil, a man-shaped clod of dirt that would fall to pieces beneath the blade of the first plow. "*All this is ours.*"

He tried to fight loose, to dig his way toward the surface, hoping that in the world he imagined outside the forest the sun would still shine, that he would be able to see to make his escape. But as he surfaced, pulling back the roots like stiff curtains, he felt the slap of freezing wind. Darkness was all there was, darkness and the moaning of the air, stirred to madness.

Then a face came to him through the tangled roots, a pale, corpse-like face. It was his own. He was not digging upward, he was digging down, and he had found his own grave.

Aelin lurched up, fighting against the strangling clutch of the forest floor, only to discover the heavy taproot that held him down was a hand across his mouth, and the face he had thought his own belonged to the young soldier Evan, eyes wide, cheeks fishbelly white with fear. He was moaning, too, or was that just the wind . . . ?

"Sir Aelin!" the youth whispered. "Wake up! Do you hear that?"

The sound that rose to his ears was not made by any wind, or if it was, it was the strangest gale that had blown since Brynioch made the skies. The high, pulsing moan seemed to have words, almost, or at least the sound of them, regular patterns that rose and fell, woven into the howling winds and thunders of a real storm but unmistakably something else. "Bagba's Herd, what is that?"

"I don't know, sir." The young soldier's face was slack with fear. "All the guards but that one have gone upstairs to see, I think." He gestured to one of the Silver Stags, who sat with his chin on his chest not far from Aelin's other soldiers, fast asleep and snoring.

"Then we follow them up," said Aelin, slipping his knife from its sheath as quietly as he could, though in truth, with the storm howling outside and the men nearby sawing and buzzing in their sleep, it would have been hard to hear a tray full of plates and cups dropped on the stone floor.

Evan drew his own blade, then followed Aelin upward past the drawing room where they had met Baron Curudan. The great room was empty now, not even a single soldier on guard, so they continued upstairs. As they made their way past rooms meant as living space and storage for the tower's usual garrison, the noise of the storm outside grew louder, not just the screech of winds but also those odd sounds threaded through the clamor, a dim sense of words and melodies, neither of them natural, neither of them familiar in any way. Aelin thought the singing in the storm felt more dreamlike than even his dream had been.

As they neared the uppermost story and the viewing gallery that commanded the entire Inniscrich valley, Aelin heard the more familiar sounds of men's voices, specifically that of Sir Samreas, Curudan's hawk-faced lieutenant. As Aelin and Evan stepped out of the stairwell the roil of wind and wet smacked them across the face.

"Shut your mouth," Samreas was telling someone. "The baron knows what he's up to. The king chose him careful."

"What if the storm just rides him down?" asked one of his men.

"Don't worry about what you don't understand," Samreas said.

Most of the Silver Stags were on the northeast side of the gallery, pressed together against the battlement as if for warmth or comfort, staring down across the mouth of the valley and the great ford that the tower protected. Because the soldiers were on the opposite side of the chamber with their attention directed outward, Aelin signaled for Evan to follow him. He stayed as much as possible in shadow as he edged toward the closest part of the battlements to try to see for himself what the Stags were watching.

It was hard to see much of the valley below—the sky was so clotted with storm that the stars were invisible, and the moon appeared and disappeared behind the streaming clouds like a winking eye. The strangest thing, though, was that the thickest part of the storm seemed to have settled on the ground, filling the river valley with tendrils of darkness like mud in a puddle of water. But not all was darkness: at the edges and in the hidden center of this ground-hugging storm, lightning flickered. During one such flash Aelin had a momentary glimpse of a single armored rider and his stamping mount, revealed on the headland above the ford. Was that Baron Curudan wearing the antlered helmet of the great god Hern? And if it wasn't him, then who was waiting there for the storm as though it were a living thing?

Evan stole silently forward, leaving the shelter of the stairwell for a better view. Aelin wanted to stop him, but dared not make a sound. Lightning raced along the top of the storm like a stone skipped on a lake's smooth surface. The lone rider did not move, but waited as the darkness seethed and loomed and at last, closed him in.

"Yes, *there* is a man!" shouted Samreas as he watched, his voice barely audible above the sharp whining of the wind. "Ah, by Murhagh's bloody wounds, is it any wonder that King Hugh loves him? *Curudan!*" he yelled, waving his fist in the air. "Hail to the baron, master of the Stags!"

Aelin could only stare, dumbfounded. What was going on here? Had the Silver Stags all lost their minds? He turned to Evan to suggest a tactical retreat, but realized after a dumbstruck second that it was not Evan at all, but one of the Silver Stags who had just come out of the stairwell. For a moment Aelin and the Stag only gaped at one another, then Curudan's man shoved hard against Aelin's chest, sending him stumbling back against the battlement so that for a moment he actually feared he might fall over into the swirling, windy black.

"Look!" cried Evan, who had not realized what had happened. He waved his hand excitedly and whispered loudly again. "Those are more than clouds! There are men in that storm . . . Men or demons!"

"Trespassers!" shouted the Stag who had shoved Aelin, loud enough to be heard above the wind. "The strangers are here!"

"Strangers!" Even as he struggled with the soldier, Aelin felt a swift flush of rage. "This is Hernystir's tower—the High Throne's border station! It is you and Curudan who are strangers and criminals!"

The rest of the Stags had turned at the soldier's cry and now came swarming back across the gallery. Aelin still held his knife, but he let them grapple him and drag him down without shedding any blood. They were the king's guard, after all, apparently on the king's orders: if he fought back, they had every right to kill him.

"Evan," he called. "Do not resist."

But the young soldier hardly seemed to be listening. A Stag had grabbed each of his arms, but Evan still stared out into the chaos at the mouth of the valley, his eyes wide with astonishment and wonder. "There are silver men in the storm!" he cried. "Were my parents wrong to deny the old gods? By all that is holy, I can see them! I think they are our ancestors, Sir Aelin! They are so tall, so fair! It must be Great Hern and his hunters!"

But Aelin had listened carefully to his great-uncle Eolair's stories of the Storm King's war. He remembered that when the Sithi had come to Hernysadharc, the king's daughter had thought they were the gods come to save the Hernystiri people. He felt sure, though, that these creatures hiding in the storm were not the Sithi but their white-skinned, dark-hearted cousins from the north, being allowed to cross Hernystiri land as though they were old allies.

Something more than ordinary treason is going on here, he realized, and in that moment Aelin wished that he had fought to the death. Because it was the Sithi's deadly cousins that the baron was welcoming onto the lands of mortals.

The Norns had come to Hernystir.

The song was so powerful that Viyeki found himself lost in it, helpless as a mariner cast from his ship and clinging to a floating spar. The singing seemed to knit together earth and sky into a single great tunnel of darkness, and hours and miles passed in mere flickering, lightning-licked moments as the world rolled away beneath their horse's hooves. Outside of the storm-song it might have been deepest night or bright day, but inside the song Viyeki saw only midnight, heard only the wail of the winds. Even the stars, which should have been constant when he could see them through the tumult of the storm, turned into glowing snail trails in the sky, smeared tracks of light that ran from horizon to horizon.

The spellmakers from the Order of Song did not cease their music even when their horses stumbled from the pace, or when the great wagons of Viyeki's builders toiled up narrow passes through the hills, and wove their melodies with such strength that their wordless song seemed to outshout the storm they had called down.

But still, Viyeki thought wildly, *no matter how great the power of their song, we cannot hope to cross the lands of mortals without anyone seeing us, even in these mostly deserted lands. And what will happen when they do? When this invasion of mortal lands is known, it must be considered a declaration of war, and this time we may not survive the mortals' anger and their far, far greater numbers.*

Viyeki had not forgotten the days after the War of Return's disastrous ending and the desperate defense of the Nakkiga Gate. The survival of his entire race had hung on the courageous sacrifice of a few hundred of his people—such a small number, yet at that moment it had seemed so large. As he and his workers from the Order of Builders had struggled to shore up the defenses while the mortals beat against the gates, he had felt sure he was living through the last moments of his people. Even in the aftermath, after the mountain fell, the gates were sealed, and the mortals retreated, it had seemed unlikely that the Hikeda'ya would ever again be more than a small, doomed tribe, a shadow of their former greatness that would wither away at last.

Why have the queen and Akhenabi set this in motion? How do they think to cause anything but the final destruction of our people?

Even as the heretical questions came to him, the music of the Singers changed tone. The riders slowed, and Viyeki, without conscious thought at first, slowed with them. He felt a superstitious flutter in his heart, the certainty of a child who had done something bad and could not escape from the knowledge of it.

The queen heard me! She heard my blasphemy and my weakness.

And just as quickly, another thought shouldered its way into his mind, the stern voices of his teachers and elders: of course Queen Utuk'ku must know what she was doing. She was the great mother of the Hikeda'ya and her every thought was for her people's safety. She of all living things had seen the Garden and knew what had been lost. Who was Viyeki to question her? A hundred High Magisters had ruled the House of Walls since Utuk'ku had first come to this land—Viyeki himself had recited the name of every one of them at his investiture. He was still but a child compared to his immortal queen.

His heart pained him as though he had been stabbed. *Forgive me, great mistress. Forgive me, Mother of All.*

The great company now slowed and halted, but the storm did not dissipate. Instead it surrounded them on all sides, growling with thunder. In a sudden new flare of lightning Viyeki could see his Builders waiting, their eyes wide but their faces rigid as masks, so that they might have been mummers at the Ceremony of the Lost Garden, acting out an ancient tragedy. The Singers still made their music, but it was muted now, as though all the riders waited in the eye of a storm.

Time passed, but nothing changed. If they had reached their destination, Viyeki wondered, why were they not making camp? If something unforeseen had stopped them, like the arrival of mortal warriors, why did he hear no sound of conflict?

He rode forward against the stiff wind until he found Buyo, the leader of the Sacrifices. "Commander, tell me what is happening," he demanded. "Why have we stopped?"

The officer bowed his head. "High Magister Viyeki. Your pardon, great one, but we have made a promise for the right to cross these lands, and must fulfill it."

"A promise?" Viyeki was growing tired of the pretense that he was in any way leading this expedition. "I do not understand."

"Nor do I, great lord. But that is all I know." Again, Buyo bowed his head, as if offering it for the ax.

Many Great Years earlier, when Viyeki was young, a Magister of one of the great houses could have had even an important officer like Buyo killed for such a vague, unsatisfying answer and no one would have thought it either unusual or unjustified. Viyeki was more open to change than many of his caste, but at the moment he could not help a nostalgic yearning for those bygone days. "How may I learn more?"

"Host Singer Sogeyu will be back soon, I am told." Buyo made a gesture toward the squall of rain and wind to the southwest. "She will doubtless answer all your questions, great lord."

Viyeki had no choice. To complain or protest would be to show himself weak, and weakness was like a fracture in rock: eventually, it would lead to collapse. He nodded. "I will wait."

High Singer Sogeyu rode back across the storm-flattened grasses to the waiting column, appearing out of the swirling dark like something summoned by ancient arts. Her face was full of cold satisfaction.

"Magister Viyeki!" she said, as if they had met by surprise near the Oil Fountains in the Queen's Square. "My storm-singers have held the winds steady for a long, unsatisfying time, I know, but now we may ride on!"

"Where did you go, Host Singer?"

Viyeki's tone had been sharp, and he thought he saw a hint of irritation flit across the Singer's features, but if he had, it was gone in an instant. "To fulfill a pledge, Magister. We ride across the lands of a mortal king, and they are jealous of their privileges. They do not sell them lightly."

"Sell them? What do you mean?"

"These lands belong to the mortal king Hugh of Hernystir. We had to buy our right to pass across them."

"Do you mean you have made a bargain with mortals so that our mission could proceed? Why was I not told?"

Sogeyu folded her hands in a gesture of peaceful cooperation between partners. "Because the bargain was made by our great queen herself, through my master, Lord Akhenabi." She watched for a moment to see what the mention of those names would do.

Viyeki maintained a stony impassivity, but inside he was shaken. He was more thoroughly in Akhenabi's power out here than he ever would have been at home. "And what was the bargain, if I may ask without intruding on Lord Akhenabi's privilege?"

"Oh, nothing of much import," Sogeyu told him. "In exchange for his turning a blind eye to our passage, we have given the mortal king a little nothing—a bauble that he coveted. But to him it shines like a drop of dew in a spider's web, and like most mortals, he is blinded by greed for shiny things."

"You gave him gold?"

"Oh, nothing so ordinary." Sogeyu shook her head. "But, please, do not concern yourself, High Magister. King Hugh is merely another player in the queen's game, although being mortal, he does not understand or appreciate his place in the greater exercise. We have done what we promised, so he will continue his useful ignorance of our presence as we make our way across his lands."

"We are passing *beyond* Hernystir, then?" Again, Viyeki was shaken. Hikeda'ya had not traveled so far from home since the great war.

"Oh, yes," said Sogeyu, content as a bird preening its feathers. "We are going somewhere where you can ply your most excellent skills in furthering the queen's design. Do not fear, Magister, your part in this is very great. When we get there, you and your laborers will astound the world!"

Viyeki overlooked the slighting word "laborers"—as if there was nothing more to the Order of Builders than digging and piling stone on stone. "And what *is* our destination, Host Foreman? Where does the queen's plan send us?"

The Singer bowed as to a superior, but her eyes seemed to tell a different story. "Trust the Mother of All, High Magister Viyeki," she said soothingly. "Trust my master, who has lived nearly as long as the queen herself. They have planned carefully, and you will learn all that is expected of you—but in their time, not your own."

"Of course I trust the queen," Viyeki replied. "She is the Mother of All." But the phrase did not feel as familiar or reassuring as it usually did.

Deep in thought, he rode silently back to his men as the Singers raised their voices again and the winds began to scream. When the company again set off through the tunnel of angry weather, he felt as though a piece of the storm had broken loose from the whole and fastened itself to him, dazzling and confusing him with lightning and turning him cold inside. He could not imagine ever being free of it as long as he rode these unfamiliar lands, among all these hidden minds.

42

Forest Music

The crowds that had seen them off from the castle and Erchester had been loud and enthusiastic and studded with nobility like a diadem. The crowds who came out during the first part of their journey north were a great deal more humble, but even more excited to see Prince Morgan and Count Eolair, the famous Hand of the Throne. In Aldhame and Draycot and other small towns shouting children lined the roads and workers came to the edge of the fields, sweating and grass-stained, to watch the procession pass. But what Morgan could not understand was how such large crowds had gathered even before they arrived.

"Post riders," Eolair explained. "Carrying the crown's letters and other important papers. Sometimes money or bills of credit as well, which is why they travel armed, as you may see. Some ride daily from Erchester out to Sistan and Falshire. Others go to Stanshire or Cellodshire, stopping on the way to change horses, so that a rider can travel from the Hayholt to the borders of Erkynland in only a day or two."

"Do you mean my grandparents are sending out letters, telling people to come and cheer for us?" Morgan liked the thought of being that important even if he didn't like the idea of the king and queen arranging it.

The count laughed. Eolair seemed in good health despite the recent attempt on his life, and showed no sign of it except the bandages he still wore on the wound to his shoulder. Morgan had seen the injury and it was not small. He was impressed by the old man's fortitude. "Your grandparents? I think not," Eolair said. "I suspect that the post riders themselves are also delivering news of their own in the form of gossip when they stop to eat and drink. A company like ours is more than enough to catch at people's attention. You are one of the royal family, and I am known a little as well."

"Perhaps your people have heard you ride with the admirable Qanuc," said Little Snenneq from atop his mighty ram. "Always in these parts people seem happy to see trolls up close. And I am well known for my impressive size."

Qina, his betrothed, thumped his arm and made a face. Binabik and Sisqi, riding nearby, both smiled.

"I am thinking that your great size, Snenneq," Qina's father said, "despite filling us with pride and delighting so many of your friends back home, is perhaps not so much to be noticed by the tall folk who live here in Erkynland."

Though Binabik said it kindly, Little Snenneq seemed saddened by the idea that the crowds had not noticed his unusual height. He stayed quiet for a while after that.

The large company rode for three days before they reached the border of Falshire and turned north off the River Road to follow the line of the forest. After they left the broad thoroughfare, the towns gave way to villages or even single crofter's huts, and nobody came to watch them pass except the occasional smallholder leaning on his hoe. It must have been a strange sight, Morgan thought, the armored knights on their horses, foot soldiers bearing the covered litter of the dying Sitha, and her bodyguard of trolls riding rams and a huge, white wolf. Those who saw it would surely remember it for the rest of their lives.

Despite the variety of mounts, the company traveled faster than Morgan had expected. The weather here was hot and dry, nor were they slowed by civilians and the massive baggage train that had attended the High Throne on its progress to Rimmersgard and back. Although he still was not happy to have been forced into this journey, Morgan had to admit that riding with Count Eolair, Sir Porto, and the rest of the soldiers was closer to the way he imagined himself: a man, doing the important things men did.

Still, as he lay on his cloak that night, disdaining a tent like Eolair's so he could watch the burning bright stars wheel overhead before they plunged at last into the black sea of nighttime forest, Morgan had to admit that he was lonely. But the strange part was that he could not say what, exactly, he missed.

He missed Lillia, of course. Because of the difference in their ages, his love for his younger sister surprised him sometimes. They had not spent much of their childhoods together; by the time she could talk he was learning how to ride and fight. Soon enough she began protesting that she too should be taught to use a sword. That had led to some sharp words between Lillia's mother, who was completely opposed to the idea, and her grandmother, who felt there was good precedent in the family for a girl learning to protect herself.

The queen had won, as queens often did, but after only a few days of instruction, Lillia had decided fighting was not as interesting as she'd thought, and wanted to learn how to ride a horse instead.

During the long trip north to Elvritshalla, Morgan had grown used to not seeing her, to not being noisily awakened by her at terrible hours of the morning, or dragged out to the garden in the middle of a game of dice to see some exceptional bird or other, and the ache of her absence had subsided enough that he barely thought of it. But seeing how much she had grown in the months he was gone frightened him a little in a way he did not understand. She had cried when he rode out this time, not even trying to hide it, which was not like the Lillia he knew, who generally wept only in frustrated anger when kept from something she badly wanted. So alive, so fierce! How could he feel so strongly about her when her own mother hardly seemed to . . .

But at least his mother loved Lillia, in her own slipshod way. Morgan's father had . . .

With a huff of breath, he pushed the memory away—that old, terrible memory. It often came to him when he was alone, and more frequently when he was both alone and sober, one of the great reasons that he hated that combination of miseries.

Will anyone else miss me? My mother? A bit, I suppose, though she did not seem overly troubled by my traveling for months with Grandmother Miriamele and Grandfather Simon. And of course she'd be wretched if I died, because who cares for the mother of a dead heir?

Morgan hoped God was not listening at this particular moment, because even as he thought it, he regretted it. It had been made very plain by Father Nulles and others over the years that loving one's parents was God's firm command. And he did his best to love his mother, he truly did. Surely God couldn't expect anything more than his best. But he couldn't understand how she could be so disinterested in her own daughter. Sometimes it seemed she scarcely saw her from one day to the next, except when Countess Rhona or one of the other women brought Lillia in to say goodnight.

But his mother, disinterested though she might be, at least would never . . . never have said . . .

Again he tried to push the memory away, but this time it would not be dismissed; it rose like some fierce, toothy thing sliding up through the water lilies in the deepest part of the Hayholt's moat—a flash from the shadows, and then it had him.

It had been a very strange day, one of the strangest of his life, and only a fortnight or so after the disturbing Midsummer's Eve when his father had caught him in the Granary Tower. First he had fallen out of the Festival Oak, where he apparently should not have been climbing for some reason he could never understand, since it was the finest climbing tree in the Inner Bailey. One knee and both elbows badly bloodied and aching, Morgan had limped into the residence, trailed by several worried chambermaids who, because he would not let them touch him, could only wipe up the red drops and smears he left behind, whispering and clucking like pigeons. His mother, interrupted in conversation with several court ladies, took one look at him and waved him off with a grand shudder, ordering her maid to take him to Lord Tiamak to be made well.

Later, after the little Wrannaman had cleaned and carefully covered the weals with lint and linen, he had given Morgan a sip of something from a small glass jar. It was sweet but strange. Tiamak said it would help him to rest easier.

The maid brought him back, and now that he was cleaned and his wounds hidden, his mother consented to let him lie on a little bed at the side of her retiring room if he kept quiet. The pain of his injuries began to retreat, only reaching out now and then to poke him and remind him not to move too much. Morgan slept a little, then woke, then slept again as his mother and her ladies spoke in quiet tones, but the second time he rose to wakefulness the retiring room was noisier. Someone was looking for John Josua, the prince was needed, Lord Tiamak was looking for him. Something about one of the chambermaids. Morgan wondered idly whether it had something to do with him, but for once he could not remember any guilty act. In any case, the bed was warm and he did not want to sit up and ask. After a bit, he drifted back down into comfortable absence.

He woke up, or half-woke, to see his father standing over him with eyes as wide and stricken as one of the martyrs on the chapel windows. This appearance was so sudden and unexpected that Morgan tried to cry out, but sleep still clung, and he made only a gasping noise. Even more astonishing, his father bent and kissed him on the side of the head and whispered into Morgan's ear, "I'm sorry. I am so sorry."

As his heart sped at this strange confidence, and he came more fully awake, Morgan heard his mother saying, "And you came here? Are you mad, John? Did you touch her? What if some contagion is on you?"

"No, I did not go near her," his father said. "But Tiamak and others did."

"Sweet Elysia! I shall not let any of them near me."

"The little Wrannaman is no fool. He said it was something else. He said it was poison."

"Oh, my dear God, protect us."

"An accident." But Morgan thought his father's voice sounded unsteady. "Bitten by a snake, perhaps." With an effort, as if he wished to change what was being discussed, his father said, "And why are you so frightened, Idela? People die here from all manner of things. Death is all around. It is God's way."

"Because I am with child," his mother said. Morgan heard what might have been triumph and anger in her voice. He was now completely awake, his heart beating swiftly, but he kept his eyes closed because his father still stood over him.

"You are . . ."

"I am carrying a child. I know it is true, and the midwives agree. Do you wonder that I take fright?"

"A child." He said it as he might have said, "a chair" or "a stone".

"Yes. But why are you so cold, John? Is this not what we wanted, another son to protect the succession?"

"I . . . I am sorry." John Josua was holding himself rigid, but his leg trembled against the bed where Morgan lay miming sleep. "It is thinking of that chambermaid—they said she vomited black bile . . ."

"John! Are you mad?"

"Oh, Lord help me. I am not myself, wife. Again, I beg your pardon."

"Give me your blessing, John. We will pray that he or she will be born safely. Hurry, John—God must think us ungrateful."

"Of course," he said, but the strange edge in his voice remained. "I pray that God will bless us all, and bless the child."

Idela kneeled in front of a picture of the Sacred Mother Elysia and began to pray, asking God's forgiveness for speaking of evil things when He had showered them with such good fortune, and would doubtless watch over all of them, and the boy would be raised as a good Aedonite—or the girl would be, of course, if it was a girl, but his mother didn't want God to think that another boy would be a burden. As she enumerated all the things she hoped God would do to protect her family, Morgan heard his father say just above him, in a low voice that he doubtless thought no other mortal could hear, *"And I pray that God will be just and the child is born dead."*

Morgan lay in horrified, rigid silence as his father went out. He could hear his mother praying—she hardly even noticed her husband's departure. Morgan wanted to cry, but couldn't, wouldn't, because it would give him away, as though he himself had done some terrible thing simply by listening.

When she finished praying, his mother rose to admit her ladies-in-waiting, who had been waiting patiently in the antechamber. They swept in like a cloud of birdsong, their voices light and sweet, talking of the beauty of the summer day beyond the windows. Morgan rolled over and pulled a blanket over his head, wishing it was something thicker, heavier, like clay or even stone, wishing he could bury himself in the earth and not hear anything again. Eventually, after a very long time, he fell back into sleep.

"Are you awake, Highness? Would you like company?"

Morgan sat up, startled to find himself in the middle of the forest instead of the bed in his mother's retiring room, and saw Sir Porto standing a short distance away. The old knight raised his hand in greeting, although none too steadily. He had stayed drinking with the soldiers longer than Morgan, which in itself told much about the prince's current mood. "Awake, yes," Morgan said. "As for company, though, I'm not certain . . ."

Missing the hint entirely, Porto seated himself on a rock nearby. "I know that look you wear, my prince."

"You do?"

"Aye, yes. I left home when I was young myself to fight against the White Foxes. Left my family behind."

"Very sad," he said, hoping that by agreeing quickly he might cut short another recitation of how the old knight had single-handedly saved the mortal race from extinction at the hands of the Norns. "They must have missed you. Your mother, all of them."

But Morgan's words seemed to startle the old man, and when he spoke again, it was to say something the prince had never heard before, as if Porto had been jolted out of one rut and into another, like a carriage wheel. "My mother?" the old man said. "No, no. My mother was long dead. I speak of my wife and child."

Morgan was surprised, and it made the memory of his father's words wriggle again just at the surface of his thoughts, making unpleasant ripples. "You have children? You've never spoken of children before. Or a wife, as far as I can recall."

"It is not a happy tale, Highness. That is why you have not heard it. I left them behind on Perdruin, which is where I was born. When I first went to war, following Prince Josua and the rest in hopes of making my fortune, my wife Sida and our little one stayed behind in her parents' house. Now, I have spoken once or twice of the Battle of Nakkiga Gate—nay, please do not make such a face, my prince, I know I have told the tale before. Astrian has chided me for it enough times. So you know I was dubbed a knight on the field of battle by Duke Isgrimnur himself."

Along with a few other men, Morgan had heard, which made it a little less impressive than it sounded, but this time he felt no urge to interrupt.

"And after I returned south, I was given a land holding by the new king and queen for my service, a parcel in Sudshire with rents worth several gold imperators every year! Not bad. More than I ever had from my own family. But when I returned to Perdruin, I found that Sida and our son had both died in the terrible sweating illness that struck there and in Nabban and in much of the south that year. You would not know, but many called it the Norn Fever, and said it was revenge for their defeat. My little boy—we called him Portinio, which means 'Little Porto'—was not even two years old. They had already been buried a month by the time I returned. I didn't even get to kiss them." His voice became hard to make out. "I never said a proper farewell . . ."

After a long silence, Morgan said, "I didn't see my father before he died, either. They wouldn't let me."

Porto looked at him but said nothing, still mired in his own grief.

"They said I shouldn't see him that way," Morgan said. "My mother said so. My grandfather and grandmother were with him . . ." He hated thinking about it, but it only took a single reminder to bring it all back in a rush.

The stairs had been wet because, a short while earlier, a maid had carried up a cloth and a sloshing bowl. Morgan had wondered why a servant was allowed in but he wasn't. He had been standing on the stairs, and Countess Rhona held his hand so tightly he could not get free, and his mother barred the stairway, her face angry. She was furious at him for trying to get past her, and the two women had stopped him and then held him like a prisoner—like a criminal— and in that moment, the door at the top of the landing, where two armored Erkynguards stood sentry, had seemed as unreachable as a mountaintop fortress. Then Tiamak had emerged from his father's chamber with a face so grave that his mother had cried out, and Morgan had instantly burst into tears at the sound.

He forced the memories away. Pointless. Foolish. He was angry at himself for speaking of it. "Tell me the rest," he said.

Porto looked up, a little startled. "What? I beg your pardon, Highness."

"What happened after you found out? About your family, I mean."

The old knight sighed. "So long ago! It's a curse to remember, sire, I tell you true. In any case, there I was with nothing left. I returned to Erkynland, but I soon sold the land I had been given there and drank the profits. Had I not fallen in with Astrian and Olveris, I suspect I would be dead now." Porto shook his head. "They have always given me a roof . . . or at least a place to huddle and be warm with them."

It had never occurred to Morgan, except in a general way, that Porto must have lived a great deal of life before he had met him. He had seen the old knight as a gentle, drunken clown without wondering what might have made him that way.

"Did you love your wife very much?" he said, although he was not entirely sure why he asked it.

"Did I what now?" Porto's thoughts had apparently wandered again. "Oh, yes, I imagine so. But it is hard to say, so many years later. Sometimes I can scarcely remember what either of them looked like. I had a miniature of her in a locket, but that was lost somewhere." He shook his head again. "Somewhere . . ."

"I hope you forget someday," Morgan said. "So the pain goes away."

"Oh, no." The old man shook his head. "I beg your pardon, Highness, but I pray it never happens. That is all I have of them." Porto levered himself upright. "Speaking of pain, my prince, the cold is creeping into my bones and making them ache. I shall set up a bit nearer the fire. Do not fret overmuch, Highness. You are a most important young man and the things that happen to others will not happen to you, I think. All those who love you will be safe and sound when you return—and you will return in glory, of that I am also sure. Trust me, the old can see things that youth cannot."

Morgan was silent as he watched the ancient knight pick his way unsteadily between the camping places of the others, like a shorebird fording a rising tide in deep mud.

"Oh, my lord Pasevalles, I am so glad you remembered!" the dowager princess said, rising as one of her serving girls showed him into her retiring room. She spread her hands as if about to receive a gift.

"How could I possibly forget such a flattering invitation, Your Highness?" The lord chancellor could not help noticing that Princess Idela had not exactly set the room ablaze with light, which would have been a more sensible approach for inspecting old books. Instead, the candles had been put out so sparingly that for some moments he did not notice the straight-backed old woman sitting on a chair in the corner, sewing.

"Lady Wilona," he said when his eyes could finally make out her face. "What a pleasure to see you, too."

The Lord Chancellor was relieved but slightly confused by the older woman's presence. Wilona was the wife of Sir Evoric of Haestall, a baron of no great family lineage or holdings, who had discovered there was more gold to be made in trade than in farming. Through a series of fortunate connections to Perdruinese relatives, Evoric had become one of the leading importers of dyed cloth from the south, and was now reputed to be richer than almost anyone. He and his wife were also great favorites of Osric, Princess Idela's father.

Lady Wilona looked up from her sewing, squinting. "Ah, it's you Lord Chancellor. Forgive me for not rising—I have an ache in my legs today that is tasking me fiercely."

"Nothing to forgive, my good lady."

"Now, what will you have to eat, Lord Pasevalles?" Princess Idela asked, then answered herself. "Meat, of course. You men!" Her smile was sweetly winning, an amused, maternal appreciation of what scamps the stronger sex could be, but Pasevalles admired Idela's skills and knew only a fool believed the artifices that attractive face could display. "I will send a servant down to the kitchens this moment," she said. "I think there must be some of that joint left from the afternoon—it was very nice and will serve admirably even cold. And we will wash down our feast with a bottle of this yellow Sandarian I have saved for just such a happy occasion."

Pasevalles could not resist poking just a little, if only to take the measure of the evening's weather. "Oh, but Princess, you were concerned for your husband's books. Should we not attend to that first, before we indulge ourselves?"

She waved a white hand at him. "Silly. We will do much better labor with full stomachs. A hard-working man like your lordship must know that."

"I bow to my lady's wisdom."

"As you should." Again the smile—flirtatious, promising. In truth, Pasevalles was not much surprised by Idela's willingness to skip past the boring business of the books. It had been quite plain to him that she cared little about the matter of her husband's library, and meant instead to reinforce her siege of Pasevalles' honor, and perhaps even finally to overthrow it. Pasevalles was by no means immune to the feelings that her pretty face, slim figure, and the pale cleft of her bosom would engender in any man, but he stood this moment in a princess's retiring room and with a lordship to his name precisely because he had negotiated each such crossroad with careful thought. He would not change that now, when the distance to fall was so much greater than it had ever been.

The servant girl returned with a platter of sliced cold meat, some cheese, several small hand loaves, and a bowl of pickled ramps. Princess Idela scolded her gently for not having brought back a sweet as well, then dismissed her. The girl disappeared into one of the other rooms of the princess's chambers.

Lady Wilona took a plate for herself and ate in her chair while the princess and the lord chancellor sat across from each other at the small table. As they ate, Idela talked animatedly of small things, events of such little matter that Pasevalles knew she was working her way toward something of greater import. At last, as he poured a second goblet of the sweet, amber Sandarian for both of them, she rounded to her point.

"I cannot tell you how much I enjoy having your company this evening, Lord Chancellor."

"Please, Princess. You must call me Pasevalles. I cannot stand on my title here, of all places."

"Very well, then, I shall do my best to call you by your Aedonite name. But you must not be naughty yourself and put me at a disadvantage. For tonight, we shall both shed our titles. I will be 'Idela.'"

"As you wish . . . Idela."

She clapped her hands. "Ah, just your man's voice is a pleasure to my ears." She leaned forward as though imparting a great secret of state, coincidentally showing him a great deal of her pale, smooth bosom. "I confess that I tire sometimes of the shrill sound of women's voices. That is all I hear! Is it any wonder I miss my son so much?"

Considering that Prince Morgan had been gone less than a sennight, and that the princess had never been known as a doting mother to either of her children, Pasevalles recognized the opening of a new gambit and generously played along. "It must have been very difficult for you, seeing him off."

"Terribly. Shatteringly." She shook her head. "I cried myself to sleep the first night."

"I am sorry for your pain, my dear lady."

She darted a glance toward Lady Wilona, who was chewing determinedly on a slice of bread and seemed to be paying them no attention at all. Idela lowered her voice again. "It is not only the fright of seeing him go off into the wild world and wondering whether he will come back—"

"He will, Idela. Count Eolair and the others will make sure of that. Eolair is as good a man as the High Ward has to show."

She made a little impatient mouth—the lord steward was not what she wanted to talk about. "It is not only the fright of seeing him ride off. I know I am a mother and will always feel my son's absence as a terrible loss. It is that I fear that growing up without a father will . . . will hinder him on that day when he must take the crown." She made the sign of the Tree. "Which we hope will be many, many years from now, of course."

"Of course," said Pasevalles, and traced the holy Tree on his own breast as well. "God protect our king and queen."

"But surely you have noticed the trouble Morgan has been in of late, Pasevalles! Surely you have seen the bad company he keeps, the fecklessness of his habits!"

"Some of his company may be less harmful than you think, Prin . . . Idela. Fighting men cannot teach smooth speech, and there is no doubt he and his companions spend too much time drinking in low establishments, but there *are* lessons that soldiers can teach him. Useful lessons. A king must not only rule his kingdom from the court, but sometimes must defend it in the field as well."

"I know! Merciful Elysia, how I know! I have horrid dreams about it. And there is not only the battlefield to worry about, but all the rest—assassins, madmen like the one who struck at Count Eolair!"

"You must know how beloved your son is by all of Erkynland, my lady. But for any man, from the least to the greatest, there is no defense against madmen but a loving God. Soothe yourself with this. There is no man in all the world who will be better guarded against ill chance than your son."

For a moment it seemed she would speak again, but instead the princess suddenly turned away from him. Her shoulders trembled a little.

"Idela? My lady? Have I said aught to offend you?"

When she turned back he thought he saw a tear in her eye, but she quickly wiped it away. "Oh, Pasevalles, no, no. You could never offend me. But that is exactly what I was told about my husband, Prince John Josua—that no man in all of Osten Ard was safer, better guarded, more protected. But all of that was worth nothing when Death reached out for him."

Pasevalles was wondering whether his words had truly made her weep, or whether the shininess on her fingertip was a bit of the acrid juice from one of the ramps that she had rubbed in her eyes to bring tears. It was hard to tell with as skilled a campaigner as the princess, but it did not matter: simple courtesy required him to reply. "I am so sorry, Idela. The pleasure and informality of our evening have made me clumsy. Of course you have more reason to worry than most mothers."

Her smile was brave. "I am greedy. I did not have him long, my kind, handsome husband, but at least it was long enough for me to give him two beautiful children." She looked down at her own hands as she wrung them together, then looked up again, eyes wide and, Pasevalles thought, quite impressively beseeching. There was no getting around it: Idela was a very, very handsome woman. "But that is why I fear for our son. He has had no father for most of his life. His schooling has been of the roughest sort. What will become of him when he must take on the responsibilities of his blood?"

Pasevalles could finally see the line of her attack, but he was still not quite sure he had perceived the object. "I will do anything I can to help, my lady. Like everyone else in this court, my concern and love for Prince Morgan is complete."

She wiped her eyes again. "You think me a fool."

"On the contrary, I think you a good, caring woman."

"Then may I confess something to you? Something unworthy, but that preys upon me nevertheless?"

"Of course."

"I fear that the king and the queen keep my son too far away from responsibility, and from those things he most needs to learn."

This was slightly astonishing—the idea that anyone was keeping responsibility from Morgan was a bit like claiming that a groom chasing a runaway horse was keeping it from its bridle—but Pasevalles only nodded. "I understand your concern."

"I did not want him sent off on this strange mission—I do not even understand all this talk of fairies and magical horns and whatnot—but it was not my place to object. Still, when he comes back"—here she allowed a tremor back into her voice—"if, God willing, he comes back safely . . . I would hope that they make better use of him, not just for his own sake, but for the sake of the kingdom itself."

Pasevalles nodded. "I think I follow you, but if you could explain for me just a bit—"

"Could he not be given something more to *do*?" The weight she gave the word told him that she had finally reached her objective. "Morgan will rule the land one day. He will be king of the entire High Ward. Nabban, Hernystir, Perdruin, all of them will bow to him. And yet he knows nothing of how to be a king."

In truth, Pasevalles thought, *there is some sense in what she says.* He doubted, though, that her reasons matched his own. "I heartily agree, my lady. He could and should be given more responsibility."

She spoke eagerly now. "His grandparents—well, there is no getting around it, Pasevalles. They are wonderful rulers, we are all grateful to them for what they have done, but they are old now—fifty years and more! Morgan could be such a help to them, if he . . . if he had a position in which he could do so."

Pasevalles nodded as if it was all just sinking in. "Ah. Do you mean if they made him . . . What would it be called? A sort of co-ruler?"

"Exactly." She reached out and clutched his hand, which caught him by surprise. Her grip was cool and dry, not in the least unpleasant. "You go beyond what I thought, but you are much wiser about these things than I am. A co-ruler—exactly! He would learn by doing, and the king and queen could teach him all he needed to know. Will you help convince them, dear Pasevalles?"

"But, Idela, are you not in a better position to do that than I am?"

"Oh, they would never understand if it came from me." She shook her head forcefully. "They would think I was meddling, that I was trying to improve my own place in things somehow."

It was hard for him not to smile. "Perhaps you're right."

"I know I am, sadly. But if it came from you, they would listen. King Simon thinks the world of you. He raised you above all those other . . . those other . . ." She faltered.

"Those other more suitable candidates? You need not fear that you will hurt my feelings, Idela. I know there are many nobles with grander names than mine, and many with larger fortunes. It is well known that my family, while never the richest to begin with, fell on hard times after the Storm King's War."

"But you were the best for the position and the king recognized that." She squeezed his hand so hard it was almost uncomfortable. "Surely he will listen to you when you suggest something that will help Morgan be a better king someday."

"I cannot promise that." He did not want her to think she had hooked him too easily. "The king and queen are both rare in the stubbornness of their minds. I say that as a compliment! They see things their own way, not as others tell them things must be. But I will try my best."

"Oh, may God bless you for your kindness!" Idela reached for the wine and, quite daringly, poured for both of them. "Say we are partners in this endeavor, and I will be the happiest woman in the Hayholt."

"I was always your partner, my lady, even if I did not know your cause, because I want the same things you want. Security for the High Ward, and happiness and health for your son."

"Pasevalles, you are the finest man I know." She drained her goblet with the vigor of a soldier just escaped from a deadly and blisteringly hot battlefield. "Come, let us take the rest of this and go and look at my husband's books."

She had caught him off balance by returning to the books, but when she stood, he did too. She took him by the hand and led him away from the table. He hesitated a little as they passed Lady Wilona's chair. The older woman was fast asleep, her plate set down carefully on the floor, her sewing muddled in her lap. "Will she not . . .?"

"Leave the poor dear be. What does she know about books that are even older than she is?" Idela giggled like a girl, then tugged at his hand. "Come away. We do not need her supervision this moment."

He let himself be led toward what he expected would be her late husband's library, or perhaps a storage room where the books were kept, but when she pulled him through the doorway, it was into a room completely without light.

"Oh, dear," she said, sounding quite undisturbed. "I seem to have led you into the wrong room. I must have had too much of this lovely wine."

"Should I go back for a candle?"

Even in the darkness, he was quite aware that she had turned to face him and was standing very close. She had let go of his hand, but now she reached up to touch his shoulder, then follow the line of his neck with her finger until her hand reached his face. "I think not," she said softly. "We can do without light and company for a little while, can we not?" She moved closer, so that he could feel her slender form touch him in several places. He could smell the wine on her breath and the floral sweetness of her scent.

"Idela . . ."

Her finger touched his lips, silencing him. "You know, it is not only a man's voice I have missed."

He kissed the finger, then gently pulled it away from his mouth. "My lady, I am only—"

"Hush. You are a man, and that is something truly wonderful. No, you are the finest man I know. Oh, and I have admired you so long!"

"But the servants—"

"Know better than to come stumbling into my chamber. Yes, I told you a lie, I confess it, my lord. This is not where my husband's books are, this is my own bedchamber. Do you hate me for my falsehood?"

"I could never hate you, dear lady. Sweet Idela." He took her hand again and kissed her fingertips, each one. He heard her breath, deep and unsteady, so he leaned forward again and found her lips. Long moments passed before he spoke again. "I could never do anything to hurt you, in any way."

"Oh, glory!" she said, and in that moment he could detect nothing false in her words. "I am all goosebumps—and my heart beats so! Here, can you feel it?" She took his hand and put it on her breast, naked now, her skin warm, the nipple nearly as hard as a cherry stone. In the darkness, she had quietly unlaced the top of her dress and pulled it down. "Can you love me, Pasevalles? Just a little?"

"Yes," was what he said, then squeezed her flesh, gently, until she gasped. "Yes, my lady, I can."

The first night they camped within sight of Aldheorte, as Binabik and the trolls were caring for the Sitha, Count Eolair waited until the knights and their squires began eating their suppers, then asked Morgan if he would like to accompany him into the forest.

"But why?" said Morgan, who had been about to go in search of Porto and the wineskin the old man generally had somewhere close by.

"To blow the horn, Highness," said Eolair, patting the wooden box tied to his saddle. "There seemed no sense in doing it while we were still within the bounds of Erchestershire."

Morgan could only say yes. He found his horse cropping contentedly in the thick, green grass, and climbed into the saddle. The mare gave him such a look that he almost felt he should apologize.

"We are not far from Hasu Vale," Eolair said as they headed their mounts toward the dark edges of the forest. "It was a dark place, once. Your grandparents were captured there and nearly killed by Fire Dancers, worshippers of the Storm King."

"I know all about the Fire Dancers," said Morgan. "Believe me, Count, I have heard all the stories." He was missing his sister and his grandmother and didn't much want to talk. He even missed his mother.

Morgan had a sudden memory of his grandfather drolly suggesting that the women in the family were conspiring to keep the king and his grandson from having any proper fun. His grandfather had wanted to go out and catch frogs in the Royal Puddle, which was his joking name for a large pond at the edge of the castle's common green. Morgan hadn't been particularly interested in catching frogs—already he was concerned to appear a young man, not a small boy—but he had been pleased his grandfather wanted to spend time with him. When had that been? After his father's death, certainly. As he thought of it now, he remembered more than a few occasions when the king had tried to interest him or amuse him.

"You and I, Morgan. That's what it will come down to, you mark your grandfather's words," the king had said. *"They'll never let you do anything if you listen to them, your mother and my wife. They're afraid you'll be hurt. But what's wrong with a bloody nose from time to time?"* Then he had told some story about Rachel, a chambermaid who had apparently frightened him badly when he was young.

His grandfather had been kind to him in those days, it was true. Why had everything changed since then? Why was the king always so angry at him now over a few foolish scrapes and mistakes?

"You have gone quiet, Highness," Eolair said, startling Morgan a little. "Is all well?"

"Yes, yes," he said, although his thoughts were so confused and uncomfortable that he truly did feel unwell. "I am just tired of talking."

So they rode silently through the trees spotted with failing afternoon light, Eolair in front and Morgan just behind him, grateful that the older man respected his wish for silence. The sun was low in the west, but such sky as Morgan could see between the branches was orange and red except for high above their heads, where it showed somber blue. In the new quiet, he could hear the sounds of the forest, or in this case, the absence of sounds. But for a few birds piping far away, safely distant, Morgan heard nothing but the soft crunching of twigs and leaves beneath their horses' hooves. The camp was only a short ride behind them, but it suddenly seemed leagues away.

"Ah, I think we can tie our mounts here," said Eolair at last. He dismounted, still impressively nimble for a man his age, and knotted his horse's reins around the slender trunk of a birch, then began to remove from his saddle the box that held the horn. Morgan tied his horse beside Eolair's, staring around at the shadowy glade.

"It's so quiet." Even to Morgan's own ears that sounded like a foolish thing to say, but Eolair only nodded.

"The forest is careful," the count replied. "It does not welcome visitors, but it does not repel them, either. At least that is what my father used to say, although he was talking about our own Grianspog woods. This forest, the Aldheorte, though . . . many say it is the oldest place there is. That is why it is named 'Oldheart'."

"How could one place be older than another?" Morgan demanded, unsettled by his recollections and by the forest stillness. Eolair had taken the velvet sack out of the box and now slid the cloth from the horn as carefully as if the strange instrument were a sleeping child. Morgan said, "I mean to say, if God made the world then He didn't make a forest first, then the rest of everything later on, did He? That doesn't make sense." The sound of his voice in the quiet clearing seemed harsh as a hectoring crow's.

"No, you are right." Eolair held the horn up to admire it in the dying daylight. "And I would be the first one to agree that we need more sense in this world."

Morgan had never seen the horn before, although it been mentioned in many stories about Sir Camaris and the Storm King's War. He was surprised to discover that it disturbed him, although he could not have said precisely why. In some ways it seemed crude, just a curving cone incised with small, precise carvings, a silver mouthpiece, and simple silver decorations around the wide end its only ornaments. But something about it held Morgan's eye, made his heart slow and then speed again.

"That's it?" he said. "That's the horn of great Camaris, like in the songs?"

"It was, but I think he was not the first to wind it—not by centuries. Do you see these marks?" The count drew his finger along the carvings. "These were made by the Sithi, and not recently, or so I have been told. This horn was crafted when the Sithi still ruled Osten Ard."

"Are you going to blow it?" Morgan asked.

"Of course. Or at least, I am going to try."

"Try?"

"The horn is like other great and powerful things, Highness—not always easy for us to understand. When Prince Josua brought it to Sir Camaris, who had lost his wits, the old man seemed at first not to recognize it, then suddenly Camaris took it up and blew it loudly and clearly. After that great blast his mind became clear again. Why should that have been? You can ask the Sithi when we meet them—if we meet them—because I doubt anyone else could say."

"Then . . . may *I* try?"

"To sound the horn? Of course, Highness." Eolair lifted the hem of his cloak and rubbed the mouthpiece until it shined.

Morgan took the horn. It was surprisingly heavy, not like something made of bone or antler at all, but more like stone. He lifted it to his lips and then lowered it, feeling the hush of the woods press in upon him. "If they hear it, the Sithi . . . they'll come?"

"No one can know," Eolair told him. "But if they do hear it, I doubt they will ignore it. Not something like Ti-tuno."

Morgan lifted it to his mouth, steadying it with his other hand. He pursed his lips and blew, but nothing came out but a splutter of air. "I didn't think it would work," he said.

"Try again," said Eolair, and for once an adult's urging did not feel like an order or a scolding. "Think of the Sithi. They have lived here since long before mortal men walked this land. Think of them in their forest deeps, listening."

Despite having seen the Sitha woman on her sickbed, and having heard many stories of the old days, it was hard for Morgan to imagine the Fair Ones. Old stories kept creeping in, stories he had heard from older children and from servants in which the pale-haired Sithi were more like ghosts than men. He closed his eyes and tried to think of the wounded Sitha's catlike eyes, which had opened once when he had gone to see her, blazing golden against her bloodless features, startling him badly. He tried to imagine eyes like that here in the forest, perhaps watching the prince and the old count this very moment, golden eyes staring from the shadows. This time, the horn gave out more spit than air, but still did not sound.

"I can't do it," he said, and held the horn out to Eolair.

"If you can't, I doubt I can either, Highness—not with these weary lungs of mine." The count shook his head. "If the horn has something of the Sithi's making in it, your claim to it is at least as great as mine. It passed from Camaris to your grandparents. Try once more."

It was strange for Morgan to think of having any claim on such a thing, especially by the mere accident of birth into the royal family. But of course, that was why he was expected to be king someday, was it not? By the accident of his birth? By the accident of surviving his father? The thought made him feel empty. He lifted the horn to his lips and blew mightily, blew until his cheeks ached, but no sound came.

"Once more, then we will return," said Eolair. "If we cannot make it sound, still we can find other ways to announce our presence. There is no shame. Please, Highness, just try once more."

Morgan wanted to argue because he knew that there *was* shame in failure. As someone who knew he had been sent to these empty, dark woods simply because he had been caught breaking rules, he knew that as well as anyone. But here in the ancient forest it suddenly seemed like something that had happened far away and long ago. He felt the weight of the horn in his hand, the substance of it, and looked at the last gleam of the setting sun burning between the trunks like a distant fire.

Snenneq's knuckle bones said that I won't get what I expect, he suddenly remembered. *What will I do then, if I don't become king?* A strange anger filled him, not the sort that scalded his heart when he didn't get his way, but another sort of feeling, a deeper rage at blind, foolish fate. *But why?* he wondered. *Why does it have to be that way? Why does anything have to be that way, just because others say that it is?*

Without even realizing, he lifted the horn to his lips, holding it with both hands like an upended wine goblet, but instead of letting the fiery taste of happiness run down his throat and fill it up, this time it was his job to do the filling—to fill this heavy thing with his own breath. To bring it to life. *What if this is the only important thing I ever do?*

And as he thought this, Morgan for the first time felt the famous horn as something more than an ancient artifact, a piece of lost history. He closed his eyes and the twilit forest vanished.

There was only Morgan and Ti-tuno, then. For an instant he thought he could feel what the horn's creator had felt, the nameless Sitha who had long ago carved the runes and polished the curving surface until it gleamed. In that instant he could even sense how the horn's triumphant music was not summoned from somewhere else, but crouched inside it like a dragon hiding in a cavern, all that fiery power coiled but awake and waiting. Somehow, even if only for the space of these few heartbeats, the horn became part of him and he, not just the air inside him, became part of the horn as well.

He blew. This time, he heard something immediately, a rattle that became a groan. His lungs and the horn became one thing, a passage of fire from his body into the horn and then out into the silent forest, a single note that grew from a moan to a stuttering howl to a deeply sounding roar, like the bellow of a huge beast. The sound climbed into the air of the forest clearing and hung there for so long that Morgan almost forgot it was he who was making it. Then it fell away, leaving only faint echoes.

Despite having been the one to urge him to try one last time, Count Eolair looked surprised—almost stunned. "You did it, Highness," he said in a voice so soft it was almost a reverent whisper.

His heart pounding with exultation, Morgan winded the horn once more, as much to feel the sensation again as anything else. Ti-tuno's call rolled out through the darkening woods, deep and throaty and astonishingly loud, the cry of some creature God had made and then forgotten. But the Sithi did not come.

Morgan still felt a sense of triumph, but though he blew two more times, nothing answered the blasts but echoes.

The prince and the count got back on their horses and returned through the forest, through an evening now alive with cricket song, back to the cookfires and the company of other mortal men.

43

Into Deeper Shadows

"Why are you here, mortal?" demanded the halfblood slave, looking her full in the face. "Here in the storerooms, we heard no mention of your coming."

His lack of courtesy was both insulting and infuriating, but Tzoja did not dare let herself be goaded into making a scene. Just the proper amount of anger was what she needed, no more, no less: the Hikeda'ya were highly sensitive to precedence and position. "How do you dare speak so to me, you low creature?" She hoped her features showed the cold fury she felt, but not her even stronger fear. "Do you not see my household sigil? Mortal or not, I am an important concubine of the High Magister of Builders, Lord Viyeki himself! I gave him a child who, despite being a halfblood like yourself, is an honored member of the Order of Sacrifice—a Queen's Talon, no less!"

Her inquisitor flinched just the tiniest bit, an infinitesimal tightening of his skin as if anticipating a blow, something Tzoja would never have noticed before living in Nakkiga. Now, she knew, it meant that her gambit had succeeded, at least in part.

"I beg your indulgence, Mistress," he said in a more guarded tone. "But I have been told that certain lowborn creatures have been making free with the Queen's pantry. I am only doing what I am bound to do."

"Mistaking me for a slave even lower than yourself, you mean?" Tzoja now felt herself on familiar ground again, since she had faced this sort of thing on many more legitimate errands. She made a sign with her fist against her throat that meant, *I will swallow my righteous fury for the moment.* "Still," she said, "since I work hard, as you do, to protect that which belongs to the Great Mother of All and to preserve the memory of the Lost Garden, I will not mention you to my lord if you quickly comply with my wishes. I need enough food for a few days' journey."

The slave, who could not have been much older than Tzoja herself but whose Norn blood, as it did for her own daughter Nezeru, gave him the look of a much more ancient creature, made a strong gesture of apology. "Again, I ask for your mercy, Mistress, but why do you need such a quantity? Your master's clan household has already had its allotment." Starvation had been a familiar companion to the Hikeda'ya in the years after the War of Return's failure. This menial had doubtless been harshly schooled in taking his guardian's role seriously.

"Fool of a slave!" she said, making her face as disapproving as she could. "Do you think yourself a temple priest teaching an ignorant child to recite the Prayer for the Queen's Strength? Or is the mortal blood in you so powerful that it stupefies the rest? Where is it written in the Hamakha Dictates that you may ask questions of a High Magister's concubine? Do you demand the details of what my husband and master wishes to do with the food as well? If so, I think the Queen's Teeth might take an interest in *your* interest."

The blow was well-aimed. The slave's face crumpled in poorly hidden fear. "No, Mistress! Please, do not misunderstand me. Usually we are informed of any such need ahead of time."

"My husband has recently left on a mission given to him by our great queen herself. He left me detailed instructions on what I was to do during his absence. You say you were not informed, but I wonder if it is possible instead that you have lost his orders?" She paused for effect. "Again, I offer to call for the Queen's Teeth, or even the nearest guards, and we will quickly find a straight path through this crooked passage."

Surrender. "No, please, Mistress. I am certain the fault was ours." The slave had the deep black eyes of his Norn blood, but the sallowness of his skin had been lightened by fear until he was almost as white as a pureblooded Hikeda'ya. "Make yourself free and do what you must." He turned to where several of the less bold kitchen slaves cowered in the background. "We all pray for your husband's safe return."

"And the triumphant fulfillment of the queen's wishes, of course," Tzoja said.

"Of course, Mistress."

It was secretly satisfying to make rude halfbloods like this one swallow their own words, but Tzoja knew that at this point someone in her position should either walk away from this undignified discussion or call the guards so that such argumentative slaves could be punished. But there might still be some small advantage she could exploit that would fall within the bounds of accepted behavior. "I am too angry now to look for myself. Here is what I have written down of my husband's orders." She held out the page on which she had made her list. "Bring me these things."

"Of course, Mistress," said the slave. His now-downcast eyes promised that there would be no further questions. "But none of us can read."

"Then I will read them to you, and you will make haste to find them all."

It was a long walk back from the order's storehouse to House Enduya, Magister Viyeki's clan compound. Tzoja had to pass several dangerous points, including the rear gate of the Order-house of Echoes, the queen's trusted communicants, and it felt like an even longer and more perilous journey because she was forced to walk slowly, carrying the two heavy sacks. She thought she must look a bit like Old Longbeard, the blue-hooded figure of Rimmersgard legend who brought gifts of food on Midwinter's Eve. Longbeard, though, rode a great gray horse; Tzoja had to bear her burdens alone, carried only by her own aching legs.

Another month from now and she would have been able to choose from many nicer things to eat, but spring and summer came late and stayed only briefly in the Nornfells, so most of what she had taken from the kitchens was the same sort of provender on which they had been living since the previous autumn—hard-baked bread, equally hard cheese, and of course a great deal of the dried fungus called "winterbread," which the Norns prepared in dozens of different ways, although Tzoja had not found one yet that she truly liked. As she trudged along, bowed beneath the weight of the sacks, it was hard not to reminisce over the food of her childhood, hot stews, berries ripe from the vine, bread so light that even the oldest of her neighbors could chew it despite having lost their teeth. It was one way that she would never be a Norn, no matter how long she lived under stony Stormspike.

She hesitated when she reached a crossing, six different featureless tunnels that came together like a crooked star. It was easy at any time to get lost in the great stone hive that was Nakkiga, with no sky overhead to orient herself, but what made it worse now was that she was not, despite her lie to the kitchen slaves, engaged in any kind of lawful activity. She was a resident of House Enduya, and could legitimately take food only from its great kitchens, which of course she dared not do—at least not in large quantities—because word would quickly make its way back to her master's wife Khimabu, the ruling lady of the clan household. Tzoja would be in even greater danger if it was discovered she had been to the Order of Builders' storerooms, of course, but Tzoja was counting on the terror of making a wrongful accusation against a noble to keep them quiet until she had finished her preparations and could flee Viyeki's house. Because if she didn't, she knew that Khimabu would have her killed: she had all but taunted Tzoja with it at their last meeting.

It was always hard to find her way through the deep darknesses of Nakkiga, even inside her own household. Even after so many years living within the mountain, her eyes had not become accustomed to the way the Norns lived, to the tiny, flickering oil lamps that lit most of the passages, especially away from the main thoroughfares, but which barely gave enough light for a mortal to see her hand before her face. Often Tzoja snuck into her husband's private garden just to stand for a moment in sunshine, however far it might have fallen from its original source and how many reflective surfaces may have redirected and diminished it along its way. After so many years here under the mountain Tzoja had come to hate the darkness, hate it like a living enemy.

After a moment's fearful consideration at the six-way crossing, she chose the passage that seemed most familiar, knowing that if she picked the wrong one she might end up somewhere she didn't belong, carrying bags of stolen food. Beloved concubine of a powerful man or not, she would immediately be imprisoned, which would be as good as a death sentence, since Khimabu could reach her anywhere in Nakkiga. That was why Tzoja had spent the last days preparing her escape to a hiding place that Khimabu would not know, a place that nobody but Viyeki himself would think to look for her. And, if the gods were willing, tonight she would take the rest of the goods and clothing she had so carefully obtained and hide herself there until her beloved returned.

To her relief, she saw she had chosen the correct corridor: the passageway led her to the wide and busy Avenue of the Fallen, which ran behind many of the great houses whose estates fronted on Great Garden Passage. Several times she passed other travelers who looked curiously at a mortal woman staggering under the burden of two enormous sacks, but each time Tzoja did her best to take on the bent, long-suffering attitude of a mere slave, and here, for once, her mortal shape and features helped her. Since the end of the Storm King's War and its terrible losses for the Hikeda'ya, the nobility had begun using mortals for many tasks that had once been done only by their own kind. Also, as with Tzoja herself, the nobles had discovered that mortal women were fertile in a way their own wives and concubines were not. Leaders like Magister Viyeki had worked hard to overturn some of the oldest taboos, to permit not just the legitimate birth of halfblood children, who in the past had nearly always been executed along with their mortal mothers, but to broaden their acceptance in places that had always been barred to them. Even so, the rise of Viyeki's own daughter Nezeru to the exalted role of Queen's Talon, especially at so young an age, had astonished many in Nakkiga, not least of whom had been Tzoja herself.

At last she reached the deepward gate of House Enduya, the back door of the clan's residence. It was guarded, of course, but she had prepared this ground earlier and felt more confident than she had in the royal kitchens.

"Greetings, Queensman Daigo," she told one of the guards as she set down her sacks. "I return as I promised."

Daigo, a sullen fellow that she had cheered a few times in the past with gifts of food she had saved for him, looked her up and down. "Haya, Mistress Tzoja," he said. "You return."

"And I have brought you something." She reached into the bag and brought out a stone jar sealed with wax. "Cloudberries. Kept under cold water all winter. Take them to your servant and have her make something nice for you." Cloudberries were picked in late summer, and were a delicacy even when they were plentiful. At this point in the circle of seasons, during Otter's Moon when the new berries were not yet ripe, they were like jewels.

The other guard, whom Tzoja recognized but did not know, made a face. "A gift for Daigo but none for me?"

Tzoja blessed the fortunate star that had warned her this might happen. "What a surprise, Queensman—I have some for you, too!"

As she handed the jar to him, he gave her a look that was a bit less grateful than she would have expected, which made her skin tighten. Had she done something to make them suspicious? "Did you see anything interesting while you were out, Mistress?" the second guard asked. "They say that Lord Akhenabi himself was seen on the Glinting Passage."

She hid a shudder—very few living things in Nakkiga frightened her more than the master of the Order of Song. The noises that echoed at night from his great mansion were heard by many, but spoken of by none.

"No," she said to change the subject, "that honor was not mine. But several men from the Order of Sacrifice threatened and insulted me when I passed them. They called me a bricklayer's bitch."

"Bricklayer?" Daigo was frowning, but not, she suspected at the idea of a Sacrifice calling her someone's bitch. "That's what they said? Bricklayer?"

"I paid little mind," she said. "Now forgive me, but I must get back to our apartments and continue my preparations." She had told Daigo something earlier about preparing a meal for Khimabu. *But if I truly did*, she thought, *I would make sure that the cloudberries and everything else were poisoned.*

Daigo and his fellow guard were already arguing over which Sacrifices might have been insulting the Order of Builders, and in which soldiers' tavern along the Glinting Passage they might be found later. She hoped she had not overdone it with her improvised tale—a fight between orders that drew the attention of the Queen's Teeth would do her own plans no good whatsoever— but there was no doubt that between the supposed jibes from the Order of Sacrifice and the gift of cloudberries, the guards were well and truly distracted. She bowed to them both, although they hardly noticed, then shouldered her sacks again.

None of the servants she passed on her way through the clan-house seemed to pay much attention to her; she made it all the way to her own door without being challenged. But as she set her sacks down to withdraw the orichalcum key hanging on its chain around her neck, she saw that her door was already open.

Tzoja's blood seemed to turn ice cold in her veins. She had not left the door so. She would never have left it so, and she specifically remembered locking it and then checking it again before she set out. Her heart beat so loudly she doubted she would hear anything else, but she leaned close to the door anyway, listening.

Male voices, quiet but forceful. More than one, and they were inside her room. If she had been innocent she might have walked in and demanded to know who they were, but carrying two heavy sacks full of contraband food-stuffs, she did not dare.

The voices grew louder. They were coming out.

Tzoja looked desperately from side to side. The sunken doorway of an un-used apartment was a dozen steps away. The door would be locked, but the doorway would be deep enough to hide her when the strangers came out, as long as they turned back toward the main hallways. If they didn't—well, no point in thinking about that or she would lose her strength and fall down right here before her own door.

She clutched her bags and huddled as far back in the doorway as she could, holding her breath as the searchers stepped out into the corridor. She could make out only a little of what they were saying but thought she heard one of them say, "she will be unhappy" and her heart slammed in her breast. Khimabu? Had her beloved's wife sent someone to kill her?

To her relief, the men turned in the other direction and their voices grew quieter. Summoning her courage, she leaned cautiously out from the doorway and looked toward the two men just before they disappeared around the corner of the passage.

White. Their armor was white. And on their heads they wore the sharply peaked helmets that proclaimed them Queen's Teeth. What could the queen's own guard want with her?

Oh, great gods, she thought. *Viyeki warned me that the queen wanted to send all mortal concubines back to the slave compounds. Have her guards come for me, then? Or is it something worse?* She remembered her secret cabinet and the things hidden there—things that would mean her death if someone saw them. She had secured them as well as she could, but had thought she only had to hide them from the servants. *Oh, merciful halls of heaven, have they found my hiding place?*

But even that terror faded into insignificance when she realized that she was no longer safe even in her master Viyeki's house. The Queen's Teeth might return any time, and then the most fortunate thing that could happen to her was that she would be returned to the slave compounds, to be raped by any noble with a taste for mortal flesh, no matter how powerful an official her beloved might be. More likely Khimabu would simply arrange for her to be killed. Because Viyeki was gone.

The time for planning and preparing was gone, too. Tzoja needed to flee for her life.

The horses could go no farther up the increasingly treacherous slopes, and Makho declared they were to be left behind before the Talons climbed any farther, so they found a cave with a freshet of water from a source deeper in the mountain. The entrance was slippery with ice where the water trickled out, but inside the cave was dry.

Nezeru found the blocks of pressed fodder at the bottom of the saddle bags and, with the mortal Jarnulf's help, crumbled a dozen of them in a corner at the back of the cave for the horses. Saomeji built a fire near the opening, and Kemme and Makho, who were both still weak from their injuries, settled next to it.

"We will warm ourselves for an hour, Singer," Makho declared. "But after that we must climb again."

"I beg you to reconsider, Chieftain," said Saomeji. "We need to rest longer—look, Kemme's wound is bleeding again. We may have dealt with the Skalijar, but there are other creatures in these mountains, not least the dragons we actually seek, who know the smell of blood."

"Also," said Jarnulf, scattering the last of the fodder, "some of us cannot climb so well in darkness. In any case, I doubt we need to keep hiding our presence by climbing only in darkness. The giant said he cannot smell any trace of the bandits or any other two-legged enemies."

"Do not seek to instruct me, mortal," the chieftain said.

"You two." Saomeji gestured at Nezeru and Jarnulf. "Go and find us something to eat. A night of full bellies will do us all much good in the morning."

Makho pushed himself up to a sitting position, his face almost as hard as Queen Utuk'ku's silver mask. "Do you give the orders here now, Singer?"

"My apologies, Hand Chieftain. Of course not."

Makho stared at Saomeji for a long moment, then turned to Jarnulf. "You and the blackbird, go out and be useful, as the Singer suggested. I am tired of looking at your faces."

"Bring back meat," said Kemme. "We are not Zida'ya, to live on flowers and bee's milk."

Jarnulf turned and walked out of the cavern, splashing through the water that spread into a tiny cataract at the cave's mouth. Nezeru followed him. Why did Makho keep throwing them together? Did he hope to entice her into some treacherous alliance with the mortal?

Goh Gam Gar was sitting just outside the cavern, his thick, yellowed pelt his only protection from the bitingly cold winds. "If you two are going out to rut," the giant said pleasantly to Nezeru, "you had better dig a hole in the snow. It will serve you for a nest, too, should you bear offspring. Still, they will be thin-blooded, mostly mortal whelps with such a father. I doubt they will survive. But perhaps it is only the rut itself you seek, eh, Sacrifice?"

Nezeru stepped around him, mindful as always of the giant's long, powerful arms. "Silence, monster," she said, but she could feel a burning in her cheeks and was sure her half-mortal skin betrayed her. "You lie to sow distrust. You accuse others of what you want for yourself."

The giant laughed and the icicles shivered above the cavern entrance. "Oh, fear not—you are safe enough from me. Goh Gam Gar would split you like a skinned rabbit on too large a stick."

She set her jaw and marched away. Jarnulf was waiting a dozen paces ahead, gazing out across the uneven peaks and the deep valleys, all covered in snow. "Such helpful traveling companions," was all he said. "We are fortunate."

Nezeru thought it would be a good idea to go back down the mountain, to places where they had seen stands of evergreens which might hide game, but Jarnulf only shook his head. "And what if we kill something large? I do not think much of having to carry it back up the mountain to the cave. No, we should go upward. We will scout a little of tomorrow's journey, and if we find anything to shoot, we can drag it back down instead of bowing our backs."

So they clambered up, trying to find the best footing they could but not always succeeding. Once Jarnulf stepped onto snow that gave way beneath him; he disappeared into a crevice so quickly he did not even have time to cry out. For a brief instant Nezeru thought him lost, but when she clambered as close as she dared to where the crust had given way, she found that he had only slipped down a few feet below the surface. She slid her pack out until he could grab it by the strap. After much slipping and sawing, he at last managed to scramble out of the hole.

"My thanks," he said, and once more displayed the expression she could not imagine from any Hikeda'ya, a broad grin. "That might have been unpleasant."

How did the giant sense my complicated feelings about this mortal? Nezeru wondered. *Not that it is lust I feel, as the beast suggested. Nothing so obvious. But I must be more careful around the others.*

At last she and Jarnulf reached a flat stone plateau at the edge of a scarp. It fell away so severely that Nezeru could see no bottom to it, only an increasingly muddled view of shadows on snow. The rest of the plateau stood on the other side of the abyss, some three dozen paces away across empty space.

Movement on the far side of the drop caught Nezeru's attention. She held her hand out to stop Jarnulf when he came up behind her, then made the signal for silence when he started to speak. She had spotted a huge mountain goat standing on the farther plateau.

"Nezeru," her companion said, slightly louder this time, but she signaled him even more violently to be quiet. In what seemed one smooth gesture, she flicked her bow from over her shoulder, raised it, nocked an arrow, and released. The shaft flew across the chasm like a beam of light and struck the goat in its side. The animal took a stumbling step, then slumped down onto the edge of the plateau, its head dangling over nothingness. It tried to lift itself a few times, as if to die on its feet, but the arrow had gone too deep and within moments it had gone still.

"I admire your eye and your aim," said Jarnulf as he looked at the dead mountain goat, its long hair set a-flutter by the stiff wind.

"You are not the only one who can hit a target," she said.

"Yes, but neither of us has wings. How do you propose we retrieve it?"

She bit back an angry response when she realized he was right—the two sides of the plateau did not join, so there was no way across the chasm to retrieve her prize. For a moment Nezeru almost felt as if she might weep like a mortal, like her own mother, great useless tears of humiliation. "I am a fool," she said at last. Between the earlier jibes of the giant and her own reactions, she had failed to make certain they could get to the other side before she shot.

"There is always more to killing than simply killing," said Jarnulf as he stared out across the gulf.

"Do not tell the others," she pleaded. "Please, say nothing."

"You think I would sell your mistake to try to gain favor with your companions?" His expression was as flatly empty as any Hikeda'ya's. "I think you do not know either them or myself very well, Sacrifice Nezeru."

Chastened and furious with herself, she now let him set the pace. Her thoughts remained tangled, but as time passed and Jarnulf said nothing, she managed to clear her mind enough to concentrate once more on the hunt. At last, they found another goat, this one in a place they could reach. Nezeru again took the shot—Jarnulf insisted—and again it struck home. A short time later, they had retrieved their kill and stood once more on relatively flat ground. Nezeru thought the huge mountains seemed to be watching them, like cloaked gods against the gray sky—perhaps wondering why such strange, tiny creatures trespassed in their domain.

"There are dark clouds on the northeastern horizon," she said. "A storm is coming."

"Right you are," Jarnulf said. "And this would be a bad place to be caught. I had hoped we might bring down a second goat to keep the giant sweet, but he will have to share with the rest of us."

Nezeru and the mortal took turns carrying their kill across their shoulders as they made their way down the mountain, but the beast was heavy and the footing became increasingly treacherous as the winds rose. Jarnulf at last dropped the carcass to the ground and began to drag it behind them, leaving a blood-tinged rut in the snow. "And now you see why we went uphill, not down," he said.

"You have made your point, mortal," Nezeru told him. "You are a better hunter than this Hikeda'ya."

"No, I am the more practiced hunter," he said. "You have a keen eye and light feet, and your aim is nearly faultless. But I have been keeping myself alive in the wild with only my own wits and my own weapons for many years. Even Makho, I think, has not had to do that."

After long moments, silent but for the *swish* of the carcass dragging across the snow, Nezeru abruptly said, "You still have not told me all the truth."

Jarnulf didn't answer immediately, which might have been because he was negotiating a difficult stretch of downhill climb, trying to keep the sliding weight of the mountain goat from dragging him over the edge. "Do you mean to ask why am I still here?" he asked at last. "I gave your chieftain an answer to that days ago, whether you heard it or not—whether any of you believed it or not."

So the slow game still continues, she thought. "Do not treat me like a fool, Rimmersman. That was no answer and you know it. Why did you save us and why are you with us? Why did that bandit of the Skalijar recognize you?"

"What do you wish me to say, woman of Sacrifice? That you have plumbed my deepest secrets? That I left my task as Queen's Huntsman, risking punishment, so I could travel with your Hand into the eastern wilderness? And why would that be? To enrich myself somehow? How would that work, pray tell?"

"I don't know. But I do know that you have not told the whole truth. You recognized that bandit, the one with but one eye, and he recognized you. I saw. Do you deny it?"

Jarnulf stopped. The dead mountain goat slid a little way farther down the slope. Its eyes were filmy, and its swollen tongue protruded from its mouth as though the creature's downhill journey had exhausted it. "Why should I? Yes. Yes, I knew him. His name was Dyrmundur. We were companions for a while, when I was young."

Her heart sped with triumph and sudden alarm. "How can that be? You grew up in the slave barracks of Nakkiga—or at least that is what you claimed."

He shook his head. "I did not lie about that, or anything else important. Yes, I grew up in a slave barn. And when I first became a queen's huntsman, I used that opportunity to escape. Would you have done differently? Well, perhaps you would have. For a while after, I lived with the Skalijar, but their anger was not mine, nor was their fight."

"What do you mean?"

"Remember, please, that we are trying to outpace a storm, Sacrifice Nezeru. If we stand here until I answer all your questions, we will die. Surely they taught you that, whatever you may think, even the queen herself does not rule the snow and wind, not here." He began to make his way down the slope, forcing her to follow him to hear what he said. "The only one who could be-spell the weather is gone, sent back to perdition at Asu'a." He smirked. "Do not look so surprised. Yes, I know of Asu'a. In fact, I have seen it, if only from a distance, which is more than I think you can say."

She wanted to know more, but he was right: the darkening sky said they had only a little time. "We shall keep moving, then, but you will not silence me. So you were of the Skalijar once, those . . . mortal bandits. Why did you leave?"

"Because they were foul and cruel, and what they wanted was meaningless. Because they nursed old hatreds that had nothing to do with me, who was not born in Rimmersgard. My ancestors were slaves of Nakkiga, and so was I. Why should I care whether Rimmersmen worship Usires the Aedon or the old gods they brought out of the lost west?"

The sky was darkening quickly now, blackness swirling overhead like the smoke from a gigantic chimney. "So you returned into what you call slavery? That makes no sense. Why would you do that?"

"Better a slave with a roof above his head, however crude, than a man lost in the wilderness, soon to starve or freeze. That was how it seemed to me." Jarnulf gave her a keen-eyed look. "But if we are to play this game of questions, then you must answer the same one that began the contest. Why are *you* here, Sacrifice?"

"That is a waste of a question, mortal." She lifted her hand to help him down a pile of snow-covered rocks and onto the ledge where she stood. For a moment, even through their gloves, she felt a strange, strong connection, and she spoke as much to cover her confusion as anything else. "I was sent by the queen herself. I am of the Order of Sacrifice. The queen's word is as the beating of our own hearts."

"I'm sure," he said, letting go of her hand and reaching back for the goat's leg. He eased the carcass over the top, down the stones, and onto the stony lip beside him. "But that is not what I mean. The queen herself chose you. A great honor—an astounding honor! And to die for the queen is, I'm sure, your fondest wish. But why should the queen, or whoever might have acted for her, choose *you*?"

"I was first among my file in the Order of Sacrifice! I defeated five others Sacrifices with only my hands!"

"Ah. And did Makho do the same?"

"In his day, yes! He is many years older than I am."

"And Kemme?"

"He is Makho's friend. He is also a fearsome warrior."

A swirl of snow began to spin past them. "Yes, he is, but otherwise not tremendously distinguished. In fact, Kemme is as stupid as a bag of stones. And Saomeji, for all his subtlety, is also young, is he not? Not to mention that he is a halfblood like yourself?"

She wiped melting snow from her eyes with her sleeve. "What do you reach for, slave-taker?"

"Just a curious thing—that this so-important mission, which has seemingly taken you across the whole of the north, to this place where some say the last dragons live, and which is commanded by Makho, undoubtedly one of the fiercest warriors of your Order of Sacrifice, should otherwise be made up of such . . . disposable minions."

She was not certain what the mortal meant to suggest, but it made her furious. "Why do you seek to undermine us, Jarnulf? What does it benefit you?"

"Ask instead what your queen wants of you, Sacrifice Sister Nezeru—or rather, I suspect, what Akhenabi wants, because from what I have seen and heard, it is his hand behind this mission, though he seems not to care if it fails."

"You dare . . . ?" she began, but never finished what she meant to say, not because she hadn't puzzled it out yet herself, but because of the sudden appearance of a snarling white shape that fell onto Jarnulf from above, as if it had dropped out of the storm. For a moment Nezeru saw nothing but a rolling, screeching ball of white that bumped and slid perilously close to the ledge's end. Some animal that had attacked them, perhaps a white wolf or a bear, but she could make out little of it in the fluttering snow except the red wetness of its maw as it tried to bite Jarnulf's face.

She could not draw her sword swiftly enough to help—already the mortal and his attacker had rolled too close to the edge, but one of her arrows had fallen from her quiver, so she snatched it up and thrust it as hard as she could into the bristling white back of Jarnulf's attacker, then pulled out another and plunged it into the hairy shape as well. She felt them both hit bone and then slide deeper, but the thing would not let go. She tried to struggle to her feet so she could draw her sword.

"My . . . knife!" Jarnulf gasped, twisting his head free from the claws of the furiously writhing animal.

Nezeru saw the weapon on his belt, but before she could reach it, the two combatants rolled again and stopped partway over the edge with Jarnulf on his back, so that nothing lay beneath his head and shoulders but a deadly fall down the scarp. Nezeru finally managed to pull her sword, but for agonizingly long moments she could not use it because man and beast were struggling so violently she feared she would stab Jarnulf instead.

Or with one shove of my foot, she suddenly thought, *I could push them both over the edge.* Just a brief instant, then it would all be over and the mortal and his questions and his lies would trouble her thoughts no longer.

Instead she leaned forward, shielding her face from the flailing attacker, and groped until her hand found living fur. Then she set the point of her sword against it and pushed hard. The thing squealed, a rasping cry of fear and pain. She shoved the blade deeper. The creature struggled for a moment, trying to fight its way up the blade toward her, and for an instant she saw its face close up, the weird, whiskery snout too long for any wolf or bear. Then Jarnulf managed to get enough of a grip to shove the thing off him and kicked out with his booted foot. The beast slid from her blade as she clung to the hilt with both hands, then it tumbled over the narrow ledge and out into the void.

For a long moment after the creature disappeared they both lay panting at the edge of the precipice. Nezeru's legs and arms felt as boneless as mushroom stalks. Jarnulf choked and wheezed, trying to get his breath, then finally sucked in enough air to crawl farther from the drop.

"What was it?" Nezeru asked at last. She rolled over and was relieved to see the dead goat still lying where they had dropped it.

"*Yukinva*, they are called by the trollfolk. A kind of giant rat of the snowy heights." He got up, absently wiping blood from his face. His skin had been torn in several places by the thing's claws and teeth. "It must have smelled the blood of our kill."

"Then let's hurry and get back down to the cave before another arrives," said Nezeru. "We'll put snow on your scratches when we reach somewhere safer."

Jarnulf got to his feet and nocked another arrow. "We won't bother," he said. "A little blood is a good sacrifice to the mountain gods, I think, and we should not spend more time out here than we need to."

Nezeru had to admit that was an even better plan.

44

Charms and Tokens

The early days of Yuven had brought a flurry of rain; it took the visitors no little time to remove their dripping cloaks. Archbishop Gervis was accompanied only by a pair of priests, clearly suggesting the meeting would be an informal one, but when he had removed his outerwear he kneeled before the king and queen and kissed each of their hands, something that Miriamele could see made Simon restless, even anxious.

"I don't know what it is with these religious fellows," Simon whispered to his wife as the archbishop retreated to his seat. "Always down on their knees kissing something."

On another day Miriamele might have smiled or even laughed, but she did not want to be distracted now. She nodded to the archbishop and said, "It is good to see you, Your Eminence. I hope no sad errand brings you to us."

"Would that it were a happier one, Your Majesty." Gervis, in all other ways almost the model of what an archbishop should look like—tall, slender, and even-featured, with a fringe of snowy white hair showing below his mitre—had a habit of gnawing at his fingernails when he was distracted or worried. As Miriamele watched, he lifted one of his hands to his mouth before remembering where he was and quickly lowering it again. "But I come to you today not as archbishop of Erchester, but as a humble servant of Mother Church and of our great father, Lector Vidian."

"And away we go," said Simon under his breath.

"As always," Miriamele said loudly, "you bring honor enough by yourself, Archbishop, but we are eager to hear what His Sacredness wishes to be made known."

"Then let me move swiftly to the matter that brings me here." Gervis was clasping his hands together as though to thwart any treacherous move one might make toward his mouth. It was clear to Miriamele that he was more than just ordinarily disturbed by something, and she began to feel it herself, as though it were a fever that could pass through the air. "You know of the troubles in Nabban, of course."

"Nabban? Nothing but trouble most of the time," Simon said. "Seems like if they're not stabbing each other in the street, they're complaining about not being allowed to stab each other."

"Yes, Archbishop, we are aware of the problems," Miriamele said with a stern look at her husband. "The king and I have spent much time discussing the current situation, especially the conflict between Duke Saluceris and his brother Drusis. Does the Sacred Father have something to say on the subject?"

"Oh, much and much, Your Majesties. He is fearful for the state of the duchy, but even more, he is fearful for the state of Mother Church and all Osten Ard."

"Please explain," said Miriamele, and reached out her hand to Simon, ostensibly in the loving gesture of a royal wife, but really with the intention of giving his knuckles a hard squeeze if he didn't stick to the course they had planned. "We are eager to hear what His Sacredness has to say."

"There is nothing to hear from me, Majesties. Lector Vidian has sent a formal envoy to you. He will arrive sometime in the next sennight, I am told." The archbishop looked a bit sheepish at this. "I was informed so that I might prepare to welcome him. I do not want to tread on the privilege of His Sacredness, but I believe it is in everyone's interest for me to tell you of this matter first, before the formal delivery of the Sancellan's request."

"And are you going to tell us what this request is?" Simon asked. "Or are we to play guessing games, like children at Aedonmansa trying to win a sweet? *Ouch!*" The king scowled. "You hurt my hand, woman."

"Many apologies, husband. I was distracted by an irritating noise." She smiled as sweetly as she could, then turned her smile on the archbishop. "Forgive us, Your Eminence, for the interruption. Please continue."

Between Simon's muttering and the seriousness of the matters discussed, it was all Archbishop Gervis could do to keep his hands away from his mouth. He pulled a ring of prayer beads from his pocket and began to tell them, one after another, around and around. "Here is the root of the matter, Majesties," he said. "In Tiyagaris month, the duke's brother Drusis is to marry Lady Turia, niece of Count Dallo Ingadaris."

"Oh," said Miriamele, genuinely surprised. "Little Turia! I thought he meant to marry the older sister. Surely Turia is not old enough to be married."

"She will have twelve years that month, Majesty, which both custom and Mother Church accept. It is not the bride's age that concerns His Sacredness, but the idea that the wedding will strengthen Drusis because he will become Count Dallo's son, and that it may be the occasion of even more serious fighting between the supporters of the Benidrivine and Ingadarine Houses."

"I know a little something about this," Simon said abruptly. "First, making Drusis his son-in-law won't change anything old Dallo's doing, because he's already backing him against his brother, the lawful duke." He held up his hand when the archbishop would have replied. "And—*and*, the lector himself, the Sacred Father, is a member of the Clavean family as I recall, who have long been allied to Dallo and the Ingadarines. So why his sudden concern?" The king turned to the queen. "You thought I was not paying attention during all those council meetings, didn't you?" The only thing missing was a childlike, "Ha!" of triumph.

Miriamele had no cheerful reply to that, so instead she turned to the archbishop. "You were about to say something, Eminence."

The beads were making a furious circuit through his fingers now. "Yes, well, the king is quite right, of course. But that is part of the problem. You see, His Sacredness is in an awkward position. Ordinarily, especially with the Sancellan Mahistrevis and the Sancellan Aedonitis such close neighbors, he would have intervened long before, when this conflict was first beginning. And do not misunderstand, Your Majesties—His Sacredness has called for peace many times in the last year, tasking all parties with the disruptions and unhappiness caused by their fighting. But things are getting worse in Nabban—just a short time ago the death of some Ingadarines led to rioting in the street, and Duchess Canthia, the Duke's wife, was caught in it. She survived without harm, thanks to our merciful God, but it was a near thing."

"Well, I agree that we can't have these bullyboy Kingfishers and Stormbirds rioting in the streets," Simon said. "But what can be done?"

"The High King and High Queen can come to the wedding," said Gervis so hurriedly that it almost seemed he tried to gasp it out with insufficient breath. "That is what the Lector's messenger will request. His Sacredness will work with Duke Saluceris and the other parties so that during your visit, all will be brought to the table together. With Your Majesties' presence to demonstrate the importance of concord, agreements can be reached that will protect the peace." He took a deep breath, then slipped his hand and the beads it held into a pocket of his robe. "That is what the Holy Father will ask. I did not wish you to be surprised."

Miriamele was, in fact, surprised, and for a moment she could think of nothing to say. A trip to Nabban was a daunting thought with so much else already swirling around the High Throne.

"Why can't the lector of Mother Church do this himself?" Simon asked. "What good is *having* a lector if he can't tell people to stop fighting? Isn't that what our faith teaches us, that the Lector is the father of the world's family? Well, that's what a father does—stops the family fighting. The good God knows I've had to do it enough times myself. Only the Lord knows how many times I've had to give Morgan a talking-to when he flouted his mother or grandmother."

And only the Lord knows how little good it ever did, thought Miriamele.

"But you see," Gervis said, "you already spoke the difficult truth at the heart of it, Majesty, when you pointed out that His Sacredness comes from a house allied with the Ingadarines. Without the help of Count Dallo, the Holy Father would never have been elected by the escritors to the Sacred Chair. Nabban is a city—an entire nation—whose history has been written by the great family houses. *'Words are less than blood,'* is one of their oldest expressions. Duke Saluceris and his supporters . . . well, they do not trust His Sacredness to be fair to both sides." The beads came out again after only moments in his pocket. "It will take someone from outside to make peace."

"But I myself am related to the Ingadarines," Miriamele pointed out.

Archbishop Gervis shook his head. "Your rulings on matters pertaining to Nabban have always been fair, Majesties, and it is known that despite your Ingadaris blood, you also have an attachment to the Benidrivines . . ."

"Because without Duke Saluceris, the whole country will turn to shit," said the king, and didn't seem to notice the archbishop nearly drop his beads. "He is the closest thing Nabban has to a man who puts what is best for the people ahead of his own desires."

This time Miriamele did smile a little, although she was not entirely pleased with her husband's contributions. Gervis clutched his beads in both hands, as if they were a floating spar and he was lost at sea. "Yes, I'm sure your Majesty is correct," the archbishop said through a wince. "But I am certain you and the queen will need to discuss this matter in private, so I will take my leave. The Holy Father's legate is already on his way."

"Do you know who it is?" Miriamele asked.

"Escritor Auxis, I am told." It was clear that the archbishop was pining for the security of St. Sutrin's. "He is a good man, godly and fair-minded."

"I'm sure," said Miriamele. "Thank you for sharing your concerns with us, Your Eminence, another of your many services to the High Throne."

When Gervis had departed, Simon turned to her and said, "Well, a lot of nonsense, isn't it? The Nabbanai are always squabbling. Rachel the Dragon used to say that the Hernystiri liked hunting best, the Erkynlanders liked fishing, but the Nabbanai preferred arguing to all other sport."

Miriamele gathered her dress and rose from her chair. "I don't think the Mistress of Chambermaids, however much she may have meant to you, is the best guide to the strife of nations."

"By all the bloody saints, what have I done now?" Simon called after her. "You are angry again, Miri, aren't you? Miri?"

29th Day of Yuven, Founding Year 1201

My dear Lord Tiamak,

Greetings to you, and I hope this finds you well. The ship that will take me to Nabban and then on to Kwanitupul leaves this afternoon, so I will try to finish this in time to give it to the royal post before I embark.

The first part of my journey was largely uneventful, but I fear I will never make a traveler. The trip down the Gleniwent had a most grievous effect on my innards, though the river pilot kept assuring me that the waters were unusually smooth and it must have been something I ate. That is not impossible, because what I was given to eat on board the river-ship seemed to be as much beetle parts as biscuit, but I fear I may suffer from a more general indisposition to traveling on water. I am not looking forward to the longer trip, although the abbot here at St. Sallimo's has kindly informed me that, except for an unusual amount of activity among the kilpa, the seas are calm at this time of year and my journey should be a good one.

I have never seen a kilpa, but I confess that after hearing some of the rivermen's tales, I am in no hurry to end my ignorance.

Lest you think that I have nothing but complaints to share, my lord, Meremund is a very goodly city, and I am pleased to have finally seen it. As we approached it I could see its white towers from a great distance, standing high above the walls. The harbor is very large, with cunning canals to allow the ships to come very close to the warehouses where most of them load and unload cargo. I could not disembark immediately because my own small pile of belongings had somehow been put behind a large quantity of barrels, and my guide, your friend Madi, was nowhere to be found. Remembering what you said about experiencing more of the world, I should mention that as I waited I was able to learn a number of new words that, although common among rivermen and dockside laborers, are not generally heard among the monks of St. Sutrin's.

At last my belongings were found and cheerfully tossed out onto the dock. As I stood beside them, waiting to see if Madi would be thrown onto the dock as well, I was accosted by two of the dirtiest children I have ever seen. So ill-kempt and filthy were they that at first I thought they might be southern apes, such as I hear the mariners sometimes make pets of, and even dress in clothes. In fact, I doubt many sailors dress their apes as poorly as these children. Even as I looked them over, these two creatures ran at me and, evidently mistaking me for someone else, began to paw and embrace me, all the time calling me "Good old uncle!" although I had never seen them before in my life. When I noticed that the smaller of the two, a girl, somehow had her hand deep in the pocket inside my robe and was attempting to lift my purse from it, while the boy had hooked one of my small trunks with his foot and was pushing it away from me even as he hugged and petted me, I realized that not only were they not confusing me with someone else, they actually meant to steal my possessions! I engaged in a struggle with the girl, and though she was but a slight thing with a wrist no wider than a Halfmansa candle, while I arrested her removal of my purse, I could not induce her to let go of it.

We stood there for long moments, and to an outsider it must have looked like some strange dance—me clutching one child by the arm while trying to yank the other back from the trunk he was trying to shove beyond my reach. At last someone called, 'Children, stop that,' and to my relief, they did, but not before the girl child made one last attempt to slip the purse out, which I thwarted forcefully enough that she kicked my shin.

My rescuer turned out to be Madi, and instead of telling me where he'd vanished to, he said, 'I see you've met my lovely young ones. Plek, Parlip, give His Worship room to breathe, my dear little fleas, or I'll smack the skin off you.'

I was a bit taken aback to learn these apes were his. He told me their full names were Plekto and Parlippa—the latter, I assume, named after beloved Saint Pelippa. I was even more startled when Madi let slip the information that they would be accompanying us on the journey to Nabban. When I said, and rather firmly, that you had told me nothing of any children, Madi sadly bowed his head and said that he had no choice, that the children's mother had demanded it. 'She's ill with the summer ague, my darling,' he explained, 'and cannot even get out of her bed. The older ones are trial enough, she says, and I'm to bring these two with me.'

I feel I must note that among his other habits, my guide refers to everyone he meets as 'darling,' 'my dear,' 'sweetness,' or 'my love.' Perhaps it is common among the Hyrka, but it seems to me an odd way to address strangers.

So it was that I was led away from the Meremund docks by Madi and his two young charges, and although the children helped me to carry my belongings, they also made free with my possessions when their father was not looking, which seemed to be often. I still have not found my candles.

Instead of leading me to Meremund's main Agarine abbey, where I had planned to spend the night and where you told me the abbot was expecting me, Madi insisted on bringing me to his own house, a ramshackle dwelling in a neighborhood called the Stews, to meet his family. This despite the apparently dreadful illness suffered by his wife—I call her such because charity demands it, but I suspect no Aedonite vows were ever exchanged. Once inside, I was reminded again of my first impression, that the children were in fact apes. The rest of the children at home were larger, but no better dressed and no better in their manners. The oldest, a homuncule of Madi himself but with wispier whiskers, asked me what terrible secrets I learned by listening to rich women giving their confessions. Madi asked me for the loan of a few coppers so that he could buy some meat for the pot, but after I gave it to him he was gone a long time, leaving me with the loud, boisterous children—their mother remained under the covers, groaning that she was dying, though with such a strong voice that I doubted it. And when he returned home he had the distinct semblance of someone who has drunken several beers. Nor did I ever see any sign of meat in the soup I was served, although the bread was hard enough, I was just as grateful not having anything else to chew, for fear my teeth would not survive the meal.

A bed was made for me in the middle of the floor, the blankets so flea-ridden that I could scarcely sleep at all. In the middle of the night I was awakened by a small hand touching my face, and when I sat up in alarm, discovered the boy Plekto, who told me that he thought there were robbers trying to get in. Worried for the family, I roused myself and looked around, but found no sign of intruders. When I returned, I found the boy rooting through my possessions again. When I demanded that he stop, he saucily asked me what I was hiding, that I was so secretive.

My good lord Tiamak, I think that your trusted guide Madi is not so trustworthy as you thought, or at least his family is not. Should I find another guide instead? I fear we will have to leave Meremund before this will reach you, but perhaps you can send a letter for me to Kwanitupul advising me what to do.

Against Madi's urging, I moved the second night to St. Agar's and found there much more comfortable surroundings. In fact, I have been at the abbey since, and this letter is written in the refectory, which is wonderfully free of vermin. Best of all, the abbot kindly gave me permission to use the abbey's library, and I found something of interest there.

The book of which we spoke before I left the Hayholt is not to be found here, of course, but I did discover a volume by Tertissis of Gemmia that discusses it. He says of it, 'the great sin of Fortis is not that he describes the devilish methods of the Old Ones'—by this he means the Norns and their cousins, the Sithi—'but that he speaks of those methods as though they can teach something to Godly men. These snares of the Devil have driven men mad before. It is said they drove Bishop Fortis himself mad, and it is rumored that he spent his last days in confinement in his own abbey.' I tell you this, Lord Tiamak, not because I think you do not know the dangers already, but because I fear for any others who might come into contact with it. Have you told the king and queen? I know they would be most anxious for any knowledge of their son, even this, but I would feel very sad if they were exposed to this dreadful book because of me.

Also, although I went to the Princess Idela to examine Prince John Josua's books on Lord Pasevalles' behalf, in the course of many distractions and worries in those days I never told Pasevalles what I found. I leave it to you whether he should know about it.

Do please advise me whether I should seek a new guide when I reach Kwanitupul. I remain your servant in God.

Etan Fratilis Ercestris

"Well?" said Aengas.

Tiamak looked up, more than a little startled. Although he had been reading aloud, he had all but forgotten that he had company. "Well what? Am I going to tell Lord Pasevalles about the *Treatise*? I think not. I think that I will speak only to those who need to know."

"Like the king and queen?"

"Yes. Eventually. But before I worry and upset them with news about their dead son, I would like to know a bit more about the book, and take time to review the rest of his library."

Aengas stretched his arms. His large wooden chair, which his servants had erected in a spare bedchamber with all the ceremony of builders raising a miniature cathedral, took up a great deal of room, and although it could be wheeled from place to place, it took two men to do so—three if Aengas was in it. This made for many complications, but Tiamak did not mind them because there were few scholars in all of Osten Ard who knew more about forbidden and ancient books than the former viscount. "In any case," Aengas went on, "all this about the book was not the question I was trying to ask you, dear fellow. I wanted to know whether you had intentionally given poor Brother Etan into the hands of Hyrka thieves."

"Oh, that." Tiamak made a sour face. "I am not pleased to hear about Madi's family, nor do I doubt I will be dunned for the miserable night's lodging he gave Brother Etan. Despite what Etan has seen, though, I think Madi is a good man. I have known him for years, ever since my first journey back to Kwani-tupul. He is a bit of a rascal, and clearly not the best father, but I swear his heart is good. I have known him a long time."

Aengas rearranged the *Treatise* atop the large board that lay on his armrests as a makeshift table. "And you are certain there is no one else you wish to bring into our discussion, like Lord Pasevalles?"

"I am fairly certain, yes. Lord Chancellor Pasevalles is a good man—a very clever man, too—but I think that the fewer folk who know we have this book, the smaller the chance of it slipping out by mischance. Beside, Pasevalles is a devout Aedonite. I do not wish to demand his secrecy and pit his faith against our friendship."

"But your own faith does not trouble you about it?"

Tiamak smiled. "My faith, old friend, applies only to Wrannamen and is all but mute on the subject of drylanders, let alone the Sithi. He Who Always Steps On Sand enjoins us to seek boldly but not to abandon caution entirely. I think that makes for a reasonable approach. Why do you ask?"

"Just curious. The book, what little of it I have managed to translate, is full of ideas both inspiring and terrifying."

"Lucky for you that you have no faith to be outraged."

"Oh, I have faith," Aengas said. "Would you hand me my cup? Bless you. I have faith that mortal Man cannot be trusted with gold or with power over other men. I have faith that learning will always frighten stupidity, and that stupidity will often strike back, sometimes murderously." He took the cup from Tiamak. Because he could not easily lift it to his lips, he sipped instead from the hollow reed, drawing watered wine to his mouth. "Now, shall we continue?"

Tiamak smiled again. "You renew my own faith that some things truly are eternal, Aengas. You are as cynical as ever you were."

"More so. My cynicism grows like a weed. Someday it will choke all the weaker flowers like charity and hope that live in my garden." He cleared his throat. "Now be quiet if you wish me to read this to you.

"Beside these great scrying-stones, which the elders only may use, there are other charms and tokens that can carry such whispers through the aetheric fluids and across great distances. It is said that some of the adepts can speak not just over earthly spans, but across the boundary or veil between the world of living and the cloudy halls of death."

"God give you good day, Your Majesty."

Simon looked up. "Ah, Lord Pasevalles. Good to see you."

"And you, Majesty. May I trouble you for your royal hand and seal on these?"

The king shuffled through the curling rolls of vellum. "What am I signing my name to?"

Pasevalles smiled. "A dozen different things, all of them rather boring, as you may see if you examine them—confirmations of land titles, a report from the royal mint, three petitions begging you for tax relief. And of course the letter from our ambassador at the Sancellan Mahistrevis about the visit of Lector Vidian's legate. I showed you that already."

The king frowned. "S'Bloody Tree! Ah, forgive me, Pasevalles, I forget myself when I'm vexed, and this matter is vexing me fiercely. Why must I sign something for our own ambassador? The damnable legate is on his way whether I want it or not."

"I took the liberty of writing a reply for you to Count Froye, thanking him for his letter. These are the things I must do with Count Eolair gone from the castle."

Simon thought he heard a note of self-pity. "And you do them very well, man. I realize we ask a great deal of you, between the Chancelry and all else that has fallen to you with the Hand of the Throne gone off with the prince. Don't think the queen and I will forget this service."

Pasevalles looked down. "You are kind, as always, my king, especially to one as unworthy as myself. I have already been given a gift by you and the queen greater than any I could have hoped to receive otherwise, just by the bestowal of your trust."

"Good God, man, you talk like all the other courtiers around here. Don't start complimenting me too much, or I won't trust you anymore. It's your honesty I crave. No king—or queen, for that matter—can live without honesty from at least one person they trust."

"I hear your rebuke, Sire." He smiled. "I will strive to tell you more unpleasant truths."

Simon laughed. "That was good! More unpleasant truths."

"But you are surely fortunate, Sire, that you have a queen who is both honest and extremely wise. And I do not say that to flatter."

"No, you're right. The problem with my Miri is that when she's angry at me, I don't want to listen to her good advice because it makes me feel like a fool."

"You have my sympathy, Majesty."

"And you have never married yourself, Pasevalles. Can you find no one who appeals? From what I hear, there are many ladies here in the court who have set their caps for you."

"I am married to my work, Your Majesty. It leaves me little time for things like a family."

"But what of the future? What of your name?"

By now his smile had vanished. "My family name, I am afraid, likely died with my uncle, the baron. Perhaps someday when my labors are over—or at least have become less all-consuming—I will think about changing that."

"There's no shame to waiting," Simon said hurriedly. "Don't get me wrong. Dear old Tiamak is older than I am, and he married only a few years ago. He's as happy as can be."

"Lady Thelía is a fine woman."

"She is, she is." But Simon was a bit confused now. Had he offended his lord chancellor? He hadn't meant to. Perhaps Pasevalles was one of those men who didn't like women. Simon had always found the idea strange himself, but it seemed too commonplace to be merely sin. God had made all kinds of people upon His Earth, from Simon's old harper Sangfugol, who even in his old age had still had an eye for attractive young men as well as women, to those like Archbishop Gervis, whom Simon had once seen walk past a drunk, half-naked woman without even noticing her as she lay singing on her back in Market Square.

Despite his own marriage and his still powerful desire for his wife, the dark secrets of the bedchamber often confused Simon. If God had meant the act to be only between married men and women, why did He fill the world with so many temptations? Why did He make the desire so strong and the act so pleasurable . . . ?

"I am sorry, Majesty, I have distracted you from your thoughts," Pasevalles said. "Please just fix your seal on these last few and I will leave you in peace."

"No, I was woolgathering," Simon said, dripping wax on the last document. "But this talk of ours has put me in mind of another thing I would discuss with you. This visit from the legate."

"I have made the arrangements, Sire. The only question remaining is whether he should stay here in the Hayholt or at St. Sutrin's, which is the usual place for important religious visitors."

"I feel no strong urge to put him up in the castle," Simon said. "But it is not the arrangements I want to discuss, it's the thing itself."

"Sire?"

"The thing itself. The wedding of the duke's brother Drusis. You have heard that the Lector is requesting the queen and myself attend, and then use the opportunity to force the two arguing sides to make peace. You are from Nabban and you know the southern mind better than I do. What do you think?"

Pasevalles stood, his arms now full of vellum rolls with dangling seals. "Well, Majesty," he began.

"Oh, sit down, man, before you drop everything," Simon said, pointing to a bench. "I want your thoughts."

Once seated, Pasevalles was quiet for some time, considering. At last he stirred and said, "If I may be perfectly truthful, my king, I think you should go. Both of you."

"Really?" Simon was pleased, but he wanted something more he could offer to Miriamele, because he knew she thought it a bad idea. "Why?"

"Because this is no mere feud between families, though feuds are nearly as common in Nabban as an afternoon meal. It stems from a real problem, but there is another cause too."

"What is this real problem, do you think?"

"For years now, the northern and eastern lords of Nabban have been pushing into the grasslands, building castles and settlements in lands the horsemen have always thought theirs. The Thrithing-folks, as you know, Sire, are a disorganized rabble, each band with its petty chieftain, and even the most powerful chief that they have, Rudur Redbeard, is only Marchthane of the Meadow Thrithing, and cannot call all the clans to war. But still there are many of them, many thousands of armed men who are raised to fight. In the past, most of their fighting has been against each other. Now they perceive two common enemies—Nabban and Erkynland."

"Erkynland?" Simon was startled. "What have we done to them?"

"Nothing like what the Nabbanai are doing, but the grasslanders have a long memory, and they still are angry about the last war they fought against us, despite it being one of their own who roused them to violence and led them into defeat. We also share a long border with their lands, and many new settlements have been built along the river road as far west as Gadrinsett, the town that had grown from a camp where Prince Josua fought against his brother, King Elias."

"Still, there has been very little fighting in the High Thrithing lately, Lord Chancellor. We have kept a close watch on those towns for exactly that reason, so as not to follow the bad example of Nabban."

"True, Majesty, but the horsemen have trouble distinguishing between the Nabbanai nobles and the High Throne here in Erkynland that permits those nobles to encroach on Thrithings land." He raised both his hands at Simon's outraged expression. "I do not say it is true, Majesty, simply what I fear the grasslanders believe." The chancellor leaned forward, his face serious. "I know these people, my king. I grew up on the verges of the Lake Thrithing. They are a fierce folk, and they not only nurse grudges, they pass them down from generation to generation. If nothing is done, one day another leader will rise among them and there will be bloodshed all along the border—not skirmishes, but all-consuming war. I am sad to say it, but I believe it is true."

"Good God, man! Good God." Simon was shaken. "But what does all this have to do with that damnable wedding?"

"It is the greatest issue dividing the two sides in Nabban. Most of Dallo Ingadaris' followers are eastern lords. They fear the Thrithings-men despite the fact that it is they themselves who have angered the horsemen. They want to punish the grasslanders so fiercely that they will give up their raids entirely. But Duke Saluceris is of a more careful mind, so the Stormbirds, Dallo's faction, call him a coward who will not defend his own people. Thus, any end to the struggle between the two factions will require some solution to the towns and great houses being built on Thrithings territory."

"Good God," said Simon again. "Now that is a poser. But I think you said there was something else at work as well? Or have I misunderstood?"

"No, Sire, you are right. And it is this: Drusis is a leader who is loved and respected by his men because he is fierce. He plays on the fears of the easterners, who live near the threatening horsemen, or perhaps he truly believes it all himself—I could not say. But I think that those who lived through the days of the Storm King's War can appreciate exactly what the problem is between him and his brother."

Simon was a little confused again. "Which is?"

"Which is that although the younger brother Drusis is bold, resolute, and never lets himself be distracted by complication of any kind, Duke Saluceris is the opposite, a man who would rather give something to everyone to keep the peace, and who will not stoop to lying for advantage." Pasevalles gave the king a significant look. "Does that remind you of any two brothers you have known?"

Simon nodded. "Of course. Our own King Elias and Prince Josua."

"Exactly, Majesty. Now imagine that Josua had been born a year earlier and was raised to the throne, while your wife's father had been given little of importance to occupy himself and his vaunting ambition. What do you think would have happened then, if Josua had been the older and Elias the younger? That is what is at the root of Nabban's problems. The brother who most think should have been the duke is *not* the duke."

Simon sat back, overwhelmed. "I have not thought of it in this way before, Pasevalles. I thank you. And you think the queen and I should attend this wedding? But I do not want my wife endangered. You make it sound like Nabban is little better than the Thrithings these days."

"It will take the full prestige of the High Throne and the High Ward, I think, to solve this problem." Pasevalles stood. "I beg pardon if I have been too forthright in my talk, but you asked to know my thoughts. Matters in Nabban are more delicate than they have been since the Storm King's War. The High Throne must take the lead, I believe, if only to remind the Nabbanai that they are part of a larger kingdom." He bowed. "Forgive me for taking so much of your time, Majesty. If you will excuse me, I must get these letters back to the Chancelry so they can be dispatched."

Pasevalles backed up several paces before turning his back on his king, always the correct courtier even in such an informal situation. After he had gone, Simon could only sit, staring at his royal seal and the stick of wax, wondering whether he and Miri were to spend the rest of their lives trying to prevent fools from harming themselves and others, and never to have a little peace for themselves.

45

A Nighttime Sun

Zhakar sucked the rest of the meat off the haunch, then threw the rabbit bones into the fire where they popped and sizzled as the marrow boiled. Before they got too hot, he plucked them out with calloused fingers and snapped the bones in half, then sucked out the contents. He wiped his forearm against his mouth, leaving a trail of grease through his beard, and made a noise of satisfaction.

"Are you finished with your meal, Stepfather? Or do I interrupt you?"

Zhakar flinched and nearly fell off the bottom step of his new wagon. He had not noticed the tall shadow looming only a short distance away. "By the Piercer, how long have you been standing there? And where have you been? I thought you had left for good, all these days missing."

"Today I have been to a wedding," his stepson said. "I did not see you there."

"Ah! May the gods curse it, is today the day? Drojan's wedding? No one sent for me." Zhakar was clearly ill at ease, and still did not look up to meet the younger man's eye. "Ah, hell's stripes on them all. How was the food? Was the food good?"

"I left before the feast."

Something in the younger man's tone finally made Zhakar look up. "Well, don't expect to share any food of mine, because it's all gone." His eyes narrowed. "What have you been doing? Your clothes are covered in dirt. And is that blood?"

"It could be. I was in a fight." Unver came forward into the full light of the fire. The sun had all but sunk in the west and the sky was striped with purple and red. "But I do not come here for food, Stepfather. I come here for answers."

The older man half-rose, putting one hand behind him for balance. "Answers? What do you mean? How dare you strut in after all those days missing and talk to me this way?"

A brief flash of firelight on metal, then the point of Unver's long knife was against his neck, pushing until Zhakar gasped in pain and terror. "Were you going to go inside your nice new wagon and lock the door against me? Do you really think that would stop me?"

"What are you doing? Have you gone mad? I am your father!"

"No, you are my stepfather, and a poor one at that. Where did this wagon come from, old man? I think Odrig sold it to you. Am I right?"

"Yes! Yes! Why do you act this way? He sold it to me for some horses!"

"But those horses were mine, old man."

"They were in my paddock! That makes them mine!" Zhakar let out a sudden screech as the knife poked deeper into the wattle of flesh beneath his beard. "What do you want?"

"I told you. Answers." Unver sank down onto the steps. "Where do I come from?"

"What nonsense is this? I told you!"

"You told me I came from a clan far away across the grasslands."

"You did!"

"Tell me their name!"

The old man gasped in pain as the blade prodded him. "I do not remember! No, wait! It was one of the clans from the High Thrithings. They sent you to us."

"You told me my father and mother were both dead. Is that true?"

"Of course—!"

"Think and answer carefully, man. It may be your final act."

The deadness in Unver's words seemed to frighten the old man more than the blade. Zhakar's staring eyes showed a great deal of white. "Perhaps . . . perhaps I misunderstood—it was such a long time ago!" He could not bear to look at Unver's face. "Your mother might have been . . . might have been alive. Yes, perhaps that was how it went. But your stepmother was so pleased to have you. Yes, that's it, I remember now, we told you your mother was dead. It was the thane's orders!"

"Thane Hurvalt would not have ordered such a thing. He was a good man before his wits were taken."

"It is the truth, I swear it, Sanver!"

"Do not call me that name!" He said it with such violence that the old man broke free and threw himself off the wagon steps and onto his knees. "That was the name my stepmother gave me, not you, Zhakar. After she died, you never spoke it once. You called me 'Unver' just like all the others—*Nobody*."

"Oh, by the spirits, what do you want? What do you want from me?"

"I want as much truth as you know, old man. How did I come to the Crane Clan? Tell me all you know or I will slit you and bleed you like an old sheep."

"Do not hurt me. If you do not care for me, think of the others in the clan. If you spill my blood, they will shun you!"

Unver laughed. It was sudden and loud, ragged as an uncleaned wound. "Will they? Do you know what I have done today, old man—stupid, selfish, lying old man? I have gone to a wedding, and I have killed the bridegroom. This here is his blood—at least so I believe." He plucked at his tattered, stained shirt.

"You killed Drojan?" The old man looked up from his knees, his terror even greater. "By all the gods, what have you done? Odrig will have your head!"

"I think not." Again, that terrible laugh, softer now but no less raw. "You see, I killed Odrig, too. I turned the wedding into a funeral. And I buried the bride as well—but her death was none of mine."

Zhakar began to weep. It was clear he believed every word. "Oh, Gods, what will we do? What will *I* do? You madman, you have destroyed us!"

"There is no *us*, not since my stepmother died. You made that clear to me time and again, when you made me beg to be fed, when you gave me all the work you did not wish to do yourself, when you mocked me with the name the others had put on me—'Nobody'. Now, if you do not wish to suffer a slower and more painful death than Thane Odrig, you'll tell me everything you know about my true clan. And stop your blubbering or I will cut off your lips and you will tell me your secrets with a bloody mouth."

It took a long time because the old man could not stop crying and lamenting his unfair fate, but at last Unver had the story from him, word by ugly, weeping word.

When he had finally finished, the old man lay on his back like a whipped dog. There were thin cuts on his cheeks and his hands, but no mortal wounds. "I have told you all I know," he sobbed. "Please, son, do not kill me. Take Deofol and go. See, I did not sell him! I knew that if you returned, you would want him. He is in the paddock."

The younger man frowned. "For the last time, do not call me son. I am no son of yours." He snorted and stood up. "Kill you? I have killed two men today. Why should I waste my blade on a sniveling creature like you? For my step-mother's sake, I will let you live, so that you may remember your shame. I hope it burns you, old man."

"Oh, may the Sky Piercer bless you!" the old man said, and would have said more, but he was silenced by a kick in the ribs.

"But before I go, I wish to see your fine new wagon that you bought with my hard work—with my horses, that would have been Kulva's bride price." He bent and took a burning brand from the fire, then walked the length of the wagon, examining the cunning fittings of leather and metal and painted wood. Then he went up the steps and stepped inside.

"Seven horses this cost you?" he called. "Truly?"

Zhakar was on his hands and knees now, trying to get to his feet, puffing and gasping from the ache in his chest. "It is a fine wagon!" he bawled. "Odrig gave me an excellent price!"

Unver appeared in the doorway. "I think he cheated you." He came down the steps and dropped the brand back into the firepit.

"Cheated?" The old man was still struggling, but at last he managed to rise. Thin streams of blood had run down his cheeks and into his beard, giving him the look of a painted clan shaman. "It is a fine wagon! Odrig's second best! How can you say I was cheated? What is wrong with it?"

"For one thing," Unver said with a hard smile, "someone seems to have set it on fire."

As Unver walked away toward the paddock the old man screeched helplessly at the evening sky, calling for help. Flames were just beginning to lick at the windows and their carefully painted trim.

By the time Unver saddled his horse and rode away, the wagon had become a ball of bright fire, visible from a great distance away, like a nighttime sun.

She went out the southern door of the Sancellan Mahistrevis. It was the least used, but guarded as closely as all the others. Jesa nodded politely as the guards called to her, but she did not find their attention flattering, only confusing. Did they not know who she was? Did they think that the Duchess's own nurse had time for flirting with soldiers, even if she wanted to? She was not even dressed to please, her hair pulled tight and wrapped in a head-scarf, her dress covered with an old cloak.

Most men are fools, she thought.

Time was pressing, so she made her way quickly through the farmer's quarter of the old city to the spice market, and bought cinnamon, nutmeg, and Harcha pepper, paying with the silver coin her mistress had given her. As she went with her bag from merchant to merchant, Jesa kept a close watch for anyone following her but saw nothing out of the ordinary. The market was full of the usual morning buyers, many of them servants of great houses like herself—although none from any greater house, she thought with pride, since there was no house in Nabban above the Sancellan Mahistrevis, except perhaps the Sancellan Aedonitis, the palace of His Sacredness, the Lector.

When she felt confident that she was not being watched, she left the market and walked quickly down Harbor Way toward the docks, through the wide commons and into the Avenue of the Saints as most called it, since the great entrance arch bore statues of several important religious figures. She only knew Saint Pelippa, the one who had given the dying Usires a drink of water from her bowl, and although the saints of Nabban were not hers, Jesa respected Pelippa as a woman who, for once, had been given praise for doing a woman's thankless job.

The Avenue of the Saints was a wide, winding road that led up from the quarter, curving around Estrenine Hill until it reached the large residences at the top, mostly owned by foreigners, rich merchants and rich nobles who liked to keep a place in the city—the greatest city in all the world, as Duke Saluceris liked to say. Jesa did not doubt it was true, at least in terms of size. Everywhere she went the roads were crowded, not just with folk going about their business, although there were plenty of those, but with others who never seemed to leave the streets at all; hawkers, layabouts, and even women who Jesa felt rather certain were the ones Canthia had told her about, those who had fallen so far from God (as the Duchess explained) that they had to sell their *samuli,* as Jesa's people named them—their "delicate flowers"—for money.

And although today everything seemed ordinary enough, even in this wealthy neighborhood she saw signs of the troubles that had beset the city lately, the riots in which she herself had nearly died. Crude pictures of wide-winged birds and the motto, "*SECUNDIS PRIMIS EDIS*"—"the second shall be the first"—had been painted on the walls of several buildings, symbols of the Stormbirds, the men who supported the duke's enemies, Dallo Ingadaris and the duke's own brother, Drusis. At the poorer end of the street, near the public market, she could even see the ruins of several houses that had been set afire. She shivered as she passed one, the blackened spaces of its windows like ghostly eyes.

When she reached the middle of the hill she looked back once more to make sure she was not being followed, then turned and walked quickly through the gate and into the ill-tended courtyard of a tall house. At the back of the courtyard she knocked on a heavy wooden door. A servant opened the slot and asked her business. Jesa whispered Duchess Canthia's name and was quickly admitted.

If the outside of the house had been disappointing for the dwelling of a man as rich as Viscount Matreu, the inside was not. Candles burned everywhere, and tapestries of many colors hung on the walls, some stitched with bright golden wire, but she had little time to admire them as she passed.

The servant silently led her upstairs to an antechamber furnished with thick, low couches and equally low tables and lit by several oil lamps. This room also was too thickly draped with fine tapestries to examine them all, but one in particular caught her attention. After the servant left, she walked closer to examine it.

Jesa had never seen anything quite like it. The design was of a male human figure wearing a crown, but the figure had the tail of a whalefish (or so she assumed, having seen such things only in pictures). The crowned man's hands were spread wide over what looked like mountains, but much of his vast body seemed to be floating in the ocean, with tiny ships surrounding him on all sides. Surely this must be a picture of Usires the Aedon, Jesa thought, the great god of Nabban, although she had never seen him portrayed in such a way. The strangest thing about the hanging, though, was the material itself. It was not stitchery that made the picture, but rather tiny little shining plates glued one beside another, like the beautiful mosaics on some of the floors of the Sancellan Mahistrevis. None of the shiny bits was much larger than baby Serasina's fingernails; as Jesa moved they caught the light and seemed to flicker and move, as if the crowned man with the tail was truly alive and watching her. This made her fearful, so she made the sign of the Tree, although it still felt strange and false to do it. Still, in a foreign land there were foreign gods and demons that needed to be appeased, and Jesa was a practical young woman.

"I see you are admiring the picture," a voice said behind her.

Jesa was as startled as if she had been caught stealing. She turned to see Viscount Matreu standing in the doorway. He wore a long housecoat, with what she thought might be the bottom of a nightdress showing above his hose and leather slippers.

"I beg your pardon, my lord!" she said.

"Why? Do you not like it?" He moved forward, smiling.

"Oh, no. I think it is very good done. No, done very good." She spread her hands helplessly, thwarted by words. "Beautiful."

"Yes, it is, I think. It was made by a great artist, one of the last on all of Spenit Island who practices the skill. Do you see the small pieces? Those are fish scales. We have many, many colors of fish in our waters." He moved up beside her and examined the strange image. "Do you know who is pictured there? That is the great Lord Nuanni, the old god of the sea. The islands bowed to Usires long ago, but my people still have a great affection for him. They call him "Ocean Father," and still sacrifice to him before beginning a long voyage." He saw her look and laughed. "Fear not! The sacrifice is not a person. Only a bit of fruit or some pretty polished stones." He kept his eyes on her face. "Do I not know you? What is your name?"

"Jesa, my lord. I am the nurse to the Duchess Canthia. To her child."

"Of course! You were in the carriage in St. Lavennin's Square the other day. That was a terrible thing. I am glad I was able to bring the duchess out safely with her child. And you, too, of course."

"Thank you, my lord. We owe you very much."

"I could have done nothing else. But, as we speak of your mistress, I believe you have brought something for me?"

"Oh!" Jesa had been so taken by being once again in the presence of this handsome, dark man—despite his size, he was so much like the men of her own tribe, at least to look at—that she had nearly forgotten. She hoped her shame did not show on her face. "Yes, my lord. Yes, of course!" She reached into the bosom of her dress and pulled it out, embarrassed to hand it to him with the warmth of her body still on the roll of parchment. "My mistress sends this to you and asks you for the kindness of a reply."

He smiled as he took it, as an adult to a charming child. "Does she want my reply now?"

"Yes, please, my lord. If you may please and do so."

"Very well. You must give me a little time, then." He gestured to one of the low couches. "Please, sit, while I attend to your mistress's letter."

Jesa sat, and did her best to look as though she did this sort of thing every day, entering the house of a wealthy nobleman without a chaperone, bearing messages from the duchess of all Nabban, but in truth she was flustered and more than a little frightened. She had no idea what the note said—she would no more have tried to read it than she would have intentionally harmed little Serasina—but since she did not know what it contained, she had no idea how the viscount would react. What if what the duchess had written made him angry? What if he beat her, or forbade her to leave?

Courage, woman, she told herself. *Remember the Green Honeybird. Your mistress the duchess honored you with this important task. Be a brave soldier for her!*

She took a deep breath and forced herself to get up and move around. The room was full of odd, interesting objects, but suddenly she was afraid to be so far from the Sancellan Mahistrevis and all that was familiar. Strange, when she was already so far from her true home!

Jesa was staring at a scowling wooden mask when the viscount said, "A fierce fellow, eh? That is the Mountain Demon. In the high hills of Spenit they still dance the story of how he stole the maiden, the chief's daughter, and how Brave Wing defeated him and brought her back to her people."

"It reminds me of something back home," Jesa said, then had to repeat herself because she had spoken too softly. "They wear masks like this for the Homecoming Boats Festival in the Wran."

"Ah, is that where you are from? I wondered. You almost look like the hill people on my island." He looked up from his writing desk and smiled. "Have you ever been to Spenit?"

"No, my lord. I have come to Kwanitupul only, before I came to Nabban."

"Then this must all be very strange to you. Even growing up in the Honsa Spenitis, I found Nabban disturbing on my first visit. So loud! So many people!"

"Yes, Lord. Very loud people."

"Very loud people indeed. I hope you are never subjected to a meeting of the Dominiate. They screech at each other like the birds they wear."

She could not help laughing. She had sometimes thought the same thing herself, that the shouting and arguing of these people seemed like harbor birds fighting over fish guts on the dock.

Viscount Matreu dripped wax, then applied his seal. After he had blotted it, he rolled up the letter. Halfway back across the room, he stopped and looked Jesa up and down. She felt her face grow hot. What did he want? What was he thinking?

"You are a beautiful young woman, Jesa of the Wran. It would do my heart good to see a woman like you as part of this household, instead of the pinched, pale faces of my other servants. Do you think I could hire you away from the duchess?" He smiled again. It was like a moment of sunshine cutting through the clouds on a cold day. "I would make you very happy, very comfortable here."

For a moment her heart beat as fast as Green Honeybird's wings, to think of spending her days in the company of this handsome, soft-spoken man. But then she remembered little Serasina, how her tiny hand would curl around Jesa's finger like a baby monkey on a high branch might clutch its mother's tail, sure of that one thing only.

"I fear I can come not to here, my lord. Not to work. I owe my lady too much. And her baby. I am the nurse, you see. I could not leave her."

He shook his head, not sternly but only regretfully. "Ah, too bad. But I admire your loyalty. I wish all of the duke's and the duchess's allies and servants were so mindful of their duty." He extended the roll of parchment. "Here. Take this back to your dear mistress. I have kept you away from your duties long enough."

She did. This time it was something warmed by Viscount Matreu's hands that she slid into the bosom of her dress, its length pressing against her chest so that she found it suddenly difficult to breathe. "You are very kind man, my lord."

"I only wish it were true." He saw that she hesitated. "I'm sorry, have I forgotten something?"

She was ashamed to say it, but a stern little voice inside her would not let Jesa stay silent. "I am sorry, my good lord, but I must have the letter of my duchess back, too."

For a moment he looked surprised and perhaps just a tiny bit annoyed, but his features quickly relaxed. "Of course. The duchess cannot be too careful. She has chosen her messenger well." He returned to his writing desk and picked up the message Jesa had brought, then handed it to her. "Take good care of both. Go straight back to the Sancellan and let no one distract you."

She wondered more than ever now what might be in the parchments, but even though the letter her mistress had written was now unsealed, she did not dream of reading it, and not only because she still had trouble with written Nabbanai. She wrapped the old letter around the new, then returned both to the bosom of her dress. "I will, my lord," was all she said.

As the servant arrived to show her out, Matreu took her hand and kissed it—kissed it!—as though she were a highborn lady like her mistress. "Farewell, Jesa. You are one messenger who is always welcome in my house. And if you should ever change your mind about the thing we discussed . . ."

The servant, a thin, pale old man, was watching them. She thought she saw a little sneer of contempt curl his lip. "You are most kind, Lord Viscount," she said loudly enough for him to hear. "Most kind and courteous to me. But my mistress needs me."

"Of course. And I am glad she has you. Go in God's grace, Jesa of the Wran."

She was so taken by the memory of the viscount kissing her hand that she was halfway back down the Avenue of the Saints before she remembered where she was.

Twilight had ended and full night had fallen, but the wolves were still howling in the hills as Unver's black horse breasted the Littlefeather and climbed dripping onto the far bank. Their cries rose and tangled, eerie as the wailing of wind spirits, before dying away as he spurred his horse toward the northeast.

For a moment, as he turned his back on the camp and the smoldering light of the burning wagon, Unver lifted his head as though he had heard someone calling his name. He reined up and swiveled in the saddle, searching the darkness. But when the wolves began to cry again, he shook his head and put his heels to Deofol's ribs, leaping forward across the grassland.

Beyond the Littlefeather the land was mostly flat, an ocean of hummocky meadows broken only by stands of low, stunted trees and islands of tall grass, the shared pasture of the entire western Lake Thrithing. The moon was not quite full, but no clouds shadowed its face, and its light made it easy to see for long distances. Anyone who wished to follow him would have found it easy, although they would have needed to ride swiftly to keep up with Deofol. And because the moon was so bright and the land so flat, it was easy for Unver to see the low, dark shapes drifting down from the nearby hills after him, singly or in twos and threes. The wolves were following him.

Any man of the plains knew that a good horse could outrun even the fastest wolves for a time. Unver leaned close to his horse's neck and let him gallop, no doubt hoping the wolves would lose interest. Deofol had a better sense of smell than Unver did; he didn't need the spurs to let him know they were in danger.

At last, after an hour's hard riding, Unver reined up on top of a small hillock. The wolves had not given up. In fact, they were close now, and Deofol was weary, his coat damp with sweat that gleamed in the strong moonlight, his breath making a fog that surrounded them. Unver had his curved sword in his hand, and his face was hard and empty, as if what was ahead of him was merely a transaction, to be weighed and added up by the gods, then life or death distributed to whoever earned them, without regard to any human desires.

The first wolf, a great gray beast with its hackles raised, charged up the slope and began to circle just a few paces below the horse. Deofol danced away from the gape-mouthed, growling beast, but other wolves followed until the hillock was surrounded by ghostlike shapes, swift and silvery in the moonlight, slipping through the bending grass like sharks around a foundering swimmer.

The largest wolf stopped on the slope just below Unver, well out of reach of his blade. Its hackles were up, the ears forward and tail lifted. The others crowded in behind the leader, less aggressive and less certain, yipping and growling among themselves. The wolf-chieftain looked around—its eyes caught the moonlight in a brief flare of flame-yellow—then it threw back its head and howled again. After a moment the other beasts joined in. The horse danced anxiously as the howls pierced the night, but Unver only stared. His face was still set in a stern mask, but his posture hinted at his confusion: this was not the way wolves behaved, especially not when they had surrounded their prey.

At last, the largest wolf ended his cry and gradually the voices of the rest faded as well. As if under a spell, Unver sat and stared at the great, gray chieftain for a long time, then slowly began to dismount. The wolves watched him. A few of the animals on the outskirts, less confident than their fellows, made little growling sounds of discomfort, but the rest merely watched Unver, eyes bright and tongues lolling.

At last Unver stood with both boots on the grassy hill, not a pace and a half from the biggest wolf. The two of them looked at each other. Deofol whinnied. Unver did not look at his mount, but raised his hand as if giving a blessing. The leader of the pack watched the hand go up, and then, as if a command had been given, the wolf lowered his own head, dipping his chest before lifting his muzzle toward Unver's upraised fingers. Then, without any further sound, the great gray leader stood up, turned, and trotted away back down the hill. The rest of the pack followed him without a backward glance at the man and his horse, and very shortly they were running back in the direction from which they'd come, across the silvered grasses, until they melted at last into moving shadows and then were gone.

Unver, his face still expressionless, climbed back into his saddle, then rode down the slope and spurred away toward the north.

When Fremur came to himself, he realized he was kneeling in the wet grass beside his horse, on a slope not two hundred paces from where the wolves had surrounded Unver. He had been sure that Unver would die in the jaws of the wolves, and he had been about to die with him, without thought even for the clan he now ruled in place of his dead brother. Fremur remembered watching the beasts surround Unver, but he did not remember dismounting, as though holy lightning had leaped from the heavens and struck him witless. He had been following Unver since just outside the camp, on the other side of the Littlefeather, and though he had called out to him several times, Unver had not heard him.

Fremur did not know exactly what he had just seen, but he was trembling all over with it, exalted, mad with fear and excitement. Everything he had suspected, everything he had dreamed, was coming true. The man he had followed was no ordinary man—no ordinary chieftain, or even clan-thane.

Fremur struggled into his saddle and turned his horse back toward the camp of the Crane Clan. He could not help himself, and he spoke as he rode, saying the same thing over and over as though someone other than his horse and the bright, sliding moon were there to hear him.

"I have seen it," he said. "I have seen with my own eyes that even the beasts of the grassland bow to him. I, Fremur, have seen the true *Shan!*"

46

River Man

As Tiyagar-month proceeded the days remained long, but Eolair and Morgan blew the horn only at dusk, so on this particular day an hour or more of daylight still remained when they finished riding and began to make camp. Bored, Morgan wandered off by himself, down to the water.

They had stopped somewhere near the border between Stanshire and Falshire, in a place where several streams that had their beginnings in the nearby Woodpecker Hills came down to join the Ymstrecca, the tributaries forming a marshy delta between the highlands and the wide river. Morgan walked for a short distance until he found a place out of sight of the camp, then waded out through the shallow water to a single tall stone standing a bit less than man-height above the slow-moving stream, surrounded by reeds and sawgrass. It looked a little like the Hayholt itself looming above the Kynslagh and Kynswood, and once he had reached the top and found a flat place to sit, Morgan turned to survey his new kingdom.

The only one I'll likely ever get, he thought. *If I believe in magic knucklebones, that is.* He found a loose stone and tossed it as far as he could. It fell midstream with a muffled *ploosh. Gone,* he thought glumly. *Just like everything else. Out in the sun for a while, then gone.*

The river gurgled around the walls of his stone fortress. Somewhere in the nearby reeds a duck quacked, then the splashing grew louder for a moment and the reeds trembled. A moment later all was silence again. The waterfowl did not appear, nor did it make any more noises.

A pike, Morgan guessed. *Sad for the duck.* He had seen the long, wolfish swimmers many times in the castle moat, water dragons as big as he was, and sometimes older too—much older, if his grandfather knew what he was talking about. The king had told him once that the oldest pikefish lived two score years or more.

What kind of life would that be? he wondered. *Forty years, as long as many men's lives, down in that dark water . . .*

"Morgan!"

His companions had come looking for him. He hunched down, hoping the reeds would shield him from whoever it was. It had been a strangely high-pitched voice, though.

"Morgan Prince, please! Please say to me you are here!"

He peered between the reeds and saw a small figure standing a few paces up the riverbank. It was Qina, the troll girl. His first urge was to remain hidden, but there was something about her worried face that shamed him into giving himself away.

"I'm here." He stood so she could see him past the reeds that surrounded his stone island.

"Daughter of the Mountains!" she said. "Oh, but I am good to see you well. You should not be here."

"You can't tell me what to do, Qina. I'm a prince, remember?"

"No, should not be here because making danger." She waved her hands in agitation. "Come back!" Her face changed, as if she had thought of something new and even worse than whatever was bothering her. "No, do not come. Stay there. I will coming to you." She backed a little way farther up the bank, then ran to the water's edge and leaped across the sizeable distance with her arms spread wide. She landed with both feet on Morgan's stone refuge, but one of her boots slipped and she began to fall backward. Irritated by the loss of his solitude but alarmed that she might hurt herself, Morgan grabbed her jacket sleeve and kept her from toppling back into the cold water.

"What are you doing?" he demanded. "And how did you jump so far?" He was almost twice her height, but he could not imagine jumping the same distance, not on the first try.

"Where I am living, many are places ice is gave way or path is breaked. Sometimes jump is only way." She never took her eyes off the water beside them. "Now I will call after Snenneq to help us back. He can be watching."

Morgan could not understand almost anything the troll girl had just said. "Watch? Snenneq needs to be here to watch us?"

"Ssshhhh!" She held her finger in front of her lips. "Not so much noise making. River Man will hear."

"River Man? Who is that?"

But instead of answering him, Qina continued to look past him, her eyes fixed worriedly on the stream. "*There*," she said in a whisper. "He has smelled of us."

Morgan wondered if this was some kind of religious ceremony. Was there a taboo on this place? Was this some kind of trollish sacred site? "Who is River Man?"

She grabbed his hand and pinched it with her strong little fingers, then again gestured him to silence. "Watch," she whispered. "See, there." She pointed.

Now Morgan saw a pattern in the ripples a few dozen paces upstream, a sort of curved, invisible obstacle around which the water flowed less evenly, an obstruction now sliding toward them through the shallows. Then he saw something else he had missed—a large gray heron, standing in the midst of a nearby patch of reeds, so motionless on its long, thin legs that it seemed to be part of the vegetation.

"That's just a bird," he told Qina, who was still staring at the spot with wide eyes. "It's a heron. They don't eat anything bigger than rabbits and frogs . . ."

He did not finish explaining about the heron's diet, because at that moment something massive, long, and flat surged up out of the shallow water and crashed into the reeds. Before he could even make out what it was, it had sucked the large, struggling bird into its impossibly broad mouth.

Morgan shouted out in shock and terror. The long body and wide, flat head was brown and green and gray, mottled like stones on a river bottom, but the belly and the underside of its massive jaw that he saw as it took the heron were white. The head was shaped like nothing he had ever seen, a great, flattened ham with two piggy eyes set far back from the vast mouth and its tiny, sharp teeth, but most upsetting of all were the thing's forepaws, which despite their mottled shininess seemed to end in wide, flat human fingers that had curled tenaciously in the heron's feathers, holding it fast even as its wings spread and beat.

The struggling heron swallowed down, the thing slid backward into the river, leaving nothing to mark that either creature had existed, except the agitated water and broken reeds.

"By the Aedon!" Morgan realized he was shaking all over. "Merciful God— *what was that?*"

"River Man," said Qina. "River Man by us he is called. He lives in such places. We have him in Blue Mud Lake where my people go, but we know his hiding holes."

"Qina!" This time Morgan recognized the voice immediately. "You are there?"

"Out here, Snenneq!" she called, her relief plain. "Qallipuk is in this water. We saw him."

"What are you doing out on the rock?" Snenneq asked as he got closer. "Qina, dear wife-to-be, I did not know you had such foolishness in you. I am worried."

"I came. Morgan Prince was on the rock." She stood. "Do not speak me with the words speaked to children. Help us to shore."

Little Snenneq cautiously made his way down to the river's edge and stood on the bank upstream from the large rock, jabbing at the water with the sharp end of his hooked staff. "I see him not," he said. "Come now."

This time Qina did not jump, but took Morgan's hand to lead him back to the shore. As they slid down into the water, he realized that although the cold but gentle current came no higher than his thighs, most of the young troll woman was going to be beneath the water. He bent down and, though she protested, lifted her up and carried her to the shore. As he took his last step in the river, he thought he felt something brush his leg. In a sudden panic, he tossed her onto the bank and scrambled out of the water as swiftly as he could.

Back at the camp, Binabik and his wife Sisqi came to make certain their daughter and Morgan were unhurt.

"It is a sobering thing to be meeting the Qallipuk," said Binabik as he examined bloody scratches on the prince's ankles. "Do not give yourself hard words, Prince Morgan. They have great fierceness, and attack from where they are not being seen first. And some of them are having twice the length of a man your size—perhaps more." He patted him on the knee. "I see nothing but small wounds coming from rocks in the stream. You have been having a luckier first encounter with the water monster than is given to some!"

Morgan didn't understand how the troll's comments were supposed to make him feel better—so the River Man he'd met was only a small one? Binabik's use of the word "sobering" troubled him too, as if the little man might be repeating something he'd been told by Morgan's grandparents.

Have they told him to keep an eye on me? That I'm a drunkard who can't be trusted?

Snenneq wrapped his beloved in a cloak and took her off to change into dry clothes. When Binabik and Sisqi returned to tending the feverish Sitha, Morgan got up and walked across the camp to take a seat by the fire where Porto sat.

The old man looked at the prince, still shivering and wet nearly to the waist, and asked, "What happened, Highness? Did you fall into the river?"

"Not quite." He leaned closer to the flames. It was summer, and even with evening coming on quickly the air was warm, but Morgan could not remember feeling so cold in a long time, even in snowy Rimmersgard. "I almost became a meal for River Man."

"Who is that?"

"The trolls call it a 'Kallypook' or something. I've never seen anything like it." He described the monster to Porto, who reacted with appropriate awe at the prince's close escape.

"That is why I never go far without my sword," Porto said, patting the hilt fondly. "The forest, all these wild lands—they are full of terrible things. Did I tell you of some of the things I saw at the Nakkiga Gate?"

Morgan was about to answer wearily—when his teeth had temporarily stopped chattering—that he had heard about Nakkiga Gate from the old knight a hundred times, but he realized that he had never heard Sir Porto talk of anything quite like this. "Were there such things at Nakkiga?" he asked. "Kallypooks?"

"I did not see your water-monster, so I cannot say. But I can promise you that we fought many kinds of demon-spawn. The Norns themselves were bad enough, with their corpse-skin and dead eyes. And silent! Like fighting ghosts. There was one I had to fight by myself in a cave on the mountainside. He was already wounded, thank merciful God. And when I cut the arm off him, he never said a word, made no cry of pain—just kept crawling toward me, blood pouring out of him like a river. I had to slice his head away, nearly, before he gave up. But it was not the Norns I feared most. No, that would have been the giants."

In his present mood, Morgan was not certain he wanted to hear any more, but he was also too cold to move away from the fire. "I have heard many stories about the northern giants," he said to the old knight. "And not just yours. My grandfather had to fight one, he told me."

"We fought more than one of them on our way to Nakkiga. Praise the Aedon there weren't more. That was the Norns' great weapon, those cursed, murdering beasts. Big as houses, strong as bulls."

Morgan remembered the tales he had heard more recently from the men who had survived the fighting on the Frostmarch Road, about the biggest giant anyone had ever seen. His guts felt like water to think of it. "How can anyone kill such a thing?"

"One man can't. Perhaps Camaris the Great could, but no other man I've met could survive long enough to make a killing blow. Great clubs those creatures had, studded with spikes, and every time they swung, men flew apart into bloody bits. I saw one giant pick a man up and squeeze him until he burst like a ripe plum crushed in your fist."

Morgan was becoming even more certain he didn't want to hear any more of Porto's tales, but he did not know how to stop him without seeming cowardly. The old man had a look on his face that Morgan had never seen, as if he was not just telling a story but seeing it happen again before him.

"One moment the poor devil was alive and screaming," the knight said, still staring at something that Morgan couldn't see and didn't want to see. "The next he was nothing but drippings and ragged skin."

It was impossible not to flinch. "God preserve us! How did you not go mad?"

Porto gave him a flat look. "Oh, Highness, I saw worse, much worse. At Nakkiga, I saw our own dead climb up out of their graves and come against us."

"Good God."

"God could not have been there that day—at least that is what I thought, many times, may the Redeemer forgive me." He made the sign of the Tree. "And even that was not the worst that came to me." Porto shook his head. As he tried to find new words, he made a sound that Morgan recognized as someone fighting tears. "But I cannot talk about that, about what they did to me— no, what they did to my friend who died at Nakkiga. They . . . he . . ." The old man shook his head again, harder, as if trying to dislodge some stinging, biting vexation. "No, I still cannot speak of it. I am sorry, Highness. But those damned, white-skinned things are not God's creatures, they are something else. Demons. Remember that if you ever face them."

"And the Sithi?" It had suddenly occurred to Morgan that the very same people they were seeking all along the edges of this dark forest were the cousins of Porto's Norns. If the Norns were demons, what did that make their relatives?

It took the old knight a moment to reply. When he did, his voice was still shaky, but more controlled than it had been. "The Sithi? What do you ask, my prince?" Porto slapped at his cloak, then looked around. "By all that is holy, why is there nothing to drink anywhere?"

Morgan was surprised to realize he hadn't had a drink himself all day. "I'll find something." He fetched his saddlebags, which he had left hanging over a branch near his grazing horse, and carried them back to the fire, nodding to the men who gave him "Good day, Highness," or "God speed you, Prince Morgan," on the way. By the time he returned to the fire he felt a little better. He enjoyed traveling with battle-hardened men who treated him as one of their own—albeit a bit more exalted—instead of as an excuse to run to his grandfather and grandmother and complain about him.

He handed Porto a silver flask that carried his princely arms in gemstones and fine enamels. "The Cuthmanite Brothers' best apple brandy. I brought it in case we became lost in the forest, or were attacked by Norns."

Porto reached out for the flask, staring at it like a child given a colorful whirligig. "What good would this do if we were attacked by Norns, Highness?"

"It would make sure we didn't care." He dropped down on the log beside the old knight.

Porto took out the stopper and sniffed the neck of the flask, eyes shut. His smile unrolled across his bearded face like a hedgehog waking from a happy dream. "Ah," he said, then offered it to the prince.

"Your health, Porto." Morgan took a warming draught. It rolled down his throat with the clean bite of the finest stuff, honeyed fire.

Porto accepted the brandy back from him reverently. He took a mouthful and savored it, puffing his cheeks as he sluiced it from side to side, so comical that Morgan laughed out loud. "It is worth some care," the old knight told him with more than a hint of pained sensibilities. "*You* may drink such stuff every day, my prince. It comes to a man like myself perhaps once in a lifetime. Your very good health, Highness." He took a proper swallow.

Morgan was still grinning, but he waited a respectful time for Porto to savor his brandy before asking him what he had been about to say of the Sithi.

"Ah, yes. So." He hesitated, then held up the flask. "Another sip, Highness?"

"For me or you? No, go on, have as much as you like." He looked up at the sky, which was beginning to darken in the east. "Well, as much as you can drink before I have to blow the Horn of Failure so the Sithi can ignore it again. I'm not such a fool as to leave the brandy with you while I'm gone."

Porto again made the sign of the Tree. "Careful how you talk, Morgan. Prince Morgan, I mean." He leaned, his breath fuming with the Cuthmanite monk's finest. "They might hear you."

"If you mean the fairies, if they can't hear that great bellowing horn we've blown every night for a fortnight or more, they're hardly going to hear me talking to you. But what were you going to say about them?"

Porto fortified himself again before beginning. "I saw the fighting at the Hayholt, Prince Morgan, as you know. Back in the Storm King's War. I saw the fairy folk, the white and the golden, the Norns and the Sithi—even saw them fighting each other, although *that* was . . ." He frowned. "Hard to explain it properly. Like hearing a song in someone else's tongue, Highness. Trying to make it out, do you see, without understanding the words."

"I don't think I do see, Porto. What do you mean?"

"It was so fast. And some of it didn't make sense. I can't find the words, and I swear it isn't this little bit of grog that's fuddled me, beautiful and welcome as it is. Watching the Fair Ones and the White Foxes fight each other was like watching someone singing a song and playing at some contest, both at the same time, and I couldn't understand either song or game. Can you compass that, Highness?"

Morgan waved his hand. "Go on."

"And they were as bold and lovely as any fairies I ever heard about when I was young, my prince. But deadly. Deadly like a hawk is deadly, which is to say no more deadly than a sword's blade, which only does what it is made to do.

"But when we went north after the Storm King failed, chasing the Norns back to Nakkiga, the Sithi did not come with us. Old Duke Isgrimnur, bless him, he was most set that the Norns should not get back to the shelter of their mountains, and he talked the king and queen into letting him take a great troop and pursue them, but the Norns moved too fast—like smoke on a brisk wind— and they made it all the way past their great walls and into their mountain. That was Nakkiga Gate, and the Sithi were not with us there. If they had been, there would be no White Foxes left."

"But if they fought their kin at the Hayholt, why didn't the Sithi fight with you that time?"

"A better man than I would have to answer that, Highness. I was only a soldier, and more concerned about having to ride all the way to the end of the world than I was about what the fairy-folk were doing. It was never certain that the Sithi *weren't* coming, at least among us men. Many of us thought they would show up for the fighting, you see, riding in a great company as they rode to Hernystir, and as many were fearful of that as were happy to think so. You'd understand if you'd been there, my prince. They were so terribly *different* than men."

"But the Sithi never did come to Nakkiga."

"No, they didn't. I heard from another fellow, who heard it from someone, that the Sithi still had some family feeling for the Norns—that they would defeat them but not destroy them. But Duke Isgrimnur, he was so set on it that he drove on regardless. Perhaps he too thought the Sithi would show up at the last. He was a great man, the duke, but even great men make mistakes."

Morgan noticed a member of the Erkynguard lurking nearby, clearly waiting to say something. "A moment, Porto."

The soldier made a half-bow. "Beg your pardon, Highness, but Count Eolair says it's time for us to go into the forest."

"Us?" said Morgan.

"Myself and some of the other men. Count said we should come along this time, Your Highness."

Morgan excused himself to Porto, made sure to retrieve his flask, then followed the guardsman.

* * *

As they led half a dozen mounted Erkynguards toward the darkening line of the forest, Morgan asked Count Eolair about the armed escort. He had grown rather fond of his rides into and out of the forest edge with the old count, who never said exactly what you expected him to say—a rare trait in old people, Morgan thought.

"It is because we have now ridden beyond the easy reach, and perhaps even the repute, of the High Ward," the count said. "Out here the Hayholt is more legend than fact, and the high king and high queen even less known. You will see it clearly if we reach New Gadrinsett. The citizens are loyal to the High Throne in theory, but the town that has built up around it is more Thrithings camp than Erkynlandish city. And the farther we go, the less anything we carry or wear will mean. Except our weapons, of course."

"Do you mean bandits?"

"All manner of things. I hear you met one of the locals earlier this afternoon."

"The River Man?" Morgan barely repressed a shudder. "Yes, and I would not like to meet him again."

They were in among the trees now. Eolair led them deeper, until the last orange and pink smears of sunset gleamed only in spots through the high trees. They stopped at last in a forest clearing, beside a stream that was on its way to join the marsh down the shallow slope behind them, but they did not dismount. Eolair handed the wooden chest containing Ti-tuno to Morgan.

"Make music, my prince," said Eolair.

Morgan took out the horn and weighed it in his hand. "Why can I blow it now, but I couldn't when I first tried?"

"Who can say?" Eolair gave the ghost of a shrug. "The things the Sithi have made are always strange to mere mortals. Or perhaps it is simply that you found the trick."

"If I found the trick, why don't I know what it is?"

Eolair smiled. "Another question I cannot answer, Your Highness. But the light is fleeing us swiftly now. May I suggest you perform that trick you don't know one more time?"

Morgan lifted the horn and sounded it, giving it all his breath, so that the mournful wail of it flew out into the deepening evening and rang and rang until the echoes died at last among the trees. The silences after the horn blew always seemed different than ordinary silences, although he could not have said why. Some quality of heightened stillness, perhaps, as though something listened and heard its call, even if the listeners were not the same ones he and Eolair sought.

Long moments passed, then Morgan winded the horn again. He had only a moment to savor the great silence after the echoes, then it was broken.

"Who are you, mortal men? And why do you carry a gift that is not yours to carry?"

The voice was not loud, but it seemed to fly straight into Morgan's ear like a bee, startling him so that he nearly dropped the horn. The soldiers who had accompanied them grasped at their swords when they heard it, but Eolair held up his hand. "Do not draw your weapons," the count said. "It would be pointless." He looked slowly around the clearing, but saw nothing, heard nothing now that the voice had fallen silent, only the trees and the plashing of the little stream.

"I am Count Eolair of Nad Mullach," the old man called, his voice only a little louder than when he had been talking to Morgan: he clearly thought that whoever had spoken was close by. "We mean no harm. I know your Prince Jiriki of old and would have words with him."

"And I am a prince, too," Morgan said, rather more loudly than he'd meant to. "I am Morgan of Erchester. King Simon and Queen Miriamele are my grandparents, and I'd like to talk to Prince Jiriki, too." His heart, he realized, was beating madly, almost as swiftly as when he'd seen the river monster leap up to take the heron. "Show yourself!"

"Do not make demands," Eolair said quietly.

A figure appeared at the edge of the clearing, so suddenly that it almost seemed to form out of the half-darkness. "Tell your men not to move," the newcomer said. "They are surrounded by my hunters."

"Nobody will move," said Eolair.

The figure came toward Morgan, who was feeling a strong impulse to ride away as fast as he could. It was not that the stranger was frightening to look at—he was slender, and the angled bones of his face and his huge, golden eyes marked him clearly as one of the Sithi—but that Morgan felt a coldness beating out from him, a disdain. He felt certain that this odd creature in rough-spun garments, with red hair that seemed unnaturally bright, even in the darkening twilight, would happily have him feathered with arrows if the need arose, regardless of his princely status.

The stranger put out a thin, long-fingered hand. It took Morgan a moment to realize he wanted Ti-tuno. He looked to Eolair, who nodded.

The stranger took the horn and handled it with obvious reverence, turning it over in his hands, his lips moving as if in prayer. "It truly is Ti-tuno," he said at last, his use of the Common Tongue almost faultless, but shaped and accented in liquid ways Morgan had never heard before. "It is a strange thing to hear its note in these dark days. We had thought it lost. Who are you?"

"I am Count Eolair, Hand of the Throne. We come from the High King and High Queen in the Hayholt—in old Asu'a. We have been sent to find Prince Jiriki and his sister Aditu, and to speak to them."

"Prince Jiriki," said the stranger, but his smile was close to a smirk. "So. And why should we take you to trouble them?"

"For old friendship's sake, if nothing else, I hope," said Eolair. "But there is another, more urgent matter—"

"Why is he asking us all these questions," Morgan demanded. "Doesn't he understand that it's the king and queen of this entire land we're talking about? That I'm the heir? Listen, you, we want to speak to this Jeekee."

"The name is Jiriki, Highness." Eolair gave him a significant look. "This is why your grandparents sent me, my prince. Please, let me . . ." The lord steward turned back to the Sitha. "We have one of your people with us, very ill and in need of care, back at our camp. You sent her to us, but she was attacked and shot with arrows—poisoned arrows."

"What?" The Sitha's catlike face sharpened into a mask of anger. "You have shot another of our people?"

Morgan was about to tell this puffed-up idiot that he didn't understand anything, but Eolair was making the face at him again, so he remained resentfully silent.

"No, we who serve the king and queen in the Hayholt did not shoot her. We do not know who did. She was found, injured and senseless, near the castle. We have nursed her as well as we can, but she has passed beyond our healers' craft."

For a moment the Sitha only stared at Eolair, his face a mask made even harder to read by the fading light. Then he let out a whistle, although Morgan did not see him purse his lips. A moment later a dozen shapes stepped from the shadows on all sides—Sithi, male and female, all dressed in similar rough clothing, all with arrows nocked on the strings of their bows.

"Send your soldiers to bring our injured kin to us. You two stay here."

"We need to speak to . . ."

"What you need will be addressed later," the flame-haired Sitha said, cutting Eolair's words short. "I am Yeja'aro of the Forbidden Hills, and you are trespassers who may not make demands. But if you bring our kinswoman swiftly, and come along without trouble, I promise to return you here safely, whether the ones you seek wish to meet you or not."

The Erkynguards looked confused, but since they were surrounded and outnumbered, they did not seem particularly eager to start a fight. "Go back to the camp and bring the Sitha-woman on her litter," Eolair told them. "Quickly."

After a bit of hesitation, the soldiers turned and rode back toward the camp.

"You two will have to leave your horses behind," Yeja'aro said. "They will not be able to travel where we go."

"Is it far?" Morgan couldn't help asking.

Yeja'aro gave him a flat look. "That depends on how it is measured."

It was growing dark quickly. Two of Yeja'aro's hunters produced sticks of wood that suddenly burst into flame, although Morgan had no idea what lit them. By this light they waited as the forest evening deepened into night. Morgan thought he had never in his life experienced anything quite as eerie as being watched for so long by all those silent Sithi.

When the soldiers finally returned, this time with the horses bearing the Sitha-woman's litter, they were accompanied by Sir Porto and all the trolls.

Porto hurried to Morgan's side. "The Erkynguard captain said he and his men are waiting just down at the edge of the trees," he whispered. "If you need them, just shout."

Count Eolair heard him and carefully shook his head. "We will not need the captain and his men, Sir Porto. And be aware—the Sithi have very good ears."

Yeja'aro had been standing over the Sitha-woman's pale, motionless form. When he looked up, his expression seemed to have tightened into an even deeper anger. "Your men would be sentencing you both to death if they attacked."

"Nobody is attacking," Eolair said. "These men are here in large part to protect Prince Morgan, our royal heir. We are a peaceful mission, and we want only to speak to your masters—"

"Masters!" said Yeja'aro with sudden fury. "Ha! Do the Zida'ya have masters now, like mortal men? Are we to have kings and slaves and such?" He stared at Morgan and Eolair for a moment, then his face turned expressionless once more. "We will take you with us now. Say your farewells."

"I would like to come too," said Binabik. "I am knowing Prince Jiriki and his sister of old, and am proud to be calling them friends."

"And I am pledged to help this mortal prince find his destiny," Snenneq said. "I must go too, because I have made a pledge!"

The Sitha looked at Binabik's wolf-steed Vaqana. It clearly puzzled him, but he only shook his head. "What you might have pledged, or how you might name the members of House Sa'onserei, means nothing to me," said Yeja'aro, and pointed to Morgan and Count Eolair. "No others will accompany us but these two." And nothing Binabik or Snenneq could say would change his mind.

To Morgan's surprise, in the midst of all the other danger and confusion surrounding them, he actually found himself feeling sorry for both Binabik and Little Snenneq, who looked absolutely miserable that they could not go along.

"But for how long will we be gone?" Eolair asked at last. "How can our men wait for us if we cannot tell them how long?"

Yeja'aro shook his head in irritation. "There is no answer. If you wish to come with us, come. If you do not wish to, do not. But if it is *you* who have harmed this woman Tanahaya," he gestured toward her litter, "and you have told us lies about it, then we will find you no matter where you are and destroy you."

Morgan was torn between wanting to tell this self-important fellow a few things and his earlier urge to get out of the vicinity as quickly as possible. Stymied, he looked to Eolair.

"We will come with you, Yeja'aro," said Eolair. "We wish to see her healed as much as you do."

Qina reached up and touched Morgan's sleeve. "Remember Sedda sent token to you, Prince Highness," she said so quietly he had to bend down to hear better. "The moon mother saw you on the mountain. She watch out for you."

Morgan did not know what to say, and only nodded his head.

"Do not fear, friend Morgan—we will all be waiting here," said Snenneq. "In the same place, until the time of your returning."

"He is speaking truth," said Binabik, his round face stern. "Your safety is being our sworn promise to your grandparents. We will be waiting."

"But hurry back, Highness," Porto added. "The king and queen will have my head if you don't."

As Morgan and the count finished their farewells, four of the Sithi took up the handles of the litter and carried it silently away into the forest shadows.

"Walk now," demanded Yeja'aro. "You two follow one of the torchbearers. I know mortal eyes are weak, especially after the sun has gone to her bed."

"You heard him," said Count Eolair with a less than happy smile. "Time to go, my prince."

Morgan was afraid to look back at old Porto and the rest as he left them behind, worried that in his fearful state he might do something that seemed unmanly. He did his best to walk like a man who was not afraid as he followed the light of the Sithi torches into the ancient forest.

47

Hidden Chambers

The climax subsiding, Idela rolled onto her back and took a deep, shuddering breath. Her breasts trembled. "Oh, sweet and merciful God. I have been without a man so long—since my poor husband died!"

Pasevalles thought the pink flush on her throat and cheeks was very moving, and did not doubt that she had deeply enjoyed their lovemaking of recent days, but he was a bit more cynical about the idea that he was the first she'd had since Prince John Josua's death. Too many rumors had come to him over the years, and he knew that Sir Zakiel of Garwynswold, the guard captain, had been frequently in Idela's company in years past—so much so that some courtiers had taken to calling him "the Widow's bed warmer".

But whatever he might think of Idela's application to chastity, Pasevalles was beginning to admire her more than he had thought he would. She had not mentioned their agreement once since she had first brought it up. In his experience, those who expected favors were prone to remind him of it far more often than necessary, but the princess had left the entire subject cloaked in dignified silence. Not that he needed to be reminded; in this respect, at least, he and Idela were of like mind. He too wanted Morgan to learn responsibility, or at least some semblance of it, so the young prince would make a fitting ruler one day.

He reached out and touched her right breast, tracing his finger up from the base to the still pouting tip. She shuddered and pushed his hand away. "Don't! You make me want to start all over again."

He smiled. "I am in no hurry."

She sat up, pulling the coverlet up to her neck, then thought better of it and let it fall. Idela was a handsome, vital young woman, something else Pasevalles could not help but admire; someone who did not sit back and wait for things to come her way but reached out for them—quite the opposite of his own mother, who had largely given up on life after Pasevalles's father had died at the battle for the Hayholt. When the fever caught her, she had not resisted—even his infant sister had fought harder, although she too had ultimately succumbed. But his mother had been like the defenders of a castle who had decided to open the gates to a superior force: The fever had barely touched her before she surrendered.

Not Idela, though. The prince's widow still had ambitions and not just for her son, Pasevalles knew: she wanted a meaningful role in things. Pasevalles might bring nothing in the way of patrimony, but he had worked hard and made himself an indispensable man here in the Hayholt. There would be no shame in John Josua's widow marrying a lord chancellor, especially one who was in line to become the next Hand of the Throne. Pasevalles was pragmatic about himself, too: he did not flatter himself that his charm or looks alone had led them to this bed on this hot afternoon. Idela knew the limits women faced, even royal women, and she wanted a partner. Pasevalles was seriously considering the partnership, although neither had spoken of the possibility out loud, or even hinted at it beyond his promise to push the king and queen for more responsibility for Prince Morgan. It was not as easy a decision as it seemed. Pasevalles had ambitions of his own, ideals he had harbored since boyhood, and Idela was a strong-willed woman who would want her own way in any marriage.

He smiled at the thought that he was even contemplating taking a princess for a wife.

"You look pleased with yourself," she said, catching his expression and smiling back. "Now that you have made a fallen woman of me."

"Angels do not fall," he said. "They fly down on their shining wings, so that we mortals may see something of perfection."

She pinched his arm. "I wish I could believe that you really thought that."

"You do not know my depths, lady, if you think me incapable of such strong feelings."

Idela laughed, but there was a hitch in it, as if for a moment real emotion had interfered with pillow talk. "You read me like a book! That is just what I thought of you for so long. So proper, so courteous! Always dressed just right, always the correct thing to say. I am glad to learn that you are not as prim as you once appeared. The things you do to me—!" She shook her head. "I could never have guessed you were such a wicked man!"

He put his mouth close to her ear. "If the angel can remain earthbound just a while longer, there are other mortal tricks I could show you." He kissed the side of her neck.

She turned and took his face between her hands and stared into his eyes, long and searchingly. "Sometimes I do not know what to think of you, Pasevalles. Truly I don't. You are such a gift." She let him go. "But I cannot stay. The queen expects me to join her this afternoon, and I had to tell a terrible lie just to steal this time." She sat up and looked around the chamber. "How strange to be so close to everyone yet so far from them, too!"

"Must you really leave?"

"Yes, I really must." She swung her legs out and set her feet on the floor. "How can it be so hot outside but these stone flags are cold as ice?"

"This room has thick walls," he said. "Because it was once part of an old fireplace flue, when this part of the residence had only one, although it was sealed off and filled in long ago. That is one reason why it is so private—even if there were people in the next room, they would hear nothing."

"Private, silent, and all but unused. How clever of you to find it."

He shrugged. "When I first came to the castle I enjoyed roaming through it, discovering bits of its history. I have long kept this room as my secret—I have the only key. There are so many chambers here in the residence that even when we are full up with guests, nobody bothers with it. Even the maids do not come in." He sat up so he could better watch her dressing. "I needed a place where I can steal some time for myself, especially when I have to exercise Count Eolair's duties as well as my own."

"And that is all you ever do here?" she said, then lifted her foot to pull on her hose, showing him the smooth length of her leg. "Truly, Lord Pasevalles?" Her flirtatious manner had a hint of something deeper, something Pasevalles could almost scent—a touch of desperation, perhaps.

"I promise you, Idela, you are the first lover I have ever brought here."

"I choose to believe you." She turned and crawled across the bed to kiss him, wearing only hose and her half-donned shift. Her curling hair draped either side of his face like the curtains on the bed canopy. She dragged her breasts slowly across his chest as their lips met.

"My mother-in-law will be furious," she said. "But I could be a little late."

"You should not," he said, pushing gently on her shoulders. "Remember, one of their chief complaints with Morgan is that he is always late—when he shows up at all. Let us not remind them of his faults in his absence."

She pouted very prettily. "I expect the man I bed to be quite mad with lust for me, not to speak with practical good sense."

"Then you should pick younger men, my beautiful one. Remember, I am quite old and that means, I fear, a certain practicality."

"Mmmmm." She leaned close again to kiss him one last time, so he could feel her skin upon his, her breasts upon his chest. "You are not so old as all that, Lord Chancellor. Oh! You have made me tingle all over, all over again, dear, dear Pasevalles."

"And you have brought something into my life that has been long missing," he said. "But now we must both get up and attend to our duties, so that we may have this in the future. Discretion, Princess, discretion! This household is a thousand mouths and two thousand ears just waiting for interesting tittle-tattle."

She sighed, but sat up and returned to hunting for her clothes, cast here and there in the heat of their first moments. "When will we be together again?"

"Soon, I pray. It will be difficult with the escritor and all his retinue coming tomorrow, but we will find time, I promise."

"You had better. I am a religious woman, but I do not consider an escritor, even when sent by His Sacredness himself, an acceptable excuse for you to stay away from me." She stood and stretched, showing him her pale ribs and belly before pulling her shift back down in mock modesty. "Goodness! I forget myself—and in front of our respectable lord chancellor, too!"

"You are truly beautiful, Highness," he said, and meant it.

"And I am yours," she said, without any mockery at all.

Their lovemaking had been stormy, almost angry. At times in the darkness he had felt as though he lay not with his wife of so many years, but some she-beast of the wild forest, all snarls and scratches. Afterward, they lay panting, side by side but not touching.

"Why?" he said again, when he could talk. "Tell me why?"

"I have already told you, and you know I am right. There is no other way."

"That wasn't what I was going to ask you."

"What, then?" She sat up. "Sweet Elysia, it is so hot." He heard her fumbling toward her table, then a moment later he heard the clink of ewer against goblet as she poured herself watered wine. He listened to her swallowing. How strange it was, to live in the dark! How different it made things. Even the familiar sounds made by his familiar wife were transformed into little mysteries.

"Why did you marry me?" he asked.

"What? That is a foolish question. I married you because I loved you as I loved no one else, before or since." But something in her tone made her words seem odd and false to his ears.

"If that is true, it doesn't explain why you are so often angry with me." He didn't mean to sound like a hurt child, but he knew that he did. At the moment, though, hidden by the darkness, he did not care. "When we argued earlier, you all but called me 'kitchen boy.' As if, despite more than thirty years of being a king, of ruling at your side, I was still a child you thought you had to instruct."

"No, no. That's not true. It's not even fair." He heard her bare feet pad across the floor, felt the bed sag slightly as she climbed back in. "It's just . . . sometimes I lose patience."

"As you would lose patience with a child. Or a simpleton."

"Simon, please. It isn't like that. Not truly." Her hand found his in the darkness and curled within it, like an exhausted animal looking for shelter. "I love you so much that it sometimes makes me think I would go mad without you. But sometimes you don't seem to think beyond what you can see, what you can reach. If someone tells you they mean well, you believe them. If someone fails you but tries hard, you never punish them, or even dismiss them."

"Isn't that what Usires taught? 'The weakest of thee, the poorest of thee, those I love the most.'"

"Usires was not a king! He did not have the safety of all the world to consider. He was a fisherman's son."

"Like me."

"By the Holy Tree, Simon, see how you do it again! These are important matters."

"And you are saying that the souls of men, which Usires tried to save, are not important?"

She pulled her hand away. "Are you being difficult by intention because you are still angry with me?"

"Oh, am I the angry one?"

"Just now you are."

He bit back what he would have said, and for long moments they lay side by side in silence.

"I'm afraid, Miri," he said at last. "I'm not angry, I'm afraid."

This time his wife's reply was careful and quiet. "What do you mean? Afraid of what?"

"Everything. That I'm a fool blind chance has made a king. Or even worse, that I may have been destined for this throne, but I have disappointed destiny."

She said nothing for a while. The darkness seemed as thick as treacle, covering everything. "Miri?" he asked at last.

"I fear being a disappointment to our people, too," she said quietly. "It would be a wicked ruler, I think, who didn't. But that is not my greatest fear. I have already seen that come true."

Simon understood, and now it was his turn to fall silent.

"I miss him too," he said at last.

"Every day," Miri replied. "And the strange thing is, I don't merely miss him in one way. I miss the clever young man who died, but I also miss the baby he was, that chortling, fat-legged cherub who used to pull my sewing box down and then sit in the middle of all those pins and needles, laughing. I miss the boy who so badly wanted to shoot a bow, and then wept when he actually shot a bird. I miss all the different John Josuas at the same time. How can that be?"

"Death is a stain," Simon said. "It leaks into everything and taints it."

"Aedon preserve me, I know the truth of that! Every memory, every keepsake. I could not even look at John Josua's possessions for a long time, and still I cannot see them as anything but things he will never use again." She laughed, short and bitter. "Perhaps that is why I sometimes dislike Idela so. Because to me she is something of his, left behind."

Simon considered. "Doctor Morgenes once told me that, in old Khand, they would kill the king's wives and concubines when he died, so that they could accompany him to the next life."

"Dear Simon," she said. "I will leave word in my testament that they are not to kill you when I die."

He smiled, but she could not see that in the dark, so he reached out and found her hand again, then squeezed it. "And I will do the same for you, dear Miri. But you may feel free to leap into my grave, as long as it's your own idea."

Miriamele giggled. "Oh, how horrible we are," she said. "What if God hears us?"

"God always hears us. But He made us, so He must know what we're capable of. That's probably God's First Rule—let nothing shock You."

After another silence, Miriamele said, "I lied to you a moment ago, Simon, but I didn't mean to. I'm not just frightened of being a disappointment. I'm afraid for Morgan. I do not like it that he has gone away into those wild lands. I'm angry I can't protect him."

"But we survived those lands when we were much the same age," he pointed out. "In even more dangerous days. And whatever you may think of me now, I would have grown to be much more foolish had I not spent that year and more fighting for my life and seeing unlikely things. The lessons I learned were hard, painful, but they serve me still."

"I know. And God Himself knows that Morgan needs experience beyond dodging his debts and cozening tavern girls. But you know you also had luck, and Morgan may not. Oh, my husband, I could not bear it if something happened to him! I don't think I could live if we lost him as we lost his father."

"I should tell you that is blasphemy," Simon said after a little while. "That we never truly lose anyone—that John Josua's soul watches us from Heaven, and that we will all meet again. And I do believe it. But a lifetime is a very long time to wait for a reunion."

"Too long. Far, far too long."

Again they fell silent, or mostly so.

"Are you crying?" he asked at last.

"A little. I do when I think of him. It can't be helped."

Simon took a breath. It felt as if he had something to say that was so important it would change everything, like a magic word from an old story but also as ordinary as wishing someone good day. "I don't want to ever lose you, Miriamele. That's another reason I'm afraid."

"The world is a frightening place, husband." He could almost hear her wiping her eyes, beginning to restore the serene, queenly face she showed to the court and, usually, even to their close friends. "Did we imagine that once we found each other, once the Storm King was thwarted, that nothing bad could ever happen again? Instead we still have war and murder, sickness and death, danger to all we love. But we of all people must go on, no matter what threatens. We are the High Queen and the High King, so we have no choice. We must be brave."

"I do not like those words," he said. "*We must be brave.* Every time I've heard them, it meant something bad was about to happen."

"We can only have what we have, we can only know what we know," she said. "Come here, Simon. Hold me and let me hold you."

Nothing had been resolved. Nothing could be resolved until all this was over and they were safe together. Possibly that could never be, on this side of the grave. But the fight was ended, at least for now, and they clung to each other in the dark.

Sometimes, thought Simon, *that really is all we can do.*

Lord Chamberlain Jeremias and his minions had been busy as bees in flowering spring, and the great throne room was almost unrecognizable. Great, swooping banners billowed between the ancient pennants, and a canopied entranceway with scalloped edges of white and gold had been built over the inside of the hall's main door, so that the lector's handpicked spokesman would walk to the table in a splendor similar to that of the Sancellan Aedonitis.

When Miriamele found her husband, he was with Jeremias, who was excitedly describing the other preparations: the cleaning of the best silver for the evening's state dinner, the aromatic spices in the hand-bowls, and the special meal now being prepared, whose highlight was an immense lamprey pie made in the shape of the Hayholt itself.

"A bit of a strange message," Miriamele said as the king's childhood friend rhapsodized over the Kynslagh full of gravy and the tiny oyster shell boats. "Are we inviting Mother Church to swallow us?"

The Lord Chamberlain looked confused. Simon laughed, despite trying not to. "Don't be cruel, wife. It sounds splendid, Jeremias. Escritor Auxis cannot fail to be impressed and honored."

"I hope so." Jeremias gave Miriamele a look that was almost a challenge. "It is to honor the church we have done all this, not just the escritor, although he is himself a famous and godly man." Jeremias ostentatiously made the sign of the Tree. "We are lucky that the Sacred Father sent him."

It was all the queen could do not to make a face. Jeremias was very pious, as Miriamele considered herself to be, but somehow his fervor always made her feel a little sour. As for Escritor Auxis, Jeremias was right when he called him famous—many thought that despite his comparative youth, he was the most likely to succeed the present Lector—but she was not as certain about the godly part. The escritor's reputation for hard bargaining and high-handedness outstripped anything known of his piety.

When the Lord Chamberlain had shot off to see to some other details, Miriamele took her husband by the arm. "Shall we go in?"

"I suppose." With Jeremias and his excitement now gone from the anteroom, the king seemed to sag. "I have told you, I think, that I do not approve of any of this?"

"A dozen times, at least. And you may tell me again if you wish—but not in front of the lector's messenger. Is that agreed?"

He sighed. "Yes, Your Majesty."

"Don't play the scolded kitchen boy with me, Seoman Snowlock. I know you too well. You get your way far more often than you deserve. Show some good grace that, for once, I have won the toss."

"It wasn't a toss. That would have been fair. You just *told* me what we were going to do."

She pulled herself closer. "But you know I am right. Now, shall we go in?"

He made a growling noise that she decided to take for assent.

Miriamele had to admit that Jeremias and his legion of helpers had done a fine job. The great chamber hadn't looked so clean in years, perhaps since Queen Inahwen's visit with young Prince Hugh more than ten years ago. *How does time slide past us so quickly?* she wondered. *There is nothing more precious in all the world, not gold, not jewels, not even love itself. So how does it so easily slip through our fingers?* A strange thought came to her. *And what of the Sithi? Or what of an eternal horror like the Norn Queen, Utuk'ku? What can time mean to those who have so much of it? Does it creep past, each moment a stretching misery, as it did for me when I was a child? As during some of those endless summer afternoons in Meremund, when I had nothing to do but stay quiet and sew?* In fact, the air was hot and still today, just like those long-ago afternoons.

What would it feel like to live forever?

But even as she thought it, she saw Jeremias's great canopy with the golden Trees of Mother Church artfully painted on it, and was ashamed of herself for such a question, which suddenly seemed like the worst sort of ingratitude. Was not Heaven itself an eternal afternoon, and had God and Usires not promised that gift to everyone?

"Perhaps if we go and sit down," Simon said, "everyone will get the hint and things can begin."

"Nothing can begin until the escritor arrives," she reminded him. "But I would not mind sitting down. It's so hot today, and this dress is very heavy."

It turned out to be a good choice, because even after the escritor left Saint Sutrin's in the city—Jeremias came to tell them of it as soon as the archbishop's messenger informed *him*—his procession through the streets to the castle took a long time, limited to the speed of the slowest priests in the procession, some of whom were extremely old. But none of them would have missed this chance, and in fact there were as many dignitaries lined up for the escritor's visit as for the only visit the lector himself had ever made, when he had come to the Hayholt to preside at John Josua's funeral.

Miriamele would not let that gloomy memory distract her. This was more than a state visit from one of the princes of the Sancellan Aedonitis. She had work to do, bargains to make, and she wanted to keep her wits sharp. She nodded as all the great and good of Erkynland filed in, Lord Constable Osric, the inescapable Count Rowson, Feran the castle's marshal and dozens of other nobles, all in their finest clothes. The queen was fairly certain that ostentation was against the church's teachings, but she also knew Auxis himself was said to have a weakness for expensive robes.

At last the procession led by Auxis and Erchester's own Archbishop Gervis reached the throne room. Miriamele and Simon went out onto the steps to greet their important guests. After a blessing was said, and the crowd gathered outside had a chance to see their monarchs and the lector's representative together, the escritor and the rest of his escort from St. Sutrin's were ushered into the throne hall so the official visit and negotiations could begin in earnest.

Escritor Auxis was surprised when he was informed of what was to come by Lord Pasevalles, acting as Hand of the Throne in Eolair's absence. "Negotiations?" Auxis turned to the king and queen, looking almost more annoyed than surprised. "What is there to negotiate, Your Majesties? I come on behalf of His Sacredness, Lector Vidian."

Miriamele had not seen the escritor for many years, although she had followed his rise through the church from a distance. He had aged much as she had imagined he would—handsomely, his bold nose and strong chin, and bushy eyebrows, along with his height, giving him more the look of a warrior-king than a mere churchman. She had to admit he cut an impressive figure in his heavy golden robes.

She saw no need to explain, not yet, but only held out her hand so that he could kiss it. She was pleased that Simon remembered to do the same—it was important to remind the escritor that he stood before the High Throne of all Osten Ard, not just that of some ordinary ruler. When Auxis had been seated and the rest of the preliminaries finished, she squeezed Simon's hand to let him know she was going to speak.

"We know why you are here, Your Eminence," she said, "and we hope we will be able to find a way to help our beloved Sacred Father, the lector."

"And His Sacredness is grateful to you for making time for his humble servant and messenger."

Miriamele almost looked around in comic confusion, because nobody would ever mistake Escritor Auxis for a servant, especially not the humble sort, but she restrained herself. It was just the sort of thing she had scolded Simon for in the past. What was it about Auxis that brought out these childish resentments in her? "We all have the same interests, Your Eminence—" she said, "— you, His Sacredness, my husband, myself. We all want peace for our people."

After that conventional opening, Auxis clearly felt he had a grip on the situation again. He nodded and began a disquisition on the current state of affairs in Nabban, one that although it stuck more or less to the truth, played down the sins of House Ingadaris and played up the efforts of the Sancellan Aedonitis to find a solution. The fact that His Sacredness owed his position largely to his connection with Count Dallo, one of the main authors of the problems, was not a part of the escritor's summation—not that Miriamele had expected it would be.

Descriptions and counter-descriptions of the exact problems went on for the best part of an hour, couched in courteous language as befitted a meeting between Mother Church and the High Throne, but Miriamele could see that Escritor Auxis was already frustrated. He had expected an agreement to the lector's request for the king and queen to attend the wedding of Drusis and Turia Ingadaris as a matter of form only, and was dismayed by the idea he might actually have to bargain for it.

"I beg both Your Majesties' pardon," he said at last, "but we have talked half the day and I fear I do not understand whether or not you will answer His Sacredness regarding the counsel he has given you."

"If by 'counsel' you mean the Sacred Father's request that the High Throne give its blessing by attending the wedding, the answer is yes." She smiled. The escritor, relieved, smiled back. He was indeed a fine-looking man when he was in a good mood, Miriamele noted. She wondered if that would still be true when his mood changed. "It is most likely that the High Throne will be present at the wedding and will work with the feuding parties in Nabban to make peace."

"I am very pleased to hear that, Majesties," Auxis said, spreading his arms as if in benediction. "And I can assure you that our Sacred Father, Lector Vidian, will be pleased, too."

"Excellent." Miriamele squeezed Simon's hand beneath the table to let him know the time had come. He made a little snorting noise.

"You always think I'll say something to spoil things," he whispered.

"Shush, husband," she said, *"the fish is almost in the net."* She raised her voice. "And the High Throne will formally agree to the invitation as soon as His Sacredness grants us a few small kindnesses in turn that would please us very greatly."

The ordinary background of murmured asides and the skritch-skratch of pens on parchment suddenly ceased.

"Are you proposing that His Sacredness should. . . *strike a deal*?" said Auxis, making it sound like the sort of thing usually done in dark alleyways. All eyes now went from his pale, strained features to the queen.

"Surely not," Miriamele said. "The Blessed Patriarch has kindly offered us advice—his *counsel*, as you so neatly put it—to which we are giving very careful thought. And since we have this splendid opportunity, due to his so generously sending a high official of the church like yourself, we have some counsel *we* would like to tender in turn." Beside her, Simon did his best to stifle a laugh, but was not entirely successful. She squeezed his hand again, slightly harder this time.

"I know, *I know*," he said so that only she could hear.

It was all Auxis could do not to glare. He leaned and whispered something to his clerks, and when he turned back to the table, his expression had been wiped clean of all emotions except patient interest. "I would be very happy to hear what counsel the High King and Queen would offer to His Sacredness."

Miriamele's smile was a little tighter this time. "Very well. The High Queen and the High King suggest that we are overdue another escritor from the north. The last three have been from Nabban or Perdruin or the islands. Surely His Sacredness would not wish his northern flock to think we are forgotten by the Sancellan Aedonitis."

"Ah," said Auxis. "I see. And would you have a suggestion for the Blessed Father?"

"How about Archbishop Gervis?" proposed Simon, a little too abruptly for Miriamele's taste.

She closed her eyes and said a little prayer, then put on a pacific smile. "Yes, how about Gervis? The lector could raise no one to the synod we favor more. He is a man of high learning and high ideals."

Archbishop Gervis, caught by surprise, stared open-mouthed from his seat as at a holy miracle.

Auxis lifted an eyebrow in a finely calibrated gesture of bemusement. "Well, of course, the archbishop is held in great esteem by His Sacredness . . ."

"Good," said Simon. "That's settled, then." Securing an escritor's golden robe for Gervis had been the part that her loyal husband had most favored.

Auxis was clearly realizing that if his master only had to raise one northern archbishop to the Escritorial Synod, it was not much to give up. Some of the tension went out of his posture, and he even smiled and nodded at Gervis, who still looked flustered.

But all this means, Miriamele thought, *is that things must be worse in Nabban than we realized. Vidian would never let anyone dictate to him, not even us, if he did not need our help badly.* That gave her a bit of a chill, but she had set her course and could not slacken now.

"So," said Auxis, in the tone of someone about to make a summary speech, "if we have heard and satisfied the desires of our revered High Monarchs . . ."

"There is yet a bit more counsel from us, Your Eminence."

The escritor turned to her, and this time his eyes were wary. "Of course, Majesty. Forgive me for anticipating."

"As far as the visit itself," she said, "if a peace between two antagonistic parties is to be brokered, the lector himself must be part of the process. And that means he must show his support by a public embrace of both parties and an equally public promise to show no favoritism between the noble houses of Nabban in any matter in which the Church has discretion." Nabbanai lectors had a centuries-old history of partisanship in holy office, which had made the lectorship a prize worth uncountable riches. "The High Ward, of course, will stand behind—and enforce—the Sacred Father's promise."

The corner of the escritor's lip twitched. He had almost smiled. "Ah. A noble idea, Majesties. I cannot say for certain, of course, but I think His Sacredness might give his assent to such a suggestion." Which meant that Auxis believed business could continue as usual in Nabban, despite the High Ward inserting itself into the process.

We'll see about that, Miriamele thought. Aloud, she said, "And that agreement would be printed in a public document, posted and read out in the churches for all in Nabban to read and understand."

This annoyed the escritor, but he was growing better at hiding his irritation. "Of course, of course, Your Majesty. I can see no impediment. Now, I hope we can begin to plan for Your Majesties' visit."

"Excellent," she said. "We will be happy to plan the High Throne's presence at the wedding—and the other matters in Nabban, of course—as soon as we have evidence that the Blessed Father has agreed to implement our royal counsel."

This struck Auxis like a thunderbolt. For the first and only time, he stumbled over his words. Again, the room had gone silent. "But, Majesties! I . . ." He forced himself toward composure. "Your Majesties, surely I misunderstand you. It is a fortnight's voyage to Nabban, even by fast ship. The wedding is only a bit more than a month away. How can I possibly provide you with lector's agreement in time for you to make the journey?"

"Surely the Blessed Father did not send his legate without authority to make some decisions," she said sweetly. "But if these matters are beyond your remit, we will certainly understand, and wait patiently to hear the lector's reply. If we cannot journey to Nabban in time for the wedding, we will still be able to come and aid in negotiations between the unhappy factions."

For the first time, Auxis looked out of his depth, even lost. Miriamele could not help feeling what was doubtless a childish satisfaction at seeing this graceful, powerful man so flummoxed. "I do not know what to say, Majesties. I fully admit that His Sacredness is very, very anxious to have the two of you in Nabban—as I'm sure you are yourself, because of the importance of peace in your largest subject country—but all this, at this very late moment."

"The two of us?" Miriamele pretended surprise. "What do you mean?" She made a show of considering it. "Ah, I see. A misunderstanding, clearly. The use of the royal 'we' is often confusing to listeners. We are not both coming to Nabban, even when these matters of advice are settled. As rulers, we have been too often absent of late from our home here in Erkynland and especially the Hayholt. Only I will come to Nabban. King Seoman will remain here at the Hayholt."

"That's true," said Simon, and if he had argued long and hard against it, he did not show it now. "And I can tell you that if you mean to dispute that decision with Queen Miriamele, you would be better off saving your breath, Escritor."

Auxis could only stare. His clerks whispered among themselves, sounding like a brisk wind through long grass.

"So, if you would like to convey all this to the His Sacredness the Lector, Your Eminence, please feel free," Miriamele said. "The sooner the better, I assume. As you pointed out, time is short."

And then she rose, and Simon rose too, a bit belatedly. The courtiers all bowed their heads. Even Auxis, in his confusion, lowered his chin to his chest, although in his case it seemed more likely he was praying for patience.

For once, Miriamele was glad to be dressed in the full panoply of state. Her dress swished and rustled and her jewelry rattled most satisfyingly as she swept from the great hall.

48

The Little Boats

Morgan followed the torches of the Sithi as best he could, but as night came on the forest itself seemed to spring to life, doing its best to confuse and mock him. The wind rose. Trees thrashed and reached for him with twiggy fingers. Sometimes he almost thought he could see faces outlined in their bark by the flickering torchlight, angry faces that wanted him gone from the forest or dead. The near silence of twilight had been replaced by a chorus of night sounds, hoots and trills and the scratching of a thousand small things. And though Morgan did his best at first to keep some idea of direction in his head, the course the Sithi led them twisted so many times, with no sign of path, track, or landmark, that he quickly gave up.

"Where do you think they're taking us?" he asked after what seemed most of an hour's walk. Eolair only shook his head.

"We will learn," the count said. "The Sithi do not share their secrets freely, especially secrets about where they live. You should ask your grandfather some time about how he had to walk out of winter into summer to reach their settlement."

Which made no sense to Morgan at all but neither had most of his grandfather's tales about the Sithi.

So they marched on and on through the woods, guided by half-seen figures who never paused, and who seemed to know their route as clearly as if they walked across a familiar city in bright day. Morgan began to feel he was dreaming, that somewhere between the afternoon and this moment he had fallen into a deep sleep—that this was only the story his sleeping mind had chosen to tell him.

As a child, when Morgan had imagined the Sithi who figured in so many of his grandparents' solemn old stories, he had always thought of them as nearly insubstantial, like ghosts, beings that might appear and disappear in a shaft of moonlight, or materialize at the foot of one's bed to grant a wish. He had come later to understand that they were actual living creatures, but his childish notions had continued to lurk at the back of his thoughts. It had never occurred to him that they would be so *real*, with bodies and clothing and hard faces that seemed to examine and judge him. But every now and then he heard a quiet snatch of song, or saw one of them vault over an obstacle with the graceful power of a stag, and they suddenly became unknowably magical once more. But when he stumbled, and hands reached out of the darkness to keep him from falling, their touch was hard and impersonal, less like a parent guiding a child and more like a warder conducting a prisoner to his place of confinement.

As the journey wore on, Morgan grew more and more anxious, and with the anxiety came anger. Were he and Eolair ambassadors or prisoners?

At one point, when a beam of moonlight found its way through the tree canopy, he looked back and saw Tanahaya being carried on her litter. In the momentary wash of blue light her face seemed still and pale as a marble effigy, and it occurred to him that perhaps for the Sithi this march was something closer to a funeral procession. What would happen to Morgan and the count if the wounded Sitha-woman died? Would the fairy-folk blame them for what had happened to her?

Be brave, he told himself. *You are a prince. If you're not brave, what are you?*

Though their way still turned and twisted along paths that were invisible to him, Morgan could sense that they were now heading consistently uphill: his tired legs were working harder, and he could see the sky more often through the trees, with here and there a bright, welcome spatter of stars visible against the blackness.

The climb seemed to lead them on a spiral path up a large hill. Morgan could hear a stream flowing past, sometimes near to where they walked, sometimes more distant, so that he could barely make out its gurgling music. Once he had to jump across it, and again hands came out of the darkness to help him land safely.

As the trees became thinner he could finally see the peak of the hill that loomed above them, its jagged shape blocking the stars. They crossed the stream again, then crossed over it once more, and then suddenly the burning brands the leaders carried were all extinguished at once, leaving them in utter dark. Surprised, Eolair stopped, but Morgan did not realize it until he stumbled into him from behind.

"Walk forward, but with care," said the red-haired leader, Yeja'aro, as they untangled themselves. "We are passing into the hill through a crevice in the rock."

Morgan put his hand on the lord steward's back and blindly followed him. Someone reached out to guide them; he felt hands on each shoulder, and then a moment later a third hand pushing gently down on his head. This startled him so that he tried to shake it loose, but only managed to bang his skull against invisible stone.

"You will hurt yourself—the roof of the passage dips very low here. Let us help you." This voice spoke more kindly than Yeja'aro had. Morgan let himself be directed, although the complete darkness was daunting: every sightless step felt as though it might lead him over a precipice. It was all he could do simply to keep moving forward and trust to the spidery touch of the Sithi guiding him.

A few moments later Eolair gave a low cry. Morgan was alarmed, but also puzzled because the count's exclamation sounded strangely like joy. Two more hesitant steps and the prince walked out of the dark into the full glow of the stars, thousands upon thousands burning brightly all across the sky, candles in a church far greater than any human cathedral. Morgan was dazzled. Not only did the sky sparkle fiercely above their heads, but humbler lights burned all across the narrow pocket valley—dozens upon dozens of campfires.

Morgan stared at this spectacle, trying to make sense of it. Somehow they had climbed through a tunnel or crevice into a small valley nestling in the top of the blocky hill he had seen from below. As his eyes grew used to the light and the blaze of stars faded he saw that the valley was full of Sithi-folk. Many wore garments as crude and basic as those of Yeja'aro's band, while others were wrapped in shimmering cloth that fluttered even in this still place like the sails of ships running before the wind.

A few of the Sithi turned to look at the newcomers, but none of them seemed alarmed or even perturbed: their large eyes settled on Morgan and the count, then turned to other things. The prince stared back, heart beating hard and fast, his fear turned almost entirely to wonder. He could hear odd, faint music coming to him from more than one spot in the valley, pipes and singing voices, and some of the figures farther up the slopes were dancing together, graceful as birds in flight. As the music and movement swirled around him like blossoms blown from the trees, the fairy stories of his childhood came back to him with all their force; in that moment, he could easily imagine a man being lured away by the Sithi-folk to live a hundred years in one night.

"Ah, yes," said Eolair, but from his tone it wasn't clear whether he was speaking to the prince or to the empty air. "I *do* remember. Oh, I remember . . ."

They might have stood there for an hour, content merely to experience this unexpected, wild beauty, but suddenly a shape appeared before them.

"You will come with me," said Yeja'aro. "*Prince* Jiriki is not here, but the . . . *princess* . . . will want to see you." He gave the word a curious, angry emphasis.

The Sitha led them up the rocky path himself, winding between the fires; this time, when Morgan or the count stumbled, nobody reached out to help them. Dozens of Sithi watched the pair of them, curiously incurious as cats, as they climbed the slope toward a single large fire burning in a pit that had been dug at the top of a mounded grass meadow, not far from one of the valley's steep walls. A single white-haired figure sat beside the fire. Her garment was full and loose, covering her body entirely from the neck down, and Morgan thought she must be some respected elder of the Sithi-folk.

Grandfather talked of the Sithi's First Grandmother, didn't he? But he seemed to remember that one had died in some terrible attack.

As they drew closer and he could see the Sitha-woman's face more clearly, he decided that not only was she much younger than the color of her hair had led him to believe, she was also one of the most beautiful creatures he had ever seen.

They had almost reached the fire when she finally looked up at them. A small, almost secretive smile curled at the edge of her mouth, and her wide eyes caught the light, glowing. Her skin seemed the same shade as the flames, as though she and the fire were part of the same thing.

"So," she said. "I had a feeling."

"Aditu, I found them at the forest's edge," Yeja'aro said, his voice less harsh than it had been. Morgan thought he almost sounded apologetic. "They carry Ti-tuno. It was the horn we heard, in truth."

When she smiled again, Morgan did not know whether he wanted to marry her on the spot or crawl into her arms and let her gently rock him to sleep. "Yes. I knew it was Ti-tuno," she said. "I can never forget when I last heard it sounding, before Asu'a." She smiled. "Count Eolair, my heart is glad to see you. It has been so long!"

"Lady Aditu." Eolair sounded as though he might weep. "Much longer for me than for you, it seems. You have not changed."

She smiled again. "Ah, but I have, as you will discover. Still, handsome boys become distinguished men—I would know you anywhere. Come, sit. And, speaking of handsome boys, who is this young one? I think I know him, but I would be told."

Morgan realized his mouth was open but was doing nothing useful. "I am Prince Morgan," he said, but it sounded strange and impolite, by itself. "My lady Aditu—Princess—I give you greetings from my grandparents."

"Yes," she said, as if he had asked a question. "Oh, yes. In the midst of such sadness, it is good to see the face of old friends again, even at several removes."

Morgan was still staring. He knew he shouldn't, but in that moment he couldn't imagine looking at anything or anyone else.

"We have much to discuss," Count Eolair began, but Aditu lifted her hand to forestall him.

"Not now, old friend. You have walked far, and walked the Sithi's ways at that, which are even more tiring." She turned to Yeja'aro, who had been standing silently by. "What of Tanahaya?"

Yeja'aro's narrow face was grim. "She is very ill. These *Sudhoda'ya* say she has been poisoned. She is with the healers now."

"Bring me word as soon as they know anything." Aditu turned back to the count. "And now you two must sleep. My brother will return tomorrow and all that must be said will be said then. Eolair, it is good to see you again, against all the world's chances. Morgan, this meeting means more to me than you can know."

"Come," said Yeja'aro, while Morgan was still puzzling out her liquid, lightly accented Westerling. He and Eolair let themselves be led away from the fire. Morgan looked back and saw that the woman named Aditu had again lowered her chin to her chest, contemplating the flames as though reading a beloved old book, a familiar but still instructive companion.

Morgan was exhausted. Suddenly the night seemed to be sagging in on top of him, and it was all he could do to put one foot after the other as Yeja'aro led them along the side of the valley to a place that had been prepared for them, two beds of moss in a frame of sticks, each with a blanket thin as a whisper, made of a slippery, cool substance that to Morgan's weary mind felt like a moth's wing looked.

Neither he nor Eolair spoke after they climbed into their beds. For all its near-insubstantiality, Morgan's blanket was very warm. He watched a patch of stars slowly spinning across the sky above his head, a wheel of lights that he thought he should recognize but didn't—just one more strangeness of this very strange day. Then, after only a very short time of listening to the sweet, strange sound of Sithi voices singing to each other across the pocket valley, he fell into a deep sleep.

Eolair had to work hard to wake the prince. Morgan complained bitterly, keeping his eyes tightly closed as though some horrifying demon stood over him instead of the Count of Nad Mullach. Eolair had only the dimmest recollection of himself at the prince's age; a few sharp memories like mountain peaks piercing a haze, but he did not believe he had ever been allowed to sleep until he woke on his own. His father, the old count, had regarded rising with the dawn to say prayers to the gods as part of a noble's duties. And Eolair's fretful, quiet mother had hardly ever seemed to sleep at all.

"Come, Highness." He gave the prince a harder shake. "Aditu's brother Jiriki has returned, and we must speak to our hosts. The sun is in the sky. Rouse yourself, please."

Morgan gave Eolair a slit-eyed stare and a frowning look meant to shame him. Instead, the lord steward laughed.

"Come. Sit up, Highness. I have brought you something to eat."

The prince reached out blindly, then hesitated when he felt what Eolair had put in his hand. He peered at it suspiciously. "What is it?"

"Bread, of a sort. Flavored with honey. It's quite nice. And there's a stream of fresh water just below the rise, over there."

"We're really here," Morgan said a moment later with his mouth full, looking around him. "With the Sithi. I didn't think it would feel like this. It's so strange . . . !" But this home of theirs was not anything as grand as Morgan had imagined—that was certain.

"It has been more than thirty years since I first saw the Peaceful Ones up close," Eolair said, "and I am still astonished each time."

While the young prince tended to his morning needs, the count sat on a toppled tree in the warm sun and watched the morning life of the Sithi camp.

It was both a smaller and less organized gathering than the Zida'ya war camp he had visited all those years ago outside Hernysadharc. At first glance everything seemed chaotic, with exotic figures coming and going from the small valley and many others engaged in quiet work, although Eolair could not always guess what they were truly doing. By daylight he could see that the hill and its hidden valley stood high above the surrounding Aldheorte. Anyone down among the forest trees would find it almost impossible to see even the valley's campfires at night, because the trees and the bulk of the hill would hide their glow.

"It seems only days since I saw you last, Eolair of Nad Mullach," someone said behind him.

Eolair turned to see Jiriki standing a short distance away at the top of the rise. His hair was long and white, like his sister's, but like her he did not look an hour older than at their last meeting. "Days to you, perhaps," the count told him. "To me, it has been a weary length of years. But whatever the length of time, it is good to see you again, Jiriki i-Sa'onserei. I heard you and your company return just before first light. I heard them singing."

"We came a long distance," the Sitha said, then sprang down the hillside as lightly as a deer. He reached Eolair's side in a moment, and looked him over with a slight frown. "Your face shows pain. Have you been wounded?"

Eolair smiled. "No—well, yes, I was, but that is not the cause of my discomfort now. My hip aches. It is what happens when we mortals age—our bodies do not last as long as our wits."

Jiriki's face remained serious. "I wish that were true for all your folk, but some appear to lose their wits very young, or never to have them at all." He shook his head; his fine hair, caught by a morning breeze, momentarily obscured his features. Something about Jiriki *was* different, Eolair thought, but not in the way he looked. He was being kind and courteous, but the count could feel a subtle chill in his manner. He would never claim to understand the Sithi well, or to be able to read their thoughts in their faces, but he had been a servant of many mortal rulers and had bargained in many courts in many lands; he recognized the signs that something was wrong.

"How is the woman we brought—Tanahaya, if I have her name right?" Eolair asked. "Our mortal healers did all they could for her, I promise you. If you remember the Wrannaman Tiamak, he and his wife struggled to save her in every way they knew."

Jiriki nodded slowly. "I can tell. And they have my gratitude for that. It is hard to say whether she will survive." He looked down the rise to where Morgan knelt, scooping water out of a stream and drinking deeply. As they both watched, the youth dunked his red-gold head into the water, then pulled it out again with a gasp of shock.

"Bloody Tree, that's cold!" he shouted.

"And is this truly the grandson of Seoman and Miriamele?" Jiriki asked.

"No, do not answer. I can see them both in him, bones and breath. What an awkward creature Simon was when I first met him!"

"I thought the same," said Eolair. "But there was always more to him than showed on the surface. Miriamele too. I suspect it will also prove true with the grandson."

"We may hope." Something in his tone made Eolair look at him again, trying to fathom what might lurk behind the placid, high-cheekboned face. "Bring the young prince back to the fire circle when you are ready," Jiriki said at last. "There is much to talk about. Not all will be to your liking—or mine, for that matter—but this has waited too long already."

Jiriki turned away, leaving Eolair to wonder what he meant, but fearing the answer.

As he led Morgan up the slope toward the fire circle, Eolair was surprised to see that a fire burned in the wide pit even on this bright, warm summer morning. Several Sithi waited there, including Aditu, who sat beside the fire as if she hadn't moved since the previous night. This time she wore a long, hooded robe dyed in many shades of blue, from pale sky to deep near-violet, modest garments completely different from the way Eolair remembered her dressing in the past— something he had never forgotten, even after so many years. In fact, every occasion on which he had met with Aditu no'e-Sa'onserei remained nearly whole and perfect in his mind. It was not just her golden beauty that made her memorable, although she was very beautiful, even to one who was not of her kind, but the lightness of her spirit—light as smoke, light as drifting ash. To be with her was to feel an odd peace. It was only after the last time they had met that Eolair had realized that Aditu seemed to have no fear whatsoever. To be in her presence, even in the most frightsome times, was to find a light in a dark place.

As they approached her, Eolair also remembered that Aditu had told him the night before that she had changed, but other than her more decorous clothing, he could see nothing different from the first time he had seen her, near the end of the Storm King's War. So what could she have meant?

Almost as if she heard his thoughts, Aditu turned and smiled. She was the only Sithi the count of Nad Mullach had ever met whose smile seemed as natural and reassuring as a mortal's, and by the undemonstrative standards of her people, Aditu smiled often and broadly. As they approached she stood up, and in doing so, let fall her blue-hued robe. Beneath it she was dressed more like the old days Eolair remembered, partly naked like a child and unconcerned with the discomfort it created for mortals. But that belly of hers, that round, golden belly as big as a sugar melon, was something decidedly new.

Eolair stumbled a little and was furious with himself, afraid that it would look like the feebleness of age. Aditu was with child. What did that mean? Did it have any bearing on the years of silence between the Sithi and the Hayholt?

By the time they reached the fire pit she had pulled on a short, flimsy jerkin that covered her down to her hips, making it a bit easier for Eolair to look at her without feeling discourteous. He took her hand in his, as he wished he had done the previous night, and brushed it with his lips.

"It is good for my heart to see you again, Lady Aditu," he said. "Or is it 'Princess'?"

"You should not call me that, Eolair," she said, but her tone was gentle. "It is not a word we use or even truly an idea that we have. That was only a bit of Yeja'aro's unhappiness coming out."

The way she said it, the suggestion that she apologized for Yeja'aro, caught Eolair's attention: it seemed he meant something to her. Could he be the father of her child? Eolair realized he knew almost nothing of how the Sithi dealt with such things. Did they marry? "Then at your insistence," he said, "but to my pleasure, it will be Aditu and Eolair." He smiled, simply because looking at her again after all these years made him want to smile. "It was good to see Jiriki, too. I thought he was going to join us here."

"We will see him very soon. But, as always, there are things that must be done, my good Eolair, and they must be done certain ways. You understand that, I think?"

"I think I understand that as well as any mortal man alive," he said, and laughed at the truth of it. "I have lived most of my life waiting for things to be done in their certain ways, in every capital in every country. As I look back, I marvel at how much ceremony I have endured without going mad."

"Our ceremonies are very different than yours," Aditu began, then interrupted herself. "Oh! Please, Prince Morgan, I ask your pardon. Count Eolair is an old friend and my heart was very full. It made me forget my manners! Welcome to H'ran Go-jao, the most easterly of the Go-jao'e."

"Go . . . jow . . .?" said Morgan.

Eolair suspected the prince was repeating the word so slowly not because he was particularly interested in it, but because he was fascinated with Aditu and a bit befuddled by her. It showed that the young man had good judgement in at least one respect, anyway.

"*Go-jao'e*—little boats," Aditu explained. "You will learn about them soon, I think, but now I see my brother waving to us. Come!" She sprang to her feet so nimbly despite her large belly that Eolair could only smile again. "I think that you, of all people, Count Eolair, are a person who understands ceremony, and the difference between those which are empty or only for show, and those which have true meaning."

"I'd like to think I do, my lady."

Aditu smiled. "So formal! Remember, we are to dispense with such things. In any case, now that my brother is ready, I think that it would be fitting for you to see our mother again."

"Likimeya?" He would never forget Jiriki's and Aditu's fierce parent, although even in memory, the leader of the Sithi still made him uneasy. "Of course. I would be grateful for the chance to pay my respects."

"Then you shall have it. Prince Morgan, you come too." Aditu placed herself between them, took the prince's arm and Eolair's, and moved toward Jiriki, who waited beside a wide crevice in the tumbled rocks of the hillside. When he saw them coming, Jiriki ducked back through the opening.

"They will be confused by you," Aditu warned them as they approached the crevice. "Do not be startled."

"Your pardon, lady," Eolair asked, "but who are are 'they'?" The black crack before him looked like the entrance to one of the old hill-tombs on the eastern part of Nad Mullach, tombs the local inhabitants claimed went back to Hern's day, in the Dawn of Time.

Aditu did not answer his question. "Do not be startled," she repeated.

She stepped ahead as they approached the opening and led them into the crevice. Eolair had only just ducked his head to follow her when suddenly the air seemed to burst into a thousand mad pieces around him. He would have shouted in surprise but so many flying things filled the air he feared they would get into his mouth. He stumbled back from the opening and the cloud of fluttering shapes followed him out, gushing past him like beer frothing out of a tumbled barrel.

Butterflies, he realized after the first few overwhelming instants. As the insects burst out into the sun they exploded into color—blue, brilliant orange, red and sunflower yellow, thousands upon thousands of butterflies all surging around and upward in a great maelstrom of shimmering wings. Beside him, Prince Morgan had stumbled backward and was now sitting on his rump, staring at the cloud as it seethed and fluttered all around them, filling the air so that Eolair could see little else. At last the creatures began to settle on the naked rock of the valley's edge and in every tree and shrub.

"Brynioch's rainbow!" said Eolair. It was not merely an oath, but also a description. On the ground beside him, Morgan goggled like a drunkard who had mistaken a second-floor window for a door.

"Come inside." Aditu's voice had an echo now.

Eolair moved forward once more, careful not to step on any of the bright gleams of color now gently fanning their wings on the ground around the entrance. After a moment, Morgan climbed to his feet and followed, but his face was pale and his progress cautiously slow. Eolair reached back and gently took the prince's arm, pretending it was to steady himself.

When he had stepped through the entrance and could lift his head, the count found himself in a wide but low cavern, dark except for an open shaft that let daylight fall through the irregular stone ceiling. All together the irregular chamber was not much larger than his own bedroom back in Nad Mullach, a beloved place he had not visited in a long time, and for which he now felt a sudden, fierce longing. He felt Morgan flinch, but kept his grip on the prince's arm. This time it was not only to steady the boy, but himself as well.

At the center of the small chamber lay a figure wrapped from head to foot in something like the kind of linen bandages in which the funeral priests of

Erkynland wrapped their kings and queens for burial. Only the face was exposed—a face he recognized as that of Jiriki and Aditu's mother, Likimeya, though her features seemed as still and lifeless as one of the statues from Nabban's Age of Gold.

"By all the gods, what is this?" he asked, his voice quiet yet raw, even to his own ears. "She is dead?"

Jiriki, who waited beside his mother's recumbent form, looked up. His face still had the same cold stillness Eolair had seen that morning. "No. Our mother sleeps the Long Sleep, but she is not dead. She has slept for a long time, though— for years—without recovering, and we do not harbor much hope she will ever wake again."

"Recovering?" Eolair let go of Morgan's arm and kneeled beside the shrouded figure. A few butterflies still remained on the cavern's walls; a few more walked delicately across Likimeya's body, slowly flexing their wings, seeming to burst into color once more whenever they crossed the shaft of falling sunlight that knifed down from the chamber's roof. When Eolair drew a little closer he could see that Likimeya was wrapped not in bandages but in layer after layer of some shining white thread, an unimaginable length of the stuff. He saw the butterflies pick their way across her sleeping form and had a sudden idea who had actually shrouded Likimeya for this strange sort of entombment. "What happened to her?"

Jiriki gave him a sharp look, as though he had said something odd, then turned away. "She was shot with an arrow in the heart."

"Murhagh's Red Eye! Who did this?"

Aditu stepped forward, but her gaze did not leave her mother's expressionless face. "We do not know for certain, except that the murderers were mortals."

"Mortals?" The count was horrified. For a time he could only stare at Likimeya's wan, golden face. "You say 'murderers,'" he said at last, "but she has not died. The gods willing, perhaps she will still recover and identify those who attacked her so they can be punished."

"They will still be murderers," said Jiriki, his voice quiet but hard as the crypt's stone walls. "They killed eleven more of our folk. Only our mother and one other survived the attack."

"Oh, gods, no." Eolair could not stare at Likimeya's empty face any longer. "No. Tell me what happened."

"We will, but not here," said Aditu. "The Yásira—this gathering place— belongs to our mother now. We will not sully it with any more talk of the cowardly beasts who attacked her."

As they moved toward the cavern's entrance, Eolair saw a few butterflies drifting back in. He thought nothing of it at first, but then had to hang back for a moment as a handful more, then dozens, flew back in.

Jiriki said something sharp to Aditu in their own musical tongue. Butterflies streamed back into the cavern in force now, circling the count's head, filling the spaces between floor and ceiling. But where was Prince Morgan? Eolair turned in sudden apprehension and saw him standing beside Likimeya's body, staring down at her with sickened fascination, an expression he had never seen the prince wear. "Morgan! Come away," he called. More and more butterflies were returning to the cavern, making it harder to see past the glimmer and shadow of their wings.

The prince said something Eolair could not hear.

"What? Come away!"

Morgan spoke louder this time. "She is trying to talk—!"

Jiriki sprang across the room and crouched beside his mother's body. "Rabbit, come to me!" he cried. "It is true."

Aditu hurried to join him. "But she has not spoken since she was first struck down, since she survived the first fever!"

Eolair too moved closer. He could see Likimeya's face moving in her silken shroud, but barely, as though a mere tremor of dream made its way to the surface. Aditu leaned very close and put her hand on her mother's breastbone, then put her ear next to Likimeya's mouth. For a moment she remained, listening intently. Then at last Aditu straightened and stood up. She curled her hands around her belly as if to protect the child within, and again spoke to her brother in their own language.

"Could you understand what your mother said?" Eolair asked her.

"*I* could," said Morgan, to the count's utter astonishment. The youth looked as though his entire world had just turned downside-up; his eyes were wide and shocked, his face pale as parchment. "I could understand her, I swear! I heard it in my head! She said, '*All the voices lie except the one that whispers. And that one will steal away the world.*'" The prince had an expression Eolair had not seen before, one of complete and frightened confusion.

Jiriki and his sister both stared at Morgan, then at each other. After an achingly long pause, Aditu turned back to Count Eolair, her face unusually blank.

"Our mother is silent again," she announced. "I do not think she will speak more. We should go from this place. We have much that is new to think about—and you two still have much to learn about all that has happened between our peoples."

Morgan could hardly feel his feet as he walked, or his head either. He might have been a smoldering flake of ash borne aloft by a fire, something lighter than air, drifting without choice or thought. The Sitha-woman's voice had echoed in his head as though she somehow spoke from inside him—as though her words had made their way out of the marrow of his own treacherous bones. He had never felt anything like it and never wanted to feel such a thing again.

Count Eolair and the other two Sithi were talking busily but quietly. At any other time Morgan would have resented the way they kept their words from him, but at this precise instant he felt poured full as a pitcher whose contents would overspill if even one single drop was added.

"But what could she have meant by that?" Eolair asked.

"If we knew, I promise we would tell you what we could," Aditu said. "As it is, we must consider this strange, unexpected message, and we must also speak to others of our people." She wrapped her arms around her belly as they walked through the forest. "Our mother spoke much in the first days after the attack, as she struggled against the poisonous fever that threatened to consume her, but it was mostly meaningless—thoughts and memories torn loose by her deadly wound and the illness it brought."

"You say poisonous." Eolair was a little short of breath; Morgan could see that the pace was not easy for him. "Could it be anything like the envoy who was attacked—Tanahaya? She said she was poisoned too."

"That is a question to be pondered," said Jiriki. "But it is a painful, difficult subject, as I fear you will learn."

"In any case, our mother has been silent since it happened," Aditu resumed—rather quickly, Morgan thought, as though she wished to avoid any more talk about the envoy just now, "as she was when you first saw her today in the Yásira. Why she should choose that precise moment to break her silence, as well as the meaning of her words—and yes, young Prince Morgan heard the same strange warning that I heard, although in some different fashion, because the words we heard were in the tongue of the Zida'ya—I'm afraid that is also beyond our understanding at this moment."

"But I fear I only have more questions for you," Eolair said. "Questions my king and queen desperately want to have answered. What has happened to your people in these last years? Why have you been silent so long?"

"We cannot speak of it yet," Jiriki told him, and would not explain further.

After the strange events in the butterfly cavern, Aditu, Jiriki, and several more Sithi had prepared quickly, almost feverishly, for a journey, gathering up water and food for Morgan and Eolair, as well as a few blankets and other things. As soon as the preparations were completed the small group—perhaps a dozen in all—had set out. Morgan thought they had been walking for at least an hour now, but was not quite sure. In fact, he was not quite sure of anything at the moment, except that the world was far stranger than he had ever guessed, stranger even than he had suspected when he looked down into the shadows of Hjeldin's Tower and saw what he felt certain (but still did not want to believe) had been the red priest Pyrates' restless, murderous spirit.

Is this what Grandfather means when he says you never know you're in a story? Am I in a story?

The Aldheorte itself seemed different to Morgan now, older and deeper than the parts he had traversed before. The shadows seemed darker too, the moments of sun less frequent. Even the trees and other vegetation seemed to huddle closer together, as if for protection.

The Sithi, though, seemed not to notice, and it certainly didn't slow them any. Jiriki walked so quickly it almost seemed like running, and his sister, despite her bulging belly, had no problem keeping up with him. But the one called Yeja'aro was the most agile of all, and also seemed in the greatest hurry. Morgan had the feeling that if Yeja'aro could have whipped them into greater speed, he would have. Not that anyone but another of his own folk could have kept up with him: at one point, while the rest trotted down into and then up out of a small canyon, Yeja'aro simply leapt from one side of the little valley to the other, dozens of paces away—an astonishing feat that none of Yeja'aro's kin seemed to notice. Meanwhile, the mortal prince and the aged lord steward had to scramble over obstacles their companions seemed barely to notice.

Yeja'aro kept looking back to Aditu and her brother. Morgan could guess nothing of Sithi feelings by their faces, but there was something noteworthy just in the frequency with which the red-haired Sitha watched the siblings. Something complicated seemed to be going on there—love, anger, hatred, perhaps all three. Whatever it was, though, was strong; Morgan felt certain about that.

At last, he caught up to Aditu (or more likely, he knew, she slowed down for him) but he was too daunted to ask about the things he had been wondering. Instead, when he had mustered enough breath, he asked, "Where are we going?"

"To T'seya Go-jao," she said. "Another of the little boats, as we call these more humble dwellings. Your grandfather saw Jao é-Tinukai'i, the Boat on the Ocean of trees, the greater refuge from which all the little boats came."

"What direction is that? Because Eolair said he thought we were traveling west—back in the direction he and I first came."

"That is true, more or less."

"But then the sun should be in our eyes, at least when we can see it through all these bloody trees. It has to be far past noon and the sun's been on the back of my neck for an hour!"

She adjusted her pace a little to match his. "Hm. Did your grandfather ever teach you to play *shent*?"

"He tried." In truth, it had been one of the most frustrating things Morgan could remember. The game had far too many pieces, or at least the pieces had too many names, and the contest seemed to have no rules that made sense. Instead it was full of useless directions such as, "Consider the point from which you started," or "Follow the wind." In the few times he had played with King Simon he had won only once and did not understand why, except that a bored, blatant attempt at cheating on his part had made his grandfather laugh. The memory brought a pang of discomfort and anger. "I could never do it right."

"It is about different ways of thinking. That is why I asked. Yes, the sun is on your neck. Yes, we are traveling west. Some things are more slippery than you think they are." She reached out and patted his arm, her touch light as a bird's wing, then sped her pace again. Morgan could only struggle to keep up.

★   ★   ★

What seemed a good part of the afternoon had passed when they finally reached a quiet lake hidden among the trees, a blue gem darker than the sky. Sithi dressed in pale green and gray waited there, tending a tiny harbor complete with what looked to Morgan like a very flimsy dock and several flatboats made of woven willow branches.

Morgan, Eolair, and all the Sithi climbed into one of the boats and were soon poling themselves silently across the lake. On the far side they slipped into a hidden river where Morgan had seen nothing but reeds, then made their way up it for some time. At last they began to pass strange structures made of willow branches and thorns that had been raised on both banks, like defensive walls but impossibly fragile. As they moved farther upstream the walls occasionally rose to join over the top of the water, so that he and his fellow passengers seemed to float through tunnels of gray wood and black thorn. Not long after that, Morgan began to notice more Sithi crouching behind these structures, watching their boat pass from expressionless golden eyes. Most of these wore colorful wooden or bone armor. Their spears and swords did not seem made from metal either, but Morgan felt sure from the cold faces watching them pass that the weapons would prove as deadly as any steel.

At last they came to a wide place in the river with a willow-wood dock and an enclosure beside it on one side that was roofed with an even more complicated arrangement of willow limbs thatched with broad leaves. A figure stood on the dock as if it had waited there years just for this moment. As they drew closer, Morgan could see this was another Sitha, with the same blaze of red hair as Yeja'aro. He wore no helm, but was armored in pale green painted wood, with a sword hanging in a scabbard on his belt. Something about his face seemed unusual, but Morgan was still too far away to make out what it was. At least a dozen Sithi warriors stood behind him in attitudes of calm expectancy.

"S'hue Khendraja'aro!" called Jiriki as he leaped lightly from the boat to the dock. "I see you have heard of our coming. We left H'ran Go-jao quiet and secure."

"You have brought mortals," said the red-haired Sitha, his arms crossed on his chest. Hearing the harshness in his words, Morgan thought that this man and Yeja'aro had more in common than just the color of their hair, their thin, prominent noses, and their high brows. Could this one be Yeja'aro's brother? Father? Morgan had already learned from quiet conversation with Count Eolair that it was nearly impossible to guess a Sitha's age.

Aditu helped Eolair from the boat to the dock, then stepped across herself, nimble as a squirrel leaping from one thin branch to another. The other Sithi followed, but did not move forward to greet or mingle with those on the dock. Morgan wondered what that meant. Something invisible seemed to hang between them, as if these two groups, all but identical to Morgan's eyes, were somehow from quite different tribes.

Jiriki turned to Morgan and Eolair. "S'hue Khendraja'aro is our mother's brother."

"More importantly," said Khendraja'aro, "I am the Protector of the Zida'ya."

Now that he was closer, Morgan could see that the protector's face was scarred. Something had cut him from the left edge of his mouth up almost to his cheekbone, and it had not healed well. Not only did the scar give him a persistent and disturbing half-smile, but at the top end it pulled his eyelid down into a squint.

"We have news, Khendraja'aro," said Aditu.

The red-haired Sitha raised his hand. "And this news meant you thought it appropriate to bring mortals here? To *me?*"

"We did what—" was all Jiriki had a chance to say before Khendraja'aro interrupted him, taking a step toward Count Eolair.

"Know that it is only the old alliance between my people and yours, Hernystirman, that prevents me from killing you both on the spot." His voice was not loud, but something hard in it carried right to Morgan's ear, like a shout. "As it is, honor demands that you two be allowed to leave this place. But that is all. Whatever knowledge you seek, whatever bargain you hope for, it is denied before you even ask. Now go, leave this forest now, or even the old, hallowed memory of your noble Sinnach and the battle of Ereb Irigú, when our people fought together, will not save your miserable lives."

49

Blood as Black as Night

Jarnulf and the Hikeda'ya had climbed well beyond Urmsheim's broad skirts, but although they had been pulling themselves upward for days now, until even the tallest of the nearby peaks lay below them, the bulk of the great mountain still towered high above.

"We shall have to go roped together soon," he said as they rested at the end of a hard day's labor, deep in a vertical crevice in the rocky mountain face.

"I decide what we do or do not do," Makho told him. The wounds the Norn chieftain had received at the hands of the Skalijar had made him even colder and more unpleasant. Jarnulf did not have the strength for an argument, though or even for a shrug. For the hundredth time, he wished he could have encountered the chieftain alone in the wilderness, so that he could have treated with the cold-eyed murderer as he deserved. He had been traveling with the Hikeda'ya so long now that sometimes he actually forgot what they had done to him, how much he loathed them all.

The crevice where they sheltered was deep enough that Jarnulf actually had room to lie down. He had long believed himself all but impervious to heights and cold, but was now wishing that he could just stay here in this place and never move again. His legs and arms throbbed from the day's effort so that he did not think he could fall asleep, and he knew that at first light their climb would begin again. The only small solace was that Makho and the other Hikeda'ya had agreed it would be safer to climb in daylight, since there was little fear of their mission being discovered now that they had traveled so far above the world.

Aching and exhausted, Jarnulf himself no longer had any true idea of what he was doing here. His great goal, his sworn purpose, had not changed, but this seemed more and more like an almost ridiculously bad way to go about achieving it.

I should have stuck to killing them off in ones and twos. Not only did it give me a certain pleasure, but I also had a lifelong vocation. Now I have risked everything on a single throw of the dice, all or nothing. Father would not have approved.

But was that true? Father had been cautious by nature, but he had also often said, *"God does not lean down to give us His hand, whatever the Church may say. He waits for us to climb as close as we can to Him first."* Certainly Jarnulf was doing as much climbing as even God could wish, but the rest of his motivations had become obscure to him, lost in the day-to-day ordinariness of traveling, even traveling with the hated Hikeda'ya. And there was Nezeru . . .

What was it about the halfblood woman that puzzled and fascinated him so? It was nothing so simple as attraction, he had told himself many times—his devotion to God and his loathing of her kind assured him of that. But he had come to care about her in some way he did not completely understand, perhaps because he saw in her unthinking slogans and stunted emotions another victim of Hikeda'ya slavery. Or perhaps because she was young he could still sense something of what she could be, before the cold, cruel ways of Nakkiga froze her forever. Whatever the case, Jarnulf could not deny the truth of his feelings. In moments of daydream he even imagined sparing her alone, out of all of them, and bringing her into the hands of a loving God—something she had never known and, without the intercession of Jarnulf White Hand, would never glimpse.

Despite his immense size, Goh Gam Gar was by far the best climber of them all, especially now that his hands were free. The Norns were graceful, agile, and sure, but the great, leathery pads on the giant's hands and feet gripped the icy stone, and his strength was so great that he could even lift his own massive weight with a single one of his arms. In fact, the monster seemed almost happy to be exercising his skills this way, although it was hard to tell with such an evil-tempered creature; the only other time he showed good cheer was when one of his companions hurt themselves.

Captors, Jarnulf reminded himself, *not companions*. Foul creature that he was, the monster still had less choice about being on this expedition than Jarnulf did. As Makho never ceased pointing out, there had been more than a few opportunities when he could have deserted the White Foxes, but the giant did not have that freedom.

Why was the giant with them? Did the Norns really think even such a huge creature was enough to defeat a dragon? And what would they do with a dragon if they found one? Makho had said they wanted its blood, but that made no sense to Jarnulf. Not to mention that no dragon was going to give its blood up without a fight—a deadly fight.

Prevented from escaping by the witchwood collar and the queen's gem, Goh Gam Gar ranged far ahead of the rest of the company now, seeking out the best routes and clearing dangerous obstacles by sheer might. Makho never let him out of sight for long, though, perhaps fearing a sudden giant-caused avalanche. The only consistent noise on the mountainside other than the crunch of snow and the hiss of breath the climbers made were the arguments between the giant and Makho on those occasions when the chieftain used a lashing of pain to summon the giant back.

Late in the afternoon, Makho shouted for Goh Gam Gar to return for perhaps the dozenth time that day, but this time the giant did not appear. After a few moments Makho took the crystal from its pouch and held it up, murmuring the words that Akhenabi had taught him. A roar of pain and fury drifted to them, but the giant did not return. Makho raised the crystal rod again, and once more Goh Gam Gar bellowed in rage but still did not reappear.

His face rigid with anger, Makho had raised the crystal a third time when Nezeru said, "Don't."

"Do you dare to give me orders, Blackbird? Your condition has made you foolish."

Jarnulf wasn't certain what that meant, but for a moment he was certain Makho would hit her, perhaps even knock her from the narrow path. In that complicated instant, as he tried to decide what he would do, Nezeru told their leader, "Perhaps the giant has fallen, or something has fallen upon him. Would it not be better to see what has happened before we torture the brute any further?"

Saomeji the Singer nodded his head. "I think she is right, Chieftain Makho. If nothing else, in his agony he might destroy what little path there is on this treacherous mountain. If you like, I will go first."

"No. The Blackbird will go." Makho's tone made it clear that there would be no further discussion.

Nezeru took the lead as nimbly as any of the pureblood Hikeda'ya. Just watching her scramble up the sloping, narrow path around the looming mountainside, nothing visible below her but fog and remorseless, empty space, made Jarnulf, despite his own well-honed skills, feel as clumsy as a fat householder.

She had only just vanished from sight when the rest of the Hand heard her call in fear and excitement for them to hurry. Kemme and Makho both drew their swords, but Jarnulf decided to wait and see what manner of challenge awaited them before surrendering the use of one of his hands.

The path was broken where Nezeru was stopped, but only a small part of it was gone, and it would be easy enough for any of them to jump to the rest of the path on other side. Since he could see no sign of the giant, Jarnulf assumed that was what Goh Gam Gar had done. As he drew closer, though, he understood why Nezeru had stopped. It was not just the path that had collapsed: a wide piece of the mountain below had slid down as well, leaving a jumble of boulders and broken tree trunks marking the place where the track had been. It also meant that something below had stopped the slide from continuing down the mountain. What that something might be was made clear a moment later, when Goh Gam Gar's harsh voice boomed up from the cluttered, wedge-shaped fall of trees, rocks, and snow.

"By the queen herself, if one of you cowardly little bugs doesn't get down here and help me, I'll pull the whole mountain out from under you!"

"Look!" said Nezeru, kneeling on the path near the place where the slide had collapsed it. "The giant is just down there. Not too far. Wedged in by broken trunks."

Makho was staring at the tumble of rocks and wood, his face set in an unhappy smirk. "And what are we to do, monster?" he shouted down, his mockery tinged with disgust. "Lean over and pull you out?"

"No, you fool!" the giant bellowed. "Climb down and get my rope. If you tie it around something strong enough up there, I can free myself."

"We should let the ugly creature die," said Kemme.

Makho had probably been considering just that, but he scowled at Kemme's words. "I told you, we will need him. You, mortal—climb down and do what he says."

Jarnulf was too surprised at first to be angry. "But I'm the worst climber of any of us!"

"You are also the least useful. Go."

Jarnulf briefly considered the odds, but Makho and Kemme had their blades drawn. For all his skills, he knew the chance he could take both Norns on a slippery mountain path were unimaginably small, even if neither Nezeru or Saomeji waded in to help their leader. He scowled, but Makho's fierce, bony face was hard as an ivory mask.

"I will need a good rope," Jarnulf said at last, by way of surrender. "I do not carry enough."

"Take mine," Nezeru said. "It was made by the weavers of the Blue Cave."

He accepted the coil of silver-white cord from her, then found a stone outcropping that he could not budge no matter how he pulled. He tied one end around it, then pulled his gloves on tightly and lowered himself over the edge.

The rockfall had taken more than rocks in its passage, and within moments Jarnulf was walking himself backward over broken trees as well as fallen boulders, a pile of large, heavy obstacles that he knew had to be supported by something below or they would have continued to slide down the slope and into the misty crevasse. He had no idea how firmly they were held, though, so he did his best to touch lightly and take most of his weight on his arms. As a result, his muscles were trembling by the time he reached the giant, who was caught in a tangle of splintered trunks and icy stones.

"I've pulled out the end of my rope," Goh Gam Gar said, his voice a soft growl that Jarnulf could still feel in his feet as he lit on one of the trees pinioning the giant's chest. The giant's face was bloodied with dozens of scratches, which did not make him any handsomer. "Tie it to yours and send it up. Tell them to wrap it around something strong."

Jarnulf considered this, but he did not want to be without a support of his own when the giant was breaking free of the rockslide. Instead he took the massive cord, wide as his forearm, and draped a single, astonishingly heavy loop of it over his shoulders, then worked his way a few yards back up the slope to where he could perch on solid mountain stone again. "Throw down another rope!" he shouted to the Talons.

It took a few moments, but another of the slender spidersilk ropes spun down from above, which Jarnulf tied around the end of the giant's rope. "Now pull it up and tie it to something that will support his weight," he called. Jarnulf wanted to be well out of the way before Goh Gam Gar began to break himself loose, so he swung a bit farther to the side of the rockfall. He missed his footing trying to land, and for a moment swung free over dizzying depths like a spider in a windstorm. By the time he had his footing again, the giant's rope had been drawn up out of sight.

A short while later Makho shouted something from the path, and although Jarnulf couldn't make out the words, the giant could: the rope tightened and creaked as the great creature put his weight on it.

A loud crash startled Jarnulf into grabbing for a handhold on the mountain's face, but it was not another slide. The giant had dislodged one of the trees supporting him and sent it spinning down into the white void. Stones and broken trees showered down too, but even as the giant struggled free, most of the slide remained in place, tons of stone, snow, and shattered timbers wedged in a huge crevice shaped like the bow of a ship, its bottom end some ten or twenty cubits beneath Goh Gam Gar. Out of the top of this pile the beast emerged like some bizarre birth, shoulder and back muscles bulging beneath his pale fur as he slowly climbed the rope, pausing only to dislodge the larger trunks and whole trees that still clung to him.

As the giant made his way upward Jarnulf had only one task, which was to watch for anything sliding from above and stay out of its way. When Goh Gam Gar had climbed past, Jarnulf braced to swing himself back into a more direct line with the anchor of his own rope, but something in the rubble down near the bottom of the slide caught his attention, a smear of yellow and rusty brown quite unlike the rest of the debris. He knew the Norns would not hesitate to leave him if he delayed them long, but his curiosity was aroused, so he swung over to where the giant had been trapped. He looked up to be sure the great beast was not going to lose his grip and come plummeting down on top of him, but Goh Gam Gar was now on secure footing and appeared to have nearly reached the top. Jarnulf let himself down a little way, then braced his feet on a bit of solid stone to rest his aching arms and see what he had found.

It was such a strange, disarticulated thing that at first he thought it was only the remains of trees and stones curiously crushed together into one mass, melded by age and elements into a single shape, but then he saw a pale, puckered blister in the largest piece and realized he was looking at the dried and frozen remains of an eye the size of his own head. A huge skeleton dressed in rags of dried flesh hung in the tangle of stone and broken trees—the bones of a massive, long-dead creature. However it had previously rested on the mountainside, the slide had dislodged it in almost one piece. The limbs and spine and long tail had been twisted into an unnatural shape by the elements, but the long, reptilian skull gave it away.

"The giant is safe!" Nezeru shouted from somewhere above, beyond his sight. "Come up!"

"And I have found a dragon!" Jarnulf shouted back. "Come down and see!"

As he waited, he reached out to touch the nearest part of the carcass, the curled bones of a mighty foot with curved talons as long as daggers. One of the claws came off in his hand. As he marveled at its size, his finger began to sting fiercely. A clot of crumbling black material at its base was burning his skin as painfully as if he had sliced the skin in a half-dozen places. Cursing, Jarnulf dropped the long claw to frantically scrape the painful substance from his fingers onto a nearby stone as the claw bounced against the pile of scree, then caromed off into emptiness. Black as a night without stars, the sticky stuff had eaten through the tip of his glove like fire.

Dragon's blood, he realized. *Mother of God, even years old and almost dry, it still burns!*

Two of the others were now slithering down from the top on ropes of their own—Makho and Saomeji the Singer, as best as Jarnulf could tell from his angle. As he waited, Jarnulf had an idea. He pulled his salt jar from his pocket and emptied out the last few grains. He used the sleeve of his jerkin to protect him as he worked another huge claw loose from the desiccated corpse, then wiped the thick, black residue from it on the inside of the witchwood jar. When the jar did not melt or burst into flame, he scooped the rest of the blood-paste off the claw, a sticky ball of the stuff about the size of a raven's egg, then scraped that into his jar and stoppered it. The claw was too big to hide easily from Makho and the rest, but if nothing else, he would take a keepsake of dragon's blood with him from this mad expedition. He might even be able to sell it to some Tungoldyr thaumaturge for a tidy sum.

He wiped the rest of the black smear from his sleeve, which was already beginning to turn black where the blood had touched it. Then, his face as calm as he could make it, Jarnulf waited for the other climbers.

"It had fur or quills along its spine—I saw them," said Saomeji as he clambered onto the edge of the broken path. Nezeru stepped well back out of his way, in large part because she simply did not much like being near him.

Kemme was still pulling up Makho, while the giant Goh Gam Gar, despite the many wounds he had taken in the slide, had insisted on being the one to pull Jarnulf back up to the path. "It must be the carcass of great Lekkija," the Singer continued, "Igjarjuk, as mortals named her—the daughter of great Hidohebhi."

"How long has the worm been dead?" Nezeru asked.

"It does not matter," said Makho as he appeared from below, scowling fiercely. "A dead, bloodless dragon is no use to us."

Despite being the last to begin the ascent, Jarnulf, reeled in by Goh Gam Gar's huge hands on the rope, came over the edge and onto the path only a moment after Makho. "And a dead giant is no use to you, either, or I think you would not have been in such a hurry to send me down after him," Jarnulf told the chieftain with a cold look, then coiled Nezeru's rope and tossed it back to her. "My thanks, Sacrifice."

Nezeru could not look him in the eye. She had seen the glance that passed between Makho and Kemme when the Rimmersman had first called, before he had spoken of finding the dead dragon. It was clear that they had been considering simply cutting his rope and letting him fall. But why? Either the mortal was useful or he was not. Why let him come so far only to murder him? It was strange beyond understanding that her loyalties were beginning to shift from her rightful chieftain—the queen's choice!—to a mortal and the monster Goh Gam Gar, but she could not deny her mistrust of Makho was growing deeper each day that passed. Jarnulf, whether he meant to or not, had cursed her with his questions about why she had been chosen and what the hand's true mission might be.

"You said you wanted a dragon," said Jarnulf, rubbing the muscles of his arms. "That was a dragon. You told us we must find dragon's blood. If you did not notice, despite my pointing it out, the carcass still had a great deal of blood on it, even if it was dry."

"Be silent, mortal" said Makho. "You know nothing. We need a living dragon. Nothing else will do."

"Hand Chieftain Makho speaks the truth," Saomeji said. "Finding the dragon's carcass is a rare thing, and I will write the tale of what we found for the Onyx Library, but it does not fulfill Lord Akhenabi's needs."

"The *queen's* needs, I think you mean," said Makho.

"Of course. As you say." Saomeji quickly made the sign for Peaceful Withdrawal from Conflict, but his face told Nezeru a more complicated story. Was the Singer losing his patience with Makho as well? "In any case," said Saomeji, "it is getting dark, and I do not like the look of the sky. We should find a place to shelter for the night."

"A good idea," said Jarnulf. "I have almost no strength left in my limbs."

"By the Voiceless Ones, does every one of you think you have the right to give orders here?" The dead dragon seemed to have put Makho in a foul mood, although his face, as always, was nearly empty of expression. "I will say when we go and when we stop. I will say what tasks we perform and for whom. Does anyone doubt this?"

Nezeru knew better than to provoke the hand chieftain when such a mood was on him. As she turned away, the slanting light, filtered through thick mountain mists, made a strange shadow on the snow above the path.

"Perhaps the mortal would like to take a faster way down the mountain," suggested Kemme. "Plenty of time to regain his strength before he hits bottom."

"Perhaps you will take that trip with me." Jarnulf dropped his hand to the hilt of his sword. "I can think of worse ways to go to my rest."

"What is that there?" Nezeru asked. Nobody replied, and when she turned to see why, the others were ignoring her, staring at each other like suspicious dogs. "Stop strutting and come here," she said. "All of you. Chieftain, I think you should see this."

Makho's tone was more disgusted than angry. "What? What now?"

"You cannot see it from there. I only noticed it because I am close. Look."

She pointed to the marks scraped in the snow. "That is the print of something's foot. Something large."

Kemme shook his head in dismissal. "We have seen many prints on this mountain. It is likely only the slot of a goat, broadened as the snow melted—"

"No goat made this," she said, "unless goats have claws and are big as wagons."

Makho's attention was finally caught. He came to stand beside her on the path, staring up the slope where she pointed. There, by itself in the middle of an undisturbed patch of snow, was the track of some large creature, longer and wider than even Goh Gam Gar's, with four clawed toes.

"By my masters," said Saomeji, joining them. "She is right!"

"Could it be something like that rat-thing we killed?" she asked Jarnulf. "A larger one?"

He shook his head. "I have seen claws like that just moments ago—although these are smaller, thank—." He hesitated for a mere instant; Nezeru thought only she noticed it. "Thank the Mother of All," he finished. "But if that is not a dragon's track, what else could it be?"

"So the creature left tracks before it fell to its death," said Kemme. "What could that matter?"

"Did you not see the dragon's carcass, Sacrifice Kemme?" said Saomeji. "It had been lying among the rocks of the mountainside for many, many years. Not just frozen, but dried like a salt fish from the Hidden Sea. And this dragon, from its prints, is far smaller."

"A quarter the size at most," agreed Jarnulf.

"It is not the difference of size that tells the most important tale," Nezeru said, surprised by her own annoyance at their pointless disputes. "Do you not understand? This print is on new snow."

Makho stared at the print, then at Nezeru, clearly interested, but irritated that it had been her to point it out. "Its maker may be close by," he said at last, conceding her point without acknowledging her. "And a living dragon is what we need, so we will search until the last of the sun is gone and only seek shelter afterward. That is what our queen would want, so that is what we will do."

Makho kept them hunting far into evening, until the mountain had become a death trap of wind, mist, flying ice, and nearly invisible precipices. They found a few more tracks before blowing whiteness covered them, all made by what seemed to be the same creature, the edges of the prints sharp enough to suggest they had been made in the last day or two. At last the Talons made camp in a sheltered spot a few hundred steps above the path where they had found the second track.

Nezeru wrapped herself in her cloak, choosing a spot near Jarnulf, not because of any softness in her heart toward him, but because she did not want to be near Makho and Kemme. Quite separate from the dishonor of it, she was disgusted that they had considered killing the mortal while he might still be useful to achieve the queen's will.

"We could search this mountainside for days and not find anything, even if the dragon is here," said Jarnulf. "We should set a trap."

"Why must I hear your voice, mortal?" Makho demanded. "This task was given to me by the queen herself. You are nothing."

Jarnulf's mouth set in a tight line but he said no more.

"In truth, what the mortal says makes some sense, Chieftain Makho," said Saomeji. "Our time here is limited by our supplies and—"

Makho whirled and lashed out so quickly that for a moment Nezeru thought he had slit Saomeji's throat, but he had only grasped the Singer's neck, his long white fingers pressing deeply into flesh. "One more word from you and it will be the last you ever speak, spellwright," Makho hissed. "I do not care that you are Akhenabi's favorite. Did you not hear me? I was chosen by the queen herself. And nobody else will suffer as I will suffer if we fail." He turned on Nezeru, who had not spoken or moved. "Do you doubt me, halfblood? Before we left Nakkiga to retrieve Hakatri's bones from their resting place, I was shown what my fate would be if I came back without them, or if I failed the Great Mother in any way."

Jarnulf took a sudden breath behind her. Nezeru guessed it was the first time the mortal had heard about what they had done on the Island of the Bones before they met him.

"I was taken down into the Cold, Slow Halls," Makho continued. "Yes, Singer, I see you have heard of that place, although I doubt much you have seen it. But *I* did. And that is where I will be taken again if we fail, whether the fault is mine or not, and where I will be made to suffer as you cannot imagine. Every cut, every burn, every blow there feels as though it lasts a thousand years." Makho roughly pushed Saomeji away from him, so that he almost fell over. Outside their shelter the world had gone white with flying snow, and the wind sounded like the voice of something hungry. "No more argument from any of you. I will decide what we do and how we do it. And I will kill without hesitation anyone who threatens our task."

Nobody spoke again for a long time. Nezeru listened to the wind groaning and shrieking around the great, rock-studded mass of Jinyaha-yu'a and wished she had been less ambitious. For the first time, it had become clear that even this deadly quest might be less dangerous than her companions, and especially her leader.

An hour had passed in silence.

"Father once told me that to hunt something you must know it, but to catch something you must *become* it," said Jarnulf. He did not say it loudly, but everyone heard him. Makho snapped a glance at him, then looked away, but Saomeji straightened up as if he had heard his name called.

"But it is not possible to know dragons," the Singer pronounced. "It is no common beast, like a cow or sheep, or even a rare but fearsome one, like a lion."

"What do you mean?" asked Nezeru.

"Dragons did not grow in these lands of their own accord, as the other beasts of the field. They came here with our ancestors, from the Garden."

"I have never heard such a thing," she said.

"The failure of your education does not make what I say any less true," Saomeji chided her. "In fact, like the changeling Tinukeda'ya, dragons were . . ." He stopped suddenly, as if someone had signaled him to be quiet, though no one had: Makho was talking with Kemme and, despite his earlier anger, did not appear to be listening. "I have a tongue that is sometimes hard to govern," Saomeji said to no one in particular. "Forgive my foolishness."

Nezeru felt certain he had been about to say something important, but she could not guess what it might have been. She looked at Jarnulf, who only shook his head, but so subtly that she doubted anyone else saw.

As Jarnulf knew well, once the Norns set their minds to a thing, they were extremely thorough and as patient as water eroding stone. Day after day, they continued to hunt the mountain for the dragon's slot until they had found enough tracks to discern what seemed to be a regular path.

"The greatest worms are all female," Makho said as they considered their next step. "The drakes are smaller, and come to the females only to mate. By its small track, this must be such a wandering drake. Perhaps something in the scent of the dead queen dragon called to him, or perhaps he was born here on this mountain and lives here still. Perhaps the dead queen was his mother. In any case, we must find a spot he often passes over and there make our trap."

"So now you agree we need a trap?" Jarnulf asked, sourly amused.

As he expected, the chieftain ignored him, but Saomeji was not so reserved. "We must take this dragon alive, mortal. It is the blood of a living dragon our queen desires."

"Alive? But even if its track tells that this is a smaller beast than the dead one, it is still far larger than any of us, even the giant!" Jarnulf said. "Have any of you hunted a dragon?"

"Silence," said Makho. "We are the Queen's Talons. We will do whatever must be done."

They chose a wide, flat plateau on what seemed to be the creature's regular route of passage. Jarnulf guessed that Makho meant to dig a pit, but there was far more rock than soil, and as Nezeru quietly pointed out, they were not even certain how large their quarry was, only of the size of its feet.

"What about a springe?" asked Jarnulf. "Some of these trees, could we bend them down, would—"

"You are a fool, mortal," Makho said. "Even with bait confusing the scent, the beast would know we were close by and never go near it."

Instead, after careful sampling of the wind over the course of an hour or two, Makho set Jarnulf and the rest at points around the chosen spot, none closer than a hundred paces, each placed behind something, a stone or a copse of trees, that could keep them hidden. Each of the hunters also held a coil of rope with a slipping noose at one end.

"When I give the word," Makho said, "you will catch the beast by the neck or foot with your rope. The other end you must hold tightly, not letting go at any cost, until you have secured the loose end around something strong, a large tree or rock."

"What if it is the kind that spits fire?" Nezeru asked.

"There are not many of those," Saomeji said.

Makho hardly seemed to hear him. "Then we will be burned up, and the queen will send another hand to redeem our failure."

Jarnulf said nothing—he had learned what the chieftain thought of questions—but as he watched Kemme bait their trap with the haunch of a goat they had killed many days before, he wondered how Makho thought four or five of them could wrestle down any full-grown dragon, even with the considerable help of Goh Gam Gar. It was nowhere near the first time since he had joined the Norn company that he had feared for his life, but Jarnulf could not help wondering whether this time he had pushed his luck farther than it would stretch.

The giant had his massive ax and his own great coil of rope, but because Makho said his stench would make the dragon fearful, he had been dispatched to a spot not just downwind but far away. Goh Gam Gar's exile made Jarnulf restless and concerned. Makho might not care if most of them were killed by an angry monster before the giant joined the game, but as one of the weaker playing pieces on Makho's *shent* board, Jarnulf felt differently.

Preparations made, they settled into a long, cold time of waiting.

It was on the cusp of morning, with the sun's light beginning to warm the sky along the eastern rim of the world, brightening it from impenetrable violet to deep blue, when Jarnulf saw the giant up on the mountainside raise his arm. At first he thought he must be mistaken, that it had been just another curl of the blowing snow he had mistaken for signals several times already. Jarnulf's head was heavy and his eyes were dry, and he had long since decided that there was no creature more stupid in all of Osten Ard than an ex-slave who would throw his fate in with the doings of his former masters. But after he blinked several times and even rubbed at his eyes with the rough sleeve of his jacket, the smear of white high above him on the slope continued to look like a hairy white arm raised in warning. Jarnulf's heart sped, and he began to move in slow, squirming movements, trying to get blood back into his limbs and feeling back into his fingers. He peered slit-eyed at the dragon-path through the murk of blowing snow and the chill mist that clung to the slope. At first he could see nothing, but after what seemed an achingly long time he finally saw movement on the northern side of the slope. What made it was nearly impossible to discern because it was the same color as the snow and ice over which it crawled, but he could see by the shadow of its movement and occasional puffs of snow that it was long and low to the ground.

Now Jarnulf's heart began to beat swiftly indeed. He couldn't make out its exact shape, but he could see that the moving whiteness must be something like ten or twelve paces long from head to tail-tip, bigger than one of the monstrous cockindrills his father had told him lived in the southern swamps, and at least two or three times even Goh Gam Gar's weight. Jarnulf had fought giants and other unnatural creatures, but almost never by choice, and the sheer folly of trying to capture a dragon, even a small one, suddenly struck him with the force of a blow.

I'm only here because of my ridiculous, swollen pride—because of an oath I made that nobody but myself and God heard—and I'll likely die here on this Godforsaken peak, fighting beside the very Hikeda'ya monsters I am sworn to destroy.

He said a prayer, then another, asking his blessed Aedon to take pity on a believer far from home. Nobody else would, that was certain. If he died here, even the halfblood would soon forget about him, though there was no guarantee she would survive either. All of them, even the giant, seemed completely expendable to their chieftain. The queen of the Norns would be satisfied as long as one of them survived to bring the dragon's blood to her, and Makho planned to be that one.

Jarnulf's hatred of Utuk'ku, which he had done his best to keep buried during his time journeying with her Talons, suddenly blazed up again.

Heartless, ancient bitch, he thought. *Murderer. She-demon. My dear God, if I am spared death today, I promise I will fulfill that oath I made so many years ago when I was little more than a boy. I understand the task You have given me, and how these cruel Norns will help me fulfill it. I will see the queen of treachery dead by my own hand.*

But if he did not join in to help the rest, Jarnulf doubted he would ever make it back down the mountain. And if he fled for his life this moment, Makho would make a point of chasing him down and killing him—no, not just a point, but a gleeful exercise.

Jarnulf wrapped his hands around the rope the Blue Cavern weavers had made, silently touched his sword hilt to make sure it slid easily in its scabbard, and waited.

As the white thing drew closer to the spot where the goat haunch lay, Jarnulf could see more of it, and it was not what he had expected, not exactly. He had never seen a living dragon, but from drake-lore he had heard over the years he had supposed it would be longer and thinner, like a snake with legs. Instead, it seemed to have a more rounded shape. Its tail was short and blunt, as was its snout.

Could it be something else? he wondered. God alone knew what other horrors might lurk here at the edge of the world. In any case, killing such a thing would be difficult enough; trying to capture it alive now seemed like the grossest folly imaginable.

The wind eased for a moment and the flurrying snow began to settle. Jarnulf could suddenly see clearly. He could no longer doubt it was a dragon of some sort—the long, toothy jaws and reptilian head proved that instantly—but its back looked to be covered with thick white bristles, or even porpentine quills. As it dipped its head to the lure, Jarnulf saw Kemme rise and step forward from the jumble of rocks where he had been hidden and let fly an arrow, all in an instant's swift movement. An eyeblink later the Norn arrow dangled from the creature's shoulder, a single black quill among the white. The dragon let out an echoing honk of pain and surprise.

Makho now shouted for the rest of them to charge, and without further thought, Jarnulf bounded down the slope with the Talons. The dragon heard its attackers before it saw them, but it was befuddled to discover enemies on all sides, and in that moment of confusion Makho reached it and threw his loop of rope over the creature's head. Kemme was only a few steps behind, but the thrashing tail struck him and flung him to one side like a chip of wood leaping from an ax-blow. Kemme somehow staggered to his feet again a few moments later and managed to throw his own noose behind one of the creature's back feet, then waited until the dragon stepped into it before he pulled the cord tight.

Nezeru had snagged a front leg as it clawed at her, then managed to pull her rope around a huge spike of stone before the worm realized it; from that moment on the dragon was anchored. Jarnulf, aiming for the other hind leg, got the tail instead, but pulled the rope as tight as he could and scrambled backward until he could belay it around a boulder. He threw his weight back against the pull of the creature, which even under restraint was astoundingly strong, and dug in his heels. The dragon bellowed in fury, a strange mixture like a lion's deep roar mingled with a donkey's bray, that made Jarnulf's ears ache. He could not imagine how they would subdue the creature, even as Goh Gam Gar came clambering down from his high hiding place and leaped up onto the creature's broad back as if to ride it. Even under the giant's weight, the dragon still thrashed and snapped, but as Makho and Kemme secured their own ropes, one to a rock, one to a wide stump mostly buried in frozen earth, the flailing white beast had increasingly little room to move. Goh Gam Gar lifted his great ax as if to dash out the dragon's brains, but Makho shouted at him not to harm it. The giant glared back at the chieftain with an expression of disgust that would have amused Jarnulf if not for the rope that vibrated in his hands like a stretched bowstring—a rope with a thrashing, jaw-snapping monster at the other end of it.

Then suddenly, as if by magic, the dragon's movements slowed and became clumsy rather than desperate. Its pale, blind-looking eyes fell shut as it strained upward against Makho's noose one more time, trying to get its teeth into the mountainous creature on its back, then it shuddered, stumbled, and collapsed.

"Fool of a giant!" Makho snarled. "What were you thinking? I told you—a living dragon! We need a living dragon! That is why Kemme shot it with an arrow dipped in precious *kei-vishaa*, to steal its wits and put it to sleep."

"I would not have hit it so hard as to kill it outright, little Norn," Goh Gam

Gar said, rising carefully from the now motionless body, the heavy legs and long claws splayed out across the snow on either side of its trunk. "There would have been time to take blood while it still lived."

Makho shook his head. "You understand nothing . . ." But he was breathing so hard that he said no more, only bent and did his best to find his breath.

Saomeji, who had never managed to employ his own noose despite several attempts, now came forward, his rope dragging along the icy slope beside him. The sun had mounted above the eastern rim of the mountains. Jarnulf saw a puzzled look twisting the Singer's face. "Giant, can you lift the tail?"

Goh Gam Gar barked a laugh at the strange request, but reached down and heaved the huge, wide tail up so that Saomeji could climb underneath. "Don't let go," the Singer begged.

"It is a trifle slippery," said the giant, showing his yellow tusks in amusement.

Saomeji spent a few moments beneath the creature's tail, staring at the base of its belly. "This is no he-dragon," he said as he clambered out. "Not as shown in any treatise I've seen. This is a female."

"So?" Makho helped Kemme to his feet. He had collapsed after the dragon had stopped fighting, and clearly, from the way he clutched his ribs, had been injured by the flailing tail. "The Mother of the People did not specify male or female, only the blood of a living dragon," Makho said, then turned to Goh Gam Gar. "Take your great rope, giant, and wrap it fast around the creature from head to tail. Hurry, or you will feel the sting of the queen's collar and think the dragon the lucky one."

Saomeji shook his head. "You do not understand, Hand Chieftain. If this creature is female, it is very young. Scarcely a year old, perhaps less."

Jarnulf could not get over the size of the thing, three or more times the length of a man and so broad through the body it must weigh somewhere between twenty and forty hundredweights—as much as two long tons. He watched the great rib cage expand and contract with each slow breath, examined claws like curved swords, and thought how lucky they were that the *keivishaa* had done its job quickly.

"What do you mean, Singer?" asked Nezeru, who also seemed stunned by the sheer size of the thing they had captured. She crouched at a respectful distance, looking at the finger-sized teeth protruding from the creature's pale jaws.

"If this is such a young she-dragon, it means it could not be the child of the monster we saw buried in the rock slide, which has plainly been dead for many years."

Makho did not even look up, too intent on watching Goh Gam Gar bind the apparently slumbering dragon. "What matter is that? Knot it there, giant. Tightly. If it has no room to struggle, it cannot break someone's leg with a twitch."

"What matter is that, you say?" Saomeji took a step back, suddenly looking all around. "Does no one understand? If this huge creature is not the child of the dead dragon, then it is the child of another."

Makho looked up at Saomeji as it finally came to him. "Another—?"

A great booming roar rolled down upon them, as if the clouds around the mountain had turned to stone and fallen from the sky. Even the echoes were earsplitting. Jarnulf and the rest looked up the mountainside in time to see the thing appear headfirst over a great outcropping, looking like some unbelievably vast serpent, though that was only its head and long, long neck. The rest of the body came into view as the dragon crawled over the rock, its claws digging deep furrows in the raw stone. This beast was white, too, wingless like its child, but much, much bigger than the creature lying trussed at their feet. It saw them, and opened its toothy maw in a hiss of fury.

Saomeji's voice seemed to come from very far away. "The mother is not very happy with us."

And then, with a roar that shook the mountainside and echoed from the surrounding peaks, the huge white thing clambered off the rocky outcrop and came scrabbling and slithering down the slope toward them in a landslide of tumbling stones, fountaining earth, and billowing snow.

50

Several Matters of State

During a brief pause between audiences with visitors and supplicants, Simon turned to his wife and said, "That was a clever gamble with the escritor—and a lucky one."

"What was?" She gave Pasevalles a sign across the heads of the milling courtiers. He nodded and said something to his clerk.

"That Auxis would be able to agree to all that by himself, without waiting to hear from the lector. Or were you hoping he wouldn't so you could avoid the wedding? It will probably be an unpleasant affair, with both sides snarling at each other."

She shook her head. "You are right—I am not looking forward to it. My teeth will be clenched the whole time I'm there."

"Poor wife. Remember, though, you were the one who decided to face it by yourself and leave me at home."

"Don't mock me, husband," she told him sternly.

"I don't mean to. In any case, you handled the negotiation well."

She recognized a peace offering. "It seemed obvious that Vidian had to have put a few concessions in the escritor's pocket, or what's the use of sending a high-ranking churchman instead of a letter? The Sancellan Aedonitis has known for a long time that we wanted another northern escritor, so it made sense that the lector would have given permission ahead of time for Auxis to accept any reasonable candidate. As for the other promise—fairer treatment of all sides by Mother Church—I felt certain Auxis had been told to accept any deal that the lector might be able to slip out of later on."

"Sweet Elysia, Mother of our Redeemer," Simon said, keeping his voice down to avoid being heard by the various courtiers and visitors Pasevalles was now herding toward the throne room's great doors. "You are more cynical about the church than I am!"

"I love God, but I know the church is composed of mere men."

The king laughed, though not entirely happily. "Well, I give you all the credit, my dear. You told me Auxis could say yes on the lector's behalf without waiting for an answer from his master, and you were right."

"It only made sense. Lector Vidian wants the dukedom of Nabban to be held by one of his allies, like Count Dallo, but not by violent rebellion, which will bring in the High Throne. Now he sees that matters have gone too far and is desperate to calm things down, and a large part of that is because his own position is shaky. It's his own fault for having so obviously favored the Ingadarines that none of the other families trust him."

Simon looked uncertain. "But even if Dallo and Drusis reach for power and fail, Lector Vidian cannot be . . . what would it be called? 'Un-elected'? See, there isn't even a word for it. Lectors serve for life!"

"You're right, my husband. So he knows that if it came to a civil war in Nabban, someone would likely kill him."

"What do you mean? Not truly."

"Yes, truly. What do you think happened to the first Larexes, or old Saqualian? Choked on a fish bone? It is well known in Nabban that his mistress poisoned his oyster stew." She paused. "In fact, even poor, brave Lector Ranessin died an unnatural death, and I should know, since I was in the Sancellan that night."

"But Ranessin was killed by Pryrates!"

"It was still a removal for political reasons." Her mouth twisted. "My father's reasons, although I pray he did not know how that cursed priest planned to do it. No, my beloved man, power struggles in Nabban are nearly always deadly." She showed him a smile, although it came with difficulty. "It's a good thing I'm the one going. It's also fitting that I'll be going there on a ship named after my mother, since it was she and my Nabbanai relatives who taught me these things."

"How did your mother teach you all this? She died when you were only a child."

"And that taught me that life is precarious. But it was her inner court and my relatives there—especially a few rare bitches among her ladies-in-waiting—who taught me how things are done in Nabban."

Which is all the more reason I should not go back to that treacherous place, though I must, she thought. *But I shall miss my kind-hearted husband so painfully while we are apart.* And almost without realizing it, she reached out and took Simon's strong, familiar hand and squeezed it as though she would never let go.

"Your visitors have all been sent away," announced Lord Chancellor Pasevalles. "But Osric, Duke of Falshire and Wentmouth is waiting, and you will want to see him. He brings news of who shall attend you on your journey, my queen."

Miri shared a wordless look of resignation with Simon; neither of them loved Duke Osric, who was doggedly old-fashioned in his ideas and relentlessly humorless. He also had a tendency to hand all the most valuable plums of office to members of his own large, greedy clan. Still, compared to many of the most powerful Erkynlandish nobles, Osric was fairly sensible and hard-working, and he was also Lillia's and Morgan's grandfather, which made him family. "By all means," Simon said, with a creditable appearance of cheer. "Usher him in, please."

Osric, in company with his clerks as well as half a dozen Erkynguardsmen, strode into the audience room. Thinking about the tangle of Nabbanai politics suddenly made Miriamele wonder which way their own Erkynguard would turn if something happened to the king. Her husband was fantastically popular with them, and they liked bluff Lord Constable Osric as well, but she doubted they felt quite the same about her.

Could I hold this kingdom together, my own grandfather's empire, without Simon? Or would they push Morgan onto the throne too early?

It was not a pleasant thought.

Osric strode to the throne and dropped to a knee, still agile and strong though he was older than Miri or Simon. The rest of his retinue did the same, eyes firmly fixed on the floor. "Majesties," said the duke, "may God give you health."

"Rise, good Wentmouth," Miri said. "It is good to see you."

"And you. But are you certain you must make this journey, Majesty?" Osric asked her. "I fear for your safety, I must confess. Nabban is a dangerous place just now."

She ignored the squeeze Simon gave her hand. "The journey must be made. But with good, strong Erkynlandish soldiers to protect me, I will feel quite safe. Are all the arrangements made?"

"The *Princess Hylissa* waits, and the boat that will take you to her is ready. All else has been prepared. A long company of the Queen's Erkynguard will accompany you—as well as the women and others of the queen's household, of course."

"And who will command my guard?" she asked.

"Chancellor Pasevalles and I have decided that the night captain, Sir Jurgen of Sturmstad, will be the best choice."

"I know him but only a little. Is he the dark one?"

"He is very dark of hair and beard, yes. He is of Rimmersgard blood, but his grandfather was Perdruinese, I think," Osric said. "Still, he was born and raised an Erkynlander and he fought with me at the Ymstrecca. A good, solid man."

"You will have no cause to complain of Sir Jurgen, Your Majesties," Pasevalles said. "He is as devoted as I am to seeing the queen safely through her visit to Nabban."

"So it is all accomplished, then?" But as Miriamele said it, she had a sudden swipe of misgiving, a cold reluctance that she had not felt for years.

"You leave the day after tomorrow, Majesty—St. Endrian's Day—as you wished. Escritor Auxis and his party will accompany you on the *Hylissa*, so you will have no lack of company and conversation," Pasevalles said.

Osric bowed again. "And now, my lady, I must leave you and the king to finish the last preparations. I will see you on St. Endrian's!"

"May I have a few more words with Your Majesties about arrangements in Nabban?" Pasevalles asked after Osric was gone.

"She will be well guarded, yes?" Simon asked. "And not just by the duke's men."

"Absolutely, Majesty. The queen will take many of the Erkynguard with her, some of our best men. Osric has already arranged it."

"Then am I needed for this discussion?" he asked. "I have a prior engagement."

Miri could see the unhappiness in Simon's long face. "What prior engagement could you possibly have?" she asked.

He looked evasive. "Nothing—nothing important. Just some things to be seen to."

Miriamele felt sure he did not want to hear her making plans for Nabban, that it made him sad. "Go then with God's grace, my husband, and do your 'nothing important.'"

When Simon had gone, Pasevalles said, "I did not wish to talk of this in front of the others—excepting the king, of course—but I wanted to give to you a name that might prove useful if you find yourself in any difficulty."

"Difficulty?" It came out mockingly, though she had meant it to be light and teasing. "In our beloved southern duchy? Yours and my dear ancestral home?"

He could not manage a smile, but he nodded. "Please, Majesty. You know as well as I do that Nabban is a bear pit covered with pretty ribbons. And matters there, I suspect, are worse than anyone is letting on."

She was afraid of just that but did not show it in her face. "And so, Lord Pasevalles . . . ?"

"I have already reminded you of Count Froye, our ambassador there, but should you find yourself in a *truly* bad situation, I want you to remember the name of a friend of mine, a very able and sensible man—Viscount Matreu."

"Matreu? That sounds like an island name."

"He is the son of old Count Millatin of Spenit. Matreu's mother came from an old island family. But all that is of little import. Matreu is a good man who has given me much useful information over recent years and done me more than a few favors."

"But Spenit is such a long journey from the capital!"

"Matreu lives most of the year in Nabban. If you need him, you have only to send a messenger and he will attend you, I promise."

"I will remember it, Lord Pasevalles, and my thanks." She looked on him for a moment with real fondness. "It is always good to have a secret ally."

"In Nabban, Majesty, you must have as many as you can find, if only to make up for all the secret enemies."

She took a sharp breath. "You are usually the mildest and most cautious of courtiers, Pasevalles. Do you really think things there are so bad?"

"I saw my family cheated of their land and name, Majesty." A hard edge was in his voice that she had not heard before. "I saw my mother humbled and treated like a servant. I left that country with only my shoes and the clothes on my back." His smile was twisted. "And that was in better times."

"Then I hear you, and I am grateful for your concern," she said. "I know that those old days were bad ones for you, loyal Pasevalles. We are lucky that your road brought you to us."

He bowed. "I deserve no credit, my queen. I think only of the High Throne." He rose, then kissed her hand. "I will pray for your safety every night, Majesty."

"Pray for Nabban," she said. "If Nabban is preserved, I'm sure I will be too."

She was trying to play jackbones with Aedonita and Aedonita's sister, Elyweld, but Elyweld was too young and spoiled everything by grabbing the bones when it wasn't even her turn.

"Stop it or I'll tell my grandmother on you." Lillia gave Elyweld a little shake, meant only to underline the seriousness of the threat, but Aedonita's sister was a blower of the lowest variety and immediately began to shriek as if she'd been slapped.

"Here, what's this?" Countess Rhona looked up from her conversation with the queen. "Why can't you three play nicely?"

"Lillia hurt me!" said Elyweld.

"She's a blower, Auntie Rhoner—a terrible liar! I hardly touched her." Lillia was particularly irritated by the hue and cry because she'd also been listening with interest to the two grown-up women's conversation. "Isn't that true, Aedonita?"

Aedonita, daughter of a Rowson relative and one of Lillia's most frequent playmates, nodded vigorously. "Ely's a terrible sniveler, Countess."

After order was restored, Elyweld was given one of Lillia's dolls to play with (and probably to destroy, was Lillia's thought). The two older girls continued with their game of jackbones and Lillia continued with her eavesdropping.

"I dread this, I truly do," the queen was saying. "It is hard enough, having Morgan so far from home, but now I must leave this little one behind, too."

Lillia knew that meant her, and although she did not like being called the "little one," she was pleased that her grandmother was worrying about her.

Auntie Rhoner laughed "She's like a weed, our Lillia. She'll be fine. And why shouldn't she be, here in the Hayholt with me and soldiers and her grandfather the king?"

"I just worry. The world seems such a dangerous place to me these days."

"Well, you know what they say, dear Miriamele—I mean Your Majesty. 'Heaven is good, but you still shouldn't dance in a small boat.' And I think that it's true. You shouldn't call down troubles you don't have yet. In Nad Glehs, we were raised most studiously to avoid such things."

"Ah. Very wise." The queen sighed loudly, which surprised Lillia, because it seemed more like the sound she, herself, would make on a boring afternoon or during a punitive banishment to her bedchamber. "But it's not just the little one I'm worrying for. It's the king as well."

"Do you think him apt to get into mischief with you gone? Shall I keep an eye on the serving girls?"

The queen laughed again. "Simon? No. He is more like a boy that way. Not in the marriage bed, where he is lusty enough, but his eye for a pretty woman shames him a bit—he thinks I would take it badly, so he looks away more than he looks *at,* if you take my meaning. God bless him, but he does not want me angry with him."

"So what is it you want, dear? What is it that has you worried?"

"Oh, everything. I'm not even certain, my lovely Rhona. I suppose I fear that the king, my Simon, will be sad with me gone. That he will be lost. And this is not a time when he can afford to be a mooncalf."

"The king—a mooncalf?"

Miriamele smiled. It was slightly grim. "You cannot even guess. Don't misunderstand me—Simon is the kindest man I know. But sometimes, I swear with the Sacred Mother as my witness, I feel more like a mother than a wife. Do you know, he wanted us to go and eat supper last night on top of Holy Tree Tower?"

"Truly? Why?"

"He wanted to talk about things he'd done when he was a boy—which tower roofs he'd been on, where he'd gotten into different kinds of mischief. I wanted to talk with him instead about what was to come, what he must watch carefully while I'm gone, many important things. All he wanted to talk about was when we were young."

"Hmmmm." Lillia saw that Auntie Rhoner was not convinced by what the queen said. "I can think of worse things, Majesty, than a husband who wants to reminisce about the days when you both were young and in love."

"To be honest, I don't think I have that much to do with it, Rhona. When he was young he knew me only as somebody he saw a few times from a distance. I knew him better than he knew me."

"You did? How could that be?"

Lillia, listening intently now, wanted to ask the same thing.

"Because I watched him and the other servants. I envied them their freedom."

"That's an odd word for it."

"Oh, I know, Rhona dear. Don't scold me. We never understand anyone but ourselves when we're young, and we don't understand ourselves very well. But I watched Simon and Jeremias, and that page, what was his name . . . ? I watched them running around, and even when they were working, they laughed and they sang." She frowned. "Izaak. That was his name. Little fellow, but he had a lovely singing voice. Not like Simon's honking."

Rhona laughed. "I stand near your husband in the chapel. I have heard him sing, my lady. When you say 'honking,' you are very kind."

"Bless him. And he does love to sing, too." She sighed again. "Oh, don't get me wrong, Rhona. I will miss him terribly. And he is not a fool, not at all—he will do very well whenever he takes time to think carefully. But I worry that something may happen that compels a sudden choice, and that is when I fear his judgement."

"I will do my best to watch over all your dear ones, Majesty," her friend said. "And don't forget, we will miss you too—and not just the ladies of the court, either. All of Erkynland will miss you until you come back to us, my queen. I'll pray every day for your safe journey and speedy return."

"Ah, you have reminded me of something else." The queen looked over toward the children, and Lillia pretended to be studying the jackbones, which had been awaiting her next throw for some moments.

"Aren't you going to go again?" Aedonita demanded, sounding almost as querulous as her little sister.

"Ssshhhh." Lillia waggled her hand, wanting to hear what else the queen had remembered.

"I have heard a number of alarming things lately about Hernystir," the queen told Auntie Rhoner. "Most of them we've talked about already, but the latest reports suggest that things have grown very strange indeed in Hernysadharc. Please, write to your friends who are still there, and without being too obvious, see what you can learn."

"About Tylleth? The woman that King Hugh is marrying?"

"About anything. About Lady Tylleth, Hugh, anything you can discover. Do not ask too specifically or too openly, but I would like some impressions of what goes on around the Hernystir throne that does not come from our envoys or other official carriers."

"Do you distrust your ambassadors?"

"I trust nobody completely, dear Rhona—except you and Simon, of course. But the news that comes to me from the Taig seems too strange not to be more generally known. Did you know that the Silver Stags have arrested and imprisoned several nobles who were friends of Queen Inahwen?"

Lillia could see that Countess Rhona looked surprised. "Truly? I have not heard it! Why?"

"I haven't been told yet. But I fear Hugh, especially since that woman got her claws into him."

"I will do my best to learn more."

"But discreetly, dear, as I said, and not just to keep my interest secret. Your husband still has many ties to Hernysadharc. Do not risk your family's safety."

"Risk their safety? Now you truly are frightening me, Majesty."

"Better that I frighten you into caution than lull you into carelessness." She smiled and raised her voice. "Now, where is my granddaughter, the one I came to see? I could have sworn she was here somewhere!"

Lillia was pleased that her turn had finally come, although slightly miffed by how much time the queen and Auntie Rhoner had spent talking first. "I'm here, Grandmother! I mean, Your Majesty!"

"You may certainly call me Grandmother, and especially today, when I have to say farewell to you for a while."

The queen beckoned to her, and Lillia got up and hurried over, then crawled into her lap. The queen always smelled of nice things. Today her dress smelled of oranges and cloves, and her hair smelled of violets. "Why do you have to go to Nabban?"

"Because there is an important wedding there, and I want to attend it."

"Why isn't King Grandfather going?"

The queen smiled. "Because he has to stay here and take care of the kingdom."

"Will you be gone long?"

"Not too long. I'll be back before St. Granis' Day."

Lillia thought. "Will you bring me back something?"

"Would you like a doll?"

"Yes. A Nabban doll. With a great long *stola*."

"They don't wear stolas in Nabban anymore, dear one," said Rhona. "Not for years and years. Centuries!"

"I don't care. I want one with a stola."

Her grandmother stroked her hair. "Look how golden you're becoming with all this sunshine. I'll do my best, lamb. I'll see what I can find."

"You can get one for Aedonita too," Lillia said generously. "But not Ely-weld. She's a terrible, terrible sniveler."

But her grandmother was talking to Auntie Rhoner again, and Lillia could only hope the queen had heard the important part at the end about not wasting a doll on little girls who blew and cried and told tales. She snuggled deeper, smelling her grandmother's smells, and wondered why people ever went anywhere far away.

"And the chapterhouse at St. Ormod's is to be rededicated on the saint's feast day—that's coming soon. The archbishop will remind you, I'm sure, but I'm telling you so you won't stay up late the night before. You know how easily you fall asleep at such events."

"I'm not a child, Miri. And I'm not such an old man, either."

"No, but you don't do well at long ceremonies. Oh, and that reminds me, Earl Gared is bringing his son for a Naming at St. Sutrin's. You don't have to be there, but it would be good to invite him and Lady Devona to an audience afterward. Just say a few nice things about Nordhithe and admire the baby, then send them on their way. Oh, and a gift. Jeremias should be able to find them a nice silver cup or some plate. Remember, Nordhithe is on Hugh's border and we need to keep Gared sweet. The Hernystiri are worrying me."

"The Hernsytiri aren't worrying me nearly as much as the Norns."

"Of course, but we've already talked about that. Which reminds me, have you sent out the muster orders?"

"No. But before you start poking at me, woman, I do know what I'm doing. We already agreed it has to be done quietly. If we start crying 'the White Foxes are coming' up and down the countryside we'll have a panic, not to mention another ten thousand people trying to get inside the walls of Erchester. God knows what it would mean farther north—farms abandoned, villages deserted, roads falling apart . . ."

"So what are we doing now? What if they come marching down out of the north when the new moon comes?"

"The Norns won't come in the middle of summer. They like fighting in the cold and dark because they know we don't. But even so, I'm sending out people I trust to talk to all the northern nobles—they'll understand the danger right away. And we'd have to warn them, anyway, so all we're really doing is keeping it among those who must know *now*."

"I'm not sure . . ."

"Miri, we met a single band of White Foxes on the Frostmarch Road, and had a letter of warning from a man we've never heard of, and the only thing we know for certain about him is that he was traveling with the Norns. I don't trust that horrid, silver-faced witch up north any more than you do, but there will still be a harvest to bring in this year."

"And if we need soldiers instead, it will take a long time to get them."

"And if we tell them we need them *this moment* and then we're wrong, how long will it take to muster them next time? Or the time after that? It will be like the Tale of the Idle Shepherd."

"I suppose."

"You know, wife, this isn't really what I thought we'd be doing on the night before you sail for Nabban."

"I'm sure that's true. Which reminds me, the Controller of the Salt Staple in Meremund has to be replaced—he's a drunk and he has his hand in the money box. Same for the Controller of Wool."

"We're not going to have any luck with Tostig. He has most of the Wool Staples in his pocket because he's smart enough to share his thefts. The Council of Erchester love him. Besides, you know he's another of Osric's cousins. Aedon bless us and protect us, that man has more cousins than a dog has fleas."

"Yes, but he's the heir's other grandfather, Simon. He feels he has the right to dip his snout into the High Throne's jar and eat as much as he pleases. And it keeps him sweet."

"Don't I know it. And without his three thousand Falshiremen and his Wentmouth levies, if it comes to a fight with the White Foxes we might as well rename ourselves Southern Nornland."

"No jests, Simon. Please, not when I have to go away. Not when everything feels so fragile."

⋆　　⋆　　⋆

"I'm sorry. I don't even know why I'm in tears. I just woke up feeling dreadful."

"Don't, Miri. Don't apologize."

"But I don't like crying. It's an excuse for people to say, 'She's just a woman.'"

"I like holding you, though. Stop wriggling."

"Oh, very well, but just for a moment. It will be time for me to get dressed soon—I have so much to do! And in any case, Jeremias will be in soon, and I don't particularly like the way he chirps around here in the morning like a fat robin."

"He is doing his duty, beloved, nothing more."

"I know. Ooh, your hands are cold."

"You don't get away so easily. Besides, you know what they say. 'Cold hands . . . warm horn.'"

"You! Stop that. We have things to talk about still—many things."

"And you're leaving tomorrow. Damn and blast, Miri, don't push me away!"

"And what will happen if I let you? Afterward, you will smile like a dog in the sun, roll over, and fall back asleep while there are still important matters to discuss."

"No. I will kiss you first, many times. Because I love you, and I'm going to miss you terribly. Don't you still love me?"

"Yes, you fool man. Most of the time I love you to distraction. The rest of the time, the distraction comes on its own. But as you know, we have other responsibilities now."

"Oh, God on His Throne, *responsibilities*! I hate that word sometimes. And I miss the days when it wasn't like this. Don't you wish we could just do what we wished? Go where we wished?"

"I don't think I could do that, Simon. I don't think I could forget all the people who count on us. And neither could you, if I remember correctly, not even when you were young. That's why you risked your life for Josua and had to flee the castle. No, don't get up. Please. Come, hold me again, but be careful with those cold hands! I have just remembered about the Perdruinese factors."

"Not them again."

"Yes, them. If I'd known I was going to Nabban I could have arranged to meet them there, but they are already coming here. They'll arrive before the end of Tiyagar-month. They say that it is unfair to set the tariff so high for their grain, because the farmers in the south have had a terrible year."

"So we will lower it."

"You cannot. Then the Northern Alliance factors will be angry. And our own grain merchants here in Erkynland will not be best pleased, either."

"Why should we argue with Perdruinese traders in the first place?"

"Because they are part of my grandfather's kingdom, part of the High Ward, and we have made promises to treat them fairly."

"No, I mean why should we tell them anything at all? Why not let them decide for themselves what prices to set?"

"Because farmers, shepherds, merchants, traders, they are all strung together like beads on a necklace. Do not pretend to be foolish, Simon. You know this. It is all one great thing, and we must pull the strands at one end to keep them tight at the other, and so on. Back and forth, back and forth."

"They could do it better for themselves, surely."

"Then they would not be under the High Ward and would soon go back to fighting and killing each other. Have you forgotten about the old days before my grandfather, when Nabban fought Erkynland and Perdruin, and Erkynland fought Hernsytir, and everyone fought with Rimmersgard and the Thrithings-Men? *That* was why my grandfather King John brought them together under one throne, and why we must rule over them all. To keep them from killing each other."

"If the High King and the High Queen must decide what every single grain factor and wool merchant is to do, it seems to me that something is wrong. It also means that all the power is vested in the High Throne."

"Yes, that's what it means."

"What if the person sitting on the throne is, pardon my saying so, more like your father than your grandfather? Or like King Hugh instead of Eolair, or like Drusis instead of his brother Saluceris?"

"Morgan will not be like any of those!"

"No? I hope not too. But what of Morgan's sons and daughters? What of the others to come? How long until a madman or a fool sits on the High Throne?"

"I'm beginning to think there is at least one fool sitting on it *now*. Not to mention an ape with no manners. Did I tell you to start pawing me again?"

"I'm sorry. You're right, Miri, I have no manners. But it feels so sweet when I squeeze you right . . . there."

"Stop, you monster."

"Yes. Yes, I am. A monster who is going to miss you so fiercely that I will pray every day and every night for you to hurry back to me. Hurry back to me, wife, so I can do this."

"Simon, please."

"Are there any other important details you need to give me? Let's call in Pasevalles and the clerks to be certain. Surely there is a thread that some weaver in Crannhyr has broken that I should replace. Or is there a fisherman on Firannos Bay who cannot earn his living until I mend his nets for him?"

"That is not a net you are paddling, ape."

"Nor are you a fisherman. So it works out well for everyone."

"Pig."

"Tyrant."

"Fool. Great clumping fool of a husband. By the sweet Mother of God, I shall miss you."

"And I shall miss you. No more talk. Kiss me. It will be dawn soon."

"Oh. Oh, what are you doing there?"

"Nothing but my duty. All this talk of duty has inspired me to send the King's Hand on a state visit."

"Simon! You really are like a child, did you know that? An irresponsible boy."

"Then who is truly the fool, High Queen Miriamele? After all, you are the one who married me. But if you are ordering me to desist . . ."

"Save your temper, husband. I called you a name, but I did not tell you to stop."

51

Stolen Scales

Count Eolair remembered the name Khendraja'aro from King Simon's stories, but he had never heard or seen anything to suggest that this bad-tempered relative would be the one giving the orders. The hierarchy of the Zida'ya had seemed quite clear to Eolair during the Storm King's War: Likimeya and her husband were the royal couple, and their children, Jiriki and Aditu were prince and princess, or at least next in the line of succession. But either he had been wrong or something had happened to change it.

"You say only our old alliance preserves our lives today, Khendraja'aro," Eolair said. "If so, we are grateful for your restraint, but I confess I am puzzled. Before you send us away, please tell me what I—or my people—have done to earn such words of scorn."

"You want to know what you mortals have done?" Khendraja'aro asked. "Lied. Betrayed. Murdered. Is that not enough to deserve those words?"

"Why is he saying that?" Morgan demanded. "That's not true! Count, what does he mean?"

"I don't know—" Eolair began.

"You saw Likimeya!" cried Yeja'aro. "You saw the mistress of Year-Dancing drowning in the Long Sleep! Your people did that!"

Aditu shot Yeja'aro a look that seemed to Eolair half-anger, half-pity. "Not all mortals know what all mortals do, *S'hue-tsa*."

"They were men of this Seoman Snowlock's own kingdom!" Yeja'aro turned to Khendraja'aro. "Uncle, you said yourself that mortal words are meaningless, useless—that those creatures do not know anything of truth."

Morgan stirred and seemed about to reply. Eolair reached out and squeezed his arm—a little harder than he had intended, but the last thing they needed was an angry young prince making things worse.

"Saying so does not make it so, Yeja'aro," Jiriki said. "And Aditu and I can both promise that although many mortals are unworthy of trust, there are others whose words are as rooted in truth as those of the Zida'ya. Seoman Snowlock and his wife Miriamele are two such mortals."

"Then tell me," demanded Khendraja'aro, "what Snowlock and his queen say about their subjects who attacked me, and who nearly killed Likimeya and may yet prove to have caused her death. And what of our messengers? First Sijandi slaughtered, now Tanahaya attacked and poisoned!" The red-haired Sitha suddenly went rigid, like a hawk spotting something vulnerable moving on the ground. "Tanahaya. Where is the scale she carried?"

Jiriki almost looked uncomfortable. "She does not have it with her." He turned to Eolair. "Did your people find her possessions?"

Eolair shook his head. "I have asked Lord Pasevalles, the one who found Tanahaya and brought her to the castle. He said her horse had vanished, and in her pack they found only some food wrapped in leaves. What is missing?"

"What Protector Khendraja'aro seeks—what we are all curious about—is a mirror small enough to fit in the hand," said Aditu. "Simon may have told you of these mirrors, which we Zida'ya use to speak to each other over a great distance. Scales of the Greater Worm, they are called, or sometimes just Witnesses."

"I know tales about such things—in legends my people called it a 'wormglass'—but I heard nothing of any mirror found with the wounded Sitha," Eolair said. "But another question is pressing me fiercely. Did you say you sent a previous messenger?"

"Some years ago, by your reckoning," said Jiriki. "When the attacks upon our folk began, we thought they must be the work of just a few ignorant mortals. But when they continued and grew more violent and yet seemed to be carefully planned, we determined to send an envoy to Simon and Miriamele to ask them if they knew why these things were happening."

"Were there truly so many attacks on your people?" Eolair was beginning to have a very, very nasty feeling.

"What are they talking about?" Morgan asked in a hoarse whisper. "Are they saying my grandparents started some kind of war?"

"Just let me talk to them, Highness," said Eolair, quickly and quietly. "I will get answers for us, but the Sithi will not be rushed, especially now."

"Do I have your permission, Protector Khendraja'aro, to answer Count Eolair's question?" Jiriki asked. "It might be useful for us to find out what these mortals know, since they are here. But that will mean sharing what *we* know with them, and it will take some time."

Khendraja'aro inspected Eolair and Morgan again. His scar-hooded eye made it look as though he doubted everything he heard, but at last he nodded and made a broad gesture with his hand. "Bring them in," he said. "Give them water and food if they need it. But not overmuch—they will not remain here long."

Eolair and Morgan were led from the dockside shelter farther into the forest camp, to a structure made entirely from a ring of living trees, which had somehow been coaxed into growing together at the top so that their branches mingled in a single leafy roof. Spiderwebs hung between all of the trunks except the two that served as gateposts, and although it seemed to Eolair that at least a few of the webs should be old or broken, they all appeared new and perfect, with each strand in place. The Sithi in this place seemed more serious than those in the first Little Boat, Eolair thought, as if this were a military camp near the front lines of a battle. He saw no one singing or dancing, and Eolair thought they watched him and Morgan much more closely than the first group of Sithi had.

Or perhaps they are simply less interested in being courteous, he thought.

He and the prince were given fruit and small loaves of bread on broad leaves that served as plates, and bowls of water so cold and lively on the tongue that it almost seemed like strong drink; when Eolair looked he could see that Morgan was enjoying the refreshment far more than he had expected to.

When they were done eating, Jiriki said, "Much has happened since you and I saw each other last, Count Eolair, at the crowning of Miriamele and Seoman. Soon after that, we had to decide whether to abandon Jao é-Tinukai'i, our last home, because it had been discovered by the Hikeda'ya, and we had been attacked there in the year of Ineluki's war."

"Ineluki was the Storm King's true name," Eolair explained to Morgan. "He was a Sitha once. Before he died."

"I know all that," said Morgan.

Eolair was grateful that at least he seemed to be paying attention. Young princes were seldom very accomplished listeners, as he knew from long experience.

"Some years ago," Jiriki continued, "as we struggled with our own disputes and concerns, we began to hear of attacks on our people in the southwestern part of the Great Forest, not far from our abandoned city of Da'ai Chikiza. This has always been important territory for our people, so when we heard that mortals were responsible—Erkynlanders, by their clothes and weapons, Seoman's and Miriamele's own people—we were disturbed, but we had known centuries of ignorance and distrust and even hatred would not evaporate simply because a mortal throne had changed hands, so though we hunted the attackers, we did not blame your king and queen."

"Which was foolish, as it turned out," said Khendraja'aro, sipping from a cup made of carved horn trimmed with silver. "As I had warned."

A swift look, the merest glance, flickered between Jiriki and Aditu before Jiriki continued. "But as years passed and more attacks happened—many of the victims were innocents out gathering necessary plants, or acting the sentry along our forest borders—we knew something was truly wrong."

"May I ask *how* mere mortals could have wounded Sithi," Eolair asked, "— especially sentries that I presume were armed and prepared to fight?"

"They were lured, Count Eolair," explained Aditu. "Their mortal attackers were not striking out in surprise and a moment's fear—they were not just angry peasants. In one case our people went to investigate a crowd of mortals felling trees in a part of the forest that, by our agreement with your High Throne, was not for mortal use. But these tree-cutters were merely the bait. Other mortals were waiting in ambush, and when our people came to see what was happening they were attacked by bowmen firing from cover."

"Elysia, Mother of God!" said Eolair in astonishment. "Someone actually set traps? To try to kill *Sithi*? How could you think this was anything to do with Simon and Miriamele?"

"Most of our people didn't," Jiriki said. "Not at first."

"And some of us still do not," Aditu added. "Because we know better."

Jiriki nodded, though Eolair thought he looked less certain than his sister. "But then we sent Sijandi of Kinao Vale," Jiriki continued, "who had once been a companion of Seoman Snowlock, your King Simon, long ago on the mountain that mortals call Urmsheim. Sijandi was directed to travel to Asu'a—the Hayholt, as you call it—and learn the truth. I confess I still hoped it was all some mistake."

"Just tell the story, Cousin." Yeja'aro's voice was tight with anger. "Tell what happened." The tale clearly meant something different to him than it did to Jiriki.

"Sijandi was sent to your king and queen," continued Jiriki, "the mortals who had promised us that things would be different—but we never heard from him again. Some two years later, as you would count it, we found the rotting remains of his saddle and equipment in a meadow south of the forest. The Scale that Sijandi carried, the sacred mirror with which he was to send us the words of the mortals, was gone. There were arrow holes in his saddlebag. No other trace of him has ever been found."

Eolair could feel the sadness as well as the anger of those gathered around him in this odd, open room made of trees. The Sithi were few, and although their long lives seemed nearly endless by human standards they could die like any other creatures. Also, they bore children only rarely, so each death further diminished the tribe.

"I am sorry to hear about Sijandi," the count said at last. "I did not know him, but I know of him from King Simon's stories. Still, I can promise you without hesitation that neither Simon nor Miriamele had anything to do with such a horror, nor know anything about it. I have to believe it is our old enemies the Norns who have the most to gain, as well as the best chance of doing such a thing."

"Have you not listened, mortal?" Yeja'aro leaped to his feet. By what Eolair had seen of the Sithi, Khendraja'aro's nephew was practically trembling with rage, dangerous as an angry young god, his hair like a holy flame. "These murderers were *mortals*—mortals like you! We would have smelled the Hikeda'ya's touch on any of these crimes. We have never stopped watching them, *especially* in the Forbidden Hills—"

"Silence!" said Khendraja'aro, and for once his anger was not directed at the intruders. "You are to remain quiet, Yeja'aro. You speak too often without thinking first."

The younger Sitha dropped back into a crouch, his golden-skinned face studiously empty once more.

This curious exchange finished, Aditu now resumed where her brother had left off. "The disappearance of Sijandi frightened us all," she explained. "And sharpened the argument about whether we should remain in Jao é-Tinukai'i, a place we all knew was no longer secret. Most disturbingly, because it had been discovered during the war by the Hikeda'ya, it led to the death of our beloved Amerasu, the mother of the Zida'ya."

The Sithi all made the same fluid hand gesture of sorrow. Eolair knew about the attack and Amerasu's death because young Simon had been present, still a captive. *What a blow that must have been,* Eolair thought, *to lose the wisdom of so many years in one treacherous blow—a blow directed by Queen Utuk'ku, Amerasu's own great-grandparent!*

"What are they talking about?" Morgan demanded of Eolair. "I don't know all these names!"

"I'll explain later," he said quietly. "Until then, listen and learn as best you can, my prince. This is a history older than mankind."

"Then, just a short year ago, while they were camped far to the west of this place," Aditu went on, "our mother Likimeya and S'hue Khendraja'aro and their company were attacked by a troop of mortals."

"Are you sure it was not merely a group of panicked huntsmen?" Eolair asked. "There are many false rumors about the Sithi that pass for truth among mortals—"

"Impossible," said Khendraja'aro.

"Our uncle is correct, I fear," Aditu told the count. "Eighty mortals, more or less, waited for a Zida'ya hunting party of a dozen. They attacked without warning, arrows flying. They chose daytime, clearly knowing the advantage we would have over them in darkness."

Khendraja'aro pointed at Eolair. The Sitha's ravaged face made every word terrible. "Know this, Hernystirman. Those killers were prepared for us—taught by someone who knew our ways and skills. The Erkynlanders lay in ambush on a trail we use but seldom, so they must have waited a long time. They had disguised their scent as well. Then they attacked without warning. We lost half our company in the first volley. Does this sound like a chance encounter?"

"No, I agree it does not." Eolair suddenly felt every one of his many years. The Sithi were right: this was no mere misunderstanding, to be softened by diplomacy and careful words. In fact, it was a puzzle he could not solve here and now, and perhaps never would. Who could have done such a thing? And why, except for this very reason—to sour the friendship between the Sithi and the mortal rulers of the High Throne? "My king and queen are innocent, I promise you, but still I grieve to hear your tale."

"Grieve?" Khendraja'aro made a gesture as dismissive as the slice of a knife. "You do not know grief, mortal. The mistress of our house—our queen, as you would have it—was cut down before my eyes. My kinsmen died all around me. I alone escaped, carrying Likimeya's arrow-pierced body across my shoulders, watering the uncaring earth with her blood and my own."

Morgan stirred at his side again. Eolair knew they were walking a very narrow path now, with disaster close on either side. Once more he grabbed Morgan's upper arm and gave a warning squeeze, then said, "I hear everything you have said, and it pierces my heart, Protector Khendraja'aro. Do not forget, unlike all but a few other mortals, I have met Likimeya. I know her wisdom and her strength. But why are you so certain that these were Erkynlanders? Did you hear them speak?"

"Hah." Khendraja'aro's laugh was pure scorn. "They did not even shout to one another as they killed us. More proof this was an ambush, pure and simple."

"But in the past the Sithi have had conflict with many mortal races—the Nabbanai of the Imperium, and closer in time the Rimmersmen when they came out of the West. Why are you so certain this attacking band was from Erkynland?"

"Because I found something," the protector said. "On the leader of our attackers, whom I killed before the rest retreated, dragging his body away."

"I will get it, Uncle!" said Yeja'aro, then rose and loped from the tree-hall. He returned a few moments later with a leather sack in his hands, which he passed to Khendraja'aro, who took the bag and turned it upside down. A cataract of gold coins slid out, clinking and chiming as it puddled on the ground before his booted feet. "See for yourself," he said.

Eolair stepped forward with Morgan close behind him. The count picked up a handful of them, felt their heaviness, saw the sharpness of their edges. "Gold thrones," he said.

"Not just that," said Jiriki, the first time he had spoken in some while. "Look closely."

Eolair lifted one up to the light that streamed through the spiderweb walls. "Bagba bite me," he murmured. "It's the Lady and the 'Lock."

Each new-minted coin had portraits stamped on both sides—Queen Miriamele on one, her husband King Simon Snowlock on the other. This particular issue of gold Thrones had been made in Erkynland under the careful rules of the High Ward, the first of them minted only a few years earlier. The count looked helplessly from Jiriki to Aditu, who could only stare back, then turned at last to Protector Khendraja'aro. "I cannot explain this," Eolair said. "But that does not mean there is no explanation."

"No matter. We do not want explanations," said Khendraja'aro. "Nor anything else your kind can offer. We want you gone from our woods and our ways, mortal. Since you so value their kind, Jiriki, you may be the one to lead them from our lands. And you, mortals, will leave the horn Ti-tuno, which has returned to its makers. That is all."

Morgan had not wanted to go on this journey into the wilderness, not at all; but as time had passed he had begun to feel differently. He had been proud to discover that he could sound the ancient Sithi horn when even noble Count

Eolair could not; later he had been excited because he, of all people, had drawn out the Sithi with it. That pleasure made it all the more galling now that not only were the Hand of the Throne and the heir-apparent being ignored and dismissed by the immortals, but evil-tempered Protector Khendraja'aro had even kept the horn.

As Jiriki led them back through the forest toward the Erkynguard camp, toward Porto and the trolls and the waiting soldiers, Morgan's anger grew. Not only had the Sithi first frightened him, then snubbed him, they had all but made his entire journey pointless. Several weeks riding and sleeping out of doors and many nights' merriment back home missed, and his only reward was to be treated like a beggar by the glorious immortals he had heard so much about.

Back at home they will say the whole trip was wasted, he thought bitterly. *And no doubt my grandparents will blame me, since they would never blame their magical Sithi friends or their old comrade Count Eolair. But who are the Sithi, after all is said? They live in the forest without houses, as poor as trappers or charcoal burners.*

Morgan looked over at Jiriki and his certainty suffered a little. The Sitha moved like a true wild creature, his strides long, even, and completely silent, while Morgan and Eolair clattered and rustled with each step as they struggled to keep up.

As they followed Jiriki, the afternoon passed its crest and began to fail. The forest air that had sparkled with dust motes bright as tiny stars now grew more opaque, and as the sun dropped lower the first mists rising from the earth gave the Aldheorte the look of a streambed seen through moving water. Morgan paid little attention, though: He was full of angry thoughts, with a heaviness in his chest that felt like grief, though no one had died.

"Why did we leave the horn?" he demanded suddenly. "My grandparents gave that horn to us! It belonged to Sir Camaris, and he wasn't any Sithi!"

"It was made by them in the first place, long, long ago," said Eolair, frowning as he struggled over a log that blocked their path. "It was simple courtesy to let them have it again, Highness. And in any case, Ti-tuno is the least of our problems."

"I would apologize for my uncle," Jiriki said, "but I think there is blame enough for all, including an ample share for my sister and myself. Even Seoman and Miriamele did not understand what they sought when they tried to make a new peace with my people. We do not change so easily, nor so lightly, and neither do the mortals who fear and hate us. Years of care and much attention were needed, and both were lacking. Now it is likely too late."

"Too late?" Eolair asked. "Why?"

"When Khendraja'aro and our mother were attacked by the mortals we had favored, our clan—the House of Year Dancing—lost favor among the rest of the Zida'ya. Khendraja'aro, as eldest of the clan, declared himself the house's protector until the threat was finished. All the clans still work together in . . . well, in certain important ways, let us say, but our old shared home, Jao é-Tinukai'i, is now gone. It's name means 'Boat on the Ocean of Trees,' as I think my sister told you. Our clans have now dispersed into many Little Boats instead. By our ancient traditions, it was the right thing to do."

"What I fear—" Count Eolair began, but Morgan was tired of listening to other people talk.

"Why do all you Sithi let your uncle tell you what to do?" he demanded of Jiriki's back. "How do we know that whatever-his-name—Khendararo, Khenjadaro—didn't do all this himself and blame it on mortals?"

"Prince Morgan!" The count seemed shocked by this, but Morgan didn't care. Hadn't the old man even considered it? After all, Eolair was the diplomat, supposedly wise in the world's ways.

"Well, he was the only one who came back to tell the story, wasn't he? And now he's in power, when it used to be the queen." Morgan thought it seemed quite obvious. "All he'd need is a purse full of new gold pieces so he could claim that these supposed attackers were carrying them."

"I apologize for the prince," Eolair said to Jiriki, which only made Morgan angrier. "We came a long way for this meeting, and of course we are disappointed . . ."

The Sitha waved his hand. "Peace, Count. We Zida'ya are not complete strangers to deceit—in fact, if you know the story of Ineluki's murder of his own father, you know we are no strangers to treachery among our own people either. But I think Prince Morgan speaks before he understands us well enough to judge us."

"Perhaps." Morgan was not in the mood to be conciliatory, however highly his grandfather and grandmother thought of the fairy-folk. "Or perhaps we've been hoping for help that was never going to come to us from these Sithi anyway."

"Help?" said Jiriki. "You said something of this before, but I thought you spoke of breaching the distance that yawns between our peoples. What do you mean? What has happened, and why is this the first you have mentioned it?"

"Because your protector, as you call him, did not give me a chance to speak of it," Eolair said, then told him of the attack on the royal progress along the North Road, and of the message they had found when the battle had ended.

"Witchwood Crown?" Jiriki said. "That is a very old phrase indeed."

"What does it mean?" asked Eolair. "Is it some weapon or object of power like the swords we sought in the Storm King's War?"

Jiriki made a gesture with clutching fingers, as though he tried to grasp something invisible. "I wish my sister were here. Aditu is a better student of the elder days than I am and would know more about such things. But 'witchwood crown'—*kei-jáyha* in our tongue—has more than one meaning. The most common, at least in elder days, signified all the groves of witchwood trees that were planted when our people first came to the new lands."

"New lands?" said Eolair.

"This place—Osten Ard, as you mortals call it. 'New' because we came here after we fled our old home, the Garden."

"Are there many groves?" the count asked. "Are they important?"

"Most of the witchwood trees are dead now," said Jiriki, and even for Morgan, unused to Sithi ways, there was no mistaking the bitterness in his voice. "Even our sacred groves in Jao é-Tinukai'i failed at last, not long after the Storm King was defeated. The living trees that remain are all in Nakkiga with the Hikeda'ya, so Utuk'ku seeking to capture *that* witchwood crown makes little sense."

"But you said the words had other meanings as well," said Eolair.

Jiriki hesitated, and Morgan wondered whether he was hiding something. "We used to bury some of our dead with a crown made of witchwood branches on their caskets or upon their brows. Because of that, it is also the name of a move in the game of *shent*."

Eolair was struggling to keep up with Jiriki's effortless pace, but Morgan could see he was clearly interested. "A move? A piece of strategy, do you mean? Could that be the meaning in the message we received?"

Jiriki seemed intent on the path before them. Morgan had decided he did not trust him at all, and was now certain the immortal was hiding something from them.

"Again," the Sitha said at last, "I doubt it could be anything to do with Utuk'ku's goal. In the game of *shent*, Witchwood Crown is a means to gain by surrendering. And I cannot think the queen of the Hikeda'ya intends surrender."

"So there is nothing else to be done about the message we received?" Eolair asked. "The Norns' plans remain a mystery and your people cannot help us? *Will* not help us?" Morgan thought the old count sounded quite pathetic, like a man begging for money from a wealthy relative. "What will we do if the Norns seek war again?"

"You don't need to ask him," Morgan said. "*My grandparents* will decide what is to be done."

Jiriki turned toward him, his severe features even more alien in the sharply angled, late-afternoon light. Gaps in the trees overhead displayed the spreading scarlet of sunset in the sky, but to Morgan's dismay it was once more in completely the opposite direction from what he thought was west. He was struck suddenly by how far he was from everything he knew, and had to fight against a pang of fearful homesickness.

"If so, Prince Morgan, your grandparents will not only have to make their own decisions," Jiriki answered calmly, "but implement them as well. The Zida'ya can do nothing because we do not agree among ourselves." He turned to the lord steward. "Count Eolair, we have almost reached our parting, and I must speak of something else while we can."

"I am listening."

"My sister and I sent the envoy Tanahaya to you, but it was completely against Khendraja'aro's wishes and he would have forbidden it if he could. What happened to her is terrible, but a graver problem disturbs me now. As we discussed, Tanahaya carried one of our Witnesses, and so did Sijandi before he was lost. Both those mirrors are now missing. But why would mere Erkynlandish bandits steal such seemingly unimportant trinkets unless they knew their real worth?"

"What *is* their worth, Jiriki?" the count asked. "I know you use them to speak to each other. Is there something more? Can they be used as weapons?"

"Here is where our tongue and yours diverge, I fear." Shadows were filling the forest now; in his dark, plain clothes, Jiriki seemed only a pale, floating half-face. "Can a Witness be a weapon? Not as such. But they are vastly powerful, for all that, and like the precious witchwood, they are vanishing out of the world. We use them to know each other's minds across distance, and because of that, across time. But in the hands of other, less careful users, they can become portals into and out of unknown places. Dangerous places. This child's grandfather once innocently looked into mine and found himself face to face with the Norn Queen herself."

This child. Morgan hunched his shoulders, struggling to keep his temper. *This child . . . !*

"But why would anyone steal such a thing, Jiriki?" the count asked. "As you said, how could mere bandits know what they were?"

"I was hoping you might have some idea. Perhaps a rumor among mortals about Sithi objects being sold, anything that might suggest the attackers had an ordinary reason for taking them, like mere greed. But more and more I fear that those who attacked Sijandi and Tanahaya—and even those who attacked our mother and uncle—might actually have been *seeking* their mirrors, not just their lives." Jiriki abruptly halted sudden and silent as a cat. "Look, we are near to the place where you summoned us. You will be with your own people soon."

Morgan saw that they had indeed returned to the same part of the forest where he had blown the horn and summoned the Sithi, and at much the same time of day, with the sun sinking behind an unseen horizon and the blue of the sky deepening where it showed through the trees..

"So there is nothing we can do to convince your people to help us?" the count asked. "More importantly, to help your old friends, Simon and Miri-amele?"

Jiriki was somber. "My sister is even now singing against the wind, trying to convince Khendraja'aro that your concerns cannot simply be dismissed because he dislikes mortals. And now that I have heard your story of this strange Rimmersman who travels with Norns and the message he sent to you, I am more than ever convinced that Aditu and I have the right of it. But unless our uncle and the rest of our people change their hearts, we can do nothing. Tell our friends in the Hayholt that I am sorry, Count Eolair."

Morgan thought it was bad enough to be rejected, but to be ignored too was almost more than he could stand. It made him feel like a child standing beside the table waiting for the grown people to finish their talk. "Whose baby does your sister carry, Jiriki?" he asked suddenly.

"Prince Morgan!" the count said. "Some tact, please."

"Don't pretend you weren't wondering, Eolair. Don't blame me because I wasn't afraid to ask."

"That is not—" The lord steward broke off at a low flutter of sound from Jiriki. It took a moment for Morgan to understand that the Sitha was laughing, which only irritated him more.

"Forgive me," Jiriki said. "We should have spoken of this earlier. I forgot that among mortals such things are often wrapped in shame and confusion. This one time at least, Eolair, Prince Morgan is correct—it is not a question that needs to be swallowed. My sister is indeed *chiru*—ready to share with the river of our people. In other, less complicated days you would have celebrated it with us, Eolair of Nad Mullach, because it is a rare and fine thing." He turned to Morgan. "And although your question is not as important as you think it is, it will be answered, young mortal. Yeja'aro, our clan cousin, is the father."

"Are they married?" Morgan asked.

Jiriki smiled. "No, it was not—is not—that kind of pairing. We have only a few births each generation, and in our house this is the first in nearly a century, as you would reckon it, so of course everyone was pleased by the tidings."

So these were his grandparents' beloved Sithi, Morgan thought in disgust—the magical creatures they always talked about as though they were angels or even gods upon the Earth. Yet they lived in the forest like bandits, could not defend themselves against a small force of mortal attackers, and their royal women bore children out of wedlock without shame or care. He felt cheated. The whole mission had turned out as he had feared—just an excuse to get him out from under his grandparents' feet for a while.

When they stopped at the edge of the clearing a cold breeze came to meet them. They could see sunset glow through the branches. "You have only a little way to walk to reach the open lands where your friends and soldiers must be waiting. Farewell."

"Farewell, Jiriki," said Eolair. "I wish our meeting had been happier."

"Do not despair, Nobody, not even the wisest, can know all ends. We may meet again in a happier hour."

Eolair smiled without conviction. "I do not think I have so many hours, Jiriki—we do not live as long as you Sithi. My gods have nearly finished with me on this earth."

For a moment Jiriki stood silent. Then he extended a hand and clasped Eolair's. "As I said, nobody can know all ends. I hope your gods spare you longer than you suppose."

"I will pray for your mother's return to health," the count said. "And for the safe birth of your sister's child."

Jiriki nodded, then turned to Morgan. "Faith," he said.

The prince was startled. "What?"

"Faith in others, Prince Morgan," he repeated. "Faith, as Eolair has, that most of your fellow mortals mean well."

"But you don't believe that!"

"Oh, but I do," said Jiriki. "And I believe it of my own folk as well. We would not be having this conversation otherwise."

"The world is full of liars."

"All the more reason to look for truth and value it when you find it. And do not forget faith in yourself! Faith is all you lack, I think, to make your grandparents proud. Good luck and farewell, seed of the *Hikka Staja*."

Before Morgan could do more than stare and wonder at what his last words meant, Jiriki turned and strode away; within a few moments he had vanished into the forest as if he had never been there at all.

"What did he mean? What was the name he called me?"

"I do not know, Highness," said Eolair. "But we had better discuss it later. Now we should make our way out onto the open grassland as quickly as we can while we have the light. We don't want to spend the night in these woods."

Morgan shivered, though he did his best to hide it. "I hope Porto's made a fire, at least."

By the time Morgan and the count reached the forest fringe, the only trace of the sun was a bright blush along the western horizon. As they emerged from the last tall stands of birch and oak and onto the shrubby slopes leading down to the riverlands, they could see a smattering of fires on the meadow before them and a tangle of smoke like scratches against the darkening sky. They hurried toward them, the long grass whispering around their knees, then slowed and stopped.

"There's no one there," Morgan said. "No one waiting. Where have our men gone? Why would they all leave?"

Eolair looked up and down the plain. "Perhaps they are out searching for us—time among the fairy-folk is said to be different. Perhaps we have been away longer than we suspect." He leaned forward, squinting now. "My eyes are too old to make out much from so far away—do you see anyone moving?"

"Nothing. Nobody."

As they drew nearer to the silent camp, Morgan felt himself go cold all over, though the summer evening was warm and there was scarcely any breeze on the meadow. He could hear the river just a short way ahead, though it was too dark now to see more than a dark line across the grass. Most of the fires had burned down almost to coals, but they were not, as Morgan had first thought, deserted cookfires or the abandoned campfires of sentry posts.

When they reached the first fire they saw the last flames were feeding wearily on splintered wheels and blackened poles. "That was the supply wagon," said Morgan. Even to his own ears, his voice sounded like a dead man's, a ghost in an old folktale predicting doom. "By the Sacred Tree, what happened here?"

Eolair walked to the far side of the burning wagon and stood looking down. After a moment, Morgan went to join him and almost stepped on the body lying at the count's feet. "Oh, Aedon preserve us," the prince said, then turned away. "His guts are out."

"There are three dead men here all together." Morgan was surprised by the steadiness of the old man's voice—the prince felt himself only a step or two from madness and terror. All around them stretched the empty grasslands. "And a dead horse, too."

"But who could do this?" Morgan asked. "These were Erkynguards." It still did not seem remotely real. "And where are the rest?" But Eolair did not answer. After a moment, the prince looked up and saw Eolair was staring out across the grassland to the north. Morgan turned and saw a troop of armored men on horseback, several dozen at least, riding along the edge of the forest toward them.

"Are they ours?" said Eolair, but the count did not sound hopeful. "My eyes are not strong enough. Can you tell?"

Morgan squinted. He could feel his blood pounding in his head. "They have no insignia I can see—no banners, either. And all of them are wearing different kinds of armor." Even as he looked, the nearest of the riders spotted them and suddenly the whole force was riding toward them, waving axes and spears above their heads.

"Bagba bite me!" Eolair cursed. "Thrithings-men—or bandits!" He grabbed Morgan's arm and gave him a push. "Run, my prince. Run to the forest!"

"Are you mad?" Morgan had already drawn his sword. "I can't leave you—"

"You can and will, curse your stubbornness! You are the heir to the High Throne, young man, and it is my duty to keep you safe. My life is nothing to that. Run to the forest and hide there. If I survive, I will come and call for you. If I do not—well, try to find the Sithi again. Go!"

"No! I won't!" The drumming of the attackers' hooves grew louder as the horsemen swept toward like a thunderstorm, only a couple of arrows' flights away and closing quickly.

Eolair shoved Morgan again, so hard that he almost stumbled and fell. The count had his own long, slender sword in his hand now. "By Murhagh's bloody stump, if you do not run, Prince Morgan, I swear I will kill you myself before letting the Thrithings-men take you. Some of the clans burn prisoners alive!"

Morgan took a step toward the forest fringe, then another, but he could not imagine leaving the old man to die. "Come—we'll both run."

"I would never reach it," the count said. "I am too slow. No, you must escape."

"But I am a prince!"

"Fire does not care about such things," Eolair cried, "and neither does a Thrithings spear." Morgan could see little in the twilight but the count's pale face. "Run, curse you, boy—run!"

Furious and terrified, caught between two impossible choices, Morgan at last turned and sprinted toward the trees.

At the edge of the forest, dodging through a stand of ash trees, he slowed and turned to look back. The grassy plain was all but dark now but he could see that the horsemen had almost reached Eolair. The old count waited almost patiently as they began to surround him, but Morgan could also see that several of the horsemen had broken off from the main group and were now heading up the sloping meadow toward where he stood watching.

For the briefest of moments he considered turning to meet them, contemplated a heroic although likely unknown and unsung death. Then a sudden thought of Lillia came to him, of her serious little face, and he could not imagine how she would bear the news. Born without a father, and now her brother gone too? He could not do that to her—not by choice.

Morgan turned and hurried on up the slope through the grove of ash trees, tripping on shrubs and tangling grasses as he reached the darkness of the forest. Within moments the light was mostly gone and he had to slow down to little more than a walk, but for all he knew the Thrithings-men who were chasing him knew the forest well, so he kept moving and did not stop until his legs and arms were so scratched and aching he did not think he could take another step.

As he stood trying to catch his breath without making too much noise he listened for the sound of pursuers, but could hear nothing except the pounding of his own heart. After a moment he realized he was standing beneath a large tree, its trunk many times wider than he was; from the knobbly feel of its bark, he guessed it was an oak.

If I can get up into it, I can rest, he thought. *The men chasing me don't have dogs— at least I didn't see or hear any. They won't find me if I'm hidden up in the branches.*

He wondered what had happened to poor Eolair, alone against a company of mounted men, but it felt too freshly raw and painful, so he felt around for a suitable branch instead, then began to climb.

He had made his way a bit more than twice his own height off the ground when he reached the first great spread of branches. He worked himself a little higher up the tree, until he had found a wide place where several of the larger limbs came together, then seated himself with his back against the rough trunk. He listened again, but heard no sounds of pursuit, no sounds at all except the rapid buzz of a nightjar and the wind sighing through the treetops high above his head.

At last, frightened but exhausted, he dozed, dreaming of black butterflies in a cloud so dense it threatened to choke him. When he woke he could see the three-quarters moon high in the sky above, like a Midsummer mask peeping through the branches, and he wondered how long he had slept, and why he was in a tree. Then the entire, horrible truth came back to him, and for a moment he wanted nothing so much as to cry like a child and then be comforted. But there was nobody to comfort him. He was alone in the dark in the forest.

Something brushed the back of his neck and the side of his face—a branch or some leaves. It happened again, and he was about to reach up and push it away when he realized by its movement that it was not leaves or twigs but something altogether different, something alive. He went deadly still, fearing some venomous thing, spider or serpent. When he realized it was neither his heart did not slow, but began to race even faster, rattling like the nightjar's call.

A hand was gently exploring his goose-pimpling skin—a hand with long, tickling fingers so thin and so cold they might have belonged to a starveling child.

52

Homecoming

"Where is my soup? Bring me soup!"

Despite the reedy thinness of his voice and the relative immensity of the wagon—it was actually two wagons joined together—the old man's words seemed always to come to her from a mere hand's breadth away. Hyara said a prayer for patience to the Grass Thunderer, and just to be careful, one to the stone-dwellers' martyred Aedon as well. "It's not ready yet," she said. "It's still warming."

"I don't care. It's warm enough."

"It is *not* warm enough. As soon as you get it you'll be complaining, so you can wait."

"I should have pulled that spiteful tongue out of your head long ago."

It was all she could do not to reply with something really unpleasant. She no longer feared the old man, but she did fear her husband, who was quick with a blow or even a kick and always took her father's side. Her older sister saw her frustration and nodded toward the wagon's main door. "Go outside, Hyara. Take them more *yerut* and bring in the bowls. I'll deal with the old fool."

Grateful, Hyara wiped her hands on her rough apron and went outside.

Her husband was out checking the paddocks to make sure the animals were secure, but the rest of his men, relatives and hangers-on, had finished their work and were gathered around the fire waiting for the thane to return. Her husband's cousin Cudberj, who for at least this moment was the most important man in the compound, was holding forth about something that Hyara felt sure he knew little about. Her husband might be a brute, she might dream of him being gored by a bull or killed in a raid on one of the Erkynlandish settlements, but at least he was not a blatherer like his cousin.

"There you are!" Cudberj shouted when she stepped down from the wagon. "Bring us more drink, woman. My friends are thirsty."

"I've sent our son to fetch more," Hyara said. "You and the others have drained what we have, and my husband will want some when he gets back."

The trees around the camp were full of crows, more than Hyara had seen gather at once in a long while. She thought they were much like her husband's men, useless and loud.

"Well, then," said another man, a young idiot with mustaches that almost reached his collar bone, "if you've no *yerut*, give us a kiss!"

Cudberj laughed loudly at this. "You'd better hope my cousin the thane doesn't hear you say that to his wife, or he'll have your guts for stirrups."

Hyara couldn't decide which she'd enjoy more at that moment, not being the thane's wife or getting to see the thane make stirrups out of the young fool's innards. "When the boy comes back with the jug," she said, "make sure you leave enough for my husband or he'll spill the offal out of all of you."

"Didn't I tell you?" Cudberj slapped his leg and chortled. "Didn't I say she had a sharp tongue on her? And her older sister is worse. The women in this family are part snake, I tell you!"

Hyara didn't say anything, but concentrated on picking up the bowls and spoons that had been discarded without a second thought all over the area around the fire. Everybody thought that because she was the thane's wife, with the largest wagon and the largest camp, her life must be enviable. But the largest wagon and camp needed the most work to keep them tidy, and her husband, his cousins, and her ancient father were like spoiled children, leaving messes and breakage behind them wherever they went.

As she thought of the heedless men she had to deal with every day, Hyara felt the darkness begin to flow over her again, as though clouds had swallowed the sun, even though the summer twilight was clear and cloudless. Sometimes the feeling was so strong that it was all she could do not to fall down and weep, to lie helpless and unmoving until the men dragged her away and ended her uselessness, as though she were a horse with a broken leg. Her sister knew this fearful, hopeless darkness too, although neither of them spoke of it. The two of them carried the secret between them, and if nothing made it stop, at least it was a tiny bit easier for Hyara knowing she was not the only one.

She stood up, stacking the bowl she had just found onto the others she had gathered, and saw that someone was approaching the camp—a man of good size, but too slender to be her burly husband. She shaded her eyes against the setting sun but still did not recognize him, though something about the way he moved caught her attention. The newcomer did not walk so much as he loped, body balanced, head steady, like a wolf calmly pacing a herd of deer.

Cudberj saw him too and stood up, his hand falling to the ax hung on his belt. A few of the other men saw this sudden movement and looked up. Hyara could feel a certain tightness in the air suddenly. A stranger was a rare thing on the High Thrithings.

The man stopped a dozen paces from the fire and calmly examined the half-dozen men sitting there. The stranger was tall and well-muscled but not as broad as Cudberj or the others, and certainly nowhere near as burly as Hyara's own husband, the thane of the Stallion Clan. "I look for the camp of Thane Fikolmij," he said. "Is this it?"

"Why?" Cudberj demanded. He had his ax out and was stroking it as though currying a prize horse. "Who are you, to walk into the March-thane's camp so bold? I do not know your face, nor does any other man here, and you wear no clan badge."

"My name is not important," the stranger said. "Until a short time ago I was part of the Crane Clan from south of the Littlefeather, down in the Lake Thrithings. They called me Unver. But I have left them now. I have no clan."

"No clan?" Cudberj shook his head and spat into the fire. "You might as well say you have no heart, no cock. What kind of man renounces his clan?"

"A man whose clan treats him badly." The tall stranger had dark hair like a clansman, but even in the late daylight Hyara could see that his eyes were unusually pale, like someone from the far north, but more gray than blue. Something else about him caught her attention, too, something about his long, narrow face that seemed almost familiar. "But my leave-taking was not a pleasant one," he went on, "and my mood is still foul, so do not keep me standing here when I have asked you a question. Is this the camp of Thane Fikolmij?" He looked past the men to the wagon. "Is that his?" He began to walk toward the steps, but Cudberj stepped out to block his path.

"Turn around," Cudberj said, hefting his ax. He might have been no match for his cousin the March-thane, but he was still a dangerous man. "Turn around, or I will send you back to those Crane Clan cowards in pieces."

The stranger ignored him and tried to walk past. Cudberj let out a hiss of rage and grabbed at the stranger's arm, at the same time drawing back his ax to deal what would no doubt have been a mortal blow, but instead the dark-haired man grabbed Cudberj's wrist and pivoted, twisting the arm until Cudberj shrieked in astonished pain and dropped his weapon. A moment later the stranger's fist hit him full in the face, knocking him to the ground as though he had been slaughtered with a horse-maul.

The others leaped up to attack the stranger, but within a time so short it seemed to Hyara like some kind of magical vision, they were nearly all down, one with his head rammed between the spokes of the nearest wagon wheel, another with his jaw clacked violently shut by a blow from the stranger's knee. A third managed to swing his curved sword once, but by the time he brought it around, the stranger was no longer where he had been. He kicked the swordsman hard behind the knee, then again in the other knee, so that the man dropped his sword and fell to the ground, howling and clutching his injured joints. The last of Cudberj's companions had seen enough and did not attack the stranger, but sprinted away from the wagons, probably to find Hyara's husband, the thane.

During the fighting Hyara herself had climbed up onto the wagon steps, and now she blocked the stranger's way. "Do you mean harm to the women or children here?" she asked. "We will fight you if we must."

"I do not hurt women," he growled. "I do not hurt children. I want answers only. I seek my mother, the woman called Vorzheva."

"By all the gods and all the saints of Sacred Mother Church!" Hyara was so astounded she muddled her prayers together again. "Vorzheva? You are my sister's child?"

He looked at her, not particularly interested. The familiar thing she had noticed was now much plainer—a likeness in the eyes, in the hawklike nose and strong jaw, that could only have come from her own family's blood. "So I've been told. Is she still alive?"

"She is alive and she is here," said Hyara. "By the Thunderer, I do not know what to say!" A sudden thought came. "But if you wish to speak to her, you had better be fast. They will bring back my husband any moment now, and he will be angry. You must leave before he gets here. He is a terrible man."

"No," said the stranger, and his face suddenly went hard, as her sister's face sometimes went hard. It was like seeing a ghost. "Your husband is strong, perhaps, or cruel, or even dangerous, but those are not the same."

"I don't understand," she said, but she fumbled off the latch and pushed the wagon's door open. "What do you mean?"

His look suddenly made her feel sick to her stomach—he was so cold, so terribly, hopelessly angry. "*I* am what a truly terrible man looks like." He vaulted up the steps and pushed his way into the wagon.

Inside Vorzheva stood waiting, a look on her face that Hyara had never seen before, a mixture of both hope and horror. "No," she said as she saw the stranger, and pawed at her iron-gray hair, still stubbornly streaked with black even after so many years. "No, go away. You cannot see me like this, covered in ashes."

The gray-eyed man looked her up and down, and if Vorzheva's face was something hard to read, his was suddenly even more so. "You are my mother," he said at last. "Why?" There was something damaged in his voice that Hyara had not heard before. "Why did you do it?" He strode forward and took Vorzheva's face in his hand, examining it as though it were some rare object, staring at each fold and wrinkle while she stood motionless but for her eyes.

She slowly lifted a hand to clutch the stranger's wrist. "By my soul, it truly is you—!"

He shook her fingers off, then pushed her back so that she thumped against the wall of the wagon. Confused and only half-awake, their father Fikolmij struggled to sit up in his corner bed and failed.

"Tell me what is happening!" the old man demanded. "Who is this?"

Vorzheva and the stranger stood eye to eye. Hyara was frightened the man would kill her sister—she could see his arms trembling where he held her prisoned against the side wall—but before she could move toward them, he let her go and his hands fell to his sides. His face seemed empty of all feeling now.

"Why did you send me away?" he asked. "They told me that you and my father were dead."

Vorzheva did not use her sudden freedom to escape him. "I had no choice. Send you away or see you killed—those were his orders. *Him!*" She pointed to the old man in the bed, who looked from his daughter to his grandson, still not understanding.

Fikolmij blinked, then looked to Hyara, his face almost pitiful in its confusion. "I don't like this. Where is my supper?"

"Shut up, you old fool!" Vorzheva cried. "This is my son, do you hear? My son! And he has come back to kill you." Her lined face was suddenly lit with some deep exhilaration. "My Deornoth has returned, and now all will be put right." She turned back to the stranger. "That is your name, your true name—Deornoth! You were named after a hero."

Her son showed his teeth like a dog. "What sort of name is that? A stone-dweller name? But it does not matter, for it is not mine. I am Unver, and Unver I will remain."

"But your father was a prince!"

"My father left us for another woman before he died—you told me so all those years ago! And where is my sister, Derra? What did you do with her, marry her to one of those smirking brutes outside?"

Old Fikolmij suddenly seemed to understand what was happening. His eyes went wide, and his nearly toothless mouth gaped in a grin of delight. "By the Thunderer, is this the wretched stonedweller's son? Is this Prince Josua's bastard come back?" He laughed, an explosion of surprised amusement that turned into a deep cough.

"Where is my sister?" Unver demanded.

"She is gone, Deornoth, my son." Vorzheva's usually guarded expression was so naked, so raw that Hyara could barely stand to look at her. "She ran away from the family that took her. Twenty years ago, and I have mourned for her every day, as I mourned for you." She lifted a hand toward Unver, but he backed away. "No, do not blame me! When your father left us, I tried to take you away to a safe place, but the grasslands were at war and we were captured—"

"Vorzheva, you cannot speak of this now," Hyara said. "Gurdig will be back any moment. I can hear them shouting for him out by the paddocks. If this truly is your son, he must go before my husband gets here."

"Run away?" Unver gave her a brief look of contempt. "After being cast out like a lame colt or a sickly hound? No. I will stay until I have answers." He turned back to Vorzheva. "Where is my father? Why did he leave us?"

"Because he was a coward," Fikolmij wheezed from his bed. "He was always a coward. And he made your mother his whore."

Vorzheva grabbed a cup from a shelf beside her and threw it at him. It sailed wide and smashed against the wall. Fikolmij laughed, as pleased with chaos as a demented child.

"Shut your mouth!" Vorzheva screamed at the old man. "You tried to drive us apart from the beginning." She turned back to Unver. "She lured him away. That Perdruinese witch Faiera, that Scrollbearer, she stole your father from us. He left to go to her and never came back. And his noble friends did *nothing* to help us." Vorzheva looked around wildly for a moment, then hurried across the wagon to a chest piled with blankets. As Unver and the rest watched, she threw the blankets onto the floor and opened the heavy chest, sinews straining in her bony arms, then lifted something long and black from inside. It was a scabbard, and as the rest of it came into view Hyara recognized it—Vorzheva's husband's sword, a slender weapon even for the blades of city folk.

"Here!" Vorzheva cried. "Here is his sword! Tell me Josua was not bespelled by that Perdruinese she-demon! Otherwise, why would he go away and leave this behind? This is the blade he used to kill Utvart and win me!"

The tumult outside was growing very loud; Hyara could hear many people shouting. She had time only to say, "I warned you—it is Gurdig—!" before the door of the wagon was yanked open so powerfully that one of the hinges snapped. A tall, wide figure shouldered its way through, and for a moment the darkening skies behind and the flames from the wagon's cookfire made it seem a kind of demon.

Not so far from the truth, thought Hyara, her stomach like a cold stone.

"Where is this stranger?" her husband bellowed but did not wait for anyone to answer his question. Gurdig crossed the wagon so quickly that Unver scarcely had time to raise his arms before the thane hit him with the back of his fist hard enough to knock him sprawling into the crockery chest, which overturned. The lid flew open and bowls and cups tumbled out onto the wagon's floor, but even as Unver struggled to find his footing, Gurdig, who must have outweighed him by a hundredweight, caught hold of his tunic and yanked him to his feet, then threw him out through the open front door of the wagon and sprang out after him.

"Kill him, Gurdig!" shouted old Fikolmij, wheezing with delight as he struggled to get out of his bed, something he had not done in many moons. "Yes! Kill the stone-dweller's whelp!"

"One thing I swear," said Vorzheva, her voice gone icy cold. "Whatever happens, you will not be there to gloat, old man." And even as Hyara watched in astonishment, her elder sister snatched the first thing that came to her hand, a long meat fork, and jabbed it into Fikolmij's wattled neck. The old man shrieked, his eyes rolling like a panicked cow's, but even as he thrashed in the tangling blanket, his long, straggling beard slowly turned red on one side, Vorzheva picked up another object, a great carving knife, and set the point of it against his nightshirt, between his ribs. "I promised myself this day," she said, leaning close to the old man's terrified face, then shoved the blade into him until it would go no farther. Fikolmij's shrieks turned into gurgles. For a moment he waved his hands to no purpose, like an infant unable to control its limbs, then he slumped sideways in his bed in a widening red stain.

Hyara fled the wagon as if demons were after her.

At first, because of the deepening twilight, she could barely make out what was happening outside the wagon. Perhaps half a dozen men had dragged Unver to the ground, with Gurdig leaning over them like a bear trying to pick fish from a river. Dozens more had crowded into the camp and surrounded the combatants, shouting and cursing in excitement. Crows, startled from their nearby nesting tree by the noise, wheeled above the mêlée in their hundreds like a squawking thundercloud.

By sheer weight of numbers the Stallion clansmen had overwhelmed the stranger, kicking and pummeling him, shouting as they did so, some of them laughing as though it were only a rough game. Hyara suddenly wished she could set all of them on fire—the brutish clansmen, her husband, the wagon and the entire camp—then fly away like a bird.

"Off him!" Gurdig bellowed. "Off him, you shit-eaters! He is mine!"

Her husband was a very large man with a terrible temper, as Hyara and the clansmen knew well; the men swiftly untangled themselves from Unver and rolled away. The last pair dragged the stranger to his feet and pushed him staggering toward Gurdig, who felled him with a single blow of his thick fist.

"How do you dare to push your way into the March-thane's wagon?" Gurdig said, standing over him. "What clan do you come from?"

Unver looked up at him, his eyes still bright in a mask of blood and dirt. "I have no clan. I came for what is mine."

One of Gurdig's followers handed him a long, curved sword. "Then die nameless," the thane said, and spat on the ground. Gurdig turned to the men who had now formed a rough circle around the two of them. "Someone give him a blade so that I will have at least a hoof-paring's less shame when I kill him."

Hyara felt someone shoulder past her, almost tumbling her off the wagon's shallow front step. It was Vorzheva, who threw something toward Unver. It struck, pommel first, and fell flat on the ground—a long, thin, straight sword. A stone-dweller sword.

"Take it!" Vorzheva cried. "Your father called it 'Naidel'."

"He named his sword a needle?" Gurdig threw back his head and laughed, the twin braids of his beard bouncing on his chest. "Good! Very good! To call a man's weapon, especially such a puny one, after a woman's tool."

Unver looked down at the sword, blood dripping from his chin, but he did not pick it up. "I want nothing of his."

Thane Gurdig laughed again. "Then I shall give you something of mine!" he said, and leaped forward, swinging his great sword in a horizontal arc meant to decapitate the other man with one stroke. Unver rolled out of the way and let Gurdig's momentum carry him past, but it was a near thing.

The March-thane turned. His smile was wolfish. "I see there is some fight left in you. That is good, by the Grass Thunderer! I will have some evening entertainment after all!" He moved toward him, this time in a more controlled way, swiping this way and that, making Unver creep backward toward the fire pit.

"Watch out for the fire!" Vorzheva cried.

"Wife!" shouted Gurdig. "Tell your sister to keep her mouth shut or I will shut it well and truly when I finish with this horse-stealer."

For the first time, Unver's face showed something other than disgust and resignation. "I am no thief. I came only for what is mine."

"But everything here is *mine*, little man," said Gurdig, slashing again. Unver leaped backward over the pit before he could be driven into the flames, but landed badly; when he turned, he could barely stand straight. Several of the other clansmen moved to shove him back toward Gurdig, but the thane waved them off and began to stalk Unver, the fire now between them.

The trees were thick with crows. Their squawking cries almost overtopped the shouts of Gurdig's men, and even in the midst of all that was happening before her, Hyara felt a moment of superstitious dread. Nesting season for the black birds was over. Where had they all come from? It was like the famous story of Edizel Shan, when the crows came from all over the world to salute the hero's birth. But sometimes they came to herald a disaster, too.

For long moments Unver kept the fire between them, but Hyara knew the stalemate could not last long: the younger man was staggering, while her husband had not only the advantage of size but was not covered with bruises and bleeding welts from a beating as his opponent was. Gurdig already seemed almost bored with the chase; after a feint first to one side and then the other, the March-thane leaped over the fire pit and landed on the other side with a thump of impact and a scatter of sparks. Now nothing lay between him and the stranger but trampled grass. Swiping his blade again and again like a scythe, Gurdig drove the other man toward the ring of spectators, but they only fell back a little way before stopping. When Unver reached them, rough hands shoved him back toward Gurdig.

"I did not come seeking a fight," he said, breathing hard, blood bubbling in the corner of his mouth. "But you and your people gave me the back of your hand."

"I don't care if you came in a wagon with golden wheels." Gurdig was now nearly within the span of his long blade. "You forced your way into the March-thane's wagon. You struck my cousin. That is enough to earn you death and a vulture's belly for your grave, No-Clan."

"Then strike," said Unver, and lowered his arms. Many of those watching gasped in surprise or perhaps disappointment. "I will be happy to leave this world behind."

Suddenly there was a vast clatter and a chorus of shrill, creaking cries. Crows came swirling out of the nearby trees like a black cyclone, swirling up and out. But instead of flying away, the birds turned and stooped abruptly on the camp, wings and beaks everywhere, crowing in their flat, urgent voices. The onlookers shouted in surprise, throwing up their hands to protect themselves as the cloud of black birds dropped on them. Some of the clansfolk broke and ran away; others fell to their knees, but the thickest part of the flock descended on Gurdig and Unver. The March-thane, suddenly blinded by wings and bright eyes, whipped his heavy blade from side to side like a horsewhip, knocking black shapes from the air. Most of those struck fell to the ground around him, but a few were batted into the fire.

"The stranger called the birds," someone cried. "He is a witch!"

"No!" roared Gurdig. "He is my meat!" Hyara's husband had been forced back almost to the fire pit by the flurry of squawking shapes. The sword Vorzheva had thrown her son lay at Unver's feet where it had fallen, still untouched. Gurdig's violent swings began to drive away the nearest of the crows. Others had taken to the sky and were barely visible against the deep evening blue, wheeling just overhead, still croaking in what sounded like outrage or warning.

Facing him, only a few paces away, Unver did not attempt to defend himself again, but looked up at the sky and the circling birds. The firelight turned his features into a stony carving, a mask of resignation or even perhaps peace. His arms still hung at his sides as Gurdig came toward him with his curved sword swept back for the killing blow. Then a blazing ball of feathers burst out of the fire pit and flew awkwardly into the air, shedding sparks like a comet, before it swooped down and flew directly into Gurdig's face. He bellowed in surprise and pain as the burning crow battered him with its fiery wings and became entangled in his beard. His efforts to knock the thing away only made it cling more fiercely, until the dying bird was screeching as loudly as the thane, whose beard now curled and smoked where the crow clung to it.

A moment later Unver lurched forward, picked the slender sword from the ground, then lunged toward Gurdig and buried the point three handspan's deep in the March-thane's burly chest.

The dead crow fell away from Gurdig's face and dropped to the ground, feathers almost extinguished, all movement ended. Gurdig's eyes bulged in disbelief as he looked from the crow to the shining length of Naidel jutting just beneath his breastbone. He opened his mouth to say something but only blood issued from his lips, then he slowly sank to his knees before toppling face first to the ground like a falling tree.

Unver stood over him, expressionless, staring at nothing. The crows overhead began to settle back into the trees around the camp, their harsh cries changing to something more muted, the branches sagging as they gathered once more.

None of the crowd touched Unver. Nobody dared to come near to either the March-thane or his killer. Instead they stood, awestruck and terrified. Someone shouted "murderer!" but another cried, "The crows knew!"

Like Edizel Shan, Hyara thought, stunned and helpless. *The birds swarmed at Edizel's birth and flew through the fire.* She stared at her husband's body, at Gurdig's sightless eyes staring up into the night, but she felt nothing. He had been her world, and a cruel world it had been. Now he was dead. She felt nothing at all. She could not understand how everything in her life had changed so much in the space between twilight and dark.

She was still standing when Vorzheva led her son back to the steps of the thane's wagon. Still as speechless as an infant, he let her seat him there. Some of those who had been watching now came forward to gather silently around the body of the March-thane. Others stared at Unver where he sat on the steps, bleeding and silent, the slender, red-smeared sword still gripped in his hand.

"My father is dead," said Vorzheva. She almost sang it, as though the words were a cradle song. "Fikolmij is dead. And Gurdig is dead." Now she raised her voice, so everyone could hear. "The March-thane Gurdig is dead, in fair combat. The gods spoke—you all saw. My son is March-thane now." She put her hand on his head, but he seemed not to feel or even notice. "And you will make them all pay, now that you have returned to me. You will show them blood and fire, my son—all the clans, and the stone-dwellers too. You will show them *blood and fire!*"

Unver remained silent. All around the camp wide-eyed clansfolk whispered to one another, looking from the thane's corpse to the black birds still watching from the trees.

At last, as if waking from one dream and passing into another, Hyara went to help her sister wash Unver's wounds and bandage them with clean white linen.

53

Their Masters' Folly

It was a terrifying journey down the wide Avenue of the Martyred Drukhi. The weight of her few belongings and the food she was carrying meant she had to go slowly—not that Tzoja would have dared to walk much faster even if she could. No slave ever wanted to attract attention so they all went at much the same pace, just fast enough not to be accused of slacking, but not so swift as to attract the attention of suspicious guards.

The thoroughfare was dazzlingly lit by Nakkiga's standards, with a torch column at every crossing, but the light for which Tzoja was usually so grateful now made her feel conspicuous and vulnerable. She pulled the hood of her cloak down as far as she dared as a trio of fully armored Sacrifices walked past. But the soldiers were discussing something and did not even look at her. When they were gone, she stepped up out of the gutter and continued on. The streets were quiet, which was not unusual—unless there was a public celebration, Nakkiga was never noisy—but also strangely empty. Something was happening, Tzoja could tell.

Nothing to me, she reminded herself. *It's nothing to me. Head down, walk straight, don't bump into any Hikeda'ya and don't look up unless someone addresses me.* It was a good thing that all slaves in Nakkiga were frightened of being noticed, because that was at least one way in which Tzoja did not have to pretend.

She turned off the broad avenue into the slightly less daunting confines of the Street of Sacred Discipline, a shadowy, narrow passage with old stone houses looming close on both sides. Some of the buildings were training dormitories for the Order of Song, which made her anxious—even the youngest Singers were strange and could be full of disturbing surprises—but at this hour of the clock they should be at their academies, and it was by far the fastest way to the city's outer roads.

So far to go! Tzoja had seldom left the residence in Clan Enduya's compound during the last years, and other than an occasional trip to the Animal Market, she only went out in Viyeki's company, borne by litter on the back of carry-men. All this walking had exhausted her already, but she could not stop to rest. Her only hope was to remain unnoticed until she reached the level of the deep lake.

The overhanging houses here oppressed her. Uniformly dark, finished in the slate that had been fashionable centuries earlier, they seemed like a row of heads leaning in to watch her pass. Low, narrow windows facing the street gave them the slit-eyed stare of something that had just been awakened and was not happy about it. It felt as if every window held a watcher she could not see, that each step she took was being silently observed and judged, and that at any moment someone would raise an alarm about the intruder in their silent neighborhood.

She passed through a grave cache at the end of the road, a kind of fenced park built around a pile of stone slabs. Beneath it lay the crypt where the Hikeda'ya interred the ashes of those who sentiment forbade dumping in the Field of the Nameless, but who had not been important enough to earn a place in a family tomb or in the death-cote of one of the great Order-houses. The grave cache was largely overgrown with grass and black creeper, but here and there the bright bloom of a blood lily burned like a candleflame. A few offerings had been left before the crypt door, loose flowers and pairs of house slippers, which made her think that at least some of those entombed here must have been students from the Order of Song. Even the idea of dead Singers made her uneasy. She decided a slave who hurried through such a place would not attract undue notice, so she walked as quickly as she could.

On the far side of the grave cache she left the park and was able to move into the network of smaller streets surrounding the center of Nakkiga. Her heart finally slowed a little. There was much less chance that one of the lower caste folk living here would stop or question a slave, because any slave might be on an errand for someone powerful; just as slaves did not want to be noticed by anyone, lower caste Hikeda'ya, both Bound and Pledged, did not want to draw the attention of the Recognized, their high caste superiors. Utuk'ku's people were reluctant to kill any of their own pure-blooded folk because they were now so few, but it was no gift for even a full-blood criminal to be allowed to live: the punishment for angering a noble was often far worse than mere death. But because of all these things, the closer Tzoja got to Nakkiga's center, the less likely it was anyone would stop her.

Terror is a weapon with a sharp edge on both sides, she thought. *That is its greatest weakness.*

A rare memory of her father pushed up into her thoughts, of him telling her, "He who rules by fear can expect at best only obedience, and even that only as long as fear remains." She had been too young to understand him at the time and had not thought of it for years, but suddenly it was as though he stood over her again. How tall he had seemed!

She had many memories of her dark-haired mother, strong and sour as vinegar, and of her second mother Valada Roskva singing wordlessly as she concocted her cures and simples, her thick, deft fingers sifting the herbs into loosecloth bags, but Tzoja could remember surprisingly little of her father, except how wonderful it felt when he came back from one of his trips to Nabban or Perdruin, how the house had seemed to glow, how easily words had become laughter—even the food had tasted better! Until that time he didn't come back.

And that is another weapon with a sharp edge on both sides, she thought. *A father's love, or a daughter's love for him.*

It took her two bells to make her way across the broad city tier and down into the lower levels because she was doing her best to look like the kind of unimportant, shuffling creature that the Hikeda'ya nobles would not concern themselves with. The second bell from Martyrs Temple was so distant she could barely hear it the second time because, instead of following the well-traveled route to the Memory Gardens down into the ultimate depths, she had chosen that rarity in Nakkiga, a comparatively new road, the clean-edged tunnel that led outward from the city and down to Dark Garden Lake, an underground body of water that her master and husband Lord Viyeki had discovered when she herself was still an infant. Viyeki had only taken her there once, but she had no fear of getting lost because it was a well-known route. During Serpent's Moon, hundreds of families would crowd this passage on their way to the lake to celebrate the end of the Days of Mourning. But more than half a year stretched between now and then: other than a few Bound and their fishing boats, Tzoja felt sure that the end of the lake where the houses of the nobility stood would be all but deserted.

The last part of her journey led her along a winding outer tunnel barely wide enough for a single noble family's litter and baggage train. Plenty of those would be jostling down the passage when Serpent's Moon returned, but just now she heard no sound but her own footfalls and what the Hikeda'ya called "the mountain's breath," the perpetual soft winds that moaned through these deep passages. She wondered how long she would have to stay hidden. A dark, anxious part of her imagined what it would be like to live here in a darkness even thicker than the city's, chasing lizards for food when her supplies were gone; she shuddered, but reminded herself how fortunate she was to have this refuge.

While carving out a deep shelter during the siege of Nakkiga, a building crew under Viyeki's command had broken through into a previously unknown cavern and found a lake there full of blind, white fish and crustaceans, more than enough of them to help save the starving population. As a reward for this accidental but invaluable service, Viyeki had been given one of the lake's first festival houses when they were built, but for some reason that Tzoja did not understand, her master had never been entirely happy about that or comfortable with the place. In fact, he had decided only a few years later to give it to his own master, High Magister Yaarike, but the house on the lake had never actually changed hands because Magister Yaarike died in a rockfall shortly after Viyeki told him of the gift. The old magister's family had not known about it, and Viyeki himself had been too busy to give it much thought after he was named Yaarike's successor as leader of the Order of Builders. Best of all, Lady

Khimabu, Viyeki's wife, had been told that the festival house by the underground lake now belonged to Yaarike's heirs in the Kinjada clan, and had never learned otherwise. Of all Viyeki's intimates, only Tzoja knew the truth, because he had told her of it and brought her for a visit in the early years of their bond. Before his work had overwhelmed him, Viyeki had hoped it would be their place, far from gossiping servants, so Tzoja alone, of all his family and intimates, had the heavy key-bar that would open the house. As she made her way now through a forest of black dripstones toward the small estate, able to see only because of all the shining grubs on long, sticky threads that dangled above the edges of the lake, she found herself immeasurably grateful that things had worked out this way.

She thought of her mother, left behind so very many years ago. *"A fox's den never has only one entrance,"* had been one of Vorzheva's favorite sayings. *"Always have an escape ready."* At least in this one way, Tzoja had proved herself her mother's true child.

Her mother had shared that bit of wisdom long before their father disappeared, when the four of them had still been living peacefully at the inn called Pelippa's Bowl in Kwanitupul and there had seemed no need even to think about such things. Now, all these years later, father and mother and brother lost to her for decades and her own original name little but a memory, Tzoja saw that her mother might have been an unhappy woman, bitter as wormwood, but she had been right about always being ready to run.

She was a long time hiking around the lake to the festival house in a darkness, illuminated only by the sparkling strands hanging above the water. The glowing grubs swayed so gently on their filaments that they appeared to flicker, which reminded her of her names both old and new.

"Derra? It means 'star,' my child," her mother had told her when she was small. And so did "Tzoja," the Hikeda'yasao name Viyeki had given to her when she had shared that little remnant of her past in the first days of their unexpected love. *Once a star, always a star,* he had told her.

Tzoja was so deep into thoughts of the past that she gasped in surprise and stumbled when she stepped out of a thicket of smooth stone columns and found the great, glittering expanse of the night-dark lake stretched before her. For a moment it seemed as though she had walked directly into the starry sky—black stone overhead, black water below, and between those two horizons, thousands upon thousands of tiny, glowing points.

She turned, and there above her, shimmering gently on one of the stony hills that seemed to prop the ceiling of Dark Garden Lake, stood the volcanic stone house that had been awarded to her master by the palace, in thanks for the discovery of this strange, beautiful place. The path to its portico led upward between pale, dimly glowing lawns of candlesnuff fungus and whitecrown to a massive front door carved with the circular wreath of leaves and grass that the Hikeda'ya used as a symbol for the Lost Garden. Tzoja knew there would be blankets and robes inside for her to sleep on, as well as water and preserved food to pad out the supplies she had brought with her. She would be able to live here in secrecy and safety for at least a while—perhaps even until Viyeki came back.

But perhaps I won't stay lucky that long, she reminded herself. She needed to start thinking about what she would do if this den were discovered, too.

Tzoja settled her bag on her shoulder for the last steep hike to safety, and began to clamber up the slope of loose stones toward the front path.

The light rain felt oddly soothing against Viyeki's skin, like the touch of a thousand small, cold fingers.

What would it be like, he wondered, *to live always beneath the sky like this? Our great mountain protects us but it also isolates us. We take our children from their mothers young to protect them from sentiment and the weakness it causes, and we avoid Mother Sun for the same reason. But is it truly weak to enjoy what the sky brings?*

It was a strange and interesting thought, the kind that he often had when he left the confines of Nakkiga, but Viyeki could not afford to follow it just now. He had too many questions he needed to ask the upstart cleric Sogeyu and the Sacrifice military commanders—something that irritated him in and of itself: Why should a high magister have to seek for information? But he could find neither the main officers nor leading Singers anywhere around the camp, although he had walked from one end to the other. And not one of the Hikeda'ya soldiers or the bestial Tinukeda'ya carry-men who remained could tell him where they had gone.

His own company of Builders and the rest of the Sacrifice troops were spread across the north side of a hill in what he guessed must be the northern marches of mortal Erkynland. No fires had been lit, and even starlight and moonlight were scarce tonight with rain clouds thronging the blueblack midnight sky. He was thankful that at least they were not making their presence on mortal lands any more obvious than was necessary. Still, as he searched for the other commanders he felt himself almost a phantom, as though it was not the other Hikeda'ya leaders who had left him, but Viyeki himself who had stepped out of the world.

These lands are so wide, he thought, looking out across a landscape that sparkled with rain. *So much room! How can the mortals stand it? How can they protect it all?*

The answer was, of course, that they couldn't. In the past, only the sheer lack of soldiers had kept the Hikeda'ya from triumphing in their battles against the mortals, who bred like rats in a midden-heap. That was why the Order of Sacrifice had declared the defeat of the old ways after the failed War of Return, and with the help of Viyeki and others had taken advantage of Queen Utuk'ku's long sleep to change the ancient laws and begin to use mortal women as brood animals.

Viyeki felt a moment of pain thinking of his lovely Tzoja that way, but as one of the queen's high magisters he could not shrink from the truth: as an individual, his mistress seemed almost as real to him as another Hikeda'ya, but as a race they were little more than vermin.

Perhaps we could save the best of them when we finally win back our land, he thought. *That would be a kindness befitting an old and generous race like ours. And that way we would save them from themselves.*

Viyeki stepped to the side of the path as a procession of brutish carry-men lumbered past pulling an empty supply wagon, silent but for their steady breathing, muscles bulging and straining. Even their overseer made no noise as he teased the creatures' thick skin with the barbed tip of his crop. The carry-men's hairless heads bobbed in rhythm with each step, as though they were one many-headed beast.

When they had passed him and gone trudging down the hill toward the main camp, Viyeki suddenly wondered where they were coming from. Why would a supply wagon be here, at the farthest edge of the camp, if not to bring someone supplies? But the supply train itself would have come in on the opposite side of the camp, trailing the soldiers' advance.

Viyeki ordered his new secretary Nonao and the clan guards back to camp because he didn't completely trust any of them, then he began to climb the slope in the direction from which the empty wagon had come. When he reached the hilltop he had time only to stand in the swirl of wind and spattering rain for a half-dozen heartbeats before a pair of Sacrifice guards appeared as if from nowhere and ordered him to remain where he was.

"What are you doing?" he asked as they approached with their spears lowered. "Could it be that you Pledged value your heads so lightly? I am High Magister Viyeki, Lord of Builders."

They looked at him with more curiosity than they had before, but kept their spears lowered. "These useless slaves beg your pardon, Magister," said one of them. "But we have orders from Host General Kikiti to let no one pass. We were told of no exceptions."

"If one of Queen Utuk'ku's high magisters is not an exception, then the queen herself will hear of it," Viyeki said, and his cold fury was only partly for effect. "I do not doubt the punishments will be dreadful. Do you know of the Cold, Slow Halls?"

Both soldiers remained stolid, but Viyeki could see by the narrowing of their eyes that his threat had struck home. "Yes, Magister," they said in ragged chorus.

"Well, then I suggest you think very, very carefully. I wish to pass. Will you try to stop me, or will you seek out your superiors and avoid a terrible mistake?"

Neither guard looked at the other, but he could feel the tension that gripped them both.

"I will go and ask our troop chieftain," said one finally. He turned and within moments had vanished down the steep slope on the far side of the hill. His companion now assumed an even more fixed and determined look, as if he hoped to redouble the threat to make up for the other guard's absence. Viyeki tamped down his anger and humiliation. These were ignorant Sacrifices, mere minions—Hikeda'ya, yes, but only a step or two up from Tinukeda'ya slaves. Letting himself feel anger at them was like hating the watchdog chained to the barn door.

It was League Commander Buyo who came back with the guard, his broad face creased in dismay. "High Magister Viyeki, what are you doing here?"

"What am *I* doing here? I go where I please, Commander. Why am I being stopped as if I were an interloper?"

"I am sorry, Magister, but the Host General and the Host Singer gave strict orders. We did not expect you."

"I suppose that you mean Kikiti and Sogeyu. Take me to them now."

Buyo hesitated for a moment, but wherever his ultimate loyalties might lie, there was no possibility in any sensible Hikeda'ya world that a mere commander could dispute with a high magister. "Of course, great lord. Follow me, please."

At first it looked as though the missing officers and Singers had built a small, separate camp for themselves on the east side of the hill, in a forest of rocky outcroppings just below the summit, but as Buyo led him down the winding path from the hillcrest, Viyeki realized that it was not just a camp but a sentry post, positioned so it could look across the wide valley at the Forbidden Hills and the great Oldheart Forest beyond.

Sogeyu greeted him there, her face solemn and her manner ingratiating. "My deepest apologies, Magister Viyeki! We would have sent for you within the matter of an hour or so even had you not come looking for us. Please forgive us."

"I cannot forgive you until I know what you have done, Host Singer," he replied with stiff formality. It was a dangerous thing to be left out of important meetings—a bad sign at best, and usually a token of fatal mistrust. "Why have I been ignored?"

"Not ignored, Magister. We delayed to summon you only to make certain that our forward position was safe for visitors."

Viyeki doubted that—he could now see the others present, several more Singers and several important Sacrifices as well, including Host General Kikiti, and they all looked quite settled. "How thoughtful," he said.

"Welcome, High Magister," said General Kikiti, lean and long-legged as a black heron in his spiky armor. "Join us, my lord. We are making our plans, and although you need take no part in them at first, soon yours will be the most important part of all."

"What do you mean?"

"Turn. Look." Kikiti swept his long arm out to indicate the uneven plain that lay below them. "What do you see?"

The dawn was just beginning to creep up behind Oldheart Forest—Viyeki could see its warning glow all along the horizon—but night's shadows still clung to everything but the very tops of the Forbidden Hills. Still, he could make out something on one of the slopes facing him, halfway down its purple-black side. He squinted. Something lay there waiting for the dawn to reveal it—a cluster of dim, boxlike shapes. "A fortress?" he guessed.

"More than just a fortress," said Sogeyu, stepping up to stand beside him. She smelled of something Viyeki could not name, something sour that made Viyeki's nostrils twitch and his mouth pucker. "What you see are the remains of what was once the infamous Slave Hold—the place the mortals call *Naglimund*."

"But it *belongs* to the mortals now!" Viyeki said, astonished. "They took it back again when we lost the War of Return." As the dawn light grew stronger he could make out the mortal settlement that stretched along the hillside below the fort. His sharp Hikeda'ya eyes could even see what looked like the movement of people and animals as the mortals' day began.

"We did not lose that war," said General Kikiti harshly, narrowing his own hawklike gaze. "Our queen was persuaded to put too much confidence in her chief ally, the undead Zida'ya princeling—"

This was an old argument, and clearly Host Singer Sogeyu did not want it to begin again because she immediately interrupted. "You are doubtless right, General, but that is not our concern. The task our beloved queen has set us is to take the fortress back, and then to hold it until we have done what we must."

It was one thing to discover that the Hikeda'ya host of which Viyeki was a commander—although not the sort of commander who was kept informed of important matters, he thought angrily—had been sneaking across mortal lands because of a bargain with the mortal king of Hernystir, but it was another entirely to learn that they were supposed to attack and overthrow a fortified military outpost that belonged to the mortals' high king and queen. "But why?" he asked. "For the love of our queen and the Garden, why? What purpose does it serve us to start a war here?"

Although Viyeki outranked him, General Kikiti barely disguised his contempt. "The war has already started, Magister. The Order of Sacrifice has known that since the queen first awakened from her sleep, already planning revenge against those who tried to destroy us. In fact, it would be more proper to say that the war never ended. But now our long retreat will truly and finally come to an end."

If Viyeki had not been so shocked he would have felt gravely insulted. "I do not understand what you are saying, General. All this way simply to attack a mortal fortress? Then why bring me? Any host-engineer of the House of Walls can lay a siege."

"Ah, but taking the fortress is only the beginning," said Sogeyu, black eyes glittering in the depths of her hood. "You see, there is a far greater task coming after the siege—one more than worthy of your eminence, High Magister. Because beneath the ancient Slave Hold, hidden under countless tons of rock, lies an object of great power. In all the years they have held their 'Naglimund,' as they call it, the mortals never knew what lies beneath. When we briefly held the place during the War of Return, the Order of Song used the power of a certain object hidden there to aid the Storm King Ineluki in his doomed quest, but we did not have the time or knowledge to find it and bring it to the surface before we were forced to retreat."

"'It'? What is this object?" Viyeki demanded. "What could be worth resuming war with the numberless mortals?"

"The armor of Ruyan the Navigator," said Sogeyu flatly, "the greatest of all the Tinukeda'ya. In that armor, he helped our people flee the Garden on the Eight Ships, and brought his own race and ours here, across all the deadly dangers of the Ocean Indefinite and Eternal. But when we have found his tomb and recovered his armor, and it has been given into the hands of the queen and her great counselor Akhenabi, it will do something even more remarkable."

"And that is?" What he had assumed was Sogeyu's pride in her own importance, or in their vital service for Queen Utuk'ku, was something more, Viyeki suddenly realized. The sound of her voice and the look on her exulting face told him Sogeyu was a fanatic even by the broad standards of the Order of Song.

"The Navigator's armor will help us to sweep the mortals and our traitorous relatives the Zida'ya from the very face of this land," she declared. "That is all any of us needs to know until our queen wishes to tell us more. Hail to the Mother of All! Our queen will live forever, and her triumph will be complete and unending."

"Hail to the Mother of All!" echoed General Kikiti. "All hail the queen!"

"All hail the queen," said Viyeki, but his secret thoughts were fearful, and his heart heavy as black granite from the deepest quarries of Nakkiga. The terrible madness that had nearly destroyed them all was sweeping through his people again. And worst of all, Viyeki knew his only child was one of the young Hikeda'ya warriors who would pay the price of their masters' folly.

The immense length of the serpentine creature scrambling down the hill stunned Nezeru as much as its daunting speed.

Her heart rattled in her ribs until it threatened to burst from her chest. The dragon they had captured seemed nothing beside this monstrous worm—like a model built in soft clay, some clumsy, miniature replica of the awesome reality.

The new beast was more slender than the captive but at least four times as long, with forelegs as exaggerated as the hind limbs of a cricket, so that it lurched from side to side as it descended, knocking loose sprays of snow and dislodging balanced stones, forcing Nezeru and her companions to dive out of the way. Even so, a tumbling boulder as big as a mine cart took an unexpected bounce and struck Goh Gam Gar on the shoulder before careening over the edge of the rocky shelf on which they stood. The giant windmilled his arms for balance, but to no effect: an instant later he had disappeared over the precipice. Another large boulder, sliding more than rolling, missed Nezeru by only a few paces and skidded to a slow halt behind her, just a short distance from the cliff's edge.

The mortal Jarnulf raised his bow and loosed a stream of arrows toward the dragon; Nezeru saw some of them hit its bristle-covered hide and bounce away. One even flew into the creature's gaping mouth, which was gray as rotted meat, but didn't seem to bother the beast at all.

"Nakkiga and the Queen!" cried Makho, waving his sword Cold Root as he clambered through the snow toward the monster.

Kemme was just behind his chieftain, sword in one hand and a rock as large as his head in the other, as though he had simply grabbed what was closest to him. "The Queen!" he shouted. Even in this moment of sheer terror, Nezeru thought he sounded almost happy.

The larger dragon had a neck like the body of a great serpent; even as it wound downslope it kept the two Hikeda'ya at a distance by coiling to strike again and again, each time with a curious, hissing rattle of the spiny hairs along its back. Its head was long and ended in a bony, fanged snout curved like a hawk's beak. The eyes, like those of the smaller beast that lay bound at Nezeru's feet, were pale blue and seemed empty as a blind beggar's.

The snapping jaws struck at Makho again, missing the hand chieftain by only a small distance, but this time as the head swung back it struck him in the leg and knocked him head over heels into the snow. Nezeru was shooting at it, but most of her arrows did not penetrate the creature's thick skin, and those that stuck only became more bristles rattling against the white hide.

Nezeru struggled to think. Goh Gam Gar had tumbled off the mountain and was gone. Makho had fallen, and although Kemme was protecting him, attacking the creature's head with a flurry of swordstrokes, the dragon seemed to have no problem evading his blows. Steam billowed from its hissing mouth, so that after a few moments Kemme and the beast seemed to be dancing in a fog bank.

None of this is going to save us, she realized. In only a few moments, they would all be dead and the mountainside would be silent again.

"Jarnulf!" she shouted. "Over here! Help me!"

Arrows spent, he tossed his bow to one side and hurried toward her, lifting his knees high as he struggled through the thick snow.

"Hold this," she shouted, throwing him one end of her coil of Blue Cavern rope. He caught it, but was distracted by a hissing bellow from the creature above them and an answering moan from the captive dragon. She grabbed the rest of the rope and scrambled along the step to where the largest boulder had skidded to a halt a few paces from the edge of the mountain.

As Nezeru scrambled up onto the boulder, trailing the length of cord behind her, Jarnulf saw what she was doing and did his best to keep the rope from getting snagged. Farther upslope Makho had climbed to his feet again, but now it was Kemme who lay sprawled and bloody in the snow. The worm's long head lashed out again and again as Makho tried to protect his fellow Sacrifice, jaws snapping only inches from his flesh.

As Nezeru reached the part of the boulder lying nearest the cliff's edge she almost overbalanced. For a moment the emptiness below seemed to leap up and surround her, but she managed to lower herself into an unsteady crouch until the wheeling dizziness passed, then continued looping her rope around the boulder.

"Make a noose!" she called to Jarnulf, but the Rimmersman had anticipated her and already held the knotted loop.

"Just tell me when you're ready!" he shouted.

In a sane world she would have had time to tie everything properly, to make sure the rope was firmly in place and that the pull would be even. Instead, she slid off the boulder with the Blue Cavern cord merely looped several times around the boulder and knotted. "Go!" she cried.

Jarnulf scrambled up the slope with his head down and his body low. The steaming clouds of the dragon's breath now made it impossible to see either Makho or Kemme. The only proof that at least one of them still lived was the continuous rising and dipping of the dragon's immense head as it struck over and over at some invisible target.

The rope left in his hands rapidly growing shorter, the mortal clambered up the last rise and then had to duck as the dragon's flailing tail appeared from the mist like some monster scythe, nearly crushing him. For a moment Nezeru could see the creature's back legs as the mist swirled up, and Jarnulf saw them too. He waited until the nearest one had lifted so the creature could drive toward Makho again, then he threw his wide noose onto the snow where the clawed foot was coming down.

As the dragon stepped into the noose Jarnulf dove back beneath the returning tail. The rope pulled tight against the boulder and the worm roared in fury to discover itself partially immobilized, but it was too busy defending itself against Makho's redoubled attacks to try to bite through the restraint. The smaller worm was awake and had broken its own rope muzzle. It screeched at the air as if imitating the larger beast.

Fog spread along the mountainside, whipped into streamers like the fluttering banners of a festival parade or the white streamers of a funeral procession. Nothing seemed entirely real. Nezeru set her back against the boulder and began trying to push the great stone the last couple of paces toward the cliff's edge, but she could not budge it. "By the Holy Garden," she screamed, "somebody *help me!*"

A moment later the mortal Jarnulf crunched awkwardly back down the snowy slope and began pushing beside her. The rope tied to the dragon's leg was between them, and Nezeru could hear its plaits creak as the dragon pulled against it, but the monster was still fixed on Makho and Kemme, snapping at them with its long jaws. She prayed they could keep distracting the worm a few moments longer, and also sent a prayer of thanks to the weavers and the pale, tireless spiders of the Blue Cavern for making the rope so strong. Still, it was becoming clear that even if the restraint held it would not be enough to save them, because she and Jarnulf didn't have the strength to budge the great boulder.

Just as despair washed over her like an icy stream, sucking away the last of her warmth and strength, Nezeru heard a scraping noise. An instant later two immense, hairy hands appeared on the edge of the precipice a short distance away; a moment later, the ugly, brutish face of Goh Gam Gar rose into view.

Nezeru did not think she had ever been so glad to see another living thing. "Help us!" she called. "Help us push!"

The giant looked at the scene with disgust as he pulled himself up, then spat a gobbet of red onto the snow, but did not waste time arguing. His whitish fur was stained in a dozen places by dirt and streaming blood, and one of his fingers was clearly broken, jutting at an odd angle, but when Goh Gam Gar was onto the slope he crossed the distance in a single stride and set his shoulder against the huge stone. The bellowing of the two dragons had now reached a terrible pitch, the older one thundering so loudly that drifts of snow broke loose on the nearby mountains, while the younger one shrieked and honked with what sounded like genuine terror.

I will fight as one already dead, Nezeru recited, *unafraid because my sacrifice was made long ago.* It was the pledge she had been taught when she had first entered her order. *I will fight as one already dead—!*

Then the great stone began to slide. It was only a small movement at first, a shudder and a slip, but the dragon felt the tug on its leg and bellowed again, this time with an edge of frustrated rage. Nezeru's entire body was trembling, muscles jumping in agony along her back and neck, but she dug in and kept pushing as hard as she could. Beside her the giant bent and set his shoulder lower against the boulder, and for a moment his massive, hideous face was only a few inches from Nezeru's own, his hot, stinking breath on her, huge eyes rolled up in his head so that all she could see were the whites, now red as blood. The stone slid again, then the edge of it scraped out over the drop and dipped sharply downward; Nezeru felt her feet go out from under her. She was stumbling, falling, following the boulder out into emptiness when Goh Gam Gar's huge hand closed around her leg and yanked her back. The boulder teetered for a brief moment, then tipped almost soundlessly over the edge, leaving behind only a puff of snow and rock dust.

The dragon's leg was yanked out from under it, and as it was dragged backward down the short slope bellowed so loud Nezeru was nearly deafened. As the boulder tumbled down the mountainside the dragon slithered backward on three legs, claws useless against the pull of the great stone, then lost its balance entirely and began to slide ponderously toward the precipice.

Nezeru only realized that the great fanged mouth had swung toward her when the bulk of the dragon was already sliding over the edge. She did not have time to dodge, or even to move. The huge jaws thumped closed just a hand's breath in front of her face with a noise like a wagon axle snapping, near enough for her to feel the waft of foul air from its missed strike, then the monster was gone.

For a moment everything around her became silence and more than silence, a humming nothingness that seemed to have descended over the world.

Sound came back slowly. Nezeru rolled away from the edge and crawled far enough back from it to feel safe before collapsing again. The mortal Jarnulf was kneeling in the snow a short distance away, gasping and quivering as if in some kind of fit. Makho and Kemme had survived too, and now came limping down the slope toward them, Saomeji trailing a short distance behind.

Goh Gam Gar stood over the smaller dragon where it lay, still bound but thrashing as though it did not realize the fight had ended. The giant stared down at it for a moment, then kicked it hard. The creature gave a grunting squeal like a stuck pig, squirming in its bonds and huffing steam.

"Call for your mother *now*, shit-worm," the giant snarled. He bent and picked his great axe out of the snow. "She'll still be just as dead, and I'll give you something you'll like even less than that kicking."

"Don't hurt it." Nezeru crawled toward the captive beast and began to wind another length of rope around its snout, careful to avoid its thrashing attempts to bite her. The small dragon's movements were still slowed by the poison that had felled it, and when Jarnulf stumbled over to help, the two of them managed to secure the rope around its toothy muzzle without too much trouble.

"Why don't we simply drain some of this thing's blood here? How are we going to wrestle this monster down the mountain? It may not be as big as its mother, but it's plenty big enough."

"I am weary of your questions, mortal," Makho snarled. "The queen and Akhenabi want a live dragon. The rituals must be performed on a living creature when taking the blood—or so Saomeji tells me." The chieftain came and crouched beside the beast, followed shortly by Kemme and the Singer. They examined its length.

Saomeji leaned close and stared into the dragon's pale-blue eye. "We have uses for you," he told the bound monster.

"We will build a sledge to carry it," said Makho. "The giant can pull it back to Nakkiga."

"But it's a long way back down to any trees big enough to make a sledge," Nezeru said.

"Then the giant will just have to go and get them," said Makho.

"Go and get them, you say?" roared Goh Gam Gar. He stood up, brandishing his axe, the curved blade big as a cart wheel, and loomed over Makho. "Is that how it is, after the mortal and the Blackbird and I saved you? I'll throw you down the mountain and then we'll see *you* drag a few trees back!" Suddenly the giant groaned and grabbed at his neck. He swayed, then dropped to his knees, gasping for breath.

"Speak so to your masters again and I will burn the heart from your body, animal." Makho lifted the crystalline rod so the giant could see it. The huge beast could only groan and roll in the snow. "This never leaves my person. Do not forget who rules here."

"Enough," wheezed Goh Gam Gar. "Enough." He leaned forward and steadied himself with one massive hand. Makho stared at the suffering giant in satisfaction, but was careful to stay out of his long reach.

Nezeru was experiencing an unexpected sympathy for Goh Gam Gar when a rattling, scraping sound suddenly caught her attention. An instant later the larger dragon's narrow, horselike head suddenly rose from below the cliff's edge, wounded and bloody but clearly alive: some obstacle on the mountainside had kept the terrible thing from sliding all the way down into the abyss. Now, before any of the Hikeda'ya could move, the head whipped forward on its long neck and snatched Kemme off the ground, the great jaws closing around his midsection. The Sacrifice had time only for a brief cry that ended as the jaws crunched down, then the great worm tossed his broken, bloody body out into the empty air and Kemme was gone.

Next the dragon—dripping red in a dozen places and with one useless foreleg—began to struggle up over the edge of the cliff. Makho thrust at its occluded eye with his sword, but the dragon caught the blade in its teeth and yanked Makho off his balance and down into the snow at its feet. Then, as the worm reared to strike at him, the giant Goh Gam Gar clambered onto his feet, roaring in wordless rage, and brought his massive axe down on the creature's long neck just behind the head, all but slicing through the spine. The worm writhed like a dying snake, the long neck fountaining black blood that fell hissing into the snow, then the great dragon lost its grip on the cliff edge, slid backward, and vanished once more.

Still stunned by the suddenness of it all, Nezeru did not even realize, for the first moments after the monster fell, that someone was screaming—long, ragged, agonized cries. It took her another moment to recognize the voice as Makho's. He was drenched in black blood from his head to his chest, and his skin was smoking.

Saomeji dove forward to snatch the crystal goad from Makho's hand, then used it to drive Goh Gam Gar backward, forcing the huge creature to howl and cower. When the giant was a safe distance away, the Singer bent and began piling snow on the wounded chieftain's burns.

"Help me, Sacrifice," he said to Nezeru. "He can still be saved, I think."

She crouched bedside him and began grabbing handfuls of snow, but she could already see Makho's skin peeling loose in blackened strips, showing reddish meat beneath. Makho had now stopped screaming and only bubbled and gasped, eyes unseeing, spirit trapped somewhere in a land of suffering. Nezeru piled the snow thickly on his face, as much to hide the terrible sight as to give the wounded chieftain comfort.

"Well," said the mortal Jarnulf with a quaver in his voice he did not try to hide, "I'm sure Queen Utuk'ku will be pleased by how well this went."

54

Voices Unheard, Faces Unseen

10th Day of Tiyagar, Founding Year 1201

My dearest husband,

Now that I have related all the business of the High Ward in the other letter, here is one just for your eyes. I pray that it finds you safe and that Our Lady and the saints keep you and our grandchildren and all the rest of our dear ones in good health as well. I feel foolish writing to you with my fears because the dread that I feel now may well pass, but I miss you so at this moment.

Last night, our first here, I had a terrible dream. I know that some say that there is no truth in dreams, that they are but tricks of the Adversary or small fevers of the mind, but you my husband know better than anyone that they can be true—that they can be a warning.

In the dream, our son came back to me. Not John Josua as he was in his last years, not the sober young father with his beard and the black scholar's robes that he always wore, but as he was in his childhood, thin and wide-eyed, the restless little boy we so loved and worried over. In the dream I walked through the Hayholt in search of something, though at first I did not know what it might be. I saw nobody else, no servants, no courtiers, only empty halls, but at times it seemed I heard voices, as though people had gathered behind closed doors. I could never find them, though, and could barely hear the sound of them speaking and singing. Once I thought I heard a great number of women weeping.

Then I saw him, although at first I did not know him. I saw only a small shape that ran just ahead of me, losing itself around corners. When I could see it more clearly, the figure was so far ahead that although I thought it a child, I could not know for certain.

Since I had seen no one else, and in my dream I was still searching for that something I cannot now remember, I hurried after the small shape. I was led up one passage and down another, through the deserted throne room and out into the Inner Bailey. I followed this apparition into the maze that was destroyed when Green Angel Tower fell, but in my dream both the maze and the fallen tower were still there, the tower in broken pieces across the maze, blocking its paths in many places.

I found my way at last to the center of the maze and there was John Josua sitting on the bench that used to be at its center—do you remember that bench? I cried out in joy, I think, but when he saw me he only looked frightened, jumped up and sped away.

I was heartbroken that our son would not stay with me, but now that I knew whom it was I followed, neither could I give up. I was such a long time dreaming, Simon! Or that is how it felt, for our John led me a chase all over the castle, as he used to when we tried to drag him back to dress for state occasions. I wish now I had never made him attend any of them. How cruel to waste any of his short life on such nonsense.

At last, after what would have been a wearying chase had it not been a dream, he led me back to the ruins of Green Angel Tower, but they had vanished. All was as it is now, in this current age, with only the broken Angel remaining to mark its memory. But the Angel had been cast down from its plinth and lay beside a ragged hole in the ground, something that looked to have been dug by some savage, hurrying beast. John Josua crouched beside it and beckoned me. I came with slow care because I was afraid he would startle again and run away, but he waited for me. Still, he would not let me embrace or kiss him, which in the dream made my heart ache so that I can still feel it. Instead he pointed at the hole, his thin little face so full of discontent and worry that I could do nothing else except what he wished. I got down onto my knees and put my head close to the hole. From it, although as from a great distance, I could hear the strangest clamor, people wailing and shouting and the noises of beasts. I was certain it must be the mouth of Hell itself, and I sat up immediately, afraid. John Josua was gone again, and I was alone in the garden.

The next moment I awoke in my bed aboard the Hylissa. My maid was beside me, almost in tears because she had tried to wake me from my dream but could not do so. I was breathless and could not speak at first, and my nightgown was damp with sweat. The Thrithings-folk say that a bad dream is the Dark pressing down upon us, kneeling on our chests, trying to squeeze out our breath. I felt that. I think John Josua, if it was his spirit that came to me, and not a trick of the Adversary, was trying to tell me, to tell us, that the Dark is close.

My good husband, perhaps you will think that as soon as we are parted I have become a fool, but I pray you will remember your own dreams during the Storm King's War, the tall Tree and the great Wheel, and what came of them. I am afraid, not just for you or myself or even our grandchildren, although I fear mightily for them, but for all our kingdom.

I will write again soon. It may even be that by the time of my next letter I will have decided that the fears I write about now were only phantoms, but please do not forget them. Please do not ignore them.

There will be no real peace for me until we are together again, dear Simon, safe with our family. Take good care, my husband. It is when we are apart that I most realize how fortunate we were to find each other, though all the world was against us.

I will write to you again on a brighter day—perhaps tomorrow, when there are not so many clouds in the sky.

"And how is the queen, may God give her good health?"

"Well enough in body, Pasevalles, but prey to fearful dreams." Simon folded the letter and slipped it into his purse. He had an ache in his stomach that felt like hunger, but he knew it was not.

"As are we all sometimes, Majesty. The land of Sleep can be a terrifying place."

The king nodded. Whatever had smothered and silenced his dreams of late, Simon knew very well the terrors that could be found on the Dream Road. "In any case, I am sorry I've kept you waiting, Lord Chancellor. You look as though something is troubling you, too."

Pasevalles shook his head. "I am not troubled, sire, but only being cautious. I am told that you have asked Tiamak and Aengas, the Northern Alliance factor, to speak to the prisoner."

"That Hernystirman kitchen servant who stabbed Eolair? Yes. Aengas speaks his tongue. Between you and me, I am concerned that he may not be the simple madman everyone has assumed."

"Majesty?"

"I told you of the strange reception we had from King Hugh. And Eolair has heard disturbing things, too."

"Of course, Majesty. I also found it troubling."

"A part of me wonders whether Hugh might fear Eolair's influence—the Lord Steward is a popular man in Hernystir."

Pasevalles looked troubled. "You think Hugh might have tried to have Eolair killed? I will be honest, sire—that little madman seems a very clumsy tool for such a dangerous task."

"I know, I know. But these are perilous times and I trust Tiamak's judgement."

"As do I," the chancellor said. "But what of Aengas? Do you trust him as well?"

The king gave him a look that was half surprise, half frustration. "What? Do you suspect him of something as well?"

Pasevalles frowned. "I suspect no one, Majesty. I am just cautious—as you would wish me to be, I think. The factor arrived from Hernystir on the same day as the attack on Eolair."

"But they say the criminal has worked here in the Hayholt kitchens for years."

"Of course, sire. I only mention it because in times like these no assumption is safe. That is why I ask what we know of Aengas."

Simon found it difficult to keep an even temper. "By the Tree, Pasevalles, you are too suspicious. I know and love Tiamak as well as I do any man, and he tells me that Aengas is worthy of our trust. Is that not enough?"

In less exalted settings than a meeting between king and chief minister, Pasevalles' small movement would have been called a shrug. "Of course, Majesty—it should be more than enough. But as you and the queen yourselves told me on your return, everything is different now. I only ask the questions my position demands that I ask. Please forgive me."

"Don't, Pasevalles. You make me ashamed. Of course you are right to be careful." He sighed. "But in the end I must trust someone or I would go mad. I trust you. I trust Eolair. I trust Tiamak. I trust the queen."

"Yes, my king. I too trust Lord Tiamak, both his goodness and his judgement. If he vouches for Aengas, that is enough."

Simon's bleak mood had returned. "Now I am worried too, but not about Aengas. I hope Tiamak will be careful of that kitchen worker, if the creature is truly mad." He was thinking of some of the moonstruck folk he had met in his youth, the peasant girl Skodi and even Miri's father, King Elias, in his last months. "Madness can lie hidden, you know. Like a snake under a rock. But when you lift the rock and the sun falls upon it . . ." He thrust his hand forward like a serpent's bite, and accidentally knocked his empty cup clattering onto the stone flags. Pasevalles silently picked it up, and when the king waved his hand for it, wiped the lip of the cup on his doublet before returning it.

When the king's cup had been refilled, he and lord chancellor finished the rest of their business. When Pasevalles had gone, Simon sat back in his chair and ignored the courtiers waiting for his attention, his thoughts on a very different path.

Miriamele's letter had made him think about their lost son—a grief no less painful for being familiar—but it had also reminded him of his own childhood, when the castle had seemed as big as the world and when nobody had paid much attention to the comings and goings of a mere kitchen boy. The memory gripped him and would not let go.

"Where is my little girl?" he muttered to himself. "Where is my lion cub?" Simon got to his feet and looked around. Courtiers leaned forward, each hoping that he or she was the one the king sought. To the king, though, the throne hall seemed strange and unfamiliar; for an instant or two Simon could almost believe he was a child-spy once more, poking his nose into places he should not be.

Yes, I will find my granddaughter, he decided, ignoring the polite, expectant faces that surrounded him. *It will do my heart good to see her and to hear her voice. My son is lost to God and my grandson has gone far away—for good or ill—but I can at least find my Lillia and keep her close.*

Tiamak found it easiest to walk behind Aengas's litter: the shoulders of its four brawny bearers all but filled the narrow corridors beneath the guardhouse. "I know nothing much beyond what I've already related," Tiamak said. "He is a kitchen worker from Crannhyr who has been here in the Hayholt for many years—long before Hugh took the throne in Hernystir. My wife attended to him back in Feyever when he fell into a fit. His name is Riggan."

"That means 'headstrong,'" said Aengas. "It may have been only a nickname, but he has certainly lived up to it."

It was a small enough jest, but Tiamak was not in the mood to be amused. In fact, almost nothing about the task pleased him, although he supposed it was a good thing to have something else to think on for a little while beside the endlessly puzzling, frequently terrifying *Treatise on the Aetheric Voices*.

"Just ahead, masters," said the shuffling jailer, a man almost as large as Lord Aengas and only slightly more nimble. "Don't know why we're still keeping him. They should have had him doing the rope dance. Murdering poor old Lord Eolair . . ."

"The count survived and was able to ride out on his horse the next day, for which we are all grateful," said Tiamak. "In any case, I'm told this man is quite mad."

"Mad? Could be. But we could do with a few less mad ones like him. You don't put a collar on a mad dog, and you don't keep a fellow like this alive."

Tiamak frowned at this easy conclusion. "If he had been hanged already, then we could not come to question him."

"Well, then, I'm sure you know best, my lords," said the jailer. "Still, what can you learn from a madman?"

What indeed? Tiamak wondered. After all, his wife Thelía had spoken to the fellow at length while the royal company traveled across the Frostmarch, but she had still been shocked to learn of Riggan's attempt on the lord steward's life. Tiamak himself thought it was doubtful this aged scullion could be a spy for the Hernystiri throne, let alone an assassin directed all the way from the Taig, but after the murderous attack on the Sitha envoy and now another against Count Eolair, he could understand why Simon was taking nothing for granted.

The prisoner was a small man, not much bigger than Tiamak himself, though stockier. He had been badly shaved by his jailers, which gave his head a crooked appearance, and was also bruised from the struggle in which he had been captured, but he did not seem to have been too badly harmed.

When Aengas questioned him his responses sounded reasonable, though Tiamak could not understand the words. "What does he say?"

"Much, but with little sense. 'How can I face her when we are all finally set free? I failed her! She summoned me!' and other complaints of that nature. In short, someone summoned him, but he failed to attend them."

"'How can I face *her*' . . . ?" Tiamak shook his head. "Who does he mean?"

Aengas laughed. "I speak Hernystiri, my friend, not the language of madness, whatever some may say about me."

Tiamak turned to the prisoner. "Riggan, I am Lord Tiamak. Can you understand me? I want to talk to you about what happened. Who summoned you?"

He shook his head violently, but when he spoke again his voice was mild.

"He says only that he has failed her," Aengas translated.

"Her, her—and this is not the first time he has spoken of 'her.'" Tiamak frowned. "He told someone else it was the Morriga who spoke to him. Ask him if he still believes that."

"The Morriga?" Aengas was clearly surprised. "The Crow Mother?"

"Yes, he spoke of her when my wife tended him. Please, ask him."

Riggan listened to Aengas' questions with worried interest, then gave a long reply, at one point raising his hands over his head and gesturing to the roof of his cramped cell.

"He says she has three faces—the Summoner, the Silence, and the Mother of Tears." Aengas paused. The jailer had leaned in to hear better, so he glared at the man until he stepped back again. "I am impressed by the madman's knowledge of old tales," Aengas continued, "but it all seems straightforward to me. He has foul dreams and thinks his dreams are true. And it is not unusual for people to believe the gods speak to them, whether the Morriga or Brynioch himself—King Lluth's own daughter suffered from a madness like this, I have heard it told."

"Perhaps, but his answer seemed longer. What else did he say?"

"I heard something about, *'Behind her are older ones, older still, old as the rain, old as the stone.'* That must be the gods."

The madman's words made Tiamak itch, although he did not know why. "I am still uncertain. Ask him to name these old ones."

Aengas gave Tiamak an odd look, but spoke to the prisoner again. Riggan, agitated, waved his hands in the air and let loose a burble of Hernystiri; Tiamak recognized a single word—*duircha,* or "darkness"—and his heart stumbled a little.

"He does not know their names, but he says their shadows are the light of other worlds, and that the stars are their eyes." The factor's wide face now creased in a frown of unease. "Tiamak, my swamp-paddling friend, where could this creature have learned such things? Could he once have been a priest or scholar? But if so, what was he doing working in the Hayholt's kitchens?"

"A king and several high and holy knights have labored in those kitchens," Tiamak said. "Do not underestimate the place." But he did not feel as light-hearted as his words made him sound. "Surely that cannot be all he said, Aengas. I heard the word 'darkness.' What was that?"

"Ah, yes," Aengas said. "It troubled me too. He said something like, *I do not know why they speak to me or who they are, but their silent voices are the true names of darkness—*" He suddenly looked not just disturbed but startled. "But hold—why does that sound familiar, dear man?"

"Because you were reading it only yesterday or the day before." Tiamak's heart seemed to grow cold in his chest. " *'The true name of Darkness is made of these silent voices,'* were the exact words. Do you remember them now?"

Aengas's broad face turned a paler shade, and despite the dank air of the cell, a sheen of sweat appeared on his brow. " *'The true name of Darkness . . .'* Gods, yes, I remember it now—*'and Darkness itself is wound all through these whisperless whispers, and even a godly man may lose his wits and even his immortal soul when they call him.'* I wish at this moment I were a more religious man, Tiamak, because I could use such comfort. Those are the words of Fortis the Recluse."

"Yes." Tiamak spoke almost in a whisper, as if someone beside the slack-faced warder might be listening. "Straight from the pages of the *Treatise*. Ask the prisoner if he can read, Aengas."

Riggan shook his head in shame. "He says he cannot," Aengas reported.

"And I believe him. Ask him if he knows the name of Bishop Fortis."

Again the prisoner shook his head, then spoke in a rush of words, looking more fearful by the moment. "He does not know it, and he says he is a man who loves the gods and does not wish to be burned. He did only what he was told, he said."

"And who told him?" Tiamak asked.

"He says it was the Morriga," said Aengas after listening to the reply. "But he says the lady of three faces whispered in his dreams for many moons, until he knew it was a true summons. He says he is not the only person who can hear her, for the whispers are grown very loud of late." Aengas took a deep breath and let it out with a shudder. "Do you know, I suddenly find myself disliking the smell and dampness of this place, friend Tiamak. I would like to leave." He gave his bearers a command; they bent to hoist the litter.

Tiamak nodded his agreement, but he knew that what they had heard here could not be so easily left behind.

Pasevalles had finished his business for King Simon, as well as some boring but important letters of his own, but it was still more than an hour until the bells in Holy Tree Tower called him to the midday meal. He decided to take advantage of this unexpected freedom to spend some time reading in his private room at the top of the residence where no one would disturb him. But he had only made it to the top of the third floor landing before he was reminded that his secret hiding-hole was no longer entirely secret.

"Lord Pasevalles! I thought I might find you here."

He was tired, distracted, and worried, not at all in the mood to dally with Idela in conversation or otherwise, but he put on a smile as she made her way up the long staircase. "And find me you did, my lady," he said as she reached him. "Your Highness is a Hound of Love, who always runs down her quarry."

She looked around quickly to make sure they were alone, then kissed him warmly upon the lips. "Since I am a woman as well as a hound, do you call me a she-hound, Lord Chancellor? It is true enough, I suppose—I am your bitch and will do as you command."

"Ssshh! My lady! Not so loud." The princess had pushed up against him, and for a moment he worried she might jostle one or both of them off the landing and down the steep staircase. "Please, sweet Idela, if you wish to talk this way, let us at least go to my room, where we do not have to worry about offending the sensibilities of those who might hear us."

"As you say, Lord Chancellor. You command me, after all. I am merely your servant—your pet." But her hand was fumbling at his buttons in a most un-servantlike way, and it was all he could do to gently detach her fingers from his jerkin.

"Enough," he said. "I am delighted to see you, dear princess, light of my heart. But not here. Let us go up."

"As you wish, although there is no one to see us. Even the chambermaids come up here but seldomly." She stepped back. "Ah, and since I am your servant, you must chastise me, dear Pasevalles."

He was relieved to have calmed the situation. "Why?"

"Because I forgot that I had something of yours." She lifted the hand that until now she had kept at her side. "See? You dropped this at the bottom of the stairs. I have carried it all this way for you."

He took the folded letter from her. His fingers trembled. "You . . . found this?"

"Yes. I saw you drop it from across the front hallway."

"But the seal is broken." He looked from the wax to the letter written on fine Perdruinese parchment. "Did you read it?"

For a moment, just a moment, something flickered in her eyes—guilt, perhaps. "No! It must have come open when you dropped it. I would not read something private of yours, beloved!"

"You are not telling me the truth, Princess."

Again he saw a flash of unease. "Very well. No, I did not read it, but I could not help noticing that it was from Nabban. From Lord Drusis, the duke's brother." She put a finger against his lips. "Ssshhh, do not scold me. I would never tell anyone, but *you* may tell *me*. Are you trying to arrange peace between him and his brother? Is it something to help the queen with her mission?" She was smiling now. "You can share with me, beloved. You know I want only to help you do what is best for the kingdom. After all, it will all be my son's kingdom someday."

"Yes, it will," he said, and took a deep breath. "Wait—look there. Is that your father coming?"

Surprised, she turned to look down to the chamber below. "I do not see him—"

Pasevalles put both hands against her back and shoved hard. Idela's arms flew up as if she were merely miming surprise. She struck first against the wall several steps below, then tumbled heels over head, rolling down the narrow, circular staircase until he could not see her anymore. He quickly made his way down the steps and found her lying some distance below, head hanging over the edge of a step, one arm bent awkwardly behind her, dress flung up, and legs splayed, precisely as if someone had dropped a child's rag doll.

He crouched beside her. The princess dowager had bloody scrapes on her face and hands and a red bubble at the corner of her mouth, now swelling outward, now shrinking back. When he leaned close he could hear the dry gasp of her breath, slow and ragged but fairly steady.

Pasevalles shook his head and then stood. He pressed the sole of his boot down on the side of Princess Idela's head, ignoring the way her eyes rolled beneath the half-closed lids, then twisted his foot until he heard the bones of her neck snap. He hid the letter from Nabban in the waistband of his hose, then began to call for help, shouting over and over until the stairwell echoed.

The funny thing was, the king thought, that although almost everything else that had loomed so large in his childhood—trees and walls and people—had shrunk as Simon himself grew, the Hayholt actually seemed larger to him now than it had when he was young. *Perhaps because I've seen so much of what's underneath. Perhaps because I have more of an idea of the secrets it holds than almost anyone else does.* It was hard to feel familiarity and comfort when you knew that the large but familiar house in which you'd grown was built over an entire separate castle, and a Sithi castle at that, unexplored for centuries and haunted by dangerous secrets.

"Aren't you going to tell us the rules, Grandfather?" demanded Lillia. "Or are you just going to stare at the ground?"

He looked up, a little startled to find himself woolgathering. "Here, now. Don't be sharp with the king, young lady, or I'll have you in the dungeon before you know it."

Lillia and her friends duly pretended to be frightened, which made him smile. His granddaughter had rounded up several playmates, a pair of Rowson girls and two boys close to Lillia's own age, young relations of Earl Osrics, both in the age between childhood and the serious business of manhood, impatient to be grown. He prayed they could retain their romantic beliefs about manhood for many years to come, that he would not be forced to send them to war.

"Well?"

"Sorry, Princess Lillia the Stern," he said. "I was thinking about how I will marry you off someday to a fat and bossy prince who will eat all the sweets and leave you none."

"No, you won't. Now tell us the rules. Why is this game called 'Holly King'?"

"Because that was the name of a Hernystiri king who long ago ruled here—ruled most of the north. And he was not an Aedonite, but a pagan!"

"Then why did God let him rule in the Hayholt?"

"Oh, eventually he lost. He's not the king now, is he? And we're not Hernystiri, are we? Now, enough questions, child. This is a hiding game, and we pretend we are Aedonite priests."

"We already know how to play hide and seek, Grandfather."

"Ah, but this is different. Priests do not betray each other." And he explained how only one person was to hide at first, while everybody else would look, and if a player found the person who was hiding they had to climb into the hiding place with them. "Then, you see, the last person becomes the Holly King, and then he—yes, Lillia, or *she*—becomes the first to hide in the next game. Do you understand?"

"But if the last person is the Holly King, why would he be the person who hides? I thought you said the Holly King was trying to catch the priests."

Simon sighed. "In truth, it is sometimes difficult trying to do things with you, Granddaughter."

One of Osric's young relations was the first to hide, and Simon, who knew the castle far better than any of the children, soon found him in the back of one of the residence's ground-floor storerooms. He whispered to the boy to keep quiet, then sat down beside him to wait for the rest to discover their hiding place. Soon, the darkness and the warmth of close quarters made the king's eyes begin to feel heavy.

It makes no sense, he thought. *When I dreamed, I would sometimes wake up many times in a night, my heart pounding like a war drum, and then I'd find it hard to get back to sleep. Some days I walked around in a fog all day from the sleep I'd missed. But now, when for some reason my dreams have deserted me, I still feel the same way, weary and stupid. Bloody Tree, it really isn't fair!*

It was strange to be playing children's games once again. His own son John Josua had seldom indulged in such things, remaining apart from the castle's other children, content to read or sometimes even just to sit by himself and think. Simon could remember him perched in a chair that was too large for him, staring solemnly out at the sky as though the firmament itself were a book and young Johnno could read what it said.

He was startled out of his memories when the older Rowson girl found them and squeezed into the small storage room. She whispered excitedly with the boy, their voices like the murmur of wind in the eaves, but Simon was already floating back to earlier times—earlier, but not always happier times.

What could we have done differently? he wondered, as he had so often over the years. *Could Miri and I have protected our son better? But who can stop sickness? Who can beat back fever? The best healers and physicians in the land all did their best, Tiamak and so many more, but it was like standing on the bank and watching him drown just beyond our reach.* The remembrance of John Josua's last days, memories so cold and so sickening they felt like poison, now threatened to overwhelm him. He forced himself back to the present, to the sound of whispering children in the darkened storeroom. The second boy had found them, and was laughing with the other two. Simon shushed them. Didn't they understand how the game was played? It was important to stay hidden as long as possible, until only one remained, one lone player, wondering where everyone else had gone.

Alone. Now that he remembered the few times he had played, he also remembered that he had never liked the game of Holly King all that much.

Because it was so lonely if you were the last to discover where the others were hidden, warm and safe and giggling quietly, secure in the company of others. So lonely . . .

The other Rowson girl found them now, a little one named Elli-something. She was crying a little from having been on her own. In between sniffs and sobs, she asked, "Where's Lillia?"

Where *was* Lillia? Simon wondered too. It was hard to believe his confident granddaughter, who strode the castle halls as boldly as any monarch ever had, could actually be the last one to find their hiding place. It reminded him of something Miri had once told him: "*You and I were never scared of the same thing. You were always afraid of being found out, but I was always afraid of being overlooked.*"

The crowding made the small storeroom even warmer. "Shush, you lot," he said, "or she'll find us." But a part of him wanted Lillia to find them, because he was feeling a little worried about her. "In any case, don't push. You'll only make it hotter in here."

It *was* getting warm—downright hot, like a summer's night when covers clung to damp legs and sleep would not come. When his dreams had been so horrible in the months after John Josua's death, Simon had nearly cried some nights just from weariness, desperate for sleep. Now sleep itself seemed like something dangerous as it pulled at him, as the quiet voices of the children around him mixed and slurred. Where had Lillia gone? He groaned and stretched, but could not free himself from the weariness that was on him. What if he fell asleep here like some old drunkard? Shouldn't he be out looking for his granddaughter?

Even as he started to nod again he heard new voices. They were distant, barely audible above the children's whispers, but Simon heard them most clearly, as if they spoke in his own thoughts.

Come to us, they said. *It is time. The time is here, for you to have again what you lost so long ago.* It seemed almost like singing, like a river of words, flowing endlessly past. *It is time to come to us. It is time . . .*

Startled, Simon sat bolt upright. That had been no child calling to him, but something else, a voice from out of his lost dreams. *It is time . . .* What could that mean?

No. It means nothing, he told himself. *It is only that I am sleepy and foolish. A warm afternoon, a tired old man.*

But he could still hear noise from outside the storeroom, new voices this time, and growing in strength.

"Quiet!" he told the children. "Let me listen!"

"*Oh, God save us!*" a woman was screaming. "*God grant us mercy! The poor princess!*"

Sweet Elysia save me, am I awake or dreaming? he wondered, but his heart banging against his ribs felt very, very real. The princess? Who could that be but . . .?

"*Lillia!*" he cried, shoving the children to either side as he rose and pushed his way through the dark toward the front of the closet. "Lillia! Oh, sweet

Elysia, please let nothing have happened to her!" He was suddenly hollow with dread. "Lillia, where are you?"

And then the door swung open and his granddaughter stood there, nothing but a silhouette, a ghost, until his eyes adjusted to the light. Lillia's face was pale, her eyes wide. "Grandfather! What's happened?" She burst into tears and rushed to wrap her arms around Simon's waist. "Why are they shouting that the princess is dead? I'm not dead!"

He could still hear people shouting, even more of them now, cries of horror and shock spreading through the residence.

"Stay with me, all you children." Something very bad had happened, he knew, and nothing would ever be the same. He held Lillia tightly. "Just stay with me, little ones. I'm the king. I'll keep you safe."

Afterword

She had found it again somehow, against all odds, and now she clasped the witchwood egg close to her breast and tried to fight her way through the chaos. She had stood outside this roiling madness once, she thought, had been able to consider her situation with something like detachment, but if that had ever been true, it had been a long time ago. Now the sky itself had turned to hot gray slush, and muddy hands reached up again and again from the bubbling muck that surrounded her, catching at her limbs and hair, trying always to pull her downward. Even the branches of the sacred willows seemed to reach out to entangle her, to force her back into the endless, all-devouring lake of steaming mud. Every step was a nightmare struggle.

Why am I even fighting? Always now this treacherous voice spoke in her thoughts, urging surrender. *The heat will only be for a little while,* it told her. *Then everything will turn cool again, cool as running water, cool as early spring grass, cool as stones deep in the ground. The fight will be over. You will rest.*

But despite her breathless weariness and her muddled thoughts, Tanahaya knew that voice was not telling the whole truth. It was the sleep of death to which she was being invited, the cool of life finally departing her body. And so she fought on.

Faces came to her as she struggled, her family, her loved ones. But instead of urging resistance they joined the treacherous inner voice, begging her to give up.

You have fought well, said ancient Himano, her clan lord. *There is no disgrace in surrender, child. No disgrace.*

It was not disgrace she feared, but obliteration. Tanahaya was neck deep in bubbling hot mud, tangled in roots, but knew she dared not give up. Her people were so few now. They could not surrender, did not surrender, would *never* surrender, no matter how terrible the odds.

We love you, as-good-as-sister, Aditu and Jiriki told her. *We will remember you when you are at rest. We will celebrate your sacrifice.*

But Tanahaya did not want to be celebrated. She wanted nothing but to see the sun again and feel its dry warmth, to drink the scents on a breeze, to hear the music of wind through forest branches. She wanted to exist.

Give up the egg. It is not worth dying for, her childhood friend Yeja'aro told her.

No, it is worth living for, she told herself—told all the voices—even as her strength flagged and she slipped deeper into the boiling mud. *It is worth living for.*

Then without warning a wind swept across the world, just a whisper of a breeze at first, then stronger, gradually stronger, cooling the mud, cooling the drippingly hot air, cooling everything. At first Tanahaya thought it only another attack, but the mud that pulled at her began to turn solid and after only a few more moments she kicked her way free. The hot mire had lost its grip, and she pulled herself out of it and onto solid land for the first time in a long, long while. When she did not sink again, when the beautiful cool continued to grow, she knew she could finally stop fighting.

The fever. It was a last thought before she let go, before she could finally, truly rest after so long. *The poison fever—it has finally broken.*

"Tanahaya. Can you hear me?"

"It's us, Aditu and Jiriki. Can you hear us?"

She opened her eyes, not without difficulty, because the lids were crusted and sore. "Where am I?" she asked.

"In H'ran Go-jao, Sister-bird," said Aditu, the beloved face bent close above her. "It gives my heart joy to see you. We feared you lost, but the healers have done their work. And not just our healers—the mortals kept you alive until they could bring you here, praise to the Garden."

"Yes," said Jiriki, and there was something in his voice that Tanahaya had not heard before, something deep and profound. "Praise to the Garden."

"Poison. My wounds were poisoned with something terrible. What was it?"

"The healers still do not know," Aditu told her. "None of them have seen its like before. We are astonished you still live, dear friend."

"But I failed my mission." Tanahaya had recovered enough to feel shame. "I let myself be ambushed before I even reached Asu'a."

"Did you see who did it?"

Tanahaya tried to shake her head but was still too weak. She felt fragile, no more substantial than dried flower petals. "They shot at me from hiding. It was more than one enemy and the arrows were black. That is all I know."

"Black like those of the Hikeda'ya?"

"Perhaps. At the time I did not closely examine their workmanship, and when I awoke later they were gone." She lay still for a moment, breathing slowly, trying to think. "How did I get here?"

"The mortals brought you. The young prince and Count Eolair, an old ally of ours."

"I wish to thank them."

Jiriki made *Lapwing's Cry* with his long fingers, the sign for a sadness that could not be helped. "They have gone. S'hue Khendraja'aro sent them back."

"But we need their help!"

Aditu sat up, her hands cradling her round belly. "Yes, and they sought help from us as well, but the time is wrong for it—perhaps wrong beyond mending. It seems the curse of our two races to be so often at cross purposes."

"So what will we do?" Despite her fear, Tanahaya felt sleep pulling powerfully at her, but she did not want to give up the world again so soon.

"What we must," Jiriki said. "Fight on. Give our lives if that is all we can do. Because if we lose this time, the ending is unthinkable. It will be worse than what Ineluki Storm King himself had planned." He made a sign against the jealous dead. "It may bring Unbeing itself."

"But you are not ready to rejoin that battle yet," Aditu told her. "Sleep, dear Tanahaya. Sleep. As we say, tomorrow the Garden may be closer."

But even as she let herself slide back toward exhausted sleep, Tanahaya knew that Aditu only meant to soothe her. The Garden was lost, as all their people knew. It would remain lost no matter what, or at least everything good it had contained was gone beyond reclaiming. That was the doom of her people.

Appendix

PEOPLE

ERKYNLANDERS

Aedonita—playmate of Princess Lillia

Agar, St.—an Aedonite saint

Avner, Father—Lord Tiamak's secretary

Begga—one of Princess Idela's ladies in waiting; trained in healing

Benamin—the royal butler of the Hayholt

Buttercup—mistress of a brothel in Erchester

Cloda—Prince Morgan's onetime nurse

Colfer, Baron—nobleman; part of the royal progress

Devona, Lady—Lord Gareth's wife; mistress of Northithe

Dregan—an innocent wanderer in the Kynswood

Eahlstan Fiskerne, St.—King Simon's ancestor and founder of the League of the Scroll; sixth king of the Hayholt; called the "Fisher King"

Elias, King—former High King; Queen Miriamele's father

Elyweld—Aedonita's sister

Etan, Brother—an Aedonite monk

Evoric, Baron—baron of Haestall

Feran, Lord—Master of Horse; Marshal of the Hayholt

Gared, Earl—nobleman of Northithe; husband of Lady Devona

Gervis, Archbishop—archbishop of Erkynland

Goda—the ostler's girl

Hatcher—owner of the *Quarely Maid*

Idela, Princess—widow of Prince John Josua; daughter of Duke Osric

Jack Mundwode—a mythical forest bandit

Jeremias, Lord—Lord Chamberlain of the Hayholt

John Josua, Prince—son of King Simon and Queen Miriamele; Prince Morgan and Princess Lillia's father; late husband of Princess Idela; called "Johnno" by King Simon

John Presbyter, King—former High King; Queen Miriamele's grandfather; also known as Prester John

Josua, Prince—King Elias' brother; Queen Miriamele's uncle

Jubal, Sir—a knight

Jurgen of Sturmstad, Sir—Night Captain of the Erkynguard

Kenrick, Sir—a young Captain Marshal of the Erkynguard

Lillia, Princess—granddaughter of King Simon and Queen Miriamele; Morgan's sister

Leleth—Queen Miriamele's former handmaid

Martha—resident maid of the Hayholt

Melkin—Prince Morgan's squire

Miriamele, Queen—High Queen of Osten Ard; wife of King Simon

Morgan, Prince—heir to the High Throne; son of Prince John Josua and Princess Idela

Morgenes, Doctor—former Scrollbearer; King Simon's onetime friend and mentor

Natan—a forester of the Kynswood

Osric, Duke—Lord Constable and Duke of Falshire and Wentmouth; Princess Idela's father

Putnam, Bishop—senior of the priests traveling with the royal party

Rachel—former Mistress of Chambermaids of the Hayholt; also known as "The Dragon"

Rinan—a young harper

Rowson, Earl—a nobleman of Glenwick

Sangfugol—a famous harper of the Hayholt

Seth of Woodsall—chief architect of the Royal Court

Shulamit, Lady—one of Queen Miriamele's court ladies

Simon, King—High King of Osten Ard and husband of Queen Miriamele; also known as "Seoman", his birth name; sometimes called "Snowlock"

Sofra—a young woman; acquaintance of Prince Morgan

Strangyeard, Father—former Scrollbearer and royal chaplain of the Hayholt

Sutrin, St.—an Aedonite saint, also known as Sutrines

Tabata—resident maid of the Hayholt

Tamar, Lady—wife of the Baron of Aynsberry; one of Queen Miriamele's chief ladies-in-waiting

Thomas Oystercatcher—mayor of Erchester

Tobiah—a guardsman of the Hayholt

Tostig, Baron—a wool merchant

Wibert, Father—Lord Chancellor Pasevalles' secretary

Wiglaf, St.—an Aedonite saint

Wilona, Lady—wife of Sir Evoric

Zakiel of Garwynswold, Sir—Captain of the Erkynguard; Sir Kenrick's commander

HERNYSTIRI

Aelin, Sir—great nephew of Count Eolair

Aengas ec-Carpilbin of Ban Farrig—former Viscount of Abaingeat; a merchant and scholar of ancient books

Airgad Oakheart—famous Hernystiri hero

Bagba—cattle god

Brannan—former monk and cook to Aengas

Brynioch of the Skies—sky god

Cadrach ec-Crannhyr—monk of indeterminate order
Cuamh Earthdog—earth god
Curudan, Baron—Commander of the Silver Stags
Deanagha of the Brown Eyes—goddess; daughter of Rhynn
Elatha—Count Eolair's sister
Eolair, Count—Lord Steward, Hand of the Throne and Count of Nad Mullach
Evan—one of Sir Aelin's men
Gwythinn, Prince—King Hugh's father; killed in the Storm King's War
Hern, King—legendary founder of Hernystir
Hugh ubh-Gwythinn, King—ruler of Hernystir
Inahwen—Dowager Queen
Jarreth—Sir Aelin's squire
Irwyn, Sir—a knight
Lluth, King—former ruler; father of Maegwin and Gwythinn
Llythinn, King—King Lluth's father
Maegwin, Princess—daughter of King Lluth; died during the Storm King's
    War
Mircha—rain goddess; wife of Brynioch
Morriga—the Maker of Orphans, the Crow Mother; an ancient war goddess
Murdo, Earl—a powerful Hernystiri noble
Murhagh One-Arm—war god
Murtach, Sir—a courtier who accompanies the royal progress to Elvritshalla
Nial, Count of Nad Glehs—Countess Rhona's husband
Riggan—a kitchen servant of the Hayholt
Rhona, Countess—noblewoman of Nad Glehs; friend to Queen Miriamele;
    guardian of Princess Lillia, who calls her "Auntie Rhoner"
Samreas, Sir—Baron Curudan's hawk-faced lieutenant
Sinnach—former prince of Hernystir, also known as "The Red Fox"
Tethtain, King—fifth king of the Hayholt; called the "Holly King"
Tylleth, Lady—widow of Earl of Glen Orrga; betrothed to King Hugh

RIMMERSMEN

Alva, Lady—Countess of Engby; Jarl (Earl) Sludig's wife
Dyrmundur—Jarnulf's companion in the Skalijar
Elvrit—first King of Rimmersgard, called "Elvrit Far-Seeing"
Fingil Bloodfist—first human ruler of the Hayholt; called "Fingil the Great"
    and "Fingil the Bloody-Handed"
Frode—Escritor of Elvritshalla
Fray, the Green Mother—goddess
Gerda, Lady—daughter of Jarl Halli
Gret—Jarnulf's sister
Grimbrand—son of Duke Isgrimnur; duke apparent

Gutfrida, St.—Aedonite saint

Gutrun, Duchess—Duke Isgrimnur's late wife

Halli, Jarl—lord of Blarbrekk Castle

Helvard, St.—Aedonite saint

Hildula, St.—a visionary nun of an earlier century; also an Aedonite saint

Hjeldin, King—second ruler of the Hayholt and King Fingil's son; called the "Mad King"

Ikferdig, King—third ruler of the Hayholt; called the "Burned King"

Isbeorn—Duke Isgrimnur's father

Isgrimnur of Elvritshalla, Duke—ruler of Rimmersgard

Ismay—Duke Isgrimnur's younger daughter

Isvarr—Grimbrand's son

Isorn—oldest son of Duke Isgrimnur and Duchess Gutrun; killed during the Storm King's War

Jarnauga—former Scrollbearer; killed during the Storm King's War

Jarngrimnur—Jarnulf's brother

Jarnulf Godtru—a Queen's Huntsman

Jormgrun Redhand—last King of Rimmersgard; killed by King John Presbyter

Loken—fire god

Lomskur—a smith in Elvritshalla

Maggi, Jarl—one of Rimmersgard's most important nobles; has large holdings along the border with Hernystir

Narvi—thane (baron) of Radfisk Foss

Olov, Brother—former royal tutor

Ragna—Jarnulf's mother

Roskva—Tzoja's surrogate mother, called "Valada" ("wise woman")

Signi—Duke Isgrimnur's elder daughter

Skodi—a witch in northeastern Rimmersgard; killed during the Storm King's War

Skali—former Thane of Kaldskryke; also known as "Sharp-nose"; deceased

Skalijar—bandits; former followers of Skali of Kaldskryke

Sludig—Jarl of Engby; friend to King Simon, Queen Miriamele, and Binabik

Sorde—Grimbrand's wife

Svana—young Rimmersgard woman in Erchester

Tonngerd of Skoggey—Ismay's husband

Valfrid—Signi's husband

QANUC

Binabik (Binbiniqegabenik)—Scrollbearer; Singing Man of the Qanuc; dear friend to King Simon

Kikkasut—legendary king of birds

Little Snenneq—Qina's betrothed; grandson of Snenneq

Qina (Qinananamookta)—daughter of Binabik and Sisqi

Sedda—moon goddess also known as Moon-Mother

Sisqi (Sisqinanamook)—daughter of the Herder and Huntress (rulers of Min-tahoq Mountain); Binabik's wife

Snenneq—herd-chief of Lower Chugik; killed at Battle of Sesuad'ra

THRITHINGS-FOLK

Bordelm—a Crane clansman

Burtan—shaman of the Crane Clan

Cudberj—Thane Gurdig's cousin

Drojan—Thane Odrig's friend

Edizel Shan—folklore hero

Fikolmij—former March-thane of the Stallion Clan and the High Thrithings; Vorzheva's father

Fremur—a Crane clansman; brother of Thane Odrig

Gezdahn Baldhead—a Crane Clan rider

Gurdig—Thane of the Stallion Clan; Hyara's husband

Hurvalt—former Thane of the Crane Clan; Fremur's father

Hyara—Thane Gurdig's wife; Vorzheva's sister

Kulva—sister of Fremur and Thane Odrig

Mother of the Green—Thrithings deity

Odrig Stonefist—Thane of the Crane Clan; brother of Fremur and Kulva

Rudur Redbeard—March-thane of the Meadow Thrithings; most powerful Thrithings chieftain

Stone Holder—a Thrithings deity

Tasdar the Anvil Smasher—one of the powerful spirits worshipped by all the grassland clans

Unver—"Nobody," a man without clan; also known as Sanver; Unver Long Legs

Utvart—Fikolmij's choice to marry his daughter Vorzheva

Vorzheva—Prince Josua's wife; daughter of Fikolmij

Zhakar—Unver's adoptive father

Zigvart—a Crane clansman; Fremur's, Kulva's, and Thane Odric's cousin

NABBANAI

Anitulles the Great—former Imperator

Ardrivis—the last Imperator; defeated at Nearulagh by King John

Astrian, Sir—a member of the Erkynguard and drinking companion of Prince Morgan

Auxis, Escritor—a church envoy from Nabban

Benidrivis—first Duke of Nabban under King John Presbyter; father of Camaris

Blasis—son of Duchess Canthia and Duke Saluceris

Brindalles—Pasevalles' father, brother of Seriddan; killed during the Storm King's War

Cais Sterna—a Nabbanai nobleman who visited Asu'a when the Sithi still ruled

Camaris-sá-Vinitta, Sir—King John's greatest knight, also known as "Camaris Benidrivis"; lost during the Storm King's War

Canthia, Duchess—noblewoman; wife of Duke Saluceris

Cornellis, St.—a military saint

Crexis the Goat—former Imperator of Nabban

Cuthman, St.—an Aedonite saint

Dallo Ingadaris, Count—Queen Miriamele's cousin

Dinan, St.—an Aedonite saint

Dinivan, Father—former Scrollbearer and secretary to Lector Ranessin; killed in Sancellan Aedonitis during the Storm King's War

Drusis, Earl—Earl of Trevinta and Eadne; Duke Saluceris' brother and rival

Endrian, St.—an Aedonite saint

Envalles—Duke Saluceris' uncle

Eogenis IV—former Lector of Mother Church

Elysia—mother of Usires Aedon; called "Mother of God"

Gervis, Archbishop—the highest religious authority in Erkynland; Lord Treasurer of the Hayholt

Granis, St.—an Aedonite saint

Hylissa, Princess—Queen Miriamele's mother

Idexes Claves, Count—Lord Chancellor of Nabban

Larexes—historic Imperator; killed by poison

Lavennin, St.—patron saint of Spenit Island

Lesta Hermis—a nobleman living on the border to Thrithings land

Matreu, Viscount—son of ruler of Spenit Island

Millatin of Spenit, Count—Matreu's father

Nuanni (Nuannis)—Father Ocean; an ancient Nabbanai sea god

Nulles, Father—royal chaplain of the Hayholt

Olveris, Sir—knight; drinking companion of Prince Morgan

Oren—Duke Saluceris' ancient valet

Pasevalles, Lord—Lord Chancellor to the High Throne

Pelippa, St.—Aedonite saint, called "Pelippa of the Island"

Pellaris, Impertor—Nabbanai Imperator (contemporary of King Tethtain)

Porto, Sir—hero of the Battle of Nakkiga Gate; drinking companion of Morgan

Pryrates—priest, alchemist, and wizard; King Elias' counselor

Ranessin—lector killed by Pryrates during the Storm King's War

Rhiappa, St.—Aedonite saint; called "Rhiap" in Erkynland

Rillian Albias, Count—the Solicitor General of Nabban; head of Albian noble house

Saqualian—historic figure

Saluceris, Duke—ruling duke of Nabban

Serasina—Duke Saluceris' infant daughter

Seriddan, Baron—former Lord of Metessa, uncle of Pasevalles; also known as "Seriddan Metessis"; killed during the Storm King's War

Sulis, Lord—the fourth ruler of the Hayholt; the "Heron King," also known as "The Apostate"

Tersian Vullis—nobleman whose daughter may wed Blasis

Thelía, Lady—Tiamak's wife; herbalist, called 'Tia-Lia" by Princess Lillia

Tiyanis Sulis—nobleman; an ally of the Ingadarines

Tunath, St.—Aedonite saint

Turia Ingadaris, Lady—Count Dallo's niece

Usires Aedon—Aedonite Son of God; also called "the Ransomer"

Vidian, Lector—Lector of Mother Church

Vultinia, St.—Aedonite saint

PERDRUINESE

Faiera, Lady—Scrollbearer; disappeared

Froye, Count—a correspondent of Pasevalles; currently residing in Nabban

Honora, St.—an Aedonite saint

Porto, Sir—a hero of the Battles of Nakkiga; one of Prince Morgan's drinking companions

Porto—Porto's son, also called "Portinio"

Sallimo, St.—a saint particularly worshipped by sailors

Sida—Sir Porto's wife

Streawé, Count—former ruler of Perdruin

Tallistro, Sir—a famous knight; member of King Prester John's Great Table

Yistrin, St.—an Aedonite saint

Yissola, Countess—Count Streawé's daughter, ruler of Perdruin

WRANNAMEN (AND WRANNAWOMEN)

He Who Always Steps on Sand—god

He Who Bends the Trees—wind god

Jesa—nurse to Duke Saluceris' infant daughter Serasina; named "Green Honeybird" by her elders

Green Honeybird—mythical Wranna spirit, Jesa's namesake

She Who Birthed Mankind—goddess

She Who Waits to Take All Back—death goddess

They Who Watch and Shape—gods

Tiamak, Lord—Scrollbearer; scholar and close friend of King Simon and Queen Miriamele; called "Uncle Timo" by Princess Lillia

Tree Python—mythical Wranna spirit

SITHI (ZIDA'YA)

Aditu no'e-Sa'onserei—daughter of Likimeya; Jiriki's sister
Amerasu y-Senditu no'e-Sa'onserei—mother of Ineluki; called "First Grand-
	mother," also known as "Amerasu Shipborn"
Hakatri—Amerasu's son who vanished into the West
Himano of the Flowering Hills—Tanahaya's clan leader
Ineluki—Amerasu's son; the "Storm King"
Jiriki i-Sa'onserei—son of Likimeya; brother of Aditu
Khendraja'aro—uncle of Jiriki and Aditu
Likimeya y-Briseyu no'e-Sa'onserei—mother of Jiriki and Aditu
Sijandi of Kinao Vale—a relative of Jiriki and Aditu; accompanied Jiriki and
	Simon during their journey to Urmsheim
Tanahaya of Shisae'ron—messenger to the High Throne; attacked in the Kynswood
Yeja'aro of the Forbidden Hills—Khendraja'aro's nephew

NORNS (HIKEDA'YA)

Akhenabi, Lord—High Magister of the Order of Song, also called "Lord of
	Song"
Buyo—commander of Viyeki's Sacrifice guards
Daigo—a house guard of Clan Enduya
Denabi sey-Xoka—a sword master
Drukhi—son of Queen Utuk'ku and Ekimeniso
Ekimeniso Blackstaff—husband of Queen Utuk'ku; father of Drukhi
Enah-gé—Singer; member of the Red Hand
Ibi-Khai—Echo, member of Makho's Talon
Inyakki—Lady Khimabu's uncle; one of the chief aides to Lord Akhenabi
Jijibo—a close descendant of Queen Utuk'ku, called "the Dreamer"
Kanikusi Tuya—a poet
Karkkaraji—Singer; member of the Red Hand
Kemme—Sacrifice in Makho's Talon
Khimabu, Lady—Lord Viyeki's wife
Kikiti—General of the Order of Sacrifice
Luk'kaya—High Gatherer of the Harvesters
Makho—Hand Chieftain of a Queen's Talon
Muyare, Marshal—High Magister of the Order of Sacrifice
Nayago—chief of Viyeki's household guard
Nezeru Seyt-Enduya—Daughter of Lord Viyeki and his mistress Tzoja; mem-
	ber of Makho's Queen's Talons
Nijika—a Host Singer
Nonao—member of Lord Viyeki's household
Ommu the Whisperer—Singer, member of the Red Hand

Riugo—chief of Lord Viyeki's household guards

Saomeji—member of the Order of Song; Sacrifice in Makho's Talon

Shun'y'asu of Blue Spirit Peak—a poet

Sogeyu—Host Singer of the Order of Song

Suno'ku—a famous general

Sutekhi—Singer; member of the Red Hand

S'yessu—a Hamakha First Armiger

Uloruzu—a Singer; member of the Red Hand

Urayeki—a court artist; Lord Vijeki's father

Utuk'ku Seyt-Hamakha—Norn Queen; Mistress of Nakkiga

Viyeki sey-Enduya, Lord—High Magister of the Order of Builders; father of
Nezeru

Yaarike sey-Kijana, Lord—former High Magister of the Order of Builders

Ya-Jalamu—a granddaughter of Marshal Muyare

Yemon—Lord Viyeki's secretary

Zuniyabe—High Magister of the Order of Celebrants

OTHERS

Adversary, the—Aedonite devil

Braxas—a pirate

Bur Yok Kar—a Hunë

Deornoth—lost son of Prince Josua and Lady Vorzheva

Derra—lost daughter of Prince Josua and Lady Vorzheva

Fortis the Recluse—a 6th century bishop on Warinsten Island; writer of an
infamous book

Gan Itai—a Niskie who died saving Queen Miriamele during the Storm King's
War

Geloë—a wise woman, called "Valada Geloë"; killed at Sesuad'ra

Goh Gam Gar—a Hunë

Hyrkas—a migrant people from east of Aldheorte

Lightless Ones—dwellers in the depths of Nakkiga; of unknown origin

Madi—a Hyrka guide

Parlippa—Madi's daughter, also known as Parlip

Plekto—Madi's son, also known as Plek

Qosei—a people of the western islands

Ruyan Ve—fabled patriarch of the Tinukeda'ya; called "The Navigator"

Tertissis of Gemmia—scholar from Warinsten Island ("Gemmia" was its Nabbanai name)

Tinukeda'ya, the—third kind of Gardenborn; eg. Niskies, Dwarrows, Pengi,
also called "Changelings"

Tzoja—Lord Viyeki's human mistress; mother of Nezeru

Vaxo of Harcha—a scholar

PLACES

Abaingeat—important trading town in Hernystir, on Barraillean River at coast
Abbey of St. Cuthman's—a monastery in Meremund
Aldhame—a small Erkynlandish town near the forest
Aldheorte—aka Oldheart; a large forest to the north and east of Erkynland
Animal Market—market in Nakkiga held and visited by mortals
Antigine—one of Nabban's hills; location of the Domos Benidriyan
Asu'a—name of the Hayholt under Sithi rule
Avenue of the Martyred Drukhi—a road in Nakkiga
Avenue of the Fallen—a street in Nakkiga which runs behind many of the great houses whose estates front on Great Garden Passage
Avenue of the Saints—a wide, winding road that leads up from the quarter, curving around Estrenine Hill, one of Nabban's Hills
Aynsberry—a barony in Erkynland
Ballydun—a city in the Frostmarch in Hernystir; home to many Rimmersmen
Birch Meadow—part of the Crane Clan's camp
Bitter Moon Castle—Norn fortress on top of Dragon's Reach Pass
Black Mirror Shrine—in Nakkiga-That-Was
Black Water Field—ceremonial gathering place in Nakkiga
Blarbrekk Castle—Home of Jarl Halli in Rimmersgard
Blood Yards—the training grounds for Sacrifices in Nakkiga
Blue Cavern—home of pale spiders and place of Norn rope production
Blue Spirit Peak—mountain near Nakkiga
Bridvattin—a lake in Rimmersgard
Carn Inbarh—castle in Hernystir; home of Earl Murdo, Eolair's ally
Cellodshire—town in Erkynland
Chamber of the Well—the heart of Nakkiga; location of The Well and The Breathing Harp
Chasu Orientis—castle belonging to Earl Drusis
Chidsik Ub Lingit—Qanuc's "House of the Ancestor," on Mintahoq in Yiqanuc
Circoille—forest north and west of Hernystir
Circus of Larexes—amphitheater in Nabban
Cold, Slow Halls—place of torture in Nakkiga
Dalchester—Erkynlandish city on the Royal Northern Road
Dark Garden Lake—an underground lake in Nakkiga discovered by Lord Viyeki, later renamed "Lake Suno'ku"
Da'ai Chikiza—abandoned Sithi city in Aldheorte; called "Tree of the Singing Wind"
Dillathi, the—hill region of western Hernystir
Dimmerskog—forest north of Rimmergard
Domos Bendriyan—the Benidrivine family palace in Nabban; built by the first Benidrivis some two hundred years ago

Dragon's Throat Pass—route in and out of Bitter Moon Castle

Draycot—small town in Erkynland

Drinas Novis—a Nabbanai settlement on the Thrithings

Drorshullven Lake—lake in the north

Dunath Tower—fortress protecting the Inniscrich Valley

Engby—Jarl Sludig's county in Rimmersgard

Eadne—large lake in Nabban

Eight Cities Bridge—landmark in Nakkiga-That-Was

Elvritshalla—ducal seat in Rimmersgard

Emettin Bay—bay located between Nabban and Perdruin

Erchester—capital of Erkynland and seat of the High Throne

Ereb Irigú—"Western Gate"; Sithi name for The Knock, a site of a famous battle in Erkynland

Erkynland—kingdom in central Osten Ard

Estrenine Hill—one of Nabban's hills, location of Matreu's house

Falshire—wool-harvesting city in Erkynland

Field of Banners—open area just outside gates of Nakkiga, anciently a place of triumphant celebration; currently the home of the so-called Animal Market

Fields of the Nameless—graveyard for the disgraced of Nakkiga

Firannos Bay—bay south of Nabban; location of many islands

Fish Way—street in Erchester

Frostmarch, the—a region in northern Hernystir/Southern Rimmersgard

Garwynswold—town in eastern Erkynland

Gemmia—ancient name of Warinsten Island

Gleniwent—a river running from Kynslagh to the ocean

Glenwick—town in Erkynland

Glen Orrga—place in Hernystir

Glittering Passage—place in Nakkiga

Goaddi—mountain on the Island of Bones

Go-jao'e—Little Boats; name for small Sithi settlements

Gratuvask—Rimmersgard river which runs past Elvritshalla

Great Garden Passage—a main street in Nakkiga

Grenburn Town—Erkynlandish town, near a river

Grianspog—mountain range in the west of Hernystir

Haestall—barony in Erkynland

Harbor Road—road from the harbor beside the Hayholt up to Erchester

Harbor Way—wide street in Nabban

Harcha—island in Bay of Firannos

Hasu Vale—valley and town in central Erkynland

Hayclif—cliffs overlooking the Kynslagh

Hayholt, the—seat of the High Throne, located above Erchester

Hawk's Path—an open circular gallery in Nakkiga where several stairwells come together on the way down to the Well

Heartwall—landmark in Nakkiga

Heartwall Stair—a stairway in Nakkiga
Hernysadharc—capital of Hernystir
Hernystir—kingdom in the west of Osten Ard
Himilfells—a mountain range east of Nakkiga
Himnhalla—heavenly home of the Rimmersgarder gods
Hjeldin's Tower—a sealed tower in the Hayholt
Honsa Spenitis—the Spenit noble house
Honor Steps—landmark coming down from Nakkiga Gate
Houses of Tears—a place in Nakkiga-That-Was
H'ran Go-jao—the most easterly of the Go-jao'e (Little Boats)
Iceflame—river in Nakkiga-That-Was
Ijsgard—legendary birthplace of Rimmersmen, across the western ocean
Inniscrich—a valley and river in northern Hernystir
Island of the Bones—an island far west of Rimmersgard
Jackdaw, the—a tavern in Erchester
Jao é-Tinukai'i—a hidden Sithi dwelling in Aldheorte, now abandoned
Kaldskryke—fiefdom in Rimmersgard
Kementari—one of the nine Gardenborn cities, now lost
Khandia—a lost and fabled land
Kiga'rasku—waterfall beneath Nakkiga, called "the Tearfall"
Kopstade, the—market district of Elvritshalla
Kwanitupul—city in the Wran
Kynslagh—lake in central Erkynland
Kynswood—small forest adjacent to the Hayholt
Lake Rumiya—lake beside Nakkiga
Littlefeather—river in the Lake Thrithings
Little Gardens of Memory—"Sojeno nigago-zhe"; graveyard for Norns too
    humble or poor to have family tombs
Little Gratuvask—a river; a tributary of the Gratuvask
Lost Garden (Venyha Do'sae)—the fabled place whose destruction the Keida'ya
    fled
Lyktenspan—Lantern Bridge crossing the Gratuvask to Elvritshalla
Mahistrevine Hill—one of Nabban's hills
Mahistrevine Road—road leading to the Sancellan Mahistrevis
Main Row—major thoroughfare in the city of Erchester
Martyrs Temple—shrine located in Nakkiga
Meremund—Erkynlandish town on the rivers Greenwade and Gleniwent,
    birthplace of Queen Miriamele
Merchants Road—a street in Nabban
Mezutu'a—the Silverhome; abandoned Sithi and Dwarrow city beneath Gri-
    anspog Mountains; original Sithi name: Mezutu'a
Mintahoq—a mountain of the Trollfells; Binabik's home village
Moon's Reach Valley—valley below Dragon's Throat Pass
M'yin Azoshai—Sithi name for Hern's Hill; location of Hernysadharc

Nabban—duchy in the southern part of Osten Ard; former seat of empire

Nad Glehs—home of Countess Rhona in Hernystir

Nad Mullach—Count Eolair's home in eastern Hernystir

Naglimund—stronghold in northern Erkynland; place of battles during the Storm King's War

Nakkiga—Gardenborn city beneath Stormspike Mountain, meaning "Mask of Tears"; home of the Hikeda'ya

Nakkiga-That-Was—city outside Nakkiga mountain; one of the Nine Cities of the Gardenborn; now abandoned

Naraxi—island in the Bay of Firannos

Naarved—city in western Rimmersgard

Nascadu—a desert land in the south

Nearulagh Gate—main entrance to the Hayholt

New Frostmarch Road—road linking the Frostmarch towns to Hernysadharc

New Moon Market—marketplace in Nakkiga

Nornfells—the northern mountains; home to the Hikeda'ya

Northithe—county in Erkynland

Old Granary Tower—roundhouse in the Inner Keep once used by Prince John Josua

Omeiyo Hamakh (the Maze Palace)—Queen Utuk'ku's labyrinthine home

Onestris—a Nabbanai valley

Onestrine Pass—pass between two Nabbanai valleys; site of many battles

Onyx Library—an archive of the Order of Song

Osten Ard—mortal kingdom (Rimmerspakk, "Eastern Land")

Osterdyr plain—a plain in Rimmersgard

Patorine Hill—one of Nabban's seven hills, location of the Ingadarine palace

Perdruin—an island in the Bay of Emettin

Purta Falessis—port town in southern Nabban

Quarely Maid, the—a tavern in Erchester; located on Badger Street near Market Square

Queen's Square—in Nakkiga

Radfisk Foss—a barony in Southern Rimmersgard

Reach, the—part of Sacrifice training grounds

Refarslod—"The Fox's Road"; a road in Rimmersgard

Rimmersgard—duchy in the north of Osten Ard

Risa—island in the Bay of Firannos

Royal North Road—king's road leading north from Erchester

Royal Way—ancient road running south from Nakkiga

Rumiya—lake beside the mountain of Nakkiga

Sacred Redeemer's Church—located in Tellis Narassi, Nabban

Saegard—town in Rimmersgard, on the coast

Sailmaker Road—a street in Nabban which runs along the Great Canal in the shadow of the walls

St. Helvard's Cathedral—a church in the center of Elvritshalla

St. Galdin's Square—a landmark in the City of Nabban

St. Lavennin's Square—a place in Nabban

St. Ormod's—a church in Erchester

St. Rhiappa's—a cathedral in Kwanitupul

St. Sutrin's—cathedral in Erchester

St. Wiglaf's Minster—a shabby old church in Erchester

St. Yistrin's—a monastery

Shisae'ron—broad meadow valley; once Sithi territory

Shimmerspine—Norn name for northern mountain range mortals call Whitefells

Sistan—village in Erkynland near Aldheorte forest

Skoggey—a town in eastern Rimmersgard

Spenit—island in Bay of Firannos

Spider Groves—place in Nakkiga

Springmarsh—a swamp in the southernmost Frostmarch

Stanshire—town in eastern Erkynland

Stefflod—a river in eastern Erkynland; also site of battleground in second Thrithings War

Stews, the—a poor district in Meremund

Stormspike—the mountain also known as Nakkiga or Sturmrspeik

Street of Martyrs—landmark in Nakkiga-That-Was

Street of Sacred Discipline—a shadowy, narrow road with ancient stone houses in Nakkiga

Sturmstad—place on the border of Erkynland and Rimmersgard

Sudshire—county in the southern part of Erkynland

Sumiyu Shisa—stream through the valley Shisae'ron

Swertclif—hill near Erchester; burial site of the kings of Erkynland

Taig Road—road leading through Hernysadharc; also known as "Tethtain's Way"

Taig, the—wooden castle; house of Hernystir's ruling family

Tearfall—huge waterfall at the heart of Nakkiga

Tellis Narassi—a poor neighborhood in the City of Nabban

Thrithings—plain of grassland in the southeast of Osten Ard

Tower of the Holy Tree—new tower in the Hayholt

Trevinta—a county in Nabban

Trollfells—human name for the home of the Qanuc

T'seya Go-jao—one of the Little Boats

Tumet'ai—one of the nine Sithi cities, lost under ice

Tungoldyr—a town in the far north of Rimmersgard

Tzaaita's Stone—landmark in Nakkiga

Venyha Do'sae—original home of Sithi, Hikeda'ya, and Tinukeda'ya; called "The Garden"

Vestvenn—river in central Rimmersgard

Vestvennby—Rimmersgard town on the Frostmarch

Vennweg—road leading to Vestvennby

Unhav—Thrithing name for Lake Eadne
Urmsbakkir—the hills surrounding Urmsheim
Urmsheim—a fabled mountain in the far northeast
Village Grove—Tiamak's home village in the Wran
Vinitta—an island in the Bay of Firannos
Warinsten—island off the West Coast; birthplace of King John Presbyter, once called "Gemmia"
Wentmouth—town in southern Erkynland; on the coast at the mouth of the Gleniwent River
Whitefells—northern mountain range
White Snail Castle—a fortress in Nakkiga-That-Was, at the foot of Stormspike
Whitstan—town in southern Erkynland
Willow Hall—Tanahaya's home
Woodsall—a village and barony in Erkynland
Woodpecker Hills—source of streams that feed the Ymstrecca
Wran, the—marsh land in southern Osten Ard
Yakh Huyeru—"Hall of Trembling"; cavern beneath Stormspike
Yásira—Sithi sacred meeting place
Yiqanuc—home of the Qanuc; also known as the Trollfells
Ymstrecca—a river in eastern Erkynland; also the site of a battlefield

CREATURES

Bukken—Rimmersgard name for diggers; called "Boghanik" by trolls; called "Furi'a" by Norns
Deofol—Unver's black horse
Diggers—small, manlike subterranean creatures
Drochnathair—Hernystiri name for dragon Hidohebhi; slain by Ineluki and Hakatri
Falku—Little Snenneq's ram
Ghants—chitinous Wran-dwelling creatures
Giants—large, shaggy, manlike creatures, called "Hunë" in the north
Hidohebhi—a dragon
Hunën—Rimmersgard name for giants
Igjarjuk—ice dragon of Urmsheim; "Likkija" in the Sithi and Norn tongues; the daughter of great worm Hidohebhi
Kilpa—manlike marine creatures
Pengi—Tinukeda'ya slaves; "changelings"
Qallipuk—"River Man"; a water monster
Qantaqa—Binabik's wolf companion during the Storm King's War
Raoni—Hikeda'ya name for "giants"
Scand—Tiamak's donkey at the Hayholt

Shurakai—fire-drake, slain beneath the Hayholt; her bones make up the
    Dragonbone Chair
Spidersilk—Tanahaya's horse
Vaqana—Binabik's current wolf companion; descendant of Qantaqa
Witiko'ya—a ferocious wolflike predator of the far north
Yukinva—a giant rodent of the snowy heights

THINGS

Age of Gold—ancient Nabbanai era
Aedonites—the followers of Usires Aedon
Aedontide—holy time celebrating birth of Usires Aedon
Albian House—one of Nabban's fifty noble families
Analita—also "analita-zé"; quicksilver liquor drunk by the Hikeda'ya
Astaline Sisters—a lay group who sponsored settlements for women
Benedrivine House—ruling family in Nabban
Black rye—a grain
Blood lily—a bright red flower like the spray from a wound
Breathing Harp, the—Master Witness in Nakkiga
Ceremony of the Lost Garden—a Hikeda'ya religious observance
Citril—an addictive root for chewing; grown in the south
Clavean House—one of Nabban's fifty noble families
Cold Root—Makho's witchwood sword
Cold Leaf—Makho's witchwood dagger
Comis—a wine from Nabban
Council of Erchester—ruling body in Erchester
Cuthmanite Brothers—a monkish order dedicated to St. Cuthman; known for
    their apple brandy
Dance of Sacrifice—Hikeda'ya term for combat
Days of Mourning—Hikeda'ya holiday
Death-cote—another Hikeda'ya name for tombs
Dominiate—Nabbanai council consisting primarily of the fifty noble families
Drukhi's Day—Nakkiga holiday
Enduya—clan of High Magister Viyeki
Erkynguard—sentries of the Hayholt
Escritorial Synod—a board of the Aedonite church
Faceless—the Nakkiga Council's secret police
Fifty Families—Nabbanai noble houses
Fire Ordeal—test in Sacrifice training
Flann's Crows—a troop of outlaws (mostly Hernystiri) in the southern Frost-
    march
Gardenborn—all Hikeda'ya who came from Venyha Do'sae

Grass Blade—a move in Hikeda'ya combat technique

Hall of Spears—test in sacrifice training

Hamakha—clan of Queen Utuk'ku

Hamakha Dictates—a set of Hikeda'ya laws created by Queen Utuk'ku

Hamakha Wormslayer Guard—the keepers of public peace in Nakkiga

Hao sa-Rashi—"the Way of the Exiles"; Hikeda'ya sign language

Harchan dittany—a herb

Hebi-kei—"the serpent"; a witchwood switch used for punishment (literally: "witchwood snake")

Hersrede—the Citizens Council in Elvritshalla

Hesitancy—a Hikeda'ya spell

High King's Ward—protection of the High Throne over the countries of Osten Ard

Hikeda'yasao—the speech of Nakkiga

Homecoming Boats festival—a holiday in the Wran

House of Year-Dancing—Sithi clan

Hovnir—the axe of Udun Rimmer, the highest pagan Rimmersgard god

Hringleit—aka Ringquest; a Black Rimmersmen ship

Ice moly—a healing ointment carried by Saomeji

Ice Ordeal—test in sacrifice training

Jarl—a Rimmersgard title equivalent to Westerling "Earl"

Jarn clan—the Iron clan (Rimmersgard)

Juya'ha—Sithi art; pictures made of woven cords

Kangkang—Qanuq liquor

Keida'ya—the Sithi and Hikeda'ya

Kei-in—the holy witchwood seed

Kei-vishaa—substance used by Gardenborn to make enemies drowsy and weak

Keta yi'indra—Hikeda'ya term, "dangerous sleep"; recuperative sleep of Queen Utuk'ku

Kinjada—Hikeda'ya clan

Kuwa—Hikeda'ya name for a slave collar

Landborn—those Hikeda'ya and Sithi born in the first generations after the arrival in Osten Ard

League of the Scroll—an exclusive and secret society of scholars, seeking and preserving knowledge

Metessan House—one of Nabban's fifty noble families; Lord Pasevalles is a member; blue crane emblem

Naidel—a slender sword, once belonging to Prince Josua, also known as "Needle"

Nonamansa—a middday Aedonite religious ceremony

Northern Alliance—a trade organization, in competition with the ancient Sindigato Perdruine

Ocean Indefinite and Eternal—the ocean crossed by the Gardenborn

Oil Fountains—a landmark in Queen's Square, in Nakkiga

On the Movement of Blood And Pneuma—a book on medicine by Rachoun

Order of the Red Drake—a royal award to knights for bravery

Otter's Moon—Hikeda'ya month in Spring

Pellarine Table—table of the Small Council of the High Throne; a gift from the Nabbanai imperator Pellaris to King Tethtain

Plesinnen—Plesinnen of Myrme, writer of a book of natural philosophy

Prayer of Loyal Servants—Hikeda'ya childhood prayer

Princess Hylissa—a ship, named after Miriamele's late mother

Puju—bread made from the white barley grown in the cold valleys below Stormspike

Queen's Stricture—Hikeda'ya prayer, almost a catechism

Queen's Teeth—Utuk'ku's personal guard

Quinis-piece—a Nabbanai coin

Rachoun—an ancient philosopher and healer

Rock Serpent retreat—a move in Hikeda'ya combat technique

Rite of Quickening—Qanuc Spring ceremony

Sacred College—Aedonite church's inquisition

Scale—Sithi device for talking over distance

Shaynat—a Hikeda'ya game, called "Shent" by the Sithi

St. Agar's Order—an Aedonite monk order

Sacrifice—a trained assassin/soldier

Sandarian—a sweet, amber-colored wine from Spenit

Scrollbearers—members of the League of the Scroll; a secret society seeking and preserving knowledge

Sea Rover's Crown—ruling insignia of Rimmersgard

Sedda's Token—the Spring full moon

Serpent's Moon—Hikeda'ya month

Shan—Thrithings word meaning "lord of lords"; ruler of all the Thrithings

Shent—a Sithi game of socializing and strategy

Silent Court of the Council—part of the Hikeda'ya elite

Silver Stags—a Hernystiri elite troop; hand-picked by King Hugh

Sindigato Perdruine—a trade organisation

Skalijar—an organized troop of brigands in northern Rimmersgard

Soldier's Cantis—an Aedonite prayer

Sotfengsel—King Elvrit's ship, buried at Skipphaven

Sovran Remedies of the Wranna Healers—a book written by Tiamak

Spinsilk—a delicate Norn fabric

Stag—emblem of Hern's House, the ruling house of Hernystir

Stormbirds—supporters of Dallo Ingadaris; the Albatross is their sign

Summer Ice—one of the Houses of Sacrifice

Tale of the Idle Shepherd—old story, similar in moral to "The Boy Who Cried Wolf"

Talon—a hand-troop of five specially trained Sacrifices

Thane—a Rimmersgard title equivalent to Westerling "Baron"

The Color of Water—a forbidden collection of poems by Shun'y'asu

The Five Fingers of the Queen's Hand—a beloved Hikeda'ya book of wisdom

Thieves' Poetry—a game

Third Green Moon—Thrithings month-name, roughly

Thrones—Erkynlandish gold coins; one issue has portraits of King Simon and Queen Miriamele

Ti-tuno—Camaris' horn; made from dragon Hidohebhi's tooth; also known as "Cellian"

Towers—Erkynlandish silver coins

Tractit Eteris Vocinnen—"A Treatise On The Aetheric Whispers"; a banned book

Tree—"Holy Tree", or "Execution Tree"; symbol of Usires Aedon's execution and the Aedonite faith

U'ituko—a predatory beast, who can cross snow without breaking even the crust

Valada—a wise woman

Vitmaers—Thrithings word for witnesses to a declaration

War of Return—Hikeda'ya name for the Storm King's War

Westerling—language originating from Waristen Island; now the common tongue of Osten Ard

White Hand—a mark left on dead Hikeda'ya

Witchwood—rare wood from trees brought from the Garden; as hard as metal

Witchwood Crown—Sithi: "kei-jáyha"; a circlet for heroes; a group of witch-wood trees; a move in Shaynat/Shent

Witness—a Sithi device to talk over long distances and enter the Road of Dreams, often times a mirror.

Wormglass—Hernystiri name for certain old mirrors

Yedade's Box—a Hikeda'ya device for testing children

Yew Tree—Aengas' ship

Yerut—fermented mare's milk that the Thrithings-folk have drunk since time before time

STAR CONSTELLATIONS

Gate—Hikeda'ya

Hare—Erkynlandish

Kingfisher—Nabbanai

Lantern—Hikeda'ya

Lobster—Nabbanai

Mantis—Hikeda'ya

Mixis the Wolf—Nabbanai

Owl—Hikeda'ya

Serpent—Nabbanai as well as Norn

Spinning Wheel—Erkynlandish

Storm's Eye—Hikeda'ya
Winged Beetle—Nabbanai
Yuvenis' Throne—Nabbanai

KNUCKLEBONES

Qanuc auguring tools
Patterns include:
  Wingless Bird
  Fish–Spear
  The Shadowed Path
  Torch at the Cave–Mouth
  Balking Ram
  Clouds in the Pass
  The Black Crevice
  Unwrapped Dart
  Circle of Stones
  Mountain Dancing
  Masterless Ram
  Slippery Snow
  Unexpected Visitor
  Unnatural Birth
  No Shadow

NORN ORDERS:

Order, Ordination, Ordinal
Order House—actual location of Order's school, offices
Orders mentioned: Sacrifices; Whisperers; Echoes; Singers; Builders; Celebrants;
  Harvesters

THRITHINGS CLANS (AND THEIR THRITHING):

Adder—Lake
Antelope—Meadow
Crane, aka "Kragni"—Lake
Dragonfly—Lake
Fitch—Lake
Kestrel—Lake
Lynx—Lake
Stallion, aka "Mehrdon"—High
White Spot Deer—Lake

HOLIDAYS

Feyever 2—Candlemansa
Marris 25—Elysiamansa
Marris 31—Fool's Night
Avrel 1—All Fool's Day
Avrel 3—St. Vultinia's Day
Avrel 24—St. Dinan's Day
Avrel 30—Stoning Night
Maia 1—Belthainn Day
Yuven 23—Midsummer's Eve
Tiyagar 15—Saint Sutrin's Day
Anitul 1—Halfmansa
Septander 29—Saint Granis' Day
Octander 30—Harrows Eve
Novander 1—Soul's Day
Decander 21—Saint Tunath's Day
Decander 24—Aedonmansa

Days of the Week
   Sunday, Moonday, Tiasday, Udunsday, Drorsday, Frayday, Satrinsday

Months of the Year
   Jonever, Feyever, Marris, Avrel, Maia, Yuven, Tiyagar, Anitul, Septander, Octander, Novander, Decander

WORDS AND PHRASES

QANUC

Amaq and kukaq—"urine" and "feces"
Falku—"Tasty white fat"; Snenneq's ram
Henimaa!—"Don't talk!" / "Shut up!"
Nihut—"Attack"
Ninit-e, Afa!—"Come on, Father!"
Nukapik—"Betrothed"
Qallipuk—"River Man"
Shummuk—"Wait"
So-hiq nammu ya—"The night of thin ice"
Ummu Bok!—"Well done!" (roughly)

SITHI (KEIDA'YASAO)

Chiru—"Pregnant"
Hikeda'ya—"Cloud Children"; Norns
Hikka Staja—"Arrow-Bearer"
S'hue—"Lord"
Sojeno nigago-zhe—"Little Gardens of Memory"
Staja-hikkada'ya—"Descendant of the arrow-bearer"
Sudhoda'ya—"Sunset Children": mortals
Tinukeda'ya—"Ocean Children": Niskies and Dwarrows
Tsa—equivalent of a human cluck noise or "tsk"
Venyha s'ahn!—"By the Garden!"
Zida'ya—"Dawn Children": Sithi

NORN (HIKEDA'YASAO)

Do'Nakkiga—the mountain where the Hikeda'ya live
Do'sae né-Sogeyu—"The Shadow Garden"; aka Osten Ard
Furi'a—"Diggers"
Hikeda'yasao—the language of Nakkiga
Kei-in—"the holy witchwood seed"
Keta-Yi'indra—a deep, decades-long sleep
K'rei!—"Hail!"
Ra'haishu—"Tunnel meeting"; signifies a mistake that could lead to sudden
    death
Rayu ata na'ara—"I hear the Queen in your voice"
San'nakuno—"Sad Little Dog"; nickname given to Jarnulf
Shu'do-tkzayha—Hikeda'ya name for mortals: "Sunset Children"
Srinyedu—Hikeda'ya name for weaving art
Z'hue—term of respect for an elder

NABBANAI

Agarine—of St. Agar
Caimentos—quicklime cement
Exsequis—a prayer
Mansa sea Cuelossan—a funeral ceremony prayer
Orxis—a giant
Podos orbiem, quil meminit—"He who remembers can make the world anew"
Secundis primis edis—"Second will be first"

HERNYSTIRI

Eolair Tarna—"Lord Eolair"
Mu' harcha!—"My love!"
Och, cawer lim!—"Help me!"

RIMMERSPAKK

Jarl—"Earl"
Refarslod—"The Fox's Road"
Valada—"Wise woman"

OTHER

Cockindrill—northern word for "crocodile"
Higdaja—giants' name for Norns
Hojun—giants' name for themselves
Samuli—"Delicate flowers"; Wranna word for female genitalia
Njar-hunë—"Corpse giant"

A GUIDE TO PRONUNCIATION

ERKYNLANDISH

Erkynlandish names are divided into two types, Old Erkynlandish (O.E.) and Warinstenner. Those names which are based on types from Prester John's native island of Warinsten (mostly the names of castle servants or John's immediate family) have been represented as variants on Biblical names (Elias—Elijah, Ebekah—Rebecca, etc.) Old Erkynlandish names should be pronounced like modern English, except as follows:

  a—always ah, as in "father"
  ae—ay of "say"
  c—k as in "keen"
  e—ai as in "air," except at the end of names, when it is also sounded, but with an eh or uh sound, i.e., Hruse—"Rooz-uh"
  ea—sounds as a in "mark," except at beginning of word or name, where it has the same value as ae

g—always hard *g*, as in "glad"
h—hard *h* of "help"
i—short *i* of "in"
j—hard *j* of "jaw"
o—long but soft *o*, as in "orb"
u—*oo* sound of "wood," never *yoo* as in "music"

HERNYSTIRI

The Hernystiri names and words can be pronounced in largely the same way as the O.E., with a few exceptions:
th—always the *th* in "other," never as in "thing"
ch—a guttural, as in Scottish "loch"
y—pronounce *yr* like "beer," *ye* like "spy"
h—unvoiced except at beginning of word or after *t* or *c*
e—*ay* as in "ray"
ll—same as single *l*: Lluth—Luth

RIMMERSPAKK

Names and words in Rimmerspakk differ from O.E. pronunciation in the following:

j—pronounced *y*: Jarnauga—Yarnauga; Hjeldin—Hyeldin (*H* nearly silent here)
ei—long *i* as in "crime"
e—*ee*, as in "sweet"
ö—*oo*, as in "coop"
au—*ow*, as in "cow"

NABBANAI

The Nabbanai language holds basically to the rules of a romance language, i.e., the vowels are pronounced "ah-eh-ih-oh-ooh," the consonants are all sounded, etc. There are some exceptions.
i—most names take emphasis on second to last syllable: Ben-i-GAR-is. When this syllable has an *i*, it is sounded long (Ardrivis: Ar-DRY-vis) unless it comes before a double consonant (Antippa: An-TIHP-pa)
es—at end of name, *es* is sounded long: Gelles—Gel-leez
y—is pronounced as a long *i*, as in "mild"

QANUC

Troll-language is considerably different than the other human languages. There are three hard "k" sounds, signified by: *c, q,* and *k*. The only difference intelligible to most non-Qanuc is a slight clucking sound on the *q,* but it is not to be encouraged in beginners. For our purposes, all three will sound with the *k* of "keep." Also, the Qanuc *u* is pronounced *uh,* as in "bug." Other interpretations are up to the reader, but he or she will not go far wrong pronouncing phonetically.

SITHI

Even more than the language of Yiqanuc, the language of the Zida'ya is virtually unpronounceable by untrained tongues, and so is easiest rendered phonetically, since the chance of any of us being judged by experts is slight (but not nonexistent, as Binabik learned). These rules may be applied, however.

i—when the first vowel, pronounced *ih,* as in "clip." When later in word, especially at end, pronounced *ee,* as in "fleet": Jiriki—Jih-REE-kee

ai—pronounced like long *i,* as in "time"

' (apostrophe)—represents a clicking sound, and should not be voiced by mortal readers.

EXCEPTIONAL NAMES

Geloë—Her origins are unknown, and so is the source of her name. It is pronounced "Juh-LO-ee" or "Juh-LOY." Both are correct.

Ingen Jegger—He is a Black Rimmersman, and the "J" in Jegger is sounded, just as in "jump."

Miriamele—Although born in the Erkynlandish court, hers is a Nabbanai name that developed a strange pronunciation—perhaps due to some family influence or confusion of her dual heritage—and sounds as "Mih-ree-uh-MEL."

Vorzheva—A Thrithings-woman, her name is pronounced "Vor-SHAY-va," with the *zh* sounding harshly, like the Hungarian *zs*.

Begin a new adventure with master storyteller Tad Williams

MEMORY, SORROW & THORN

OTHERLAND

SHADOWMARCH

THE BOBBY DOLLAR TRILOGY

  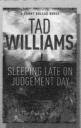

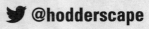